**Books by John Irving**

The 158-Pound Marriage
Setting Free the Bears
The Water-Method Man
The World According to Garp

Published by POCKET BOOKS

John Irving

# The World According to Garp

TURKEYFOOT LENDING
LIBRARY

PUBLISHED BY POCKET BOOKS NEW YORK

The author wishes to express his gratitude to the Guggenheim Foundation.

Grateful acknowledgment is made for permission to reprint "The Plot against the Giant." Copyright 1923, 1951 by Wallace Stevens. Reprinted from *The Collected Poems of Wallace Stevens* by permission of Alfred A. Knopf, Inc.

Portions of this book have appeared in different form in the following magazines: *Antaeus, Esquire, Gallery, Penthouse, Playboy, Ploughshares,* and *Swank.*

POCKET BOOKS, a Simon & Schuster division of
GULF & WESTERN CORPORATION
1230 Avenue of the Americas, New York, N.Y. 10020

*for Colin and Brendan*

# Chapters

# The World
# According to
# Garp

# 1

❘❘-❘❘-❘❘-❘❘-❘❘-❘❘-❘❘

# Boston Mercy

GARP'S mother, Jenny Fields, was arrested in Boston in 1942 for wounding a man in a movie theater. This was shortly after the Japanese had bombed Pearl Harbor and people were being tolerant of soldiers, because suddenly everyone *was* a soldier, but Jenny Fields was quite firm in her intolerance of the behavior of men in general and soldiers in particular. In the movie theater she had to move three times, but each time the soldier moved closer to her until she was sitting against the musty wall, her view of the newsreel almost blocked by some silly colonnade, and she resolved she would not get up and move again. The soldier moved once more and sat beside her.

Jenny was twenty-two. She had dropped out of college almost as soon as she'd begun, but she had finished her nursing-school program at the head of her class and she enjoyed being a nurse. She was an athletic-looking young woman who always had high color in her cheeks; she had dark, glossy hair and what her mother called a mannish way of walking (she swung her arms), and her rump and hips were so slender and hard that, from behind, she resembled a young boy. In Jenny's opinion, her breasts were too large; she thought the ostentation of her bust made her look "cheap and easy."

1

She was nothing of the kind. In fact, she had dropped out of college when she suspected that the chief purpose of her parents' sending her to Wellesley had been to have her dated by and eventually mated to some well-bred man. The recommendation of Wellesley had come from her older brothers, who had assured her parents that Wellesley women were not thought of loosely and were considered high in marriage potential. Jenny felt that her education was merely a polite way to bide time, as if she were really a cow, being prepared only for the insertion of the device for artificial insemination.

Her declared major had been English literature, but when it seemed to her that her classmates were chiefly concerned with acquiring the sophistication and the poise to deal with men, she had no trouble leaving literature for nursing. She saw nursing as something that could be put into immediate practice, and its study had no ulterior motive that Jenny could see (later she wrote, in her famous autobiography, that too many nurses put themselves on display for too many doctors; but then her nursing days were over).

She liked the simple, no-nonsense uniform; the blouse of the dress made less of her breasts; the shoes were comfortable, and suited to her fast pace of walking. When she was at the night desk, she could still read. She did not miss the young college men, who were sulky and disappointed if you wouldn't compromise yourself, and superior and aloof if you would. At the hospital she saw more soldiers and working boys than college men, and they were franker and less pretentious in their expectations; if you compromised yourself a little, they seemed at least grateful to see you again. Then, suddenly, everyone was a soldier—and full of the self-importance of college boys—and Jenny Fields stopped having anything to do with men.

"My mother," Garp wrote, "was a lone wolf."

The Fields' family fortune was in shoes, though Mrs. Fields, a former Boston Weeks, had brought some

2

money of her own to the marriage. The Fields family had managed well enough with footwear to have removed themselves from the shoe factories years ago. They lived in a large, shingled house on the New Hampshire shore at Dog's Head Harbor. Jenny went home for her days and nights off—mainly to please her mother, and to convince the grande dame that although Jenny was "slumming her life away as a nurse," as her mother remarked, she was not developing slovenly habits in her speech or in her moral person.

Jenny frequently met her brothers at the North Station and rode home on the train with them. As all members of the Fields family were bidden to do, they rode on the right-hand side of the Boston and Maine when the train left Boston and sat on the left when they returned. This complied with the wishes of the senior Mr. Fields, who admitted that the ugliest scenery lay out that side of the train, but he felt that all Fieldses should be forced to face the grimy source of their independence and higher life. On the right-hand side of the train, leaving Boston, and on the left as you returned, you passed the Fields Factory Outlet in Haverhill, and the vast billboard with the huge work shoe taking a firm step toward you. The billboard towered above the railroad yard and was reflected in countless miniatures in the windows of the shoe plant. Beneath this menacing, advancing foot were the words:

*FIELDS* FOR YOUR FEET
IN THE FACTORY OR IN
THE FIELDS!

There was a Fields line of nursing shoe, and Mr. Fields gave his daughter a free pair whenever she came home; Jenny must have had a dozen pairs. Mrs. Fields, who insisted on equating her daughter's leaving Wellesley with a sordid future, also gave Jenny a present every time she came home. Mrs. Fields gave her daughter a hot-water bottle, or so she said—and so Jenny assumed;

she never opened the packages. Her mother would say, "Dear, do you still have that hot-water bottle I gave you?" And Jenny would think a minute, believing she had left it on the train or thrown it away, and she'd say, "I *may* have lost it, Mother, but I'm sure I don't need another one." And Mrs. Fields, bringing the package out from hiding, would press it on her daughter; it was still concealed in the drugstore paper. Mrs. Fields would say, *"Please,* Jennifer, be more careful. And *use* it, please!"

As a nurse, Jenny saw little use for the hot-water bottle; she assumed it to be a touching, odd device of old-fashioned and largely psychological comfort. But some of the packages made it back to her small room near Boston Mercy Hospital. She kept them in a closet, which was nearly full of boxes of nursing shoes—also unopened.

She felt detached from her family, and thought it strange how they had lavished so much attention on her, as a child, and then at some appointed, prearranged time they seemed to stop the flow of affection and begin the expectations—as if, for a brief phase, you were expected to absorb love (and get enough), and then, for a much longer and more serious phase, you were expected to fulfill certain obligations. When Jenny had broken the chain, had left Wellesley for something as common as nursing, she had dropped her family—and they, as if they couldn't help themselves, were in the process of dropping her. In the Fields family, for example, it would have been more appropriate if Jenny had become a doctor, or if she'd stayed in college until she *married* one. Each time she saw her brothers, her mother, and her father, they were more uncomfortable in one another's presence. They were involved in that awkward procedure of getting to unknow each other.

That must be how families are, thought Jenny Fields. She felt if she ever had children she would love them no less when they were twenty than when they were two; they might need you more at twenty, she thought. What do you really need when you're two? In the hos-

4

pital, the babies were the easiest patients. The older they got, the more they needed; and the less anyone wanted or loved them.

Jenny felt she had grown up on a large ship without having seen, much less understood, the engine room. She liked how the hospital reduced everything to what one ate, if it helped one to have eaten it, and where it went. As a child she had never seen the dirty dishes; in fact, when the maids cleared the table, Jenny was sure they were throwing the dishes away (it was some time before she was even allowed in the kitchen). And when the milk truck brought the bottles every morning, for a while Jenny thought that the truck brought the day's dishes, too—the sound, that glassy clatter and bang, being so like the sound of the maids in the closed kitchen, doing whatever they did to the dishes.

Jenny Fields was five before she saw her father's bathroom. She tracked it down one morning by following the scent of her father's cologne. She found a steamy shower stall—quite modern, for 1925—a private toilet, a row of bottles so unlike her mother's bottles that Jenny thought she had discovered the lair of a secret man living undetected in their house for years. In fact, she *had*.

In the hospital, Jenny knew where everything went—and she was learning the unmagical answers to where almost everything came from. At Dog's Head Harbor, when Jenny had been a girl, the family members had their own baths, their own rooms, their own doors with their own mirrors on the backs. In the hospital, privacy was not sacred; nothing was a secret; if you wanted a mirror, you had to ask a nurse.

The most mysterious thing she had been allowed to investigate on her own, when Jenny was a child, had been the cellar and the great pottery crock which every Monday was filled with clams. Jenny's mother sprinkled cornmeal on the clams at night, and every morning they were rinsed in fresh sea water from a long pipe that ran into the basement from the sea itself. By the weekend the clams were fat and free of sand, they were growing too big for their shells, and their great, obscene necks lolled on the salt water. Jenny would help the cook sort through them on Fridays; the dead ones did not retract their necks when touched.

Jenny asked for a book about clams. She read all about them: how they ate, how they bred, how they grew. It was the first live thing she understood completely—its life, its sex, its death. At Dog's Head Harbor, human beings were not that accessible. In the hospital, Jenny Fields felt she was making up for lost time; she was discovering that people weren't much more mysterious, or much more attractive, than clams.

"My mother," Garp wrote, "was not one for making fine distinctions."

One striking difference she might have seen between clams and people was that most people had some sense of humor, but Jenny was not inclined toward humor. There was a popular joke among the nurses in Boston at that time, but it was not funny to Jenny Fields. The joke involved one of the other hospitals in Boston. The hospital Jenny worked in was Boston Mercy Hospital, which was called Boston Mercy; there was also Massachusetts General Hospital, which was called the Mass General. And another hospital was the Peter Bent Brigham, which was called the Peter Bent.

One day, the joke goes, a Boston cab driver had his taxi hailed by a man who staggered off the curb toward him, almost dropping to his knees in the street. The man was purple in the face with pain; he was either strangling or holding his breath, so that talking was clearly difficult for him, and the cabby opened the door and helped him inside, where the man lay face down on the floor alongside the back seat, tucking his knees up to his chest.

"Hospital! Hospital!" he cried.

"The Peter Bent?" the cabby asked. That was the closest hospital.

"It's worse than *bent*," the man moaned. "I think Molly bit it *off!*"

Few jokes were funny to Jenny Fields, and certainly not this one; no peter jokes for Jenny, who was staying clear of the issue. She had seen the trouble peters could get into; babies were not the worst of it. Of course she saw people who didn't want to have babies, and they were sad that they were pregnant; they shouldn't *have* to have babies, Jenny thought—though she mainly felt sorry for the babies who were born. She saw people who wanted to have their babies, too, and they made *her* want to have one. One day, Jenny Fields thought, she would like to have a baby—just one. But the trouble was that she wanted as little to do with a peter as possible, and nothing whatsoever to do with a man.

Most peter treatment that Jenny saw was done to soldiers. The U.S. Army would not begin to benefit from the discovery of penicillin until 1943, and there were many soldiers who didn't get penicillin until 1945. At Boston Mercy, in the early days of 1942, peters were usually treated with sulfa and arsenic. Sulfathiazole was for the clap—with lots of water recommended. For syphilis, in the days before penicillin, they used neoarsphenamine; Jenny Fields thought that this was the epitome of all that sex could lead to—to introduce *arsenic* into the human chemistry, to try to clean the chemistry up.

The other peter treatment was local and also required a lot of fluid. Jenny frequently assisted with this method of disinfecting, because the patient required lots of attention at the time; sometimes, in fact, he needed to be held. It was a simple procedure that could force as much as one hundred cc's of fluid up the penis and through the surprised urethra before it all came back, but the procedure left everyone feeling a bit raw. The man who invented a device for this method of treatment was named Valentine, and his device was called the Valentine irrigator. Long after Dr. Valentine's irrigator was improved, or replaced with another irrigation device, the nurses at Boston Mercy still referred to the procedure as the Valentine treatment—an appropriate punishment for a lover, thought Jenny Fields.

"My mother," Garp wrote, "was not romantically inclined."

When the soldier in the movie theater first started changing seats—when he made his first move for her— Jenny Fields felt that the Valentine treatment would be just the thing for him. But she didn't have an irrigator with her; it was much too large for her purse. It also required the considerable cooperation of the patient. What she *did* have with her was a scalpel; she carried it with her all the time. She had not stolen it from surgery, either; it was a castaway scalpel with a deep nick taken out of the point (it had probably been dropped on the floor, or in a sink)—it was no good for fine work, but it was not for fine work that Jenny wanted it.

At first it had slashed up the little silk pockets of her purse. Then she found part of an old thermometer container that slipped over the head of the scalpel, capping it like a fountain pen. It was this cap she removed when the soldier moved into the seat beside her and stretched his arm along the armrest they were (absurdly) meant to share. His long hand dangled off the end of the armrest; it twitched like the flank of a horse shuddering the flies away. Jenny kept her hand on the scalpel inside her purse; with her other hand, she held the purse tightly in her white lap. She was imagining that her nurse's uniform shone like a holy shield, and for some perverse reason this vermin beside her had been attracted by her light.

"My mother," Garp wrote, "went through her life on the lookout for purse-snatchers and snatch-snatchers."

In the theater, it was not her purse that the soldier wanted. He touched her knee. Jenny spoke up fairly

8

clearly. "Get your stinking hand off me," she said. Several people turned around.

"Oh, come on," the soldier moaned, and his hand shot quickly under her uniform; he found her thighs locked tightly together—he found his whole arm, from his shoulder to his wrist, suddenly sliced open like a soft melon. Jenny had cut cleanly through his insignia and his shirt, cleanly through his skin and muscles, baring his bones at the joint of his elbow. ("If I'd wanted to kill him," she told the police, later, "I'd have slit his wrist. I'm a nurse. I know how people bleed.")

The soldier screamed. On his feet and falling back, he swiped at Jenny's head with his uncut arm, boxing her ear so sharply that her head sang. She pawed at him with the scalpel, removing a piece of his upper lip the approximate shape and thinness of a thumbnail. ("I was *not* trying to slash his throat," she told the police, later. "I was trying to cut his nose off, but I missed.")

Crying, on all fours, the soldier groped his way to the theater aisle and headed toward the safety of the light in the lobby. Someone else in the theater was whimpering, in fright.

Jenny wiped her scalpel on the movie seat, returned it to her purse, and covered the blade with the thermometer cap. Then she went to the lobby, where keen wailings could be heard and the manager was calling through the lobby doors over the dark audience, "Is there a doctor here? Please! Is someone a doctor?"

Someone *was* a nurse, and she went to lend what assistance she could. When the soldier saw her, he fainted; it was not really from loss of blood. Jenny knew how facial wounds bled; they were deceptive. The deeper gash on his arm was of course in need of immediate attention, but the soldier was not bleeding to death. No one but Jenny seemed to know that—there was so much blood, and so much of it was on her white nurse's uniform. They quickly realized she had done it. The theater lackeys would not let her touch the fainted soldier, and someone took her purse from her. The mad nurse! The crazed slasher! Jenny Fields was calm. She thought it was only a matter of waiting for the true authorities to comprehend the situation. But the police were not very nice to her, either.

"You been dating this guy long?" the first one asked her, en route to the precinct station.

And another one asked her, later, "But how did you know he was going to *attack* you? He says he was just trying to introduce himself."

"That's a real mean little weapon, honey," a third told her. "You shouldn't carry something like that around with you. That's asking for trouble."

So Jenny waited for her brothers to clear things up. They were law-school men from Cambridge, across the river. One was a law student, the other one taught in the law school.

"Both," Garp wrote, "were of the opinion that the *practice* of law was vulgar, but the *study* of it was sublime."

They were not so comforting when they came.

"Break your mother's heart," said one.

"If you'd only stayed at Wellesley," said the other.

"A girl alone has to protect herself," Jenny said. "What could be more proper?"

But one of her brothers asked her if she could prove that she had not had previous relations with the man.

"Confidentially," whispered the other one, "have you been dating this guy long?"

Finally, things were cleared up when the police discovered that the soldier was from New York, where he had a wife and child. He had taken a leave in Boston and, more than anything else, he feared the story would get back to his wife. Everyone seemed to agree that *would* be awful—for everyone—so Jenny was released without charges. When she made a fuss that the police had not given her back her scalpel, one of her brothers said, "For God's sake, Jennifer, you can steal another one, can't you?"

"I didn't *steal* it," Jenny said.

"You should have some friends," a brother told her.

"At Wellesley," they repeated.

"Thank you for coming when I called you," Jenny said.

"What's a family for?" one said.

"Blood runs thick," said the other. Then he paled, embarrassed at the association—her uniform was so besmirched.

"I'm a good girl," Jenny told them.

"Jennifer," said the older one, and her life's earliest model—for wisdom, for all that was right. He was rather solemn. He said, "It's best not to get involved with married men."

"We won't tell Mother," the other one said.

"And certainly not Father!" said the first. In an awkward attempt at some natural warmth, he winked at her—a gesture that contorted his face and for a moment convinced Jenny that her life's earliest model had developed a facial tic.

Beside the brothers was a mailbox with a poster of Uncle Sam. A tiny soldier, all in brown, was climbing down from Uncle Sam's big hands. The soldier was going to land on a map of Europe. The words under the poster said: SUPPORT OUR BOYS! Jenny's oldest brother looked at Jenny looking at the poster.

"And don't get involved with soldiers," he added, though in a very few months he would be a soldier himself. He would be one of the soldiers who wouldn't come home from the war. He would break his mother's heart, an act he once spoke of with distaste.

Jenny's only other brother would be killed in a sailboat accident long after the war was over. He would be drowned several miles offshore from the Fields' family estate at Dog's Head Harbor. Of his grieving wife, Jenny's mother would say, "She's still young and attractive, and the children aren't obnoxious. At least not yet. After a decent time, I'm sure she'll be able to find someone else." It was to Jenny that her brother's

11

widow eventually spoke, almost a year after the drowning. She asked Jenny if she thought a "decent time" had passed and she could begin whatever had to be begun "to find someone else." She was anxious about offending Jenny's mother. She wondered if Jenny thought it would be all right to emerge from mourning.

"If you don't *feel* like mourning, what are you mourning for?" Jenny asked her. In her autobiography, Jenny wrote: "That poor woman needed to be told what to *feel*."

"That was the stupidest woman my mother said she ever met," Garp wrote. "And she had gone to Wellesley."

But Jenny Fields, when she said good-night to her brothers at her small rooming house near Boston Mercy, was too confused to be properly outraged. She was also sore—her ear, where the soldier had cuffed her, hurt her; and there was a deep muscle cramp between her shoulder blades, which made it hard for her to sleep. She thought she must have wrenched something in there when the theater lackeys had grabbed her in the lobby and pulled her arms behind her back. She remembered that hot-water bottles were supposed to be good for sore muscles and she got out of bed and went to her closet and opened one of her mother's gift packages.

It was not a hot-water bottle. That had been her mother's euphemism for something her mother couldn't bring herself to discuss. In the package was a douche bag. Jenny's mother knew what they were for, and so did Jenny. She had helped many patients at the hospital use them, though at the hospital they were not much used to prevent pregnancies after lovemaking; they were used for general feminine hygiene, and in venereal cases. To Jenny Fields a douche bag was a gentler, more commodious version of the Valentine irrigator.

Jenny opened all her mother's packages. In each one was a douche bag. "Please *use* it, dear!" her mother had begged her. Jenny knew that her mother, though she meant well, assumed that Jenny's sexual activity was considerable and irresponsible. No doubt, as her mother would put it, "since Wellesley." Since Wellesley, Jenny's mother thought that Jenny was fornicating (as she would also put it) "to beat the band."

Jenny Fields crawled back to bed with the douche bag filled with hot water and snuggled between her shoulder blades; she hoped the clamps that kept the water from running down the hose would not allow a leak, but to be sure she held the hose in her hands, a little like a rubber rosary, and she dropped the nozzle with the tiny holes into her empty water glass. All night long Jenny lay listening to the douche bag leak.

In this dirty-minded world, she thought, you are either somebody's wife or somebody's whore—or fast on your way to becoming one or the other. If you don't fit either category, then everyone tries to make you think there is something wrong with you. But, she thought, there is nothing wrong with me.

That was the beginning, of course, of the book that many years later would make Jenny Fields famous. However crudely put, her autobiography was said to bridge the usual gap between literary merit and popularity, although Garp claimed that his mother's work had "the same literary merit as the Sears, Roebuck catalog."

But what made Jenny Fields vulgar? Not her legal brothers, not the man in the movie theater who stained her uniform. Not her mother's douche bags, though these were responsible for Jenny's eventual eviction. Her landlady (a fretful woman who for obscure reasons of her own suspected that every woman was on the verge of an explosion of lasciviousness) discovered that there were nine douche bags in Jenny's tiny room and bath. A matter of guilt by association: in the mind of the troubled landlady, such a sign indicated a fear of contamination beyond even the landlady's fear. Or worse, this profusion of douche bags represented an actual and awesome *need* for douching, the conceivable reasons for which penetrated the worst of the landlady's dreams.

Whatever she made of the twelve pairs of nursing shoes cannot even be hinted. Jenny thought the matter so absurd—and found her own feelings toward her parents' provisions so ambiguous—that she hardly protested. She moved.

But this did not make her vulgar. Since her brothers, her parents, and her landlady assumed a life of lewdness for her—regardless of her own, private example— Jenny decided that all manifestations of her innocence were futile and appeared defensive. She took a small apartment, which prompted a new assault of packaged douche bags from her mother and a stack of nursing shoes from her father. It struck her that they were thinking: If she is to be a whore, let her at least be clean and well shod.

In part, the war kept Jenny from dwelling on how badly her family misread her—and kept her from any bitterness and self-pity, too; Jenny was not a "dweller." She was a good nurse, and she was increasingly busy. Many nurses were joining up, but Jenny had no desire for a change of uniform, or for travel; she was a solitary girl and she didn't want to have to meet a lot of new people. Also, she found the system of *rank* irritating enough at Boston Mercy; in an army field hospital, she assumed, it could only be worse.

First of all, she would have missed the babies. That was really why she stayed, when so many were leaving. She was at her best as a nurse, she felt, to mothers and their babies—and there were suddenly so many babies whose fathers were away, or dead or missing; Jenny wanted most of all to encourage these mothers. In fact, she envied them. It was, to her, the ideal situation: a mother alone with a new baby, the husband blown out of the sky over France. A young woman with her own child, with a life ahead of them—just the two of them. A baby with no strings attached, thought Jenny Fields.

14

An almost virgin birth. At least, no *future* peter treatment would be necessary.

These women, of course, were not always as happy with their lot as Jenny thought she would have been. They were grieving, many of them, or abandoned (many others); they resented their children, some of them; they wanted a husband and a father for their babies (many others). But Jenny Fields was their encourager—she spoke up for solitude, she told them how lucky they were.

"Don't you believe you're a good woman?" she'd ask them. Most of them thought they were.

"And isn't your baby beautiful?" Most of them thought their babies were.

"And the father? What was he like?" A bum, many thought. A swine, a lout, a liar— a no-good run-out fuck-around of a man! But he's *dead!* sobbed a few.

"Then you're better off, aren't you?" Jenny asked.

Some of them came around to seeing it her way, but Jenny's reputation at the hospital suffered for her crusade. The hospital policy toward unwed mothers was not generally so encouraging.

"Old Virgin Mary Jenny," the other nurses said. "Doesn't want a baby the easy way. Why not ask God for one?"

In her autobiography, Jenny wrote: "I wanted a job and I wanted to live alone. That made me a sexual suspect. Then I wanted a baby, but I didn't want to have to share my body or my life to have one. That made me a sexual suspect, too."

And that was what made her vulgar, too. (And that was where she got her famous title: *A Sexual Suspect,* the autobiography of Jenny Fields.)

Jenny Fields discovered that you got more respect from shocking other people than you got from trying to live your own life with a little privacy. Jenny *told* the other nurses that she would one day find a man to make her pregnant—just that, and nothing more. She did not entertain the possibility that the man would need to try more than once, she told them. They, of course, couldn't wait to tell everyone they knew. It was not long before Jenny had several proposals. She had to make a sudden decision: she could retreat, ashamed that her secret was out; or she could be brazen.

A young medical student told her he would volunteer on the condition that he could have at least six chances over a three-day weekend. Jenny told him that he obviously lacked confidence; she wanted a child who would be more secure than that.

An anesthesiologist told her he would even pay for the baby's education—through college—but Jenny told him that his eyes were too close together and his teeth were poorly formed; she would not saddle her would-be child with such handicaps.

One of the other nurses' boyfriends treated her most cruelly; he frightened her in the hospital cafeteria by handing her a milk glass nearly full of a cloudy, viscous substance.

"Sperm," he said, nodding at the glass. "All that's *one* shot—I don't mess around. If one chance is all anyone gets, I'm your man." Jenny held up the horrid glass and inspected it coolly. God knows what was actually in the glass. The nurse's boyfriend said, "That's just an indication of what kind of stuff I've got. Lots of seeds," he added, grinning. Jenny dumped the contents of the glass into a potted plant.

"I want a baby," she said. "I don't want to start a sperm farm."

Jenny knew this was going to be hard. She learned to take a ribbing, and she learned to respond in kind.

So they decided Jenny Fields was crude, that she was going too far. A joke was a joke, but Jenny seemed too determined about it. Either she was sticking to her guns, just to be stubborn—or worse, she really meant it. Her hospital colleagues couldn't make her laugh, and they couldn't get her to bed. As Garp wrote of his mother's dilemma: "Her colleagues detected that she

16

felt herself to be superior to them. Nobody's colleagues appreciate this."

So they initiated a get-tough policy with Jenny Fields. It was a staff decision—"for her own good," of course. They decided to get Jenny away from the babies and the mothers. She's got babies on her brain, they said. No more obstetrics for Jenny Fields. Keep her away from the incubators—she's got too soft a heart, or a head.

Thus they separated Jenny Fields from the mothers and their babies. She's a good nurse, they all said; let her try some intensive care. It was their experience that a nurse in Boston Mercy's intensive care quickly lost interest in her own problems. Of course Jenny knew why they had sent her away from the babies; she only resented that they thought so little of her self-control. Because what she wanted was strange to them, they assumed that she also had slim restraint. There is no logic to people, Jenny thought. There was lots of time to get pregnant, she knew. She was in no hurry. It was just part of an eventual plan.

Now there was a war. In intensive care, she saw a little more of it. The service hospitals sent them their special patients, and there were always the terminal cases. There were the usual elderly patients, hanging by the usual threads; there were the usual industrial accidents, and automobile accidents, and the terrible accidents to children. But mainly there were soldiers. What happened to them was no accident.

Jenny made her own divisions among the non-accidents that happened to the soldiers; she came up with her own categories for them.

1. There were the men who'd been burned; for the most part, they'd been burned on board ship (the most complicated cases came from Chelsea Naval Hospital), but they'd also been burned in airplanes and on the ground. Jenny called them the Externals.

2. There were the men who'd been shot or damaged in bad places; internally, they were in trouble, and Jenny called them the Vital Organs.

3. There were the men whose injuries seemed almost mystical, to Jenny; they were men who weren't "there" anymore, whose heads or spines had been tampered with. Sometimes they were paralyzed, sometimes they were merely vague. Jenny called them the Absentees. Occasionally, one of the Absentees had External or Vital Organ damage as well; all the hospital had a name for them.

4. They were Goners.

"My father," Garp wrote, "was a Goner. From my mother's point of view, that must have made him very attractive. No strings attached."

Garp's father was a ball turret gunner who had a non-accident in the air over France.

"The ball turret gunner," Garp wrote, "was a member of the bomber's crew who was among the most vulnerable to anti-aircraft fire from the ground. That was called flak; flak often looked to the gunner like fast-moving ink flung upward and spread on the sky as if the sky were a blotter. The little man (for in order to fit in the ball turret, a man was better off if he was small) crouched with his machine guns in his cramped nest—a cocoon in which he resembled one of those insects trapped in glass. This ball turret was a metal sphere with a glass porthole; it was set into the fuselage of a B-17 like a distended navel—like a nipple on the bomber's belly. In this tiny dome were two fifty-caliber machine guns and a short, small man whose chore was to track in his gunsights a fighter plane attacking his bomber. When the turret moved, the gunner revolved with it. There were wooden handles with buttons on the tops to fire the guns; gripping these trigger sticks, the ball turret gunner looked like some dangerous fetus suspended in the bomber's absurdly exposed amniotic sac, intent on protecting his mother. These handles also steered the turret—to a cut-off point, so that the ball turret gunner would not shoot off the props forward.

"With the sky *under* him, the gunner must have felt especially cold, appended to the plane like an afterthought. Upon landing, the ball turret was retracted—usually. Upon landing, an *un*retracted ball turret would send up sparks—as long and violent as automobiles—off the old tarmac."

Technical Sergeant Garp, the late gunner whose familiarity with violent death cannot be exaggerated, served with the Eighth Air Force—the air force that bombed the Continent from England. Sergeant Garp had experience as a nose gunner in the B-17C and a waist gunner in the B-17E before they made him a ball turret gunner.

Garp did not like the waist gun arrangements on the B-17E. There were two waist gunners tucked into the rib cage of the plane, their gunports opposite each other, and Garp was always getting clouted in the ears when his mate swiveled his gun at the same time Garp was moving with his. In later models, precisely because of this interference between the waist gunners, the gunports would be staggered. But this innovation would happen too late for Sergeant Garp.

His first combat mission was a daylight sortie by B-17Es against Rouen, France, on August 17, 1942, which was accomplished without losses. Technical Sergeant Garp, at his waist gun position, was clouted once on the left ear by his gunner mate and twice on the right. A part of the problem was that the other gunner, compared to Garp, was so large; the man's elbows were level with Garp's ears.

In the ball turret the first day over Rouen was a man named Fowler who was even smaller than Garp. Fowler had been a jockey before the war. He was a better shot than Garp, but the ball turret was where Garp wished he could be. He was an orphan but he must have liked being alone, and he sought some escape from the crowding and elbowing of his fellow waist gunner. Of course, like a great many gunners, Garp dreamed of his fiftieth mission or so, whereafter he hoped to be transferred to the Second Air Force—the bomber training command—where he could retire safely as a gunnery instructor. But until Fowler was killed, Garp envied Fowler his private place, his jockey's sense of isolation.

"It's a foul spot to be in if you fart a lot," Fowler maintained. He was a cynical man with a dry, irritating tickle of a cough and a vile reputation among the nurses at the field hospital.

Fowler was killed during a crash landing on an unpaved road. The landing struts were shorn off in a pothole and the whole landing gear collapsed, dropping the bomber into a hard belly slide that burst the ball turret with all the disproportionate force of a falling tree hitting a grape. Fowler, who'd always said he had more faith in machines than he had in horses or in human beings, was crouched in the unretracted ball turret when the plane landed on him. The waist gunners, including Sergeant Garp, saw the debris skid away from under the belly of the bomber. The squadron adjutant, who was the closest ground observer of the landing, threw up in a Jeep. The squadron commander did not have to wait for Fowler's death to become official in order to replace him with the squadron's next-smallest gunner. Tiny Technical Sergeant Garp had always wanted to be a ball turret gunner. In September of 1942, he became one.

"My mother was a stickler for detail," Garp wrote. When they would bring in a new casualty, Jenny Fields was the first to ask the doctor how it happened. And Jenny classified them, silently: the Externals, the Vital Organs, the Absentees, and the Goners. And she found little gimmicks to help her remember their names and their disasters. Thus: Private Jones fell off his bones, Ensign Potter stopped a whopper, Corporal Estes lost his testes, Captain Flynn has no skin, Major Longfellow is short on answers.

Sergeant Garp was a mystery. On his thirty-fifth flight over France, the little ball turret gunner stopped shooting. The pilot noticed the absence of machine-gun fire from the ball turret and thought that Garp had taken a hit. If Garp had, the pilot had not felt it in the belly of his plane. He hoped Garp hadn't felt it much, either. After the plane landed, the pilot hurried to have Garp transferred to the sidecar of a medic's motorcycle; all the ambulances were in use. Once seated in the sidecar, the tiny technical sergeant began to play with himself. There was a canvas canopy that covered the sidecar in foul weather; the pilot snapped this covering in place. The canopy had a porthole, through which the medic, the pilot, and the gathering men could observe Sergeant Garp. For such a small man, he seemed to have an especially large erection, but he fumbled with it only a little more expertly than a child—not nearly so expertly as a monkey in the zoo. Like the monkey, however, Garp looked out of his cage and stared frankly into the faces of the human beings who were watching him.

"Garp?" the pilot said. Garp's forehead was freckled with blood, which was mostly dry, but his flight hat was plastered to the top of his head and dripping; there didn't seem to be a mark on him. "Garp!" the pilot shouted at him. There had been a gash in the metal sphere where the fifty-caliber machine guns had been; it appeared that some flak had hit the barrels of the guns, cracking the gun housing and even loosening the trigger handles, though there was nothing wrong with Garp's hands—they just seemed to be clumsy at masturbation.

"Garp!" cried the pilot.

"Garp?" said Garp. He was mimicking the pilot, like a smart parrot or a crow. "Garp," said Garp, as if he had just learned the word. The pilot nodded to Garp, encouraging him to remember his name. Garp smiled. "Garp," he said. He seemed to think this was how people greeted each other. Not hello, hello!—but Garp, Garp!

"Jesus, Garp," the pilot said. Some holes and glass cracks had been visible in the porthole of the ball turret. The medic now unzipped the porthole of the sidecar's canopy and peered into Garp's eyes. Something was wrong with Garp's eyes, because they rolled around independently of each other; the medic thought that the world, for Garp, was probably looming up, then going by, then looming up again—if Garp could see at all. What the pilot and the medic couldn't know, at the time, was that some sharp and slender shards from the flak blast had damaged one of the oculomotor nerves in Garp's brain—and other parts of his brain as well. The oculomotor nerve consists chiefly of motor fibers that innervate most of the muscles of the eyeball. As for the rest of Garp's brain, he had received some cuts and slashes a lot like a prefrontal lobotomy—though it was rather careless surgery.

The medic had a great fear of *how* carelessly a lobotomy had been performed on Sergeant Garp, and for that reason he thought against taking off the blood-sodden flight hat which was stuck to Garp and yanked down to where it touched a taut, shiny knob that appeared, now, to be growing on his forehead. Everyone looked around for the medic's motorcyclist, but he was off vomiting somewhere and the medic supposed he would have to find someone to sit in the sidecar with Garp while he drove the motorcycle himself.

"Garp?" Garp said to the medic, trying his new word.

"Garp," the medic confirmed. Garp seemed pleased. He had both his small hands on his impressive erection when he successfully masturbated.

"Garp!" he barked. There was joy in his voice, but also surprise. He rolled his eyes at his audience, begging the world to loom up and hold still. He was unsure of what he'd done. "Garp?" he asked, doubtfully.

The pilot patted his arm and nodded to the others of the flight and landing crew, as if to say: Let's give a bit of support to the sergeant, men. Please, let's make him feel at home. And the men, respectfully dumb-struck by Garp's ejaculation, all said, "Garp! Garp!

Garp!" to him—a reassuring, seallike chorus intent on putting Garp at ease.

Garp nodded his head, happily, but the medic held his arm and whispered anxiously to him, "No! Don't move your head, okay? Garp? Please don't move your head." Garp's eyes roamed past the pilot and the medic, who waited for them to come around again. "Easy does it, Garp," the pilot whispered. "Just sit tight, okay?"

Garp's face radiated pure peace. With both hands holding his dying erection, the little sergeant looked as if he had done just the thing that the situation called for.

They could do nothing for Sergeant Garp in England. He was lucky to have been brought home to Boston long before the end of the war. Some senator was actually responsible. An editorial in a Boston newspaper had accused the U.S. Navy of transporting wounded servicemen back home only if the wounded came from wealthy and important American families. In an effort to quell such a vile rumor, a U.S. senator claimed that if *any* of the severely wounded were lucky enough to get back to America, "even an *orphan* would get to make the trip—just like anyone else." There was then some scurrying around to come up with a wounded orphan, to prove the senator's point, but they came up with a perfect person.

Not only was Technical Sergeant Garp an orphan; he was an idiot with a one-word vocabulary, so he was not complaining to the press. And in all the photographs they took, Gunner Garp was smiling.

When the drooling sergeant was brought to Boston Mercy, Jenny Fields had trouble categorizing him. He was clearly an Absentee, more docile than a child, but she wasn't sure how much else was wrong with him.

"Hello. How are you?" she asked him, when they wheeled him—grinning—into the ward.

"Garp!" he barked. The oculomotor nerve had been partially restored, and his eyes now leapt, rather than rolled, but his hands were wrapped in gauze mittens, the result of Garp's playing in an accidental fire that broke out in the hospital compound aboard his transport ship. He'd seen the flames and had reached out his hands to them, spreading some of the flames up to his face; he'd singed off his eyebrows. He looked a lot like a shaved owl, to Jenny.

With the burns, Garp was an External and an Absentee all at once. Also, with his hands so heavily bandaged, he had lost the ability to masturbate, an activity that his papers said he pursued frequently and successfully—and without any self-consciousness. Those who'd observed him closely, since his accident with the ship's fire, feared that the childish gunner was becoming depressed—his one adult pleasure taken from him, at least until his hands healed.

It was possible, of course, that Garp had Vital Organ damage as well. Many fragments had entered his head; many of them were too delicately located to be removed. Sergeant Garp's brain damage might not stop with his crude lobotomy; his internal destruction could be progressing. "Our general deterioration is complicated enough," Garp wrote, "without the introduction of flak to our systems."

There'd been a patient before Sergeant Garp whose head had been similarly penetrated. He'd been fine for months, just talking to himself and occasionally peeing in his bed. Then he started to lose his hair; he had trouble completing his sentences. Just before he died, he began to develop breasts.

Given the evidence, the shadows, and the white needles in the X rays, Gunner Garp was probably a Goner. But to Jenny Fields he looked very nice. A small, neat man, the former ball turret gunner was as innocent and straightforward in his demands as a two-year-old. He cried "Garp!" when he was hungry and "Garp!" when he was glad; he asked "Garp?" when something puzzled him, or when addressing strangers, and he said "Garp" without the question mark when he recognized you. He usually did what he was told, but he couldn't be trusted; he forgot easily, and if one time he was as obedient as a six-year-old, another time he was as mindlessly curious as if he were one and a half.

His depressions, which were well documented in his transport papers, seemed to occur simultaneously with his erections. At these moments he would clamp his poor, grown-up peter between his gauzy, mittened hands and weep. He wept because the gauze didn't feel as good as his short memory of his hands, and also because it hurt his hands to touch anything. It was then that Jenny Fields would come sit with him. She would rub his back between his shoulder blades until he tipped back his head like a cat, and she'd talk to him all the while, her voice friendly and full of exciting shifts of accent. Most nurses droned to their patients—a steady, changeless voice intent on producing sleep, but Jenny knew that it wasn't sleep Garp needed. She knew he was only a baby, and he was bored—he needed some distraction. So Jenny entertained him. She played the radio for him, but some of the programs upset Garp; no one knew why. Other programs gave him terrific erections, which led to his depressions, and so forth. One program, just once, gave Garp a wet dream, which so surprised and pleased him that he was always eager to *see* the radio. But Jenny couldn't find that program again, she couldn't repeat the performance. She knew that if she could plug poor Garp into the wet-dream program, her job and his life would be much happier. But it wasn't that easy.

She gave up trying to teach him a new word. When she fed him and she saw that he liked what he was eating, she'd say, "Good! That's *good.*"

"Garp!" he'd agree.

And when he spat out food on his bib and made a terrible face, she'd say, "Bad! That stuff's *bad,* right?"

"Garp!" he'd gag.

The first sign Jenny had of his deterioration was when

25

he seemed to lose the G. One morning he greeted her with an "Arp."

"*G*arp," she said firmly to him. "G-arp."

"Arp," he said. She knew she was losing him.

Daily he seemed to grow younger. When he slept, he kneaded the air with his wriggling fists, his lips puckering, his cheeks sucking, his eyelids trembling. Jenny had spent a lot of time around babies; she knew that the ball turret gunner was nursing in his dreams. For a while she contemplated stealing a pacifier from maternity, but she stayed away from that place now; the jokes irritated her ("Here's Virgin Mary Jenny, swiping a phony nipple for her child. Who's the lucky father, Jenny?"). She watched Sergeant Garp suckle in his sleep and tried to imagine that his ultimate regression would be peaceful, that he would turn into his fetus phase and no longer breathe through his lungs; that his personality would blissfully separate, half of him turning to dreams of an egg, half of him to dreams of sperm. Finally, he simply wouldn't *be* anymore.

It was almost like that. Garp's nursing phase became so severe that he seemed to wake up like a child on a four-hour feeding schedule; he even cried like a baby, his face scarlet, his eyes springing tears in an instant, and in an instant being pacified—by the radio, by Jenny's voice. Once, when she rubbed his back, he burped. Jenny burst into tears. She sat at his bedside wishing him a swift, painless journey back into the womb and beyond.

If only his hands would heal, she thought. Then he could suck his thumb. When he woke from his suckling dreams, hungry to nurse, or so he imagined, Jenny would put her own finger to his mouth and let his lips tug at her. Though he had real, grown-up teeth, in his *mind* he was toothless and he never bit her. It was this observation that led Jenny, one night, to offer him her breast, where he sucked inexhaustibly and didn't seem to mind that there was nothing to be had there. Jenny thought that if he kept nursing at her, she *would* have

milk; she felt such a firm tug in her womb, both maternal
and sexual. Her feelings were so vivid—she believed
for a while that she could possibly *conceive* a child
simply by suckling the baby ball turret gunner.

It was almost like that. But Gunner Garp was not
*all* baby. One night, when he nursed at her, Jenny
noticed he had an erection that lifted the sheet; with his
clumsy, bandaged hands he fanned himself, yelping
frustration while he wolfed at her breast. And so one
night she helped him; with her cool, powdered hand she
took hold of him. At her breast he stopped nursing, he
just nuzzled her.

"Ar," he moaned. He had lost the *P*.

Once a Garp, then an Arp, now only an Ar; she
knew he was dying. He had just one vowel and one
consonant left.

When he came, she felt his shot wet and hot in her
hand. Under the sheet it smelled like a greenhouse in
summer, absurdly fertile, growth gotten out of hand.
You could plant *anything* there and it would blossom.
Garp's sperm struck Jenny Fields that way: if you
spilled a little in a greenhouse, *babies* would sprout out
of the dirt.

Jenny gave the matter twenty-four hours of thought.

"Garp?" Jenny whispered.

She unbuttoned the blouse of her dress and brought
forth the breasts she had always considered too large.
"Garp?" she whispered in his ear; his eyelids fluttered,
his lips reached. Around them was a white shroud, a curtain on runners, which enclosed them in the ward. On
one side of Garp was an External—a flame-thrower
victim, slippery with salve, swaddled in gauze. He had
no eyelids, so it appeared he was always watching, but
he was blind. Jenny took off her sturdy nurse's shoes,
unfastened her white stockings, stepped out of her dress.
She touched her finger to Garp's lips.

On the other side of Garp's white-shrouded bed was
a Vital Organ patient on his way to becoming an Ab-

sentee. He had lost most of his lower intestine and his rectum; now a kidney was giving him trouble and his liver was driving him crazy. He had terrible nightmares that he was being forced to urinate and defecate, though this was ancient history for him. He was actually quite unaware when he did those things, and he did them through tubes into rubber bags. He groaned frequently and, unlike Garp, he groaned in whole words.

"Shit," he groaned.

"Garp?" Jenny whispered. She stepped out of her slip and her panties; she took off her bra and pulled back the sheet.

"Christ," said the External, softly; his lips were blistered with burns.

"Goddamn shit!" cried the Vital Organ man.

"Garp," said Jenny Fields. She took hold of his erection and straddled him.

"Aaa," said Garp. Even the *r* was gone. He was reduced to a vowel sound to express his joy or his sadness. "Aaa," he said, as Jenny drew him inside her and sat on him with all her weight.

"Garp?" she asked. "Okay? Is that good, Garp?"

*"Good,"* he agreed, distinctly. But it was only a word from his wrecked memory, thrown clear for a moment when he came inside her. It was the first and last true word that Jenny Fields heard him speak: good. As he shrank and his vital stuff seeped from her, he was once again reduced to Aaa's; he closed his eyes and slept. When Jenny offered him her breast, he wasn't hungry.

"God!" called the External, being very gentle with the *d;* his tongue had been burned, too.

"Piss!" snarled the Vital Organ man.

Jenny Fields washed Garp and herself with warm water and soap in a white enamel hospital bowl. She wasn't going to douche, of course, and she had no doubt that the magic had worked. She felt more receptive than prepared soil—the nourished earth—and she had felt Garp shoot up inside her as generously as a hose in summer (as if he could water a lawn).

She never did it with him again. There was no reason. She didn't enjoy it. From time to time she helped him with her hand, and when he cried for it, she gave him her breast, but in a few weeks he had no more erections. When they took the bandages off his hands, they noticed that even the healing process seemed to be working in reverse; they wrapped him back up again. He lost all interest in nursing. His dreams struck Jenny as the dreams a fish might have. He was back in the womb, Jenny knew; he resumed a fetal position, tucked up small in the center of the bed. He made no sound at all. One morning Jenny watched him kick with his small, weak feet; she imagined she felt a kick *inside*. Though it was too soon for the real thing, she knew the real thing was on its way.

Soon Garp stopped kicking. He still got his oxygen by breathing air with his lungs, but Jenny knew this was simply an example of human adaptability. He wouldn't eat; they had to feed him intravenously, so once again he was attached to a kind of umbilical cord. Jenny anticipated his last phase with some anxiousness. Would there be a struggle at the end, like the sperm's frantic struggle? Would the sperm shield be lifted and the naked egg wait, expectantly, for death? In little Garp's return trip, how would his *soul* at last divide? But the phase passed without Jenny's observation. One day, when she was off duty, Technical Sergeant Garp died.

"When *else* could he have died?" Garp has written. "With my mother off duty was the only way he could escape."

"Of course I *felt* something when he died," Jenny Fields wrote in her famous autobiography. "But the best of him was inside me. That was the best thing for both of us, the only way he could go on living, the only way I wanted to have a child. That the rest of the world finds this an immoral act only shows me that the rest of the world doesn't respect the rights of an individual."

It was 1943. When Jenny's pregnancy was apparent,

she lost her job. Of course, it was all that her parents and brothers had expected; they weren't surprised. Jenny had long ago stopped trying to convince them of her purity. She moved through the big corridors in the parental estate at Dog's Head Harbor like a satisfied ghost. Her composure alarmed her family, and they left her alone. Secretly, Jenny was quite happy, but with all the musing she must have done about this expected child, it's a wonder she never gave a thought to names.

Because, when Jenny Fields gave birth to a nine-pound baby boy, she had no name in mind. Jenny's mother asked her what she wanted to name him, but Jenny had just delivered and had just received her sedative; she was not cooperative.

"Garp," she said.

Her father, the footwear king, thought she had burped, but her mother whispered to him, "The name is *Garp*."

"Garp?" he said. They knew they might find out who this baby's father was, this way. Jenny, of course, had not admitted a thing.

"Find out if that's the son of a bitch's first name or last name," Jenny's father whispered to Jenny's mother.

"Is that a first name or a last name, dear?" Jenny's mother asked her.

Jenny was very sleepy. "It's Garp," she said. "Just Garp. That's the whole thing."

"I think it's a last name," Jenny's mother told Jenny's father.

"What's his *first* name?" Jenny's father asked crossly.

"I never knew," Jenny mumbled. This is true; she never did.

"She never knew his first name!" her father roared.

"Please, dear," her mother said. "He *must* have a first name."

"Technical Sergeant Garp," said Jenny Fields.

"A goddamn soldier, I knew it!" her father said.

"Technical Sergeant?" Jenny's mother asked her.

30

"T. S.," Jenny Fields said. "T. S. Garp. That's my baby's name." She fell asleep.

Her father was furious. "T. S. Garp!" he hollered. "What kind of a name for a baby is *that?*"

"All his own," Jenny told him, later. "It's his *own* goddamn name, all his own."

"It was great fun going to school with a name like that," Garp has written. "The teachers would ask you what the initials stood for. First I used to say that they were *just* initials, but they never believed me. So I'd have to say, 'Call my mom. She'll tell you.' And they would. And old Jenny would give them a piece of her mind."

Thus was the world given T. S. Garp: born from a good nurse with a will of her own, and the seed of a ball turret gunner—his last shot.

# 2

⊰⊱⊰⊱⊰⊱⊰⊱⊰⊱⊰⊱

# Blood and Blue

T. S. GARP always suspected he would die young. "Like my father," Garp wrote, "I believe I have a knack for brevity. I'm a one-shot man."

Garp narrowly escaped growing up on the grounds of an all-girls' school, where his mother was offered the position of school nurse. But Jenny Fields saw the possibly harrowing future that would have been involved in this decision: her little Garp surrounded by women (Jenny and Garp were offered an apartment in one of the dorms). She imagined her son's first sexual experience: a fantasy inspired by the sight and feel of the all-girls' laundry room, where, as a game, the girls would bury the child in soft mountains of young women's underwear. Jenny would have liked the job, but it was for Garp's sake that she turned down the offer. She was hired instead by the vast and famous Steering School, where she would be simply one more school nurse among many, and where the apartment offered her and Garp was in the cold, prison-windowed wing of the school's infirmary annex.

"Never mind," her father told her. He was irritated with her that she chose to work at all; there was money enough, and he'd have been happier if she'd gone into hiding at the family estate in Dog's Head Harbor until her bastard son had grown up and moved away. "If the child has any native intelligence," Jenny's father told her, "he should eventually *attend* Steering, but in the meantime, I suppose, there's no better atmosphere for a boy to be raised in."

"Native intelligence" was one of the ways her father had of referring to Garp's dubious genetic background. The Steering School, where Jenny's father and brothers had gone, was at that time an all-boys' school. Jenny believed that if she could endure her confinement there—through young Garp's prep school years—she would be doing her best for her son. "To make up for denying him a father," as her father put it to her.

"It's odd," Garp wrote, "that my mother, who perceived herself well enough to know that she wanted nothing to do with living with a man, ended up living with eight hundred boys."

So young Garp grew up with his mother in the infirmary annex of the Steering School. He was not exactly treated as a "faculty brat"—the students' term for all the underage children of the faculty and staff. A school nurse was not considered in quite the same class or category as a faculty member. Moreover, Jenny made no attempt to invent a mythology for Garp's father—to make up a marriage story for herself, to legitimize her son. She was a Fields, she made a point of telling you her name. Her son was a Garp. She made a point of telling you *his* name. "It's his own name," she said.

Everyone got the picture. Not only were certain kinds of arrogance tolerated by the society of the Steering School, certain kinds were encouraged; but acceptable arrogance was a matter of taste and style. *What* you were arrogant about had to appear worthy—of higher purpose—and the manner in which you were arrogant was supposed to be charming. Wit did not come naturally to Jenny Fields. Garp wrote that his mother "never chose to be arrogant but was only arrogant under duress." Pride was well loved in the community of the Steering School, but Jenny Fields appeared to be proud of an illegitimate child. Nothing to hang her head about, perhaps; however, she might show a *little* humility.

But Jenny was not only proud of Garp, she was especially pleased with the manner in which she had gotten him. The world did not know that manner, yet; Jenny had not brought out her autobiography—she hadn't begun to write it, in fact. She was waiting for Garp to be old enough to appreciate the story.

The story Garp knew was all that Jenny would tell anyone who was bold enough to ask. Jenny's story was a sober three sentences long.

1. The father of Garp was a soldier.
2. The war killed him.
3. Who took the time for weddings when there was a war?

Both the precision and mystery of this story might have been interpreted romantically. After all, given the mere facts, the father might have been a war hero. A doomed love affair could be imagined. Nurse Fields might have been a field nurse. She might have fallen in love "at the front." And the father of Garp might have felt he owed one last mission "to the men." But Jenny Fields did not inspire the imagination of such a melodrama. For one thing, she seemed too pleased with her aloneness; she didn't appear in the least misty about the past. She was never distracted, she was simply all for little Garp—and for being a good nurse.

Of course, the Fields name was known at the Steering School. The famous footwear king of New England was a generous alumnus, and whether or not it was suspected at the time, he would even become a trustee. His was not the oldest but not the newest of New England money, and his wife, Jenny's mother—a former Boston Weeks—was perhaps still better known at Steering. Among the older faculty there were those who could remember years and years, without interruption, when there had always been a graduating Weeks. Yet, to the Steering School, Jenny Fields didn't seem to have inherited all the credentials. She was handsome, they would admit, but she was plain; she wore her nurse's uniform when she could have dressed in something smarter. In fact, this whole business of being a nurse—of which she also appeared too proud—was curious. Considering her family. Nursing was not enough of a profession for a Fields or a Weeks.

Socially, Jenny had that kind of graceless seriousness which makes more frivolous people uncomfortable. She read a lot and was a great ransacker of the Steering library; the book someone wanted was always discovered to be checked out to Nurse Fields. Phone calls were politely answered; Jenny frequently offered to deliver the book directly to the party who wanted it, as soon as she finished it. She finished such books promptly, but she had nothing to say about them. In a school community, someone who reads a book for some secretive purpose, other than discussing it, is strange. What was she reading for?

That she attended classes in her off-duty hours was stranger still. It was written in the constitution of the Steering School that faculty and staff and/or their spouses could attend, free of charge, any course offered at Steering, simply by securing the permission of the instructor. Who would turn away a nurse?—from the Elizabethans, from the Victorian Novel, from the History of Russia until 1917, from an Introduction to Genetics, from Western Civilization I and II. Over the years Jenny Fields would march from Caesar to Eisenhower—past Luther and Lenin, Erasmus and mitosis, osmosis and Freud, Rembrandt and chromosomes and van Gogh—from the Styx to the Thames, from Homer to Virginia Woolf. From Athens to Auschwitz, she never said a word. She was the only woman in the classes. In her white uniform she listened so quietly that the boys and finally the teacher forgot her and relaxed; they went on with the learning process while she sat keenly white and still among them, a witness to everything—maybe determining nothing, possibly judging it all.

Jenny Fields was getting the education she had waited for; now the time seemed ripe. But her motives were not wholly selfish; she was screening the Steering School for her son. When Garp was old enough to attend, she'd be able to give him lots of advice—she'd know the deadweights in every department, those courses that meandered and those that sang.

Her books spilled out of the tiny wing apartment in the infirmary annex. She spent ten years at the Steering School before discovering that the bookstore offered a 10 percent discount to the faculty and staff (which the bookstore had never offered her). This made her angry. She was generous with her books, too—eventually shelving them in every room of the bleak infirmary annex. But they outgrew the shelf space and slid into the main infirmary, into the waiting room, and into X-ray, first covering and then replacing the newspapers and the magazines. Slowly, the sick of the Steering School learned what a serious place Steering was—not your ordinary hospital, crammed with light reading and the media trash. While you waited to see the doctor, you could browse through *The Waning of the Middle Ages;* waiting for your lab results, you could ask the nurse to bring you that invaluable genetics manual, *The Fruit Fly Handbook.* If you were seriously ill, or might be visiting the infirmary for a long time, there was sure to be a copy of *The Magic Mountain.* For the boy with the broken leg, and all the athletically wounded, there were the good heroes and their meaty adventures—there were Conrad and Melville instead of *Sports Illustrated;* instead of *Time* and *Newsweek,* there were Dickens and Hemingway and Twain. What a wet dream for the lovers of literature, to lie sick at Steering! At last, a hospital with something good to read.

When Jenny Fields had spent twelve years at Steering, it was a habit among the school librarians, upon

recognizing that they didn't have a book which someone sought, to say, "Perhaps the infirmary has it."

And at the bookstore, when something was out of
stock or out of print, they might recommend that you
"find Nurse Fields over at the infirmary; *she* might have
it."

And Jenny would frown upon hearing the request,
and say, "I believe that's in twenty-six, at the annex, but
McCarty is reading it. He has the flu. Perhaps when
he's through, he'll be glad to let you have it." Or she
might respond, "I last saw that one down at the whirlpool bath. It might be a little wet, in the beginning."

It is impossible to judge Jenny's influence on the
quality of education at Steering, but she never got over
her anger at being cheated out of the 10 percent discount for ten years. "My mother supported that bookstore," Garp wrote. "By comparison, nobody else at
Steering ever read anything."

When Garp was two, the Steering School offered
Jenny a three-year contract; she was a good nurse,
everyone agreed, and the slight distaste that everyone
felt toward her had not increased in those first two
years. The baby, after all, was like *any* baby; perhaps
a little darker-skinned in summer than most, and a little
sallow-skinned in winter—and a little fat. There was
something rounded about him, like a bundled Eskimo,
even when he wasn't actually bundled. And those
younger faculty who had just gotten over the last war
remarked that the shape of the child was as blunt as a
bomb. But illegitimate children are still children, after
all. The irritation at Jenny's oddness was acceptably
mild.

She accepted the three-year contract. She was learning, improving herself but also preparing the way
through Steering for her Garp. "A superior education"
is what the Steering School could offer, her father had
said. Jenny thought she'd better make sure.

When Garp was five, Jenny Fields was made head nurse. It was hard to find young, active nurses who could tolerate the freshness and wild behavior of the boys; it was hard to find anyone willing to live in, and Jenny seemed quite content to stay in her wing of the infirmary annex. In this sense she became a mother to many: up in the night when one of the boys threw up, or buzzed her, or smashed his water glass. Or when the occasionally bad boys fooled around in the dark aisles, raced their hospital beds, engaged in gladiatorial combat in wheelchairs, stole conversations with girls from the town through the iron-grate windows, attempted to climb down, or up, the thick rungs of ivy that laced the old brick buildings of the infirmary and its annex.

The infirmary was connected to the annex by an underground tunnel, wide enough for a bed-on-wheels with a slim nurse on either side of it. The bad boys occasionally *bowled* in the tunnel, the sound reaching Jenny and Garp in their faraway wing—as if the test rats and rabbits in the basement laboratory had overnight grown terribly large and were rolling the rubbish barrels deeper underground with their powerful snouts.

But when Garp was five—when his mother was made head nurse—the Steering School community noticed something strange about him. What could be exactly different about a five-year-old boy is not clear, but there was a certain sleek, dark, wet look to his head (like the head of a seal), and the exaggerated compactness of his body brought back the old speculations about his genes. Temperamentally, the child appeared to resemble his mother: determined, possibly dull, aloof but eternally watchful. Although he was small for his age, he seemed unnaturally mature in other ways; he had a discomforting calmness. Close to the ground, like a well-balanced animal, he seemed unusually well coordinated. Other mothers noted, with occasional alarm, that the child could *climb* anything. Look at jungle gyms, swing sets, high slides, bleacher seats, the most dangerous trees: Garp would be at the top of them.

One night after supper, Jenny could not find him. Garp was free to wander through the infirmary and the annex, talking to the boys, and Jenny normally paged him on the intercom when she wanted him back in the apartment. "GARP HOME," she'd say. He had his instructions: which rooms he was not to visit, the contagious cases, the boys who felt really rotten and would prefer to be left alone. Garp liked the athletic injuries best; he liked looking at casts and slings and big bandages, and he liked listening to the cause of the injury, over and over again. Like his mother, perhaps— a nurse at heart—he was happy to run errands for the patients, deliver messages, sneak food. But one night, when he was five, Garp did not respond to the GARP HOME call. The intercom was broadcast through every room of the infirmary and the annex, even those rooms Garp was under strict orders not to be in—the lab, surgery, and X-ray. If Garp couldn't hear the GARP HOME message, Jenny knew that he was either in trouble or not in the buildings. She quickly organized a search party among the healthier and more mobile patients.

It was a foggy night in the early spring; some boys went outside and called through the damp forsythia and the parking lot. Others poked through the dark, empty nooks and the forbidden equipment rooms. Jenny indulged her first fears first. She checked the laundry chute, a slick cylinder that for four floors dropped straight down to the basement (Garp was not allowed even to put laundry down the chute). But beneath where the chute shot through the ceiling, and spewed its contents on the basement floor, there was only laundry on the cold cement. She checked the boiler room and the scalding, huge, hot-water furnace, but Garp had not been cooked there. She checked the stairwells, but Garp was instructed not to play on the stairs and he wasn't lying broken at the bottom of any of the four-story wells. Then she started in on her unexpressed fears that little Garp would fall victim to a secret sex violator among the Steering School boys. But in the early spring there were too many boys in the infirmary for Jenny to keep track of them all—much less know them well enough to suspect their sexual tastes. There were the fools who went swimming on that first sunny day, even before the snow was off the ground. There were the last victims of drag-on winter colds, their various resistances worn down. There were the culminating winter-sports injuries and the first to be injured in spring-sports practice.

One such person was Hathaway, who, Jenny heard, was buzzing her now from his room on the fourth floor of the annex. Hathaway was a lacrosse player who had done ligament damage to his knee; two days after they put him in a cast and turned him loose on crutches, Hathaway had gone out in the rain and his crutch tips had slipped at the top of the long marble stairs of Hyle Hall. In the fall, he had broken his other leg. Now Hathaway, with both his long legs in casts, sprawled in his bed on the fourth floor of the infirmary annex, a lacrosse stick held fondly in his large-knuckled hands. He had been put out of the way, almost all by himself on the fourth floor of the annex, because of his irritating habit of flinging a lacrosse ball across his room and letting it carom off the wall. Then he snared the hard, bouncy ball in the looping basket on the end of his lacrosse stick and flicked it back against the wall. Jenny could have put a stop to this, but she had a son of her own, after all, and she recognized the need in boys to devote themselves, mindlessly, to a repetitious physical act. It seemed to relax them, Jenny had noticed—whether they were five, like Garp, or seventeen, like Hathaway.

But it made her furious that Hathaway was so clumsy with his lacrosse stick that he was always losing his ball! She had gone out of her way to put him where other patients would not complain about the thumping,

41

but whenever Hathaway lost his ball, he buzzed for someone to fetch it for him; although there was an elevator, the fourth floor of the annex was out of everyone's way. When Jenny saw the elevator was in use, she went up the four flights of stairs too quickly, and was out of breath, as well as angry, when she got to Hathaway's room.

"I *know* how much your game means to you, Hathaway," Jenny said, "but right now Garp is lost and I don't really have time to retrieve your ball."

Hathaway was an ever-pleasant, slow-thinking boy with a slack, hairless face and a forward-falling flop of reddish-blond hair, which partially hid one of his pale eyes. He had a habit of tipping his head back, perhaps so that he could see out from under his hair, and for this reason, and the fact that he was tall, everyone who looked at Hathaway looked up his wide nostrils.

"Miss Fields?" he said. Jenny noticed he was not holding his lacrosse stick.

"What *is* it, Hathaway?" Jenny asked. "I'm sorry I'm in a rush, but Garp is lost. I'm looking for *Garp*."

"Oh," Hathaway said. He looked around his room—perhaps for Garp—as if someone had just asked him for an ashtray. "I'm sorry," Hathaway said. "I wish I could help you look for him." He stared helplessly at both his casts.

Jenny rapped lightly on one of his plastered knees, as if she were knocking on a door behind which someone might be asleep. "Don't worry, please," she said; she waited for him to tell her what he wanted, but Hathaway seemed to have forgotten that he'd buzzed her. "Hathaway?" she asked, again knocking on his leg to see if anyone was home. "What did you *want*? Did you lose your ball?"

"No," Hathaway said. "I've lost my *stick*." Mechanically, they both took a moment to look around Hathaway's room for the missing lacrosse stick. "I was asleep," he explained, "and when I woke up, it was gone."

42

Jenny first thought of Meckler, the menace of the second-floor annex. Meckler was a sarcastically brilliant boy who was in the infirmary at least four days out of every month. He was a chain smoker at sixteen, he edited most of the school's student publications, and he had twice won the annual Classics Cup. Meckler scorned dining-hall food and lived on coffee and fried-egg sandwiches from Buster's Snack and Grill, where he actually wrote most of his long and long-overdue, but brilliant, term papers. Collapsing in the infirmary each month to recover from his physical self-abuse, and his brilliance, Meckler's mind turned to hideous pranks that Jenny could never quite prove him guilty of. Once there were boiled polliwogs in the teapot sent down to the lab technicians, who complained of the fishiness of the tea; once, Jenny was sure, Meckler had filled a prophylactic with egg whites and slipped its snug neck over the doorknob to her apartment. She knew the filling had been egg whites only because she later found the shells. In her purse. And it had been Meckler, Jenny was sure, who had organized the third floor of the infirmary during the chicken pox epidemic of a few years ago: the boys were beating off, in turn, and rushing with their hot spunk in their hands to the microscopes in the infirmary lab—to see if they were sterile.

But Meckler's style, Jenny thought, would have been to cut a hole in the netting of the lacrosse stick—and to have left the useless stick in the sleeping Hathaway's hands.

"I'll bet Garp has it," Jenny told Hathaway. "When we find Garp, we'll find your stick." She resisted, for the hundredth time, the impulse to take her hand and brush back the flop of hair that nearly hid one of Hathaway's eyes; instead, she gently squeezed Hathaway's big toes where they thrust out of his casts.

If Garp was going to play lacrosse, Jenny thought, where would he go? Not out, because it's dark; he'd lose the ball. And the only place he might not have heard the intercom was in the underground tunnel between the annex and the infirmary—a perfect place for flinging that ball, Jenny knew. It had been done before; once Jenny had broken up an after-midnight scrimmage. She took the elevator directly to the basement. Hathaway is a sweet boy, she was thinking; Garp could do worse than grow up to be like that. But he could do better, too.

However slowly, Hathaway was thinking. He hoped little Garp was all right; he sincerely wished he could get up to help find the child. Garp was a frequent visitor to Hathaway's room. A crippled athlete with two casts was better than average. Hathaway had allowed Garp to draw all over his plastered legs; over and through the signatures of friends were the looping, crayoned faces and monsters of Garp's imagination. Hathaway now looked at the child's drawings on his casts and worried about Garp. That was why he saw the lacrosse ball, between his thighs; he had not felt it, through the plaster. It lay there as if it were Hathaway's own egg, keeping warm. How could Garp play lacrosse without a ball?

When he heard the pigeons, Hathaway knew Garp wasn't playing lacrosse. The pigeons! he remembered. He had complained about them to the boy. The pigeons kept Hathaway awake at night with their damn cooing, their cluckish fussing under the eaves and in the rain gutter beneath the steep slate roof. That was a problem with the sleeping conditions on the fourth and topmost floor; that was a problem for every top-floor sleeper at the Steering School—*pigeons* seemed to rule the campus. The maintenance men had caged off most of the eaves and perches with chicken wire, but the pigeons roosted in the rain gutters, in dry weather, and found niches under the roofs, and perches on the old gnarled ivy. There was no way to keep them off the buildings. And how they could coo! Hathaway hated them. He'd told Garp that if he had even *one* good leg, he would get them.

"How?" Garp asked.

"They don't like to fly at night," Hathaway told the boy. It was in Bio. II that Hathaway had learned about the habits of pigeons; Jenny Fields had taken the same course. "I could get up on the roof," Hathaway told Garp, "at night—when it wasn't raining—and trap them in the rain gutter. That's all they do, just sit in the rain gutter and coo and crap all night."

"But *how* would you trap them?" Garp asked.

And Hathaway twirled his lacrosse stick, cradling the ball. He rolled the ball between his legs, he dropped the net of the stick gently over Garp's little head. "Like that," he said. "With this, I'd get them easy—with my lacrosse stick. One by one, until I got them all."

Hathaway remembered how Garp had smiled at him—this big friendly boy with his two heroic casts. Hathaway looked out the window, saw that it was indeed dark and not raining. Hathaway rang his buzzer. "Garp!" he cried out. "Oh, God." He held his thumb on the buzzer button and did not let up.

When Jenny Fields saw it was the fourth-floor light that was flashing, she could only think that Garp had brought Hathaway's lacrosse equipment back to him. What a good boy, she thought, and rode the elevator, up again, to the fourth floor. She ran squeakily on her good nurse's shoes to Hathaway's room. She saw the lacrosse ball in Hathaway's hand. His one eye, which was clearly in view, looked frightened.

"He's on the roof," Hathaway told her.

"On the roof!" Jenny said.

"He's trying to capture pigeons with my lacrosse stick," Hathaway said.

A full-grown man, if he stood on the fourth-floor fire-escape landing, could reach over the rim of the rain gutter with his hands. When the Steering School cleaned its rain gutters, only after all the leaves were fallen and before the heavy spring rains, only *tall* men were sent to do the job because the shorter men complained of reaching into the rain gutters and touching things they couldn't see—dead pigeons and well-rotted squirrels and unidentifiable glop. Only the tall men could stand on the fire-escape landings and peek into the rain gutters before they reached. The gutters were as wide and nearly as deep as pig troughs, but they were not as strong —and they were old. In those days, *everything* at the Steering School was old.

When Jenny Fields went out the fourth-floor fire door and stood on the fire escape, she could barely reach the rain gutter with her fingertips; she could not see over the rain gutter to the steep slate roof—and in the darkness and fog, she could not even see the underside of the rain gutter as far down as either corner of the building. She could not see Garp at all.

"Garp?" she whispered. Four stories below, among the shrubbery and the occasional glint from the hood or roof of a parked car, she could hear some of the boys calling him, too. "Garp?" she whispered, a little louder.

"Mom?" he asked, startling her—although his whisper was softer than hers. His voice came from somewhere close, almost within her reach, she thought, but she couldn't see him. Then she saw the netted basket end of the lacrosse stick silhouetted against the foggy moon like the strange, webbed paw of some unknown, nocturnal animal; it jutted out from the rain gutter, almost directly above her. Now, when she reached up, she was frightened to feel Garp's leg, broken through the corroded gutter, which had torn his pants and cut him, wedging him there, one leg through the gutter up to his hip, the other leg sprawled out in the gutter behind him, along the edge of the steep slate roof. Garp lay on his belly in the creaky rain gutter.

When he had broken through the gutter, he'd been too scared to cry out; he could feel that the whole flimsy trough was rotted through and ready to tear apart. His *voice,* he thought, could make the roof fall down. He lay with his cheek in the gutter, and through a tiny rusted hole he watched the boys in the parking lot and bushes, four stories below him, looking for him.

The lacrosse stick, which had indeed held a surprised pigeon, had swung out over the edge of the gutter, releasing the bird.

The pigeon, despite being captured and freed, had not moved. It squatted in the gutter, making its small, stupid sounds. Jenny realized that Garp could never have reached the rain gutter from the fire escape, and she shuddered to think of him climbing up the ivy to the roof with the lacrosse stick in one hand. She held his leg very tightly; his bare, warm calf was slightly sticky with blood, but he had not cut himself badly on the rusty gutter. A tetanus shot, she was thinking; the blood was almost dry and Jenny did not think he would need stitches—though, in the darkness, she could not clearly make out the wound. She was trying to think how she could get him down. Below her, the forsythia bushes winked in the light from the downstairs windows; from so far away, the yellow flowers looked (to her) like the tips of small gas flames.

"Mom?" Garp asked.

"Yes," she whispered. "I've got you."

"Don't let go," he said.

"Okay," she told him. As if triggered by her voice, a little more of the gutter gave way.

"Mom!" Garp said.

"It's okay," Jenny said. She wondered if the best way would be to yank him down, hard, and hope that she could pull him right through the rotten gutter. But then the whole gutter could possibly rip free of the roof—and *then* what? she thought. She saw them both swept off the fire escape and falling. But she knew no one could actually go up *on* the rain gutter and pull the child out of the hole, and then lower him to her over the edge. The gutter could barely support a five-year-old; it certainly couldn't support a grownup. And Jenny knew that she would not let go of Garp's leg long enough to let someone try.

It was the new nurse, Miss Creen, who saw them from the ground and ran inside to call Dean Bodger. Nurse

Creen was thinking of Dean Bodger's spotlight, fastened to the dean's dark car (which cruised the campus each night in search of boys out after curfew). Despite the complaints of the grounds' crew, Bodger drove down the footpaths and over the soft lawns, flashing his spotlight into the deep shrubs alongside the buildings, making the campus an unsafe place for lurkers—or for lovers, with no indoor place to go.

Nurse Creen also called Dr. Pell, because her mind, in a crisis, always ran to people who were supposed to take charge. She did not think of the fire department, a thought that was crossing Jenny's mind; but Jenny feared they would take too long and the gutter would collapse before they arrived; worse, she imagined, they would insist she let *them* handle everything and make her let go of Garp's leg.

Surprised, Jenny looked up at Garp's small, soggy sneaker, which now dangled in the sudden and ghastly glare of Dean Bodger's spotlight. The light was disturbing and confusing the pigeons, whose perception of dawn was probably not the best and who appeared almost ready to come to some decision in the rain gutter; their cooing and the scrabbling sounds of their claws grew more frantic.

Down on the lawn, running around Dean Bodger's car, the boys in their white hospital smocks appeared to have been bedlamized by the experience—or by Dean Bodger's sharp orders to run here or run there, fetch this or fetch that. Bodger called all the boys "men." As in "Let's have a line of mattresses under the fire escape, men! Double-quick!" he barked. Bodger had taught German for twenty years at Steering before being appointed dean; his commands sounded like the rapid-fire conjugating of German verbs.

The "men" piled mattresses and oogled through the skeletal fire escape at Jenny's marvelous white uniform in the spotlight. One of the boys stood flush to the building, well under the fire escape, and his view up Jenny's skirt and her spotlit legs must have dazzled him because he appeared to forget the crisis and he just *stood* there. "Schwarz!" Dean Bodger yelled at him, but his name was Warner and he did not respond. Dean Bodger had to shove him to make him stop staring. "More mattresses, Schmidt!" Bodger told him.

A piece of the gutter, or a particle of leaf, stuck in Jenny's eye and she had to spread her legs wider apart, for balance. When the gutter gave way, the pigeon Garp had caught was launched out of the broken end of the trough and forced into brief and frenzied flight. Jenny gagged at her first thought: that the pigeon blurring past her vision was the falling body of her son; but she reassured herself with her grip on Garp's leg. She was first knocked into a deep squat, and then thrown to one hip on the fire-escape landing, by the weight of a substantial chunk of the rain gutter that still contained Garp. Only when she realized that they were both safe on the landing, and sitting down, did Jenny let go of Garp's leg. An elaborate bruise, in the near-perfect form of her fingerprints, would be on his calf for a week.

From the ground, the scene was confusing. Dean Bodger saw a sudden movement of bodies above him, he heard the sound of the rain gutter ripping, he saw Nurse Fields fall. He saw a three-foot hunk of the rain gutter drop into the darkness, but he never saw the child. He saw what looked like a pigeon dart into and through the beam of his spotlight, but he did not follow the flight of the bird—blinded by the light, then lost in the night. The pigeon struck the iron edge of the fire escape and broke its neck. The pigeon wrapped its wings around itself and spiraled straight down, like a slightly soft football falling well out of the line of mattresses Bodger had ordered for the ultimate emergency. Bodger saw the bird falling and mistook its small, fast-moving body for the child.

Dean Bodger was a basically brave and tenacious man, the father of four rigorously raised children. His devotion to campus police work was not so much motivated by his desire to prevent people from having fun as stemming from his conviction that almost every accident was unnecessary and could, with cunning and industry, be avoided. Thus Bodger believed he could catch the falling child, because in his ever-anxious heart he was prepared for just such a situation as plucking a plummeting body out of the dark sky. The dean was as short-haired and muscular and curiously proportioned as a pit bull, and shared with that breed of dog a similar smallness of the eyes, which were always inflamed, as red-lidded and squinty as a pig's. Like a pit bull, too, Bodger was good at digging in and lunging forward, which he now did, his fierce arms outstretched, his piggy eyes never leaving the descending pigeon. "I've got you, son!" Bodger cried, which terrified the boys in their hospital smocks. They were unprepared for anything like this.

Dean Bodger, on the run, dove for the bird, which struck his chest with an impact even Bodger was not wholly prepared for. The pigeon sent the dean reeling, rolled him over on his back, where he felt the wind socked out of him and he lay gasping. The battered bird was hugged in his arms; its beak poked Bodger's bristly chin. One of the frightened boys cranked the spotlight down from the fourth floor and shone the beam directly on the dean. When Bodger saw that he clutched a pigeon to his breast, he threw the dead bird over the heads of the gaping boys and into the parking lot.

There was much fussing in the admittance room of the infirmary. Dr. Pell had arrived and he treated little Garp's leg—it was a ragged but superficial wound that needed a lot of trimming and cleaning, but no stitches. Nurse Creen gave the boy a tetanus shot while Dr. Pell removed a small, rusty particle from Jenny's eye; Jenny had strained her back supporting the weight of Garp and the rain gutter, but was otherwise fine. The aura of the admittance room was hearty and jocular, except when Jenny was able to catch her son's eye; in public, Garp was a kind of heroic survivor, but he must have been anxious about how Jenny would deal with him back in their apartment.

Dean Bodger became one of the few people at the Steering School to endear himself to Jenny. He beckoned her aside and confided to her that, if she thought it useful, he would be glad to reprimand the boy—if Jenny thought that, coming from Bodger, it would make a more lasting impression than any reprimand she could deliver. Jenny was grateful for the offer, and she and Bodger agreed upon a threat that would impress the boy. Bodger then brushed the feathers off his chest and tucked in his shirt, which was escaping, like a cream filling, from under his tight vest. He announced rather suddenly to the chattering admittance room that he would appreciate a moment alone with young Garp. There was a hush. Garp tried to leave with Jenny, who said, "No. The *dean* would like to speak to you." Then they were alone. Garp didn't know what a dean was.

"Your mother runs a tight ship over here, doesn't she, boy?" Bodger asked. Garp didn't understand, but he nodded. "She runs things very well, if you ask me," Dean Bodger said. "She should have a son whom she can *trust*. Do you know what *trust* means, boy?"

"No," Garp said.

"It means: Can she believe you'll be where you *say* you'll be? Can she believe you'll never do what you're not supposed to do? *That's* trust, boy," Bodger said. "Do you believe your mother can trust you?"

"Yes," Garp said.

"Do you like living here?" Bodger asked him. He knew perfectly well that the boy loved it; Jenny had suggested that this be the point Bodger touch.

"Yes," Garp said.

"What do you hear the boys call me?" the dean asked.

" 'Mad Dog'?" asked Garp. He *had* heard the boys in the infirmary call *someone* "Mad Dog," and Dean Bodger looked like a mad dog to Garp. But the dean

51

was surprised; he had many nicknames, but he had never heard that one.

"I meant that the boys call me sir," Bodger said, and was grateful that Garp was a sensitive child—he caught the injured tone in the dean's voice.

"Yes, sir," Garp said.

"And you *do* like living here?" the dean repeated.

"Yes, sir," Garp said.

"Well, if you *ever* go out on that fire escape, or anywhere near that roof again," Bodger said, "you won't be *allowed* to live here anymore. Do you understand?"

"Yes, sir," Garp said.

"Then be a good boy for your mother," Bodger told him, "or you'll have to move to some place strange and far away."

Garp felt a darkness surround him, akin to the darkness and sense of being far away that he must have felt while lying in the rain gutter, four stories above where the world was safe. He started to cry, but Bodger took his chin between one stumpish, deanly thumb and forefinger; he waggled the boy's head. "Don't *ever* disappoint your mother, boy," Bodger told him. "If you do, you'll feel as bad as this all your life."

"Poor Bodger meant well," Garp wrote. "I *have* felt bad most of my life, and I *did* disappoint my mother. But Bodger's sense of what *really* happens in the world is as suspect as anyone's sense of that."

Garp was referring to the illusion poor Bodger embraced in his later life: that it had been little Garp he caught falling from the annex roof, and not a pigeon. No doubt, in his advancing years, the moment of catching the bird had meant as much to the good-hearted Bodger as if he *had* caught Garp.

Dean Bodger's grasp of reality was often warped. Upon leaving the infirmary, the dean discovered that someone had removed the spotlight from his car. He went raging through every patient's room—even the contagious cases. "That light will one day shine on him who took it!" Bodger claimed, but no one came forward. Jenny was sure it had been Meckler, but she couldn't prove it. Dean Bodger drove home without his light. Two days later he came down with someone's flu and was treated as an outpatient at the infirmary. Jenny was especially sympathetic.

It was another four days before Bodger had reason to look in his glove compartment. The sneezing dean was out cruising the nighttime campus, with a new spotlight mounted on his car, when he was halted by a freshly recruited patrolman from campus security.

"For God's sake, I'm the dean," Bodger told the trembling youth.

"I don't know that for sure, sir," the patrolman said. "They told me not to let anyone drive on the footpaths."

"They should have told you not to tangle with Dean Bodger!" Bodger said.

"They told me that, too, sir," the patrolman said, "but I don't *know* that you're Dean Bodger."

"Well," said Bodger, who was secretly very pleased with the young patrolman's humorless devotion to his duty, "I can certainly prove who I *am*." Dean Bodger then remembered that his driver's license had expired, and he decided to show the patrolman his automobile registration instead. When Bodger opened the glove compartment, there was the deceased pigeon.

Meckler had struck again; and, again, there was no proof. The pigeon was not excessively ripe, not writhing with maggots (yet), but Dean Bodger's glove compartment was infested with lice. The pigeon was so dead that the lice were looking for a new home. The dean found his automobile registration as quickly as possible, but the young patrolman could not take his eyes off the pigeon.

"They told me they were a real problem around here," the patrolman said. "They told me how they got into everything."

"The *boys* get into everything," Bodger crooned. "The pigeons are relatively harmless, but the *boys* bear watching."

For what seemed to Garp like a long and unfair time, Jenny kept a very close watch on *him*. She really had always watched him closely, but she had learned to trust him, too. Now she made Garp prove to her that he could be trusted again.

In a community as small as Steering, news spread more easily than ringworm. The story of how little Garp climbed to the roof of the infirmary annex, and how his mother didn't know he was there, cast suspicion on them both—on Garp as a child who could ill influence other children, on Jenny as a mother who did not look after her son. Of course, Garp sensed no discrimination for a while, but Jenny, who was quick to recognize discrimination (and quick to anticipate it, too), felt once again that people were making unfair assumptions. Her five-year-old had gotten loose on the roof; therefore, she never looked after him properly. And, therefore, he was clearly an *odd* child.

A boy without a father, some said, has dangerous mischief forever on his mind.

"It's odd," Garp wrote, "that the family who would convince *me* of my own uniqueness was never close to my mother's heart. Mother was practical, she believed in evidence and in results. She believed in Bodger, for example, for what a dean did was at least clear. She believed in *specific* jobs: teachers of history, coaches of wrestling—nurses, of course. But the family who convinced me of my own uniqueness was never a family my mother respected. Mother believed that the Percy family *did* nothing."

Jenny Fields was not entirely alone in her belief. Stewart Percy, although he did have a title, did not have a real job. He was called the Secretary of Steering School, but no one ever saw him typing. In fact, he had his own secretary, and no one was very sure *what* she could have to type. For a while Stewart Percy appeared to have some connection with the Steering Alumni Association, a body of Steering graduates so

powerful with wealth and sentimental with nostalgia
that they were highly esteemed by the administration
of the school. But the Director of Alumni Affairs
claimed that Stewart Percy was too unpopular with the
young alumni to be of use. The young alumni remembered Percy from the days when they had been students.

Stewart Percy was not popular with students, who
themselves suspected Percy of doing nothing.

He was a large, florid man with the kind of false
barrel chest that at any moment can reveal itself to
be merely a stomach—the kind of bravely upheld chest
that can drop suddenly and forcefully burst open the
tweed jacket containing it, lifting the regimental-striped
tie with the Steering School colors. "Blood and blue,"
Garp always called them.

Stewart Percy, whom his wife called Stewie—although a generation of Steering schoolboys called him
Paunch—had a flat-top head of hair the color of Distinguished Silver. The boys said that Stewart's flat-top
was meant to resemble an aircraft carrier, because
Stewart had been in the Navy in World War II. His
contribution to the curriculum at Steering was a single
course he taught for fifteen years—which was as long
as it took the History Department to develop the nerve
and necessary disrespect to forbid him to teach it. For
fifteen years it was an embarrassment to them all. Only
the most unsuspecting freshmen at Steering were ever
suckered into taking it. The course was called "My Part
of the Pacific," and it concerned only those naval battles of World War II which Stewart Percy had personally fought in. There had been two. There were no texts
for the course; there were only Stewart's lectures and
Stewart's personal slide collection. The slides had been
created from old black and white photographs—an
interestingly blurred process. At least one memorable
class week of slides concerned Stewart's shore leave in
Hawaii, where he met and married his wife, Midge.

"Mind you, boys, she was not a *native,*" he would
faithfully tell his class (although, in the gray slide, it

55

was hard to tell *what* she was). "She was just *visiting* there, she didn't *come* from there," Stewart would say. And there would follow an endless number of slides of Midge's gray-blond hair.

All the Percy children were blond, too, and one suspected they would one day become Distinguished Silver, like Stewie, whom the Steering students of Garp's day named after a dish served them in the school dining halls at least once every week: Fat Stew. Fat Stew was made from another of the weekly Steering dining-hall dishes: Mystery Meat. But Jenny Fields used to say that Stewart Percy was made entirely of Distinguished Silver hair.

And whether they called him Paunch or Fat Stew, the boys who took Stewart Percy's "My Part of the Pacific" course were supposed to know already that Midge was not a Hawaiian native, though some of them really did have to be told. What the smarter boys knew, and what every member of the Steering community was nearly born knowing—and committed thereafter to silent scorn—was that Stewart Percy had married Midge *Steering*. She was the last Steering. The unclaimed princess of the Steering School—no headmaster had yet come her way. Stewart Percy married into so much money that he didn't *have* to be able to do anything, except stay married.

Jenny Fields' father, the footwear king, used to think of Midge Steering's money and shake in his shoes.

"Midge was such a dingbat," Jenny Fields wrote in her autobiography, "that she went to Hawaii for a *vacation* during World War II. And she was such a *total* dingbat," Jenny wrote, "that she actually fell in love with Stewart Percy, and she began to have his empty, Distinguished Silver children almost immediately—even before the war was over. And when the war *was* over, she brought him and her growing family back to the Steering School. And she told the school to give her Stewie a job."

"When I was a boy," Garp wrote, "there were already

three or four little Percys, and more—seemingly always more—on the way."

Of Midge Percy's many pregnancies, Jenny Fields made up a nasty rhyme.

> *What lies in Midge Percy's belly,*
> *so round and exceedingly fair?*
> *In fact, it is really nothing*
> *but a ball of Distinguished Silver hair.*

"My mother was a bad writer," Garp wrote, referring to Jenny's autobiography. "But she was an even worse poet." When Garp was five, however, he was too young to be told such poems. And what made Jenny Fields so unkind concerning Stewart and Midge?

Jenny knew that Fat Stew looked down on her. But Jenny said nothing, she was just wary of the situation. Garp was a playmate of the Percy children, who were not allowed to visit Garp in the infirmary annex. "Our house is really better for children," Midge told Jenny once, on the phone. "I mean"—she laughed—"I don't think there's anything they can *catch*."

Except a little stupidity, Jenny thought, but all she said was, "I know who's contagious and who isn't. And nobody plays on the roof."

To be fair: Jenny knew that the Percy house, which had been the Steering family house, was a comforting house to children. It was carpeted and spacious and full of generations of tasteful toys. It was rich. And because it was cared for by servants, it was also casual. Jenny resented the casualness that the Percy family could afford. Jenny thought that neither Midge nor Stewie had the brains to worry about their children as much as they should; they also had so *many* children. Maybe when you have a *lot* of children, Jenny pondered, you aren't so anxious about each of them?

Jenny was actually worried for her Garp when he was off playing with the Percy children. Jenny had grown up in an upper-class home, too, and she knew perfectly well that upper-class children were not magically protected from danger just because they were somehow born safer, with hardier metabolisms and charmed genes. Around the Steering School, however, there were many who seemed to believe this—because, superficially, it often *looked* true. There *was* something special about the aristocratic children of those families: their hair seemed to stay in place, their skin did not break out. Perhaps they did not appear to be under any stress because there was nothing they wanted, Jenny thought. But then she wondered how she'd escaped being like them.

Her concern for Garp was truly based on her specific observations of the Percys. The children ran free, as if their own mother believed them to be charmed. Almost albino-like, almost translucent-skinned, the Percy kids really *did* seem more magical, if not actually healthier, than other children. And despite the feeling most faculty families had toward Fat Stew, they felt that the Percy children, and even Midge, had obvious "class." Strong, protective genes were at work, they thought.

"My mother," Garp wrote, "was at *war* with people who took genes this seriously."

And one day Jenny watched her small, dark Garp go running across the infirmary lawn, off toward the more elegant faculty houses, white and green-shuttered, where the Percy house sat like the oldest church in a town full of churches. Jenny watched this tribe of children running across the safe, charted footpaths of the school—Garp the fleetest. A string of clumsy, flopping Percys was in pursuit of him—and the other children who ran with this mob.

There was Clarence DuGard, whose father taught French and smelled as if he never washed; he never opened a window all winter. There was Talbot Mayer-Jones, whose father knew more about all of America's history than Stewart Percy knew about his small part of the Pacific. There was Emily Hamilton, who had eight brothers and would graduate from an inferior all-girls' school just a year before Steering would vote to admit women; her mother would commit suicide, not necessarily as a result of this vote but simultaneously with its announcement (causing Stewart Percy to remark that *this* was what would come of admitting girls to Steering: more suicide). And there were the Grove brothers, Ira and Buddy, "from the town"; their father was with the maintenance department of the school, and it was a delicate case—whether the boys should even be encouraged to attend Steering, and how well it could be expected they would do.

Down through the quadrangles of bright green grass and fresh tar paths, boxed in by buildings of a brick so worn and soft it resembled pink marble, Jenny watched the children run. With them, she was sorry to note, ran the Percy family dog—to Jenny's mind, a mindless oaf of an animal who for years would defy the town leash law the way the Percys would flaunt their casualness. The dog, a giant Newfoundland, had grown from a puppy who spilled garbage cans, and the witless thief of baseballs, to being *mean*.

One day when the kids had been playing, the dog had mangled a volleyball—not an act of viciousness, usually. A mere bumble. But when the boy who owned the deflated ball had tried to remove it from the great dog's mouth, the dog bit him—deep puncture wounds in the forearm: not the type of bite, a nurse knew, that was only an accident, a case of "Bonkers getting a little excited, because he loves playing with the children so much." Or so said Midge Percy, who had named the dog Bonkers. She told Jenny that she'd gotten the dog shortly after the birth of her fourth child. The word *bonkers* meant "a little crazy," she told Jenny, and that's how Midge said she still felt about Stewie after their first four children together. "I was just *bonkers* about him," Midge said to Jenny, "so I named the poor dog Bonkers to prove my feelings for Stew."

"Midge Percy was bonkers, all right," wrote Jenny Fields. "That dog was a killer, protected by one of the many thin and senseless bits of logic that the upper classes in America are famous for: namely, that the children and pets of the aristocracy couldn't possibly be *too* free, or hurt anybody. That *other* people should not overpopulate the world, or be allowed to release *their* dogs, but that the dogs and children of rich people have a right to run free."

"The curs of the upper class," Garp would call them, always—both the dogs and the children.

He would have agreed with his mother that the Percys' dog, Bonkers, the Newfoundland retriever, was dangerous. A Newfoundland is a breed of oily-coated dog resembling an all-black Saint Bernard with webbed feet; they are generally slothful and friendly. But on the Percys' lawn, Bonkers broke up a touch football game by hurling his one hundred and seventy pounds on five-year-old Garp's back and biting off the child's left ear-lobe—and part of the rest of Garp's ear, as well. Bonkers would probably have taken *all* the ear, but he was a dog notably lacking concentration. The other children fled in all directions.

"Bonkie bit someone," said a younger Percy, pulling Midge away from the phone. It was a Percy family habit to put a *-y* or an *-ie* at the end of almost every family member's name. Thus the children—Stewart (Jr.), Randolph, William, Cushman (a girl), and Bainbridge (another girl)—were called, within the family, Stewie Two, Dopey, Shrill Willy, Cushie, and Pooh. Poor Bainbridge, whose name did not convert easily to a *-y* or an *-ie* ending, was also the last in the family to be in diapers; thus, in a cute attempt to be both descriptive and literary, *she* was Pooh.

It was Cushie at Midge's arm, telling her mother that "Bonkie bit someone."

"Who'd he get this time?" said Fat Stew; he seized a squash racket, as if he were going to take charge of the matter, but he was completely undressed; it was Midge who drew her dressing gown together and prepared to be the first grownup to run outside to inspect the damage.

Stewart Percy was frequently undressed at home. No one knows why. Perhaps it was to relieve himself of the strain of how *very* dressed he was when he strolled the Steering campus with nothing to do, Distinguished Silver on display, and perhaps it was out of necessity— for all the procreation he was responsible for, he *must* have been frequently undressed at home.

"Bonkie bit Garp," said little Cushie Percy. Neither Stewart nor Midge noticed that Garp was there, in the doorway, the whole side of his head bloody and chewed.

"Mrs. Percy?" Garp whispered, not loud enough to be heard.

"So it was Garp?" Fat Stew said. Bending to return the squash racket to the closet, he farted. Midge looked at him. "So Bonkie bit Garp," Stewart mused. "Well, at least the dog's got good taste, doesn't he?"

"Oh, Stewie," Midge said; a laughter light as spit escaped her. "Garp's still just a little boy." And there he was, in fact, near-to-fainting and bleeding on the costly hall carpet, which actually spread, without a tuck or a ripple, through four of the monstrous first-floor rooms.

Cushie Percy, whose young life would terminate in childbirth while she tried to deliver what would have been only her first child, saw Garp bleeding on the Steering family heirloom: the remarkable rug. "Oh, gross!" she cried, running out the door.

"Oh, I'll have to call your mother," Midge told Garp, who felt dizzy with the great dog's growl and slobber still singing in his partial ear.

For years Garp would mistakenly interpret Cushie Percy's outcry of "Oh, gross!" He thought she was *not* referring to his gnawed and messy ear but to her father's great gray nakedness, which filled the hall. *That* was what was gross to Garp: the silver, barrel-bellied navy man approaching him in the nude from the well of the Percys' towering spiral staircase.

Stewart Percy knelt down in front of Garp and peered curiously into the boy's bloody face; Fat Stew did not appear to be directing his attention to the mauled ear, and Garp wondered if he should advise the enormous, naked man concerning the whereabouts of his injury. But Stewart Percy was not looking for where Garp was hurt. He was looking at Garp's shining brown eyes, at their color and at their shape, and he seemed to convince himself of something, because he nodded austerely and said to his foolish blond Midge, "Jap."

It would be years before Garp would fully comprehend this, too. But Stewie Percy said to Midge, "I spent enough time in the Pacific to recognize Jap eyes when I see them. I *told* you it was a Jap." The *it* Stewart Percy referred to was whoever he had decided was Garp's father. That was a frequent, speculative game around the Steering community: guessing who Garp's father was. And Stewart Percy, from his experience in his part of the Pacific, had decided that Garp's father was Japanese.

"At that moment," Garp wrote, "I thought 'Jap' was a word that meant my ear was all gone."

"No sense in calling his mother," Stewie said to Midge. "Just take him over to the infirmary. She's a nurse, isn't she? *She'll* know what to do."

Jenny knew, all right. "Why not bring the dog over here?" she asked Midge, while she gingerly washed around what was left of Garp's little ear.

"Bonkers?" Midge asked.

"Bring him here," Jenny said, "and I'll give him a shot."

"An injection?" Midge asked. She laughed. "Do you mean there's actually a *shot* to make him so he won't bite any more people?"

"No," Jenny said. "I mean you could save your money—instead of taking him to a vet. I mean there's a shot to make him *dead*. *That* kind of an injection. *Then* he won't bite any more people."

"Thus," Garp wrote, "was the Percy War begun. For my mother, I think, it was a class war, which she later said all wars were. For me, I just knew to watch out for Bonkers. And for the rest of the Percys."

Stewart Percy sent Jenny Fields a memo on the stationery of the Secretary of the Steering School: "I cannot believe you actually want us to have Bonkers put to sleep," Stewart wrote.

"You bet your fat ass I do," Jenny said to him, on the phone. "Or at least tie him up, forever."

"There's no point in having a dog if the dog can't run free," Stewart said.

"Then kill him," Jenny said.

"Bonkers has had all his shots, thank you just the same," Stewart said. "He's a gentle dog, really. Only if he's provoked."

"Obviously," Garp wrote, "Fat Stew felt that Bonkers had been provoked by my *Jap*ness."


"What's 'good taste' mean?" little Garp asked Jenny. At the infirmary, Dr. Pell sewed up his ear; Jenny reminded the doctor that Garp had recently had a tetanus shot.

"Good taste?" Jenny asked. The odd-looking amputation of the ear forced Garp always to wear his hair long, a style he often complained about.

"Fat Stew said that Bonkers has got 'good taste,'" Garp said.

"To bite you?" Jenny asked.

"I guess so," Garp said. "What's it mean?"

Jenny knew, all right. But she said, "It means that Bonkers must have known you were the best-tasting kid in the whole pile of kids."

"Am I?" Garp asked.

"Sure," Jenny said.

"How did Bonkers know?" Garp asked.

"*I* don't know," Jenny said.

"What's 'Jap' mean?" Garp asked.

"Did Fat Stew say that to you?" Jenny asked him.

"No," Garp said. "I think he said it about my ear."

"Oh yes, your ear," Jenny said. "It means you have *special* ears." But she was wondering whether to tell him what she felt about the Percys, *now,* or whether he was enough like her to profit at some later, more important time from the experience of anger. Perhaps, she thought, I should save this morsel for him, for a time when he could *use* it. In her mind, Jenny Fields saw always more and larger battles ahead.

"My mother seemed to need an enemy," Garp wrote. "Real or imagined, my mother's enemy helped her see the way *she* should behave, and how she should instruct me. She was no natural at motherhood; in fact, I think my mother doubted that *any*thing happened naturally. She was self-conscious and deliberate to the end."

It was the world according to Fat Stew that became Jenny's enemy in those early years for Garp. That phase might be called "Getting Garp Ready for Steering."

She watched his hair grow and cover the missing parts of his ear. She was surprised at his handsomeness, because handsomeness had not been a factor in her relationship with Technical Sergeant Garp. If the sergeant had been handsome, Jenny Fields hadn't really noticed. But young Garp was handsome, she could see, though he remained small—as if he were born to fit in the ball turret installation.

The band of children (who coursed the Steering footpaths and grassy quadrangles and playing fields) grew more awkward and self-conscious as Jenny watched them grow. Clarence DuGard soon needed glasses, which he was always smashing; over the years Jenny would treat him many times for ear infections and once for a broken nose. Talbot Mayer-Jones developed a lisp; he had a bottle-shaped body, though a lovely disposition, and low-grade chronic sinusitis. Emily Hamilton grew so tall that her knees and elbows were forever raw and bleeding from all her stumbling falls, and the way her small breasts asserted themselves made Jenny wince—occasionally wishing she had a daughter. Ira and Buddy Grove, "from the town," were thick in the ankles and wrists and necks, their fingers smudged and mashed from messing around in their father's maintenance department. And up grew the Percy children, blond and metallically clean, their eyes the color of the dull ice on the brackish Steering River that seeped through the salt marshes to the nearby sea.

Stewart, Jr., who was called Stewie Two, graduated from Steering before Garp was even of age to enter the school; Jenny treated Stewie Two twice for a sprained ankle and once for gonorrhea. He later went through Harvard Business School, a staph infection, and a divorce.

Randolph Percy was called Dopey until his dying day (of a heart attack, when he was only thirty-five; he was a procreator after his fat father's heart, himself the father of five). Dopey never managed to graduate from Steering, but successfully transferred to some other prep school and graduated after a while. Once Midge cried out in the Sunday dining room, "Our Dopey's dead!" His nickname sounded so awful in that context that the family, after his death, finally spoke of him as Randolph.

William Percy, Shrill Willy, was embarrassed by his stupid nickname, to his credit, and although he was three years older than Garp, he befriended Garp in a very decent fashion while he was an upperclassman at Steering and Garp was just starting out. Jenny always liked William, whom she called William. She treated him many times for bronchitis and was moved enough by the news of his death (in a war, immediately following his graduation from Yale) that she even wrote a long letter of commiseration to Midge and Fat Stew.

As for the Percy girls, Cushie would get hers (and Garp would even get to play a small part; they were near the same age). And poor Bainbridge, the youngest Percy, who was cursed to be called Pooh, would be spared *her* encounter with Garp until Garp was in his prime.

All these children, and her Garp, Jenny watched grow. While Jenny waited for Garp to get ready for Steering, the black beast Bonkers grew very old, and slower—but not toothless, Jenny noticed. And always Garp watched out for him, even after Bonkers stopped running with the crowd; when he lurked, hulking by the Percys' white front pillars—as matted and tangled and nasty as a thorn bush in the dark—Garp still kept his eye on him. An occasional younger child, or someone new in the neighborhood, would get too close and be chomped. Jenny kept track of the stitches and missing bits of flesh for which the great slathering dog was accountable, but Fat Stew endured all Jenny's criticisms and Bonkers lived.

"I believe my mother grew fond of that animal's presence, although she would never have admitted it," Garp wrote. "Bonkers was the Percy Enemy come alive—made into muscle and fur and halitosis. It must have pleased my mother to watch the old dog slowing down while I was growing up."

By the time Garp was ready for Steering, black Bonkers was fourteen years old. By the time Garp entered the Steering School, Jenny Fields had a few Distinguished Silver hairs of her own. By the time Garp started Steering, Jenny had taken all the courses that were worth taking and had listed them in order of universal value and entertainment. By the time Garp was a Steering student, Jenny Fields had been awarded the traditional gift for faculty and staff enduring fifteen years of service: the famous Steering dinner plates. The

stern brick buildings of the school, including the infirmary annex, were baked into the big-eating surfaces of
the plates, vividly rendered in the Steering School colors.
Good old blood and blue.

# 3

⊰⊱⊰⊱⊰⊱⊰⊱⊰⊱⊰⊱⊰⊱

# What He Wanted to Be
# When He Grew Up

IN 1781 the widow and children of Everett Steering founded Steering Academy, as it was first called, because Everett Steering had announced to his family, while carving his last Christmas goose, that his only disappointment with *his* town was that he had not provided his boys with an academy capable of preparing them for a higher education. He did not mention his girls. He was a shipbuilder in a village whose life-link to the sea was a doomed river; Everett knew the river was doomed. He was a smart man, and not usually playful, but after Christmas dinner he indulged in a snowball fight with both his boys and his girls. He died of apoplexy before nightfall. Everett Steering was seventy-two; even his boys and his girls were too old for snowball fights, but he had a right to call the town of Steering *his* town.

It had been named after him in a glut of enthusiasm for the town's independence following the Revolutionary War. Everett Steering had organized the installation of mounted cannons at strategic points along the river shore; these cannons were meant to discourage an attack that never came—from the British, who were expected to sail up the river from the sea at Great Bay. The river was called Great River then, but after the war it was called the Steering River; and the town, which had no proper name—but had always been called The Meadows, because it lay in the salt- and freshwater marshes only a few miles inland from Great Bay—was also called Steering.

Many families in Steering were dependent on shipbuilding, or on other business that came up the river from the sea; since it was first called The Meadows, the village had been a backup port to Great Bay. But along with his wishes to found a boys' academy, Everett Steering told his family that Steering would *not* be a port for very long. The river, he noticed, was choking with silt.

In all his life, Everett Steering was known to tell only one joke, and only to his family. The joke was that the only river to have been named after him was full of mud; and it was getting fuller by the minute. The land was all marsh and meadow, from Steering to the sea, and unless people decided that Steering was worth maintaining as a port, and gouged a deeper channel for the river, Everett knew that even a rowboat would eventually have trouble making it from Steering to Great Bay (unless there was a very high tide). Everett knew that the tide would one day fill in the riverbed from his home town to the Atlantic.

In the next century, the Steering family was wise to stake its life-support system on the textile mills they constructed to span the waterfall on the freshwater part of the Steering River. By the time of the Civil War the *only* business in the town of Steering, on the Steering River, was the Steering Mills. The family got out of boats and into textiles when the time was ripe.

Another shipbuilding family in Steering was not so lucky; this family's last ship made it only half the way from Steering to the sea. In a once-notorious part of the river, called The Gut, the last ship made in Steering settled into the mud forever, and for years it could be seen from the road, half out of the water at high tide and completely dry at low tide. Kids played in it until it listed to its side and crushed someone's dog. A pig farmer named Gilmore salvaged the ship's masts to raise his barn. And by the time young Garp attended Steering, the varsity crew could row their shells on the river only at high tide. At low tide the Steering River is one wet mudflat from Steering to the sea.

It was, therefore, due to Everett Steering's instincts about water that a boys' academy was founded in 1781. After a century or so, it flourished.

"Over all those years," Garp wrote, "the shrewd Steering genes must have suffered some dilution; the family instincts regarding water went from good to very bad." Garp enjoyed referring to Midge Steering Percy in this way. "A Steering whose water instincts had run their course," he said. Garp thought it wonderfully ironic "that the Steering genes for water sense ran out of chromosomes when they got to Midge. *Her* sense of water was so perverse," Garp wrote, "that it attracted her first to Hawaii and then to the United States Navy— in the form of Fat Stew."

Midge Steering Percy was the end of the bloodline. The Steering School itself would become the last Steering after her, and perhaps old Everett foresaw that, too; many families have left less, or worse, behind. In Garp's day, at least, the Steering School was still relentless and definite in its purpose: "the preparing of young men for a higher education." And in Garp's case, he had a mother who also took that purpose seriously. Garp himself took the school so seriously that even Everett Steering, with his one joke in a lifetime, would have been pleased.

Garp knew what to take for courses and whom to have for teachers. That is often the difference between doing well or poorly in a school. He was not really a gifted student, but he had direction; many of his courses were still fresh in Jenny's mind, and she was a good drillmaster. Garp was probably no more of a natural at intellectual pursuits than his mother, but he had Jenny's powerful discipline; a nurse *is* a natural at establishing a routine, and Garp believed in his mother.

If Jenny was remiss in her advice, it was in only one area. She had never paid any attention to the sports at Steering; she could offer Garp no suggestions as to what games he might like to play. She could tell him that he would like East Asian Civilization with Mr. Merrill more than he would like Tudor England with Mr. Langdell. But, for example, Jenny did not know the differences in pleasure and pain between football and soccer. She had observed only that her son was small, strong, well balanced, quick, and solitary; she assumed he already knew what games he liked to play. He did not.

Crew, he thought, was stupid. Rowing a boat in unison, a galley slave dipping your oar in foul water— and the Steering River was indeed foul. The river was afloat with factory scum and human turds—and always the after-tide, saltwater slime was on the mudflats (a muck the texture of refrigerated bacon fat). Everett Steering's river was full of more than mud, but even if it had been sparkling clean, Garp was no oarsman. And no tennis player, either. In one of his earliest essays—his freshman year at Steering—Garp wrote: "I do not care for balls. The ball stands between the athlete and his exercise. So do hockey pucks and badminton birdies—and skates, like skis, intrude between the body and the ground. And when one further removes one's body from the contest by an extension device—such as a racket, a bat, or a stick—all purity of movement, strength, and focus is lost." Even at fifteen, one could sense his instinct for a personal aesthetic.

Since he was too small for football, and soccer certainly involved a ball, he ran long distance, which was called cross-country, but he stepped in too many puddles and suffered all fall from a perpetual cold.

When the winter sports season opened, Jenny was distressed at how much restlessness her son exhibited; she criticized him for making too much of a mere athletic decision—why didn't he know what form of exercise he might prefer? But sports did not feel like recreation to Garp. *Nothing* felt like recreation to Garp. From the beginning, he appeared to believe there was something strenuous to achieve. ("Writers do not read for fun," Garp would write, later, speaking for himself.) Even before young Garp knew he was going to be a writer, or knew *what* he wanted to be, it appears he did nothing "for fun."

Garp was confined to the infirmary on the day he was supposed to sign up for a winter sport. Jenny would not let him get out of bed. "You don't know what you want to sign up for, anyway," she told him. All Garp could do was cough.

"This is silly beyond mortal belief," Jenny told him. "Fifteen years in this snotty, rude community and you fall to pieces trying to decide what *game* you're going to play to occupy your afternoons."

"I haven't found my sport, Mom," Garp croaked. "I've *got* to have a sport."

"Why?" Jenny asked.

"I don't know," he moaned. He coughed and coughed.

"God, listen to you," Jenny complained. *"I'll* find you a sport," she said. "I'll go over to the gym and sign you up for something."

"No!" Garp begged.

And Jenny pronounced what was for Garp, in his four years at Steering, her litany. "I know more than you do, don't I?" she said. Garp fell back on his sweaty pillow.

"Not about *this,* Mom," he said. "You took all the courses but you never played on any of the *teams.*"

If Jenny Fields recognized this as a rare oversight, she did not admit it. It was a typical Steering December day, the ground glassy with frozen slush and the snow gray and muddy from the boots of eight hundred boys. Jenny Fields bundled up and trudged across the winter-grim campus like the convinced and determined mother she was. She looked like a nurse resigned to bring what slim hope she could to the bitter Russian front. In such a manner Jenny Fields approached the Steering gym. In her fifteen years at Steering, Jenny had never been there; she had not known it was important. At the far end of the Steering campus, ringed by the acres of playing fields, the hockey rinks, the tennis courts like the cross section of a huge, human hive, Jenny saw the giant gymnasium loom out of the dirty snow like a battle she had not anticipated, and her heart filled with worry and with gloom.

The Seabrook Gymnasium and Field House—and the Seabrook Stadium, and the Seabrook Ice Hockey Rinks—were named after the superb athlete and World War I flying ace Miles Seabrook, whose face and massive torso greeted Jenny in a triptych of photographs enshrined in the display case in the gym's vast entranceway. Miles Seabrook, '09, his head in a leather football helmet, his shoulder pads probably unnecessary. Beneath the photo of old No. 32 was the near-demolished jersey itself: faded and frequently under the attack of moths, the jersey lay in a heap in the locked trophy case under the first third of Miles Seabrook's triptych photograph. A sign said: HIS ACTUAL SHIRT.

The center shot in the triptych showed Miles Seabrook as a hockey goalie—in those old days the goalies wore pads, but the brave face was naked, the eyes clear and challenging, the scar tissue everywhere. Miles Seabrook's bulk filled the dwarfed net. How could anyone have scored on Miles Seabrook, his cat-quick and bear-sized leather paws, his clublike stick and swollen chest protector, his skates like the long claws of a giant anteater? Beneath the football and the hockey pictures were the scores of the annual *big* games: in every Steering sport, the season ended in the traditional contest with Bath Academy, nearly as old and famous as Steering, and every Steering schoolboy's hated rival. The vile Bath boys in their gold and green (in Garp's day, these colors were called puke and babyshit). STEERING 7, BATH 6; STEERING 3, BATH 0. Nobody scored on Miles.

*Captain* Miles Seabrook, as he was called in the third photo in the triptych, stared back at Jenny Fields in a uniform all too familiar to her. It was a flyboy's suit, she saw in an instant; although the costumes changed between world wars, they did not change so much that Jenny failed to recognize the fleece-lined collar of the flight jacket, turned up at a cocky angle, and the confident, untied chin strap of the flight cap, the tipped-up earmuffs (Miles Seabrook's ears could never get cold!), and the goggles pushed carelessly up off the forehead. At his throat, the pure white scarf. No score was cited beneath this portrait, but if anyone in the Steering Athletic Department had possessed a sense of humor, Jenny might have read: UNITED STATES 16, GERMANY 1. Sixteen was the number of planes Miles Seabrook shot down before the Germans scored on him.

Ribbons and medals lay dusty in the locked trophy case, like offerings at an altar to Miles Seabrook. There was a battered wooden thing, which Jenny mistook for part of Miles Seabrook's shot-down plane; she was prepared for *any* tastelessness, but the wood was only all that remained of his last hockey stick. Why not his jock? thought Jenny Fields. Or, like a keepsake of a dead baby, a lock of his hair? Which was, in all three photos, covered by a helmet or a cap or a big striped sock. Perhaps, Jenny thought—with characteristic scorn —Miles Seabrook was hairless.

Jenny resented the implications lying honored in that dusty case. The warrior-athlete, merely undergoing another change of uniform. Each time the body was offered only a pretense of protection: as a Steering School nurse, Jenny had seen fifteen years of football and hockey injuries, in spite of helmets, masks, straps,

75

buckles, hinges, and pads. And Sergeant Garp, and the others, had shown Jenny that men at war had the most illusory protection of all.

Wearily, Jenny moved on; when she passed the display cases, she felt she was moving toward the engine of a dangerous machine. She avoided the arena-sized spaces in the gymnasium, where she could hear the shouts and grunts of contest. She sought the dark corridors, where, she supposed, the offices were. Have I spent fifteen years, she thought, to lose my child to *this?*

She recognized a part of the smell. Disinfectant. Years of strenuous scrubbing. No doubt that a gym was a place where germs of monstrous potential lay waiting for a chance to breed. That part of the smell reminded her of hospitals, and of the Steering infirmary—bottled, postoperative air. But here in the huge house built to the memory of Miles Seabrook there was *another* smell, as distasteful to Jenny Fields as the smell of sex. The complex of gym and field house had been erected in 1919, less than a year before she was born: what Jenny smelled was almost forty years of the forced farts and the sweat of boys under stress and strain. What Jenny smelled was *competition,* fierce and full of disappointment. She was such an outsider, it had never been part of *her* growing up.

In a corridor that seemed separated from the central areas of the gym's various energies, Jenny stood still and listened. Somewhere near her was a weight-lifting room; she heard the iron bashing and the terrible heaves of hernias in progress—a nurse's view of such exertion. In fact, it seemed to Jenny that the whole building groaned and pushed, as if every schoolboy at Steering suffered constipation and sought relievement in the horrid gym.

Jenny Fields felt undone, the way only a person who has been careful can feel when confronted by a mistake.

The bleeding wrestler was at that instant upon her.

Jenny was not sure how the groggy, dripping boy had surprised her, but a door opened off this corridor of small, innocuous-appearing rooms, and the matted face of the wrestler was smack in front of her with his ear guards pulled so askew on his head that the chin strap had slipped to his mouth, where it tugged his upper lip into a fishlike sneer. The little bowl of the strap, which had once cupped his chin, now brimmed with blood from his streaming nose.

As a nurse, Jenny was not overimpressed with blood, but she cringed at her anticipated collision with the thick, wet, hard-looking boy, who somehow dodged her, lunging sideways. With admirable trajectory and volume, he vomited on his fellow wrestler who was struggling to support him. "Excuse me," he burbled, for most of the boys at Steering were well brought up.

His fellow wrestler did him the favor of pulling his head gear off, so that the hapless puker would not choke or strangle; quite unmindful of his own bespattering, he called loudly back into the open door of the wrestling room, "Carlisle didn't make it!"

From the door of that room, whose heat beckoned Jenny in the way a tropical greenhouse might be alluring in midwinter, a man's clear tenor voice responded. "Carlisle! You had *two* helpings of that dining-hall slop for lunch, Carlisle! *One* helping and you deserve to lose it! *No sympathy,* Carlisle!"

Carlisle, for whom there was no sympathy, continued his lurching progress down the corridor; he bled and barfed his way to a door, through which he made his smeared escape. His fellow wrestler, who in Jenny's opinion had also withheld his sympathy, dropped Carlisle's headgear in the corridor with the rest of Carlisle's muck; then he followed Carlisle to the lockers. Jenny hoped that he was going somewhere to change his clothes.

She looked at the wrestling room's open door; she breathed deeply and stepped inside. Immediately, she felt off-balance. Underfoot was a soft fleshy feel, and the wall sank under her touch when she leaned against it; she was inside a padded cell, the floor and the wall mats warm and yielding, the air so stifling hot and stench-full of sweat that she hardly dared to breathe.

"Shut the door!" said the man's tenor voice—because wrestlers, Jenny would later know, *love* the heat and their own sweat, especially when they're cutting weight, and they *thrive* when the walls and floors are as hot and giving as the buttocks of sleeping girls.

Jenny shut the door. Even the door had a mat on it, and she slumped against it, imagining someone might open the door from the outside and mercifully release her. The man with the tenor voice was the coach and Jenny, through the shimmering heat, watched him pace against the long room's wall, unable to stand still while he squinted at his struggling wrestlers. "Thirty seconds!" he screamed to them. The couples on the mat bucked as if they were electrically stimulated. The batches of twosomes around the wrestling room were each locked in some violent tangle, the intent of each wrestler, in Jenny's eye, as deliberate and as desperate as rape.

"Fifteen seconds!" the coach screamed. *"Push* it!"

The twisted pair nearest Jenny suddenly came apart, their limbs unknotting, the veins on their arms and necks popping. A breathless cry and a string of saliva broke from one boy's mouth as his opponent broke free of him and they uncoupled, bashing into the padded wall.

"Time's up!" the coach screamed. He did not use a whistle. The wrestlers went suddenly limp, untying each other from each other with great slowness. A half dozen of them now lumbered toward Jenny at the door; they had the water fountain and fresh air on their minds, though Jenny assumed they were all heading for the hall in order to throw up, or bleed in peace—or both.

Jenny and the coach were the only standing bodies left in the wrestling room. Jenny observed that the coach was a neat, small man, as compact as a spring; she also observed he was nearly blind, because the coach now squinted in her direction, recognizing that her whiteness and her shape were foreign to the wrestling room. He began to grope for his glasses, which he usually stashed above the wall mats, at about head level—where they would not be so easily crushed by a wrestler who was flung upon them. Jenny observed that the coach was about her age, and that she had never seen him on or about the Steering campus before—with or without his glasses.

The coach was new at Steering. His name was Ernie Holm, and so far he had found the Steering community to be just as snotty as Jenny had found it. Ernie Holm had been a two-time Big Ten wrestling champion at the University of Iowa, but he had never won a national title and he had coached in high schools all over Iowa for fifteen years while trying to raise his only child, a daughter, all by himself. He was bone-tired of the Midwest, as he would have said it himself, and he had come East to assure his daughter of a classy education—as he would also have said it. She was the brains of the family, he was fond of saying—and she had her mother's fine looks, which he never mentioned.

Helen Holm, at fifteen, had spent a lifetime of three-hour afternoons sitting in wrestling rooms, from Iowa to Steering, watching boys of many sizes sweat and throw each other around. Helen would remark, years later, that spending her childhood as the only girl in a wrestling room had made her a reader. "I was brought up to be a spectator," Helen said. "I was raised to be a voyeur."

She was such a good and nonstop reader, in fact, that Ernie Holm had moved East just for her. He took the job at Steering for Helen's sake, because he had read in his contract that the children of the faculty and staff could attend the Steering School for free—or they could receive a comparable sum of money toward their tuition at another private school. Ernie Holm was a bad reader, himself; he had somehow overlooked the fact that Steering admitted only boys.

He found himself moving into the chilly Steering community in the fall, with his brainy daughter once more enrolled in a small, bad public school. In fact, the public school in the town of Steering was probably worse than most public schools because the smart boys in the town went to Steering, and the smart girls went away. Ernie Holm hadn't figured he'd have to send his daughter away from him—that had been why he'd moved: to stay with her. So while Ernie Holm was getting used to his new duties at Steering, Helen Holm wandered the fringes of the great school, devouring its bookstore and its library (hearing stories, no doubt, of the community's *other* great reader: Jenny Fields); and Helen continued to be bored, as she had been bored in Iowa, by her boring classmates in her boring public school.

Ernie Holm was sensitive to people who were bored. He had married a nurse sixteen years earlier; when Helen had been born, the nurse gave up her nursing to be a full-time mother. After six months she wanted to be a nurse again, but there were no day-care centers in Iowa in those years, and Ernie Holm's new wife grew gradually more distant under the strain of being a full-time mother and an ex-nurse. One day she left him. She left him with a full-time daughter and no explanation.

So Helen Holm grew up in wrestling rooms, which are very safe for children—being padded everywhere, and always warm. Books had kept Helen from being bored, although Ernie Holm worried how long his daughter's studiousness could continue to be nourished in a vacuum. Ernie was sure that the *genes* for being bored were in his daughter.

Thus he came to Steering. Thus Helen, who also wore glasses—as needfully as her father—was with him that day Jenny Fields walked into the wrestling room. Jenny didn't notice Helen; few people noticed Helen, when Helen was fifteen. Helen, however, noticed Jenny right away; Helen was unlike her father in that she didn't wrestle with the boys, or demonstrate moves and holds, and so she kept her glasses *on*.

Helen Holm was forever on the lookout for nurses

because she was forever on the lookout for her disappeared mother, whom Ernie had made no attempt to find. With women, Ernie Holm had some experience at taking no for an answer. But when Helen had been small, Ernie had indulged her with a speculative fable he no doubt liked to imagine himself—it was a story that had always intrigued Helen, too. "One day," went the story, "you might see a pretty nurse, sort of looking like she doesn't know where she *is* anymore, and she might look at you like she doesn't know who *you* are, either—but she might look curious to find out."

"And that will be my mom?" Helen used to ask her father.

"And that will be your mom!" Ernie used to say.

So when Helen Holm looked up from her book in the Steering wrestling room, she thought she saw her mother. Jenny Fields in her white uniform was forever appearing out of place; there on the crimson mats of the Steering School, she looked dark and healthy, strong-boned and handsome if not exactly pretty, and Helen Holm must have thought that no other woman would have ventured into this soft-floored inferno where her father worked. Helen's glasses fogged, she closed her book; in her anonymous gray sweat suit, which hid her gawky fifteen-year-old frame—her hard hips and her small breasts—she stood up awkwardly against the wrestling-room wall and waited for her father's sign of recognition.

But Ernie Holm was still groping for his glasses; in a blur he saw the white figure—vaguely womanly, perhaps a nurse—and his heart paused at the possibility he had never really believed in: his wife's return, her saying, "Oh, how I've missed you and our daughter!" What *other* nurse would enter his place of employment?

Helen saw her father's fumbling, she took this to be the necessary sign. She stepped toward Jenny across the blood-warm mats, and Jenny thought: My God, that's a *girl!* A pretty girl with glasses. What's a pretty girl doing in a place like this?

"Mom?" the girl said to Jenny. "It's *me,* Mom! It's *Helen,*" she said, bursting into tears; she flung her slim arms around Jenny's shoulders and pressed her wet face to Jenny's throat.

"Jesus Christ!" said Jenny Fields, who was never a woman who liked to be touched. Still, she was a nurse and she must have felt Helen's need; she did not shove the girl away from her, though she knew very well she was not Helen's mother. Jenny Fields thought that having been a mother *once* was enough. She coolly patted the weeping girl's back and looked imploringly at the wrestling coach, who had just found his glasses. "I'm not *your* mother, either," Jenny said politely to him, because he was looking at her with the same brief relief in his face that Jenny had seen in the face of the pretty girl.

What Ernie Holm thought was that the resemblance went deeper than the uniform and the coincidence of a wrestling room in two nurses' lives; but Jenny stopped short of being as pretty as Ernie's runaway wife, and Ernie was reflecting that even fifteen years would not have made his wife as plain and merely handsome as Jenny. Still, Jenny looked all right to Ernie Holm, who smiled an unclear, apologetic smile that his wrestlers were familiar with, when they lost.

"My daughter thought you were her mother," Ernie Holm said to Jenny. "She hasn't seen her mother in quite a while."

*Obviously,* thought Jenny Fields. She felt the girl tense and spring out of her arms.

"That's not your mom, darlin'," Ernie Holm said to Helen, who retreated to the wrestling-room wall; she was a tough-minded girl, not at all in the habit of emotionally displaying herself—not even to her father.

"And did you think I was your *wife?*" Jenny asked Ernie, because it had looked to her, for a moment, that Ernie had mistaken her, too. She wondered how long a "while" Mrs. Holm had been missing.

"You fooled me, for a minute," Ernie said, politely; he had a shy grin, which he used sparingly.

Helen crouched in a corner of the wrestling room, fiercely eyeing Jenny as if Jenny were deliberately responsible for her embarrassment. Jenny felt moved by the girl; it had been years since Garp had hugged her like that, and it was a feeling that even a very selective mother, like Jenny, remembered missing.

"What's your name?" she asked Helen. "My name is Jenny Fields."

It was a name Helen Holm knew, of course. She was the other mystery reader around the Steering School. Also, Helen had not previously given to anyone the feelings she reserved for a mother; even though it had been an accident that she'd flung those feelings around Jenny, Helen found it hard to call them back entirely. She had her father's shy smile and she looked thankfully at Jenny; oddly, Helen felt she would like to hug Jenny again, but she restrained herself. There were wrestlers shuffling back into the room, gasping from the drinking fountain, where those who were cutting weight had only rinsed their mouths.

"No more practice," Ernie Holm told them, waving them out of the room. "That's it for today. Go run your laps!" Obediently, even relieved, they bobbed in the doorway of the crimson room; they picked up their headgear, their rubber sweat suits, their spools of tape. Ernie Holm waited for the room to clear, while his daughter and Jenny Fields waited for him to explain; at the very least, an explanation was in order, he felt, and there was nowhere Ernie felt as comfortable as he felt in a wrestling room. For him it was the natural place to tell someone a story, even a difficult story with no ending—and even to a stranger. So when his wrestlers had left to run their laps, Ernie very patiently began his father-and-daughter tale, the brief history of the nurse who left them, and of the Midwest they only recently had left. It was a story Jenny could appreciate, of course, because Jenny did not know another single parent with a single child. And although she may have felt tempted to tell them *her* story—there being interesting similarities, and differences—Jenny merely repeated her standard version: the father of Garp was a soldier, and so forth. And who takes the time for weddings when there is a war? Though it was not the whole story, it clearly appealed to Helen and Ernie, who had met no one else in the Steering community as receptive and frank as Jenny.

There in the warm red wrestling room, on the soft mats, surrounded by those padded walls—in such an environment, sudden and inexplicable closeness is possible.

Of course Helen would remember that first hug her whole life; however her feelings for Jenny might change, and change back, from that moment in the wrestling room Jenny Fields was more of a mother to Helen than Helen had ever had. Jenny would also remember how it felt to be hugged like a mother, and would even note, in her autobiography, how a daughter's hug was different from a son's. It is at least ironic that her one experience for making such a pronouncement occurred that December day in the giant gymnasium erected to the memory of Miles Seabrook.

It is unfortunate if Ernie Holm felt any desire toward Jenny Fields, and if he imagined, even briefly, that here might be another woman with whom he might live his life. Because Jenny Fields was given to no such feelings; she thought only that Ernie was a nice, good man—perhaps, she hoped, he would be her friend. If he would be, he would be her first.

And it must have perplexed Ernie and Helen when Jenny asked if she could stay a moment, in the wrestling room, just by herself. What for? they must have wondered. Ernie then remembered to ask her why she had come.

"To sign my son up for wrestling," Jenny said quickly. She hoped Garp would approve.

"Well, sure," Ernie said. "And you'll turn out the

lights, and the heaters, when you leave? The door locks itself."

Thus alone, Jenny turned off the lights and heard the great blow heaters hum down to stillness. There in the dark room, the door ajar, she took off her shoes and she paced the mat. Despite the apparent violence of this sport, she was thinking, why do I feel so *safe* here? Is it him? she wondered, but Ernie passed quickly through her mind—simply a small, neat, muscular man with glasses. If Jenny thought of men at all, and she never really did, she thought they were more tolerable when they were small and neat, and she preferred men *and* women to have muscles—to be strong. She enjoyed people with glasses the way only someone who doesn't need to wear glasses can enjoy glasses on other people—can find them "nice." But mostly it is this *room,* she thought—the red wrestling room, huge but contained, padded against pain, she imagined. She dropped thud! to her knees, just to hear the way the mats received her. She did a somersault and split her dress; then she sat on the mat and looked at the heavy boy who loomed in the doorway of the blackened room. It was Carlisle, the wrestler who'd lost his lunch; he had changed his equipment and come back for more punishment, and he peered across the dark crimson mats at the glowing white nurse who crouched like a she-bear in her cave.

"Excuse me, ma'am," he said. "I was just looking for someone to work out with."

"Well, don't look at *me,*" Jenny said. "Go run your laps!"

"Yes, ma'am," Carlisle said, and he trotted off.

When she closed the door and it locked behind her, she realized she'd left her shoes inside. A janitor did not seem able to find the right key, but he lent her a large boy's basketball shoes that had turned up in Lost and Found. Jenny trudged across the frozen slush to the infirmary, feeling that her first trip to the world of sports had left her more than a little changed.

In the annex, in his bed, Garp still coughed and coughed. "Wrestling!" he croaked. "Good God, Mother, are you trying to get me killed?"

"I think you'll like the coach," Jenny said. "I met him, and he's a nice man. I met his daughter, too."

"Oh, Jesus," Garp groaned. "His *daughter* wrestles?"

"No, she reads a lot," Jenny said, approvingly.

"Sounds exciting, Mom," Garp said. "You realize that setting me up with the wrestling coach's daughter may cost me my neck? Do you want that?"

But Jenny was innocent of such a scheme. She really had only been thinking about the wrestling room, and Ernie Holm; her feelings for Helen were entirely motherly, and when her crude young son suggested the possibility of matchmaking—of *his* taking an interest in young Helen Holm—Jenny was rather alarmed. She had not previously thought of the possibility of her son's being interested in anyone, in that way—at least, she'd thought, he wouldn't be interested for a long time. It was very disquieting to her and she could only say to him, "You're only fifteen years old. Remember that."

"Well, how old is the daughter?" Garp asked. "And what's her name?"

"Helen," Jenny answered. "She's only fifteen, too. And she wears *glasses*," she added, hypocritically. After all, she knew what *she* thought of glasses; maybe Garp liked them, too. "They're from *Iowa*," she added, and felt she was being a more terrible snob than those hated dandies who thrived in the Steering School community.

"God, *wrestling*," Garp groaned, again, and Jenny felt relieved that he had passed on from the subject of Helen. Jenny was embarrassed at herself for how much she clearly objected to the possibility. The girl *is* pretty, she thought—though not in an obvious way; and don't young boys like only *obvious* girls? And would I prefer it if Garp were interested in one of those?

As for *those* kind of girls, Jenny had her eye on Cushie Percy—a little too saucy with her mouth, a little too slack about her appearance; and should a fifteen-year-old of Cushman Percy's breeding be so *developed* already? Then Jenny hated herself for even thinking of the word *breeding*.

It had been a confusing day for her. She fell asleep, for once untroubled by her son's coughing because it seemed that more serious troubles might lie ahead for him. Just when I was thinking we were home free! Jenny thought. She must discuss *boys* with someone—Ernie Holm, maybe; she hoped she'd been right about him.

She was right about the wrestling room, it turned out—and what intense comfort it gave to her Garp. The boy liked Ernie, too. In that first wrestling season at Steering, Garp worked hard and happily at learning his moves and his holds. Though he was soundly trounced by the varsity boys in his weight class, he never complained. He knew he had found his sport and his pastime; it would take the best of his energy until the writing came along. He loved the singleness of the combat, and the frightening confines of that circle inscribed on the mat; the terrific conditioning; the mental constancy of keeping his weight down. And in that first season at Steering, Jenny was relieved to note, Garp hardly mentioned Helen Holm, who sat in her glasses, in her gray sweat suit, reading. She occasionally looked up, when there was an unusually loud slam on the mat or a cry of pain.

It had been Helen who returned Jenny's shoes to the infirmary annex, and Jenny embarrassed herself by not even asking the girl to come in. For a moment, they had seemed so close. But Garp had been in. Jenny did not want to introduce them. And besides—Garp had a cold.

One day, in the wrestling room, Garp sat beside Helen. He was conscious of a pimple on his neck and how much he was sweating. Her glasses looked so fogged, Garp doubted she could see what she was reading. "You sure read a lot," he said to her.

"Not as much as your mother," Helen said, not looking at him.

Two months later Garp said to Helen, "Maybe you'll wreck your eyes, reading in a hot place like this." She looked at him, her glasses very clear this time and magnifying her eyes in a way that startled him.

"I've already got wrecked eyes," she said. "I was *born* with ruined eyes." But to Garp they looked like very nice eyes; so nice, in fact, that he could think of nothing further to say to her.

Then the wrestling season was over. Garp got a junior varsity letter and signed up for track and field events, his listless choice for a spring sport. His condition from the wrestling season was good enough so that he ran the mile; he was the third-best miler on the Steering team, but he would never get any better. At the end of a mile, Garp felt he was just getting started. ("A novelist, even then—though I didn't know it," Garp would write, years later.) He also threw the javelin, but not far.

The javelin throwers at Steering practiced behind the football stadium, where they spent much of their time spearing frogs. The upper, freshwater reaches of the Steering River ran behind Seabrook Stadium; many javelins were lost there, and many frogs were slain. Spring is no good, thought Garp, who was restless, who missed wrestling; if he couldn't have wrestling, at least let the summer come, he thought, and he would run long-distance on the road to the beach at Dog's Head Harbor.

One day, in the top row of empty Seabrook Stadium, he saw Helen Holm alone with a book. He climbed up the stadium stairs to her, clicking his javelin against the cement so that she wouldn't be startled by seeing him so suddenly beside her. She wasn't startled. She had been watching him and the other javelin throwers for weeks.

"Killed enough little animals for today?" Helen asked him. "Hunting something else?"

"From the very beginning," Garp wrote, "Helen knew how to get the words in."

"With all the reading you do, I think you're going to be a writer," Garp told Helen; he was trying to be casual, but he guiltily hid the point of his javelin with his foot.

"No chance," Helen said. She had no doubt about it.

"Well, maybe you'll *marry* a writer," Garp said to her. She looked up at him, her face very serious, her new prescription sunglasses better suited to her wide cheekbones than her last pair that always slid down her nose.

"If I marry *anybody,* I'll marry a writer," Helen said. "But I doubt I'll marry anybody."

Garp had been trying to joke; Helen's seriousness made him nervous. He said, "Well, I'm sure you won't marry a *wrestler.*"

"You can be *very* sure," Helen said. Perhaps young Garp could not conceal his pain, because Helen added, "Unless it's a wrestler who's also a writer."

"But a writer first and foremost," Garp guessed.

"Yes, a *real* writer," Helen said, mysteriously—but ready to define what she meant by that. Garp didn't dare ask her. He let her go back to her book.

It was a long walk down the stadium stairs, dragging his javelin behind him. Will she ever wear anything but that gray sweat suit? he wondered. Garp wrote later that he first discovered he had an imagination while trying to imagine Helen Holm's body. "With her always in that damn sweat suit," he wrote, "I *had* to imagine her body; there was no other way to see it." Garp imagined that Helen had a very good body—and nowhere in his writing does he say he was disappointed when he finally saw the real thing.

It was that afternoon in the empty stadium, with frog gore on the point of his javelin, when Helen Holm provoked his imagination and T. S. Garp decided he was going to be a writer. A *real* writer, as Helen had said.

# 4

⊰⊱⊰⊱⊰⊱⊰⊱⊰⊱⊰⊱⊰⊱

# Graduation

T. S. GARP wrote a short story every month he was at Steering, from the end of his freshman year until his graduation, but it wasn't until his junior year that he showed anything he wrote to Helen. After her first year as a spectator at Steering, Helen was sent to Talbot Academy for girls, and Garp saw her only on occasional weekends. She would sometimes attend the home wrestling meets. It was after one such match that Garp saw her and asked her to wait for him until he'd showered; he had something in his locker he wanted to give her.

"Oh boy," Helen said. "Your old elbow pads?"

She didn't come to the wrestling room anymore, even if she was home from Talbot on a long vacation. She wore dark green knee socks and a gray flannel skirt, with pleats; often her sweater, always a dark and solid color, matched her knee socks, and always her long dark hair was up, twirled in a braid on top of her head, or complexly pinned. She had a wide mouth with very thin lips and she never wore lipstick. Garp knew that she always smelled nice, but he never touched her. He did not imagine that anyone did; she was as slender

91

and nearly as tall as a young tree—she was taller than Garp by two inches or more—and she had sharp, almost painful-looking bones in her face, although her eyes behind her glasses were always soft and large, and a rich honey-brown.

"Your old wrestling shoes?" Helen asked him, inquiring of the large-sized, lumpy envelope that was sealed.

"It's something to read," Garp said.

"I've got plenty to read," Helen said.

"It's something I wrote," Garp told her.

"Oh boy," Helen said.

"You don't have to read it now," Garp told her. "You can take it back to school and write me a letter."

"I've got plenty to write," Helen said. "I've got papers due all the time."

"Then we can talk about it, later," Garp said. "Are you going to be here for Easter?"

"Yes, but I have a date," Helen said.

"Oh boy," said Garp. But when he reached to take back his story, the knuckles of her long hand were very white and she would not let go of the package.

In the 133-pound class, his junior year, Garp finished the season with a won-lost record of 12–1, losing only in the finals of the New England championships. In his senior year, he would win everything—captain the team, be voted Most Valuable Wrestler, and take the New England title. His team would represent the beginning of an almost twenty-year dominance of New England wrestling by Ernie Holm's Steering teams. In this part of the country, Ernie had what he called an Iowa advantage. When Ernie was gone, Steering wrestling would go downhill. And perhaps because Garp was the first of many Steering stars, he was always special to Ernie Holm.

Helen couldn't have cared less. She was glad when her father's wrestlers won, because that made her father happy. But in Garp's senior year, when he captained the Steering team, Helen never attended a single match.

She did return his story, though—in the mail from Talbot, with this letter.

> *Dear Garp,*
>     *This story shows promise, although I do think, at this point, you are more of a wrestler than a writer. There is a care taken with the language, and a feeling for people, but the situation seems rather contrived and the ending of this story is pretty juvenile. I do appreciate you showing it to me, though.*
>
>                             *Yours,*
>                             *Helen*

There would be other rejection letters in Garp's writing career, of course, but none would mean as much to him as this one. Helen had actually been kind. The story Garp gave her was about two young lovers who are murdered in a cemetery by the girl's father, who thinks they are grave robbers. After this unfortunate error, the lovers are buried side by side; for some completely unknown reason, their graves are promptly robbed. It is not certain what becomes of the father— not to mention the grave robber.

Jenny told Garp that his first efforts at writing were rather unreal, but Garp was encouraged by his English teacher—the closest thing Steering had to a writer-in-residence, a frail man with a stutter whose name was Tinch. He had very bad breath, remindful to Garp of the dog breath of Bonkers—a closed room of dead geraniums. But what Tinch said, though odorous, was kind. He applauded Garp's imagination, and he taught Garp, once and for all, good old grammar and a love of exact language. Tinch was called Stench by the Steering boys of Garp's day, and messages were constantly left for him about his halitosis. Mouthwash deposited on his desk. Toothbrushes in the campus mail.

It was after one such message—a package of spearmint breath fresheners taped to the map of Literary

England—that Tinch asked his composition class if they thought he had bad breath. The class sat as still as moss, but Tinch singled out young Garp, his favorite, his most trusted, and he asked him directly, "Would *you* say, Garp, that my b-b-breath was bad?"

Truth moved in and out of the open windows on this spring day of Garp's senior year. Garp was known for his humorless honesty, his wrestling, his English composition. His other grades were indifferent to poor. From an early age, Garp later claimed, he sought perfection and did not spread himself thin. His test scores, for general aptitude, showed that he wasn't very apt at anything; he was no natural. This came as no surprise to Garp, who shared with his mother a belief that *nothing* came naturally. But when a reviewer, after Garp's second novel, called Garp "a born writer," Garp had a fit of mischief. He sent a copy of the review to the testing people in Princeton, New Jersey, with a note suggesting that they double-check their previous ratings. Then he sent a copy of his test scores to the reviewer, with a note that said: "Thank you very much, but I wasn't 'born' anything." In Garp's opinion, he was no more a "born" writer than he was a born nurse or a born ball turret gunner.

"G-G-Garp?" stuttered Mr. Tinch, bending close to the boy—who smelled the terrible truth in Senior Honors English Composition. Garp knew he would win the annual creative writing prize. The sole judge was always Tinch. And if he could just pass third-year math, which he was taking for the second time, he would respectably graduate and make his mother very happy.

"Do I have b-b-bad breath, Garp?" Tinch asked.

" 'Good' and 'bad' are matters of opinion, sir," Garp said.

"In *your* opinion, G-G-Garp?" Tinch said.

"In *my* opinion," Garp said, without batting an eye, "you've got the best breath of any teacher at this school." And he looked hard across the classroom at Benny Potter from New York—a *born* wise-ass, even

Garp would agree—and he stared Benny's grin off Benny's face because Garp's eyes said to Benny that Garp would break Benny's neck if he made a peep.

And Tinch said, "Thank you, Garp," who won the writing prize, despite the note submitted with his last paper.

*Mr. Tinch: I lied in class because I didn't want those other assholes to laugh at you. You should know, however, that your breath is really pretty bad. Sorry.*

*T. S. Garp*

"You know w-w-what?" Tinch asked Garp when they were alone together, talking about Garp's last story.

"What?" Garp said.

"There's nothing I can d-d-do about my breath," Tinch said. "I think it's because I'm d-d-dying," he said, with a twinkle. "I'm r-r-rotting from the inside out!" But Garp was not amused and he watched for news of Tinch for years after his graduation, relieved that the old gentleman did not appear to have anything terminal.

Tinch would die in the Steering quadrangle one winter night of causes wholly unrelated to his bad breath. He was coming home from a faculty party, where it was admitted that he'd possibly had too much to drink, and he slipped on the ice and knocked himself unconscious on the frozen footpath. The night watchman did not find the body until almost dawn, by which time Tinch had frozen to death.

It is unfortunate that wise-ass Benny Potter was the first to tell Garp the news. Garp ran into Potter in New York, where Potter worked for a magazine. Garp's low opinion of Potter was enhanced by Garp's low opinion of magazines, and by Garp's belief that Potter always envied Garp for Garp's more significant output as a writer. "Potter is one of those wretches who has a dozen novels hidden in his drawers," Garp wrote, "but he wouldn't dare show them to anybody."

In Garp's Steering years, however, Garp was also not outgoing at showing his work around. Only Jenny and Tinch got to see his progress—and there was the one story he gave Helen Holm. Garp decided he wouldn't give Helen another story until he wrote one that was so good she wouldn't be able to say anything bad about it.

"Did you hear?" Benny Potter asked Garp in New York.

"What?" Garp said.

"Old Stench kicked off," Benny said. "He f-f-froze to death."

"What did you say?" Garp said.

"Old Stench," Potter said. Garp had never liked that nickname. "He got drunk and went wobbling home through the quad—fell down and cracked his noggin, and never woke up in the morning."

"You asshole," Garp said.

"It's the truth, Garp," Benny said. "It was fucking fifteen-below. Although," he added, dangerously, "I'd have thought that old furnace of a mouth of his would have kept him w-w-warm."

They were in the bar of a nice hotel, somewhere in the Fifties, somewhere between Park Avenue and Third; Garp never knew where he was when he was in New York. He was meeting someone else for lunch and had run into Potter, who had brought him here. Garp picked Potter up by his armpits and sat him on the bar.

"You little gnat, Potter," Garp said.

"You never liked me," Benny said.

Garp tipped Benny Potter backward on the bar so that the pockets of Potter's open suit jacket were dipped into the bar sink.

"Leave me alone!" Benny said. "You were always old Stench's favorite ass-wipe!"

Garp shoved Benny so that Benny's rump slouched into the bar sink; the sink was full of soaking glasses, and the water sloshed up on the bar.

"Please don't sit on the bar, sir," the bartender said to Benny.

"Jesus Christ, I'm being assaulted, you moron!" Benny said. Garp was already leaving and the bartender had to pull Benny Potter out of the sink and set him down, off the bar. "That son of a bitch, my *ass* is all wet!" Benny cried.

"Would you please watch your language here, sir?" the bartender said.

"My fucking wallet is soaked!" Benny said, wringing out the seat of his pants and holding up his sodden wallet to the bartender. "Garp!" Benny hollered, but Garp was gone. "You always had a lousy sense of humor, Garp!"

It *is* fair to say, especially in Garp's Steering days, that he was at least rather humorless about his wrestling and his writing—his favorite pastime and his would-be career.

"How do you know you're going to be a writer," Cushie Percy asked him once.

It was Garp's senior year and they were walking out of town along the Steering River to a place Cushie said she knew. She was home for the weekend from Dibbs. The Dibbs School was the fifth prep school for girls that Cushie Percy had attended; she'd started out at Talbot, in Helen's class, but Cushie had disciplinary problems and she'd been asked to leave. The disciplinary problems had repeated themselves at three other schools. Among the boys at Steering, the Dibbs School was famous—and popular—for its girls with disciplinary problems.

It was high tide on the Steering River and Garp watched an eight-oared shell glide out on the water; a sea gull followed it. Cushie Percy took Garp's hand. Cushie had many complicated ways of testing a boy's affection for her. Many of the Steering boys were willing to handle Cushie when they were alone with her, but most of them did not like to be *seen* demonstrating any affection for her. Garp, Cushie noticed, didn't care. He held her hand firmly; of course, they had grown up together, but she did not think they were very good or close friends. At least, Cushie thought, if Garp wanted what the others wanted, he was not embarrassed to be seen pursuing it. Cushie liked him for this.

"I thought you were going to be a wrestler," Cushie said to Garp.

"I *am* a wrestler," Garp said. "I'm *going* to be a writer."

"And you're going to marry Helen Holm," Cushie teased him.

"Maybe," Garp said; his hand went a little limp in hers. Cushie knew this was another humorless topic with him—Helen Holm—and she should be careful.

A group of Steering boys came up the river path toward them; they passed, and one of them called back, "What are you getting into, Garp?"

Cushie squeezed his hand. "Don't let them bother you," she said.

"They don't bother me," Garp said.

"What are you going to write about?" Cushie asked him.

"I don't know," Garp said.

He didn't even know if he was going to college. Some schools in the Midwest had been interested in his wrestling, and Ernie Holm had written some letters. Two places had asked to see him and Garp had visited them. In their wrestling rooms, he had not felt so much outclassed as he had felt out*wanted*. The college wrestlers seemed to want to beat him more than he wanted to beat them. But one school had made him a cautious offer—a little money, and no promises beyond the first year. Fair enough, considering he was from New England. But Ernie had told him this already. "It's a different sport out there, kid. I mean, you've got the ability—and if I do say so myself, you've had the coaching. What you haven't had is the competition.

And you've got to be hungry for it, Garp. You've got to really be interested, you know."

And when he asked Tinch about where he should go to school, for his *writing,* Tinch had appeared at a typical loss. "Some g-g-good school, I guess," he said. "But if you're going to w-w-write," Tinch said, "won't you d-d-do it anywhere?"

"You have a nice body," Cushie Percy whispered to Garp, and he squeezed her hand back.

"So do *you,*" he told her, honestly. She had, in fact, an absurd body. Small but wholly bloomed, a compact blossom. Her name, Garp thought, should not have been Cushman but *Cushion*—and since their childhood together, he had sometimes called her that. "Hey, Cushion, want to take a walk?" She said she knew a place.

"Where are you taking me?" Garp asked her.

"Ha!" she said. *"You're* taking *me.* I'm just showing you the way. And the place," she said.

They went off the path by the part of the Steering River that long ago was called The Gut. A ship had been mired there once, but there was no visible evidence. Only the shore betrayed a history. It was at this narrow bend that Everett Steering had imagined obliterating the British—and here were Everett's cannons, three huge iron tubes, rusting into the concrete mountings. Once they had swiveled, of course, but the later-day town fathers had fixed them forever in place. Beside them was a permanent cluster of cannon balls, grown together in cement. The balls were greenish and red with rust, as if they belonged to a vessel long undersea, and the concrete platform where the cannons were mounted was now littered with youthful trash—beer cans and broken glass. The grassy slope leading down to the still and almost empty river was trampled, as if nibbled by sheep—but Garp knew it was merely pounded by countless Steering schoolboys and their dates. Cushie's choice of a place to go was not very original, though it was like her, Garp thought.

Garp liked Cushie, and William Percy had always

treated Garp well. Garp had been too young to know Stewie Two, and Dopey was Dopey. Young Pooh was a strange, scary child, Garp thought, but Cushie's touching brainlessness was straight from her mother, Midge Steering Percy. Garp felt dishonest with Cushie for not mentioning what he took to be the utter assholery of her father, Fat Stew.

"Haven't you ever been here before?" Cushie asked Garp.

"Maybe with my mother," Garp said, "but it's been a while." Of course he knew what "the cannons" were. The pet phrase at Steering was "getting banged at the cannons"—as in "I got banged at the cannons last weekend," or "You should have seen old Fenley blasting away at the cannons." Even the cannons themselves bore these informal inscriptions: "Paul banged Betty, '58," and "M. Overton, '59, shot his wad here."

Across the languid river Garp watched the golfers from the Steering Country Club. Even far away, their ridiculous clothing looked unnatural against the green fairway and beyond the marsh grass that grew down to the mudflats. Their madras prints and plaids among the green-brown, gray-brown shoreline made them look like cautious and out-of-place land animals following their hopping white dots across a lake. "Jesus, golf is silly," Garp said. His thesis of games with balls and clubs, again; Cushie had heard it before and wasn't interested. She settled down in a soft place—the river below them, bushes around them, and over their shoulders the yawning mouths of the great cannons. Garp looked up into the mouth of the nearest cannon and was startled to see the head of a smashed doll, one glassy eye on him.

Cushie unbuttoned his shirt and lightly bit his nipples.

"I like you," she said.

"I like *you,* Cushion," he said.

"Does it spoil it?" Cushie asked him. "Us being old friends?"

"Oh no," he said. He hoped they would hurry ahead to "it" because *it* had never happened to Garp before, and he was counting on Cushie for her experience. They kissed wetly in the well-pounded grass; Cushie was an open-mouthed kisser, artfully jamming her hard little teeth into his.

Honest, even at this age, Garp tried to mumble to her that he thought her father was an idiot.

"Of course he is," Cushie agreed. "Your mother's a little strange, too, don't you think?"

Well, yes, Garp supposed she was. "But I like her anyway," he said, most faithful of sons. Even then.

"Oh, *I* like her, too," Cushie said. Thus having said what was necessary, Cushie undressed. Garp undressed, but she asked him, suddenly, "Come on, where is it?"

Garp panicked. Where was *what?* He'd thought she was holding it.

"Where's your *thing?*" Cushie demanded, tugging what Garp thought *was* his thing.

"What?" Garp said.

"Oh wow, didn't you bring any?" Cushie asked him. Garp wondered what he was supposed to have brought.

"What?" he said.

"Oh, Garp," Cushie said. "Don't you have any *rubbers?*"

He looked apologetically at her. He was only a boy who'd lived his whole life with his mother, and the only rubber he'd seen had been slipped over the doorknob of their apartment in the infirmary annex, probably by a fiendish boy named Meckler—long since graduated and gone on to destroy himself.

Still, he should have known: Garp had heard much conversation of rubbers, of course.

"Come here," Cushie said. She led him to the cannons. "You've never done this, have you?" she asked him. He shook his head, honest to his sheepish core. "Oh, Garp," she said. "If you weren't such an old friend." She smiled at him, but he knew she wouldn't let him do it, now. She pointed into the mouth of the

101

middle cannon. "Look," she said. He looked. A jewel-like sparkle of ground glass, like pebbles he imagined might make up a tropical beach; and something else—not so pleasant. "Rubbers," Cushie told him.

The cannon was crammed with old condoms. Hundreds of prophylactics! A display of arrested reproduction. Like dogs urinating around the borders of their territory, the boys of the Steering School had left their messes in the mouth of the mammoth cannon guarding the Steering River. The modern world had left its stain upon another historical landmark.

Cushie was getting dressed. "You don't know anything," she teased him, "so what are you going to write about?" He had suspected this would pose a problem for a few years—a kink in his career plans.

He was about to get dressed but she made him lie down so that she could look at him. "You *are* beautiful," she said. "And it's all right." She kissed him.

"I can go *get* some rubbers," he said. "It wouldn't take long, would it? And we could come back."

"My train leaves at five," Cushie said, but she smiled sympathetically.

"I didn't think you had to be back at any special time," Garp said.

"Well, even Dibbs has *some* rules, you know," Cushie said; she sounded hurt by her school's lax reputation. "And besides," she said, "you see Helen. I know you do, don't you?"

"Not like this," he admitted.

"Garp, you shouldn't tell anybody everything," Cushie said.

It was a problem with his writing, too; Mr. Tinch had told him.

"You're too serious, all the time," Cushie said, because for once she was in a position where she could lecture him.

On the river below them an eight-oared shell sleeked through the narrow channel of water remaining in The Gut and rowed toward the Steering boathouse before the tide went out and left them without enough water to get home on.

Then Garp and Cushie saw the golfer. He had come down through the marsh grass on the other side of the river; with his violet madras slacks rolled up above his knees, he waded into the mud flats where the tide had already receded. Ahead of him, on the wetter mud flats, lay his golf ball, perhaps six feet from the edge of the remaining water. Gingerly, the golfer stepped forward, but the mud now rose above his calf; using his golf club for balance, he dipped the shiny head into the muck and swore.

"Harry, come back!" someone called to him. It was his golfing partner, a man dressed with equal vividness, knee-length shorts of a green that no grass ever was—and yellow knee socks. The golfer called Harry grimly stepped closer to his ball. He looked like a rare aquatic bird pursuing its egg in an oil slick.

"Harry, you're going to *sink* in that shit!" his friend warned him. It was then that Garp recognized Harry's partner: the man in green and yellow was Cushie's father, Fat Stew.

"It's a new ball!" Harry yelled; then his left leg disappeared, up to the hip; trying to turn back, Harry lost his balance and sat down. Quickly, he was mired to his waist, his frantic face very red above his powder-blue shirt—bluer than any sky. He waved his club but it slipped out of his hand and sailed into the mud, inches from his ball, impossibly white and forever out of Harry's reach.

"Help!" Harry screamed. But on all fours he was able to move a few feet toward Fat Stew and the safety of shore. "It feels like eels!" he cried. He moved forward on the trunk of his body, using his arms the way a seal on land will use its flippers. An awful *slorp*ing noise pursued him through the mud flats, as if beneath the mud some mouth was gasping to suck him in.

Garp and Cushie stifled their laughter in the bushes. Harry made his last lunge for shore. Stewart Percy, trying to help, stepped on the mud-flats with just one foot and promptly lost a golf shoe and a yellow sock to the suction.

"Ssshhh! And lie *still*," Cushie demanded. They both noticed Garp was erect. "Oh, that's too bad," Cushie whispered, looking sadly at his erection, but when he tried to tug her down in the grass with him, she said, "I don't want babies, Garp. Not even yours. And yours might be a *Jap* baby, you know," Cushie said. "And I surely don't want one of those."

"What?" Garp said. It was one thing not to know about rubbers, but what's this about Jap babies? he wondered.

"Ssshhh," Cushie whispered. "I'm going to give you something to write about."

The furious golfers were already slashing their way through the marsh grass, back to the immaculate fairway, when Cushie's mouth nipped the edge of Garp's tight belly button. Garp was never sure if his actual memory was jolted by that word *Jap,* and if at that moment he truly recalled bleeding in the Percys' house—little Cushie telling her parents that "Bonkie bit Garp" (and the scrutiny the child Garp had undergone in front of the naked Fat Stew). It may have been then that Garp remembered Fat Stew saying he had Jap eyes, and a view of his personal history clicked into perspective; regardless, at this moment Garp resolved to ask his mother for more details than she had offered him up to now. He felt the need to know more than that his father had been a soldier, and so forth. But he also felt Cushie Percy's soft lips on his belly, and when she took him suddenly into her warm mouth, he was very surprised and his sense of resolve was as quickly blown as the rest of him. There under the triple barrels of the Steering family cannons, T. S. Garp was first treated to sex in this relatively safe and nonreproductive manner. Of course, from Cushie's point of view, it was nonreciprocal, too.

They walked back along the Steering River holding hands.

"I want to see you next weekend," Garp told her. He resolved he would not forget the rubbers.

"I know you really love Helen," Cushie said. She probably hated Helen Holm, if she really knew her at all. Helen was such a snob about her brains.

"I still want to see you," Garp said.

"You're nice," Cushie told him, squeezing his hand. "And you're my oldest friend." But they both must have known that you can know someone all your life and never quite be friends.

"Who told you my father was Japanese?" Garp asked her.

"I don't know," Cushie said. "I don't know if he really is, either."

"I don't either," Garp admitted.

"I don't know why you don't ask your mother," Cushie said. But of course he *had* asked, and Jenny was absolutely unwavering from her first and only version.

When Garp phoned Cushie at Dibbs, she said, "Wow, it's *you!* My father just called and told me I was not to see you or write to you or talk to you. Or even read your letters—as if you wrote any. I think some golfer saw us leaving the cannons." She thought it was very funny, but Garp only saw that his future at the cannons had slipped from him. "I'll be home that weekend you graduate," Cushie told him. But Garp wondered: If he bought the condoms now, would they still be usable for graduation? Could rubbers go bad? In how many weeks? And should you keep them in the refrigerator? There was no one to ask.

Garp thought of asking Ernie Holm, but he was already fearful that Helen would hear of his being with Cushie Percy, and although he had no real relationship with Helen that he could be unfaithful to, Garp did have his imagination and his plans.

He wrote Helen a long confessional letter about his

105

"lust," as he called it—and how it did not compare to his higher feelings for her, as he referred to them. Helen replied promptly that she didn't know why he was telling *her* all this, but that in her opinion he *wrote* about it very well. It was better writing than the story he'd shown her, for example, and she hoped he would continue to show her his writing. She added that her opinion of Cushie Percy, from what little she knew of the girl, was that she was rather *stupid*. "But pleasant," Helen wrote. And if Garp was given to this lust, as he called it, wasn't he fortunate to have someone like Cushie around?

Garp wrote back that he would not show her another story until he wrote one that was good enough for her. He also discussed his feelings for not going to college. First, he thought, the only reason to go to college was to wrestle, and he wasn't sure he cared enough about it to wrestle at *that* level. He saw no point in simply continuing to wrestle at some small college where the sport wasn't emphasized. "It's only worth doing," Garp wrote to Helen, "if I'm going to try to be the best." He thought that trying to be the best at wrestling was not what he wanted; also, he knew, it was not likely he *could* be the best. And whoever heard of going to college to be the best at *writing*?

And where did he get this idea of wanting to be the best?

Helen wrote him that he should go to Europe, and Garp discussed this idea with Jenny.

To his surprise, Jenny had never thought he *would* go to college; she did not accept that this was what prep schools were *for*. "If the Steering School is supposed to give everyone such a first-rate education," Jenny said, "what on earth do you need *more* education for? I mean, if you've been paying attention, now you're educated. Right?" Garp didn't feel educated but he said he supposed he was. He thought he had been paying attention. As for Europe, Jenny was interested. "Well,

I'd certainly like to try that," she said. "It beats staying here."

It was then that Garp realized his mother meant to stay *with* him.

"I'll find out the best place for a writer to go in Europe," Jenny said to him. "I was thinking of writing something myself."

Garp felt so awful he went to bed. When he got up, he wrote Helen that he was doomed to be followed by his mother the rest of his life. "How can I write," he wrote to Helen, "with my mom looking over my shoulder?" Helen had no answers for that one; she said she would mention the problem to her father, and maybe Ernie would give Jenny some advice. Ernie Holm liked Jenny; he occasionally took her to a movie. Jenny had even become something of a wrestling fan, and although there couldn't have been anything more than friendship between them, Ernie was very sensitive to the unwed mother story—he had heard and accepted Jenny's version as all *he* needed to know, and he defended Jenny rather fiercely to those in the Steering community who suggested they were curious to know more.

But Jenny took her advice on cultural matters from Tinch. She asked him where a boy and his mother could go in Europe—which was the most artistic climate, the best place to write. Mr. Tinch had last been to Europe in 1913. He had stayed only for the summer. He had gone to England first, where there were several living Tinches, his British ancestry, but his old family frightened him by asking him for money—they asked for so much, and so rudely, that Tinch quickly fled to the Continent. But people were rude to him in France, and loud to him in Germany. He had a nervous stomach and was afraid of Italian cooking, so Tinch had gone to Austria. "In Vienna," Tinch told Jenny, "I found the *real* Europe. It was c-c-contemplative and artistic," Tinch said. "You could sense the sadness and the g-g-grandness."

A year later, World War I began. In 1918 the Spanish
107

grippe would kill many of the Viennese who had survived the war. The flu would kill old Klimt, and it would kill young Schiele and Schiele's young wife. Forty percent of the remaining male population would not survive World War II. The Vienna that Tinch would send Jenny and Garp to was a city whose life was over. Its tiredness could still be mistaken for a c-c-contemplative nature, but Vienna was hard-put to show much g-g-grandness anymore. Among the half-truths of Tinch, Jenny and Garp would still sense the sadness. "And *any* place can be artistic," Garp later wrote, "if there's an artist working there."

"Vienna?" Garp said to Jenny. He said it in the way he had said "Wrestling?" to her, over three years ago, lying on his sickbed and doubtful of her ability to pick out a sport for him. But he remembered she had been right then, and he knew nothing about Europe, and very little about anyplace else. Garp had taken three years of German at Steering, so there was some help, and Jenny (who was not good with languages) had read a book about the strange bedfellows of Austrian history: Maria Theresa and fascism. *From Empire to Anschluss!* was the name of the book. Garp had seen it in the bathroom, for years, but now no one could find it. Perhaps it was lost to the whirlpool bath.

"The last person I saw with it was Ulfelder," Jenny told Garp.

"Ulfelder graduated three years ago, Mom," Garp reminded her.

When Jenny told Dean Bodger that she would be leaving, Bodger said that Steering would miss her and would always be glad to have her back. Jenny did not want to be impolite, but she mumbled that one could be a nurse almost anywhere, she supposed; she did not know, of course, that she would never be a nurse again. Bodger was puzzled by Garp's not going to college. In the dean's opinion, Garp had not been a disciplinary problem at Steering since he had survived the roof of the infirmary annex at the age of five, and Bodger's fondness for the role he played in that rescue had always given him a fondness for Garp. Also, Dean Bodger was a wrestling fan, and one of Jenny's few admirers. But Bodger accepted that the boy seemed convinced by "the writing business," as Bodger called it. Jenny did not tell Bodger, of course, that she planned to do some writing of her own.

This part of the plan made Garp the most uncomfortable, but he did not even say a word of it to Helen. Everything was happening very fast and Garp could express his apprehension only to his wrestling coach, Ernie Holm.

"Your mom knows what she's doing, I'm sure," Ernie told him. "You just be sure about *you*."

Even old Tinch was full of optimism for the plan. "It's a little ec-ec-eccentric," Tinch told Garp, "but many good ideas are." Years later Garp would recall that Tinch's endearing stutter was like a message to Tinch from Tinch's body. Garp wrote that Tinch's body was trying to tell Tinch that he was going to f-f-freeze to death one day.

Jenny was saying that they would leave shortly after graduation, but Garp had hoped to stay around Steering for the summer.

"What on earth for?" Jenny asked him.

For Helen, he wanted to tell her, but he had no stories good enough for Helen; he had already said so. There was nothing to do but go away and write them. And he could never expect Jenny to stay another summer in Steering so that he could keep his appointment at the cannons with Cushie Percy; perhaps that was not meant to be. Still, he was hopeful that he could connect with Cushie on graduation weekend.

For Garp's graduation, it rained. The rain washed over the soggy Steering campus in sheets; the storm sewers bogged and the out-of-state cars plowed through the streets like yachts in a squall. The women looked helpless in their summer dresses; the loading of station wagons was hurried and miserable. A great crimson tent was erected in front of the Miles Seabrook Gymnasium and Field House, and the diplomas were handed out in this stale circus air; the speeches were lost in the rain beating the crimson canvas overhead.

Nobody stayed around. The big boats left town. Helen had not come because Talbot had its graduation the following weekend and she was still taking exams. Cushie Percy had been in attendance at the disappointing ceremony, Garp was sure; but he had not seen her. He knew she would be with her ridiculous family and Garp was wise to keep a safe distance from Fat Stew—an outraged father was still a father, after all, even if Cushman Percy's honor had long ago been lost.

When the late-afternoon sun came out, it hardly mattered. Steering was steamy and the ground—from Seabrook Stadium to the cannons—would be sodden for days. Garp imagined the deep ruts of water that he knew would be coursing through the soft grass at the cannons; even the Steering River would be swollen. The cannons themselves would be overflowing; the barrels were tilted up, and they filled with water every time it rained. In such weather, the cannons dribbled streams of broken glass and left slick puddles of old condoms on the stained concrete. There would be no enticing Cushie to the cannons this weekend, Garp knew.

But the three-pack of prophylactics crackled in his pocket like a tiny, dry fire of hope.

"Look," said Jenny. "I bought some beer. Go ahead and get drunk, if you want to."

"Jesus, Mom," Garp said, but he drank a few with her. They sat by themselves on his graduation night, the infirmary empty beside them, and every bed in the annex was empty and stripped of linen, too—except for the beds they would sleep in. Garp drank the beer and wondered if *everything* was an anticlimax; he reassured himself by thinking of the few good stories he had read, but though he had a Steering education, he was no reader—no match for Helen, or Jenny, for example.

Garp's way with a story was to find one he liked and read it again and again; it would spoil him for reading any other story for a long while. When he was at Steering he read Joseph Conrad's "The Secret Sharer" thirty-four times. He also read D. H. Lawrence's "The Man Who Loved Islands" twenty-one times; he felt ready to read it again, now.

Outside the windows of the tiny apartment in the infirmary annex, the Steering campus lay dark and wet and deserted.

"Well, look at it this way," Jenny said; she could see he was feeling let down. "It took you only four years to graduate from Steering, but *I've* been going to this damn school for eighteen." She was not much of a drinker, Jenny: half the way through her second beer, she fell asleep. Garp carried her into her bedroom; she had already taken off her shoes, and Garp removed only her nurse's pin—so that she wouldn't roll over and stick herself with it. It was a warm night, so he didn't cover her.

He drank another beer and then took a walk.

Of course he knew where he was going.

The Percy family house—originally the Steering family house—sat on its damp lawn not far from the infirmary annex. Only one light was on in Stewart Percy's house, and Garp knew whose light it was: little Pooh Percy, now fourteen, could not sleep with her light out. Cushie had also told Garp that Bainbridge was still inclined to wear a diaper—perhaps, Garp thought, because her family still insisted on calling her Pooh.

"Well," Cushie said, "I don't see what's *wrong* with it. She doesn't *use* the diapers, you know; I mean, she's *housebroken,* and all that. Pooh just likes to *wear* diapers—occasionally."

Garp stood on the misty grass beneath Pooh Percy's window and tried to remember which room was Cushie's. Since he couldn't remember, he decided to wake up Pooh; she was sure to recognize him, and she

111

was sure to tell Cushie. But Pooh came to her window like a ghost; she did not immediately appear to recognize Garp, who clung tenaciously to the ivy outside her window. Bainbridge Percy had eyes like a deer paralyzed in a car's headlights, about to be hit.

"For Christ's sake, Pooh, it's *me,*" Garp whispered to her.

"You want Cushie, don't you?" Pooh asked him, sullenly.

"Yes!" Garp grunted. Then the ivy tore and he fell into the hedges below. Cushie, who slept in her bathing suit, helped extricate him.

"Wow, you're going to wake up the whole house," she said. "Have you been drinking?"

"I've been *falling,*" Garp said, irritably. "Your sister is really weird."

"It's wet outside, all over," Cushie said to him. "Where can we go?"

Garp had thought of that. In the infirmary, he knew, were sixty empty beds.

But Garp and Cushie were not even past the Percy porch when Bonkers confronted them. The black beast was already out of breath, from descending the porch stairs, and his iron-gray muzzle was flecked with froth; his breath reached Garp like old sod flung in his face. Bonkers was growling, but even his growl had slowed down.

"Tell him to beat it," Garp whispered to Cushie.

"He's deaf," Cushie said. "He's very old."

"I know how old he is," Garp said.

Bonkers barked, a creaky and sharp sound, like the hinge of an unused door being forced open. He was thinner, but he easily weighed one hundred and forty pounds. A victim of ear mites and mange, old dog bite and barbed wire, Bonkers sniffed his enemy and held Garp cornered against the porch.

"Go *away,* Bonkie!" Cushie hissed.

Garp tried to sidestep the dog and noticed how slowly Bonkers reacted.

"He's half-*blind*," Garp whispered.

"And his nose doesn't smell much anymore," Cushie said.

"He ought to be dead," Garp whispered to himself, but he tried to step around the dog. Dimly, Bonkers followed. His mouth still reminded Garp of a steam shovel's power, and the loose flap of muscle on his black and shaggy chest indicated to Garp how hard the dog could lunge—but long ago.

"Just ig*nore* him," Cushie suggested, just as Bonkers lunged.

The dog was slow enough so that Garp could spin behind him; he pulled the dog's forepaws from under him and dropped his own weight, from his chest, on the dog's back. Bonkers buckled forward, he slid into the ground nose first—his hind legs still clawing. Garp now controlled the crumpled forepaws but the great dog's head was held down only by the weight of Garp's chest. A terrifying snarling developed as Garp bore down on the animal's spine and drove his chin into the dog's dense neck. In the scuffle, an *ear* appeared—in Garp's mouth—and Garp bit it. He bit as hard as he could, and Bonkers howled. He bit Bonker's ear in memory of his own missing flesh, he bit him for the four years he'd spent at Steering—and for his mother's eighteen years.

It was only when lights came on in the Percy house that Garp let old Bonkers go.

"Run!" Cushie suggested. Garp grabbed her hand and she came with him. A vile taste was in his mouth. "Wow, did you have to *bite* him?" Cushie asked.

"He bit me," Garp reminded her.

"I remember," Cushie said. She squeezed his hand and he led her where he wanted to go.

"What the hell is going on here?" they heard Stewart Percy yelling.

"It's Bonkie, it's Bonkie!" Pooh Percy called into the night.

"Bonkers!" called Fat Stew. "Here, Bonkers! Here,

113

Bonkers!" And they all heard the deaf dog's resounding caterwaul.

It was a commotion capable of carrying across an empty campus. It woke Jenny Fields, who peered out her window in the infirmary annex. Fortunately for Garp, he saw her turn on a light. He made Cushie hide behind him, in a corridor of the unoccupied annex, while he sought Jenny's medical advice.

"What happened to you?" Jenny asked him. Garp wanted to know if the blood running down his chin was his own or entirely Bonkers'. At the kitchen table, Jenny washed away a black scablike thing that was stuck to Garp. It fell off Garp's throat and landed on the table—it was the size of a silver dollar. They both stared at it.

"What *is* it?" Jenny asked.

"An ear," Garp said. "Or part of one."

On the white enamel table lay the black leathery remnant of an ear, curling slightly at the edges and cracked like an old, dry glove.

"I ran into Bonkers," Garp said.

"An ear for an ear," said Jenny Fields.

There was not a mark on Garp; the blood belonged solely to Bonkers.

When Jenny went back to her bedroom, Garp snuck Cushie into the tunnel that led to the main infirmary. For eighteen years he had learned the way. He took her to the wing farthest from his mother's apartment in the annex; it was over the main admittance room, near the rooms for surgery and anesthesia.

Thus sex for Garp would forever be associated with certain smells and sensations. The experience would remain secretive but relaxed: a final reward in harrowing times. The odor would stay in his mind as deeply personal and yet vaguely *hospital*. The surroundings would forever seem to be deserted. Sex for Garp would remain in his mind as a solitary act committed in an abandoned universe—sometime after it had rained. It was always an act of terrific optimism.

Cushie, of course, evoked for Garp many images of cannons. When the third condom of the three-pack was exhausted, she asked if that was all he had—if he'd bought only one package. A wrestler loves nothing so much as hard-earned exhaustion; Garp fell asleep to Cushie complaining.

"The first time you don't have any," she was saying, "and now you run out? It is lucky we're such old friends."

It was still dark and far from dawn when Stewart Percy woke them. Fat Stew's voice violated the old infirmary like an unnamable disease. "Open up!" they heard him hollering, and they crept to the window to see.

On the green, green lawn, in his bathrobe and slippers—and with Bonkers leashed beside him—Cushie's father bleated at the windows of the infirmary annex. It was not long before Jenny appeared in the light.

"Are you ill?" she asked Stewart.

"I want my daughter!" Stewart yelled.

"Are you drunk?" Jenny asked.

"You let me in!" Stewart screamed.

"The doctor is out," said Jenny Fields, "and I doubt there is anything I can treat you for."

"Bitch!" Stewart bellowed. "Your bastard son has seduced my daughter! I know they're in there, in that fucking infirmary!"

It *is* a fucking infirmary now, Garp thought, delighting in the touch and scent of Cushie trembling beside him. In the cool air, through the dark window, they shivered in silence.

"You should see my *dog!*" Stewart screeched to Jenny. "Blood everywhere! The dog hiding under the hammock! Blood on the porch!" Stewart croaked. "What the hell did that bastard do to Bonkers?"

Garp felt Cushie flinch beside him when his mother spoke. What Jenny said must have made Cushie Percy remember *her* remark, thirteen years earlier. What Jenny Fields said was, "Garp bit Bonkie." Then her light went out, and in the darkness cast over the infirmary and its annex only Fat Stew's breathing was audible with the runoff from the rain—washing over the Steering School, rinsing everything clean.

# 5

## In the City Where
## Marcus Aurelius Died

WHEN JENNY took Garp to Europe, Garp was
better prepared for the solitary confinement of
a writer's life than most eighteen-year-olds. He
was already thriving in a world of his own imagination; after all, he had been brought up by a woman who
thought that solitary confinement was a perfectly natural
way to live. It would be years before Garp noticed that
he didn't have any friends, and this oddity never struck
Jenny Fields as odd. In his distant and polite fashion,
Ernie Holm was the first friend Jenny Fields ever had.

Before Jenny and Garp found an apartment, they
lived in more than a dozen pensions all over Vienna.
It was Mr. Tinch's idea that this would be the ideal
way for them to choose the part of the city they liked
best: they would live in all the districts and decide for
themselves. But short-term life in a pension must have
been more pleasant for Tinch in the summer of 1913;
when Jenny and Garp came to Vienna, it was 1961;
they quickly tired of lugging their typewriters from
pension to pension. It was this experience, however, that

gave Garp the material for his first major short story, "The Pension Grillparzer." Garp hadn't even known what a pension *was* before he came to Vienna, but he quickly discovered that a pension had somewhat less to offer than a hotel; it was always smaller, and never elegant; it sometimes offered breakfast, and sometimes not. A pension was sometimes a bargain and sometimes a mistake. Jenny and Garp found pensions that were clean and comfortable and friendly, but they were often seedy.

Jenny and Garp wasted little time deciding that they wanted to live within or near the Ringstrasse, the great round street that circles the heart of the old city; it was the part of the city where almost everything was, and where Jenny could manage a little better without speaking any German—it was the more sophisticated, cosmopolitan part of Vienna, if there really is such a part of Vienna.

It was fun for Garp to be in charge of his mother; three years of Steering German made Garp their leader, and he clearly enjoyed being Jenny's boss.

"Have the schnitzel, Mom," he would tell her.

"I thought this Kalbsnieren sounded interesting," Jenny said.

"Veal kidney, Mom," Garp said. "Do you like kidney?"

"I don't know," Jenny admitted. "Probably not."

When they finally moved into a place of their own, Garp took over the shopping. Jenny had spent eighteen years eating in the Steering dining halls; she had never learned how to cook, and now she couldn't read the directions. It was in Vienna that Garp learned how he loved to cook, but the first thing he claimed to like about Europe was the W.C.—the water closet. In his time spent in pensions, Garp discovered that a water closet was a tiny room with nothing but a toilet in it; it was the first thing about Europe that made sense to Garp. He wrote Helen that "it is the wisest system—to urinate and move your bowels in one place, and to brush your teeth in another." The W.C., of course, would also feature prominently in Garp's story, "The Pension Grillparzer," but Garp would not write that story, or anything else, for a while.

Although he was unusually self-disciplined for an eighteen-year-old, there were simply too many things to see; together with those things he was suddenly responsible for, Garp was very busy and for months the only satisfying writing he did was to Helen. He was too excited with his new territory to develop the necessary routine for writing, although he tried.

He tried to write a story about a family; all he knew when he began was that the family had an interesting life and the members were all close to each other. That was not enough to know.

Jenny and Garp moved into a cream-colored, high-ceilinged apartment on the second floor of an old building on the Schwindgasse, a little street in the fourth district. They were right around the corner from the Prinz-Eugen-Strasse, the Schwarzenbergplatz, and the Upper and Lower Belvedere. Garp eventually went to all the art museums in the city, but Jenny never went to any except the Upper Belvedere. Garp explained to her that the Upper Belvedere contained only the nineteenth- and twentieth-century paintings, but Jenny said that the nineteenth and twentieth centuries were enough for her. Garp explained that she could at least walk through the gardens to the Lower Belvedere and see the baroque collection, but Jenny shook her head; she had taken several art history courses at Steering—she'd had enough education, she said.

"And the Brueghels, Mom!" Garp said. "You just take the Strassenbahn up the Ring and get off at Mariahilferstrasse. The big museum across from the streetcar stop is the Kunsthistorisches."

"But I can *walk* to the Belvedere," Jenny said. "Why take a streetcar?"

She could also walk to the Karlskirche, and there were

some interesting-looking embassy buildings a short distance up Argentinierstrasse. The Bulgarian Embassy was right across the street from their apartment on the Schwindgasse. Jenny said she liked staying in her own neighborhood. There was a coffeehouse a block away and she sometimes went there and read the newspapers in English. She never went out to eat anywhere unless Garp took her; and unless he cooked for her in their apartment, she didn't eat anything at home. She was completely taken with the idea of writing something— more taken, at this phase, than Garp.

"I don't have time to be a tourist at this point in my life," she told her son. "But *you* go ahead, soak up the culture. That's what you *should* be doing."

"Absorb, ab-ab-absorb," Tinch had told them. That seemed to Jenny to be just what Garp should do; for herself, she found she'd already absorbed enough to have plenty to say. Jenny Fields was forty-one. She imagined that the interesting part of her life was behind her; all she wanted to do was write about it.

Garp gave her a piece of paper to carry with her. It had her address written on it, in case she got lost: Schwindgasse 15/2, Wien IV. Garp had to teach her how to pronounce her address—a tedious lesson. *"Schwindgassefünfzehnzwei!"* Jenny spat.

"Again," Garp said. "Do you want to *stay* lost when you get lost?"

Garp investigated the city by day and found places to take Jenny to at night, and in the late afternoons when she was through her writing; they would have a beer, or a glass of wine, and Garp would describe his whole day to her. Jenny listened politely. Wine or beer made her sleepy. Usually they ate a nice dinner somewhere and Garp escorted Jenny home on the Strassenbahn; he took special pride in never using taxis, because he had learned the streetcar system so thoroughly. Sometimes he went to the open markets in the morning and came home early and cooked all afternoon. Jenny never complained; it didn't matter to her whether they ate in or out.

"This is a Gumpoldskirchner," Garp would say, explaining the wine. "It goes very well with the Schweine-braten."

"What funny words," Jenny remarked.

In a typical evaluation of Jenny's prose style, Garp later wrote: "My mother had such a struggle with her English, it's no wonder she never bothered to learn German."

Although Jenny Fields sat every day at her type-writer, she did not know how to write. Although she was—physically—writing, she did not enjoy reading over what she'd written. Before long, she tried to re-member the good things she'd read and what made them different from her own first-draft attempt. She'd simply begun at the beginning. "I was born," and so forth. "My parents wanted me to stay at Wellesley; how-ever . . ." And, of course: "I decided I wanted a child of my own and eventually got one in the following manner. . . ." But Jenny had read enough good stories to know that hers didn't *sound* like the good stories in her memory. She wondered what could be wrong, and she frequently sent Garp on errands to the few book-stores that sold books in English. She wanted to look more closely at how books began; she had quickly pro-duced over three hundred typed pages, yet she felt that her book never really *started*.

But Jenny suffered her writing problems silently; she was cheerful with Garp, even if she was rarely very attentive. Jenny Fields felt all her life that things began and came to an end. Like Garp's education—like her own. Like Sergeant Garp. She had not lost any affection for her son, but she felt that a phase of her mothering him was over; she felt she had brought Garp along this far, and now she should let him find something to do by himself. She could not go through their lives signing him up for wrestling, or for something else. Jenny liked living with her son; in fact, it didn't occur to her that they would ever live apart. But Jenny expected Garp to entertain himself every day in Vienna, and so Garp did.

He had gotten no further with his story about a close, interesting family except that he had found something interesting for them to do. The father of the family was some sort of inspector and his family went with him when he did his job. The job involved scrutinizing all the restaurants and hotels and pensions in Austria—evaluating them and giving them a rating according to A, B, C. It was a job Garp imagined that *he'd* like to have. In a country like Austria, so dependent on tourism, the classification and reclassification of the places the tourists ate in and slept in *should* have a kind of desperate importance, but Garp couldn't imagine what could be important about it—or for whom. So far all he had was this family: they had a funny job. They exposed flaws; they gave out the grades. So what? It was easier to write to Helen.

That late summer and early fall, Garp walked and rode the trolleys all over Vienna, meeting no one. He wrote Helen that "a part of adolescence is feeling that there's no one else around who's enough like yourself to understand you"; Garp wrote that he believed Vienna enhanced that feeling in him "because in Vienna there really *isn't* anyone like myself around."

His perception was at least numerically correct. There were very few people in Vienna who were even the same age as Garp. Not many Viennese were born in 1943; for that matter, not many Viennese were born from the start of the Nazi occupation in 1938 through the end of the war in 1945. And although there were a surprising number of babies born out of rapes, not many Viennese *wanted* babies until after 1955—the end of the Russian occupation. Vienna was a city occupied by foreigners for seventeen years. To most Viennese, it is understandable, those seventeen years did not seem like a good and wise time to have children. It was Garp's experience to live in a city that made him feel peculiar to be eighteen years old. This must have made him grow older faster, and this must have contributed to his increasing sense that Vienna was more of "a museum housing a dead city"—as he wrote Helen—than it was a city that was still alive.

Garp's observation was not offered as criticism. Garp *liked* wandering around in a museum. "A more real city might not have suited me so well," he later wrote. "But Vienna was in its death phase; it lay still and let me look at it, and think about it, and look again. In a *living* city, I could never have noticed so much. Living cities don't hold still."

Thus T. S. Garp spent the warm months *noticing* Vienna, writing letters to Helen Holm, and managing the domestic life of his mother, who had added the isolation of writing to her chosen life of solitude. "My mother, the writer," Garp referred to her, facetiously, in countless letters to Helen. But he envied Jenny, that she was writing at all. He felt stuck with his story. He realized he could go on giving his made-up family one adventure after another, but where were they going? To one more B restaurant with such a weakness in their desserts that an A rating was a lifetime out of reach; to one more B hotel, sliding to C as surely as the mildew smell in the lobby would never go away. Perhaps someone in the inspector's family could be poisoned, in a class A restaurant, but what would it *mean?* And there could be crazy people, or even criminals, hiding out in one of the pensions, but what would they have to do with the scheme of things?

Garp knew that he did not have a scheme of things.

He saw a four-member circus unload from Hungary, or Yugoslavia, at a railroad station. He tried to imagine *them* in his story. There had been a bear who rode a motorcycle, around and around a parking lot. A small crowd gathered and a man who walked on his hands collected money for the bear's performance in a pot balanced on the soles of his feet; he fell, occasionally, but so did the bear.

Finally, the motorcycle wouldn't start anymore. It never became clear what the two other members of this circus did; just as they were trying to take over for the bear and the man who walked on his hands the police came and asked them to fill out a lot of forms. That had not been interesting to watch and the crowd—what there was of one—had gone away. Garp had stayed the longest, not because he was interested in further performances by this decrepit circus but because he was interested in getting them into his story. He couldn't imagine how. As Garp was leaving the railroad station, he could hear the bear throwing up.

For weeks Garp's only progress with his story was a title: "The Austrian Tourist Bureau." He didn't like it. He went back to being a tourist instead of a writer.

But when the weather grew colder, Garp tired of tourism; he took to carping at Helen for not writing him back enough—a sign he was writing to her too much. She was much busier than he was; she was in college, where she'd been accepted with sophomore standing, and she was carrying more than double the average load of courses. If Helen and Garp were similar, in these early years, it was that they both behaved as if they were going somewhere in a *hurry*. "Leave poor Helen alone," Jenny advised him. "I thought you were going to write something beside letters." But Garp did not like to think of competing in the same apartment with his mother. Her typewriter never paused for thought; Garp knew that its steady pounding would probably end his career as a writer before he could properly begin. "My mother never knew about the silence of revision," Garp once remarked.

By November Jenny had six hundred manuscript pages, but still she had the feeling that she had not really begun. Garp had no subject that could spill out of him in this fashion. Imagination, he realized, came harder than memory.

His "breakthrough," as he would call it when he wrote Helen, occurred one cold and snowy day in the

Museum of the History of the City of Vienna. It was a museum within easy walking distance of the Schwindgasse; somehow he had skipped seeing it, knowing he could walk there any day. Jenny told him about it. It was one of the two or three places she had actually visited herself, only because it was right across the Karlsplatz and well within what she called her neighborhood.

She mentioned there was a writer's room in the museum; she forgot whose. She'd thought having a writer's room in a museum was an interesting idea.

"A writer's *room*, Mom?" Garp asked.

"Yes, it's a whole room," Jenny said. "They took all the writer's furniture, and maybe the walls and floor, too. I don't know how they did it."

"I don't know *why* they did it," Garp said. "The whole room is in the museum?"

"Yes, I think it was a bedroom," Jenny said, "but it was also where the writer actually *wrote*."

Garp rolled his eyes. It sounded obscene to him. Would the writer's toothbrush be there? And the chamber pot?

It was a perfectly ordinary room, but the bed looked too small—like a child's bed. The writing table looked small, too. Not the bed or the table of an expansive writer, Garp thought. The wood was dark; everything looked easily breakable; Garp thought his mother had a better room to write in. The writer whose room was enshrined in the Museum of the History of the City of Vienna was named Franz Grillparzer; Garp had never heard of him.

Franz Grillparzer died in 1872; he was an Austrian poet and dramatist, whom very few people outside Austria have ever heard of. He is one of those nineteenth-century writers who did not survive the nineteenth century with any enduring popularity, and Garp would later argue that Grillparzer did not deserve to survive the nineteenth century. Garp was not interested in plays and poems, but he went to the library and read what is considered to be Grillparzer's outstanding prose work: the long short story "The Poor Fiddler." Perhaps, Garp thought, his three years of Steering German were not enough to allow him to appreciate the story; in German, he hated it. He then found an English translation of the story in a secondhand bookstore on Habsburgergasse; he still hated it.

Garp thought that Grillparzer's famous story was a ludicrous melodrama; he also thought it was ineptly told and baldly sentimental. It was only vaguely remindful to him of nineteenth-century Russian stories, where often the character is an indecisive procrastinator and a failure in every aspect of practical life; but Dostoevsky, in Garp's opinion, could compel you to be interested in such a wretch; Grillparzer bored you with tearful trivia.

In the same secondhand bookstore Garp bought an English translation of the *Meditations* of Marcus Aurelius; he had been made to read Marcus Aurelius in a Latin class at Steering, but he had never read him in English before. He bought the book because the bookstore owner told Garp that Marcus Aurelius had died in Vienna.

"In the life of a man," Marcus Aurelius wrote, "his time is but a moment, his being an incessant flux, his sense a dim rushlight, his body a prey of worms, his soul an unquiet eddy, his fortune dark, his fame doubtful. In short, all that is body is as coursing waters, all that is of the soul as dreams and vapors." Garp somehow thought that Marcus Aurelius must have lived in Vienna when he wrote that.

The subject of Marcus Aurelius's dreary observations was certainly the *subject* of most serious writing, Garp thought; between Grillparzer and Dostoevsky the difference was not subject matter. The difference, Garp concluded, was intelligence and grace; the difference was art. Somehow this obvious discovery pleased him. Years later, Garp read in a critical introduction to Grillparzer's work that Grillparzer was "sensitive, tortured, fitfully paranoid, often depressed, cranky, and choked with melancholy; in short, a complex and modern man."

"Maybe so," Garp wrote. "But he was also an extremely bad writer."

Garp's conviction that Franz Grillparzer was a "bad" writer seemed to provide the young man with his first real confidence as an artist—even before he had written anything. Perhaps in every writer's life there needs to be that moment when some other writer is attacked as unworthy of the job. Garp's killer instinct in regard to poor Grillparzer was almost a wrestling secret; it was as if Garp had observed an opponent in a match with another wrestler; spotting the weaknesses, Garp *knew* he could do better. He even forced Jenny to read "The Poor Fiddler." It was one of the few times he would seek her *literary* judgment.

"Trash," Jenny pronounced it. "Simplistic. Maudlin. Cream puff."

They were *both* delighted.

"I didn't like his room, really," Jenny told Garp. "It was just not a writer's room."

"Well, I don't think that matters, Mom," Garp said.

"But it was a very cramped room," Jenny complained. "It was too dark, and it looked very *fussy*."

Garp peered into his mother's room. Over her bed and dresser, and taped to her wall mirror—nearly obscuring his mother's own image—were the scattered pages of her incredibly long and messy manuscript. Garp didn't think his mother's room looked very much like a writer's room, either, but he didn't say so.

He wrote Helen a long, cocky letter, quoting Marcus Aurelius and slamming Franz Grillparzer. In Garp's opinion, "Franz Grillparzer died forever in 1872 and like a cheap local wine does not travel very far from Vienna without spoiling." The letter was a kind of muscle-flexing; perhaps Helen knew that. The letter was calisthenics; Garp made a carbon copy of it and decided he liked it so well that he kept the original and sent

Helen the carbon. "I feel a little like a library," Helen wrote him. "It's as if you intend to use me as your file drawer."

Was Helen really complaining? Garp was not sensitive enough to Helen's own life to bother to ask her. He merely wrote back that he was "getting ready to write." He was confident she would like the results. Helen may have felt warned away from him, but she didn't indicate any anxiety; at college, she was gobbling courses at nearly triple the average rate. Approaching the end of her first semester, she was about to become a second-semester junior. The self-absorption and ego of a young writer did not frighten Helen Holm; she was moving at her own remarkable pace, and she appreciated someone who was determined. Also, she liked Garp's writing to her; she had an ego, too, and his letters, she kept telling him, were awfully well written.

In Vienna, Jenny and Garp went on a spree of Grillparzer jokes. They began to uncover little signs of the dead Grillparzer all over the city. There was a Grillparzergasse, there was a Kaffeehaus des Grillparzers; and one day in a pastry shop they were amazed to find a sort of layer cake named after him: Grillparzertorte! It was much too sweet. Thus, when Garp cooked for his mother, he asked her if she wanted her eggs soft-boiled or Grillparzered. And one day at the Schönbrunn Zoo they observed a particularly gangling antelope, its flanks spindly and beshitted; the antelope stood sadly in its narrow and foul winter quarters. Garp identified it: der Gnu des Grillparzers.

Of her own writing, Jenny one day remarked to Garp that she was guilty of "doing a Grillparzer." She explained that this meant she had introduced a scene or a character "like an alarm going off." The scene she had in mind was the scene in the movie house in Boston when the soldier had approached her. "At the movie," wrote Jenny Fields, "a soldier consumed with lust approached me."

"That's awful, Mom," Garp admitted. The phrase

"consumed with lust" was what Jenny meant by "doing a Grillparzer."

"But that's what it *was*," Jenny said. "It was lust, all right."

"It's better to say he was *thick* with lust," Garp suggested.

"Yuck," Jenny said. Another Grillparzer. It was the *lust* she didn't care for, in general. They discussed lust, as best they could. Garp confessed his lust for Cushie Percy and rendered a suitably tame version of the consummation scene. Jenny did not like it. "And Helen?" Jenny asked. "Do you feel that for Helen?"

Garp admitted he did.

"How terrible," Jenny said. She did not understand the feeling and did not see how Garp could ever associate it with pleasure, much less with affection.

" 'All that is body is as coursing waters,' " Garp said lamely, quoting Marcus Aurelius; his mother just shook her head. They ate dinner in a very red restaurant in the vicinity of Blutgasse. "Blood Street," Garp translated for her, happily.

"Stop translating everything," Jenny told him. "I don't want to know everything." She thought the decor of the restaurant was *too* red and the food was too expensive. The service was slow and they started for home too late. It was very cold and the gay lights of the Kärntnerstrasse did little to warm them.

"Let's get a taxi," Jenny said. But Garp insisted that in another five blocks they could take a streetcar just as easily. "You and your damn Strassenbahns," Jenny said.

It was clear that the subject of "lust" had spoiled their evening.

The first district glittered with Christmas gaudiness; between the towering spires of Saint Stephen's and the massive bulk of the opera house lay seven blocks of shops and bars and hotels; in those seven blocks, they could have been anywhere in the world at wintertime. "Some night we've got to go to the opera, Mom," Garp suggested. They had been in Vienna for six months without going to the opera, but Jenny did not like to stay up late at night.

"Go by yourself," Jenny said. She saw, ahead of them, three women standing in long fur coats; one of them had a matching fur muff and she held the muff in front of her face and breathed into it to warm her hands. She was quite elegant to look at, although there was something of the tinsel of Christmas about the other two women with her. Jenny envied the woman her muff. "That's what I want," Jenny announced. "Where can I get one of those?" She pointed to the women ahead of them, but Garp didn't know what she meant.

The women, he knew, were whores.

When the whores saw Jenny coming up the street with Garp, they were puzzled at the relationship. They saw a handsome boy with a plain but handsome woman who was old enough to be his mother; but Jenny hooked Garp's arm rather formally when she walked with him, and there was something like tension and confusion in the conversation Garp and Jenny were having—which made the whores think Jenny could *not* have been Garp's mother. Then Jenny pointed at them and they were angry: they thought Jenny was another whore who was working their territory and had snagged a boy who looked well-off and not sinister—a pretty boy who might have paid *them*.

In Vienna, prostitution is legal and complexly controlled. There is something like a union; there are medical certificates, periodical checkups, identification cards. Only the best-looking prostitutes are allowed to work the posh streets in the first district. In the outlying districts, the prostitutes are uglier or older, or both; they are also cheaper, of course. District by district, their prices are supposed to be fixed. When the whores saw Jenny, they stepped out on the sidewalk to block Jenny's and Garp's way. They had quickly decided that Jenny was not quite up to the standard of a first-district prostitute, and that she was probably working independently—which is illegal—or had stepped out of her assigned district to try to pull a little more money; that would get her in a lot of trouble with the other prostitutes.

In truth, Jenny would not have been mistaken for a prostitute by most people, but it is hard to say exactly what she looked like. She had dressed as a nurse for so many years that she did not really know how to dress in Vienna; she tended to overdress when she went out with Garp, perhaps in compensation for the old bathrobe in which she wrote. She had no experience in buying clothes for herself, and in a foreign city all the clothes looked slightly different to her. With no particular taste in mind, she simply bought the more expensive things; after all, she *did* have money and she did not have the patience or the interest for any comparative shopping. As a consequence, she looked new and shiny in her clothes, and beside Garp she did not look as if she came from the same family. Garp's constant dress, at Steering, had been a jacket and tie and comfortable pants—a kind of sloppy city standard uniform that made him anonymous almost anywhere.

"Would you ask that woman where she got that muff?" Jenny said to Garp. To her surprise, the women blocked the sidewalk to meet them.

"They're *whores,* Mom," Garp whispered to her.

Jenny Fields froze. The woman with the muff spoke sharply to her. Jenny didn't understand a word, of course; she stared at Garp for a translation. The woman spoke a stream of things to Jenny, who never took her eyes off her son.

"My mother wanted to ask you where you got your pretty muff," Garp said in his slow German.

"Oh, they're *foreigners,*" said one.

"God, it's his *mother,*" said another.

The woman with the muff stared at Jenny, who now stared at the woman's muff. One of the whores was a young girl with her hair piled very high and sprinkled with little gold and silver stars; she also had a green star tattoo on one cheek and a scar, which pulled her upper lip only slightly out of line—so that, for a mo-

131

ment, you didn't know *what* was wrong with her face, only that something was wrong. There was nothing at all wrong with her body, though; she was tall and lean and very hard to look at, though Jenny now found herself staring at her.

"Ask her how old she is," Jenny said to Garp.

*"Ich bin* eighteen," the girl said. "I know good English."

"That's how old my son is," Jenny said, nudging Garp. She did not understand that they had mistaken *her* for one of them; when Garp told her, later, she was furious—but only at herself. "It's my clothes!" she cried. "I don't know how to dress!" And from that moment on, Jenny Fields would never dress as anything but a nurse; she put her uniform back on and wore it everywhere—as if she were forever on duty, though she would never be a nurse again.

"May I see your muff?" Jenny asked the woman who had one; Jenny had assumed that they all spoke English, but only the young girl knew the language. Garp translated and the woman reluctantly removed her muff— a scent of perfume emerging from the warm nest where her long hands, sparkling with rings, had been clutched together.

The third whore had a pockmark on her forehead, like an impression made with a peach pit. Aside from this flaw, and a small fat mouth like the mouth of an overweight child, she was standardly ripe—in her twenties, Garp guessed; she probably had an enormous bosom, but under her black fur coat it was hard to be sure.

The woman with the muff, Garp thought, was beautiful. She had a long, potentially sad face. Her body, Garp imagined, was serene. Her mouth was very calm. Only her eyes and her bare hands in the cold night let Garp see that she was his mother's age, at least. Maybe she was older. "It was a gift," she said to Garp, about the muff. "It came with the coat." They were a silver-blond fur, very sleek.

"It is the real thing," said the young whore who spoke English; she obviously admired everything about the older prostitute.

"Of course, you can buy something, not quite so expensive, almost anywhere," the pockmarked woman told Garp. "Go to Stef's," she said, in a queer slang that Garp barely understood, and she pointed up the Kärntnerstrasse. But Jenny didn't look and Garp only nodded and continued to gaze at the older woman's long bare fingers twinkling with rings.

"My hands are cold," she said softly to Garp, and Garp took the muff from Jenny and gave it back to the whore. Jenny seemed in a daze.

"Let's *talk* to her," Jenny told Garp. "I want to ask her about it."

"About *what*, Mom?" Garp said. "Jesus Christ."

"What we were talking about," Jenny said. "I want to ask her about *lust*."

The two older whores looked at the one who knew English, but her English was not fast enough to catch any of this.

"It's cold, Mom," Garp complained. "And it's late. Let's just go home."

"Tell her we want to go to some place warm, just to sit and talk," Jenny said. "She'll let us pay her for *that*, won't she?"

"I suppose so," Garp groaned. "Mom, *she* doesn't know anything about lust. They probably don't feel anything very much like that."

"I want to know about *male* lust," Jenny said. "About *your* lust. She must know something about *that*."

"For God's sake, Mom!" Garp said.

*"Was macht's?"* the lovely prostitute asked him. "What's the matter?" she asked. "What's going on here? Does she want to buy the muff?"

"No, no," Garp said. "She wants to buy *you*."

The older whore looked stunned; the whore with the pockmark laughed.

"No, no," Garp explained. "Just to *talk*. My mother just wants to ask you some questions."

"It's cold," the whore told him, suspiciously.

"Some place inside?" Garp suggested. "Anyplace you like."

"Ask her what she charges," Jenny said.

*"Wie viel kostet?"* mumbled Garp.

"It costs five hundred schillings," the whore said, "usually." Garp had to explain to Jenny that this was about twenty dollars. Jenny Fields would live for more than a year in Austria and never learn the numbers, in German, or the money system.

"Twenty dollars, just to talk?" Jenny said.

"No, no, Mom," Garp said, "that's for the *usual*." Jenny thought. Was twenty dollars a lot for the usual? She didn't know.

"Tell her we'll give her ten," Jenny said, but the whore looked doubtful—as if talk, for her, might be more difficult than the "usual." Her indecision was influenced by more than price, however; she didn't trust Garp and Jenny. She asked the young whore who spoke English if they were British or American. Americans, she was told: this seemed to relieve her, slightly.

"The British are often perverse," she told Garp, simply. "Americans are usually ordinary."

"We just want to *talk* with you," Garp insisted, but he could see that the prostitute firmly imagined some mother-and-son act of monstrous oddity.

"Two hundred and fifty schillings," the lady with the mink muff finally agreed. "And you buy my coffee."

So they went to the place all the whores went to get warm, a tiny bar with miniature tables; the phone rang all the time but only a few men lurked sullenly by the coat rack, looking the women over. There was some rule that the women could not be approached when they were in this bar; the bar was a kind of home base, a time-out zone.

"Ask her how old she is," Jenny said to Garp; but when he asked her, the woman softly shut her eyes and shook her head. "Okay," said Jenny, "ask her why she thinks men like her." Garp rolled his eyes. "Well, you *do* like her?" Jenny asked him. Garp said he did. "Well, what *is* it about her that you *want?*" Jenny asked him. "I don't mean just her sex parts, I mean is there something else that's satisfying? Something to imagine, something to think about, some kind of *aura?*" Jenny asked.

"Why don't you pay *me* two hundred and fifty schillings and not ask her any questions, Mom," Garp said tiredly.

"Don't be fresh," Jenny said. "I want to know if it degrades her to feel *wanted* in that way—and then to be *had* in that way, I suppose—or whether she thinks it only degrades the men?" Garp struggled to translate this. The woman appeared to think very seriously about it; or else she didn't understand the question, or Garp's German.

"I don't know," she finally said.

"I have other questions," Jenny said.

For an hour, it continued. Then the whore said she had to get back to work. Jenny seemed neither satisfied nor disappointed by the interview's lack of concrete results; she just seemed insatiably curious. Garp had never wanted anyone as much as he wanted the woman.

"Do you want her?" Jenny asked him, so suddenly that he couldn't lie. "I mean, after all this—and looking at her, and talking with her—do you really want to have sex with her, too?"

"Of course, Mom," Garp said, miserably. Jenny looked no closer to understanding lust than she was before dinner. She looked puzzled and surprised at her son.

"All right," she said. She handed him the 250 schillings that they owed the woman, and another 500 schillings. "You do what you want to do," she told him, "or what you *have* to do, I guess. But please take me home first."

The whore had watched the money change hands;

135

she had an eye for recognizing the correct amount. "Look," she said to Garp, and touched his hand with her fingers, as cold as her rings. "It's all right with me if your mother wants to buy me for you, but she can't come along with us. I will *not* have her watch us, absolutely not. I'm still a Catholic, believe it or not," she said, "and if you want anything funny like that, you'll have to ask Tina."

Garp wondered who Tina was; he gave a shudder at the thought that nothing must be too "funny" for her. "I'm going to take my mother home," Garp told the beautiful woman. "And I won't be back to see you." But she smiled at him and he thought his erection would burst through his pocket of loose schillings and worthless groschen. Just one of her perfect teeth— but it was a big front upper tooth—was all gold.

In the taxi (that Garp agreed to take home) Garp explained to his mother the Viennese system of prostitution. Jenny was not surprised to hear that prostitution was legal; she was surprised to learn that it was *illegal* in so many other places. "Why shouldn't it be legal?" she asked. "Why can't a woman use her body the way she wants to? If someone wants to pay for it, it's just one more crummy deal. Is twenty dollars a lot of money for it?"

"No, that's pretty good," Garp said. "At least, it's a very low price for the good-looking ones."

Jenny slapped him. "You know all about it!" she said. Then she said she was sorry—she had never struck him before, she just didn't understand this fucking lust, lust, lust! at all.

At the Schwindgasse apartment, Garp made a point of *not* going out; in fact, he was in his own bed and asleep before Jenny, who paced through her manuscript pages in her wild room. A sentence boiled in her, but she could not yet see it clearly.

Garp dreamed of other prostitutes; he had visited two or three of them in Vienna—but he had never paid the first-district prices. The next evening, after an early

136

supper at the Schwindgasse, Garp went to see the woman with the mink muff streaked with light.

Her working name was Charlotte. She was not surprised to see him. Charlotte was old enough to know when she'd successfully hooked someone, although she never did tell Garp exactly how old she was. She had taken very fine care of herself, and only when she was completely undressed was her age apparent anywhere except in the veins on her long hands. There were stretch marks on her belly and her breasts, but she told Garp that the child had died a long time ago. She did not mind if Garp touched the Cesarean scar.

After he had seen Charlotte four times at the fixed first-district rate, he happened to run into her at the Naschmarkt on a Saturday morning. She was buying fruit. Her hair was probably a little dirty; she'd covered it with a scarf and wore it like a young girl's—with bangs and two short braids. The bangs were slightly greasy against her forehead, which seemed paler in the daylight. She had no makeup on and wore a pair of American jeans and tennis sneakers and a long coat-style sweater with a high roll collar. Garp would not have recognized her if he hadn't seen her hands clutching the fruit; she had all her rings on.

At first she wouldn't answer him when he spoke to her, but he had already told her that he did all the shopping, and the cooking, for himself and his mother, and she found this amusing. After her irritation at meeting a customer in her off-duty hours, she seemed good-humored. It did not become clear to Garp, for a while, that he was the same age as Charlotte's child would have been. Charlotte took some vicarious interest in the way Garp was living with his mother.

"How's your mother's writing coming?" Charlotte would ask him.

"She's still pounding away," Garp would say. "I don't think she's solved the lust problem yet."

But only to a point did Charlotte allow Garp to joke about his mother.

Garp was insecure enough about himself with Charlotte that he never told her *he* was trying to write, too; he knew she would think he was too young. Sometimes, he thought so, too. And his story wasn't ready to tell someone about. The most he had done was change the title. He now called it "The Pension Grillparzer," and that title was the first thing about it that solidly pleased him. It helped him to focus. Now he had a place in mind, just *one* place where almost everything that was important was going to happen. This helped him to think in a more focused way about his characters, too— about the family of classifiers, about the other residents of one small, sad pension somewhere (it would *have* to be small and sad, and in Vienna, to be named after Franz Grillparzer). Those "other residents" would include a kind of circus; not a very good kind, either, he imagined, but a circus with no other place to stay. No other place would have them.

In the world of ratings, the whole thing would be a kind of C experience. This kind of imagining got Garp started, slowly, in what he thought was a real direction; he was right about that, but it was too new to write it down—or even to write about it. Anyway, the more he wrote to Helen the less he wrote in other, important ways; and he couldn't discuss this with his mother: imagination was not her greatest strength. Of course, he'd have felt foolish discussing *any* of this with Charlotte.

Garp often met Charlotte at the Naschmarkt on Saturdays. They shopped and sometimes they ate lunch together in a Serbian place not far from the Stadtpark. On these occasions Charlotte paid for herself. At one such lunch Garp confessed to her that the first-district rate was hard for him to pay regularly without admitting to his mother where this steady flow of money was going. Charlotte was angry at him for bringing up business when she wasn't working. She would have been angrier if he'd admitted that he was seeing less of her, professionally, because the sixth-district prices of someone whom he met at the corner of Karl Schweighofer-gasse and Mariahilfer were much easier to conceal from Jenny.

Charlotte had a low opinion of her colleagues who operated out of the first district. She'd once told Garp she was planning to retire at the first sign that her first-district appeal was slipping. She would never do business in the outer districts. She had a lot of money saved, she told him, and she was going to move to Munich (where nobody knew she was a whore) and marry a young doctor who could take care of her, in every way, until she died; it was unnecessary for her to explain to Garp that she had always appealed to younger men, but Garp thoroughly resented her assumption that doctors were—in the long run—desirable. It may be this early exposure to the desirability of doctors that caused Garp, in his literary career, often to people his novels and stories with such unlikable characters from the medical profession. If so, it didn't occur to him until later. There is no doctor in "The Pension Grillparzer." In the beginning there is very little about death, either, although that is the subject the story would come to. In the beginning Garp had only a *dream* of death, but it was a whale of a dream and he gave it to the oldest person alive in his story: a grandmother. Garp guessed this meant that she would be the first to die.

## THE PENSION GRILLPARZER

My father worked for the Austrian Tourist Bureau. It was my mother's idea that our family travel with him when he went on the road as a Tourist Bureau spy. My mother and brother and I would accompany him on his secretive missions to uncover the discourtesy, the dust, the badly cooked food, the shortcuts taken by Austria's restaurants and hotels and pensions. We were instructed to create difficulties whenever we could, never to order exactly what was on the menu, to imitate a foreigner's odd requests—the hours we would like to have our baths, the need for aspirin and directions to the zoo. We were instructed to be civilized but troublesome; and when the visit was over, we reported to my father in the car.

My mother would say, "The hairdresser is always closed in the morning. But they make suitable recommendations outside. I guess it's all right, provided they don't claim to have a hairdresser actually *in* the hotel."

"Well, they *do* claim it," my father would say. He'd note this in a giant pad.

I was always the driver. I said, "The car is parked off the street, but someone put fourteen kilometers on the gauge between the time we handed it over to the doorman and picked it up at the hotel garage."

"That is a matter to report directly to the management," my father said, jotting it down.

"The toilet leaked," I said.

"I couldn't open the door to the W.C.," said my brother, Robo.

"Robo," Mother said, "you always have trouble with doors."

"Was that supposed to be Class C?" I asked.

"I'm afraid not," Father said. "It is still listed as Class B." We drove for a short while in silence; our most serious judgment concerned changing a hotel's or a pension's rating. We did not suggest reclassification frivolously.

"I think this calls for a letter to the management," Mother suggested. "Not too nice a letter, but not a really rough one. Just state the facts."

"Yes, I rather liked him," Father said. He always made a point of getting to meet the managers.

"Don't forget the business of them driving our car," I said. "That's really unforgivable."

"And the eggs were bad," said Robo; he was not yet ten and his judgments were not considered seriously.

We became a far harsher team of evaluators when my grandfather died and we inherited Grandmother—my mother's mother, who thereafter accompanied us on our travels.

140

A regal dame, Johanna was accustomed to Class A travel, and my father's duties more frequently called for investigations of Class B and Class C lodgings. They were the places, the B and C hotels (and the pensions), that most interested the tourists. At restaurants we did a little better. People who couldn't afford the classy places to sleep were still interested in the best places to eat.

"I shall not have dubious food tested on me," Johanna told us. "This strange employment may give you all glee about having free vacations, but I can see there is a terrible price paid: the anxiety of not knowing what sort of quarters you'll have for the night. Americans may find it charming that we still have rooms without private baths and toilets, but I am an old woman and I'm not charmed by walking down a public corridor in search of cleanliness and my relievement. Anxiety is only half of it. Actual diseases are possible—and not only from food. If the bed is questionable, I promise I shan't put my head down. And the children are young and impressionable; you should think of the clientele in some of these lodgings and seriously ask yourselves about the influences." My mother and father nodded; they said nothing. "Slow down!" Grandmother said sharply to me. "You're just a young boy who likes to show off." I slowed down. "Vienna," Grandmother sighed. "In Vienna I always stayed at the Ambassador."

"Johanna, the Ambassador is not under investigation," Father said.

"I should think not," Johanna said. "I suppose we're not even headed toward a Class A place?"

"Well, it's a B trip," my father admitted. "For the most part."

"I trust," Grandmother said, "that you mean there is one A place en route?"

"No," Father admitted. "There is one C place."

"It's okay," Robo said. "There are fights in Class C."

"I should imagine so," Johanna said.

"It's a Class C pension, very small," Father said, as if the size of the place forgave it.

"And they're applying for a B," said Mother.

141

"But there have been some complaints," I added.

"I'm sure there have," Johanna said.

"And animals," I added. My mother gave me a look.

"Animals?" said Johanna.

"Animals," I admitted.

"A *suspicion* of animals," my mother corrected me.

"Yes, be fair," Father said.

"Oh, wonderful!" Grandmother said. "A suspicion of animals. Their hair on the rugs? Their terrible waste in the corners! Did you know that my asthma reacts, severely, to any room in which there has recently been a cat?"

"The complaint was not about cats," I said. My mother elbowed me sharply.

"Dogs?" Johanna said. "Rabid dogs! Biting you on the way to the bathroom."

"No," I said. "Not dogs."

"Bears!" Robo cried.

But my mother said, "We don't know for sure about the bear, Robo."

"This isn't serious," Johanna said.

"Of course it's not serious!" Father said. "How could there be bears in a pension?"

"There was a letter saying so," I said. "Of course, the Tourist Bureau assumed it was a crank complaint. But then there was another sighting—and a second letter claiming there had been a bear."

My father used the rear-view mirror to scowl at me, but I thought that if we were all supposed to be in on the investigation, it would be wise to have Grandmother on her toes.

"It's probably not a real bear," Robo said, with obvious disappointment.

"A man in a bear suit!" Johanna cried. "What unheard-of perversion is *that*? A *beast* of a man sneaking about in disguise! Up to what? It's a man in a bear suit, I know it is," she said. "I want to go to that one *first*. If there's going to be a Class C experience on this trip, let's get it over with as soon as possible."

"But we haven't got reservations for tonight," Mother said.

"Yes, we might as well give them a chance to be at their best," Father said. Although he never revealed to his victims that he worked for the Tourist Bureau, Father believed that reservations were simply a decent way of allowing the personnel to be as prepared as they could be.

"I'm sure we don't need to make a reservation in a place frequented by men who disguise themselves as animals," Johanna said. "I'm sure there is *always* a vacancy there. I'm sure the guests are regularly dying in their beds—of fright, or else of whatever unspeakable injury the madman in the foul bear suit does to them."

"It's probably a *real* bear," Robo said, hopefully—for in the turn the conversation was taking, Robo certainly saw that a real bear would be preferable to Grandmother's imagined ghoul. Robo had no fear, I think, of a real bear.

I drove us as inconspicuously as possible to the dark, dwarfed corner of Planken and Seilergasse. We were looking for the Class C pension that wanted to be a B.

"No place to park," I said to Father, who was already making note of that in his pad.

I doubled-parked and we sat in the car and peered up at the Pension Grillparzer; it rose only four slender stories between a pastry shop and a Tabak Trafik.

"See?" Father said. "No bears."

"No *men*, I hope," said Grandmother.

"They come at night," Robo said, looking cautiously up and down the street.

We went inside to meet the manager, a Herr Theobald, who instantly put Johanna on her guard. "Three generations traveling together!" he cried. "Like the old days," he added, especially to Grandmother, "before all these divorces and the young people wanting apartments by themselves. This is a *family* pension! I just wish you had made a reservation—so I could put you more closely together."

"We're not accustomed to sleeping in the same room," Grandmother told him.

"Of course not!" Theobald cried. "I just meant that I

wished your *rooms* could be closer together." This worried Grandmother, clearly.

"How far apart must we be put?" she asked.

"Well, I've only two rooms left," he said. "And only one of them is large enough for the two boys to share with their parents."

"And my room is how far from theirs?" Johanna asked coolly.

"You're right across from the W.C.!" Theobald told her, as if this were a plus.

But as we were shown to our rooms, Grandmother staying with Father—contemptuously to the rear of our procession—I heard her mutter, "This is not how I conceived of my retirement. Across the hall from a W.C., listening to all the visitors."

"Not one of these rooms is the same," Theobald told us. "The furniture is all from my family." We could believe it. The one large room Robo and I were to share with my parents was a hall-sized museum of knickknacks, every dresser with a different style of knob. On the other hand, the sink had brass faucets and the headboard of the bed was carved. I could see my father balancing things up for future notation in the giant pad.

"You may do that later," Johanna informed him. "Where do *I* stay?"

As a family, we dutifully followed Theobald and my grandmother down the long, twining hall, my father counting the paces to the W.C. The hall rug was thin, the color of a shadow. Along the walls were old photographs of speed-skating teams—on their feet the strange blades curled up at the tips like court jesters' shoes or the runners of ancient sleds.

Robo, running far ahead, announced his discovery of the W.C.

Grandmother's room was full of china, polished wood, and the hint of mold. The drapes were damp. The bed had an unsettling ridge at its center, like fur risen on a dog's spine—it was almost as if a very slender body lay stretched beneath the bedspread.

Grandmother said nothing, and when Theobald reeled out of the room like a wounded man who's been told he'll live, Grandmother asked my father, "On what basis can the Pension Grillparzer hope to get a B?"

"Quite decidedly C," Father said.

"Born C and will die C," I said.

"I would say, myself," Grandmother told us, "that it was E or F."

In the dim tearoom a man without a tie sang a Hungarian song. "It does not mean he's Hungarian," Father reassured Johanna, but she was skeptical.

"I'd say the odds are not in his favor," she suggested. She would not have tea or coffee. Robo ate a little cake, which he claimed to like. My mother and I smoked a cigarette; she was trying to quit and I was trying to start. Therefore, we shared a cigarette between us—in fact, we'd promised never to smoke a whole one alone.

"He's a great guest," Herr Theobald whispered to my father; he indicated the singer. "He knows songs from all over."

"From Hungary, at least," Grandmother said, but she smiled.

A small man, clean-shaven but with that permanent gun-blue shadow of a beard on his lean face, spoke to my grandmother. He wore a clean white shirt (but yellow from age and laundering), suit pants, and an unmatching jacket.

"Pardon me?" said Grandmother.

"I said that I tell dreams," the man informed her.

"You *tell* dreams," Grandmother said. "Meaning, you *have* them?"

"Have them and tell them," he said mysteriously. The singer stopped singing.

"Any dreams you want to know," said the singer. "He can tell it."

"I'm quite sure I don't want to know any," Grandmother said. She viewed with displeasure the ascot of dark hair bursting out at the open throat of the singer's shirt. She would not regard the man who "told" dreams at all.

"I can see you are a lady," the dream man told Grandmother. "You don't respond to just every dream that comes along."

"Certainly not," said Grandmother. She shot my father one of her how-could-you-have-let-this-happen-to-me? looks.

"But I know one," said the dream man; he shut his eyes. The singer slipped a chair forward and we suddenly realized he was sitting very close to us. Robo, though he was much too old for it, sat in Father's lap. "In a great castle," the dream man began, "a woman lay beside her husband. She was wide awake, suddenly, in the middle of the night. She woke up without the slightest idea of what had awakened her, and she felt as alert as if she'd been up for hours. It was also clear to her, without a look, a word, or a touch, that her husband was wide awake too—and just as suddenly."

"I hope this is suitable for the child to hear, ha ha," Herr Theobald said, but no one even looked at him. My grandmother folded her hands in her lap and stared at them—her knees together, her heels tucked under her straight-backed chair. My mother held my father's hand.

I sat next to the dream man, whose jacket smelled like a zoo. He said, "The woman and her husband lay awake listening for sounds in the castle, which they were only renting and did not know intimately. They listened for sounds in the courtyard, which they never bothered to lock. The village people always took walks by the castle; the village children were allowed to swing on the great courtyard door. What had woken them?"

"Bears?" said Robo, but Father touched his fingertips to Robo's mouth.

"They heard horses," said the dream man. Old Johanna, her eyes shut, her head inclined toward her lap, seemed to shudder in her stiff chair. "They heard the breathing and stamping of horses who were trying to keep still," the dream man said. "The husband reached out and touched his wife. 'Horses?' he said. The woman got out of bed and went to the courtyard window. She would swear to this day that

146

the courtyard was full of soldiers on horseback—but what soldiers they were! They wore *armor!* The visors on their helmets were closed and their murmuring voices were as tinny and difficult to hear as voices on a fading radio station. Their armor clanked as their horses shifted restlessly under them.

"There was an old dry bowl of a former fountain, there in the castle's courtyard, but the woman saw that the fountain was flowing; the water lapped over the worn curb and the horses were drinking it. The knights were wary, they would not dismount; they looked up at the castle's dark windows, as if they knew they were uninvited at this watering trough—this rest station on their way, somewhere.

"In the moonlight the woman saw their big shields glint. She crept back to bed and lay rigidly against her husband.

" 'What is it?' he asked her.

" 'Horses,' she told him.

" 'I thought so,' he said. 'They'll eat the flowers.'

" 'Who built this castle?' she asked him. It was a very old castle, they both knew that.

" 'Charlemagne,' he told her; he was going back to sleep.

"But the woman lay awake, listening to the water which now seemed to be running all through the castle, gurgling in every drain, as if the old fountain were drawing water from every available source. And there were the distorted voices of the whispering knights—*Charlemagne's* soldiers speaking their dead language! To this woman, the soldiers' voices were as morbid as the eighth century and the people called Franks. The horses kept drinking.

"The woman lay awake a long time, waiting for the soldiers to leave; she had no fear of actual attack from them —she was sure they were on a journey and had only stopped to rest at a place they once knew. But for as long as the water ran she felt that she mustn't disturb the castle's stillness or its darkness. When she fell asleep, she thought Charlemagne's men were still there.

"In the morning her husband asked her, 'Did you hear water running, too?' Yes, she had, of course. But the fountain was dry, of course, and out the window they could see

147

that the flowers weren't eaten—and everyone knows horses eat flowers.

" 'Look,' said her husband; he went into the courtyard with her. 'There are *no* hoofprints, there are no droppings. We must have *dreamed* we heard horses.' She did not tell him that there were soldiers, too; or that, in her opinion, it was unlikely that two people would dream the same dream. She did not remind him that he was a heavy smoker who never smelled the soup simmering; the aroma of horses in the fresh air was too subtle for him.

"She saw the soldiers, or dreamed them, twice more while they stayed there, but her husband never again woke up with her. It was always sudden. Once she woke with the taste of metal on her tongue as if she'd touched some old, sour iron to her mouth—a sword, a chest plate, chain mail, a thigh guard. They were out there again, in colder weather. From the water in the fountain a dense fog shrouded them; the horses were snowy with frost. And there were not so many of them the next time—as if the winter or their skirmishes were reducing their numbers. The last time the horses looked gaunt to her, and the men looked more like unoccupied suits of armor balanced delicately in the saddles. The horses wore long masks of ice on their muzzles. Their breathing (or the men's breathing) was congested.

"Her husband," said the dream man, "would die of a respiratory infection. But the woman did not know it when she dreamed this dream."

My grandmother looked up from her lap and slapped the dream man's beard-gray face. Robo stiffened in my father's lap; my mother caught her mother's hand. The singer shoved back his chair and jumped to his feet, frightened, or ready to fight someone, but the dream man simply bowed to Grandmother and left the gloomy tearoom. It was as if he'd made a contract with Johanna that was final but gave neither of them any joy. My father wrote something in the giant pad.

"Well, wasn't *that* some story?" said Herr Theobald. "Ha

ha." He rumpled Robo's hair—something Robo always hated.

"Herr Theobald," my mother said, still holding Johanna's hand, *"my father died of a respiratory infection."*

"Oh, dear shit," said Herr Theobald. "I'm sorry, *meine Frau*," he told Grandmother, but old Johanna would not speak to him.

We took Grandmother out to eat in a Class A restaurant, but she hardly touched her food. "That person was a gypsy," she told us. "A satanic being, and a Hungarian."

"Please, Mother," my mother said. "He couldn't have known about Father."

"He knew more than *you* know," Grandmother snapped.

"The schnitzel is excellent," Father said, writing in the pad. "The Gumpoldskirchner is just right with it."

"The Kalbsnieren are fine," I said.

"The eggs are okay," said Robo.

Grandmother said nothing until we returned to the Pension Grillparzer, where we noticed that the door to the W.C. was hung a foot or more off the floor, so that it resembled the bottom half of an American toilet-stall door or a saloon door in the Western movies. "I'm certainly glad I used the W.C. at the restaurant," Grandmother said. "How revolting! I shall try to pass the night without exposing myself where every passerby can peer at my ankles!"

In our family room Father said, "Didn't Johanna live in a castle? Once upon a time, I thought she and Grandpa rented some castle."

"Yes, it was before I was born," Mother said. "They rented Schloss Katzelsdorf. I saw the photographs."

"Well, *that's* why the Hungarian's dream upset her," Father said.

"Someone is riding a bike in the hall," Robo said. "I saw a wheel go by—under our door."

"Robo, go to sleep," Mother said.

"It went 'squeak squeak,' " Robo said.

"Good night, boys," said Father.

"If you can talk, we can talk," I said.

"Then talk to each other," Father said. "I'm talking to your mother."

"I want to go to sleep," Mother said. "I wish no one would talk."

We tried. Perhaps we slept. Then Robo whispered to me that he had to use the W.C.

"You know where it is," I said.

Robo went out the door, leaving it slightly open; I heard him walk down the corridor, brushing his hand along the wall. He was back very quickly.

"There's someone *in* the W.C.," he said.

"Wait for them to finish," I said.

"The light wasn't on," Robo said, "but I could see under the door. Someone is in there, in the dark."

"I prefer the dark myself," I said.

But Robo insisted on telling me exactly what he'd seen. He said that under the door was a pair of *hands*.

"Hands?" I said.

"Yes, where the feet should have been," Robo said; he claimed that there was a hand on either side of the toilet— instead of a foot.

"Get out of here, Robo!" I said.

"Please come see," he begged. I went down the hall with him but there was no one in the W.C. "They've gone," he said.

"Walked off on their hands, no doubt," I said. "Go pee. I'll wait for you."

He went into the W.C. and peed sadly in the dark. When we were almost back to our room together, a small dark man with the same kind of skin and clothes as the dream man who had angered Grandmother passed us in the hall. He winked at us, and smiled. I had to notice that he was walking on his hands.

"You see?" Robo whispered to me. We went into our room and shut the door.

"What is it?" Mother asked.

"A man walking on his hands," I said.

"A man *peeing* on his hands," Robo said.

"Class C," Father murmured in his sleep; Father often dreamed that he was making notes in the giant pad.

"We'll talk about it in the morning," Mother said.

"He was probably just an acrobat who was showing off for you, because you're a kid," I told Robo.

"How did he know I was a kid when he was in the W.C.?" Robo asked me.

"Go to *sleep*," Mother whispered.

Then we heard Grandmother scream down the hall.

Mother put on her pretty green dressing gown; Father put on his bathrobe and his glasses; I pulled on a pair of pants, over my pajamas. Robo was in the hall first. We saw the light coming from the W.C. door. Grandmother was screaming rhythmically in there.

"Here we are!" I called to her.

"Mother, what is it?" my mother asked.

We gathered in the broad slot of light. We could see Grandmother's mauve slippers and her porcelain-white ankles under the door. She stopped screaming. "I heard whispers when I was in my bed," she said.

"It was Robo and me," I told her.

"Then, when everyone seemed to have gone, I came into the W.C.," Johanna said. "I left the light off. I was very quiet," she told us. "Then I saw and heard the wheel."

"The *wheel?*" Father asked.

"A wheel went by the door a few times," Grandmother said. "It rolled by and came back and rolled by again."

Father made his fingers roll like wheels alongside his head; he made a face at Mother. "Somebody needs a new set of wheels," he whispered, but Mother looked crossly at him.

"I turned on the light," Grandmother said, "and the wheel went away."

"I told you there was a bike in the hall," said Robo.

"Shut up, Robo," Father said.

"No, it was not a bicycle," Grandmother said. "There was only *one* wheel."

Father was making his hands go crazy beside his head. "She's got a wheel or two *missing*," he hissed at my mother, but she cuffed him and knocked his glasses askew on his face.

"Then someone came and looked *under* the door," Grandmother said, "and *that* is when I screamed."

"Someone?" said Father.

"I saw his hands, a man's hands—there was hair on his knuckles," Grandmother said. "His hands were on the rug right outside the door. He must have been looking *up* at me."

"No, Grandmother," I said. "I think he was just standing out here on his hands."

"Don't be fresh," my mother said.

"But we saw a man walking on his hands," Robo said.

"You did *not*," Father said.

"We *did*," I said.

"We're going to wake everyone up," Mother cautioned us.

The toilet flushed and Grandmother shuffled out the door with only a little of her former dignity intact. She was wearing a gown over a gown over a gown; her neck was very long and her face was creamed white. Grandmother looked like a troubled goose. "He was evil and vile," she said to us. "He knew terrible magic."

"The man who looked at you?" Mother asked.

"That man who told my *dream*," Grandmother said. Now a tear made its way through her furrows of face cream. "That was *my* dream," she said, "and he told everyone. It is unspeakable that he even knew it," she hissed to us. "My dream—of Charlemagne's horses and soldiers—*I* am the only one who should know it. I had that dream before you were born," she told Mother. "And that vile evil magic man told my dream as if it were *news*.

"I never even told your father all there was to that dream. I was never sure that it *was* a dream. And now there are men on their hands, and their knuckles are hairy, and there are magic wheels. I want the boys to sleep with me."

So that was how Robo and I came to share the large family room, far away from the W.C., with Grandmother, who lay on my mother's and father's pillows with her creamed face shining like the face of a wet ghost. Robo lay awake watching her. I do not think Johanna slept very well; I imagine she was dreaming her dream of death again —reliving the last winter of Charlemagne's cold soldiers with their strange metal clothes covered with frost and their armor frozen shut.

When it was obvious that I had to go to the W.C., Robo's round, bright eyes followed me to the door.

There was someone in the W.C. There was no light shining from under the door, but there was a unicycle parked against the wall outside. Its rider sat in the dark W.C.; the toilet was flushing over and over again—like a child, the unicyclist was not giving the tank time to refill.

I went closer to the gap under the W.C. door, but the occupant was not standing on his or her hands. I saw what were clearly feet, in almost the expected position, but the feet did not touch the floor; their soles tilted up to me—dark, bruise-colored pads. They were *huge* feet attached to short, furry shins. They were a *bear's* feet, only there were no claws. A bear's claws are not retractable, like a cat's; if a bear had claws, you would see them. Here, then, was an imposter in a bear suit, or a declawed bear. A domestic bear, perhaps. At least—by its presence in the W.C.—a *housebroken* bear. For by its smell I could tell it was no man in a bear suit; it was all bear. It was real bear.

I backed into the door of Grandmother's former room, behind which my father lurked, waiting for further disturbances. He snapped open the door and I fell inside, frightening us both. Mother sat up in bed and pulled the feather quilt over her head. "Got him!" Father cried, dropping down on me. The floor trembled; the bear's unicycle slipped against the wall and fell into the door of the W.C., out of which the bear suddenly shambled, stumbling over its unicycle and lunging for its balance. Worriedly, it stared across the hall, through the open door, at Father sitting on my chest. It picked up the unicycle in its front paws. "Grauf?" said the bear. Father slammed the door.

Down the hall we heard a woman call, "Where are you, Duna?"

"*Harf!*" the bear said.

Father and I heard the woman come closer. She said, "Oh, Duna, practicing again? Always practicing! But it's better in the daytime." The bear said nothing. Father opened the door.

"Don't let anyone else in," Mother said, still under the featherbed.

In the hall a pretty, aging woman stood beside the bear, who now balanced in place on its unicycle, one huge paw on the woman's shoulder. She wore a vivid red turban and a long wrap-around dress that resembled a curtain. Perched on her high bosom was a necklace strung with bear claws; her earrings touched the shoulder of her curtain-dress and her other, bare shoulder where my father and I stared at her fetching mole. "Good evening," she said to Father. "I'm sorry if we've disturbed you. Duna is forbidden to practice at night—but he loves his work."

The bear muttered, pedaling away from the woman. The bear had very good balance but he was careless; he brushed against the walls of the hall and touched the photographs of the speed-skating teams with his paws. The woman, bowing away from Father, went after the bear calling, "Duna, Duna," and straightening the photographs as she followed him down the hall.

"*Duna* is the Hungarian word for the Danube," Father told me. "That bear is named after our beloved *Donau*." Sometimes it seemed to surprise my family that the Hungarians could love a river, too.

"Is the bear a *real* bear?" Mother asked—still under the featherbed—but I left Father to explain it all to her. I knew that in the morning Herr Theobald would have much to explain, and I would hear everything reviewed at that time.

I went across the hall to the W.C. My task there was hurried by the bear's lingering odor, and by my suspicion of bear hair on everything; it was only my suspicion, though, for the bear had left everything quite tidy—or at least neat for a bear.

"I saw the bear," I whispered to Robo, back in our room, but Robo had crept into Grandmother's bed and had fallen asleep beside her. Old Johanna was awake, however.

"I saw fewer and fewer soldiers," she said. "The last time they came there were only nine of them. Everyone looked so hungry; they must have eaten the extra horses. It was so cold. Of course I wanted to help them! But we weren't alive at the same time; how could I help them if I wasn't even born? Of course I knew they would die! But it took such a long time.

"The last time they came, the fountain was frozen. They used their swords and their long pikes to break the ice into chunks. They built a fire and melted the ice in a pot. They took bones from their saddlebags—bones of all kinds—and threw them in the soup. It must have been a very thin broth because the bones had long ago been gnawed clean. I don't know what bones they were. Rabbits, I suppose, and maybe a deer or a wild boar. Maybe the extra horses. I do not choose to think," said Grandmother, "that they were the bones of the missing soldiers."

"Go to sleep, Grandmother," I said.

"Don't worry about the bear," she said.

And *then* what? Garp wondered. What can happen next? He wasn't altogether sure what *had* happened, or why. Garp was a natural storyteller; he could make things up, one right after the other, and they seemed to fit. But what did they mean? That dream and those desperate entertainers, and what would happen to them all—everything had to connect. What sort of explanation would be natural? What sort of ending might make them all part of the same world? Garp knew he did not know enough; not yet. He trusted his instincts; they had brought him this far with "The Pension Grillparzer"; now he had to trust the instinct that told him not to go any further until he knew much more.

What made Garp older and wiser than his nineteen

years had nothing to do with his experience or with what he had learned. He had some instincts, some determination, better than average patience; he loved to work hard. Altogether, with the grammar Tinch had taught him, that was all. Only two facts impressed Garp: that his mother actually believed she could write a book and that the most meaningful relationship in his present life was with a whore. These facts contributed greatly to the young man's developing sense of humor.

He put "The Pension Grillparzer"—as they say—aside. It will come, Garp thought. He knew he had to know more; all he could do was look at Vienna and learn. It was holding still for him. Life seemed to be holding still for him. He made a great many observations of Charlotte, too, and he noticed everything his mother did, but he was simply too young. What I need is *vision,* he knew. An overall scheme of things, a vision all his own. It will come, he repeated to himself, as if he were training for another wrestling season—jumping rope, running laps on a small track, lifting weights, something almost that mindless but that necessary.

Even Charlotte has a vision, he thought; he certainly knew that his mother had one. Garp had no parallel wisdom for the absolute clarity of the world according to Jenny Fields. But he knew it would take only time to imagine a world of his own—with a little help from the real world. The real world would soon cooperate.

# 6

✥✥✥✥✥✥✥

# The Pension Grillparzer

W HEN spring came to Vienna, Garp had still
not finished "The Pension Grillparzer"; he had
not, of course, even written to Helen about his
life with Charlotte and her colleagues. Jenny had kicked
her writing habit into yet a higher gear; she had found
the sentence that had been boiling in her since that
night she discussed lust with Garp and Charlotte: it was
an old sentence, actually, from her life long ago, and it
was the sentence with which she truly *began* the book
that would make her famous.

"In this dirty-minded world," Jenny wrote, "you are
either somebody's wife or somebody's whore—or fast
on your way to becoming one or the other." The sentence set a tone for the book, which the book had
been lacking; Jenny was discovering that when she
began with that sentence, an aura was cast over her
autobiography that bound the disharmonious parts of
her life's story together—the way fog shrouds an un-
even landscape, the way heat reaches through a rambling
house into every room. That sentence inspired others
like it, and Jenny wove them as she might have woven

a bright and binding thread of brilliant color through a sprawling tapestry of no apparent design.

"I wanted a job and I wanted to live alone," she wrote. "That made me a sexual suspect." And that gave her a title, too. *A Sexual Suspect,* the autobiography of Jenny Fields. It would go through eight hard-cover printings and be translated into six languages even before the paperback sale that could keep Jenny, and a regiment of nurses, in new uniforms for a century.

"Then I wanted a baby, but I didn't want to have to share my body or my life to have one," Jenny wrote. "That made me a sexual suspect, too." Thus Jenny had found the string with which to sew her messy book together.

But when spring came to Vienna, Garp felt like a trip; maybe Italy; possibly, they could rent a car.

"Do you know how to drive?" Jenny asked him. She knew perfectly well that he hadn't ever learned; there had never been a need. "Well, I don't know how, either," she told him. "And besides, I'm working; I can't stop now. If you want to take a trip, take a trip by yourself."

It was in the American Express office, where Garp and Jenny got their mail, that Garp met his first traveling young Americans. Two girls who had formerly gone to Dibbs, and a boy named Boo who had gone to Bath. "Hey, how about us?" one of the girls said to Garp, when they had all met. "We're all prep school stuff."

Her name was Flossie and it appeared to Garp that she had a relationship with Boo. The other girl was called Vivian, and under the tiny café table on the Schwarzenbergplatz, Vivian squeezed Garp's knee between her own and drooled while sipping her wine. "I just went to a *dent*hisht," she explained to him. "Got so much Novocain in my goddamn mouth I don't know whether it's open or shut."

"Sort of half and half," Garp said to her. But he thought: Oh, what the hell. He missed Cushie Percy, and his relationships with prostitutes were beginning to make *him* feel like a sexual suspect. Charlotte, it was now clear, was interested in mothering him; though he tried to imagine her on another level, he knew, sadly, that this level would never carry beyond the professional.

Flossie and Vivian and Boo were all going to Greece but they let Garp show them Vienna for three days. In that time Garp slept twice with Vivian, whose Novocain finally wore off; he also slept once with Flossie, while Boo was out cashing travelers' checks and changing the oil in the car. There was no love lost between Steering and Bath boys, Garp knew; but Boo had the last laugh.

It is impossible to know whether Garp got gonorrhea from Vivian or from Flossie, but Garp was convinced that the *source* of the dose was Boo. It was, in Garp's opinion, "Bath clap." By the time of the first symptoms, of course, the threesome had left for Greece and Garp faced the dripping and the burning alone. There could be no worse a case of clap to catch in all of Europe, he thought. "I caught a dose of Boo's goo," he wrote, but much later; it was not funny when it happened, and he didn't dare seek his mother's professional advice. He knew she would refuse to believe that he hadn't caught it from a whore. He got up the nerve to ask Charlotte to recommend a doctor who was familiar with the matter; he thought she would know. He thought later that Jenny would possibly have been *less* angry with him.

"You'd think Americans would know a little simple hygiene!" Charlotte said furiously. "You should think of your mother! I'd expect you to have better taste. People who give it away for free to someone they hardly know—well, they should make you suspicious, shouldn't they?" Once again, Garp had been caught without a condom.

Thus Garp winced his way to Charlotte's personal physician, a hearty man named Thalhammer who was missing his left thumb. "And I was once left-handed," Herr Doktor Thalhammer told Garp. "But everything is surmountable if we have energy. We can learn anything we can set our minds to!" he said, with firm good cheer; he demonstrated for Garp how he could write the prescription, with an enviable penmanship, with his right hand. It was a simple and painless cure. In Jenny's day, at good old Boston Mercy, they would have given Garp the Valentine treatment and he'd have learned, more emphatically, how not all rich kids are clean kids.

He didn't write Helen about this, either.

His spirits slumped; spring wore on, the city opened in many small ways—like buds. But Garp felt he had walked Vienna out. He could barely get his mother to stop writing long enough to eat dinner with him. When he sought out Charlotte, her colleagues told him she was sick; she hadn't worked for weeks. For three Saturdays, Garp did not see her at the Naschmarkt. When he stopped her colleagues one May evening on the Kärntnerstrasse, he saw they were reluctant to discuss Charlotte. The whore whose forehead appeared to have been pockmarked by a peach pit merely told Garp that Charlotte was sicker than she first thought. The young girl, Garp's age, with the misshapen lip and the half-knowledge of English, tried to explain to him. "Her *sex* is sick," she said.

That was a curious way to put it, Garp thought. Garp was not surprised to hear that *anyone's* sex was sick, but when he smiled at the remark, the young whore who spoke English frowned at him and walked away.

"You don't understand," said the overlush prostitute with the pockmark. "Forget Charlotte."

It was mid-June, and Charlote had still not come back, when Garp called Herr Doktor Thalhammer and asked where he could find her. "I doubt that she wants to see anybody," Thalhammer told him, "but human beings can adjust to almost anything."

Very near Grinzing and the Vienna Woods, out in the nineteenth district where the whores don't go, Vienna looks like a village imitation of itself; in these suburbs, many of the streets are still cobblestoned and trees grow along the sidewalks. Unfamiliar with this part of the city, Garp rode the No. 38 Strassenbahn too far out the Grinzinger Allee; he had to walk back to the corner of Billrothstrasse and Rudolfinergasse to the hospital.

The Rudolfinerhaus is a private hospital in a city of socialized medicine; its old stone walls are the same Maria Theresa yellow as the palace at Schönbrunn, or the Upper and Lower Belvedere. Its own gardens are enclosed in its own courtyard, and it costs as much as almost any hospital in the United States. The Rudolfinerhaus does not normally provide pajamas for its patients, for example, because its patients usually prefer their own nightclothes. The well-to-do Viennese treat themselves to the luxury of being sick there—and most foreigners who are afraid of socialized medicine end up there, where they are shocked at the prices.

In June, when Garp went there, the hospital struck him as full of pretty young mothers who'd just delivered babies. But it was also full of well-off people who'd come there to get seriously well again, and it was partially full of well-off people, like Charlotte, who'd come there to die.

Charlotte had a private room because, she said, there was no reason to save her money now. Garp knew she was dying as soon as he saw her. She had lost almost thirty pounds. Garp saw that she wore what was left of her rings on her index and middle fingers; her other fingers were so shrunken that her rings would slide off. Charlotte was the color of the dull ice on the brackish Steering River. She did not appear very surprised to see Garp, but she was so heavily anesthetized that Garp imagined Charlotte was fairly unsurprised in general. Garp had brought a basket of fruit; since they had shopped together, he knew what Charlotte liked to eat, but she had a tube down her throat for several hours each day and it left her throat too sore to swallow anything but liquid. Garp ate a few cherries while Charlotte

161

enumerated the parts of her body that had been removed. Her sex parts, she thought, and much of her
digestive tract, and something that had to do with the
process of elimination. "Oh, and my breasts, I think,"
she said, the whites of her eyes very gray and her hands
held above her chest where she flattered herself to
imagine her breasts used to be. To Garp it appeared that
they had not touched her breasts; under the sheet, there
was still something there. But he later thought that
Charlotte had been such a lovely woman that she could
hold her body in such a way as to inspire the *illusion*
of breasts.

"Thank God I've got money," Charlotte said. "Isn't
this a Class A place?"

Garp nodded. The next day he brought a bottle of
wine; the hospital was very relaxed about liquor and
visitors; perhaps this was one of the luxuries one paid
for. "Even if I got out," Charlotte said, "what could
I do? They cut my purse out." She tried to drink some
wine, then fell asleep. Garp asked a nurse's aide to
explain what Charlotte meant by her "purse," though
he thought he knew. The nurse's aide was Garp's age,
nineteen or maybe younger, and she blushed and looked
away from him when she translated the slang.

A purse was a prostitute's word for her vagina.

"Thank you," Garp said.

Once or twice when he visited Charlotte he encountered her two colleagues, who were shy and girlish
with Garp in the daylight of Charlotte's sunny room.
The young one who spoke English was named Wanga;
she had cut her lip that way as a child when she tripped
while running home from the store with a jar of mayon-
naise. "We were on a picnic going," she explained, "but
my whole family had me instead to the hospital to
bring."

The riper, sulkish woman with the peach pit pockmark on her forehead, and the breasts like two full pails,
did not offer to explain *her* scar; she was the notorious
"Tina," for whom nothing was too "funny."

Occasionally Garp ran into Herr Doktor Thalhammer there, and once he walked with Thalhammer to Thalhammer's car; they happened to be leaving the hospital together. "Do you want a lift?" Thalhammer offered him, pleasantly. In the car was a pretty young schoolgirl whom Thalhammer introduced to Garp as his daughter. They all talked easily about *Die Vereinigten Staaten* and Thalhammer assured Garp it was no trouble to drive Garp all the way to his doorstep at the Schwindgasse. Thalhammer's daughter reminded Garp of Helen, but he could not even imagine asking to see the girl again; that her father had recently treated him for clap seemed to Garp to be an insurmountable awkwardness—despite Thalhammer's optimism that people can adjust to *anything*. Garp doubted that Thalhammer could have adjusted to that.

All around Garp, now, the city looked ripe with dying. The teeming parks and gardens reeked of decay to him, and the subject of the great painters in the great museums was always death. There were always cripples and old people riding the No. 38 Strassenbahn out to Grinzinger Allee, and the heady flowers planted along the pruned paths of the courtyard in the Rudolfinerhaus reminded Garp only of funeral parlors. He recalled the pensions he and Jenny had stayed in when they first arrived, over a year ago: the faded and unmatched wallpaper, the dusty bric-a-brac, the chipped china, the hinges crying for oil. "In the life of a man," wrote Marcus Aurelius, "his time is but a moment . . . his body a prey of worms. . . ."

The young nurse's aide whom Garp had embarrassed by asking about Charlotte's "purse" was increasingly snotty to him. One day when he arrived early, before visitors were permitted, she asked him a little too aggressively what he was to Charlotte, anyway. A member of the family? She had seen Charlotte's other visitors— her gaudy colleagues—and she assumed Garp was just an old hooker's customer. "She's my mother," Garp said; he didn't know why, but he appreciated the shock of the young nurse's aide, and her subsequent respect.

"What did you tell them?" Charlotte whispered to him, a few days later. "They think you're my *son*." He confessed his lie; Charlotte confessed she had done nothing to correct it. "Thank you," she whispered. "It's nice to trick the swine. They think they're so superior." And mustering her former and fading lewdness, she said, "I'd let you have it once for free, if I still had the equipment. Maybe twice for half price," she said.

He was touched and cried in front of her.

"Don't be a baby," she said. "What *am* I to you, really?" When she was asleep, he read on her hospital chart that she was fifty-one.

She died a week later. When Garp went to her room, it was whisked clean, the bed stripped back, the windows wide open. When he asked for her, there was a nurse in charge of the floor whom he didn't recognize— an iron-gray maiden who kept shaking her head. "Fräulein Charlotte," Garp said. "She was Herr Doktor Thalhammer's patient."

"He has lots of patients," said the iron-gray maiden. She was consulting a list, but Garp did not know Charlotte's real name. Finally, he could think of no other way to identify her.

"The whore," he said. "She was a whore." The gray woman regarded him coolly; if Garp could detect no satisfaction in her expression, he could detect no sympathy either.

"The prostitute is dead," the old nurse said. Perhaps Garp only imagined that he heard a little triumph in her voice.

"One day, *meine Frau*," he said to her, "you will be dead, too."

And that, he thought—leaving the Rudolfinerhaus— was a properly Viennese thing to say. Take that, you old gray city, you dead bitch, he thought.

He went to his first opera that night; to his surprise, it was in Italian, and since he understood none of it, he took the whole performance to be a kind of religious service. He walked in the night to the lit spires of Saint Stephen's; the south tower of the cathedral, he read on some plaque, was started in the middle of the fourteenth century and completed in 1439. Vienna, Garp thought, was a cadaver; all Europe, maybe, was a dressed-up corpse in an open coffin. "In the life of a man," wrote Marcus Aurelius, "his time is but a moment . . . his fortune dark. . . ."

In this mood Garp walked home on the Kärntner-strasse, where he met the notorious Tina. Her deep pockmark, harboring the neon of the city lights, was a greenish blue.

*"Guten Abend,* Herr Garp," she said. "Guess what?"

Tina explained that Charlotte had bought Garp a favor. The favor was that Garp could have Tina and Wanga for free; he could have them one at a time or both together. Tina explained. Together, Tina thought, was more interesting—and quicker. But perhaps Garp did not like both of them. Garp admitted that Wanga did not appeal to him; she was too close to his own age, and though he would never say this if she were here and her feelings could be hurt, he did not care for the way the mavonnaise jar had pulled her lip askew.

"Then you can have me twice," Tina said, cheerfully. "Once now, and once," she added, "after you've had a long time to catch your breath. Forget Charlotte," Tina said. Death happened to everyone, Tina explained. Even so, Garp politely declined the offer.

"Well it's here," Tina said. "When you want it." She reached out and frankly cupped him in her warm palm; her big hand was an ample codpiece for him, but Garp only smiled and bowed to her—as the Viennese do—and walked home to his mother.

He enjoyed his slight pain. He took pleasure in this silly self-denial—and more pleasure in his *imagination* of Tina, he suspected, then he ever could have derived from her vaguely gross flesh. The silvery gouge on her

165

forehead was nearly as big as her mouth; her pockmark looked to Garp like a small, open grave.

What Garp was savoring was the beginning of a writer's long-sought trance, wherein the world falls under one embracing tone of voice. "All that is body is as coursing waters," Garp remembered, "all that is of the soul as dreams and vapors." It was July when Garp went back to work on "The Pension Grillparzer." His mother was finishing up the manuscript that would soon change both their lives.

It was August when Jenny finished her book and announced that *she* was ready to travel, to at last see something of Europe—maybe Greece? she suggested. "Let's take the train somewhere," she said. "I always wanted to take the Orient Express. Where's it go?"

"From Paris to Istanbul, I think," Garp said. "But *you* take it, Mom. I've got too much work to do."

Tit for tat, Jenny had to admit. She was so sick of *A Sexual Suspect* that she couldn't even proofread it one more time. She didn't even know what to do with it, now; did one just go to New York and hand over one's life story to a stranger? She wanted Garp to read it, but she saw that Garp was at last engrossed in a task of his own; she felt she shouldn't bother him. Besides, she was unsure; a large part of her life story was *his* life story, too—she thought the story might upset him.

Garp worked through August on the conclusion of his short story, "The Pension Grillparzer." Helen, exasperated, wrote to Jenny. "Is Garp dead?" she asked. "Kindly send details." That Helen Holm is a bright girl, Jenny thought. Helen got more of an answer than she counted on. Jenny sent her a copy of the manuscript of *A Sexual Suspect* with a note explaining that this was what she'd been doing all year, and now Garp was writing something, too. Jenny said she would appreciate Helen's candid opinion of the manuscript. Perhaps, said Jenny, some of Helen's college teachers would know what one *did* with a finished book?

Garp relaxed, when he wasn't writing, by going to the zoo; it was a part of the great grounds and gardens surrounding the Schönbrunn Palace. It appeared to Garp that many of the buildings in the zoo were war ruins, three-quarters destroyed; they had been partially restored to house the animals. This gave Garp the eerie impression that the zoo still existed in Vienna's war period; it also interested him in the period. To fall asleep at night he took to reading some very specific, historical accounts of Vienna during the Nazi and the Russian occupations. This was not unrelated to the death themes that haunted his writing of "The Pension Grillparzer." Garp discovered that when you are writing something, everything seems related to everything else. Vienna was dying, the zoo was not as well restored from the war damage as the homes the *people* lived in; the history of a city was like the history of a family—there is closeness, and even affection, but death eventually separates everyone from each other. It is only the vividness of memory that keeps the dead alive forever; a writer's job is to imagine everything so personally that the fiction is as vivid as our personal memories. He felt the holes from the machine-gun fire in the stone walls of the lobby of the apartment on the Schwindgasse.

Now he knew what the grandmother's dream meant.

He wrote Helen that a young writer needs desperately to live with someone and he had decided that he wanted to live with her; even *marry* her, he offered, because sex was simply necessary but it took too much of one's time if one had to be constantly *planning* how one was going to get it. Therefore, Garp reasoned, it is better to live with it!

Helen revised several letters before she finally sent him one that said he could, so to speak, go stick it in his ear. Did he think she was going through college so rigorously so that she could provide him with sex that was not even necessary to *plan?*

He did not revise, at all, his letter back to her; he

said he was too busy writing to take the time to explain it to her; she would have to read what he was working on and judge for herself how serious he was.

"I don't doubt that you're quite serious," she told him. "And right now I have more to read than I need to know."

She did not tell him that she was referring to Jenny's book, *A Sexual Suspect;* it was 1,158 manuscript pages long. Though Helen would later agree with Garp that it was no literary jewel, she had to admit that it was a very compelling story.

While Garp put the finishing touches on his much shorter story, Jenny Fields plotted her next move. In her restlessness she had bought an American news magazine at a large Vienna newsstand; in it she had read that a courageous New York editor at a well-known publishing house had just rejected the manuscript submitted by an infamous former member of the government who had been convicted of stealing government money. The book was a thinly disguised "fiction" of the criminal's own sordid, petty, political dealings. "It was a lousy novel," the editor was quoted as saying. "The man can't write. Why should he make any money off his crummy life?" The book, of course, would be published elsewhere, and it would eventually make its despicable author and its publisher lots of money. "Sometimes I feel it is my responsibility to say no," the editor was quoted as saying, "even if I know people *do* want to read this slop." The slop, eventually, would be treated to several serious reviews, just as if it were a serious book, but Jenny was greatly impressed with the editor who had said no and she clipped the article out of the news magazine. She drew a circle around the editor's name—a plain name, almost like an actor's name, or the name of an animal in a children's book: John Wolf. There was a picture of John Wolf in the magazine; he looked like a man who took care of himself, and he was very well dressed; he looked like any number of people who work and live in

New York—where good business and good sense suggest that you'd *better* take care of yourself and dress as well as you can—but to Jenny Fields he looked like an angel. He was going to be *her* publisher, she was sure. She was convinced that *her* life was *not* "crummy," and that John Wolf would believe she deserved to make money off it.

Garp had other ambitions for "The Pension Grillparzer." It would never make him much money; it would first appear in a "serious" magazine where almost no one would read it. Years later, when he was better known, it would be published in a more attentive way, and several appreciative things would be written about it, but in his lifetime "The Pension Grillparzer" wouldn't make Garp enough money to buy a good car. Garp, however, expected more than money or transportation from "The Pension Grillparzer." Very simply, he expected to get Helen Holm to live with him—even marry him.

When he finished "The Pension Grillparzer," he announced to his mother that he wanted to go home and see Helen; he would send her a copy of the story and she could have read it by the time he arrived back in the United States. Poor Helen, Jenny thought; Jenny knew that Helen had a lot to read. Jenny also worried how Garp referred to Steering as "home"; but she had reasons of her own for wanting to see Helen, and Ernie Holm would not mind their company for a few days. There was always the parental mansion at Dog's Head Harbor—if Garp and Jenny needed a place to recover, or to make their plans.

Garp and Jenny were such singularly obsessed people that they did not pause to wonder why they had seen so little of Europe, and now they were leaving. Jenny packed her nursing uniforms. There remained, in Garp's mind, only the favors that Charlotte had left up to Tina's devising.

Garp's imagination of these favors had sustained him

during the writing of "The Pension Grillparzer," but as he would learn all his life, the demands of writing and of real life are not always similar. His imagination sustained him when he was writing; now that he *wasn't* writing, he wanted Tina. He went to look for her on the Kärntnerstrasse, but the mayonnaise-jar whore, who spoke English, told him that Tina had moved from the first district.

"So goes it," Wanga said. "Forget Tina."

Garp found that he *could* forget her; lust, as his mother called it, was tricky that way. And time, he discovered, had softened his dislike of Wanga's mayonnaise-jar lip; suddenly, he liked it. And so he had *her,* twice, and as he would learn all his life, nearly everything seems a letdown after a writer has finished writing something.

Garp and Jenny had spent fifteen months in Vienna. It was September. Garp and Helen were only nineteen, and Helen would be going back to college very soon. The plane flew from Vienna to Frankfurt. The slight tingling (that was Wanga) quietly left Garp's flesh. When Garp thought of Charlotte, he imagined that Charlotte had been happy. After all, she had never had to leave the first district.

The plane flew from Frankfurt to London; Garp reread "The Pension Grillparzer" and hoped that Helen would not turn him down. From London to New York, Jenny read her son's story. In terms of what *she'd* spent more than a year doing, Garp's story struck Jenny as rather unreal. But her taste for literature was never keen and she marveled at her son's imagination. Later she would say that "The Pension Grillparzer" was just the sort of story she'd expect a boy without a proper family to make up.

Maybe so. Helen would later say that it is in the conclusion of "The Pension Grillparzer" that we can glimpse what the world according to Garp would be like.

## THE PENSION GRILLPARZER [Conclusion]

In the breakfast room of the Pension Grillparzer we confronted Herr Theobald with the menagerie of his other guests who had disrupted our evening. I knew that (as never before) my father was planning to reveal himself as a Tourist Bureau spy.

"Men walking about on their hands," said Father.

"Men looking under the floor of the W.C.," said Grandmother.

"*That* man," I said, and pointed to the small, sulking fellow at the corner table, seated for breakfast with his cohorts—the dream man and the Hungarian singer.

"He does it for his living," Herr Theobald told us, and as if to demonstrate that this was so, the man who stood on his hands began to stand on his hands.

"Make him stop that," Father said. "We know he can do it."

"But did you know that he can't do it any other way?" the dream man asked suddenly. "Did you know his legs were useless? He has no shinbones. It is wonderful that he can walk on his hands! Otherwise, he wouldn't walk at all." The man, although it was clearly hard to do while standing on his hands, nodded his head.

"Please sit down," Mother said.

"It is perfectly all right to be crippled," Grandmother said, boldly. "But you are evil," she told the dream man. "You know things you have no right to know. He knew my *dream*," she told Herr Theobald, as if she were reporting a theft from her room.

"He is a *little* evil, I know," Theobald admitted. "But not usually! And he behaves better and better. He can't help what he knows."

"I was just trying to straighten you out," the dream man told Grandmother. "I thought it would do you good. Your husband has been dead quite a while, after all, and it's about time you stopped making so much of that dream. You're not the only person who's had such a dream."

"Stop it," Grandmother said.

"Well, you ought to know," said the dream man.

"No, be quiet, please," Herr Theobald told him.

"I am from the Tourist Bureau," Father announced, probably because he couldn't think of anything else to say.

"Oh my God shit!" Herr Theobald said.

"It's not Theobald's fault," said the singer. "It's *our* fault. He's nice to put up with us, though it costs him his reputation."

"They married my sister," Theobald told us. "They are *family*, you see. What can I do?"

" 'They' married your sister?" Mother said.

"Well, she married *me* first," said the dream man.

"And then she heard *me* sing!" the singer said.

"She's never been married to the *other* one," Theobald said, and everyone looked apologetically toward the man who could only walk on his hands.

Theobald said, "They were once a circus act, but politics got them in trouble."

"We were the best in Hungary," said the singer. "You ever hear of the Circus Szolnok?"

"No, I'm afraid not," Father said, seriously.

"We played in Miskolc, in Szeged, in Debrecen," said the dream man.

"*Twice* in Szeged," the singer said.

"We would have made it to Budapest if it hadn't been for the Russians," said the man who walked on his hands.

"Yes, it was the Russians who removed his shinbones!" said the dream man.

"Tell the truth," the singer said. "He was *born* without shinbones. But it's true that we couldn't get along with the Russians."

"They tried to jail the bear," said the dream man.

"Tell the truth," Theobald said.

"We rescued his sister from them," said the man who walked on his hands.

"So of course I must put them up," said Herr Theobald,

"and they work as hard as they can. But who's interested in their act in this country? It's a Hungarian thing. There's no *tradition* of bears on unicycles here," Theobald told us. "And the damn dreams mean nothing to us Viennese."

"Tell the truth," said the dream man. "It is because I have told the wrong dreams. We worked a nightclub on the Kärntnerstrasse, but then we got banned."

"You should never have told *that* dream," the singer said gravely.

"Well, it was your wife's responsibility, too!" the dream man said.

"She was *your* wife, then," the singer said.

"Please stop it," Theobald begged.

"We get to do the balls for children's diseases," the dream man said. "And some of the state hospitals—especially at Christmas."

"If you would only do more with the bear," Herr Theobald advised them.

"Speak to your sister about that," said the singer. "It's *her* bear—she's trained him, she's let him get lazy and sloppy and full of bad habits."

"He is the only one of you who never makes fun of me," said the man who could only walk on his hands.

"I would like to leave all this," Grandmother said. "This is, for me, an awful experience."

"Please, dear lady," Herr Theobald said, "we only wanted to show you that we meant no offense. These are hard times. I need the B rating to attract more tourists, and I can't—in my heart—throw out the Circus Szolnok."

"*In his heart*, my ass!" said the dream man. "He's afraid of his sister. He wouldn't dream of throwing us out."

"If he dreamed it, you would know it!" cried the man on his hands.

"I am afraid of the *bear*," Herr Theobald said. "It does everything she tells it to do."

"Say 'he,' not 'it,'" said the man on his hands. "He is a fine bear, and he never hurt anybody. He has no claws, you know perfectly well—and very few teeth, either."

"The poor thing has a terribly hard time eating," Herr Theobald admitted. "He is quite old, and he's messy."

Over my father's shoulder, I saw him write in the giant pad: "A depressed bear and an unemployed circus. This family is centered on the sister."

At that moment, out on the sidewalk, we could see her tending to the bear. It was early morning and the street was not especially busy. By law, of course, she had the bear on a leash, but it was a token control. In her startling red turban the woman walked up and down the sidewalk, following the lazy movements of the bear on his unicycle. The animal pedaled easily from parking meter to parking meter, sometimes leaning a paw on the meter as he turned. He was very talented on the unicycle, you could tell, but you could also tell that the unicycle was a dead end for him. You could see that the bear felt he could go no further with unicycling.

"She should bring him off the street now," Herr Theobald fretted. "The people in the pastry shop next door complain to me," he told us. "They say the bear drives their customers away."

"That bear makes the customers come!" said the man on his hands.

"It makes some people come, it turns some away," said the dream man. He was suddenly somber, as if his profundity had depressed him.

But we had been so taken up with the antics of the Circus Szolnok that we had neglected old Johanna. When my mother saw that Grandmother was quietly crying, she told me to bring the car around.

"It's been too much for her," my father whispered to Theobald. The Circus Szolnok looked ashamed of themselves.

Outside on the sidewalk the bear pedaled up to me and handed me the keys; the car was parked at the curb. "Not everyone likes to be given the keys in that fashion," Herr Theobald told his sister.

"Oh, I thought he'd rather like it," she said, rumpling my hair. She was as appealing as a barmaid, which is to say

174

that she was more appealing at night; in the daylight I could see that she was older than her brother, and older than her husbands too—and in time, I imagined, she would cease being lover and sister to them, respectively, and become a mother to them all. She was already a mother to the bear.

"Come over here," she said to him. He pedaled listlessly in place on his unicycle, holding on to a parking meter for support. He licked the little glass face of the meter. She tugged his leash. He stared at her. She tugged again. Insolently, the bear began to pedal—first one way, then the next. It was as if he took interest, seeing that he had an audience. He began to show off.

"Don't try anything," the sister said to him, but the bear pedaled faster and faster, going forward, going backward, angling sharply and veering among the parking meters; the sister had to let go of the leash. "Duna, stop it!" she cried, but the bear was out of control. He let the wheel roll too close to the curb and the unicycle pitched him hard into the fender of a parked car. He sat on the sidewalk with the unicycle beside him; you could tell that he hadn't injured himself, but he looked very embarrassed and nobody laughed. "Oh, Duna," the sister said, scoldingly, but she went over and crouched beside him at the curb. "Duna, Duna," she reproved him, gently. He shook his big head; he would not look at her. There was some saliva strung on the fur near his mouth and she wiped this away with her hand. He pushed her hand away with his paw.

"Come back again!" cried Herr Theobald, miserably, as we got into our car.

Mother sat in the car with her eyes closed and her fingers massaging her temples; this way she seemed to hear nothing we said. She claimed it was her only defense against traveling with such a contentious family.

I did not want to report on the usual business concerning the care of the car, but I saw that Father was trying to maintain order and calm; he had the giant pad spread on his lap as if we'd just completed a routine investigation. "What does the gauge tell us?" he asked.

"Someone put thirty-five kilometers on it," I said.

"That terrible bear has been in here," Grandmother said. "There are hairs from the beast on the back seat, and I can *smell* him."

"I don't smell anything," Father said.

"And the perfume of that gypsy in the turban," Grandmother said. "It is hovering near the ceiling of the car." Father and I sniffed. Mother continued to massage her temples.

On the floor by the brake and clutch pedals I saw several of the mint-green toothpicks that the Hungarian singer was in the habit of wearing like a scar at the corner of his mouth. I didn't mention them. It was enough to imagine them all—out on the town, in our car. The singing driver, the man on his hands beside him—waving out the window with his feet. And in back, separating the dream man from his former wife—his great head brushing the upholstered roof, his mauling paws relaxed in his large lap—the old bear slouched like a benign drunk.

"Those poor people," Mother said, her eyes still closed.

"Liars and criminals," Grandmother said. "Mystics and refugees and broken-down animals."

"They were trying hard," Father said, "but they weren't coming up with the prizes."

"Better off in a zoo," said Grandmother.

"I had a good time," Robo said.

"It's hard to break out of Class C," I said.

"They have fallen past Z," said old Johanna. "They have disappeared from the human alphabet."

"I think this calls for a letter," Mother said.

But Father raised his hand—as if he were going to bless us—and we were quiet. He was writing in the giant pad and wished to be undisturbed. His face was stern. I knew that Grandmother felt confident of his verdict. Mother knew it was useless to argue. Robo was already bored. I steered us off through the tiny streets; I took Spiegelgasse to Lobkowitzplatz. Spiegelgasse is so narrow that you can see the reflection of your own car in the windows of the shops you pass, and I felt our movement through Vienna was superimposed (like that)—like a trick with a movie camera, as if we made a fairy-tale journey through a toy city.

When Grandmother was asleep in the car, Mother said, "I don't suppose that in this case a change in the classification will matter very much, one way or another."

"No," Father said, "not much at all." He was right about that, though it would be years until I saw the Pension Grillparzer again.

When Grandmother died, rather suddenly and in her sleep, Mother announced that she was tired of traveling. The real reason, however, was that she began to find herself plagued by Grandmother's dream. "The horses are so thin," she told me, once. "I mean, I always knew they would be thin, but not *this* thin. And the soldiers—I knew they were miserable," she said, "but not *that* miserable."

Father resigned from the Tourist Bureau and found a job with a local detective agency specializing in hotels and department stores. It was a satisfactory job for him, though he refused to work during the Christmas season—when, he said, some people ought to be allowed to steal a little.

My parents seemed to me to relax as they got older, and I really felt they were fairly happy near the end. I know that the strength of Grandmother's dream was dimmed by the *real* world, and specifically by what happened to Robo. He went to a private school and was well liked there, but he was killed by a homemade bomb in his first year at the university. He was not even "political." In his last letter to my parents he wrote: "The self-seriousness of the radical factions among the students is much overrated. And the food is execrable." Then Robo went to his history class, and his classroom was blown apart.

It was after my parents died that I gave up smoking and took up traveling again. I took my second wife back to the Pension Grillparzer. With my first wife, I never got as far as Vienna.

The Grillparzer had not kept Father's B rating very long, and it had fallen from the ratings altogether by the time I returned to it. Herr Theobald's sister was in charge of the place. Gone was her tart appeal and in its place was the sexless cynicism of some maiden aunts. She was shapeless and her hair was dyed a sort of bronze, so that her head resembled one of those copper scouring pads that you use on a pot. She did not remember me and was suspicious of my questions. Because I appeared to know so much about her past associates, she probably knew I was with the police.

The Hungarian singer had gone away—another woman thrilled by his voice. The dream man had been *taken* away—to an institution. His own dreams had turned to nightmares and he'd awakened the pension each night with his horrifying howls. His removal from the seedy premises, said Herr Theobald's sister, was almost simultaneous with the loss of the Grillparzer's B rating.

Herr Theobald was dead. He had dropped down clutching his heart in the hall, where he ventured one night to investigate what he thought was a prowler. It was only Duna, the malcontent bear, who was dressed in the dream man's pin-striped suit. Why Theobald's sister had dressed the bear in this fashion was not explained to me, but the shock of the sullen animal unicycling in the lunatic's left-behind clothes had been enough to scare Herr Theobald to death.

The man who could only walk on his hands had also fallen into the gravest trouble. His wristwatch snagged on a tine of an escalator and he was suddenly unable to hop off; his necktie, which he rarely wore because it dragged on the ground when he walked on his hands, was drawn under the step-off grate at the end of the escalator—where he was strangled. Behind him a line of people formed—marching in place by taking one step back and allowing the escalator to carry them forward, then taking another step back. It was quite a while before anyone got up the nerve to step over him. The world has many unintentionally cruel mechanisms that are not designed for people who walk on their hands.

After that, Theobald's sister told me, the Pension Grillparzer went from Class C to much worse. As the burden of management fell more heavily on her, she had less time for Duna and the bear grew senile and indecent in his habits. Once he bullied a mailman down a marble staircase at such a ferocious pace that the man fell and broke his hip; the attack was reported and an old city ordinance forbidding unrestrained animals in places open to the public was enforced. Duna was outlawed at the Pension Grillparzer.

For a while, Theobald's sister kept the bear in a cage in the courtyard of the building, but he was taunted by dogs and children, and food (and worse) was dropped into his cage from the apartments that faced the courtyard. He grew unbearlike and devious—only pretending to sleep—and he ate most of someone's cat. Then he was poisoned twice and became afraid to eat anything in this perilous environment. There was no alternative but to donate him to the Schönbrunn Zoo, but there was even some doubt as to his acceptability. He was toothless and ill, perhaps contagious, and his long history of having been treated as a human being did not prepare him for the gentler routine of zoo life.

His outdoor sleeping quarters in the courtyard of the Grillparzer had inflamed his rheumatism, and even his one talent, unicycling, was irretrievable. When he first tried it in the zoo, he fell. Someone laughed. Once anyone laughed at something Duna did, Theobald's sister explained, Duna would never do that thing again. He became, at last, a kind of charity case at Schönbrunn, where he died a short two months after he'd taken up his new lodgings. In the opinion of Theobald's sister, Duna died of mortification—the result of a rash that spread over his great chest, which then had to be shaved. A shaved bear, one zoo official said, is embarrassed to death.

In the cold courtyard of the building I looked in the bear's empty cage. The birds hadn't left a fruit seed, but in a corner of his cage was a looming mound of the bear's ossified droppings—as void of life, and even odor, as the corpses captured by the holocaust at Pompeii. I couldn't help thinking of Robo; of the bear, there were more remains.

In the car I was further depressed to notice that not one kilometer had been added to the gauge, not one kilometer had been driven in secret. There was no one around to take liberties anymore.

"When we're a safe distance away from your precious Pension Grillparzer," my second wife said to me, "I'd like you to tell me why you brought me to such a shabby place."

"It's a long story," I admitted.

I was thinking I had noticed a curious lack of either enthusiasm or bitterness in the account of the world by Theobald's sister. There was in her story the flatness one associates with a storyteller who is accepting of unhappy endings, as if her life and her companions had never been exotic to *her*—as if they had always been staging a ludicrous and doomed effort at reclassification.

# 7

# More Lust

A ND so she married him; she did what he asked. Helen thought it was a pretty good story for a start. Old Tinch liked it, too. "It is rich with lu-lu-lunacy and sorrow," Tinch told Garp. Tinch recommended that Garp send "The Pension Grillparzer" to Tinch's favorite magazine. Garp waited three months for this reply:

> *The story is only mildly interesting, and it does nothing new with language or with form. Thanks for showing it to us, though.*

Garp was puzzled and he showed the rejection to Tinch. Tinch was also puzzled.

"I guess they're interested in n-n-*new*er fiction," Tinch said.

"What's that?" Garp asked.

Tinch admitted he didn't really know. "The new fiction is interested in language and in f-f-form, I guess," Tinch said. "But I don't understand what it's really about. Sometimes it's about it-it-itself, I think," Tinch said.

181

"About itself?" Garp said.

"It's sort of fiction about fi-fi-*fiction*," Tinch told him.

Garp still didn't understand, but what mattered to Garp was that Helen liked the story.

Almost fifteen years later, when Garp published his third novel, that same editor at Tinch's favorite magazine would write Garp a letter. The letter would be very flattering to Garp, and to his work, and it would ask Garp to submit anything *new* he might have written to Tinch's favorite magazine. But T. S. Garp had a tenacious memory and the indignation of a badger. He found the old rejection note that had called his Grillparzer story "only mildly interesting"; the note was crusty with coffee stains and had been folded so many times that it was torn at the creases, but Garp enclosed it with a letter to the editor at Tinch's favorite magazine. Garp's letter said:

> *I am only mildly interested in your magazine, and I am still doing nothing new with language or with form. Thanks for asking me, though.*

Garp had a foolish ego that went out of its way to remember insults to and rejections of his work. It is fortunate for Helen that she had a ferocious ego of her own, for if she hadn't highly esteemed herself, she would have ended up hating him. As it was, they were lucky. Many couples live together and discover they're not in love; some couples never discover it. Others marry, and the news comes to them at awkward moments in their lives. In the case of Garp and Helen, they hardly knew each other but they had their hunches —and in their stubborn, deliberate ways they fell in love with each other sometime after they had married.

Perhaps because they were so busy pursuing their singular careers they did not overscrutinize their relationship. Helen would graduate from college two years after she began; she would have a Ph.D. in English literature when she was only twenty-three, and her first job—an assistant professor at a women's college—when she was twenty-four. It would take Garp five years to finish his first novel, but it would be a good novel and it would earn him a respectable reputation for a young writer—even if it wouldn't make him any money. By then, Helen would be making money for them. All the time that Helen went to school, and Garp was writing, Jenny took care of the money.

Jenny's book was more of a shock to Helen, when she first read it, than it was to Garp—who, after all, had lived with his mother and was unsurprised by her eccentricity; it had become commonplace to him. Garp, however, *was* shocked by the book's success. He had not counted on becoming a public figure—a leading character in someone else's book before he'd even written a book of his own.

The editor, John Wolf, would never forget the first morning at his office where he met Jenny Fields.

"There's a nurse to see you," his secretary said, rolling her eyes—as if this might be a paternity suit that her boss had on his hands. John Wolf and his secretary could not have known that a manuscript of 1,158 typed pages was what made Jenny's suitcase so heavy.

"It's about me," she told John Wolf, opening her suitcase and hefting the monster manuscript to the top of his desk. "When can you read it?" It looked to John Wolf as if the woman intended to stay in his office *while* he read it. He glanced at the first sentence ("In this dirty-minded world . . ."), and he thought: Oh boy, how do I get rid of *this* one?

Later, of course, he was panic-stricken when he could not find a phone number for her; when he wanted to tell her that yes!—they would certainly publish *this!*—he could not have known that Jenny Fields was the proper guest of Ernie Holm at Steering, where Jenny and Ernie talked into the night, every night (the usual parental concern when parents discover that their nineteen-year-old children plan to get married).

"Where can they go every night?" Jenny asked.

"They don't come back here until two or three, and last night it rained. It rained all night, and they don't even have a car."

They went to the wrestling room. Helen, of course, had a key. And a wrestling mat was as comfortable and familiar to them as any bed. And much bigger.

"They say they want children," Ernie complained. "Helen should finish her education."

"Garp will never finish a book, with children," Jenny said. After all, she was thinking that she'd had to wait eighteen years to *begin* her book.

"They're both hard workers," Ernie said, to reassure himself and Jenny.

"They'll *have* to be," Jenny said.

"I don't know why they can't just *live* together," Ernie said. "And if it works out, *then* let them get married; then let them have a baby."

"I don't know why *any*one wants to live with anyone else," said Jenny Fields. Ernie looked a little hurt.

"Well, you like Garp living with you," he reminded her, "and I like Helen living with me. I really miss her when she's away at school."

"It's *lust,*" Jenny said, ominously. "The world is sick with lust."

Ernie felt worried about her; he didn't know she was about to become rich and famous forever. "Do you want a beer?" he asked Jenny.

"No, thank you," Jenny said.

"They're good kids," Ernie reminded her.

"But lust gets them all, in the end," said Jenny Fields, morosely, and Ernie Holm walked delicately to his kitchen and opened another beer for himself.

It was the "lust" chapter of *A Sexual Suspect* that especially embarrassed Garp. It was one thing to be a famous child born out of wedlock, quite another to be a famous case history of adolescent need—his private randiness become a popular story. Helen thought it was very funny, though she confessed to not understanding his attraction to whores.

"Lust makes the best men behave out of character," wrote Jenny Fields—a line that particularly infuriated Garp.

"What the hell does *she* know about it?" he screamed. "She never felt it, not once. Some authority *she* is! It's like listening to a plant describe the motives of a mammal!"

But other reviewers were kinder to Jenny; though the more serious journals occasionally chided her for her actual writing, the media, in general, felt warmly toward the book. "The first truly feminist autobiography that is as full of celebrating one kind of life as it is full of putting down another," somebody wrote. "This brave book makes the important assertion that a woman can have a whole life without a sexual attachment of *any* kind," wrote somebody else.

"These days," John Wolf had forewarned Jenny, "you're either going to be taken as the right voice at the right time, or you're going to be put down as all wrong." She was taken as the right voice at the right time, but Jenny Fields, sitting whitely in her nurse's uniform—in the restaurant where John Wolf took only his favorite writers—felt discomfort at the word *feminism.* She was not sure what it meant, but the *word* reminded her of feminine hygiene and the Valentine treatment. After all, her formal training had been nursing. She said shyly that she'd only thought she made the right choice about how to live her life, and since it had not been a popular choice, she'd felt goaded into saying something to defend it. Ironically, a rash of young women at Florida State University in Tallahassee found Jenny's choice *very* popular; they generated a small controversy by plotting their own pregnancies. For a while, in New York, this syndrome among singular-minded women was called "doing a Jenny Fields." But Garp always called it "doing a Grillparzer." As for Jenny, she felt only that women—just like men—should at least be able to make conscious decisions about the course of their lives; if that made her a feminist, she said, then she guessed she *was* one.

John Wolf liked Jenny Fields very much, and he did what he could to warn her that she might not understand either the attacks or the praise her book would receive. But Jenny never wholly understood how "political" a book it was—or how it would be used as such a book.

"I was trained to be a nurse," she said later, in one of her disarming interviews. "Nursing was the first thing I took to, and the first thing I ever wanted to do. It simply seemed very practical, to me, for someone who was healthy—and I have always been healthy—to help people who weren't healthy or who couldn't help themselves. I think it was simply in that spirit that I wanted to write a book, too."

In Garp's opinion, his mother never stopped being a nurse. She had nursed him through the Steering School; she had been a plodding midwife to her own strange life story; finally, she became a kind of nurse to women with problems. She became a figure of famous strength; women sought her advice. With the sudden success of *A Sexual Suspect,* Jenny Fields uncovered a nation of women who faced making choices about how to live; these women felt encouraged by Jenny's own example of making unpopular decisions.

She could have started an advice column for any newspaper, but Jenny Fields felt through with writing, now—just as she'd decided, once before, that she was through with education; just as she'd decided she was through with Europe. In a way, she was *never* through with nursing. Her father, the shocked shoe king, died of a heart attack shortly after the publication of *A Sexual Suspect;* although Jenny's mother never blamed Jenny's book for the tragedy—and Jenny never blamed herself—Jenny knew that her mother could not live alone. Unlike Jenny Fields, Jenny's mother had developed a habit of living with someone else; she was old now, and Jenny thought of her as rattling about in the great rooms at Dog's Head Harbor, purposeless and wholly without her few remaining wits in the absence of her mate.

Jenny went to care for her, and it was at the Dog's Head Harbor mansion that Jenny first began her role as counselor to the women who sought some comfort from her no-nonsense ability to make decisions.

"Even *weird* decisions!" Garp wailed, but he was happy, and taken care of. He and Helen had their first child, almost immediately. It was a boy named Duncan. Garp often joked that the reason his first novel was written with so many short chapters was because of Duncan. Garp wrote between feedings and naps and changes of diapers. "It was a novel of short takes," he claimed, later, "and the credit is wholly Duncan's." Helen was at school every day; she had agreed to have a child only if Garp would agree to take care of it. Garp loved the idea of never having to go out. He wrote and took care of Duncan; he cooked and wrote and took care of Duncan some more. When Helen came home, she came home to a reasonably happy homemaker; as long as Garp's novel progressed, no routine, however mindless, could upset him. In fact, the more mindless, the better. He left Duncan for two hours every day with the woman in the downstairs apartment; he went to the gym. He later became an oddity at the women's college where Helen taught—running endless laps around the field hockey field, or jumping rope for half an hour in a corner of the gymnasium reserved for gymnastics. He missed wrestling and complained to Helen that she should have gotten a job somewhere where there was a wrestling team; Helen complained that the English Department was too small, and she disliked having no male students in her classes, but it was a good job and she would keep it until something better came along.

Everything in New England is at least near everything else. They got to visit Jenny at the shore and Ernie at Steering. Garp would take Duncan to the Steering wrestling room and roll him around like a ball. "This is where your daddy wrestled," he told him.

"It's where your daddy did *everything*," Helen told Duncan, referring -of course—to Duncan's own conception, and to her first rainy night with Garp in the locked and empty Seabrook Gymnasium, on the warm crimson mats stretching wall to wall.

"Well, you finally got me," Helen had whispered to him, tearfully, but Garp had sprawled there, on his back on the wrestling mat, wondering who had gotten *whom*.

When Jenny's mother died, Jenny visited Helen and Garp more frequently, though Garp objected to what he called his mother's "entourage." Jenny Fields traveled with a small core of adorers, or with occasional other figures who felt they were part of what would be called the women's movement; they often wanted Jenny's support or her endorsement. There was often a case or a cause that needed Jenny's pure white uniform on the speaker's platform, although Jenny rarely spoke very much or for very long.

After the other speeches, they would introduce the author of *A Sexual Suspect*. In her nurse's uniform, she was instantly recognizable. Into her fifties, Jenny Fields would remain an athletically attractive woman, crisp and plain. She would rise and say, "This is right." Or, sometimes, "This is wrong"—depending on the occasion. She was the decision maker who'd made the hard choices in her own life and therefore she could be counted on to be on the right side of a woman's problem.

The logic behind all this made Garp fume and stew for days, and once an interviewer from a women's magazine asked if she could come interview him about what it was like to be the son of a famous feminist. When the interviewer discovered Garp's chosen life, his "housewife's role," as she gleefully called it, Garp blew up at her.

"I'm doing what I want to do," he said. "Don't call

it by any other name. I'm just doing what I want to do—
and that's all my mother ever did, too. Just what *she*
wanted to do."

The interviewer pressed him; she said he sounded
bitter. Of course, it must be hard, she suggested, being
an unknown writer with a mother whose book was
known around the world. Garp said it was mainly
painful to be misunderstood, and that he did not resent
his mother's success; he only occasionally disliked her
new associates. "Those stooges who are living off her,"
he said.

The article in the women's magazine pointed out that
*Garp* was also "living off" his mother, very comfortably,
and that he had no right to be hostile toward the wom-
en's movement. That was the first time Garp heard of
it: "the women's movement."

It was not many days after this that Jenny came
to visit him. One of her goons, as Garp called them,
was with her: a large, silent, sullen woman who lurked
in the doorway of Garp's apartment and declined to
take her coat off. She looked warily at little Duncan, as
if she awaited, with extreme displeasure, the moment
when the child might touch her.

"Helen's at the library," Garp told Jenny. "I was
going to take Duncan for a walk. You want to come?"
Jenny looked questioningly at the big woman with her;
the woman shrugged. Garp thought that his mother's
greatest weakness, since her success, was to be, in his
words, "used by all the crippled and infirm women who
wished they'd written *A Sexual Suspect,* or something equally successful."

Garp resented standing cowed in his own apartment
by his mother's speechless companion, a woman large
enough to be his mother's bodyguard. Perhaps that's
what she is, he thought. And an unpleasant image of
his mother with a tough dyke escort crossed his mind—
a vicious killer who would keep the men's hands off
Jenny's white uniform.

"Is there something the matter with that woman's

*tongue,* Mom?" Garp whispered to Jenny. The superiority of the big woman's silence outraged him; Duncan was trying to talk with her, but the woman merely fixed the child with a quieting eye. Jenny quietly informed Garp that the woman wasn't talking because the woman was without a tongue. Literally.

"It was cut off," Jenny said.

"Jesus," Garp whispered. "How'd it happen?"

Jenny rolled her eyes; it was a habit she'd picked up from her son. "You really read nothing, don't you?" Jenny asked him. "You just never have bothered to keep up with what's going on." What was "going on," in Garp's opinion, was never as important as what he was making up—what he was working on. One of the things that upset him about his mother (since she'd been adopted by women's politics) was that she was always discussing the *news.*

"This is *news,* you mean?" Garp said. "It's such a famous tongue accident that I should have heard about it?"

"Oh, God," Jenny said wearily. "Not a famous accident. Very deliberate."

"Mother, did someone cut her tongue off?"

"Precisely," Jenny said.

"Jesus," Garp said.

"You haven't heard of Ellen James?" Jenny asked.

"No," Garp admitted.

"Well, there's a whole *society* of women now," Jenny informed him, "because of what happened to Ellen James."

"What happened to her?" Garp asked.

"Two men raped her when she was eleven years old," Jenny said. "Then they cut her tongue off so she couldn't tell anyone who they were or what they looked like. They were so stupid that they didn't know an eleven-year-old could *write.* Ellen James wrote a very careful description of the men, and they were caught, and they were tried and convicted. In jail, someone murdered them."

"Wow," Garp said. "So *that's* Ellen James?" he whispered, indicating the big quiet woman with new respect.

Jenny rolled her eyes again. "No," she said. "That is someone from the Ellen James *Society*. Ellen James is still a child; she's a wispy-looking little blond girl."

"You mean this Ellen James Society goes around not talking," Garp said, "as if *they* didn't have any tongues?"

"No, I mean they *don't* have any tongues," Jenny said. "People in the Ellen James Society have their tongues cut *off*. To protest what happened to Ellen James."

"Oh boy," Garp said, looking at the large woman with renewed dislike.

"They call themselves Ellen Jamesians," Jenny said.

"I don't want to hear any more of this shit, Mom," Garp said.

"Well, that woman there is an Ellen Jamesian," Jenny said. "You wanted to know."

"How old is Ellen James now?" Garp asked.

"She's twelve," Jenny said. "It happened only a year ago."

"And these Ellen Jamesians," Garp asked, "do they have meetings, and elect presidents and treasurers and stuff like that?"

"Why don't you ask her?" Jenny said, indicating the lunk by the door. "I thought you didn't want to hear any more about it."

"How can I ask her if she doesn't have a tongue to answer me?" Garp hissed.

"She *writes*," Jenny said. "All Ellen Jamesians carry little note pads around with them and they *write* you what they want to say. You know what writing is, don't you?"

Fortunately, Helen came home.

Garp would see more of the Ellen Jamesians. Although he felt deeply disturbed by what had happened to Ellen James, he felt only disgust at her grown-up,

191

sour imitators whose habit was to present you with a card. The card said something like:

*Hello, I'm Martha. I'm an Ellen Jamesian. Do you know what an Ellen Jamesian is?*

And if you didn't know, you were handed another card.

The Ellen Jamesians represented, for Garp, the kind of women who lionized his mother and sought to use her to help further their crude causes.

"I'll tell you something about those women, Mom," he said to Jenny once. "They were probably all lousy at talking, anyway; they probably never had a worthwhile thing to say in their lives—so their tongues were no great sacrifice; in fact, it probably saves them considerable embarrassment. If you see what I mean."

"You're a little short on sympathy," Jenny told him.

"I have *lots* of sympathy—for Ellen James," Garp said.

"These women must have suffered, in other ways, themselves," Jenny said. "That's what makes them want to get closer to each other."

"And inflict more suffering on themselves, Mom?"

"Rape is every woman's problem," Jenny said. Garp hated his mother's "everyone" language most of all. A case, he thought, of carrying democracy to an idiotic extreme.

"It's every man's problem, too, Mom. The next time there's a rape, suppose I cut my *prick* off and wear it around my neck. Would you respect *that,* too?"

"We're talking about *sincere* gestures," Jenny said.

"We're talking about *stupid* gestures," Garp said.

But he would always remember his first Ellen Jamesian—the big woman who came to his apartment with his mother; when she left, she wrote Garp out a note and slipped it into his hand as if it were a tip.

"Mom's got a new bodyguard," Garp whispered to

Helen as they waved good-bye. Then he read the body-guard's note.

*Your mother is worth 2 of you,*

the note said.

But he couldn't really complain about his mother; for the first five years Garp and Helen were married, Jenny paid their bills.

Garp joked that he called his first novel *Procrastination* because it had taken him so long to write it, but he had worked on it steadily and carefully; Garp was rarely a procrastinator.

The novel was called "historical." It is set in the Vienna of the war years, 1938–45, and through the period of the Russian occupation. The main character is a young anarchist who has to lie low, after the Anschluss, waiting for just the right blow he can strike against the Nazis. He waits too long. The point being, he should better have struck before the Nazi takeover; but there is nothing he can be sure of, then, and he is too young to recognize what is happening. Also, his mother—a widow—cherishes her private life; unconcerned with politics, she hoards her dead husband's money.

Through the war years, the young anarchist works as a zookeeper at Schönbrunn. When the population of Vienna begins seriously starving, and midnight raids on the zoo are a common source of stolen food, the anarchist decides to liberate the remaining animals—who are, of course, innocent of his country's own procrastination and its acquiescence to Nazi Germany. But by then the animals themselves are starving; when the anarchist frees them, they eat him. "That was only natural," Garp wrote. The animals, in turn, are slaughtered easily by a starving mob now roaming Vienna for food—just ahead of the Russian forces. That, too, was "only natural."

The anarchist's mother survives the war and lives in the Russian zone of occupation (Garp gave her the same apartment he and his mother shared on the Schwindgasse); the miserly widow's tolerance is finally wearied by the repeated atrocities she now sees committed by the Soviets—rape, chief among them. She watches the city restored to moderation and complacency, and she remembers her own inertia during the Nazi rise to power with great regret. Finally, the Russians leave; it is 1956, and Vienna retreats into itself again. But the woman mourns her son and her damaged country; she strolls the partially rebuilt and once again healthy zoo at Schönbrunn every weekend, recalling her secretive visits to her son there, during the war. It is the Hungarian Revolution that prompts the old lady's final action. Hundreds of thousands of new refugees come into Vienna.

In an effort to awaken the complacent city—that it must not sit back and watch things develop again—the mother tries to do what her son did: she releases the animals in the Schönbrunn Zoo. But the animals are well fed and content now; only a few of them can even be goaded into leaving their cages, and those who do wander out are easily confined in the Schönbrunn paths and gardens; eventually they're returned to their cages, unharmed. One elderly bear suffers a bout of violent diarrhea. The old woman's gesture of liberation is well intended but it is completely meaningless and totally unrealized. The old woman is arrested and an examining police doctor discovers that she has cancer; she is a terminal case.

Finally, and ironically, her hoarded money is of some use to her. She dies in luxury—in Vienna's only private hospital, the Rudolfinerhaus. In her death dream she imagines that some animals escape from the zoo: a couple of young Asiatic Black Bears. She imagines them surviving and multiplying so successfully that they become famous as a new animal species in the valley of the Danube.

But this is only her imagination. The novel ends—after the old woman's death—with the death of the diarrhetic bear in the Schönbrunn Zoo. "So much for revolution in modern times," wrote one reviewer, who called *Procrastination* "an anti-Marxist novel."

The novel was praised for the accuracy of its historical research—a point of no particular interest to Garp. It was also cited for originality and for having unusual scope for a first novel by such a young author. John Wolf had been Garp's publisher, and although he had agreed with Garp *not* to mention on the jacket flap that this was the first novel by the son of the feminist heroine Jenny Fields, there were few reviewers who failed to sound that chime.

"It is amazing that the now-famous son of Jenny Fields," wrote one, "has actually grown up to be what he said he wanted to be when he grew up." This, and other irrelevant cuteness concerning Garp's relationship to Jenny, made Garp very angry that his book couldn't be read and discussed for its own faults and/or merits, but John Wolf explained to him the hard fact that most readers were probably more interested in who he was than in what he'd actually written.

"Young Mr. Garp is still writing about bears," chided one wit, who'd been energetic enough to uncover the Grillparzer story from its obscure publication. "Perhaps, when he grows up, he'll write something about people."

But altogether, it was a literary debut more astonishing than most—and more noticed. It was, of course, never a popular book, and it hardly made T. S. Garp into a brand name; it would not make him "the household product"—as he called her—that his mother had become. But it was not that kind of book; he was not that kind of writer, and never would be, John Wolf told him.

"What do you expect?" John Wolf wrote him. "If you want to be rich and famous, get in another line. If you're serious about it, don't bitch. You wrote a serious book, it was published seriously. If you want to make a *living* off it, you're talking about another world. And remember: you're twenty-four years old. I think you'll write a lot more books."

John Wolf was an honorable and intelligent man, but Garp wasn't sure—and he wasn't content. He had made a little money, and now Helen had a salary; now that he didn't *need* Jenny's money, Garp felt all right about accepting some when she simply gave it out. And he felt he'd at least earned another reward to himself: he asked Helen to have another baby. Duncan was four; he was old enough to appreciate a brother or a sister. Helen agreed, knowing how easy Garp had made it for her to have Duncan. If he wanted to change diapers between the chapters of his next book, that was up to him.

But it was actually more than merely wanting a second child that prompted Garp to reproduce again. He knew he was an overwatchful, worrisome father and he felt he might relieve Duncan of some of the pressure of fatherly fears if there was *another* child to absorb some of Garp's excess anxiety.

"I'm very happy," Helen told him. "If you want another baby, we'll make one. I just wish you'd *relax*, I wish you'd be happier. You wrote a good book, now you'll write another one. Isn't it just what you always wanted?"

But he bitched about the reviews of *Procrastination,* and he moaned about the sales. He carped at his mother, and roared about her "sycophantic friends." Finally Helen said to him, "You want too much. Too much unqualified praise, or love—or *something* that's unqualified, anyway. You want the world to say, 'I love your writing, I love you,' and that's too much to want. That's really sick, in fact."

"That's what *you* said," he reminded her. " 'I love your writing, I love you.' That's exactly what you said."

"But there can only be one of me," Helen reminded him.

Indeed, there would only be one of her, and he

loved her very much. He would always call her "the wisest of my life's decisions." He made some unwise decisions, he would admit; but in the first five years of his marriage to Helen, he was unfaithful to her only once—and it was brief.

It was a baby-sitter from the college where Helen taught, a freshman girl from Helen's Freshman English class; she was nice with Duncan, though Helen said that the girl was not a very special student. Her name was Cindy; she had read Garp's *Procrastination,* and she'd been properly awed. When he drove her home, she would ask him one question after another about his writing: How did you think of THAT? and what made you do it THIS way? She was a tiny thing, all flutters and twitches and coos—as trusting, as constant, and as stupid as a Steering pigeon. "Little Squab Bones," Helen called her, but Garp was attracted; he called her nothing. The Percy family had given him a permanent dislike of nicknames. And he liked Cindy's questions.

Cindy was dropping out of school because she felt a women's college was not right for her; she needed to live with grownups, and with men, she said, and although the college allowed her to move off-campus—into her own apartment, in the second semester of her freshman year—still she felt the college was too "restricted" and she wanted to live in a "more real environment." She imagined that Garp's Vienna had been a "more real environment," though Garp struggled to assure her that it had not been. Little Squab Bones, Garp thought, was puppy-brained, and as soft and as easily influenced as a banana. But he wanted her, he realized, and he saw her as simply available—like the whores on the Kärntnerstrasse, she would be there when he asked her. And she would cost him only lies.

Helen read him a review from a famous news magazine; the review called *Procrastination* "a complex and moving novel with sharp historic resonances . . . the drama encompasses the longings and agonies of youth."

"Oh *fuck* 'the longings and agonies of youth,'" Garp

said. One of those youthful longings was embarrassing him now.

As for the "drama": in the first five years of his marriage to Helen, T. S. Garp experienced only one real-life drama, and it did not have that much to do with him.

Garp had been running in the city park when he found the girl, a naked ten-year-old running ahead of him on the bridle path. When she realized he was gaining on her, she fell down and covered her face, then covered her crotch, then tried to hide her insubstantial breasts. It was a cold day, late fall, and Garp saw the blood on the child's thighs and her frightened, swollen eyes. She screamed and screamed at him.

"What happened to you?" he asked, though he knew very well. He looked all around them, but there was no one there. She hugged her raw knees to her chest and screamed. "I won't hurt you," Garp said. "I want to help you." But the child wailed even louder. My God, of course! Garp thought: the terrible molester had probably said those very words to her, not long ago. "Where did he go?" Garp asked her. Then he changed his tone, trying to convince her he was on her side. "I'll kill him for you," he told her. She stared quietly at him, her head shaking and shaking, her fingers pinching and pinching the tight skin on her arms. "Please," Garp said, "can you tell me where your clothes are?" He had nothing to give her to wear except his sweaty T-shirt. He was dressed in his running shorts, his running shoes. He pulled his T-shirt off over his head and felt instantly cold: the girl cried out, awfully loud, and hid her face. "No, don't be frightened, it's for you to put on," Garp told her. He let the T-shirt drop on her but she writhed out from under it and kicked at it; then she opened her mouth very wide and bit her own fist.

"She was not old enough to be Boy or Girl yet," Garp wrote. "Only in the pudginess around her nipples was there anything faintly girlish. There was certainly no visible sex about her hairless pudenda, and she had a child's sexless hands. Perhaps there was something sensual about her mouth—her lips were puffy—but she had not done that to herself."

Garp began to cry. The sky was gray, dead leaves were all around them, and when Garp began to wail aloud, the girl picked up his T-shirt and covered herself with it. They were in this queer position to each other—the child crouched under Garp's T-shirt, cringing at Garp's feet with Garp crying over her—when the mounted park police, a twosome, rode up the bridle path and spotted the apparent child molester with his victim. Garp wrote that one of the policemen split the girl and Garp apart by steering his horse between them, "nearly trampling the girl." The other policeman brought his billy down on Garp's collarbone; one side of his body, he wrote, felt paralyzed—"but not the other." With "the other," Garp unseated the policeman and tipped him from the saddle. "It's not *me*, you son of a bitch!" Garp howled. "I just found her, just here—just a minute ago."

The policeman, sprawled in the leaves, held his drawn gun very still. The other policeman, mounted and prancing, shouted to the girl. "Is it *him?*" he yelled. The child seemed terrified of the horses. She stared back and forth from the horses to Garp. She probably isn't sure what *happened,* Garp thought—much less who. But the girl, violently, shook her head. "Where'd he go?" said the policeman on his horse. But the girl still looked at Garp. She tugged her chin and rubbed her cheeks—she tried to talk to him with her hands. Apparently, her words were gone; or her *tongue,* Garp thought, recalling Ellen James.

"It's the *beard,*" said the cop in the leaves; he had gotten to his feet but he had not holstered his gun. "She's telling us there was a beard." Garp had a beard then.

"It was *someone* with a beard," said Garp. "Like

*mine?"* he asked the girl, stroking his dark, round beard, glossy with sweat. But she shook her head and ran her fingers over her sore upper lip.

"A mustache!" cried Garp, and the girl nodded.

She pointed back the way Garp had come, but Garp remembered seeing no one near the entrance to the park. The policeman hunched on his horse and through the thrown leaves he rode away from them. The other policeman was calming his horse, but he had not remounted. "Cover her, or find her clothes," Garp said to him; he started to run down the bridle path after the first policeman; he knew there were things you could see from ground level that you couldn't see on a horse. Also, Garp was such a fool about his running that he imagined he could outlast, if not outrun, any horse.

"Hey, you better wait here!" the policeman called after him, but Garp was in stride and clearly not stopping.

He followed the great rents in the ground that the horse had made. He had not gone even half a mile back along the path before he saw the bent figure of a man, maybe twenty-five yards off the path and almost hidden by the trees. Garp yelled at the figure, an elderly gentleman with a white mustache, who looked over his shoulder at Garp with an expression so surprised and ashamed that Garp was sure he'd found the child molester. He thundered through the vines and small, whiplike trees to the man, who had been peeing and was hastening to fold himself back into his trousers. He looked very much like a man caught doing something he shouldn't have done.

"I was just . . ." the man began, but Garp was upon him and thrust his stiff, cropped beard into the man's face. Garp sniffed him over like a hound.

"If it's you, you bastard, I can *smell* it on you!" Garp said. The man flinched away from this half-naked brute, but Garp seized both the man's wrists and snapped the man's hands up under his nose. He sniffed again, and the man cried out as if he feared Garp was going to bite him. "Hold still!" Garp said. "Did you do it? Where are the child's clothes?"

"Please!" the man piped. "I was just going to the bathroom." He had not had time to close his fly and Garp eyed his crotch suspiciously.

"There is no smell like sex," Garp wrote. "You cannot disguise it. It is as rich and clear as spilled beer."

So Garp dropped to his knees in the woods and unbuckled the man's belt and tore open the man's pants and yanked the man's undershorts straight down to the man's ankles; he stared at the man's frightened equipment.

"Help!" the old gentleman screamed. Garp took a deep sniff and the man collapsed in the young trees; staggering like a puppet strung under the arms, he thrashed in a thicket of slender trunks and branches too dense to allow him to fall. "Help, *God!*" he cried, but Garp was already running back out to the bridle path, his legs digging through the leaves, his arms pummeling the air, his struck collarbone throbbing.

At the entrance to the park the mounted policeman clattered about the parking lot, peering in parked cars, circling the squat brick hut where the rest rooms were. A few people watched him, sensing his eagerness. "No mustaches," the policeman called to Garp.

"If he got back here before you did, he could have driven away," Garp said.

"Go look in the men's room," the policeman said, riding toward a woman with a baby carriage piled high with blankets.

Every men's room made Garp remember every W.C.; at the door to this sour place, Garp passed a young man who was just leaving. He was clean-shaven, his upper lip so smooth that it almost shone; he looked like a college kid. Garp entered the men's room like a dog with his hair standing up on the back of his neck and his hackles curling. He checked for feet under the crapper-stall doors; he would not have been surprised to see a pair of hands—or a bear. He looked for backs turned toward him at the long urinal—or for anyone at the dirty brown sinks, peering into the pitted mirrors. But there was no one in the men's room. Garp sniffed. He had worn a full but trimmed beard for a long time and the smell of shaving cream was not instantly recognizable to him. He just knew he smelled something foreign to this dank place. Then he looked in the nearest sink: he saw the gobs of lather, he saw the whiskers rimming the bowl.

The young, clean-shaven man who looked like a college kid was crossing the parking lot, quickly but calmly, when Garp came out the men's room door. "It's *him!*" Garp hollered. The mounted cop looked at the young molester, puzzled.

"*He* doesn't have a mustache," the policeman said.

"He just shaved it off!" Garp cried; he ran across the lot, straight at the kid, who began to run toward the maze of paths lacing the park. A litter of things flew out from under his jacket as he ran: Garp saw the scissors, a razor, a shaving cream can, and then came the little batches of clothes—the girl's, of course. Her jeans with a ladybug sewn at the hip, a jersey with the beaming face of a frog on the breast. Of course there was no bra; there was no need. It was her panties that got to Garp. They were simply cotton, and a simple blue; stitched at the waistband was a blue flower, sniffed at by a blue bunny.

The mounted policeman simply rode over the kid who was running away. The chest of the horse pounded the kid face forward into the cinder entry path and one rear hoof took a U-shaped bite of flesh out of the kid's calf; he curled, fetal, on the ground, holding his leg. Garp came up then, the girl's blue-bunny panties in his hand; he gave them to the mounted cop. Other people— the woman with the blanketed carriage, two boys on bikes, a thin man carrying a newspaper—approached them. They brought the cop the other things the kid had dropped. The razor, the rest of the girl's clothes.

Nobody spoke. Garp wrote later that at that moment he saw the short history of the young child molester spread out at the horse's hooves: the scissors, the shaving cream can. Of course! The kid would grow a mustache, attack a child, shave the mustache (which would be all most children would remember).

"Have you done this before?" Garp asked the kid.

"You're not supposed to ask him anything," the policeman said.

But the kid grinned stupidly at Garp. "I've never been *caught* before," he told him, cockily. When he smiled, Garp saw that the young man had no upper front teeth; the horse had kicked them out. There was just a bleeding flap of gum. Garp realized that something had probably happened to this kid so that he didn't *feel* very much—not much pain, not much of anything else.

Out of the woods at the end of the bridle path the second policeman came walking his horse—the child in the saddle, covered by the policeman's coat. She clutched Garp's T-shirt in her hands. She did not seem to recognize anybody. The policeman led her right up to where the molester lay on the ground, but she didn't really look at him. The first policeman dismounted; he went to the molester and tilted his bleeding face up toward the child. "Him?" he asked her. She stared at the young man, blankly. The molester gave a short laugh, spat out a mouthful of blood; the child made no response. Then Garp gently touched his finger to the molester's mouth; with the blood on his finger, Garp lightly smeared a mustache on the young man's upper lip. The child began to scream and scream. The horses needed quieting. The child kept screaming until the second policeman took the molester away. Then she stopped screaming and gave Garp back his T-shirt. She kept patting the thick ridge of black hair on the back of the horse's neck as if she had never been on a horse before.

Garp thought it must have hurt her to sit on horseback, but suddenly she asked, "Can I have another ride?" Garp was at least glad to hear that she had a tongue.

It was then that Garp saw the nattily dressed, elderly gentleman whose mustache had been innocent; he was making his meek way out of the park, coming cautiously into the parking lot, looking anxiously about for the madman who'd so savagely snatched his pants down and sniffed him like some dangerous omnivore. When the man saw Garp standing beside the policeman, he seemed relieved—he assumed Garp had been apprehended—and he more boldly walked toward them. Garp contemplated running—to avoid the confusion, the explanation—but just then the policeman said, "I have to get your name. And what it is that you do. Besides run in the park." He laughed.

"I'm a writer." Garp told him. The policeman was apologetic that he hadn't heard of Garp, but at the time Garp hadn't published anything except "The Pension Grillparzer"; there was very little the policeman *could* have read. This seemed to puzzle the policeman.

"An unpublished writer?" he asked. Garp was rather glum about it. "Then what do you do for a living?" the policeman said.

"My wife and my mother support me," Garp admitted.

"Well, I have to ask you what *they* do," the policeman said. "For the record, we like to know how everyone makes a living."

The offended gentleman with the white mustache, who had overheard only the last bits of this interrogation, said. "Just as I would have thought! A vagrant, a despicable bum!"

The policeman stared at him. In his early, unpublished years Garp felt angry whenever he was forced to admit how he had enough to live on; he felt more like inviting confusion at this moment than he felt moved to clear things up.

"I'm glad to see you've caught him, anyway," the

old gentleman said. "This used to be a nice park, but the people who get in here these days—you ought to patrol it more closely," he told the policeman, who guessed that the old man was referring to the child molester. The cop didn't want the business discussed in front of the child, so he rolled his eyes up toward her—she sat rigid in the saddle—and tried to indicate to the old gentleman why he shouldn't continue.

"Oh no, he didn't do it to that *child!*" the man cried, as if he'd just noticed her, mounted beside him, or just noticed she was not dressed under the policeman's coat—her small clothes hugged in her arms. "How vile!" he cried, glaring at Garp. "How disgusting! You'll want my name, of course?" he asked the policeman.

"What for?" the policeman said. Garp had to smile.

"Look at him smirking there!" the old man cried. "Why, as a *witness*, of course—I'd tell my story to any court in the country, if it could condemn such a man as that!"

"But what were you a witness to?" the policeman said.

"Why, he did that . . . thing . . . to *me*, too!" the man said.

The policeman looked at Garp; Garp rolled his eyes. The policeman still clung to the sanity that the old gentleman was referring to the child molester, but he didn't understand why Garp was being treated with such abuse. "Well, sure," the policeman said, to humor the old fool. He took his name and address.

*Months* later Garp was buying a package of three prophylactics when this same old gentleman walked into the drugstore.

"What?! It's *you!*" the old man shouted. "They let you out already, did they? I thought they'd put you away for *years!*"

It took Garp a moment to recognize the person. The druggist assumed that the old codger was a lunatic. The gentleman in his trimmed, white mustache advanced cautiously on Garp.

"What's the law coming to?" he asked. "I suppose

205

you're out on good behavior? No old men or young girls to *sniff* in prison, I suppose! Or some lawyer got you off on some slick technicality? That poor child traumatized for all her years and you're free to roam the parks!"

"You've made a mistake," Garp told him.

"Yes, this is Mr. Garp," the druggist said. He didn't add, "the writer." If he'd considered adding anything, Garp knew, it would have been "the hero," because the druggist had seen the ludicrous newspaper headlines about the crime and capture in the park.

UNSUCCESSFUL WRITER NO FAILURE AS HERO!
CITIZEN CATCHES PARK PERVERT;
SON OF FAMOUS FEMINIST HAS KNACK FOR
HELPING GIRLS . . .

Garp was unable to write for months because of it, but the article impressed all the locals who knew Garp only from the supermarket, the gymnasium, the drugstore. In the meantime, *Procrastination* had been published—but almost no one seemed to know. For weeks, clerks and salespeople would introduce him to other customers: "Here's Mr. Garp, the one who nabbed that molester in the park."

"What molester?"

"That one in city park. The Mustache Kid. He went after little girls."

"Children?"

"Well, Mr. Garp here is the one who got him."

"Well, actually," Garp would say, "it was the policeman on his horse."

"Knocked all his teeth down his throat, too!" they would crow with delight—the druggist and the clerk and the salespeople here and there.

"Well, that was actually the horse," Garp admitted, modestly.

And sometimes someone would ask, "And what is it you *do*, Mister Garp?"

206

The following silence would pain Garp, as he stood thinking that it was probably best to say that he *ran*— for a living. He cruised the parks, a molester-nabber by profession. He hung around phone booths, like that man in the cape—waiting for disasters. Any of this would make more sense to them than what he really did.

"I write," Garp would finally admit. Disappointment—even suspicion—all over their once-admiring faces.

In the drugstore—to make matters worse—Garp *dropped* the package of three prophylactics.

"A-*ha!*" the old man cried. "Look there! What's he up to with those?"

Garp wondered what options there were for what he *could* be up to with those.

"A pervert on the loose," the old man assured the druggist. "Looking for innocence to violate and defile!"

The old geezer's self-righteousness was irritating to the point that Garp had no desire to settle the misunderstanding; in fact, he rather enjoyed the memory of unpantsing the old bird in the park and he was not in the least sorry for the accident.

It was some time later when Garp realized that the old gentleman had no monopoly on self-righteousness. Garp took Duncan to a high school basketball game and was appalled that the ticket-taker was none other than the Mustache Kid—the real molester, the attacker of that helpless child in the city park.

"You're *out*," Garp said, amazed. The pervert smiled openly at Duncan.

"One adult, one kiddy," he said, tearing off tickets.

"How'd you ever get free?" Garp asked; he felt himself tremble with violence.

"Nobody proved nothing," the kid said, haughtily. "That dumb girl wouldn't even *talk*." Garp thought again of Ellen James with her tongue cut off at eleven.

He felt a sudden sympathy for the madness of the old man he had so unpleasantly unpantsed. He felt such a terrible sense of injustice that he could even imagine some very unhappy woman despairing enough to cut off her own tongue. He knew that he wanted to hurt the Mustache Kid, on the spot—in front of Duncan. He wished he could arrange a maiming as a kind of moral lesson.

But there was a crowd wanting basketball tickets; Garp was holding things up.

"Move along, hair pie," the kid said to Garp. In the kid's expression, Garp thought he recognized the leer of the world. On the kid's upper lip was the insipid evidence that he was growing *another* mustache.

It was *years* later when he saw the child, a girl grown up; it was only because she recognized him that he recognized her. He was coming out of a movie theater in another town; she was in the line waiting to come in. Some of her friends were with her.

"Hello, how are you?" Garp asked. He was glad to see she had friends. That meant, to Garp, that she was normal.

"Is it a good movie?" the girl asked.

"You've certainly grown!" Garp said; the girl blushed and Garp realized what a stupid thing he'd said. "Well, I mean it's been a long time—and it was a time well worth forgetting!" he added, heartily. Her friends were moving inside the movie theater and the girl gave a quick look after them to make sure she was really alone with Garp.

"Yes, I'm graduating this month," she said.

"High school?" Garp wondered aloud. Could it have been *that* long ago?

"Oh no, *junior* high," the girl said, laughing nervously.

"Wonderful!" Garp said. And without knowing why, he said, "I'll try to come."

But the girl looked suddenly stricken. "No, please," she said. *"Please* don't come."

"Okay, I won't," Garp agreed quickly.

He saw her several times after this meeting, but she

never recognized him again because he shaved off his beard. "Why don't you grow another beard?" Helen occasionally asked him. "Or at least a mustache." But whenever Garp encountered the molested girl, and escaped unrecognized, he was convinced he should remain clean-shaven.

"I feel uneasy," Garp wrote, "that my life has come in contact with so much rape." Apparently, he was referring to the ten-year-old in the city park, to the eleven-year-old Ellen James and her terrible society—his mother's wounded women with their symbolic, self-inflicted speechlessness. And later he would write a novel, which would make Garp more of "a household product," which would have much to do with rape. Perhaps rape's offensiveness to Garp was that it was an act that disgusted him with himself—with his own very male instincts, which were otherwise so unassailable. He never felt like raping anyone; but rape, Garp thought, made men feel guilt by association.

In Garp's own case, he likened his guilt for the seduction of Little Squab Bones to a rapelike situation. But it was hardly a rape. It was deliberate, though. He even bought the condoms weeks in advance, knowing what he would use them for. Are not the worst crimes premeditated? It would not be a sudden passion for the baby-sitter that Garp would succumb to; he would plan, and be ready when Cindy succumbed to *her* passion for him. It must have given him a twinge, then, to *know* what those rubbers were for when he dropped them in front of the gentleman from the city park and heard the old man accuse him: "Looking for innocence to violate and defile!" How true.

Still, he arranged obstacles in the path of his desire for the girl; he twice hid the prophylactics, but he also remembered where he'd hidden them. And the day of the last evening that Cindy would baby-sit for them, Garp made desperate love to Helen in the late afternoon. When they should have been dressing for dinner, or fixing Duncan's supper, Garp locked the bedroom and wrestled Helen out of her closet.

"Are you crazy?" she asked him. "We're going out."

"Terrible lust," he pleaded. "Don't deny it."

She teased him. *"Please,* sir, I make a point of never doing it before the hors d'oeuvres."

*"You're* the hors d'oeuvres," Garp said.

"Oh, *thanks,"* said Helen.

"Hey, the door's locked," Duncan said, knocking.

"Duncan," Garp called, "go tell us what the weather is doing."

"The weather?" Duncan said, trying to force the bedroom door.

"I think it's snowing in the backyard!" Garp called. "Go see."

Helen stifled her laughter, and her other sounds, against his hard shoulder; he came so quickly he surprised her. Duncan trotted back to the bedroom door, reporting that it was springtime in the backyard, and everywhere else. Garp let him in the bedroom now that he was finished.

But he wasn't finished. He knew it—driving home with Helen from the party, he knew exactly where the rubbers were: under his typewriter, quiet these dull months since the publication of *Procrastination.*

"You look tired," Helen said. "Want me to take Cindy home?"

"No, that's okay," he mumbled. "I'll do it."

Helen smiled at him and nuzzled her cheek against his mouth. "My wild afternoon lover," she whispered. "You can *always* take me out to dinner that way, if you like."

He sat a long time with Little Squab Bones in the car outside her dark apartment. He had chosen the time well—the college was letting out; Cindy was leaving town. She was already upset at having to say goodbye to her favorite writer; he was, at least, the only writer she'd actually met.

"I'm sure you'll have a good year, next year, Cindy,"

he said. "And if you come back to see anyone, please stop and see us. Duncan will miss you." The girl stared into the cold lights of the dashboard, then looked over at Garp, miserably—tears and the whole flushed story on her face.

"I'll miss *you*," she whined.

"No, no," Garp said. *"Don't* miss me."

"I *love* you," she whispered, and let her slim head bump awkwardly against his shoulder.

"No, don't say that," he said, not touching her. Not yet.

The three-pack of condoms nestled patiently in his pocket, coiled like snakes.

In her musty apartment, he used only one of them. To his surprise, all her furniture had been moved out; they jammed her lumpy suitcases together and made an uncomfortable bed. He was careful not to stay a second more than necessary, lest Helen think he'd spent too long a time for even a *literary* good-bye.

A thick swollen stream ran through the women's college grounds and Garp discarded the remaining two prophylactics there, throwing them furtively out the window of his moving car—imagining that an alert campus cop might have seen him and would already be scrambling down the bank to retrieve the evidence: the rubbers plucked out of the current! The discovered weapon that leads back to the crime for which it was used.

But no one saw him, no one found him out. Even Helen, already asleep, would not have found the smell of sex peculiar; after all, only hours before, he had legitimately acquired the odor. Even so, Garp showered, and slipped cleanly into his own safe bed; he curled against Helen, who murmured some affection; instinctively, she thrust one long thigh over his hip. When he failed to respond, she forced her buttocks back against him. Garp's throat ached at her trust, and at his love for her. He felt fondly the slight swell of Helen's pregnancy.

Duncan was a healthy, bright child. Garp's first novel had at least made him what he said he wanted to be. Lust still troubled Garp's young life, but he was fortunate that his wife still lusted for him, and he for her. Now a second child would join their careful, orderly adventure. He felt Helen's belly anxiously—for a kick, a sign of life. Although he'd agreed with Helen that it would be nice to have a girl, Garp *hoped* for another boy.

Why? he thought. He recalled the girl in the park, his image of the tongueless Ellen James, his own mother's difficult decisions. He felt fortunate to be with Helen; she had her own ambitions and he could not manipulate her. But he remembered the Kärntnerstrasse whores, and Cushie Percy (who would die making a baby). And now—her scent still on him, or at least on his mind, although he had washed—the plundered Little Squab Bones. Cindy had cried under him, her back bent against a suitcase. A blue vein had pulsed at her temple, which was the translucent temple of a fair-skinned child. And though Cindy still had her tongue, she'd been *unable* to speak to him when he left her.

Garp didn't want a daughter because of *men*. Because of *bad* men, certainly; but even, he thought, because of men like *me*.

# 8

Second Children, Second
Novels, Second Love

IT was a boy; their second son. Duncan's brother was
called Walt—it was never Walter, and never the
German *Valt;* he was simply a *t* at the end of a wall.
Walt: like a beaver's tail smacking water, like a well-hit
squash ball. He dropped into their lives and they had
two boys.

Garp tried to write a second novel. Helen took her
second job; she became an associate professor of English at the state university, in the town next-door to the
women's college. Garp and his boys had a boys' gym
to play in, and Helen had an occasional bright graduate
student to relieve her of the monotony of younger people; she also had more, and more interesting, colleagues.

One of them was Harrison Fletcher; his field was the
Victorian Novel, but Helen liked him for other reasons—among them: he was also married to a writer.
Her name was Alice; she was also working on her second novel, although she'd never finished her first. When
the Garps met her, they thought she could easily be
mistaken for an Ellen Jamesian—she simply didn't talk.

Harrison, whom Garp called Harry, had never been called Harry before—but he liked Garp and he appeared to enjoy his new name as if it were a present Garp had given him. Helen would continue to call him Harrison, but to Garp he was Harry Fletcher. He was Garp's first friend, though Garp and Harrison both sensed that Harrison preferred Helen's company.

Neither Helen nor Garp knew what to make of Quiet Alice, as they called her. "She must be writing one hell of a book," Garp often said. "It's taken all her words away."

The Fletchers had one child, a daughter whose age put her awkwardly between Duncan and Walt; it was implied that they wanted another. But the book, Alice's second novel, came first; when it was over, they would have a second child, they said.

The couples had dinner together occasionally, but the Fletchers were strictly cookout people—which is to say, neither of them cooked—and Garp was in a period where he baked his own bread, he had a stockpot always simmering on the stove. Mostly, Helen and Harrison discussed books, teaching, and their colleagues; they ate lunch together at the university union, they conversed—at length—in the evening, on the phone. And Garp and Harry went to the football games, the basketball games, and the wrestling meets; three times a week they played squash, which was Harry's game—his only sport—but Garp could play even with him simply because Garp was a better athlete, in better shape from all his running. For the pleasure of these games, Garp suppressed his dislike of balls.

In the second year of this friendship, Harry told Garp that Alice liked to go to movies. "I *don't*," Harry admitted, "but if you do—and Helen said that you did—why not take Alice?"

Alice Fletcher giggled at movies, especially serious movies; she shook her head in disbelief at almost everything she saw. It took months for Garp to realize that Alice had something of an impediment or a nervous defect in her speech; perhaps it was psychological. At first Garp thought it was the popcorn.

"You have a speech problem, I think, Alice," he said, driving her home one night.

"Yeth," she said, nodding her head. Often it was a simple lisp; sometimes it was completely different. Occasionally, it wasn't there. Excitement seemed to aggravate it.

"How's the book coming?" he asked her.

"Good," she said. At one movie she had blurted out that she'd liked *Procrastination*.

"Do you want me to read any of your work?" Garp asked her.

"Yeth," she said, her small head bobbing. She sat with her short, strong fingers crushing her skirt in her lap, the way Garp had seen her daughter crinkle her clothes—the child would sometimes roll her skirt, like a window shade, right up above her panties (though Alice stopped short of this).

"Was it an accident?" Garp asked her. "Your speech problem. Or were you born with it?"

"Born with," Alice said. The car stopped at the Fletchers' house and Alice tugged Garp's arm. She opened her mouth and pointed inside, as if this would explain everything. Garp saw the rows of small, perfect teeth and a tongue that was fat and fresh-looking like the tongue of a child. He could see nothing peculiar, but it was dark in the car, and he wouldn't have known what was peculiar if he'd seen it. When Alice closed her mouth, he saw she was crying—and also smiling, as if this act of self-exposure had required enormous trust. Garp nodded his head as if he understood everything.

"I see," he mumbled. She wiped her tears with the back of one hand, squeezed his hand with her other.

"Harrithon is having an affair," she said.

Garp knew that Harry wasn't having an affair with Helen, but he didn't know what poor Alice thought.

"Not with Helen," Garp said.

"Na, na," Alice said, shaking her head. "Thumone *elth.*"

"Who?" Garp asked.

"A thtudent!" Alice wailed. "A thtupid little twat!"

It had been a couple of years since Garp had molested Little Squab Bones, but in that time he had indulged himself in one other baby-sitter; to his shame, he had even forgotten her name. He felt, honestly, that baby-sitters were an appetite he was forever through with. Yet he sympathized with Harry—Harry was his friend, and he was an important friend to Helen. He also sympathized with Alice. Alice was alertly lovable; a kind of terminal vulnerability was clearly a part of her, and she wore it as visibly as a too-tight sweater on her compact body.

"I'm sorry," Garp said. "Can I do anything?"

"Tell him to *thtop*." Alice said.

It had never been hard for Garp to stop, but he had never been a teacher—with "thtudents" on his mind, or on his hands. Perhaps what Harry was involved with was something else. The only thing Garp could think of—that would perhaps make Alice feel better—was to confess his own mistakes.

"It happens, Alice." he said.

"Not to you," Alice said.

"Twice to me," Garp said. She looked at him, shocked.

"Tell the *truth*," she insisted.

"The truth." he said, "is that it happened twice. A baby-sitter, both times."

"Jesuth Chritht," said Alice.

"But they weren't important," Garp said. "I love Helen."

"*Thith* is important," Alice said. "He hurth me. And I can't *white*."

Garp knew about writers who couldn't *white*; this made Garp love Alice, on the spot.

"Fucking Harry is having an affair," Garp told Helen.

"I know," Helen said. "I've told him to stop, but he keeps going back for more. She's not even a very good student."

"What can we do?" Garp asked her.

"Fucking *lust*," Helen said. "Your mother was right. It *is* a man's problem. *You* talk to him."

"Alice told me about your baby-sitters," Harry told Garp. "It's not the same. This is a special girl."

"A *student*, Harry," Garp said. "Jesus Christ."

"A *special* student," Harry said. "I'm not like you. I've been honest, I've told Alice from the first. She's just got to accommodate it. I've told her she's free to do this, too."

"She knows *you*," Harry told him. "And she's in love with you."

"What can we do?" Garp asked Helen. "He's trying to set me up with Alice so he'll feel better about what he's doing."

"At least he's been honest with her," Helen told Garp. There was one of those silences wherein a family can identify its separate, breathing parts in the night. Open doors off an upstairs hall: Duncan breathing lazily, an almost-eight-year-old with lots of time to live; Walt breathing those tentative two-year-old breaths, short and excited; Helen, even and cool. Garp held his breath. He knew she knew about the baby-sitters.

"Harry told you?" he asked.

"You might have told me before you told Alice," Helen said. "Who was the second one?"

"I forget her name," Garp admitted.

"I think it's shabby," Helen said. "It's really beneath me; it's beneath *you*. I hope you've outgrown it."

"Yes, I have," Garp said. He meant he had outgrown baby-sitters. But lust itself? Ah, well. Jenny Fields had fingered a problem at the heart of her son's heart.

"We've got to help the Fletchers," Helen said. "We're too fond of them to do nothing about this."

Helen, Garp marveled, moved through their life together as if it were an essay she was structuring—with an introduction, a presentation of basic priorities, then the thesis.

"Harry thinks the student is *special*," Garp pointed out.

"Fucking *men*," Helen said. "You look after Alice. *I'll* show Harrison what's special."

So one night, after Garp had cooked an elegant Paprika Chicken and spätzle, Helen said to Garp, "Harrison and I will do the dishes. You take Alice home."

"Take her home?" Garp said. "Now?"

"Show him your novel," Helen said to Alice. "Show him *everything* you want. I'm going to show your husband what an asshole he is."

"Hey, come on," Harry said. "We're all friends, we all want to *stay* friends, right?"

"You simple son of a bitch," Helen told him. "You fuck a student and call her special—you insult your wife, you insult me. *I'll* show you what's special."

"Go easy, Helen," Garp said.

"Go with Alice," Helen said. "And let Alice drive her own baby-sitter home."

"Hey, come on!" Harrison Fletcher said.

"Shuth up, Harrithon!" Alice said. She grabbed Garp's hand and stood up from the table.

"Fucking *men*," said Helen. Garp, as speechless as an Ellen Jamesian, took Alice home.

"I can take the baby-sitter home, Alice," he said.

"Jutht get back *fatht*," Alice said.

"Very fast, Alice," Garp said.

She made him read the first chapter of her novel aloud to her. "I want to *hear* it," she told him, "and I can't *thay* it mythelf." So Garp said it to her; it read, he was relieved to hear, beautifully. Alice wrote with such fluency and care that Garp could have *sung* her sentences, unselfconsciously, and they would have sounded fine.

"You have a lovely voice, Alice," he told her, and she cried. And they made love, of course, and despite what everyone knows about such things, it *was* special.

"Wasn't it?" asked Alice.

"Yes, it *was*," Garp admitted.

Now, he thought, *here* is trouble.

"What can we do?" Helen asked Garp. She had made Harrison Fletcher forget his "special" student; Harrison now thought that *Helen* was the most special thing in his life.

"You started it," Garp said to her. "If it's going to stop, you've got to stop it, I think."

"That's easy to say," Helen said. "I *like* Harrison; he's my best friend, and I don't want to lose that. I'm just not very interested in sleeping with him."

"*He's* interested," Garp said.

"God, I know," Helen said.

"He thinks you're the best he's had," Garp told her.

"Oh, great," Helen said. "That must be lovely for Alice."

"Alice isn't thinking about it," Garp said. Alice was thinking about *Garp*, Garp knew; and Garp was afraid the whole thing would stop. There were times when Garp thought that Alice was the best he'd ever had.

"And what about you?" Helen asked him. ("Nothing is equal," Garp would write, one day.)

"I'm fine," Garp said. "I like Alice, I like you, I like Harry."

"And Alice?" Helen asked.

"Alice likes me," Garp said.

"Oh boy," Helen said. "So we all like each other, except that I don't care that much for *sleeping* with Harrison."

"So it's over," Garp said, trying to hide the gloom in his voice. Alice had cried to him that it could *never* be over. ("Could it? Could it?" she had cried. "I can't jutht *thtop!*")

"Well, isn't it still better than it *was?*" Helen asked Garp.

"You made your point," Garp said. "You got Harry off his damn student. Now you've just got to let him down easy."

"And what about you and Alice?" Helen asked.

"If it's over for one of us, it's over for all of us," Garp said. "That's only fair."

"I know what's *fair*," Helen said. "I also know what's *human*."

The good-byes that Garp imagined conducting with Alice were violent scenarios, fraught with Alice's incoherent speech and always ending in desperate lovemaking—another failed resolution, wet with sweat and sweet with the lush stickum of sex, oh yeth.

"I think Alice is a little *loony*," Helen said.

"Alice is a pretty good writer," Garp said. "She's the real thing."

"Fucking *writers*," Helen mumbled.

"Harry doesn't appreciate how talented Alice is," Garp heard himself say.

"Oh boy," Helen murmured. "This is the last time I try to save anyone's marriage except my own."

It took six months for Helen to let Harry down easy, and in that time Garp saw as much of Alice as he could, while still trying to forewarn her that their foursome was going to be short-lived. He also tried to forewarn himself, because he dreaded the knowledge that he would have to give Alice up.

"It's not the same, for all four of us," he told Alice. "It will have to stop, and pretty soon."

"Tho what?" Alice said. "It hasn't thtopped yet, has it?"

"Not yet," Garp admitted. He read all her written words aloud to her, and they made love so much he stung in the shower and couldn't stand to wear a jock when he ran.

"We've got to do and *do* it," Alice said, fervently. "Do it while we can."

"You know, this *can't* last," Garp tried to warn Harry, while they were playing squash.

"I know, I know," Harry said, "but it's great *while* it lasts, isn't it?"

"Isn't it?" Alice demanded. Did Garp love Alice? Oh yeth.

"Yes, yes," Garp said, shaking his head. He thought he did.

But Helen, enjoying it the least of them, suffered it the most; when she finally called an end to it, she couldn't help but show her euphoria. The other three couldn't help but show their resentment: that she should appear so uplifted while they were cast into such gloom. Without formal imposition there existed a six-month moratorium on the couples' seeing each other, except by chance. Naturally. Helen and Harry ran into each other at the English Department. Garp encountered Alice in the supermarket. Once she deliberately crashed her shopping cart into his; little Walt was jarred among the produce and the juice cans, and Alice's daughter looked equally alarmed at the collision.

"I felt the need of thum *contact,*" Alice said. And she called the Garps one night, very late, after Garp and Helen had gone to bed. Helen answered the phone.

"Is Harrithon there?" she asked Helen.

"No, Alice," Helen said. "Is something wrong?"

"He's not *here,*" Alice said. "I haven't theen Harrithon all night!"

"Let me come over and sit with you," Helen suggested. "Garp can go look for Harrison."

"Can't *Garp* come over and thit with me?" Alice asked. *"You* look for Harrithon."

"No, *I'll* come over and sit with you," Helen said. "I think that's better. Garp can go look for Harrison."

"I want Garp," Alice said.

"I'm sorry that you can't have him," Helen said.

"I'm thorry, Helen," Alice said. She cried into the phone and said a stream of things that Helen couldn't understand. Helen gave the phone to Garp.

Garp talked to Alice, and listened to her, for about an hour. Nobody looked for "Harrithon." Helen felt she had done a good job of holding herself together for the six months she'd allowed it all to continue; she expected them all to at least control themselves adequately, now that it was over.

"If Harrison is out screwing students, I'm *really* going to cross him off," Helen said. "That *asshole!* And if Alice calls herself a writer, why isn't she writing? If she's got so much to *thay,* why waste saying it on the phone?"

Time, Garp knew, would ease everything. Time would also prove him wrong about Alice's writing. She may have had a pretty voice but she couldn't complete anything; she never finished her second novel, not in all the years that the Garps would know the Fletchers— or in all the years after. She could say everything beautifully, but—as Garp remarked to Helen, when he was finally exasperated with Alice—she couldn't get to the end of anything. She couldn't *thtop.*

Harry, too, would not play his cards wisely or well. The university would deny him tenure—a bitter loss for Helen, because she truly loved having Harrison for a friend. But the student Harry had thrown over for Helen had not been let down so easy; she bitched about her seduction to the English Department—although, of course, it was her jilting that really made her bitch. This raised eyebrows among Harry's colleagues. And, of course, *Helen's* support of Harrison Fletcher's case for tenure was quietly not taken seriously—*her* relationship with Harry having also been made clear by the jilted student.

Even Garp's mother, Jenny Fields—with all she stood up for, for women—agreed with Garp that Helen's own tenure at the university, so easily granted her when she was younger than poor Harry, had been a token gesture on the part of the English Department. Someone had probably told them that they needed a woman on the department at the associate professor level, and Helen had come along. Although Helen did not doubt her own qualifications, she knew it hadn't been her quality that had gotten her tenure.

But Helen had not slept with any students; not yet. Harrison Fletcher had, unforgivably, allowed his sex life to be more special to him than his job. He got another job, anyway. And perhaps what remained of the friendship between the Garps and the Fletchers was actually saved by the Fletchers' having to move away. This way, the couples saw each other about twice a year; distance diffused what might have been hard feelings. Alice could speak her flawless prose to Garp— in letters. The temptation to touch each other, even to bash their shopping carts together, was removed from them, and they all settled into being the kind of friends many old friends become: that is, they were friends when they heard from each other—or when, occasionally, they got together. And when they were not in touch, they did not think of one another.

Garp threw away his second novel and began a *second* second novel. Unlike Alice, Garp was a real writer—not because he wrote more beautifully than she wrote but because he knew what every artist should know: as Garp put it, "You only grow by coming to the end of something and by beginning something else." Even if these so-called endings and beginnings are illusions. Garp did not write faster than anyone else, or *more;* he simply always worked with the *idea* of completion in mind.

His second book was swollen, he knew, with the energy he had left over from Alice.

It was a book full of wounding dialogue and sex that left the partners smarting; sex in the book also left the partners guilty, and usually wanting more sex. This paradox was cited by several reviewers who called the phenomenon, alternately, "brilliant" and "dumb." One reviewer called the novel "bitterly truthful," but he hastened to point out that the bitterness doomed the novel to the status of "only a minor classic." If more of the bitterness had been "refined away," the reviewer theorized, "a purer truth would have emerged."

More nonsense was compiled concerning the novel's "thesis." One reviewer struggled with the idea that the novel seemed to be saying that *only* sexual relationships could profoundly reveal people to themselves; yet it was during sexual relationships that people appeared to lose what profundity they had. Garp said he never had a thesis and he grumpily told an interviewer that he had written "a serious comedy about marriage, but a sexual farce." Later he wrote that "human sexuality makes farcical our most serious intentions."

But no matter what Garp said—or the reviewers, either—the book was not a success. Titled *Second Wind of the Cuckold,* the novel confused nearly everyone; even its reviews were confusing. It undersold *Procrastination* by a few thousand copies, and even though John Wolf assured Garp that this was what often happened to second novels, Garp—for the first time in his life—felt he had failed.

John Wolf, who was a good editor, protected Garp from one particular review until he feared Garp would see the review by accident; then Wolf reluctantly sent the clipping, from a West Coast newspaper, with the attached note that he'd heard the reviewer suffered a hormone imbalance. The review remarked, curtly, that it was sordid and pathetic that T. S. Garp, "the talentless son of the famous feminist, Jenny Fields, has written a sexist novel that wallows in sex—and not even instructively." And so forth.

Growing up with Jenny Fields had not made Garp the sort of person who was easily influenced by other people's opinions of him, but even Helen did not like *Second Wind of the Cuckold.* And even Alice Fletcher, in all her loving letters, never once mentioned the book's existence.

*Second Wind of the Cuckold* was about two married couples who have an affair.

224

"Oh boy," Helen said, when she first learned what the book was about.

"It's not about *us*," Garp said. "It's *not* about any of that. It just *uses* that."

"And you're always telling me," Helen said, "that autobiographical fiction is the *worst* kind."

"This *isn't* autobiographical," Garp said. "You'll see."

She didn't. Though the novel was not about Helen and Garp and Harry and Alice, it *was* about four people whose finally unequal and sexually striving relationship is a bust.

Each person in the foursome is physically handicapped. One of the men is blind. The other man has a stutter of such monstrous proportions that his dialogue is infuriatingly difficult to read. Jenny blasted Garp for taking a cheap shot at poor departed Mr. Tinch, but writers, Garp sadly knew, were just observers—good and ruthless imitators of human behavior. Garp had meant no offense to Tinch; he was just using one of Tinch's habits.

"I don't know how you could have done such a thing to Alice," Helen despaired.

Helen meant the handicaps, especially the women's handicaps. One has muscle spasms in her right arm— her hand is always lashing out, striking wineglasses, flowerpots, children's faces, once nearly emasculating her husband (accidentally) with a pruning hook. Only her lover, the other woman's husband, is able to soothe this terrible, uncontrollable spasm—so that the woman is, for the first time in her life, the possessor of a flawless body, entirely intentional in its movement, truly ruled and contained by herself alone.

The other woman suffers unpredictable, unstoppable flatulence. The farter is married to the stutterer, the blind man is married to the dangerous right arm.

Nobody in the foursome, to Garp's credit, is a writer. ("We should be grateful for small favors?" Helen asked.) One of the couples is childless, and wants to be. The other couple is trying to have a child; this woman conceives, but her elation is tempered by everyone's anxiety concerning the identity of the natural father. Which one was it? The couples watch for telltale habits in the newborn child. Will it stutter, fart, lash out, or be blind? (Garp saw this as his ultimate comment—on his mother's behalf—on the subject of *genes*.)

It is to some degree an optimistic novel, if only because the friendship between the couples finally convinces them to break off their liaison. The childless couple later separates, disillusioned with each other—but not necessarily as a result of the experiment. The couple with the child succeeds as a couple; the child develops without a detectable flaw. The last scene in the novel is the chance meeting of the two women; they pass on an escalator in a department store at Christmastime, the farter going up, the woman with the dangerous right arm going down. Both are laden with packages. At the moment they pass each other, the woman stricken with uncontrollable flatulence releases a keen, treble fart—the spastic stiff-arms an old man on the escalator in front of her, bowling him down the moving staircase, toppling a sea of people. But it's Christmas. The escalators are jam-packed and noisy; no one is hurt and everything, in season, is forgivable. The two women, moving apart on their mechanical conveyors, seem to serenely acknowledge each other's burdens; they grimly smile at each other.

"It's a comedy!" Garp cried out, over and over again. "No one got it. It's supposed to be very *funny*. What a film it would make!"

But no one even bought the paperback rights.

As could be seen by the fate of the man who could only walk on his hands, Garp had a thing about escalators.

Helen said that no one in the English Department ever spoke to her about *Second Wind of the Cuckold;* in the case of *Procrastination,* many of her well-meaning colleagues had at least attempted a discussion. Helen said that the book was an invasion of her privacy and she hoped the whole thing had been a kick that Garp would soon be off.

"Jesus, do they think it's *you?*" Garp asked her. "What the hell's the matter with your dumb colleagues, anyway? Do *you* fart in the halls over there? Does your shoulder drop out of socket in department meetings? Was poor Harry a stutterer in the classroom?" Garp yelled. "Am I blind?"

"*Yes,* you're blind," Helen said. "You have your own terms for what's fiction, and what's fact, but do you think other people know your system? It's all your *experience*—somehow, however much you make up, even if it's only an *imagined* experience. People *think* it's me, they *think* it's you. And sometimes I think so, too."

The blind man in the novel is a geologist. "Do they see me playing with rocks?" Garp hollered.

The flatulent woman does volunteer work in a hospital; she is a nurse's aide. "Do you see my mother complaining?" Garp asked. "Does she write me and point out that she never once farted in a hospital—only at home, and always under control?"

But Jenny Fields *did* complain to her son about *Second Wind of the Cuckold.* She told him he had chosen a disappointingly narrow subject of little universal importance. "She means sex," Garp said. "This is classic. A lecture on what's universal by a woman who's never once felt sexual desire. And the Pope, who takes vows of chastity, decides the issue of contraception for millions. The world *is* crazy!" Garp cried.

Jenny's newest colleague was a six-foot-four transsexual named Roberta Muldoon. Formerly Robert Muldoon, a standout tight end for the Philadelphia Eagles, Roberta's weight had dropped from 235 to 180 since her successful sex-change operation. The doses of estrogen had cut into her once-massive strength and some of her endurance; Garp guessed also that Robert Muldoon's former and famous "quick hands" weren't so quick anymore, but Roberta Muldoon was a formidable companion to Jenny Fields. Roberta worshiped Garp's mother. It had been Jenny's book, *A Sexual Suspect,* that had given Robert Muldoon the courage to have the sex-change operation—one winter as he lay recovering from knee surgery in a Philadelphia hospital.

Jenny Fields was now supporting Roberta's case with the television networks, who, Roberta claimed, had secretly agreed not to hire her as a sports announcer for the football season. Roberta's *knowledge* of football had not decreased one drop since all the estrogen, Jenny was arguing; waves of support from the college campuses around the country had made the six-foot-four Roberta Muldoon a figure of striking controversy. Roberta was intelligent and articulate, and of course she knew her football; she'd have been an improvement on the usual morons who commented on the game.

Garp liked her. They talked about football together and they played squash. Roberta always took the first few games from Garp—she was more powerful than he was, and a better athlete—but her stamina was not quite up to his, and being the much bigger person in the court, she wore down. Roberta would also tire of her case against the television networks, but she would develop great endurance for other, more important things.

"You're certainly an improvement on the Ellen James Society, Roberta," Garp would tell her. He enjoyed his mother's visits better when Jenny came with Roberta. And Roberta tossed a football for hours with Duncan. Roberta promised to take Duncan to an Eagles game, but Garp was anxious about that. Roberta was a target figure; she had made some people very angry. Garp imagined various assaults and bomb threats on Roberta—and Duncan disappearing in the vast and roaring football stadium in Philadelphia, where he would be defiled by a child molester.

It was the fanaticism of some of Roberta Muldoon's hate mail that gave Garp such an imagination, but when Jenny showed him some hate mail of her own, Garp was anxious about that, too. It was an aspect of the publicity of his mother's life that he had not considered: some people truly hated her. They wrote Jenny that they wished she had cancer. They wrote Roberta Muldoon that they hoped his or her parents were no longer living. One couple wrote Jenny Fields that they would like to artificially inseminate her, with elephant sperm—and blow her up from the inside  That note was signed: "A Legitimate Couple."

One man wrote Roberta Muldoon that he had been an Eagles fan all his life, and even his grandparents had been born in Philadelphia, but now he was going to be a Giants or a Redskins fan, and drive to New York or Washington—"or even Baltimore, if necessary"—because Roberta had perverted the entire Eagles offensive line with his pansy ways.

One woman wrote Roberta Muldoon that she hoped Roberta would get gang-banged by the Oakland Raiders. The woman thought that the Raiders were the most disgusting team in football; maybe they would show Roberta how much fun it was to be a woman.

A high school tight end from Wyoming wrote Roberta Muldoon that she had made him ashamed to be a tight end anymore and he was changing his position—to linebacker. So far, there were no transsexual linebackers.

A college offensive guard from Michigan wrote Roberta that if she were ever in Ypsilanti, he would like to fuck her with her shoulder pads on.

"This is nothing," Roberta told Garp. "Your mother gets much worse. Lots more people hate *her*."

"Mom," Garp said. "Why don't you drop out for a while? Take a vacation. Write another book." He never thought he'd ever hear himself suggesting such a thing to her, but he suddenly saw Jenny as a potential victim, exposing herself, through other victims, to all the hatred and cruelty and violence in the world.

When asked by the press, always, Jenny would say that she *was* writing another book; only Garp and Helen and John Wolf knew this was a lie. Jenny Fields wasn't writing a word.

"I've done all I want to do about *me,* already," Jenny told her son. "Now I'm interested in other people. You just worry about *you,*" she said, gravely, as if in her opinion her son's introversion—his imaginative life—was the more dangerous way to live.

Helen actually feared this, too—especially when Garp wasn't writing; and for more than a year after *Second Wind of the Cuckold,* Garp didn't write. Then he wrote for a year and threw it all away. He wrote letters to his editor: they were the most difficult letters John Wolf ever had to read, much less answer. Some of them were ten and twelve pages long; most of them accused John Wolf of not "pushing" *Second Wind of the Cuckold* as hard as he could have.

"Everyone *hated* it," John Wolf reminded Garp. "How could we have pushed it?"

"You never supported the book," Garp wrote.

Helen wrote John Wolf that he must be patient with Garp, but John Wolf knew writers pretty well and he was as patient and as kind as he could be.

Eventually, Garp wrote letters to other people. He answered some of his mother's hate mail—those rare cases with return addresses. He wrote long letters trying to talk these people out of their hatred. "You're becoming a social worker," Helen told him. But Garp even offered to answer some of Roberta Muldoon's hate mail; Roberta had a new lover, however, and her hate mail was rolling off her like water.

"Jesus," Garp complained to her, "first a sex reassignment and now you're in love. For a tight end with tits, you're really boring, Roberta." They were very good friends and they played squash fervently whenever Roberta and Jenny came to town, but this was not frequently enough to occupy all of Garp's restless time. He spent hours playing games with Duncan—and waiting for Walt to get old enough to play games, too. He cooked up a storm.

"The third novel's the big one," John Wolf told Helen, because he sensed she was wearying of Garp's restlessness and she was in need of a pep talk. "Give him time, it will come."

"How's *he* know the third novel's the big one?" Garp fumed. "My third novel doesn't even exist. And the way it was published, my second novel might as well not exist. These editors are full of myths and self-fulfilling prophecies! If he knows so much about third novels, why doesn't he write his *own* third novel? Why doesn't he write his *first?*"

But Helen smiled and kissed him and took up going to the movies with him, although she hated movies. She was happy with her job; the kids were happy. Garp was a good father and a good cook and he made love to her more elaborately when he wasn't writing than he did when he was hard at work. Let it come, Helen thought.

Her father, good old Ernie Holm, had shown signs of early heart trouble, but her father was happy at Steering. He and Garp took a trip together, every winter, to see one of those big wrestling matches out in Iowa. Helen was sure that Garp's writing block was a small thing to endure.

"It will come," Alice Fletcher told Garp, on the phone. "You can't *forth* it."

"I'm not trying to *force* anything," he assured her. "There's just nothing there." But he thought that desirable Alice, who could never finish anything—not even her love for him—was a poor one to understand what he meant.

Then Garp got some hate mail of his own. He was addressed in a lively letter by someone who took offense at *Second Wind of the Cuckold*. It was not a blind, stuttering, spastic farter—as you might imagine— either. It was just what Garp needed to lift himself out of his slump.

*Dear Shithead,*

[wrote the offended party]

> *I have read your novel. You seem to find other
> people's problems very funny. I have seen your
> picture. With your fat head of hair I suppose you
> can laugh at bald persons. And in your cruel book
> you laugh at people who can't have orgasms, and
> people who aren't blessed with happy marriages,
> and people whose wives and husbands are unfaith-
> ful to each other. You ought to know that persons
> who have these problems do not think everything
> is so* funny. *Look at the world, shithead—it is a
> bed of pain, people suffering and nobody believing
> in God or bringing their children up right. You
> shithead, you don't have any problems so you can
> make fun of poor people who do!*
>
> > Yours sincerely,
> > (Mrs.) I. B. Poole
> > Findlay, Ohio

That letter stung Garp like a slap; rarely had he felt
so importantly misunderstood. Why did people insist
that if you were "comic" you couldn't also be "serious"?
Garp felt most people confused being profound with
being sober, being earnest with being deep. Apparently,
if you *sounded* serious, you were. Presumably, other
animals could not laugh at themselves, and Garp believed that laughter was related to sympathy, which we
were always needing more of. He had been, after all, a
humorless child—and never religious—so perhaps he
now took comedy more seriously than others.

But for Garp to see his vision interpreted as making
*fun* of people was painful to him; and to realize that
his art had made him appear cruel gave Garp a keen
sense of failure. Very carefully, as if he were speaking
to a potential suicide high up in a foreign and unfamiliar hotel, Garp wrote to his reader in Findlay, Ohio.

*Dear Mrs. Poole:*

*The world is a bed of pain, people suffer terribly, few of us believe in God or bring up our children very well; you're right about that. It is also true that people who have problems do not, as a rule, think their problems are "funny."*

*Horace Walpole once said that the world is comic to those who think and tragic to those who feel. I hope you'll agree with me that Horace Walpole somewhat simplifies the world by saying this. Surely both of us think and feel; in regard to what's comic and what's tragic, Mrs. Poole, the world is all mixed up. For this reason I have never understood why "serious" and "funny" are thought to be opposites. It is simply a truthful contradiction to me that people's problems are often funny and that the people are often and nonetheless sad.*

*I am ashamed, however, that you think I am laughing at people, or making fun of them. I take people very seriously. People are all I take seriously, in fact. Therefore, I have nothing but sympathy for how people behave—and nothing but laughter to console them with.*

*Laughter is my religion, Mrs. Poole. In the manner of most religions, I admit that my laughter is pretty desperate. I want to tell you a little story to illustrate what I mean. The story takes place in Bombay, India, where many people starve to death every day; but not all the people in Bombay are starving.*

*Among the nonstarving population of Bombay, India, there was a wedding, and a party was thrown in honor of the bride and groom. Some of the wedding guests brought elephants to the party. They weren't really conscious of showing off, they were just using the elephants for transportation. Although that may strike us as a big-shot way to travel around, I don't think these wedding guests saw themselves that way. Most of them were prob-*

233

*ably not directly responsible for the vast numbers of their fellow Indians who were starving all around them; most of them were just calling "time out" from their own problems, and the problems of the world, to celebrate the wedding of a friend. But if you were a member of the starving Indians, and you hobbled past that wedding party and saw all those elephants parked outside, you probably would have felt some disgruntlement.*

*Furthermore, some of the revelers at the wedding got drunk and began feeding beer to their elephant. They emptied an ice bucket and filled it with beer, and they went tittering out to the parking lot and fed their hot elephant the whole bucket. The elephant liked it. So the revelers gave him several more buckets of beer.*

*Who knows how beer will affect an elephant? These people meant no harm, they were just having fun—and chances are fairly good that the rest of their lives weren't one hundred percent fun. They probably needed this party. But the people were also being stupid and irresponsible.*

*If one of those many starving Indians had dragged himself through the parking lot and seen these drunken wedding guests filling up an elephant with beer, I'll bet he would have felt resentful. But I hope you see I am not making fun of anyone.*

*What happens next is that the drunken revelers are asked to leave the party because their behavior with their elephant is obnoxious to the other wedding guests. No one can blame the other guests for feeling this way; some of them may have actually thought that they were preventing things from getting "out of hand," although people have never been very successful at preventing this.*

*Huffy and brave with beer, the revelers struggled up on their elephant and veered away from the parking lot—a large exhibition of happiness, surely—bumping into a few other elephants and things, because the revelers' elephant plowed from side to side in a lumbering wooze, bleary and bloated with buckets of beer. His trunk lashed back and forth like a badly fastened artificial limb. The great beast was so unsteady that he struck an electric utility pole, shearing it cleanly and bringing down the live wires on his massive head—which killed him, and the wedding guests who were riding him, instantly.*

*Mrs. Poole, please believe me: I don't think that's "funny." But along comes one of those starving Indians. He sees all the wedding guests mourning the death of their friends, and their friends' elephant; much wailing, rending of fine clothes, spilling of good food and drink. The first thing he does is to take the opportunity to slip into the wedding while the guests are distracted and steal a little of the good food and drink for his starving family. The second thing he does is start to laugh himself sick about the manner in which the revelers disposed of themselves and their elephant. Alongside death by starvation, this method of enormous dying must seem funny, or at least quick, to the undernourished Indian. But the wedding guests don't see it that way. It is already a tragedy to them; they are already talking about "this tragic event," and although they could perhaps forgive the presence of a "mangy beggar" at their party—and even have tolerated his stealing their food—they cannot forgive him for laughing at their dead friends and their dead friends' elephant.*

*The wedding guests—outraged at the beggar's behavior (at his laughter, not his thievery and not his rags)—drown him in one of the beer buckets that the late revelers used to water their elephant. They construe this to represent "justice." We see that the story is about the class struggle—and, of course, "serious," after all. But I like to consider*

*it a comedy about a natural disaster: they are just
people rather foolishly attempting to "take charge"
of a situation whose complexity is beyond them—
a situation composed of eternal and trivial parts.
After all, with something as large as an elephant,
it could have been much worse.*

*I hope, Mrs. Poole, that I have made what I
mean clearer to you. In any case, I thank you
for taking the time to write to me, because I appreciate hearing from my audience—even critically.*

> *Yours truly,*
> *"Shithead"*

Garp was an excessive man. He made everything
baroque, he believed in exaggeration; his fiction was
also extremist. Garp never forgot his failure with Mrs.
Poole; she worried him, often, and her reply to his
pompous letter must have upset him further.

*Dear Mr. Garp,*

[Mrs. Poole replied]

> *I never thought you would take the trouble to
> write me a letter. You must be a sick man. I can see
> by your letter that you believe in yourself, and I
> guess that's good. But the things you say are mostly
> garbage and nonsense to me, and I don't want you
> to try to explain anything to me again, because
> it is boring and an insult to my intelligence.*

> *Yours,*
> *Irene Poole*

Garp was, like his beliefs, self-contradictory. He was
very generous with other people, but he was horribly
impatient. He set his own standards for how much of
his time and patience everyone deserved. He could be
painstakingly sweet, until he decided he'd been sweet

enough. Then he turned and came roaring back the other way.

*Dear Irene:*

[Garp wrote to Mrs. Poole]

*You should either stop trying to read books, or you should try a lot harder.*

*Dear Shithead,*

[wrote Irene Poole]

*My husband says that if you write to me again, he'll beat your brains to a pulp.*

> *Very sincerely,*
> *Mrs. Fitz Poole*

*Dear Fitzy & Irene:*

[Garp shot right back]

*Fuck you.*

Thus was his sense of humor lost, and his sympathy taken from the world.

In "The Pension Grillparzer" Garp had somehow struck the chord of comedy (on the one hand) and compassion (on the other). The story did not belittle the *people* in the story—either with forced cuteness or with any other exaggeration rationalized as necessary for making a point. Neither did the story sentimentalize the people, or otherwise cheapen their sadness.

But the balance of this power in storytelling felt lost to Garp now. His first novel, *Procrastination*—in his opinion—suffered from the pretentious weight of all that fascist history he had taken no real part in. His second novel suffered his failure at imagining *enough*—

that is, he felt he had not imagined far enough beyond his own fairly ordinary experience. *Second Wind of the Cuckold* came off rather coldly to him; it seemed just another "real" but rather common experience.

In fact, it seemed to Garp now that he was too full of his own lucky life (with Helen and their children). He felt he was in danger of limiting his ability as a writer in a fairly usual way: writing, essentially, about himself. Yet when he looked very far outside himself, Garp saw there only the invitation to pretention. His imagination was failing him—"his sense a dim rushlight." When anyone asked him how his writing was coming, he managed only a short, cruel imitation of poor Alice Fletcher.

"I've *thtopped*," Garp said.

# 9

❊❊❊❊❊❊❊

# The Eternal Husband

IN the Yellow Pages of Garp's phone directory, Marriage was listed near Lumber. After Lumber came Machine Shops, Mail Order Houses, Manholes, Maple Sugar, and Marine Equipment; then came Marriage and Family Counselors. Garp was looking for Lumber when he discovered Marriage; he had some innocent questions to ask about two-by-fours when Marriage caught his eye and raised more interesting and disturbing questions. Garp had never realized, for example, that there were more marriage counselors than lumberyards. But this surely depends on where you live, he thought. In the country, wouldn't people have more to do with lumber?

Garp had been married nearly eleven years; in that time he had found little use for lumber, still less for counsel. It was not for personal problems that Garp took an interest in the long list of names in the Yellow Pages; it was because Garp spent a lot of time trying to imagine what it would be like to have a job.

There was the Christian Counseling Center and the Community Pastoral Counseling Service; Garp imagined hearty ministers with their dry, fleshy hands constantly

239

rubbing together. They spoke round, moist sentences, like soap bubbles, saying things like, "We have no illusions that the Church can be of very much assistance to individual problems, such as your own. Individuals must seek individual solutions, they must retain their individuality; however, it *is* our experience that many people have *identified* their own special individuality *in* the church."

There sat the baffled couple who had hoped to discuss the simultaneous orgasm—myth or reality?

Garp noticed that members of the clergy went in for counseling; there was a Lutheran Social Service, there was a Reverend Dwayne Kuntz (who was "certified") and a Louise Nagle who was an "All Souls Minister" associated with something called the United States Bureau of Marriage & Family Counselors (who had "certified" her). Garp took a pencil and drew little zeroes beside the names of the marriage counselors with religious affiliations. They would all offer fairly optimistic counsel, Garp believed.

He was less sure of the point of view of the counselors with more "scientific" training; he was less sure of the training, too. One was a "certified clinical psychologist," another simply followed his name with "M.A., Clinical"; Garp knew that these things could mean anything, and that they could also mean nothing. A graduate student in sociology, a former business major. One said "B.S."— perhaps in Botany. One was a Ph.D.—in marriage? One was a "Doctor"—but a medical doctor or a Doctor of Philosophy? At marriage counseling, who would be better? One specialized in "group therapy"; someone, perhaps less ambitious, promised only "psychological evaluation."

Garp selected two favorites. The first was Dr. O. Rothrock—"self-esteem workshop; bank cards accepted."

The second was M. Neff—"by appointment only." There was just a phone number after M. Neff's name. No qualifications, or supreme arrogance? Perhaps both.

If *I* needed anybody, Garp thought, I would try M. Neff first. Dr. O. Rothrock with his bank cards and his self-esteem workshop was clearly a charlatan. But M. Neff was serious; M. Neff had a vision, Garp could tell.

Garp wandered a bit past Marriage in the Yellow Pages. He came to Masonry, Maternity Apparel, and Mat Refinishing (only one listing, an out-of-town, Steering phone number: Garp's father-in-law, Ernie Holm, refinished wrestling mats as a slightly profitable hobby. Garp hadn't been thinking about his old coach; he passed over Mat Refinishing to Mattresses without recognizing Ernie's name). Then came Mausoleums and Meat Cutting Equipment—"See Saws." That was enough. The world was too complicated. Garp wandered back to Marriage.

Then Duncan came home from school. Garp's older son was now ten years old; he was a tall boy with Helen Garp's bony, delicate face and her oval yellow-brown eyes. Helen had skin of a light-oak color and Duncan had her wonderful skin, too. From Garp he had gotten his nervousness, his stubbornness, his moods of black self-pity.

"Dad?" he said. "Can I spend the night at Ralph's? It's very important."

"What?" Garp said. "No. When?"

"Have you been reading the phone book again?" Duncan asked his father. Whenever Garp read a phone book, Duncan knew, it was like trying to wake him up from a nap. He read the phone book often, for names. Garp got the names of his characters out of the phone book; when his writing was stuck, he read the phone book for more names; he revised the names of his characters over and over again. When Garp traveled, the first thing he looked for in the motel room was the phone book; he usually stole it.

"Dad?" Duncan said; he assumed his father was in his phone book trance, living the lives of his fictional people. Garp had actually forgotten that he had nonfictional business with the phone book today; he had forgotten about the lumber and was thinking only about the audacity of M. Neff and what it would be like to *be* a marriage counselor. "Dad!" Duncan said. "If I don't call Ralph back before supper, his mother won't let me come over."

"Ralph?" said Garp. "Ralph isn't here." Duncan tipped his fine jaw up and rolled his eyes; it was a gesture Helen had, too, and Duncan had her same lovely throat.

"Ralph is at *his* house," Duncan said, "and I am at *my* house and I would like to go spend the night at Ralph's house—with Ralph."

"Not on a school night," Garp said.

"It's Friday," Duncan said. "Jesus."

"Don't swear, Duncan," Garp said. "When your mother comes home from work, you can ask her." He was stalling, he knew; Garp was suspicious of Ralph— worse, he was afraid for Duncan to spend the night at Ralph's house, although Duncan had done it before. Ralph was an older boy whom Garp distrusted; also, Garp didn't like Ralph's mother—she went out in the evening and left the boys alone (Duncan had admitted that). Helen had once referred to Ralph's mother as "slatternly," a word that had always intrigued Garp (and a look, in women, that had its appeal to him). Ralph's father didn't live at home, so the "slatternly" look of Ralph's mother was enhanced by her status as a woman alone.

"I *can't* wait for Mom to get home," Duncan said. "Ralph's mother says she has to know before supper, or I can't come over." Supper was Garp's responsibility and the idea of it distracted him; he wondered what time it was. Duncan seemed to come home from school at no special time.

"Why not ask Ralph to spend the night here?" Garp said. A familiar ploy. Ralph usually spent the night with Duncan, thus sparing Garp his anxiety about the carelessness of *Mrs.* Ralph (he could never remember Ralph's last name).

"Ralph *always* spends the night here," Duncan said. "I want to stay *there*." And do *what*? Garp wondered. Drink, smoke dope, torture the pets, spy on the sloppy lovemaking of Mrs. Ralph? But Garp knew that Duncan was ten years old and very sane—very careful. The two boys probably enjoyed being alone in a house where Garp wasn't smiling over them, asking them if there was anything they wanted.

"Why not call Mrs. Ralph and ask her if you can wait until your mother comes home before you say whether you'll come or not?" Garp asked.

"Jesus, '*Mrs.* Ralph'!" Duncan groaned. "Mom is just going to say. 'It's all right with *me*. Ask your father.' That's what she always says."

Smart kid, Garp thought. He was trapped. Short of blurting out that he was terrified Mrs. Ralph would kill them all by burning them up in the night when her cigarette, with which she slept, set fire to her hair. Garp had nothing more he *could* say. "Okay, go ahead," he said, sulkily. He didn't even know if Ralph's mother smoked. He simply disliked her, on sight, and he suspected Ralph—for no better reason than that the child was older than Duncan and therefore, Garp imagined, capable of corrupting Duncan in terrible ways.

Garp suspected most people to whom his wife and children were drawn; he had an urgent need to protect the few people he loved from what he imagined "everyone else" was like. Poor Mrs. Ralph was not the only victim perhaps slandered by his paranoid assumptions. I should get out more, Garp thought. If I had a job, he thought—a thought he had every day, and rethought every day, since he wasn't writing.

There was almost no job in the world that appealed to Garp, and certainly nothing he was qualified for; he was qualified, he knew, for very little. He could write; *when* he was writing, he believed he wrote very well. But one reason he thought about getting a job was that he felt he needed to know more about other people; he wanted to get over his distrust of them. A job would at least force him to come into contact—and if he weren't forced to be with other people, Garp would stay home.

It was for his writing, in the beginning, that he had never taken the idea of a job seriously. Now it was for his writing that he was thinking he needed a job. I am running out of people I can imagine, he thought, but perhaps it was really that there had never been many people he *liked;* and he hadn't written anything he liked in too many years.

"I'm going now!" Duncan called to him, and Garp stopped dreaming. The boy was wearing a bright orange rucksack on his back; a yellow sleeping bag was rolled and tied under the pack. Garp had chosen them both, for visibility.

"I'll give you a ride," Garp said, but Duncan rolled his eyes again.

"Mom has the car, Dad," he said, "and she's still at work."

Of course; Garp grinned foolishly. Then he saw that Duncan was going to take his bicycle and he called out the door to him. "Why don't you *walk,* Duncan?"

"Why?" Duncan said, exasperated.

So your spine won't be severed when a car driven by a crazed teen-ager, or a drunken man suffering a heart attack, swipes you off the street, Garp thought—and your wonderful, warm chest is cracked against the curbstone, your special skull split open when you land on the sidewalk, and some asshole wraps you in an old rug as if you were somebody's pet discovered in the gutter. Then the dolts from the suburbs come out and guess who owns it ("That green and white house on the corner of Elm and Dodge, I think"). Then someone drives you home, rings the bell and says to me, "Uh, sorry"; and pointing to the spillage in the bloody back seat, asks, "Is it yours?" But all Garp said was, "Oh, go ahead, Duncan, *take* the bike. Just be careful!"

He watched Duncan cross the street, pedal up the next block, look before he turned *(Good boy; note the careful hand signal—but perhaps this is only for my benefit)*. It was a safe suburb of a small, safe city; comfortable green plots, one-family houses—mostly university families, with an occasional big house broken into apartments for graduate students. Ralph's mother, for example, appeared certain to be a graduate student forever, though she had a whole house to herself—and although she was older than Garp. Her former husband taught one of the sciences and presumably paid her tuition. Garp remembered that Helen had been told the man was living with a student.

Mrs. Ralph is probably a perfectly good person, Garp thought; she has a child, and she no doubt loves him. She is no doubt serious about wanting to do something with her life. If she were just more *careful!* Garp thought. You must be careful; people didn't realize. It's so easy to blow everything, he thought.

"Hello!" someone said, or he *thought* someone said. He looked around, but whoever had spoken to him was gone—or was never there. He realized he was barefoot (his feet were cold; it was an early spring day), standing on the sidewalk in front of his house, a phone book in his hand. He would have liked to go on imagining M. Neff and the business of marriage counseling, but he knew it was late—he had to prepare the evening meal and he hadn't even been shopping. A block away he could hear the hum of the engines that powered the big freezers in the supermarket (that was why they had moved into this neighborhood—so that Garp could walk to the store and shop while Helen took the car to work. Also, they were nearer to a park for him to run in). There were fans on the back of the supermarket and Garp could hear them sucking the still air out of the aisles and blowing faint food smells over the block. Garp liked it. He had a cook's heart.

He spent his day writing (or trying to write), running, and cooking. He got up early and fixed breakfast for himself and the children; nobody was home for lunch and Garp never ate that meal; he fixed dinner for his family every night. It was a ritual he loved, but the ambition of his cooking was controlled by how good a day he'd had writing, and how good a run he'd had. If the writing went poorly, he took it out on himself with a long, hard run; or, sometimes, a bad day with his writing would exhaust him so much that he could barely run a mile; then he tried to save the day with a splendid meal.

Helen could never tell what sort of day Garp had experienced by what he cooked for them; something special might mean a celebration, or it might mean that the food was the *only* thing that had gone well, that the cooking was the only labor keeping Garp from despair. "If you are careful," Garp wrote, "if you use good ingredients, and you don't take any shortcuts, then you can usually cook something very good. Sometimes it is the only worthwhile product you can salvage from a day: what you make to eat. With writing, I find, you can have all the right ingredients, give plenty of time and care, and still get nothing. Also true of love. Cooking, therefore, can keep a person who tries hard sane."

He went into the house and looked for a pair of shoes. About the only shoes he owned were running shoes—many pairs. They were in different phases of being broken in. Garp and his children wore clean but rumpled clothes; Helen was a smart dresser, and although Garp did her laundry, he refused to iron anything. Helen did her own ironing, and an occasional shirt for Garp; ironing was the only task of conventional housewifery that Garp rejected. The cooking, the kids, the basic laundry, the cleaning up—he did them. The cooking, expertly; the kids, a little tensely but conscientiously; the cleaning up, a little compulsively. He swore at errant clothes, dishes, and toys, but he left nothing lie; he was a maniac for picking things up. Some mornings, before he sat down to write, he raced over the house with a vacuum cleaner, or he cleaned the oven. The house never looked untidy, was never dirty, but there was always a certain haste to the neatness of it. Garp threw a lot of things away and the house was always missing things. For months at a time he would allow most of the light bulbs to burn out, unreplaced, until Helen would realize that they were living in almost total darkness, huddled around the two lamps that worked. Or when he remembered the lights, he forgot the soap and the toothpaste.

Helen brought certain touches to the house, too, but Garp took no responsibilities for these: plants, for example; either Helen remembered them, or they died. When Garp saw that one appeared to be drooping, or was the slightest bit pale, he would whisk it out of the house and into the trash. Days later, Helen might ask, "Where is the red arronzo?"

"That foul thing," Garp would remark. "It had some disease. I saw worms on it. I caught it dropping its little spines all over the floor."

Thus Garp functioned at housekeeping.

In the house Garp found his yellow running shoes and put them on. He put the phone book away in a cabinet where he kept the heavy cooking gear (he stashed phone books all over the house—then would tear the house down to find the one he wanted). He put some olive oil in a cast-iron skillet; he chopped an onion while he waited for the oil to get hot. It was late to be starting supper; he hadn't even gone shopping. A standard tomato sauce, a little pasta, a fresh green salad, a loaf of his good bread. That way he could go to the market after he started the sauce and he'd only need to shop for greens. He hurried the chopping (now some fresh basil) but it was important not to throw anything into the skillet until the oil was just right, very hot but not smoking. There are some things about cooking, like writing, that you don't hurry, Garp knew, and he never hurried them.

When the phone rang, it made him so angry that he threw a handful of onions into the skillet and burned himself with the spattering oil. "Shit!" he cried; he kicked the cabinet beside the stove, snapping the little hinge on the cabinet door; a phone book slid out and he stared at it. He put all the onions and the fresh basil into the oil and lowered the flame. He ran his hand under cold water, and, reaching off-balance, wincing at the pain of the burn, he picked up the phone in his other hand.

(Those fakers, Garp thought. What qualifications *could* there be for marriage counseling? No doubt, he thought, it is one more thing that those simplistic shrinks claim expertise in.)

"You caught me right in the fucking middle of something," he snapped to the phone; he eyed the onions wilting in the hot oil. There was no one who could be calling whom he feared he might offend; this was one of several advantages of being unemployed. His editor, John Wolf, would only remark that Garp's manner of answering the phone simply confirmed his notion of Garp's vulgarity. Helen was used to how he answered the phone; and if the call were for Helen, her friends and colleagues already pictured Garp as rather bearish. If it were Ernie Holm, Garp would experience a momentary twinge; the coach always apologized too much, which embarrassed Garp. If it were his mother, Garp knew, she would holler back at him, "Another lie! You're *never* in the middle of anything. You live on the fringes." (Garp hoped it *wasn't* Jenny.) At the moment, there was no other woman who would have called him. Only if it were the day-care center, reporting an accident to little Walt; only if it were Duncan, calling to say that the zipper on his sleeping bag was broken, or that he'd just broken his leg, would Garp feel guilty for his bullying voice. One's children certainly have a right to catch one in the middle of something—they usually do.

"Right in the middle of *what*, darling?" Helen asked him. "Right in the middle of *whom*? I hope she's nice."

Helen's voice on the phone had a quality of sexual teasing in it; this always surprised Garp—how she sounded—because Helen was not like that, she was not even flirtatious. Though he found her, privately, very

248

arousing, there was nothing of the sexy come-on about her dress or her habits in the outer world. Yet on the telephone she sounded bawdy to him, and always had.

"I've burned myself," he said, dramatically. "The oil is too hot and the onions are scorching. What the fuck is it?"

"My poor man," she said, still teasing him. "You didn't leave any message with Pam." Pam was the English Department secretary; Garp struggled to think what message he was supposed to have left with her. "Are you burned badly?" Helen asked him.

"No." He sulked. *"What* message?"

"The two-by-fours," said Helen. *Lumber,* Garp remembered. He was going to call the lumberyards to price some two-by-fours cut to size; Helen would pick them up on her way home from school. He remembered now that the marriage counseling had distracted him from the lumberyards.

"I forgot," he said. Helen, he knew, would have an alternative plan; she had known this much before she even made the phone call.

"Call them now," Helen said, "and I'll call you back when I get to the day-care center. Then I'll go pick up the two-by-fours with Walt. He likes lumberyards." Walt was now five; Garp's second son was in this day-care or preschool place—whatever it was, its aura of general irresponsibility gave Garp some of his most exciting nightmares.

"Well, all right," Garp said. "I'll start calling now." He was worried about his tomato sauce, and he hated hanging up on a conversation with Helen when he was in a state so clearly preoccupied and dull. "I've found an interesting job," he told her, relishing her silence. But she wasn't silent long.

"You're a writer, darling," Helen told him. "You *have* an interesting job." Sometimes it panicked Garp that Helen seemed to want him to stay at home and "just write"—because that made the domestic situation

249

the most comfortable for her. But it was comfortable for him, too; it was what he thought he wanted.

"The onions need stirring," he said, cutting her off. "And my burn hurts," he added.

"I'll try to call back when you're in the middle of something," Helen said, brightly teasing him, that vampish laughter barely contained in her saucy voice; it both aroused him and made him furious.

He stirred the onions and mashed half a dozen tomatoes into the hot oil; then he added pepper, salt, oregano. He called only the lumberyard whose address was closest to Walt's day-care center; Helen was too meticulous about some things—comparing the prices of everything, though he admired her for it. Wood was wood, Garp reasoned; the best place to have the damn two-by-fours cut to size was the nearest place.

A *marriage* counselor! Garp thought again, dissolving a tablespoon of tomato paste in a cup of warm water and adding this to his sauce. Why are all the serious jobs done by quacks? What could be more serious than marriage counseling? Yet he imagined a marriage counselor was somewhat lower on a scale of trust than a chiropractor. In the way that many doctors scorned chiropractors, would psychiatrists sneer at marriage counselors? There was no one Garp tended to sneer at as much as he sneered at psychiatrists—those dangerous simplifiers, those thieves of a person's complexity. To Garp, psychiatrists were the despicable end of all those who couldn't clean up their own messes.

The psychiatrist approached the mess without proper respect for the mess, Garp thought. The psychiatrist's objective was to clear the head; it was Garp's opinion that this was usually accomplished (*when* it was accomplished) by throwing away all the messy things. That is the simplest way to clean up, Garp knew. The trick is to *use* the mess—to make the messy things work for you. "That's easy for a *writer* to say," Helen had told him. "Artists *can* 'use' a mess; most people can't, and they just don't want messes. I know *I* don't. What a psychiatrist you'd be! What would you do if a poor man who had no use for his mess came to you, and he just wanted his mess to go away? I suppose you'd advise him to *write* about it?" Garp remembered this conversation about psychiatry and it made him glum; he knew he oversimplified the things that made him angry, but he was convinced that psychiatry oversimplified everything.

When the phone rang, he said, "The lumberyard off Springfield Avenue. That's close to you."

"I know where it is," Helen said "Is that the only place you called?"

"Wood is wood," Garp said. "Two-by-fours are two-by-fours. Go to Springfield Avenue and they'll have them ready."

"*What* interesting job have you found?" Helen asked him; he knew she would have been thinking about it.

"Marriage counseling," Garp said; his tomato sauce bubbled—the kitchen filled with its rich fumes. Helen maintained a respectful silence on her end of the phone. Garp knew she would find it difficult to ask, this time, what qualifications he thought he had for such a thing.

"You're a writer," she told him.

"Perfect qualifications for the job," Garp said. "Years spent pondering the morass of human relationships; hours spent divining what it is that people have in common. The failure of love," Garp droned on, "the complexity of compromise, the need for compassion."

"So *write* about it," Helen said. "What more do you want?" She knew perfectly well what was coming next.

"Art doesn't help anyone," Garp said. "People can't really use it: they can't eat it, it won't shelter or clothe them—and if they're sick, it won't make them well." This, Helen knew, was Garp's thesis on the basic uselessness of art; he rejected the idea that art was of any social value whatsoever—that it could be, that it should be. The two things mustn't be confused, he thought: there was art, and there was helping people. Here he was, fumbling at both—his mother's son, after all. But, true to his thesis, he saw art and social responsibility as two distinct acts. The messes came when certain jerks attempted to combine these fields. Garp would be irritated all his life by his belief that literature was a luxury item; he desired for it to be more basic—yet he hated it, when it was.

"I'll go get the two-by-fours now," Helen said.

"And if the peculiarities of my art weren't qualification enough," Garp said, "I have, as you know, been married myself." He paused. "I've had children." He paused again. "I've had a variety of marriage-related experiences—we both have."

"Springfield Avenue?" Helen said. "I'll be home soon."

"I have more than enough experience for the job," he insisted. "I've known financial dependency, I've experienced infidelity."

"Good for you," Helen said. She hung up.

But Garp thought: Maybe marriage counseling is a charlatan field even if a genuine and qualified person is giving the advice. He replaced the phone on the hook. He knew he could advertise himself in the Yellow Pages most successfully—even without lying.

MARRIAGE PHILOSOPHY
& FAMILY ADVICE—
T. S. GARP

author of *Procrastination* and *Second Wind of the Cuckold*

Why add that they were novels? They sounded, Garp realized, like marriage-counsel manuals.

But would he see his poor patients at home or in an office?

Garp took a green pepper and propped it in the center of the gas burner; he turned up the flame and the pepper began to burn. When it was black all over, Garp would let it cool, then scrape off all the charred skin. Inside would be a roasted pepper, very sweet, and he would slice it and let it marinate in oil and vinegar and a little marjoram. That would be his dressing for the salad. But the main reason he liked to make dressing this way was that the roasting pepper made the kitchen smell so good.

He turned the pepper with a pair of tongs. When the pepper was charred, Garp snatched it up with the tongs and flipped it into the sink. The pepper hissed at him. "Talk all you want to," Garp told it. "You don't have much time left."

He was distracted. Usually he liked to stop thinking about other things while he cooked—in fact, he forced himself to. But he was suffering a crisis of confidence about marriage counseling.

"You're suffering a crisis of confidence about *your* *writing*," Helen told him, walking into the kitchen with even more than her usual authority—the freshly cut two-by-fours slung over and under her arm like matching shotguns.

Walt said, "Daddy burned something."

"It was a pepper and Daddy *meant* to," Garp said.

"Every time you can't write you do something stupid," Helen said. "Though I'll confess this is a better idea for a diversion than your last diversion."

Garp had expected her to be ready, but he was surprised that she was *so* ready. What Helen called his last "diversion" from his stalled writing had been a baby-sitter.

Garp drove a wooden spoon deep into his tomato sauce. He flinched as some fool took the corner by the house with a roaring downshift and a squeal of tires that cut through Garp with the sound of a struck cat. He looked instinctively for Walt, who was right there—safe in the kitchen.

Helen said, "Where's Duncan?" She moved to the door but Garp cut in front of her.

"Duncan went to Ralph's," he said; he was not worried, *this* time, that the speeding car meant Duncan had been hit, but it was Garp's habit to chase down speeding cars. He had properly bullied every fast driver in the neighborhood. The streets around Garp's house were cut in squares, bordered every block by stop signs; Garp could usually catch up to a car, on foot, provided that the car obeyed the stop signs.

He raced down the street after the sound of the car. Sometimes, if the car was going really fast, Garp would need three or four stop signs to catch up to it. Once he sprinted five blocks and was so out of breath when he caught up to the offending car that the driver was sure there'd been a murder in the neighborhood and Garp was either trying to report it or had done it himself.

Most drivers were impressed with Garp, and even if they swore about him later, they were polite and apologetic to his face, assuring him they would not speed in the neighborhood again. It was clear to them that Garp was in good physical shape. Most of them were high school kids who were easily embarrassed—caught hot-rodding around with their girl friends, or leaving little smoking-rubber stains in front of their girl friends' houses. Garp was not such a fool as to imagine that he changed their ways; all he hoped to do was make them speed somewhere else.

The present offender turned out to be a woman (Garp saw her earrings glinting, and the bracelets on her arm, as he ran up to her from behind). She was just ready to pull away from a stop sign when Garp rapped the wooden spoon on her window, startling her. The spoon, dribbling tomato sauce, looked at a glance as if it had been dipped in blood.

Garp waited for her to roll down her window, and was already phrasing his opening remarks ("I'm sorry I startled you, but I wanted to ask you a personal favor . . .") when he recognized that the woman was Ralph's mother—the notorious Mrs. Ralph. Duncan and Ralph were not with her; she was alone, and it was obvious that she had been crying.

"Yes, what is it?" she said. Garp couldn't tell if she recognized him as Duncan's father, or not.

"I'm sorry I startled you," Garp began. He stopped. What else could he say to her? Smeary-faced, fresh from a fight with her ex-husband or a lover, the poor woman looked to be suffering her approaching middle age like the flu; her body looked rumpled with misery, her eyes were red and vague. "I'm sorry," Garp mumbled; he was sorry for her whole life. How could he tell her that all he wanted was for her to slow down?

"What is it?" she asked him.

"I'm Duncan's father," Garp said.

"I *know* you are," she said. "I'm Ralph's mother."

"I know," he said; he smiled.

"Duncan's father meets Ralph's mother," she said, caustically. Then she burst into tears. Her face flopped forward and struck the horn. She sat up straight, suddenly hitting Garp's hand, resting on her rolled-down window; his fingers opened and he dropped the long-handled spoon into her lap. They both stared at it; the tomato sauce produced a stain on her wrinkled beige dress.

"You must think I'm a rotten mother," Mrs. Ralph said. Garp, ever-conscious of safety, reached across her knees and turned off the ignition. He decided to leave the spoon in her lap. It was Garp's curse to be unable to conceal his feelings from people, even from strangers; if he thought contemptuous thoughts about you, somehow you *knew*.

"I don't know anything about what kind of mother you are," Garp told her. "I think Ralph's a nice boy."

"He can be a real shit," she said.

"Perhaps you'd rather Duncan not stay with you tonight?" Garp asked—Garp *hoped*. To Garp, she didn't appear to know that Duncan *was* spending the night with Ralph. She looked at the spoon in her lap. "It's tomato sauce," Garp said. To his surprise, Mrs. Ralph picked up the spoon and licked it.

"You're a cook?" she asked.

"Yes, I like to cook," Garp said.

"It's very good," Mrs. Ralph told him, handing him his spoon. "I should have gotten one like you—some muscular little prick who likes to cook."

Garp counted in his head to five; then he said, "I'd be glad to go pick up the boys. They could spend the night with us, if you'd like to be alone."

"Alone!" she cried. "I'm *usually* alone. I *like* having the boys with me. And *they* like it, too," she said. "Do you know why?" Mrs. Ralph looked at him wickedly.

"Why?" Garp said.

"They like to watch me take a bath," she said. "There's a crack in the door. Isn't it sweet that Ralph likes to show off his old mother to his friends?"

"Yes," Garp said.

"You don't approve, do you, Mr. Garp?" she asked him. "You don't approve of me at all."

"I'm sorry you're so unhappy," Garp said. On the seat beside her in her messy car was a paperback of Dostoevsky's *The Eternal Husband;* Garp remembered that Mrs. Ralph was going to school. "What are you majoring in?" he asked her, stupidly. He recalled she was a never-ending graduate student; her problem was probably a thesis that wouldn't come.

Mrs. Ralph shook her head. "You really keep your nose clean, don't you?" she asked Garp. "How long have you been married?"

"Almost eleven years," Garp said. Mrs. Ralph looked more or less indifferent; Mrs. Ralph had been married for twelve.

"Your kid's safe with me," she said, as if she were suddenly irritated with him, and as if she were reading his mind with utter accuracy. "Don't worry, I'm quite harmless—with children," she added. "And I don't smoke in bed."

"I'm sure it's good for the boys to watch you take a bath," Garp told her, then felt immediately embarrassed for saying it, though it was one of the few things he'd told her that he meant.

256

"I don't know," she said. "It didn't seem to do much good for my husband, and *he* watched me for years." She looked up at Garp, whose mouth hurt from all his forced smiles. Just touch her cheek, or pat her hand, he thought; at least *say* something. But Garp was clumsy at being kind, and he didn't flirt.

"Well, husbands *are* funny," he mumbled. Garp the marriage counselor, full of advice. "I don't think many of them know what they want."

Mrs. Ralph laughed bitterly. "My husband found a nineteen-year-old *cunt*," she said. "He seems to want *her*."

"I'm sorry," Garp told her. The marriage counselor is the I'm-sorry man, like a doctor with bad luck—the one who gets to diagnose all the terminal cases.

"You're a writer," Mrs. Ralph said to him, accusingly; she waved her copy of *The Eternal Husband* at him. "What do you think of this?"

"It's a wonderful story," Garp said. It was fortunately a book he remembered—neatly complicated, full of perverse and human contradiction.

"I think it's a *sick* story," Mrs. Ralph told him. "I'd like to know what's so special about Dostoevsky."

"Well," Garp said, "his characters are so complex, psychologically and emotionally; and the situations are so ambiguous."

"His women are *less* than objects," Mrs. Ralph said, "they don't even have any *shape*. They're just ideas that men talk about and play with." She threw the book out the window at Garp; it hit his chest and fell by the curb. She clenched her fists in her lap, staring at the stain on her dress, which marked her crotch with a tomato-sauce bull's-eye. "Boy, that's me all over," she said, staring at the spot.

"I'm sorry," Garp said again. "It may leave a permanent stain."

"Everything leaves a stain!" Mrs. Ralph cried out. A laughter so witless escaped her that it frightened Garp.

He didn't say anything and she said to him, "I'll bet you think that all I need is a good *lay*."

To be fair, Garp rarely thought this of people, but when Mrs. Ralph mentioned it, he *did* think that, in *her* case, this oversimple solution might apply.

"And I'll bet you think I'd let *you* do it," she said, glaring at him. Garp, in fact, *did* think so.

"No, I don't think you would," he said.

"Yes, you think I would *love* to," Mrs. Ralph said.

Garp hung his head. "No," he said.

"Well, in *your* case," she said, "I just *might*." He looked at her and she gave him an evil grin. "It might make you a little less smug," she told him.

"You don't know me well enough to talk to me like this," Garp said.

"I know that you're *smug*," Mrs. Ralph said. "You think you're so superior." True, Garp knew; he *was* superior. He would make a lousy marriage counselor, he now knew.

"Please drive carefully," Garp said; he pushed himself away from her car. "If there's anything I can do, please call."

"Like if I need a good *lover*?" Mrs. Ralph asked him, nastily.

"No, not that," Garp said.

"Why did you stop me?" she asked him.

"Because I thought you were driving too fast," he said.

"I think you're a pompous fart," she told him.

"I think you're an irresponsible slob," Garp told her. She cried out as if she were stabbed.

"Look, I'm sorry," he said (again), "but I'll just come pick up Duncan."

"No, *please*," she said. "I can look after him, I really *want* to. He'll be all right—I'll look after him like he was my own!" This didn't truly comfort Garp. "I'm not *that* much of a slob—with *kids*," she added; she managed an alarmingly attractive smile.

"I'm sorry," Garp said—his litany.

"So am I," said Mrs. Ralph. As if the matter were resolved between them, she started her car and drove past the stop sign and through the intersection without looking. She drove away—slowly, but more or less in the middle of the road—and Garp waved his wooden spoon after her.

Then he picked up *The Eternal Husband* and walked home.

# 10

◆━◆━◆━◆━◆

# The Dog in the Alley,
# the Child in the Sky

WE'VE got to get Duncan out of that mad
woman's house," Garp told Helen.

"Well, you do it," Helen said. "You're the
one who's worried."

"You should have seen how she drove," Garp said.

"Well," said Helen, "presumably Duncan isn't going
to be riding around with her."

"She may take the boys out for a pizza," Garp said.
"I'm sure she can't cook."

Helen was looking at *The Eternal Husband*. She said,
"It's a strange book for a woman to give to another
woman's husband."

"She didn't give it to me, Helen. She *threw* it at me."

"It's a wonderful story," Helen said.

"She said it was just *sick*," Garp said, despairingly.
"She thought it was unfair to women."

Helen looked puzzled. "I wouldn't say that was even
an issue," she said.

"Of course it isn't!" Garp yelled. "This woman is an
idiot! My mother would love her."

"Oh, poor Jenny," Helen said. "Don't start on her."

"Finish your pasta, Walt," Garp said.

"Up your wazoo," Walt said.

"Nice talk," Garp said. "Walt, I don't *have* a wazoo."

"Yes, you do," Walt said.

"He doesn't know what it means," Helen said. "I'm not sure what it means, either."

"Five years old," Garp said. "It's not nice to say that to people," Garp told Walt.

"He heard it from Duncan, I'm sure," Helen said.

"Well, Duncan gets it from Ralph," Garp said, "who no doubt gets it from his goddamn mother!"

"Watch your own language," Helen said. "Walt could as easily have gotten his 'wazoo' from you."

"Not from me, he couldn't have," Garp declared. *"I'm* not sure what it means, either. I never use that word."

"You use plenty just like it," Helen said.

"Walt, eat your pasta," Garp said.

"Calm down," Helen said.

Garp eyed Walt's uneaten pasta as if it were a personal insult. "Why do I bother?" he said. "The child eats nothing."

They finished their meal in silence. Helen knew Garp was thinking up a story to tell Walt after dinner. She knew Garp did this to calm himself whenever he was worried about the children—as if the act of imagining a good story for children was a way to keep children safe forever.

With the children Garp was instinctively generous, loyal as an animal, the most affectionate of fathers; he understood Duncan and Walt deeply and separately. Yet, Helen felt sure, he saw nothing of how his anxiety for the children made the children anxious—tense, even immature. On the one hand he treated them as grownups, but on the other hand he was so protective of them that he was not allowing them to grow up. He did not accept that Duncan was ten, that Walt was five; sometimes the children seemed fixed, as three-year-olds, in his mind.

Helen listened to the story Garp made up for Walt with her usual interest and concern. Like many of the stories Garp told the children, it began as a story for the children and ended up as a story Garp seemed to have made up for Garp. You would think that the children of a writer would have more stories read to them than other children, but Garp preferred that his children listen only to *his* stories.

"There was a dog," Garp said.

"What kind of dog?" said Walt.

"A big German shepherd dog," said Garp.

"What was his name?" Walt asked.

"He didn't have a name," Garp said. "He lived in a city in Germany, after the war."

"What war?" said Walt.

"World War II," Garp said.

"Oh sure," Walt said.

"The dog had been in the war," Garp said. "He had been a guard dog, so he was very fierce and very smart."

"Very *mean*," said Walt.

"No," Garp said, "he wasn't mean and he wasn't nice, or sometimes he was both. He was whatever his master trained him to be, because he was trained to do whatever his master told him to do."

"How did he know who his master was?" Walt asked.

"I don't know," Garp said. "After the war, he got a new master. This master owned a café in the city; you could get coffee and tea and drinks there, and read the newspapers. At night the master would leave one light on, inside the café, so that you could look in the windows and see all the wiped-off tables with the chairs upside-down on the table tops. The floor was swept clean, and the big dog paced back and forth across the floor every night. He was like a lion in his cage at the zoo, he was never still. Sometimes people would see him in there and they'd knock on the window to get his attention. The dog would just stare at them—he wouldn't bark, or even growl. He'd just stop pacing and stare, until whoever it was went away. You had the feeling that if you stayed too long, the dog might jump through the window at you. But he never did; he never did anything, in fact, because no one ever broke into that café at night. It was enough just having the dog there; the dog didn't have to *do* anything."

"The dog *looked* very mean," said Walt.

"Now you've got the picture," Garp told him. "Every night was the same for that dog, and every day he was tied up in an alley beside the café. He was tied to a long chain, which was tied to the front axle of an old army truck, which had been backed into the alley and left there—for good. This truck didn't have any wheels.

"And you know what cinder blocks are," Garp said. "The truck was set on blocks so it wouldn't roll an inch on its axles. There was just enough room for the dog to crawl under the truck and lie down out of the rain and the sun. The chain was just long enough so that the dog could walk to the end of the alley and watch the people on the sidewalk and the cars in the street. If you were coming along the sidewalk, you could sometimes see the dog's nose poking out of the alley; that was as far as the chain would reach, and no farther.

"You could hold out your hand to the dog and he would sniff you, but he didn't like to be touched and he never licked your hand the way some dogs do. If you tried to pat him, he would duck his head and slink back into the alley. The way he stared at you made you think it would not be a very good idea to follow him into the alley, or to try very hard to pat him."

"He would bite you," Walt said.

"Well, you couldn't be sure," Garp said. "He never bit anyone, actually, or I never heard about it if he did."

"You were there?" Walt said.

"Yes," Garp said; he knew that the storyteller was always "there."

"Walt!" called Helen; it irritated Garp that she eavesdropped on the stories he told the children. "That is what they mean by 'a dog's life,' " Helen called.

But neither Walt nor his father appreciated her interruption. Walt said, "Go on with the story. What happened to the dog?"

The responsibilities loomed for Garp, every time. What is the instinct in people that makes them expect something to *happen?* If you begin a story about a person or a dog, something must be going to happen to them. "Go on!" Walt cried impatiently. Garp, caught up in his art, frequently forgot his audience.

He went on. "If too many people held out their hands for the dog to sniff, the dog would walk back down the alley and crawl under the truck. You could often see the tip of his black nose poking out from under the truck. He was either under the truck or at the sidewalk end of the alley; he never stopped in between. He had his habits and nothing disturbed them."

"Nothing?" Walt asked, disappointed—or else worried that nothing was going to happen.

"Well, *almost* nothing," Garp admitted, and Walt perked up. *"Something* bothered him; there was just one thing. It alone could make the dog furious. It was the only thing that could even make the dog bark. It really drove him crazy."

"Oh sure, a *cat!"* cried Walt.

"A *terrible* cat," said Garp in a voice that made Helen stop rereading *The Eternal Husband* and hold her breath. Poor Walt, she thought.

"Why was the cat terrible?" Walt asked.

"Because he teased the dog," Garp said. Helen was relieved that this was, apparently, all that was "terrible."

"Teasing isn't nice," Walt said, with knowledge; Walt was Duncan's victim in the area of teasing. *Duncan* should be hearing this story, Helen thought. A lesson about teasing is clearly wasted on Walt.

"Teasing is *terrible,"* Garp said. "But this cat *was* terrible. He was an old cat, off the streets, dirty and mean."

"What was his name?" Walt asked.

"He didn't have a name," Garp said. "Nobody owned him; he was hungry all the time, so he stole food. Nobody could blame him for that. And he had lots of fights with other cats, and nobody could blame him for that either, I suppose. He had only one eye; the other eye had been missing for so long that the hole had closed and the fur had grown over where the eye had been. He didn't have any ears. He must have had to fight all the time."

"The poor thing!" Helen cried.

"Nobody could blame that cat for the way he was," Garp said, "except that he teased the dog. That was wrong; he didn't have to do that. He was hungry, so he had to be sneaky, and nobody took care of him, so he had to fight. But he didn't *have* to tease the dog."

"Teasing isn't nice," Walt said again. Very definitely Duncan's story, Helen thought.

"Every day," said Garp, "that cat would walk down the sidewalk and stop to wash himself at the end of the alley. The dog would come out from under the truck, running so hard that the chain wriggled behind him like a snake that's just been run over in the road. You ever seen that?"

"Oh sure," Walt said.

"And when the dog got to the end of his chain, the chain would snap the dog's neck back and the dog would be tugged off his feet and land on the pavement of the alley, sometimes knocking his wind out or hitting his head. The cat would never move. The cat *knew* how long the chain was and he would sit there washing himself with his one eye staring at the dog. The dog went crazy. He barked and snapped and struggled against his chain until the owner of the café, his master, would have to come out and shoo the cat away. Then the dog would crawl back under the truck.

"Sometimes the cat would come right back, and the dog would lie under the truck for as long as he could stand it, which was not very long. He'd lie under there

266

while the cat licked himself all over out on the sidewalk, and pretty soon you could hear the dog begin to whimper and whine, and the cat would just stare down the alley at him and go on washing himself. And pretty soon the dog would start to howl under the truck, and thrash around there as if he were covered with bees, but the cat would just go on washing himself. And finally the dog would lunge out from under the truck and charge up the alley again, snapping his chain behind him—even though he knew what would happen. He knew that the chain would rip him off his feet and choke him, and throw him on the pavement, and that when he got up the cat would still be sitting there, inches away, washing himself. And he'd bark himself hoarse until his master, or someone else, would shoo the cat away.

"That dog *hated* that cat," Garp said.

"So do *I,*" Walt said.

"And so did I," said Garp. Helen felt herself turn against the story—it had such an obvious conclusion. She said nothing.

"Go on," Walt said. Part of telling a story to a child, Garp knew, is telling (or pretending to tell) a story with an obvious conclusion.

"One day," said Garp, "everybody thought the dog had finally lost his mind. For one whole day he ran out from under the truck and all the way up the alley until the chain jerked him off his feet; then he'd do it again. Even when the cat wasn't there, the dog just kept charging up the alley, throwing his weight against the chain and heaving himself to the pavement. It startled some of the people walking on the sidewalk, especially the people who saw the dog coming at them and didn't know that there *was* a chain.

"And that night the dog was so tired that he didn't pace around the café; he slept on the floor as if he were sick. Anyone could have broken into the café that night; I don't think that dog would have woken up. And the next day he did the same thing, although you could tell his neck was sore because he cried out every time the chain snapped him off his feet. And that night he slept in the café as if he were a dead dog who'd been murdered there on the floor.

"His master called a vet," Garp said, "and the vet gave the dog some shots—I guess to calm him down. For two days the dog lay on the floor of the café at nighttime and under the truck in the daytime, and even when the cat walked by on the sidewalk, or sat washing himself at the end of the alley, that dog wouldn't move. That poor dog," Garp added.

"He was sad," Walt said.

"But do you think he was *smart?*" Garp asked.

Walt was puzzled but he said, "I *think* he was."

"He was," Garp said, "because all the time he'd been running against the chain, he'd been moving the truck he was tied to—just a little. Even though that truck had sat there for years, and it was rusted solid on those cinder blocks and the buildings could fall down around it before that truck would budge—*even so,*" Garp said, "that dog made the truck *move.* Just a little.

"Do you think the dog moved the truck *enough?*" Garp asked Walt.

"I think so," Walt said. Helen thought so, too.

"He needed just a few inches to reach that cat," Garp said. Walt nodded. Helen, confident of the gory outcome, plunged back into *The Eternal Husband.*

"One day," Garp said, slowly, "the cat came and sat down on the sidewalk at the end of the alley and began to lick his paws. He rubbed his wet paws into his old ear holes where his ears had been, and he rubbed his paws over his old grown-together eye hole where his other eye used to be, and he stared down the alley at the dog under the truck. The cat was getting bored now that the dog wouldn't come out anymore. And then the dog came out."

"I think the truck moved enough," Walt said.

"The dog ran up the alley faster than ever before, so that the chain behind him was dancing off the ground, and the cat never moved although *this* time the dog could reach him. Except," said Garp, "the chain didn't *quite* reach." Helen groaned. "The dog got his mouth over the cat's head but the chain choked him so badly that he couldn't close his mouth; the dog gagged and was jerked back—like before—and the cat, realizing that things had changed, sprang away."

"God!" Helen cried.

"Oh no." Walt said.

"Of course, you couldn't fool a cat like that twice," Garp said. "The dog had one chance, and he blew it. That cat would never let him get close enough again."

"What a terrible story!" Helen cried.

Walt, silent, looked as if he agreed.

"But something *else* happened," Garp said. Walt looked up, alert. Helen, exasperated, held her breath again. "The cat was so scared he ran into the street—without looking. No matter what happens," Garp said, "you don't run into the street without looking, do you, Walt?"

"No," Walt said.

"Not even if a dog is going to bite you," Garp said. "Not *ever*. You *never* run into the street without looking."

"Oh sure, I know," Walt said. "What happened to the cat?"

Garp slapped his hands together so sharply that the boy jumped. "He was killed like that!" Garp cried. "Smack! He was dead. Nobody could fix him. He'd have had a better chance if the dog had gotten him."

"A car hit him?" Walt asked.

"A truck," Garp said, "ran right over his head. His brains came out his old ear holes, where his ears used to be."

"Squashed him?" Walt asked.

"Flat," said Garp, and he held up his hand, palm level, in front of Walt's serious little face. Jesus, Helen thought, it was Walt's story after all. *Don't run into the street without looking!*

"The end," said Garp.

"Good night," Walt said.

"Good night," Garp said to him. Helen heard them kiss.

"*Why* didn't the dog have a name?" Walt asked.

"I don't know," Garp said. "Don't run into the street without looking."

When Walt fell asleep, Helen and Garp made love. Helen had a sudden insight regarding Garp's story.

"That dog could never move that truck," she said. "Not an inch."

"Right," Garp said. Helen felt sure he had actually been there.

"So how'd you move it?" she asked him.

"I couldn't move it either," Garp said. "It wouldn't budge. So I cut a link out of the dog's chain, at night when he was patrolling the café, and I matched the link at a hardware store. The next night I *added* some links— about six inches."

"And the cat never ran into the street?" Helen asked.

"No, that was for Walt," Garp admitted.

"Of course," Helen said.

"The chain was plenty long enough," Garp said. "The cat didn't get away."

"The dog killed the cat?" Helen asked.

"He bit him in half," Garp said.

"In a city in Germany?" Helen said.

"No, Austria," Garp said. "It was Vienna. I never lived in Germany."

"But how could the dog have been in the war?" Helen asked. "He'd have been twenty years old by the time you got there."

"The dog wasn't in the war," Garp said. "He was just a dog. His *owner* had been in the war—the man who owned the café. That's why he knew how to train the dog. He trained him to kill anybody who walked in the café when it was dark outside. When it was light outside, anybody could walk in; when it was dark, even the master couldn't get in."

"That's nice!" Helen said. "Suppose there was a fire? There seems to me to be a number of drawbacks to that method."

"It's a war method, apparently," Garp said.

"Well," Helen said, "it makes a better story than the *dog's* being in the war."

"You think so, really?" Garp asked her. It seemed to her that he was alert for the first time during their conversation. "That's interesting," he said, "because I just this minute made it up."

"About the owner's being in the war?" Helen asked.

"Well, more than that," Garp admitted.

"What part of the story did you make up?" Helen asked him.

"All of it," he said.

They were in bed together and Helen lay quietly there, knowing that this was one of his trickier moments.

"Well, *almost* all of it," he added.

Garp never tired of playing this game, though Helen certainly tired of it. He would wait for her to ask: *Which* of it? Which of it is true, which of it is made up? Then he would say to her that it didn't matter; she should just tell him what she didn't *believe*. Then he would change that part. Every part she believed was true; every part she didn't believe needed work. If she believed the whole thing, then the whole thing was true. He was very ruthless as a storyteller, Helen knew. If the truth suited the story, he would reveal it without embarrassment; but if any truth was unsuccessful in a story, he would think nothing of changing it.

"When you're through playing around," she said, "I'd just be curious to know what *really* happened."

"Well, *really*," said Garp, "the dog was a beagle."

"A beagle!"

"Well, actually, a schnauzer. He *was* tied up in the alley all day, but not to an army truck."

"To a Volkswagen?" Helen guessed.

"To a garbage sled," Garp said. "The sled was used to pull the garbage cans out to the sidewalk in the winter, but the schnauzer, of course, was too small and weak to pull it—at any time of the year."

"And the café owner?" Helen asked. "He was *not* in the war?"

*"She,"* Garp said. "She was a widow."

"Her husband had been killed in the war?" Helen guessed.

"She was a *young* widow," Garp said. "Her husband had been killed crossing the street. She was very attached to the dog, which her husband had given her for their first anniversary. But her new landlady would not allow dogs in her apartment, so the widow set the dog loose in the café each night.

"It was a spooky, empty space and the dog was nervous in there; in fact, he crapped all night long. People would stop and peer in the window and laugh at all the messes the dog made. This laughter made the dog more nervous, so he crapped more. In the morning the widow came early—to air out the place and clean up the messes—and she spanked the dog with a newspaper and dragged him cowering out into the alley, where he was tied up to the garbage sled all day."

"And there was no cat?" Helen asked.

"Oh, there were lots of cats," Garp said. "They came into the alley because of the garbage cans for the café. The dog would never touch the garbage, because he was afraid of the widow, and the dog was *terrified* of cats; whenever there was a cat in the alley, raiding the garbage cans, the dog crawled under the garbage sled and hid there until the cat was gone."

"My God," said Helen. "So there was no teasing, either?"

"There is always teasing," Garp said, solemnly. "There was a little girl who would come to the end of the alley and call the dog out to the sidewalk, except that the dog's chain wouldn't reach the sidewalk and the dog would yap! and yap! and yap! at the little girl, who stood on the sidewalk and called, 'Come on, come on,' until someone rolled down a window and yelled at her to leave the poor mutt alone."

"You were there?" Helen said.

*"We* were there," Garp said. "Every day my mother wrote in a room, the only window of which faced that alley. That dog's yapping drove her nuts."

"So *Jenny* moved the garbage sled," Helen said, "and the dog *ate* the little girl, whose parents complained to the police, who had the dog put to sleep. And *you,* of course, were a great comfort to the grieving widow, who was perhaps in her early forties."

"Her late thirties," Garp said. "But that's not how it happened."

*"What* happened?" Helen asked.

"One night, in the café," Garp said, "the dog had a stroke. A number of people claimed to have been responsible for scaring the dog so badly that they caused his stroke. There was a kind of competition in regard to this in the neighborhood. They were always doing things like creeping up to the café and hurling themselves against the windows and doors, shrieking like huge cats—creating a frenzy of bowel movements by the frightened dog."

"The stroke *killed* the dog, I hope," Helen said.

"Not quite," Garp said. "The stroke paralyzed the dog's hindquarters, so that he could only move his front end and wag his head. The widow, however, clung to the life of this wretched dog as she clung to the memory of her late husband, and she had a carpenter, with whom she was sleeping, build a little cart for the dog's rear end. The cart had wheels on it, so the dog just walked on his front legs and towed his dead hindquarters around on the little cart."

"My God," Helen said.

"You wouldn't believe the *noise* of those little wheels," Garp said.

"Probably not," said Helen.

"Mother claimed she couldn't hear it," Garp said, "but the rolling sound was so pathetic, it was worse

273

than the dog's yapping at the stupid little girl. And the dog couldn't turn a corner very well, without skidding. He'd hop along and then turn, and his rear wheels would slide out beside him, faster than he could keep hopping, and he'd go into a roll. When he was on his side, he couldn't get up again. It seemed I was the only one to see him in this predicament—at least, *I* was always the one who went into the alley and tipped him upright again. As soon as he was back on his wheels, he'd try to bite me," Garp said, "but he was easy to outrun."

"So one day," Helen said, "you untied the schnauzer, and he ran into the street without looking. No, excuse me: he *rolled* into the street without looking. And everyone's troubles were over. The widow and the carpenter were married."

"Not so," said Garp.

"I want the truth," Helen said, sleepily. "What happened to the damn schnauzer?"

"I don't know," Garp said. "Mother and I came back to this country, and you know the rest."

Helen, giving in to sleep, knew that only her silence might get Garp to reveal himself. She knew that this story might be as made up as the other versions, or that the other versions might be largely true—even that *this* one might be largely true. Any combination was possible with Garp.

Helen was already asleep when Garp asked her, "Which story do you like better?" But lovemaking made Helen sleepy, and she found the sound of Garp's voice, going on and on, enhancing to her drowsiness; it was her most preferred way to fall asleep: after love, with Garp talking.

This frustrated Garp. At bedtime his engines were almost cold. Lovemaking seemed to rev him up and rouse him to moods of marathon talk, eating, all-night reading, general prowling about. In this period he rarely tried to write, though he would sometimes write messages to himself about what he would write later.

But not this night. He instead pulled back the covers

and watched Helen sleep; then he covered her again. He went to Walt's room and watched him. Duncan was sleeping at Mrs. Ralph's; when Garp shut his eyes he saw a glow on the suburban horizon, which he imagined was the dreaded house of Ralph—in flames.

Garp watched Walt, and this calmed him. Garp relished having such close scrutiny of the child; he lay beside Walt and smelled the boy's fresh breath, remembering when Duncan's breath had turned sour in his sleep in that grownup's way. It had been an unpleasant sensation for Garp, shortly after Duncan turned six, to smell that Duncan's breath was stale and faintly foul in his sleep. It was as if the process of decay, of slowly dying, was already begun in him. This was Garp's first awareness of the mortality of his son. There appeared with this odor the first discolorations and stains on Duncan's perfect teeth. Perhaps it was just that Duncan was Garp's firstborn child, but Garp worried more about Duncan than he worried about Walt—even though a five-year-old seems more prone (than a ten-year-old) to the usual childhood accidents. And what are *they?* Garp wondered. Being hit by cars? Choking to death on peanuts? Being stolen by strangers? Cancer, for example, was a stranger.

There was so much to worry about, when worrying about children, and Garp worried so much about everything; at times, especially in these throes of insomnia, Garp thought himself to be psychologically unfit for parenthood. Then he worried about *that,* too, and felt all the more anxious for his children. What if their most dangerous enemy turned out to be *him?*

He soon fell asleep beside Walt, but Garp was a fearful dreamer; he was not asleep for long. Soon he was moaning; his armpit hurt. He woke up suddenly, Walt's little fist was snagged in his armpit hair. Walt was moaning, too. Garp untangled himself from the whimpering child, who seemed to Garp to be suffering the same dream Garp had suffered—as if Garp's trembling body had communicated Garp's dream to Walt. But Walt was having his own nightmare.

It would not have occurred to Garp that his instructional story of the war dog, the teasing cat, and the inevitable killer truck could have been terrifying to Walt. But in his dream Walt saw the great abandoned army truck, more the size and shape of a tank, guns and inexplicable tools and evil-looking attachments all over it—the windshield was a slit no bigger than a letter slot. It was all black, of course.

The dog who was tied to the truck was the size of a pony, though leaner and much more cruel. He was loping, in slow motion, toward the end of the alley, his weak-looking chain spiraling behind him. The chain hardly looked strong enough to hold back the dog. At the end of the alley, with his legs all buttery and stumbling over himself, hopelessly clumsy and unable to flee, little Walt bumbled in circles, but he couldn't seem to get himself *going*—to get himself away from that terrible dog. When the chain snapped, the great truck lurched forward as if someone had started it, and the dog was on him. Walt grabbed the dog's fur, sweaty and coarse (his father's armpit), but somehow he lost his grip. The dog was at his throat but Walt was running again, into the street, where trucks like the abandoned army truck rolled heavily past, their massive rear wheels in rows stacked together like giant doughnuts on their sides. And because of the mere gun slits (for windshields) the drivers couldn't see, of course; they couldn't see little Walt.

Then his father kissed him and Walt's dream slipped away, for now. He was somewhere safe again; he could smell his father and feel his father's hands, and he heard his father say, "It's just a dream, Walt."

In Garp's dream, he and Duncan had been riding on an airplane. Duncan had to go to the bathroom. Garp pointed down the aisle; there were doors down there, a small kitchen, the pilot's cabin, the lavatory. Duncan wanted to be taken there, to be shown *which* door, but Garp was cross with him.

"You're ten years old, Duncan," Garp said. "You can read. Or ask the stewardess." Duncan crossed his knees and sulked. Garp shoved the child into the aisle. "Grow up, Duncan," he said. "It's one of those doors down there. Go on."

Moodily, the child walked down the aisle toward the doors. A stewardess smiled at him and rumpled his hair as he passed her, but Duncan, typically, would ask nothing. He got to the end of the aisle and glared back at Garp; Garp waved to him, impatiently. Duncan shrugged his shoulders, helplessly. *Which* door?

Exasperated, Garp stood up. *"Try* one!" he shouted down the aisle to Duncan, and people looked at Duncan standing there. Duncan was embarrassed and opened a door immediately—the one nearest him. He gave a quick, surprised, but uncritical look back to his father before he seemed to be drawn through the door he'd opened. The door slammed itself after Duncan. The stewardess screamed. The plane gave a little dip in altitude, then corrected itself. Everyone looked out the windows; some people fainted, some threw up. Garp ran down the aisle, but the pilot and another official-looking person prevented Garp from opening the door.

"It should always be kept locked, you stupid bitch!" the pilot shouted to the sobbing stewardess.

"I thought it *was* locked!" she wailed.

"Where's it go?" Garp cried. *"God,* where's it go?" He saw that nothing was written on any of the doors.

"I'm sorry, sir," the pilot said. "It couldn't be helped." But Garp shoved past him, he bent a plainclothesman against the back of a seat, he smacked the stewardess out of the aisle. When he opened the door, Garp saw that it went outside—into the rushing sky—and before he could cry aloud for Duncan, Garp was sucked through the open door and into the heavens, where he hurtled after his son.

# 11

❧❧❧❧❧❧❧

# Mrs. Ralph

I F Garp could have been granted one vast and naïve
wish, it would have been that he could make the
world *safe*. For children and for grownups. The
world struck Garp as unnecessarily perilous for both.

After Garp and Helen made love, and Helen fell
asleep—after the dreams—Garp got dressed. When he
sat on his bed to tie his track shoes, he sat on Helen's
leg and woke her up. She reached out her hand to
touch him, then felt his running shorts.

"Where are you going?" she asked him.

"To check on Duncan," he said. Helen stretched up
on her elbows, she looked at her watch. It was after
one in the morning and she knew Duncan was at Ralph's
house.

"*How* are you going to check on Duncan?" she asked
Garp.

"I don't know," Garp said.

Like a gunman hunting his victim, like the child
molester the parent dreads, Garp stalks the sleeping
spring suburbs, green and dark; the people snore and
wish and dream, their lawn mowers at rest; it is too

279

cool for their air conditioners to be running. A few windows are open, a few refrigerators are humming. There is the faint, trapped warble from some televisions tuned in to *The Late Show,* and the blue-gray glow from the picture tubes throbs from a few of the houses. To Garp this glow looks like cancer, insidious and numbing, putting the world to sleep. Maybe television *causes* cancer, Garp thinks; but his real irritation is a *writer's* irritation: he knows that wherever the TV glows, there sits someone who isn't *reading.*

Garp moves lightly along the street; he wants to meet no one. His running shoes are loosely laced, his track shorts flap; he hasn't worn a jock because he hasn't planned to run. Though the spring air is cool, he wears no shirt. In the blackened houses an occasional dog *snorfles* as Garp passes by. Fresh from lovemaking, Garp imagines that his scent is as keen as a cut strawberry. He knows the dogs can smell him.

These are well-policed suburbs and for a moment Garp is apprehensive that he might be caught—in violation of some unwritten dress code, at least guilty of carrying no identification. He hurries, convinced he's coming to Duncan's aid, rescuing his son from the randy Mrs. Ralph.

A young woman on an unlighted bicycle almost collides with him, her hair floating behind her, her knees bare and shiny, her breath striking Garp as a startling mixture of a fresh-cut lawn and cigarettes. Garp crouches—she cries out and wobbles her bike around him; she stands up on her pedals and pumps fast away from him, not looking back. Perhaps she thinks he is a would-be exhibitionist—there with his torso and legs bare, ready to drop his shorts. Garp thinks she is coming from some place she shouldn't have been; she is headed for trouble, he imagines. But, thinking of Duncan and Mrs. Ralph, Garp has trouble on his mind at this hour.

When Garp first sees Ralph's house, he believes it should be given the Light of the Block award; every window is glaring, the front door is open, the cancerous television is violently loud. Garp suspects Mrs. Ralph is having a party, but as he creeps closer—her lawn festooned with dog messes and mangled sports equipment—he feels the house is deserted. The television's lethal rays pulsate through the living room, clogged with piles of shoes and clothes; and crammed against the sagging couch are the casual bodies of Duncan and Ralph, half in their sleeping bags, asleep (of course), but looking as if the television has murdered them. In the sickly TV light their faces look drained of blood.

But where is Mrs. Ralph? Out for the evening? Gone to bed with all the lights on and the door open, leaving the boys to be bathed by the television? Garp wonders if she's remembered to shut the oven off. The living room is pockmarked with ashtrays; Garp fears for cigarettes still smoldering. He stays behind the hedges and slinks to the kitchen window, sniffing for gas.

There is a litter of dishes in the sink, a bottle of gin on the kitchen table, the sour smell of slashed limes. The cord to the overhead light, at one time too short, has been substantially lengthened by one sheer leg and hip of a woman's pair of panty hose—severed up the middle, the whereabouts of the other half unclear. The nylon foot, spotted with translucent stains of grease, dangles in the breeze above the gin. There is nothing burning that Garp can smell, unless there's a slow fire under the cat, who lies neatly on top of the stove, artfully spread between burners, its chin resting on the handle of a heavy skillet, its furry belly warmed by the pilot lights. Garp and the cat stare at each other. The cat blinks.

But Garp believes that Mrs. Ralph hasn't the necessary concentration to turn herself into a cat. Her home—her *life*—in utter disarray, the woman appears to have abandoned ship, or perhaps passed out upstairs. Is she in bed? Or in the bathtub, drowned? And where is the beast whose dangerous droppings have made a mine field out of the lawn?

Just then there is a thunderous approach down the back staircase of a heavy, falling body that bashes open the stairway entrance door to the kitchen, startling the cat into flight, skidding the greasy iron skillet to the floor. Mrs. Ralph sits bare-assed and wincing on the linoleum, a kimono-style robe wide open and roughly tugged above her thick waist, a miraculously unspilled drink in her hand. She looks at the drink, surprised, and sips it; her large, down-pointing breasts shine— they slouch across her freckled chest as she leans back on her elbows and burps. The cat, in a corner of the kitchen, yowls at her, complaining.

"Oh, shut up, Titsy," Mrs. Ralph says to the cat. But when she tries to get up, she groans and lies down flat on her back. Her pubic hair is wet and glistens at Garp; her belly, furrowed with stretch marks, looks as white and parboiled as if Mrs. Ralph has been under- water for a long time. "I'll get you out of here if it's the last thing I do," Mrs. Ralph tells the kitchen ceiling, though Garp assumes she's speaking to the cat. Per- haps she's broken an ankle and is too drunk to feel it, Garp thinks; perhaps she's broken her back.

Garp glides alongside the house to the open front door. He calls inside. "Anybody home?" he shouts. The cat bolts between his legs and is gone outside. Garp waits. He hears grunts from the kitchen—the strange sounds of flesh slipping.

"Well, as I live and breathe," says Mrs. Ralph, veer- ing into the doorway, her robe of faded flowers more or less drawn together; somewhere, she's ditched her drink.

"I saw all the lights on and thought there might be trouble," Garp mumbles.

"You're too late," Mrs. Ralph tells him. "Both boys are dead. I should never have let them play with that bomb." She probes Garp's unchanging face for any signs of a sense of humor there, but she finds him rather humorless on this subject. "Okay, you want to see the bodies?" she asks. She pulls him toward her by the elastic waistband of his running shorts. Garp, aware he's not wearing a jock, stumbles quickly after his pants, bumping into Mrs. Ralph, who lets him go with a snap and wanders into the living room. Her odor confuses him—like vanilla spilled in the bottom of a deep, damp paper bag.

Mrs. Ralph seizes Duncan under his arms and with astonishing strength lifts him in his sleeping bag to the mountainous, lumpy couch; Garp helps her lift Ralph, who's heavier. They arrange the boys, foot to foot on the couch, tucking their sleeping bags around them and setting pillows under their heads. Garp turns off the TV and Mrs. Ralph stumbles through the room, killing lights, gathering ashtrays. They are like a married couple, cleaning up after a party. "Night-y night!" Mrs. Ralph whispers to the suddenly dark living room, as Garp trips over a hassock, groping his way toward the kitchen lights. "You can't go yet," Mrs. Ralph hisses to him. "You've got to help me get someone *out* of here." She takes his arm, drops an ashtray; her kimono opens wide. Garp, bending to pick up the ashtray, brushes one of her breasts with his hair. "I've got this lummox up in my bedroom," she tells Garp, "and he won't *go*. I can't make him leave."

"A lummox?" Garp says.

"He's a real oaf," says Mrs. Ralph, "a fucking wingding."

"A wingding?" Garp says.

"Yes, please make him go," she asks Garp. She pulls out the elastic waistband of his shorts again, and this time she takes an unconcealed look. "God, you don't *wear* too much, do you?" she asks him. "Aren't you cold?" She lays her hand flat on his bare stomach. "No, you're not," she says, shrugging.

Garp edges away from her. "Who is he?" Garp asks, fearing he might get involved in evicting Mrs. Ralph's former *husband* from the house.

"Come on, I'll show you," she whispers. She draws him up the back staircase through a narrow channel that passes between the piled laundry and enormous sacks of pet food. No wonder she fell down here, he thinks.

In Mrs. Ralph's bedroom Garp looks immediately at the sprawled black Labrador retriever on Mrs. Ralph's undulating water bed. The dog rolls listlessly on his side and thumps his tail. Mrs. Ralph mates with her dog, Garp thinks, and she can't get him out of her bed. "Come on, boy," Garp says. "Get out of here." The dog thumps his tail harder and pees a little.

"Not *him*," Mrs. Ralph says, giving Garp a terrific shove; he catches his balance on the bed, which sloshes. The great dog licks his face. Mrs. Ralph is pointing to an easy chair at the foot of the bed, but Garp first sees the young man reflected in Mrs. Ralph's dressing-table mirror. Sitting naked in the chair, he is combing out the blond end of his thin ponytail, which he holds over his shoulder and sprays with one of Mrs. Ralph's aerosol cans. His belly and thighs have the same slick buttered look that Garp saw on the flesh and fur of Mrs. Ralph, and his young cock is as lean and arched as the backbone of a whippet.

"Hey, how you doing?" the kid says to Garp.

"Fine, thank you," Garp says.

"Get rid of him," says Mrs. Ralph.

"I've been trying to get her to just *relax,* you know?" the kid asks Garp. "I'm trying to get her to just sort of go *with* it, you know?"

"Don't let him talk to you," Mrs. Ralph says. "He'll bore the shit out of you."

"Everyone's so tense," the kid tells Garp; he turns in the chair, leans back, and puts his feet on the water bed; the dog licks his long toes. Mrs. Ralph kicks his legs off the bed. "You see what I mean?" the kid asks Garp.

"She wants you to leave," Garp says.

"You her husband?" the kid asks.

"That's right," says Mrs. Ralph, "and he'll pull your scrawny little prick off if you don't get out of here."

"You better go," Garp tells him. "I'll help you find your clothes."

The kid shuts his eyes, appears to meditate. "He's really great at that shit," Mrs. Ralph tells Garp. "All this kid's good for is shutting his damn eyes."

"Where are your clothes?" Garp asks the boy. Perhaps he's seventeen or eighteen, Garp thinks. Maybe he's old enough for college, or a war. The boy dreams on and Garp gently shakes him by the shoulder.

"Don't touch me, man," the boy says, eyes still closed. There is something foolishly threatening in his voice that makes Garp draw back and look at Mrs. Ralph. She shrugs.

"That's what he said to me, too," she says. Like her smiles, Garp notices, Mrs. Ralph's shrugs are instinctual and sincere. Garp grabs the boy's ponytail and tugs it across his throat and around to the back of his neck; he snaps the boy's head into the cradle of his arm and holds him tightly there. The kid's eyes open.

"Get your clothes, okay?" Garp tells him.

"Don't touch me," the boy repeats.

"I *am* touching you," Garp says.

"Okay, okay," says the boy. Garp lets him get up. The boy is several inches taller than Garp, but easily ten pounds lighter. He looks for his clothes but Mrs. Ralph has already found the long purple caftan, absurdly heavy with brocade. The boy climbs into it like armor.

"It was nice balling you," he tells Mrs. Ralph, "but you should learn to relax more." Mrs. Ralph laughs so harshly that the dog stops wagging his tail.

"You should go back to day one," she tells the kid, "and learn everything all over again, from the beginning." She stretches out on the water bed beside the Labrador, who lolls his head across her stomach. "Oh, cut it out, Bill!" she tells the dog crossly.

"She's very unrelaxed," the kid informs Garp.

"You don't know shit about *how* to relax anybody," Mrs. Ralph says.

Garp steers the young man out of the room and down

the treacherous back staircase, through the kitchen to the open front door.

"You know, *she* asked me in," the boy explains. "It was *her* idea."

"She asked you to leave, too," Garp says.

"You know, you're as unrelaxed as she is," the boy tells him.

"Did the children know what was up?" Garp asks him. "Were they asleep when you two went upstairs?"

"Don't worry about the kids," the boy says. "Kids are beautiful, man. And they know much more than grownups think they know. Kids are just perfect people until grownups get their hands on them. The kids were just fine. Kids are *always* just fine."

"You *have* kids?" Garp can't help but mutter; until now Garp has felt great patience toward the young man, but Garp isn't patient on the subject of children. He accepts no other authority there. "Good-bye," Garp tells the boy. "And don't come back." He shoves him, but lightly, out the open door.

"Don't push me!" the kid shouts, but Garp ducks under the punch and comes up with his arms locked around the kid's waist; to Garp it feels that the kid weighs seventy-five, maybe eighty pounds, though of course he's heavier than that. He bear-hugs the boy and pins his arms behind his back; then he carries him out to the sidewalk. When the kid stops struggling, Garp puts him down.

"You know where to go?" Garp asks him. "Do you need any directions?" The kid breathes deeply, feels his ribs. "And don't tell your friends where they can come sniffing around after it," Garp says. "Don't even use the phone."

"I don't even know her name, man," the kid whines.

"And don't call me 'man' again," says Garp.

"Okay, man," the kid says. Garp feels a pleasant dryness in his throat, which he recognizes as his readiness to touch someone, but he lets the feeling pass.

"Please walk away from here," Garp says.

A block away, the boy calls, "Good-bye, man!" Garp knows how quickly he could run him down; anticipation of such a comedy appeals to him, but it would be disappointing if the boy weren't scared and Garp feels no pressing need to hurt him. Garp waves good-bye. The boy raises his middle finger and walks away, his silly robe dragging—an early Christian lost in the suburbs.

Look out for the lions, kid, Garp thinks, sending a blessing of protection after the boy. In a few years, he knows, Duncan will be that age; Garp can only hope that he'll find it easier to communicate with Duncan.

Back inside, Mrs. Ralph is crying. Garp hears her talking to the dog. "Oh, Bill," she sobs. "I'm sorry I abuse you, Bill. You're so nice."

"Good-bye!" Garp calls up the stairs. "Your friend's gone, and I'm going too."

"Chickenshit!" yells Mrs. Ralph. "How can you leave me like this?" Her wailing grows louder; soon, Garp thinks, the dog will start to bay.

"What can I do?" Garp calls up the stairs.

"You could at least stay and talk to me!" Mrs. Ralph shouts. "You goody-goody chickenshit wingding!"

What's a wingding? Garp wonders, navigating the stairs.

"You probably think this happens to me all the time," says Mrs. Ralph, in utter rumplement upon the water bed. She sits with her legs crossed, her kimono tight around her, Bill's large head in her lap.

Garp, in fact, *does* think so, but he shakes his head.

"I don't get my rocks off by humiliating myself, you know," Mrs. Ralph says. "For God's sake, sit down." She pulls Garp to the rocking bed. "There's not enough water in the damn thing," Mrs. Ralph explains. "My husband used to fill it all the time, because it leaks."

"I'm sorry," Garp says. The marriage-counsel man.

"I hope you never walk out on *your* wife," Mrs. Ralph tells Garp. She takes his hand and holds it in her lap; the dog licks his fingers. "It's the shittiest thing a man can do," says Mrs. Ralph. "He just told me he'd been

287

faking his interest in me, 'for years'! he said. And *then* he said that almost *any* other woman, young or old, looked better to him than I did. That's not very nice, is it?" Mrs. Ralph asks Garp.

"No, it isn't," Garp agrees.

"Please believe me, I never messed around with anyone until he left me," Mrs. Ralph tells him.

"I believe you," Garp says.

"It's very hard on a woman's confidence," Mrs. Ralph says. "Why shouldn't I try to have some fun?"

"You *should,*" Garp says.

"But I'm so *bad* at it!" Mrs. Ralph confesses, holding her hands to her eyes, rocking on the bed. The dog tries to lick her face but Garp pushes him away; the dog thinks Garp is playing with him and lunges across Mrs. Ralph's lap. Garp whacks the dog's nose—too hard— and the poor beast whines and slinks away. "Don't you hurt Bill!" Mrs. Ralph shouts.

"I was just trying to help you," Garp says.

"You don't help *me* by hurting *Bill,*" Mrs. Ralph says. "Jesus, is *every*one bananas?"

Garp slumps back on the water bed, eyes shut tight; the bed rolls like a small sea, and Garp groans. "I don't know *how* to help you," he confesses. "I'm very sorry about your troubles, but there's really nothing I can do, is there? If you want to tell me anything, go ahead," he says, his eyes still shut tight, "but nobody can help the way you feel."

"That's a cheerful thing to say to someone," Mrs. Ralph says. Bill is breathing in Garp's hair. There is a tentative lick at his ear. Garp wonders: Is it Bill or Mrs. Ralph? Then he feels her hand grab him under his track shorts, and he thinks, coldly: If I didn't really *want* her to do that, why did I lie down on my back?

"Please don't do that," he says. She can certainly feel he's not interested, and she lets him go. She lies down beside him, then rolls away, putting her back to him. The bed sloshes violently as Bill tries to wriggle between them, but Mrs. Ralph elbows him so hard in his thick rib cage that the dog coughs and abandons the bed for the floor.

"Poor Bill. I'm sorry," Mrs. Ralph says, crying softly. Bill's hard tail thumps the floor. Mrs. Ralph, as if to complete her self-humiliation, farts. Her sobbing is steady, like the kind of rain Garp knows can last all day. Garp, the marriage counselor, wonders what could give the woman a little *confidence*.

"Mrs. Ralph?" Garp says—then tries to bite back what he's said.

"What?" she says. "What'd you say?" She struggles up to her elbows and turns her head to glare at him. She heard him, he knows. "Did you say 'Mrs. Ralph'?" she asks him. "Jesus, 'Mrs. Ralph'!" she cries. "You don't even know my *name!*"

Garp sits up on the edge of the bed; he feels like joining Bill on the floor. "I find you very attractive," he mumbles to Mrs. Ralph, but he's facing Bill. "Really I do."

"Prove it," Mrs. Ralph says. "You goddamn liar. Show me."

"I can't show you," Garp says, "but it's not because I don't find you attractive."

"I don't even give you an erection!" Mrs. Ralph shouts. "Here I am half-naked, and when you're beside me—on my goddamn bed—you don't even have a respectable hard-on."

"I was trying to conceal it from you," Garp says.

"You succeeded," Mrs. Ralph says. "What's my name?"

Garp feels he has never been so aware of one of his terrible weaknesses: how he needs to have people like him, how he wants to be appreciated. With every word, he knows, he is deeper in trouble, and deeper into an obvious lie. Now he knows what a wingding is.

"Your husband must be crazy," Garp says. "You look better to *me* than most women."

"Oh, please stop it," says Mrs. Ralph. "You must be sick."

I *must* be, Garp agrees, but he says, "You should have confidence in your sexuality, believe me. And more important, you should develop confidence in yourself in other ways."

"There never were any other ways," Mrs. Ralph admits. "I was never so hot at anything but sex, and now I'm not so hot at sex either."

"But you're going to school," Garp says, groping.

"I'm sure I don't know *why*," Mrs. Ralph says. "Or is that what you mean by developing confidence in other ways?" Garp squints hard, wishes for unconsciousness; when he hears the water bed sound like surf, he senses danger and opens his eyes. Mrs. Ralph has undressed, has spread herself out on the bed naked. The little waves are still lapping under her rough-tough body, which confronts Garp like a sturdy rowboat moored on choppy water. "Show me you've got a hard-on and you can go," she says. "Show me your hard-on and I'll believe you like me."

Garp tries to think of an erection; in order to do this, he shuts his eyes and thinks of someone else.

"You bastard," says Mrs. Ralph, but Garp discovers he is already hard; it was not nearly so difficult as he imagined. Opening his eyes, he's forced to recognize that Mrs. Ralph is not without allure. He pulls down his track shorts and shows himself to her. The gesture itself makes him harder; he finds himself liking her damp, curly hair. But Mrs. Ralph seems neither disappointed nor impressed with the demonstration; she is resigned to being let down. She shrugs. She rolls over and turns her great round rump to Garp.

"Okay, so you can actually get it up," she tells him. "Thank you. You can go home now."

Garp feels like touching her. Sickened with embarrassment, Garp feels he could come by just looking at her. He blunders out the door, down the wretched staircase. Is the woman's self-abuse all over for *this* night? he wonders. Is Duncan safe?

He contemplates extending his vigil until the comforting light of dawn. Stepping on the fallen skillet and clanging it against the stove, he hears not even a sigh from Mrs. Ralph and only a moan from Bill. If the boys were to wake up and need anything, he fears Mrs. Ralph wouldn't hear them.

It's 3:30 A.M. in Mrs. Ralph's finally quiet house when Garp decides to clean the kitchen, to kill the time until dawn. Familiar with a housewife's tasks, Garp fills the sink and starts to wash the dishes.

When the phone rang, Garp knew it was Helen. It suddenly occurred to him—all the terrible things she could have on her mind.

"Hello," Garp said.

"Would you tell me what's going on, please?" Helen asked. Garp knew she had been awake a long time. It was four o'clock in the morning.

"Nothing's going on, Helen," Garp said. "There was a little trouble here, and I didn't want to leave Duncan."

"Where is that woman?" Helen asked.

"In bed," Garp admitted. "She passed out."

"From *what?*" Helen asked.

"She'd been drinking," Garp said. "There was a young man here, with her, and she wanted me to get him to leave."

"So then you were alone with her?" Helen asked.

"Not for long," Garp said. "She fell asleep."

"I don't imagine it would take very long," Helen said, "with her."

Garp let there be silence. He had not experienced Helen's jealousy for a while, but he had no trouble remembering its surprising sharpness.

"Nothing's going on, Helen," Garp said.

"Tell me what you're doing, exactly, at this moment," Helen said.

"I'm washing the dishes," Garp told her. He heard her take a long, controlled breath.

"I wonder why you're still there," Helen said.

"I didn't want to leave Duncan," Garp told her.

291

"I think you should bring Duncan home," Helen said. "Right now."

"Helen," Garp said. "I've been good." It sounded defensive, even to Garp; also, he knew he hadn't been quite good enough. "Nothing has happened," he added, feeling a little more sure of the truth of that.

"I won't ask you why you're washing her filthy dishes," Helen said.

"To pass the time," Garp said.

But in truth he had not examined what he was doing, until now, and it seemed pointless to him—waiting for dawn, as if accidents only happened when it was dark. "I'm waiting for Duncan to wake up," he said, but as soon as he spoke he felt there was no sense to that either.

"Why not just wake him up?" Helen asked.

"I'm good at washing dishes," Garp said, trying to introduce some levity.

"I know all the things you're good at," Helen told him, a little too bitterly to pass as a joke.

"You'll make yourself sick, thinking like this," Garp said. "Helen, really, please stop it. I haven't done anything wrong." But Garp had a puritan's niggling memory of the hard-on Mrs. Ralph had given him.

"I've already made myself sick," Helen said, but her voice softened. "Please come home now," she told him.

"And leave Duncan?"

"For Christ's sake, wake him up!" she said. "Or *carry* him."

"I'll be right home," Garp told her. "Please don't worry, don't think what you're thinking. I'll tell you everything that happened. You'll probably love this story." But he knew he would have trouble telling her *all* this story, and that he would have to think very carefully about the parts to leave out.

"I feel better," Helen said. "I'll see you, soon. Please don't wash another dish." Then she hung up and Garp reviewed the kitchen. He thought that his half hour of work hadn't made enough of a difference for Mrs. Ralph to notice that any effort to approach the debris had even been begun.

Garp sought Duncan's clothes among the many, forbidding clots of clothing flung about the living room. He knew Duncan's clothes but he couldn't spot them anywhere; then he remembered that Duncan, like a hamster, stored things in the bottom of his sleeping bag and crawled into the nest with them. Duncan weighed about eighty pounds, plus the bag, plus his junk, but Garp believed he could carry the child home; Duncan could retrieve his bicycle another day. At least, Garp decided, he would not wake Duncan up inside Ralph's house. There might be a scene; Duncan would be fussy about leaving. Mrs. Ralph might even wake up.

Then Garp thought of Mrs. Ralph. Furious at himself, he knew he wanted one last look; his sudden, recurring erection reminded him that he wanted to see her thick, crude body again. He moved quickly to the back staircase. He could have found her fetid room with his nose.

He looked straight at her crotch, her strangely twisted navel, her rather small nipples (for such big breasts). He should have looked first at her eyes; then he might have realized she was wide-awake and staring back at him.

"Dishes all done?" asked Mrs. Ralph. "Come to say good-bye?"

"I wanted to see if you were all right," he told her.

"Bullshit," she said. "You wanted another look."

"Yes," he confessed; he looked away. "I'm sorry."

"Don't be," she said. "It's made my day." Garp tried to smile.

"You're too 'sorry' all the time," Mrs. Ralph said. "What a *sorry* man you are. Except to your wife," Mrs. Ralph said. "You never once said you were sorry to *her*."

There was a phone beside the water bed. Garp felt he had never so badly misread a person's condition as he had misread Mrs. Ralph's. She was suddenly no drunker than Bill; or she had become miraculously undrunk, or she was enjoying that half hour of clarity between stupor and hangover—a half hour Garp had read about, but had always believed was a myth. Another illusion.

"I'm taking Duncan home," Garp told her. She nodded.

"If I were you," she said, "I'd take him home, too."

Garp fought back another "I'm sorry," suppressing it after a short but serious struggle.

"Do me one favor?" said Mrs. Ralph. Garp looked at her; she didn't mind. "Don't tell your wife *everything* about me, okay? Don't make me out to be such a pig. Maybe you could draw a picture of me with a little sympathy."

"I have pretty good sympathy," Garp mumbled.

"You have a pretty good *rod* on, too," said Mrs. Ralph, staring at Garp's elevated track shorts. "You better not bring *that* home." Garp said nothing. Garp the puritan felt he deserved to take a few punches. "Your wife really looks after you, doesn't she?" said Mrs. Ralph. "I guess you haven't *always* been a good boy. You know what my husband would have called you?" she asked. "My husband would have called you 'pussy-whipped.'"

"Your husband must have been some asshole," Garp said. It felt good to get a punch in, even a weak punch, but Garp felt foolish that he had mistaken this woman for a slob.

Mrs. Ralph got off the bed and stood in front of Garp. Her tits touched his chest. Garp was anxious that his hard-on might poke her. "You'll be back," Mrs. Ralph said. "Want to bet on it?" Garp left her without a word.

He wasn't farther than two blocks from Mrs. Ralph's house—Duncan crammed down in the sleeping bag, wriggling over Garp's shoulder—when the squad car pulled to the curb and its police-blue light flickered over him where he stood *caught*. A furtive, half-naked kidnapper sneaking away with his bright bundle of stolen goods and stolen looks—and a stolen child.

"What you got there, fella?" a policeman asked him.

There were two of them in the squad car, and a third person who was hard to see in the back seat.

"My son," Garp said. Both policemen got out of the car.

"Where are you going with him?" one of the cops asked Garp. "Is he all right?" He shined a flashlight in Duncan's face. Duncan was still trying to sleep; he squinted away from the light.

"He was spending the night at a friend's house," Garp said. "But it didn't work out. I'm carrying him home." The policeman shined his light over Garp—in his running costume. Shorts, shoes with racing stripes, no shirt.

"You got identification?" the policeman asked. Garp set Duncan and the sleeping bag, gently, on someone's lawn.

"Of course not," Garp said. "If you give me a ride home, I'll show you something." The policemen looked at each other. They had been called into the neighborhood, hours ago, when a young woman had reported that she was approached by an exhibitionist—at least, by a streaker. Possibly it was a matter of attempted rape. She had escaped him on a bicycle, she said.

"You been out here a long time?" one of the policemen asked Garp.

The third person, in the back seat of the police car, looked out the window at what was going on. When he saw Garp, he said, "Hey, man, how you doing?" Duncan started to wake up.

"Ralph?" Duncan said.

One policeman knelt beside the boy and pointed the flashlight up at Garp. "Is this your father?" the cop asked Duncan. The boy was rather wild-eyed; he darted his eyes from his father to the cops to the blue light flashing on the squad car.

The other policeman went over to the person in the back seat of the car. It was the boy in the purple caftan. The police had picked him up while they were cruising the neighborhood for the exhibitionist. The boy hadn't been able to tell them where he lived—because he didn't

295

really live anywhere. "Do you know that man with the child there?" the policeman asked the boy.

"Yeah, he's a real tough guy," the kid said.

"It's all right, Duncan," Garp said. "Don't be scared. I'm just taking you home."

"Son?" the policeman asked Duncan. "Is this your father?"

"You're scaring him," Garp told the cop.

"I'm not scared," Duncan said. "Why are you taking me home?" he asked his father. It seemed that everyone wanted to hear this.

"Ralph's mother was upset," Garp said; he hoped that would be enough, but the rejected lover in the police car started to laugh. The policeman with the flashlight shone his light on the lover boy and asked Garp if he knew him. Garp thought: There is no end to this in sight.

"My name is Garp," Garp said, irritably. "T. S. Garp. I am married. I have two children. One of them—this one, named Duncan, the older—was spending the night with a friend. I was convinced that this friend's mother was unfit to look after my son. I went to the house and took my son home. Or, I'm still trying to *get* home.

"*That* boy," Garp said, pointing to the police car, "was visiting the mother of the friend of my son when I arrived. The mother wanted the boy to leave—*that* boy," Garp said, again pointing at the kid in the police car, "and he left."

"What is this mother's name?" a policeman asked; he was trying to write everything down in a giant pad. After a polite silence, the policeman looked up at Garp.

"Duncan?" Garp asked his son. "What is Ralph's name?"

"Well, it's being changed," Duncan said. "He used to have his father's name, but his mother's trying to get it changed."

"Yes, but what *is* his father's name?" Garp asked.

"Ralph," Duncan said. Garp shut his eyes.

"Ralph Ralph?" the policeman with the pad said.

"No, Duncan, please think," Garp said. "Ralph's *last* name is what?"

"Well, I think that's the name being changed," Duncan said.

"Duncan, what is it being changed *from?*" Garp asked.

"You could ask Ralph," Duncan suggested. Garp wanted to scream.

"Did you say *your* name was Garp?" one of the policemen asked.

"Yes," Garp admitted.

"And the initials are T. S.?" the policeman asked. Garp knew what would happen next; he felt very tired.

"Yes, T. S.," he said. "Just T. S."

"Hey, Tough Shit!" howled the kid in the car, falling back in the seat, swooning with laughter.

"What does the first initial stand for, Mr. Garp?" the policeman asked.

"Nothing," Garp said.

"Nothing?" the policeman said.

"They're just initials," Garp said. "They're all my mother gave me."

"Your first name is *T?*" the policeman asked.

"People call me Garp," Garp said.

"What a story, man!" cried the boy in the caftan, but the policeman nearest the squad car rapped on the roof at him.

"You put your dirty feet on that seat again, sonny," he said, "and I'll have you licking the crud off."

"Garp?" said the policeman interviewing Garp. "I know who you are!" he cried suddenly. Garp felt very anxious. "You're the one who got that molester in that park!"

"Yes!" said Garp. "That was me. But it wasn't here, and it was years ago."

"I remember it as if it were yesterday," the policeman said.

"What's this?" the other policeman asked.

"You're too young," the cop told him. "This is the

297

man named Garp who grabbed that molester in that
park—where was it? That *child* molester, that's who it
was. And what was it you did?" he asked Garp, curiously. "I mean, there was something funny, wasn't
there?"

"Funny?" said Garp.

"For a *living,*" the policeman said. "What did you do
for a living?"

"I'm a writer," Garp said.

"Oh, yeah," the policeman remembered. "Are you
still a writer?"

"Yes," Garp confessed. He knew, at least, that he
wasn't a marriage counselor.

"Well, I'll be," the policeman said, but something
was still bothering him; Garp could tell something was
wrong.

"I had a beard then," Garp offered.

"That's it!" the policeman cried. "And you've shaved
it off?"

"Right," said Garp.

The policemen had a conference in the red glow of
the taillights of the squad car. They decided to give
Garp and Duncan a ride home, but they said Garp
would still have to show them some information regarding his identity.

"I just don't recognize you—from the pictures—without the beard," the older policeman said.

"Well, it *was* years ago," Garp said, sadly, "and in
another town."

Garp felt uneasy that the young man in the caftan
would get to see the house the Garps lived in. Garp
imagined the young man would show up one day, asking for something.

"You remember me?" the kid asked Duncan.

"I don't think so," Duncan said, politely.

"Well, you were almost asleep," the boy admitted.
To Garp he said, "You're too uptight about children,
man. Children make it just fine. This your only child?"

"No, I have another one," Garp said.

"Man, you ought to have a *dozen* other ones," the boy said. "Then maybe you wouldn't get so uptight about just one, you know?" This sounded to Garp like what his mother called the Percy Theory of Children.

"Take your next left," Garp told the policeman who was driving, "then a right, and it's on the corner." The other policeman handed Duncan a lollipop.

"Thank you," Duncan said.

"What about me?" the kid in the caftan asked. "*I* like lollipops." The policeman glared; when he turned his back, Duncan gave the kid his lollipop. Duncan was no fan of lollipops, he never had been.

"Thank you," the boy whispered. "You see, man?" he said to Garp. "Kids are just beautiful."

So is Helen, Garp thought—in the doorway with the light behind her. Her blue, floor-length robe had a high, roll-up collar; Helen had the collar turned up as if she were cold. She also had her glasses on, so that Garp knew she'd been watching for them.

"Man," whispered the kid in the caftan, elbowing Garp as he got out of the car. "What's that lovely lady like when she gets her glasses off?"

"Mom! We got arrested," Duncan called to Helen. The squad car waited at the curb for Garp to get his identification.

"We did *not* get arrested," Garp said. "We got a *ride,* Duncan. Everything's *fine,*" he said angrily, to Helen. He ran upstairs to find his wallet among his clothes.

"Is that how you went out?" Helen called after him. "Dressed like that?"

"The police thought he was kidnapping me," Duncan said.

"Did they come to the house?" Helen asked him.

"No, Dad was carrying me home," Duncan said. "Boy, is Dad weird."

Garp thundered down the stairs and ran out the door. "A case of mistaken identity," Garp muttered to

299

Helen. "They must have been looking for someone else. For God's sake, don't get upset."

"I'm *not* upset," Helen said, sharply.

Garp showed the police his identification.

"Well, I'll be," the older policeman said. "It *is* just T. S., isn't it? I suppose it's easier that way."

"Sometimes it isn't," Garp said.

As the police car was leaving, the kid called out to Garp, "You're not a bad guy, man, if you'd just learn to *relax!*"

Garp's impression of Helen's body, lean and tense and shivering in the blue robe, did not relax him. Duncan was wide-awake and jabbering; he was hungry, too. So was Garp. In the predawn kitchen, Helen coolly watched them eat. Duncan told the plot of a long TV movie; Garp suspected that it was actually two movies, and Duncan had fallen asleep before one was over and woken up after the other one had begun. He tried to imagine where and when Mrs. Ralph's activities fitted into Duncan's movies.

Helen didn't ask any questions. In part, Garp knew, this was because there was nothing she could say in front of Duncan. But in part, like Garp, she was severely editing what she wanted to say. They were both grateful for Duncan's presence; by the time they got to speak freely to each other, the long wait might make them kinder, and more careful.

At dawn they couldn't wait any longer and they began to talk to each other through Duncan.

"Tell Mommy what the kitchen looked like," Garp said. "And tell her about the dog."

"Bill?"

"Right!" Garp said. "Tell her about old Bill."

"What was Ralph's mother wearing while you were there?" Helen asked Duncan. She smiled at Garp. "I hope she wore more clothes than Daddy."

"What did you have for supper?" Garp asked Duncan.

"Are the bedrooms upstairs or downstairs?" Helen

asked. "Or both?" Garp tried to give her a look that said: Please don't get started. He could feel her edging the old, worn weapons into easy reach. She had a baby-sitter or two she could recall for him, and he felt her moving the baby-sitters into place. If she brought up one of the old, wounding names, Garp had no names ready for retaliation. Helen had no baby-sitters against her; not yet. In Garp's mind, Harrison Fletcher didn't count.

"How many telephones are there?" Helen asked Duncan. "Is there a phone in the kitchen and one in the bedroom? Or is the only phone in the bedroom?"

When Duncan finally went to his room, Helen and Garp were left with less than half an hour before Walt would wake up. But Helen had the names of her enemies ready. There is plenty of time to do damage when you know where the war wounds are.

"I love you so much, and I know you so well," Helen began.

# 12

❖❖❖❖❖❖❖

# It Happens to Helen

LATE-NIGHT phone calls—those burglar alarms
in the heart—would frighten Garp all his life. Who
is it that I love? Garp's heart would cry, at the
first ring—who's been blasted by a truck, who's drowned
in the beer or lies sideswiped by an elephant in the terrible darkness?

Garp feared the receiving of such after-midnight calls,
but he once made one—unknowingly—himself. It had
been one evening when Jenny was visiting them; his
mother had let it slip how Cushie Percy had ruptured
in childbirth. Garp had not heard of it, and although
he occasionally joked with Helen about his old passion
for Cushie—and Helen teased him about her—the news
of Cushie *dead* was nearly crippling to Garp. Cushman
Percy had been so active—there had been such a hot
juiciness about her—it seemed impossible. News of an
accident to Alice Fletcher could not have upset him
more; he felt more prepared for something happening
to her. Sadly, he knew, things *would* always be happening to Quiet Alice.

Garp wandered into the kitchen and without really
noticing the time, or remembering when he opened an-

other beer, he discovered that he had dialed the Percys' number; the phone was ringing. Slowly, Garp could imagine the long way back from sleep that Fat Stew had to travel before he could answer the phone.

"God, who are you calling?" Helen asked, coming into the kitchen. "It's quarter of two!"

Before Garp could hang up, Stewart Percy answered the phone.

"Yes?" Fat Stew asked, worriedly, and Garp could imagine frail and brainless Midge sitting up in bed beside him, as nervous as a cornered hen.

"I'm sorry I woke you," Garp said. "I didn't realize it was so late." Helen shook her head and walked abruptly out of the kitchen. Jenny appeared in the kitchen doorway; on her face was the kind of critical look only a mother can give a son. That is a look with more disappointment in it than the usual anger.

"Who the hell is this?" Stewart Percy said.

"This is Garp, sir," Garp said, a little boy again, apologizing for his genes.

"Holy shit," said Fat Stew. "What do *you* want?"

Jenny had neglected to tell Garp that Cushie Percy had died *months* ago; Garp thought he was offering condolences on a fresh disaster. Thus he faltered.

"I'm sorry, very sorry," Garp said.

"You said so, you *said* so," Stewart said.

"I just heard about it," Garp said, "and I wanted to tell you and Mrs. Percy how truly sorry I was. I may not have demonstrated it, to *you*, sir, but I was really very fond of—"

"You little swine!" said Stewart Percy. "You mother humper, you Jap ball of shit!" He hung up the phone.

Even Garp was unprepared for this much loathing. But he misunderstood the situation. It would be years before he realized the circumstances of his phone call. Poor Pooh Percy, batty Bainbridge, would one day explain it to Jenny. When Garp called, Cushie had been dead for so long that Stewart did not realize Garp was commiserating with him on *Cushie's* loss. When Garp called, it was the midnight of the dark day when the black beast, Bonkers, had finally expired. Stewart Percy thought that Garp's call was a cruel joke—false condolences for the dog Garp had always hated.

And now, when Garp's phone rang, Garp was conscious of Helen's grip emerging instinctively from her sleep. When he picked up the phone, Helen had his leg clamped fast between her knees—as if she were holding tight to the life and safety that his body was to her. Garp's mind ran through the odds. Walt was home asleep. And so was Duncan; he was *not* at Ralph's.

Helen thought: It is my father; it's his heart. Sometimes she thought: They've finally found and identified my mother. In a morgue.

And Garp thought: They have murdered Mom. Or they are holding her for ransom—men who will accept nothing less than the public rape of forty virgins before releasing the famous feminist, unharmed. And they'll also demand the lives of my children, and so forth.

It was Roberta Muldoon on the phone, and that only convinced Garp that the victim was Jenny Fields. But the victim was Roberta.

"He's left me," Roberta said, her huge voice swollen with tears. "He's thrown me over. *Me!* Can you believe it?"

"Jesus, Roberta," Garp said.

"Oh, I never knew what *shits* men were until I became a woman," Roberta said.

"It's Roberta," Garp whispered to Helen, so that she could relax. "Her lover's flown the coop." Helen sighed, released Garp's leg, rolled over.

"You don't even care, do you?" Roberta asked Garp, testily.

"Please, Roberta," Garp said.

"I'm sorry," Roberta said. "But I thought it was too late to call your mother." Garp found this logic astonishing, since he knew that Jenny stayed up later than he

305

did; but he also liked Roberta, very much, and she had certainly had a hard time.

"He said I wasn't *enough* of a woman, that I confused him, sexually—that *I* was confused sexually!" Roberta cried. "Oh, God, that *prick*. All he wanted was the novelty of it. He was just showing off for his friends."

"I'll bet you could have taken him, Roberta," Garp said. "Why didn't you beat the shit out of him?"

"You don't understand," Roberta said. "I don't *feel* like beating the shit out of anyone, anymore. I'm a *woman!*"

"Don't women ever feel like beating the shit out of someone?" Garp asked. Helen reached over to him and pulled his cock.

"I don't know *what* women feel like," Roberta wailed. "I don't know what they're *supposed* to feel like, anyway. I just know what *I* feel like."

"What's that?" Garp asked, knowing she wanted to tell him.

"I feel like beating the shit out of him *now,*" Roberta confessed, "but when he was dumping all over me, I just sat there and took it. I even cried. I've been crying all day!" she cried, "and he even called me up and told me that if I was *still* crying I was faking myself."

"The hell with him," Garp said.

"All he wanted was a great big lay," Roberta said. "Why are men like that?"

"Well," Garp said.

'Oh, I know *you're* not," Roberta said. "I'm not even attractive to you, probably."

"Of course you're attractive, Roberta," Garp said.

"But not to *you*," Roberta said. "Don't lie. I'm not sexually attractive, am I?"

"Not really to *me*," Garp confessed, "but to lots of *other* men, yes. Of course you are."

"Well, you're a good friend, that's more important," Roberta said. "You're not really sexually attractive to me, either."

"That's perfectly all right," Garp said.

"You're too short," Roberta said. "I like *longer*-looking people—I mean, sexually. Don't be hurt."

"I'm not hurt," Garp said. "Don't *you* be, either."

"Of course not," Roberta said.

"Why not call me in the morning," Garp suggested. "You'll feel better."

"I won't," Roberta said, sulkily. "I'll feel *worse*. And I'll feel ashamed that I called you."

"Why not talk to your doctor?" Garp said. "The urologist? The fellow who did your operation—he's your friend, isn't he?"

"I think he wants to fuck me," Roberta said, seriously. "I think that's all he *ever* wanted to do to me. I think he recommended this whole operation just because he wanted to seduce me, but he wanted to make me a woman first. They're notorious for that—a friend was telling me."

"A *crazy* friend, Roberta," Garp said. *"Who's* notorious for that?"

"Urologists," Roberta said. "Oh, I don't know—isn't urology a little creepy to you?" It *was,* but Garp didn't want to upset Roberta any further.

"Call Mom," he heard himself say. *"She'll* cheer you up, she'll think of something."

"Oh, she *is* wonderful," Roberta sobbed. "She always *does* think of something, but I feel I've used her for so much."

"She loves to help, Roberta," Garp said, and knew it was, at least, the truth. Jenny Fields was full of sympathy and patience, and Garp only wanted to sleep. "A good game of squash might help, Roberta," Garp suggested, weakly. "Why not come over for a few days and we'll really hit the ball around." Helen rolled into him, frowned at him, and bit his nipple; Helen liked Roberta, but in the early phase of her sex reassignment Roberta could talk only about herself.

"I just feel so *drained,"* Roberta said. "No energy, no nothing. I don't even know if I could play."

"Well, you should *try*, Roberta," Garp said. "You should make yourself do something." Helen, exasperated with him, rolled away from him.

But Helen was affectionate with Garp when he answered these late-night calls; she said they frightened her and she didn't want to be the one to find out what the calls were about. It was strange, therefore, that when Roberta Muldoon called a second time, a few weeks later, *Helen* was the one who answered the phone. It surprised Garp because the phone was on his side of the bed and Helen had to reach over him to pick it up; in fact, this time, she lunged across him and whispered quickly to the phone, "Yes, what is it?" When she heard it was Roberta, she passed the phone quickly to Garp; it was not as if she'd been trying to let him sleep.

And when Roberta called a third time, Garp felt an absence when he picked up the phone. Something was missing. "Oh, hello, Roberta," Garp said. It was Helen's usual grip on his leg: it wasn't there. *Helen* wasn't there, he noticed. He talked reassuringly to Roberta, felt the cold side of his unshared bed, and noted the time was 2 A.M.—Roberta's favorite hour. When Roberta finally hung up, Garp went downstairs to look for Helen, finding her all alone on the living-room couch, sitting up with a glass of wine and a manuscript in her lap.

"Couldn't sleep," she said, but there was a look on her face—it was a look Garp couldn't immediately place. Although he thought he recognized that look, he also thought he had never seen that look on Helen.

"Reading papers?" he asked; she nodded, but there was only one manuscript in front of her. Garp picked it up.

"It's just student work," she said, reaching for it.

The student's name was Michael Milton. Garp read a paragraph of the paper. "It sounds like a story," Garp said. "I didn't know you assigned *fiction* writing to your students."

"I don't," Helen said, "but they sometimes show me what they do, anyway."

Garp read another paragraph. He thought that the writer's style was self-conscious and forced, but there were no errors on the page; it was, at least, competent writing.

"He's one of my graduate students," Helen said. "He's very bright, but . . ." She shrugged, but her gesture had the sudden mock casualness of an embarrassed child.

"But what?" Garp said. He laughed—that Helen could look so girlish at this late hour.

But Helen took her glasses off and showed him that *other* look again, that look he had first seen and couldn't place. Anxiously, she said, "Oh, I don't know. *Young,* maybe. He's just young, you know. Very bright, but young."

Garp flipped a page, read half of another paragraph, gave the manuscript back to her. He shrugged. "It's all shit to me," he said.

"No, it's not shit," Helen said, seriously. Oh, Helen the judicious teacher, Garp thought, and announced he was going back to bed. "I'll be up in a little while," Helen told him.

Then Garp saw himself in the mirror in the upstairs bathroom. That was where he finally identified that look he'd seen, strangely out of place, on Helen's face. It was a look Garp recognized because he'd seen it before—on his own face, from time to time, but never on Helen's. The look Garp recognized was *guilty,* and it puzzled him. He lay awake a long time but Helen did not come up to bed. In the morning Garp was surprised that although he'd only glanced at the graduate student's manuscript, the name of Michael Milton was the first thing to come to his mind. He looked cautiously at Helen, now lying awake beside him.

"Michael Milton," Garp said quietly, not to her, but loud enough for her to hear. He watched her unresponding face. Either she was daydreaming, and far away, or she simply had not heard him. Or, he thought, the name of Michael Milton was already on her mind, so that when Garp uttered it, it was the name that she was

309

*already* saying—to herself—and she had not noticed that Garp had spoken it.

Michael Milton, a third-year graduate student in comparative literature, had been a French major at Yale, where he graduated with indifferent distinction; he had earlier graduated from the Steering School, though he tended to play down his prep school years. Once he knew that *you* knew he had gone to Yale, he tended to play that down, too, but he never played down his Junior Year Abroad—in France. To listen to Michael Milton, you would not guess that he'd spent only a year in Europe because he managed to give you the impression that he'd lived in France all his young life. He was twenty-five.

Though he'd lived so briefly in Europe, it appeared that he'd bought all the clothes for his lifetime there: the tweed jackets had wide lapels and flared cuffs, and both the jackets and the slacks were cut to flatter the hips and the waist; they were the kind of clothes that even the Americans of Garp's days at Steering referred to as "Continental." The collars of Michael Milton's shirts, which he wore open at the throat (always with *two* unbuttoned buttons), were floppy and wide with a kind of Renaissance flair: a manner betraying both carelessness and intense perfection.

He was as different from Garp as an ostrich is different from a seal. The body of Michael Milton was an elegant body, when dressed; unclothed, he resembled no animal so much as he resembled a heron. He was thin and tallish, with a slouch his tailored tweed jackets concealed. He had a body like coat hangers—the perfect body to hang clothes on. Stripped, he had barely a body at all.

He was Garp's opposite in almost every way, except that Michael Milton had in common with Garp a tremendous self-confidence; he shared with Garp the virtue, or the vice, of arrogance. Like Garp, he was aggressive in the way only someone who believes totally in himself can be aggressive. It had been these qualities, long ago, that had first attracted Helen to Garp.

Now here were the qualities, newly attired; they manifested themselves in a much different form, yet Helen recognized them. She was not usually attracted to rather dandified young men who dressed and spoke as if they had grown world-weary and wisely sad in Europe, when, in fact, they had spent most of their short lives in the back seats of cars in Connecticut. But, in her girlhood, Helen had not *usually* been attracted to wrestlers, either. Helen liked confident men, provided that their confidence was not absurdly misplaced.

What attracted Michael Milton to Helen was what attracted many men and few women to her. She was, in her thirties, an alluring woman not simply because she was beautiful but because she was perfect-looking. It is an important distinction to note that she looked not only as if she had taken good care of herself, but that she had good reason to have done so. This frightening but fetching look, in Helen's case, was not misleading. She was a very successful woman. She looked to be in such total possession of her life that only the most confident men could continue to look at her if she looked back at them. Even in bus stations, she was a woman who was stared at only until she looked back.

In the corridors surrounding the English Department, Helen was not used to being stared at at all; everyone looked when they could, but the looks were furtive. She was, therefore, unprepared for the long, frank look that young Michael Milton gave her one day. He simply stopped in the hall and watched her walking toward him. It was actually Helen who turned her eyes away from his; he turned and watched her walk away from him, down the hall. He said to someone beside him, loud enough for Helen to hear: "Does she teach here or *go* here? What's she *do* here, anyway?" Michael Milton asked.

In the second semester of that year, Helen taught a course in Narrative Point of View; it was a seminar for

311

graduate students, and for a few advanced undergraduates. Helen was interested in the development and sophistication of narrative technique, with special attention to point of view, in the modern novel. In the first class she noticed the older-looking student with the thin, pale mustache and the nice shirt with the two buttons unbuttoned; she turned her eyes away from him and distributed a questionnaire. It asked, among other questions, why the students thought they were interested in this particular course. In answer to that question, a student named Michael Milton wrote: "Because, from the first time I saw you, I wanted to be your lover."

After that class, alone in her office, Helen read that answer to her questionnaire. She thought she knew which one of the people in the class Michael Milton was; if she'd known it was someone else, some boy she hadn't even noticed, she would have shown the questionnaire to Garp. Garp might have said, "Show me the fucker!" Or: "Let's introduce him to Roberta Muldoon." And they would both have laughed, and Garp would have teased her about leading her students on. Because the intentions of the boy, whoever he was, would have been aired between them, there would have been no possibility of actual connection; Helen knew that. When she didn't show the questionnaire to Garp, she felt already guilty—but she thought that if Michael Milton was who she thought he was, she would like to see this go a little further. At that moment, in her office, Helen honestly did not foresee it going *more* than a little further. What would have been the harm of a little?

If Harrison Fletcher had still been her colleague, she would have shown *him* the questionnaire. Regardless—whoever Michael Milton was, even if he *was* that disturbing-looking boy—she would have brought up the matter with Harrison. Harrison and Helen, in the past, had some secrets of this kind, which they kept from Garp and Alice; they were permanent but innocent secrets. Helen knew that sharing Michael Milton's interest in her with Harrison would have been another way to avoid any actual connection.

But she did not mention Michael Milton to Garp, and Harrison, of course, had left to seek his tenure elsewhere. The handwriting on the questionnaire was black, eighteenth-century calligraphy, the kind that can only be carved with a special pen; Michael Milton's written message looked more permanent than print, and Helen read it over and over again. She noted the other answers to the questionnaire: date of birth, years in school, previous courses in the Department of English or in comparative literature. She checked his transcript; his grades were good. She called two colleagues who'd had Michael Milton in courses last semester; she derived from them both that Michael Milton was a good student, aggressive and proud to the point of being vain. She gathered from both her colleagues, though they did not actually say so, that Michael Milton was both gifted and unlikable. She thought of the deliberately unbuttoned buttons on his shirt (she was *sure,* now, that it was he) and she imagined buttoning them up. She thought of that wispy mustache, a thin trace upon his lip. Garp would later comment on Michael Milton's mustache, saying that it was an insult to the world of hair and to the world of lips; Garp thought it was so much the merest imitation of a mustache that Michael Milton would do his face a favor to shave it off.

But Helen liked the strange little mustache on the lip of Michael Milton.

"You just don't like *any* mustaches," Helen said to Garp.

"I don't like *that* mustache," he said. "I've got nothing against mustaches, in general," Garp insisted, though in truth Helen was right: Garp hated all mustaches, ever since his encounter with the Mustache Kid. The Mustache Kid had spoiled mustaches for Garp, forever.

Helen also liked the length of Michael Milton's sideburns, curly and blondish; Garp's sideburns were cropped level to his dark eyes, almost at the tops of his ears—although his hair was thick and shaggy, and always just long enough to cover the ear that Bonkers ate.

Helen also noticed that her husband's eccentricities were beginning to bother her. Perhaps she just noticed them more, now that he was so fitfully involved in his writing slump; when he was writing, perhaps he had less time to devote to his eccentricities? Whatever the reason, she found them irksome. His driveway trick, for example, infuriated her; it was even contradictory. For someone who fussed and worried so much about the safety of the children—about reckless drivers, about leaking gas, and so forth—Garp had a way of entering their driveway and garage, after dark, that terrified Helen.

The driveway turned sharply uphill off a long downhill road. When Garp knew the children were in bed, asleep, he would cut the engine *and* the lights and coast *up* the black driveway; he would gather enough momentum from leaving the downhill road to roll over the lip at the top of the driveway and down into their dark garage. He said he did it so that the engine and the headlights would not wake up the children. But he had to start the car to turn it around to drive the baby-sitter home, anyway; Helen said his trick was simply for a thrill—it was puerile and dangerous. He was always running over toys left in the blackened driveway, and crashing into bicycles not moved far enough to the rear of the garage.

Once a baby-sitter had complained to Helen that she hated coasting *down* the driveway with the engine and the headlights out (*another* trick: he would pop the clutch and snap on the lights just before they reached the road).

Am *I* the one who's restless? Helen wondered. She had not thought of herself as restless until she thought of *Garp's* restlessness. And for how long had she really been irritated by Garp's routines and habits? She didn't know. She only knew that she *noticed* she was irritated by them almost from the moment she read Michael Milton's questionnaire.

Helen was driving to her office, wondering what she would say to the rude and conceited boy, when the gear knob of the Volvo's stick shift came off in her hand—the exposed shaft scratched her wrist. She swore as she pulled the car over and examined the damage to herself and to the gearshift.

The knob had been falling off for weeks, the screw threads were stripped, and Garp had several times attempted to make the knob stay on the stick-shift shaft with tape. Helen had complained about this half-assed method of repair, but Garp never claimed to be handy and the care of the car was one of Helen's domestic responsibilities.

This division of labor, though largely agreed upon, was sometimes confusing. Although Garp was the homemaker among them, Helen did the ironing ("because," Garp said, "it's *you* who cares about pressed clothes"), and Helen got the car serviced ("because," Garp said, "you're the one who drives it every day; you know best when something has to be fixed"). Helen accepted the ironing, but she felt that Garp should deal with the car. She did not like accepting a ride in the service truck from the garage to her office—sitting in the greasy cab with some young mechanic who paid less than adequate attention to his driving. The garage where the car was fixed was a friendly enough place to Helen, but she resented having to be there at all; and the comedy of *who* would drive her to work after she dropped off the car had finally worn thin. "Who's free to take Mrs. Garp to the university?" the boss mechanic would cry into the dank and oily darkness of the vehicle pits. And three or four boys, eager but begrimed, would drop their wrenches and their needle-nosed pliers, would lug and heave themselves out of the pits, would bolt forward and volunteer to share—for a brief, heady moment—that tight cab aclank with auto parts, which would take the slender Professor Garp to work.

Garp pointed out to Helen that when *he* took the car, the volunteers were slow to appear; he frequently waited in the garage for an hour, finally coaxing some laggard to drive him home. His morning's work thus shot, he decided the Volvo was Helen's chore.

They had both procrastinated about the gearshift knob. "If you just call to order a new one," Helen told him, "I'll drive there and let them screw it on while I wait. But I *don't* want to leave the car for a day while they fart around trying to fix *this* one." She had tossed the knob to him, but he'd carried it out to the car and had taped it, precariously, back on the shaft.

Somehow, she thought, it always fell off when *she* was driving; but, of course, she drove the car more than he did.

"Damn," she said, and drove to her office with the ugly gearshift uncovered. It hurt her hand every time she had to shift the car, and her scratched wrist bled a little on the fresh skirt of her suit. She parked the car and carried the gear knob with her, across the parking lot, toward her office building. She contemplated throwing it down a storm sewer, but it had little numbers printed on it; in her office she could call the garage and tell them what the little numbers were. *Then* she could throw it away, wherever she liked; or, she thought, I can *mail* it to Garp.

It was in this mood, beset with trivia, that Helen encountered the smug young man slouched in the hall by her office door with the top two buttons of his nice shirt unbuttoned. The shoulders of his tweed jacket were, she noticed, slightly padded; his hair was a bit too lank, and too long, and one end of his mustache—as thin as a knife—drooped too far down at the corner of his mouth. She was not sure if she wanted to love this young man or *groom* him.

"You're up early," she told him, handing him the gearshift knob so that she could unlock her office door.

316

"Have you hurt yourself?" he asked. "You're bleeding." Helen would think later that it was as if he had a nose for blood, because the slight scratch on her wrist had almost stopped bleeding.

"Are you going to be a doctor?" she asked him, letting him inside her office.

"I *was* going to be," he said.

"What stopped you?" she asked, still not looking at him, but moving about her desk, straightening what was straight already; and adjusting the venetian blind, which had been left exactly as she wanted it. She took her glasses off, so that when she looked at him he was soft and fuzzy.

"Organic chemistry stopped me," he said. "I dropped the course. And besides, I wanted to live in France."

"Oh, you've lived in France?" Helen asked him, knowing that's what she was supposed to ask him, knowing it was one of the things he thought was special about himself, and he didn't hesitate to slip it in. He had even slipped it in the questionnaire. He was *very* shallow, she saw right away; she hoped he was the slightest bit intelligent, but she felt curiously relieved by his shallowness—as if this made him less dangerous to her, and left her a little freer.

They talked about France, which was fun for Helen, because she talked about France as well as Michael Milton talked about it, and she had never been to Europe. She also told him that she thought he had a poor reason for taking her course.

"A poor reason?" he pressed her, smiling.

"First of all," Helen said, "it's a totally unrealistic expectation to have for the course."

"Oh, you already *have* a lover?" Michael Milton asked her, still smiling.

Somehow he was so frivolous that he didn't insult her; she didn't snap at him that it was enough to have a husband, that it was none of his business, or that she was out of his league. She said, instead, that for what he wanted he should at least have registered for independent study. He said he'd be glad to switch courses. She said she never took on any new independent study students in the second semester.

She knew she had not entirely discouraged him, but she had not been exactly encouraging, either. Michael Milton talked to her, seriously, for an hour—about the subject of her course in narration. He discussed Virginia Woolf's *The Waves* and *Jacob's Room* very impressively, though he was not so good on *To the Lighthouse* and Helen knew he only pretended to have read *Mrs. Dalloway*. When he left, she was forced to agree with her two colleagues who'd evaluated Michael Milton previously: he was glib, he was smug, he was facile, and all that was unlikable; but he had a certain brittle smartness, however shiny and thin it was—and it was *also,* somehow, unlikable. What her colleagues had overlooked was his audacious smile and his way of wearing clothes as if he were defiantly undressed. But Helen's colleagues were men; they could not have been expected to define the precise audacity of Michael Milton's smile the way Helen could define it. Helen recognized it as a smile that said to her: I already know you, and I know everything you like. It was an infuriating smile, but it tempted her; she wanted to wipe it off his face. One way of wiping it off, Helen knew, would be to show Michael Milton that he *didn't* know her—or what she really liked—at all.

She also knew that not too many ways of showing him were open to her.

When she first shifted the Volvo, driving home, the point of the uncovered stick-shift shaft dug sharply into the heel of her hand. She knew exactly where Michael Milton had left the gear knob—on the window ledge above the wastebasket, where the janitor would find it and probably throw it away. It looked as if it *ought* to be thrown away, but Helen remembered that she had not phoned in the little numbers to the car garage. That would mean that she, or Garp, would have to call the car garage and try to order a new knob *without* the goddamn numbers—giving the year and model of the car, and so forth, and inevitably ending up with a knob that wasn't right.

But Helen decided she was not going back to her office, and she had enough on her mind already without trying to remember to call the janitor and tell him not to throw away the knob. Besides, it might already be too late.

And anyway, Helen thought, it's not just *my* fault. It's Garp's fault, too. Or, she thought, it's really nobody's fault. It's just one of those things.

But she did not *quite* feel guiltless; not yet. When Michael Milton gave her his papers to read—his old papers, from his other courses—she accepted them and read them, because at least this was an allowable, still-innocent subject for them to discuss: his work. When he grew bolder, and more attached to her, and he showed her even his *creative* work, his short stories and pathetic poems about France, Helen still felt that their long conversations were guided by the critical, constructive relationship between a student and a teacher.

It was all right to have lunch together; they had his *work* to talk about. Perhaps both of them knew that the work was not so special. For Michael Milton, *any* topic of conversation that justified his being with Helen was all right. For Helen, she was still anxious about the obvious conclusion—when he simply ran out of work; when they had consumed all the papers he'd had time to write; when they'd mentioned every book they had in common. Then Helen knew they would need a new subject. She also knew that this was only *her* problem—that Michael Milton already knew what the inevitable subject between them was. She knew he was smugly and irritatingly waiting for her to make up her mind; she occasionally wondered if he would be bold enough to raise his original answer to her questionnaire again, but she didn't think so. Perhaps both of them knew that he wouldn't have to—that the next move was hers. He would show her how grown-up he was by being patient. Helen wanted, above all, to surprise him.

But among these feelings that were new to her, there was one she disliked; she was most unused to feeling guilty—for Helen Holm always felt right about everything she did, and she needed to feel guiltless about this, too. She felt close to achieving this guilt-free state of mind, but she did not quite have it; not yet.

It would be Garp who provided her with the necessary feeling. Perhaps he sensed he had competition; Garp got started as a writer out of a sense of competition, and he finally broke out of his writing slump with a similar, competitive surge.

Helen, he knew, was *reading* someone else. It did not occur to Garp that she might be contemplating more than literature, but he saw with a typical writer's jealousy that someone else's *words* were keeping her up at night. Garp had first courted Helen with "The Pension Grillparzer." Some instinct told him to court her again.

If that had been an acceptable motive to get a young writer *started,* it was a dubious motive for his writing now—especially after he'd been stopped for so long. He might have been in a necessary phase, rethinking everything, letting the well refill, preparing a book for the future with a proper period of silence. Somehow the new story he wrote for Helen reflected the forced and unnatural circumstances of its conception. The story was written less out of any real reaction to the viscera of life than it was written to relieve the anxieties of the writer.

It was possibly a necessary exercise for a writer who had not written in too long, but Helen did not care for the urgency with which Garp shoved the story at her. "I finally finished something," he said. It was after dinner; the children were asleep; Helen wanted to go to bed with him—she wanted long and reassuring lovemaking, because she had come to the end of what Michael Milton had written; there was nothing more for her to read, or for them to talk about. She knew she should not show the slightest disappointment in the manuscript Garp gave her, but her tiredness overwhelmed her and she stared at it, crouching between dirty dishes.

"I'll do the dishes alone," Garp offered, clearing the way to his story for her. Her heart sank; she had read too much. *Sex,* or at least romance, was the subject she had at last come to; Garp had better provide it or Michael Milton would.

"I want to be loved," Helen told Garp; he was gathering up the dishes like a waiter who was confident of a large tip. He laughed at her.

"Read the story, Helen," he said. *"Then* we'll get laid."

She resented *his* priorities. There could be no comparison between Garp's *writing* and the student work of Michael Milton; though gifted among students, Michael Milton, Helen knew, would only be a *student* of writing all his life. The issue was not writing. The issue is *me,* Helen thought; I want someone paying attention to me. Garp's manner of courtship was suddenly offensive to her. The *subject* being courted was somehow Garp's writing. That is *not* the subject between us, Helen thought. Because of Michael Milton, Helen was way ahead of Garp at considering the spoken and unspoken subjects between people. "If people only told each other what was on their minds," wrote Jenny Fields—a naïve but forgivable lapse; both Garp and Jenny knew how difficult it was for people to do that.

Garp cautiously washed the dishes, waiting for Helen to read his story. Instinctively—the trained teacher—Helen took out her red pencil and began. That is *not* how she should read my story, Garp thought; I'm not one of her students. But he went on quietly washing the dishes. He saw there was no stopping her.

## Vigilance

### by T. S. Garp

Running my five miles a day, I frequently encounter some smart-mouthed motorist who will pull alongside me and ask (from the safety of the driver's seat), "What are you in training for?"

Deep and regular breathing is the secret; I am rarely out of breath; I never pant or gasp when I respond. "I am staying in shape to chase cars," I say.

At this point the responses of the motorists vary; there are degrees of stupidity as there are degrees of everything else. Of course, they never realize that I don't mean them —I'm not staying in shape to chase *their* cars; not out on the open road, at least. I let them go out there, though I sometimes believe that I *could* catch them. And I do not run on the open road, as some motorists believe, to attract attention.

In my neighborhood there is no place to run. One must leave the suburbs to be even a middle-distance runner. Where I live there are four-way stop signs at every intersection; the blocks are short, and those tight-angle corners are hard on the balls of the feet. Also, the sidewalks are threatened by dogs, festooned with the playthings of children, intermittently splashed with lawn sprinklers. And just when there's some running room, there's an elderly person taking up the whole sidewalk, precarious on crutches or armed with quacking canes. With good conscience one does not yell "Track!" to such a person. Even passing the aged at a safe distance, but with my usual speed, seems to alarm them; and it's not my intention to cause heart attacks.

So it's the open road for training, but it's the suburbs I'm in training for. In my condition I am more than a match for a car caught speeding in my neighborhood. Provided they make an even halfhearted halt at the stop signs, they cannot hit over fifty before they have to brake for the next intersection. I always catch up to them. I can travel across lawns, over porches, through swing sets and the children's wading pools; I can burst through hedges, or hurdle them. And since *my* engine is quiet—and steady, and always in tune—I can *hear* if other cars are coming; *I* don't have to stop at the stop signs.

In the end I run them down, I wave them over; they always stop. Although I am clearly in impressive car-chasing condition, that is not what intimidates the speeders. No, they are almost always intimidated by my *parenthood*, because they are almost always young. Yes, my parenthood is what sobers them, almost every time. I begin simply. "Did you see my children back there?" I ask them, loudly and anxiously. Veteran speeders, upon being asked such a question, are immediately frightened that they have *run* over my children. They are instantly defensive.

"I have two young children," I tell them. The drama is deliberate in my voice—which, with this sentence, I allow to tremble a little. It is as if I am holding back tears, or unspeakable rage, or both. Perhaps they think I am hunting a kidnapper, or that I suspect them of being child molesters.

"What happened?" they invariably ask.

"You *didn't* see my children, did you?" I repeat. "A little boy pulling a little girl in a red wagon?" This is, of course, a fiction. I have two boys, and they're not so little; they have no wagon. They may have been watching television at the time, or riding their bikes in the park—where it's safe, where there are no cars.

"No," the bewildered speeder says. "I saw children, *some* children. But I don't think I saw *those* children. *Why?*"

"Because you almost killed them," I say.

"But I didn't see them!" the speeder protests.

"You were driving too fast to see them!" I say. This is sprung on them as if it were proof of their guilt; I always pronounce this sentence as if it were hard evidence. And they're never sure. I've rehearsed this part so well. The sweat from my hard sprint, by now, drips off my mustache and the point of my chin, streaking the driver's-side door. They know only a father who genuinely fears for his children would run so hard, would stare like such a maniac, would wear such a cruel mustache.

"I'm sorry," they usually say.

"This is a neighborhood *full* of children," I always tell them. "You have other places you can drive fast, don't you? *Please*, for the children's sake, don't speed here anymore." My voice, now, is never nasty; it is always beseeching. But they see that a restrained fanatic resides behind my honest, watering eyes.

Usually it's just a young kid. Those kids have a need to dribble a little oil; they want to race the frantic pace of the music on their radios. And I don't expect to change their ways. I only hope they'll do it somewhere else. I concede that the open road is theirs; when I train there, I keep my place. I run in the stuff of the soft shoulder, in the hot sand and gravel, in the beer-bottle glass—among the mangled cats, the maimed birds, the mashed condoms. But in my neighborhood, the car is not king; not yet.

Usually they learn.

After my five-mile run I do fifty-five push-ups, then five hundred-yard dashes, followed by fifty-five situps, followed by fifty-five neck bridges. It's not that I care so much for the number five; it's simply that strenuous and mindless exertion is easier if one doesn't have to keep track of too many different numbers. After my shower (about five o'clock), through the late afternoon, and in the course of the evening, I allow myself *five* beers.

I do not chase cars at night. Children should not be playing outside at night—in my neighborhood, or in any other neighborhood. At night, I believe, the car is king of the whole modern world. Even the suburbs.

At night, in fact, I rarely leave my house, or allow the members of my family to venture out. But once I went to investigate an obvious accident—the darkness suddenly streaked with headlights pointing straight up and exploding; the silence pierced with a metal screaming and the shriek of ground glass. Only half a block away, in the dark and perfect middle of my street, a Land Rover lay upside-down and bleeding its oil and gas in a puddle so deep and still I could see the moon in it. The only sound: the *ping* of heat in the hot pipes and the dead engine. The Land Rover looked like a tank tumbled by a land mine. Great juts and tears in the pavement revealed that the auto had rolled over and over before coming to rest here.

The driver's-side door could be opened only slightly, but enough to miraculously turn on the door light. There in the lit cab, still behind the steering wheel—still upside-down and still alive—was a fat man. He looked unharmed. The top of his head rested gingerly on the ceiling of the cab, which of course was now the floor, but the man seemed only dimly sensitive to this change in his perspective. He looked puzzled, chiefly, by the presence of a large brown bowling ball that sat alongside his head, like another head; he was, in fact, cheek to cheek with this bowling ball, which he perhaps felt touching him as he might have felt the presence of a lover's severed head—formerly resting on his shoulder.

"Is that you, Roger?" the man asked. I couldn't tell whether he was addressing me or the bowling ball.

"It is not Roger," I said, answering for us both.

"That Roger is a moron," the man explained. "We crossed our balls."

That the fat man was referring to a bizarre sexual experience seemed unlikely. I assumed that the fat man referred to bowling.

"This is Roger's ball," he explained, indicating the brown globe against his cheek. "I should have known it wasn't my ball because it wouldn't fit in my bag. My ball will fit in anyone's bag, but Roger's ball is really strange. I was trying to fit it in my bag when the Land Rover went off the bridge."

Although I knew there was no bridge in my entire neighborhood, I tried to visualize the occurrence. But I was distracted by the gurgle of spilling gasoline, like beer down a thirsty man's throat.

"You should get out," I told the upside-down bowler.

"I'll wait for Roger," he replied. "Roger will be right along."

And sure enough, along came another Land Rover, as if

they were a separated twosome from a column of an army on the move. Roger's Land Rover came along with its headlights out and did not stop in time; it plowed into the fat bowler's Land Rover and together, like coupled boxcars, they jarred each other another tough ten yards down the street.

It appeared that Roger *was* a moron, but I merely asked him the expected question: "Is that you, Roger?"

"Yup," said the man, whose throbbing Land Rover was dark and creaking; little fragments of its windshield and headlights and grille dropped to the street like noisy confetti.

"That could *only* be Roger!" groaned the fat bowler, still upside-down—and still alive—in his lit cab. I saw that his nose bled slightly; it appeared that the bowling ball had bashed him.

"You moron, Roger!" he called out. "You've got my *ball!*"

"Well, someone's got *my* ball, then," Roger replied.

"*I've* got your ball, you moron," the fat bowler declared.

"Well, that's not the answer to everything," Roger said. "You've got *my* Land Rover." Roger lit a cigarette in the blackened cab; he did not appear interested in climbing out of the wreck.

"You should set up flares," I suggested to him, "and that fat man should get out of your Land Rover. There's gasoline everywhere. I don't think you should smoke." But Roger only continued smoking and ignoring me in the cavelike silence of the second Land Rover, and the fat bowler again cried out—as if he were having a dream that was starting over, at the beginning—"Is that *you*, Roger?"

I went back to my house and called the police. In the daytime, in my neighborhood, I would never have tolerated such mayhem, but people who go bowling in each other's Land Rovers are not the usual suburban speeders, and I decided they were legitimately lost.

"Hello, Police?" I said.

I have learned what you can and what you can't expect of the police. I know that they do not really support the notion of citizen arrest; when I have reported speeders to them, the results have been disappointing. They don't seem interested in learning the details. I am told there are people whom the police are interested in apprehending, but I believe the police are basically sympathetic to speeders; and they do not appreciate citizens who make arrests for them.

I reported the whereabouts of the bowlers' accident, and when the police asked, as they always ask, who was calling, I told them, "Roger."

That, I knew—knowing the police—would be interesting. The police are always more interested in bothering the person who reports the crime than they are interested in bothering the criminals. And sure enough, when they arrived, they went straight after Roger. I could see them all arguing under the streetlamps, but I could catch only snatches of their conversation.

"He's Roger," the fat bowler kept saying. "He's Roger through and through."

"I'm not the Roger who called you fuckers," Roger told the police.

"That's true," the fat bowler declared. "*This* Roger wouldn't call the police for anything."

And after a while they began to call out into our dark suburb for another Roger. "Is there another Roger here?" one policeman called.

"Roger!" screamed the fat bowler, but my dark house and the dark houses of my neighbors were appropriately silent. In daylight, I knew, they would all be gone. Only their oil slicks and their broken glass would remain.

Relieved—and, as always, *pleased* with the destruction of automotive vehicles—I watched until almost dawn, when the hulking, coupled Land Rovers were finally separated and towed away. They were like two exhausted rhinos caught fornicating in the suburbs. Roger and the fat bowler stood arguing, and swinging their bowling balls, until the streetlamps in our block were extinguished; then, as if on signal, the bowlers shook hands and departed in different directions—on foot, and as if they knew where they were going.

327

The police came interrogating in the morning, still concerned with the possibility of another Roger. But they learned nothing from me—just as they learn nothing, apparently, whenever I report a speeder to them. "Well, if it happens again," they tell me, "be sure to let us know."

Fortunately, I have rarely needed the police; I am usually effective with first offenders. Only once have I had to stop the *same* driver—and him, only twice. He was an arrogant young man in a blood-red plumber's truck. Lurid-yellow lettering advertised on the cab that the plumber handled Roto-Rootering needs and all plumbing services:

### O. FECTEAU, OWNER & HEAD PLUMBER

With two-time offenders I come more quickly to the point.

"I'm calling the cops," I told the young man. "And I'm calling your boss, old O. Fecteau; I should have called him the last time."

"I'm my own boss," the young man said. "It's *my* plumbing business. Fuck off."

And I realized I was facing O. Fecteau himself—a runty but successful youth, unimpressed with standard authority.

"There are children in this neighborhood," I said. "Two of them are mine."

"Yeah, you already told me," the plumber said; he revved his engine as if he were clearing his throat. There was a hint of menace in his expression, like the trace of pubic beard he was growing on his young chin. I rested my hands on the door—one on the handle, one on the rolled-down window.

"Please don't speed here," I said.

"Yeah, I'll try," said O. Fecteau. I might have let it go at that, but the plumber lit a cigarette and smiled at me. I thought I saw on his punk's face *the leer of the world*.

"If I catch you driving like that again," I said, "I'll stick your Roto-Rooter up your ass."

We stared at each other, O. Fecteau and I. Then the plumber gunned his engine and popped his clutch; I had to leap back to the curb. In the gutter I saw a little metal dump truck, a child's toy; the front wheels were missing. I snatched it up and ran after O. Fecteau. Five blocks later I was close enough to throw the dump truck, which struck the plumber's cab; it made a good noise but it bounced off harmlessly. Even so, O. Fecteau slammed on his brakes; about five long pipes were flipped out of the pickup part of the truck, and one of those metal drawers sprang open, disgorging a screwdriver and several spools of heavy wire. The plumber jumped down from his cab, banging the door after himself; he had a Stillson wrench in his hand. You could tell he was sensitive about collecting dents on his blood-red truck. I grabbed one of the fallen pipes: It was about five feet long and I quickly smashed the truck's left taillight with it. For some time now, things have just been coming naturally to me in fives. For example, the circumference, in inches, of my chest (expanded): fifty-five.

"Your taillight's broken," I pointed out to the plumber. "You shouldn't be driving around that way."

"I'm going to call the cops on you, you crazy bastard!" said O. Fecteau.

"This is a citizen arrest," I said. "You broke the speed limit, you're endangering the lives of my children. We'll go see the cops together." And I poked the long pipe under the truck's rear license plate and folded the plate like a letter.

"You touch my truck again," the plumber said, "and you're in trouble." But the pipe felt as light in my hands as a badminton racket; I swung it easily and shattered the other taillight.

"You're already in trouble," I pointed out to O. Fecteau. "You ever drive in this neighborhood again, you better stay in first gear and use your flasher." First, I knew (swinging the pipe), he would need to *repair* his flasher.

There was an elderly woman, just then, who came out of her house to observe the commotion. She recognized me immediately. I catch up to a lot of people at her corner. "Oh, good for you!" she called. I smiled to her and she tottered toward me, stopping and peering into her well-groomed lawn where the toy dump truck arrested her attention. She seized it, with obvious distaste, and carried it over to me. I put the toy and the pieces of broken glass and plastic from the taillights and the flasher into the back of the pickup. It is a clean neighborhood; I despise litter. On the open road, in training, I see nothing but litter. I put the other pipes in back, too, and with the long pipe I still held (like a warrior's javelin) I nudged the screwdriver and the spools of wire that had fallen by the curb. O. Fecteau gathered them up and returned them to the metal drawer. He is probably a better plumber than a driver, I thought; the Stillson wrench looked very comfortable in his hand.

"You should be ashamed of yourself," the old woman told O. Fecteau. The plumber glared at her.

"He's one of the worst ones," I told her.

"Imagine that," the old lady said. "And you're a big boy," she told the plumber. "You should know better."

O. Fecteau edged back to the cab, looking as if he would hurl his wrench at me, then leap into his truck and back over the old biddy.

"Drive carefully," I told him. When he was safely in the cab, I slid the long pipe into the pickup. Then I took the old woman's arm and helped her along the sidewalk.

When the truck tore away from the curb, with that stink of scorched rubber and a noise as raw as bones leaving their sockets, I felt the old lady tremble through the frail point of her elbow; something of her fear passed into me, and I realized how risky it was to make anyone as angry as I had made O. Fecteau. I could hear him, maybe five blocks away, driving furiously fast, and I prayed for all the dogs and cats and children who might be near the street. Surely, I thought, modern life is about five times as difficult as life used to be.

I should stop this crusade against speeders, I thought. I go too far with them, but they make me so angry—with their carelessness, their dangerous, sloppy way of life, which I view as so directly threatening to my own life and the lives of my children. I have always hated cars, and hated people who drove them stupidly. I feel such anger toward people who take such risks with other people's lives. Let them race their cars—but in the desert! We would not allow an outdoor rifle range in the suburbs! Let them jump out of airplanes, if they want—but over the ocean! *Not* where my children live.

"What would this neighborhood be like without you?" the old woman wondered aloud. I can never remember her name. Without me, I thought, this neighborhood would probably be *peaceful*. Perhaps deadlier, but peaceful. "They all drive so fast," the old lady said. "If it weren't for you, I sometimes think they'd be having their smashups right in my living room." But I felt embarrassed that I shared such anxiety with eighty-year-olds—that my fears are more like their nervous, senile worries than they are the normal anxieties of people my own young middle age.

What an incredibly dull life I have! I thought, aiming the old woman toward her front door, steering her over the cracks in the sidewalk.

Then the plumber came back. I thought the old woman was going to die in my arms. The plumber drove over the curb and hurtled past us, over the old woman's lawn, flattening a whiplike young tree and nearly rolling over when he wheeled the truck into a U-turn that uprooted a sizable hedge and tore divots from the ground the size of five-pound steaks. Then down to the sidewalk the truck fled—an explosion of tools flying free of the pickup as the rear wheels jounced over the curb. O. Fecteau was off up the street, once more terrorizing my neighborhood; I saw the violent plumber jump the curb again at the corner of Dodge and Furlong—where he grazed the back of a parked car, springing open the car's trunk on impact and leaving it flapping.

Helping the shaken old lady inside, I called the police—and my wife, to tell her to keep the children indoors. The plumber was berserk. This is how I help the neighborhood, I thought: I drive mad men madder.

The old woman sat in a paisley chair in her cluttered living room, as carefully as a plant. When O. Fecteau returned—this time driving within inches of the living room bay window, and through the gravel beds for the baby trees, his horn blaring—the old woman never moved. I stood at the door, awaiting the ultimate assault, but I thought it wiser not to show myself. I knew that if O. Fecteau saw me, he would attempt to drive *in* the house.

By the time the police arrived, the plumber had rolled his truck in an attempt to avoid a station wagon at the intersection of Cold Hill and North Lane. He had broken his collarbone and was sitting upright in the cab, though the truck lay on its side; he wasn't able to climb out the door above his head, or he hadn't tried. O. Fecteau appeared calm; he was listening to his radio.

Since that time, I have tried to provoke the offending drivers less; if I sense them taking offense at my stopping them and presuming to criticize their vile habits, I simply tell them I am informing the police and quickly leave.

That O. Fecteau turned out to have a long history of violent overreactions to social situations did not allow me to forgive myself. "Look, it's all the better you got that plumber off the road," my wife told me—and she usually criticizes my meddlesomeness in the behavior of others. But I could only think that I had driven a workingman off his rocker, and that *during* his outburst, *if* O. Fecteau had killed a child, whose fault would it have been? Partly mine, I think.

In modern times, in my opinion, either everything is a moral question or there are no more moral questions. Nowadays, there are no compromises or there are only compromises. Never influenced, I keep my vigil. There is no letting up.

*Don't say anything*, Helen told herself. Go kiss him and rub against him; get him upstairs as fast as you can, and talk about the damn story later. *Much* later, she warned herself. But she knew he wouldn't let her.

The dishes were done and he sat across the table from her.

She tried her nicest smile and told him, "I want to go to bed with you."

"You don't like it?" he asked.

"Let's talk in bed," she said.

"Goddamn it, Helen," he said. "It's the first thing I've finished in a long time. I want to know what you think of it."

She bit her lip and took her glasses off; she had not made a single mark with her red pencil. "I love you," she said.

"Yes, yes," he said, impatiently. "I love you, too, but we can *fuck* anytime. What about the *story?*" And she finally relaxed; she felt he had released her, somehow. *I tried,* she thought; she felt hugely relieved.

"Fuck the story," she said. "No, I *don't* like it. And I don't want to talk about it, either. You don't care to regard what *I* want, obviously. You're like a little boy at the dinner table—you serve yourself first."

"You don't like it?" Garp said.

"Oh, it's not *bad,*" she said, "it's just not much of anything. It's a trifle, it's a little ditty. If you're warming up to something, I'd like to see what it is—when you get to it. But this is nothing, you must know that. It's a toss-off, isn't it? You can do tricks like this with your left hand, can't you?"

"It's *funny,* isn't it?" Garp asked.

"Oh, it's *funny,*" she said, "but it's funny like *jokes* are funny. It's all one-liners. I mean, what *is* it? A self-parody? You're not old enough, and you haven't written enough, to start mocking yourself. It's self-serving, it's self-justifying; and it's not about anything except yourself, really. It's cute."

"Son of a bitch," said Garp. *"Cute?"*

"You're always talking about people who write well but don't have anything to say," Helen said. "Well, what do you call this? It's no 'Grillparzer,' certainly; it isn't worth a fifth of what 'Grillparzer' is worth. It isn't worth a *tenth* of that story," Helen said.

" 'The Pension Grillparzer' is the first big thing I wrote," Garp said. "This is completely different; it's another kind of fiction altogether."

"Yes, one is about something and one is about nothing," Helen said. "One is about people and one is about only *you*. One has mystery *and* precision, and one has only wit." When Helen's critical faculties were engaged, they were difficult to disengage.

"It's not fair to compare them," Garp said. "I know this is *smaller*."

"Then let's not talk anymore about it," Helen said.

Garp sulked for a minute.

"You didn't like the *Second Wind of the Cuckold*, either," he said, "and I don't suppose you'll like the next one any better."

*"What* next one?" Helen asked him. "Are you writing another novel?"

He sulked some more. She *hated* him, making her do this to him, but she wanted him and she knew she loved him, too.

"Please," she said. "Let's go to bed."

But now he saw *his* chance for a little cruelty—and/ or a little truth—and his eyes shone at her brightly.

"Let's not say another word," she begged him. "Let's go to bed."

"You think 'The Pension Grillparzer' is the best thing I've written, don't you?" he asked her. He knew already what she thought of the second novel, and he knew that, despite Helen's fondness for *Procrastination*, a first novel is a first novel. Yes, she *did* think "Grillparzer" was his best.

"So far, yes," she said, softly. "You're a *lovely* writer, you *know* I think so."

"I guess I just haven't lived up to my potential," Garp said, nastily.

"You will," she said; the sympathy and her love for him were draining from her voice.

They stared at each other; Helen looked away. He started upstairs. "Are you coming to bed?" he asked. His back was to her; his intentions were hidden from her—his feelings for her, too: either hidden from her or buried in his infernal *work*.

"Not right now," she said.

He waited on the stairs. "Got something to *read?*" he asked.

"No, I'm through reading for a while," she said.

Garp went upstairs. When she came up to him, he was already asleep, which made her despair. If he'd had her on his mind at all, how *could* he have fallen asleep? But, actually, he'd had so much on his mind, he'd been confused; he had fallen asleep because he was bewildered. If he'd been able to focus his feelings on any *one* thing, he'd still have been awake when she came upstairs. They might have saved a lot of things, then.

As it was, she sat beside him on the bed and watched his face with more fondness than she thought she could stand. She saw he had a hard-on, as severe as if he *had* been waiting up for her, and she took him into her mouth and sucked him softly until he came.

He woke up, surprised, and he was very guilty-looking—when he appeared to realize where he was, and with whom. Helen, however, was not in the least guilty-looking; she looked only sad. Garp would think, later, that it was as if Helen had *known* he had been dreaming of Mrs. Ralph.

When he came back from the bathroom, she was asleep. She had quickly drifted off. Guiltless at last, Helen felt freed to have her dreams. Garp lay awake beside her, watching the astonishing innocence upon her face—until the children woke her.

# 13

❊⊱◈⊰❊⊱◈⊰❊⊱◈⊰❊

# Walt Catches Cold

**W**HEN Walt caught colds, Garp slept badly. It was as if he were trying to breathe for the boy, and for himself. Garp would get up in the night to kiss and nuzzle the child; anyone seeing Garp would have thought that he could make Walt's cold go away by catching it himself.

"Oh, God," Helen said. "It's just a cold. Duncan had colds all winter when he was five." Nearing eleven, Duncan seemed to have outgrown colds; but Walt, at five, was fully in the throes of cold after cold—or it was one long cold that went away and came back. By the March mud season, Walt's resistance struck Garp as altogether gone; the child hacked himself and Garp awake each night with a wet, wrenching cough. Garp sometimes fell asleep listening to Walt's chest, and he would wake up, frightened, when he could no longer hear the thump of the boy's heart; but the child had merely pushed his father's heavy head off his chest so that he could roll over and sleep more comfortably.

Both the doctor and Helen told Garp, "It's just a cough."

But the imperfection in Walt's nightly breathing

scared Garp right out of his sleep. He was usually awake, therefore, when Roberta called; the late-night anguish of the large and powerful Ms. Muldoon was no longer frightening to Garp—he had come to expect it— but Garp's own fretful sleeplessness made Helen short-tempered.

"If you were back at work, on a book, you'd be too tired to lie awake half the night," she said. It was his imagination that was keeping him up, Helen told him; one sign that he hadn't been writing enough, Garp knew, was when he had too much imagination left over for other things. For example, the onslaught of dreams: Garp now dreamed *only* of horrors happening to his children.

In a dream, there was one horror that took place while Garp was reading a pornographic magazine. He was just looking at the same picture, over and over again; the picture was very pornographic. The wrestlers on the university team, with whom Garp occasionally worked out, had a peculiar vocabulary for such pictures. This vocabulary, Garp noted, had not changed since his days at Steering, when the wrestlers on Garp's team spoke of such pictures in the same fashion. What had changed was the increased availability of the pictures, but the names were the same.

The picture Garp looked at in the dream was considered among the highest in the rankings of pornographic pictures. Among pictures of naked women, there were names for how much you could see. If you could see the pubic hair, but not the sex parts, that was called a bush shot—or just a bush. If you could see the sex parts, which were sometimes partially hidden by the hair, that was a beaver; a beaver was better than just a bush; a beaver was the whole thing: the hair and the parts. If the parts were *open,* that was called a *split* beaver. And if the whole thing *glistened,* that was the best of all, in the world of pornography: that was a wet, split beaver. The wetness implied that the woman was not only naked and exposed and open, but she was also *ready*.

In his dream, Garp was looking at what the wrestlers called a wet, split beaver when he heard children crying. He did not know whose children they were, but Helen and his mother, Jenny Fields, were with them; they all came down the stairs and filed past him, where he struggled to hide from them what he'd been looking at. They had been upstairs and something terrible had awakened them; they were on their way farther downstairs—going to the basement as if the basement were a bomb shelter. And with that thought, Garp heard the dull *crump* of bombing—he noted the crumbling plaster, he saw the flickering lights—and he grasped the terror of what was approaching them. The children, two by two, marched whimpering after Helen and Jenny, who led them to the bomb shelter as soberly as nurses. If they looked at Garp at all, they regarded him with vague sadness and with scorn, as if he had let them all down and was powerless to help them now.

Perhaps he had been looking at the wet, split beaver instead of watching for enemy planes? This, true to the nature of dreams, was forever unclear: precisely *why* he felt so guilty, and *why* they looked at him as if they'd been so abused.

At the end of the line of children were Walt and Duncan, holding hands; the so-called buddy system, as it is employed at summer camps, appeared in Garp's dream to be the natural reaction to a disaster among children. Little Walt was crying, the way Garp had heard him cry when he was caught in the grip of a nightmare, unable to wake up. "I'm having a bad dream," he sniveled. He looked at his father and almost shouted to him, "I'm having a bad dream!"

But in Garp's dream, Garp could not wake the child from *this* one. Duncan looked stoically over his shoulder at his father, a silent and bravely doomed expression on his beautiful young face. Duncan was appearing very grown-up lately. Duncan's look was a secret between

Duncan and Garp: that they both knew it was *not* a dream, and that Walt could not be helped.

"Wake me up!" Walt cried, but the long file of children was disappearing into the bomb shelter. Twisting in Duncan's grip (Walt came to about the height of Duncan's elbow), Walt looked back at his father. "I'm having a *dream!*" Walt screamed, as if to convince himself. Garp could do nothing; he said nothing; he made no attempt to follow them—down these last stairs. And the dropping plaster coated everything white. The bombs kept falling.

"You're having a dream!" Garp screamed after little Walt. "It's just a bad dream!" he cried, though he knew he was lying.

Then Helen would kick him and he'd wake up.

Perhaps Helen feared that Garp's run-amuck imagination would turn away from Walt and turn on her. Because if Garp had given half the worry to Helen that he seemed compelled to give to Walt, Garp might have realized that something was going on.

Helen thought she was in control of what was going on; she at least had controlled how it began (opening her office door, as usual, to the slouching Michael Milton, and bidding him enter her room). Once inside, she closed the door behind him and kissed him quickly on the mouth, holding his slim neck so that he couldn't even escape for breath, and grinding her knee between his legs; he kicked over the wastebasket and dropped his notebook.

"There's nothing more to discuss," Helen said, taking a breath. She raced her tongue across his upper lip; Helen was trying to decide if she liked his mustache. She decided she liked it; or, at least, she liked it for now. "We'll go to your apartment. Nowhere else," she told him.

"It's across the river," he said.

"I know where it is," she said. "Is it clean?"

"Of course," he said. "And it's got a great view of the river."

"I don't care about the view," Helen said. "I want it clean."

"It's pretty clean," he said. "I can clean it better."

"We can only use your car," she said.

"I don't have a car," he said.

"I know you don't," Helen said. "You'll have to get one."

He was smiling now; he'd been surprised, but now he was feeling sure of himself again. "Well, I don't have to get one *now*, do I?" he asked, nuzzling his mustache against her neck; he touched her breasts. Helen unattached herself from his embrace.

"Get one whenever you want," she said. "We'll never use mine, and I won't be seen walking with you all over town, or riding on the buses. If *any*one knows about this, it's over. Do you understand?" She sat down at her desk, and he did not feel invited to walk around her desk to touch her; he sat in the chair her students usually sat in.

"Sure, I understand," he said.

"I love my husband and will never hurt him," Helen told him. Michael Milton knew better than to smile.

"I'll get a car, right away," he said.

"And clean your apartment, or *have* it cleaned," she said.

"Absolutely," he said. Now he dared to smile, a little. "What kind of car do you want me to get?" he asked her.

"I don't care about that," she told him. "Just get one that runs; get one that isn't in the garage all the time. And don't get one with bucket seats. Get one with a long seat in front." He looked more surprised and puzzled than ever, so she explained to him: "I want to be able to lie down, comfortably, across the front seat," she said. "I'll put my head in your lap so that no one will see me sitting up beside you. Do you understand?"

"Don't worry," he said, smiling again.

"It's a small town," Helen said. "No one must know."

"It's not *that* small a town," Michael Milton said, confidently.

"Every town is a small town," Helen said, "and this one is smaller than you think. Do you want me to tell you?"

"Tell me what?" he asked her.

"You're sleeping with Margie Tallworth," Helen said. "She's in my Comp. Lit. 205; she's a junior," Helen said. "And you see another *very* young undergraduate —she's in Dirkson's English 150; I think she's a *freshman,* but I don't know if you've slept with her. Not for lack of trying, if you haven't," Helen added. "To my knowledge you've not touched any of your fellow graduate students; not yet," Helen said. "But there's surely someone I've missed, or there *has* been."

Michael Milton was both sheepish and proud at the same time, and the usual command he held over his expressions escaped him so completely that Helen didn't like the expression she saw on his face and she looked away.

*"That's* how small this town, and every town, is," Helen said. "If you have me," she told him, "you can't have any of those others. I know what young girls notice, and I know how much they're inclined to *say."*

"Yes," Michael Milton said; he appeared ready to take notes.

Helen suddenly thought of something, and she looked momentarily startled. "You *do* have a driver's license?" she asked.

"Oh yes!" Michael Milton said. They both laughed, and Helen relaxed again; but when he came around her desk to kiss her, she shook her head and waved him back.

"And you won't ever touch me here," she said. "There will be nothing intimate in this office. I don't lock my door. I don't even like to have it shut. Please open it, now," she asked him, and he did as he was told.

He got a car, a huge Buick Roadmaster, the *old* kind of station wagon—with real wooden slats on the side.

It was a 1951 Buick Dynaflow, heavy and shiny with pre-Korea chrome and real oak. It weighed 5,550 pounds, or almost three tons. It held seven quarts of oil and nineteen gallons of gasoline. Its original price was $2,850 but Michael Milton picked it up for less than six hundred dollars.

"It's a straight-eight cylinder, three-twenty cubic, power steering, with a single-throat Carter carb," the salesman told Michael. "It's not too badly rusted."

In fact, it was the dull, inconspicuous color of clotted blood, more than six feet wide and seventeen feet long. The front seat was so long and deep that Helen could lie across it, almost without having to bend her knees— or without having to put her head in Michael Milton's lap, though she did this anyway.

She did not put her head in his lap because she *had* to; she liked her view of the dashboard, and being close to the old smell of the maroon leather of the big, slick seat. She put her head in his lap because she liked feeling Michael's leg stiffen and relax, his thigh shifting just slightly between the brake and the accelerator. It was a quiet lap to put your head in because the car had no clutch; the driver needed to move just one leg, and just occasionally. Michael Milton thoughtfully carried his loose change in his left front pocket, so there were only the soft wales of his corduroy slacks, which made a faint impression on the skin of Helen's cheek—and sometimes his rising erection would touch her ear, or reach up into the hair on the back of her neck.

Sometimes she imagined taking him into her mouth while they drove across town in the big car with the gaping chrome grille like the mouth of a feeding fish— *Buick Eight* in script across the teeth. But that, Helen knew, would not be safe.

The first indication that the whole thing might not be safe was when Margie Tallworth dropped Helen's Comp. Lit. 205, without so much as a note of explanation concerning what she might not have liked about the course. Helen feared it was not the course that Margie hadn't liked, and she called the young Miss Tallworth into her office to ask her for an explanation.

Margie Tallworth, a junior, knew enough about school to know that no explanation was required; up to a certain point in any semester, a student was free to drop any course without the instructor's permission. "Do I have to have a reason?" the girl asked Helen, sullenly.

"No, you don't," Helen said. "But if you *had* a reason, I just wanted to hear it."

"I don't have to have a reason," Margie Tallworth said. She held Helen's gaze longer than most students could hold it; then she got up to leave. She was pretty and small and rather well dressed for a student, Helen thought. If there was any consistency to Michael Milton's former girl friend and his present taste, it appeared only that he liked women to wear nice clothes.

"Well, I'm sorry it didn't work out," Helen said, truthfully, as Margie was leaving; she was still fishing for what the girl might actually *know*.

She knew, Helen thought, and quickly accused Michael.

"You've blown it already," she told him coldly, because she *could* speak coldly to him—over the phone. "Just *how* did you drop Margie Tallworth?"

"Very gently," Michael Milton said, smugly. "But a drop is a drop, no matter how different the ways of doing it are." Helen did not appreciate it when he attempted to instruct her—except sexually; she indulged the boy that, and he seemed to need to be dominant there. That was different for her, and she didn't really mind. He was sometimes rough, but not ever dangerous, she thought; and if she firmly resisted something, he stopped. Once she had had to tell him, "No! I don't like that, I won't do that." But she had added, "Please," because she wasn't *that* sure of him. He had stopped; he had been forceful with her, but in another way—in a way that was all right with her. It was exciting that she couldn't trust him completely. But not trusting him to

344

be *silent* was another matter; if she knew he had talked about her, that would be that.

"I didn't tell her anything," Michael insisted. "I said, 'Margie, it's all over,' or something like that. I didn't even tell her there was another woman, and I *certainly* said nothing about you."

"But she's probably heard you talk about me, before," Helen said. "Before this started, I mean."

"She never liked your course, anyway," Michael said. "We *did* talk about that once."

"She never liked the course?" Helen said. This truly surprised her.

"Well, she's not very bright," Michael said, impatiently.

"She'd better not know," Helen said. "I mean it: you better find out."

But he found out nothing. Margie Tallworth refused to speak to him. He tried to tell her, on the phone, that it was all because an old girl friend had come back to him—she had arrived from out of town; she'd had no place to stay; one thing had led to another. But Margie Tallworth had hung up on him before he could polish the story.

Helen smoked a little more. She watched Garp anxiously for a few days—and once she felt actual guilt, when she made love to Garp; she felt guilty that she had made love to him not because she wanted to but because she wanted to reassure him, *if* he had been thinking that anything was wrong.

He hadn't been thinking, not much. Or: he *had* thought, but only once, about the bruises on the small, tight backs of Helen's thighs; though he was strong, Garp was a very gentle man with his children and his wife. He also knew what fingermark bruises looked like because he was a wrestler. It was a day or so later that he noticed the same small fingermark bruises on the backs of Duncan's arms—just where Garp held him when Garp wrestled with the boy—and Garp concluded that he gripped the people he loved harder than he meant to.

He concluded that the fingermarks on Helen were also his.

He was too vain a man to be easily jealous. And the name he had woken with—on his lips, one morning —had eluded him. There were no more papers by Michael Milton around the house, keeping Helen up at night. In fact, she was going to bed earlier and earlier; she needed her rest.

As for Helen, she developed a fondness for the bare, sharp shaft of the Volvo's stick shift; its bite at the end of the day, driving home from her office, felt good against the heel of her hand, and she often pressed against it until she felt it was only a hair away from the pressure necessary to break her skin. She could bring tears to her eyes, this way, and it made her feel clean again, when she arrived home—when the boys would wave and shout at her, from the window where the TV was; and when Garp would announce what dinner he had prepared for them all, when Helen walked into the kitchen.

Margie Tallworth's possible knowledge had frightened Helen, because although Helen had said to Michael— and to herself—that it would be over the instant anyone knew, Helen now knew that it would be more difficult to end than she had first imagined. She hugged Garp in his kitchen and hoped for Margie Tallworth's ignorance.

Margie Tallworth *was* ignorant, but she was not ignorant of Michael Milton's relationship with Helen. She was ignorant of many things but she knew about that. She was ignorant in that she thought her own shallow infatuation with Michael Milton had "surpassed," as she would say, "the sexual"; whereas, she assumed, Helen was merely amusing herself with Michael. In truth, Margie Tallworth had absolutely *wallowed* in, as she would say, "the sexual"; it is difficult, in fact, to know what *else* her relationship with Michael Milton had been about. But she was not altogether wrong in assuming that this was what Helen's relation-

ship with Michael Milton was also about. Margie Tallworth was ignorant in that she assumed too much, too
much of the time; but in this case she had assumed cor-
rectly.

Back when Michael Milton and Helen were actually
talking about Michael's "work," Margie assumed—even
then—that they were fucking. Margie Tallworth did not
believe there was another kind of relationship that one
could have with Michael Milton. In this one way, she
was not ignorant. She may have known the kind of relationship Helen had with Michael before Helen knew
it herself.

And through the one-way glass of the fourth-floor
ladies' room, in the English and Literature Building, it
was possible for Margie Tallworth to look through the
tinted windshield of the three-ton Buick, gliding like
the coffin of a king out of the parking lot. Margie could
see Mrs. Garp's slender legs stretched along the long
front seat. It was a peculiar way to ride in a car with
other than the best of friends.

Margie knew their habits better than she understood
her own; she took long walks, to try to forget Michael
Milton, and to familiarize herself with the whereabouts
of Helen's house. She was soon familiar with the habits
of Helen's husband, too, because Garp's habits were
much more constant than *any*one's: he padded back
and forth, from room to room, in the mornings; perhaps
he was out of a job. That fitted Margie Tallworth's assumptions of the likely cuckold: a man who was out of
work. At midday he burst out the door in track clothes
and ran away; miles later, he returned and read his
mail, which nearly always came when he was gone. Then
he padded back and forth in the house again; he undressed, in pieces, on the way to the shower, and he
was slow to dress when he was out of the shower. One
thing did not fit her image of the cuckold: Garp had
a good body. And why did he spend so much time in
the kitchen? Margie Tallworth wondered if perhaps he
was an unemployed cook.

Then his children came home and they broke Margie Tallworth's soft little heart. He looked quite nice when he played with his children, which also fitted Margie's assumptions of what a cuckold was like: someone who had witless good fun with his children while his wife was out getting *planked*. "Planked" was also a word that the wrestlers Garp knew used, and they had used it back at those blood-and-blue days at Steering, too. Someone was always bragging about planking a wet, split beaver.

So one day, when Garp burst out the door in his track clothes, Margie Tallworth waited only as long as it took him to run away; then she went up on the Garps' porch with a perfumed note, which she intended to drop in his mail. She had thought very carefully that he would have time to read the note and (hopefully) recover himself before his children came home. This was how she assumed such news was absorbed: suddenly! Then there was a reasonable period of recovery and one got ready to face the children. Here was another case of something Margie Tallworth was ignorant of.

The note itself had given her trouble because she was not good with words. And it was perfumed not by intention but simply because every piece of paper Margie Tallworth owned was perfumed; if she had thought about it, she would have realized perfume was inappropriate to this note, but that was another of the things she was ignorant of. Even her schoolwork was perfumed; when Helen had read Margie Tallworth's first essay for Comp. Lit. 205, she had cringed at its *scent*.

What Margie's note to Garp said was:

*Your Wife Is "Involved with" Michael Milton*

Margie Tallworth would grow up to be the sort of person who said that someone "passed away" instead of died. Thus she sought delicacy with the words that Helen was "involved with" Michael Milton. And she had this sweetly smelling note in her hand, and she was poised on the Garps' porch with it, when it began to rain.

Nothing made Garp turn back from a run faster than rain. He hated getting his running shoes wet. He would run in the cold, and run in the snow, but when it rained, Garp ran home, swearing, and cooked for an hour in a foul-weather mood. Then he put on a poncho and caught the bus to the gym in time for wrestling practice. On the way, he picked up Walt from day care and took Walt to the gym with him; he called home when he got to the gym to see if Duncan was back from school. Sometimes he gave Duncan instructions, if the meal was still cooking, but usually he just cautioned Duncan about riding his bike and he quizzed him about emergency phone numbers: did Duncan know what to dial in case of fire, explosion, armed robbery, mayhem in the streets?

Then he wrestled, and after practice he popped Walt into the shower with himself; by the time he called home again, Helen was there to come pick them up.

Therefore, Garp did not like rain; although he enjoyed wrestling, rain complicated his simple plans. And Margie Tallworth was unprepared to see him suddenly panting and angry behind her on the porch.

"Aaahhh!" she cried; she clutched her scented note as tightly as if it were the main artery of an animal whose blood flow she wished she could *stop*.

"Hello," said Garp. She looked like a baby-sitter to him. He had trained himself off baby-sitters some time ago. He smiled at her with frank curiosity—that is all.

"Aaa," said Margie Tallworth; she couldn't speak. Garp looked at the crushed message in her hand; she shut her eyes and held the note out to him, as if she were putting her hand into a fire.

If at first Garp had thought she was one of Helen's students, wanting something, now he thought something else. He saw that she couldn't speak, and he saw the extreme self-consciousness of her handing him the note.

Garp's experience with speechless women who handed out notes self-consciously was limited to Ellen Jamesians, and he suppressed a momentary flame of anger—that another creepy Ellen Jamesian was introducing herself to him. Or had she come to bait him about something—the reclusive son of the exciting Jenny Fields?

*Hi! I'm Margie. I'm an Ellen Jamesian,*

her stupid note would say.

*Do You Know What an Ellen Jamesian Is?*

The next thing you know, Garp thought, they'll be organized like the religious morons who bring those righteous pamphlets about Jesus to one's very door. It sickened him, for example, that the Ellen Jamesians were now reaching girls as young as this one; she was too young to know, he thought, whether she wanted a tongue in her life or not. He shook his head and waved the note away.

"Yes, yes, I know, I know," Garp said. "So what?"

Poor Margie Tallworth was unprepared for this. She had come like an avenging angel—her terrible duty, and what a burden it was to her!—to bring the bad news that somehow must be made known. But he *knew* already! And he didn't even care.

She clutched her note in both hands, so tightly to her pretty, trembling breasts that more of the perfume was *expressed* from it—or from *her*—and a wave of her young-girl smell passed over Garp, who stood glaring at her.

"I said, 'So what?'" Garp said. "Do you actually expect me to have respect for someone who cuts her own tongue off?"

Margie forced a word out. "What?" she said; she was frightened now. *Now* she guessed why the poor man

350

padded around his house all day, out of work: he was insane.

Garp had distinctly heard the word; it was not a gagged "Aaahhh" or even a little "Aaa"—it was not the word of an amputated tongue. It was a whole word.

"What?" he said.

"What?" she said, again.

He stared at the note she held against herself.

"You can *talk?*" he said.

"Of course," she croaked.

"What's *that?*" he asked, and pointed to her note. But now she was afraid of him—an insane cuckold. God knows what he might do. Murder the children, or murder her; he looked strong enough to murder Michael Milton with one arm. And every man looked evil when he was questioning you. She backed away from him, off the porch.

"Wait!" Garp cried. "Is that a note for *me?* What *is* that? Is it something for Helen? Who are you?"

Margie Tallworth shook her head. "It's a mistake," she whispered, and when she turned to flee, she collided with the wet mailman, spilling his bag and knocking herself back into Garp. Garp had a vision of Duna, the senile bear, bowling a mailman down a Viennese staircase—outlawed forever. But all that happened to Margie Tallworth was that she fell to the floor of the porch; her stockings tore and she skinned one knee.

The mailman, who assumed he'd arrived at an awkward moment, fumbled for Garp's mail among his strewn letters, but Garp was now only interested in what message the crying girl had for him. "What *is* it?" he asked her, gently; he tried to help her to her feet, but she wanted to sit where she was. She kept sobbing.

"I'm sorry," Margie Tallworth said. She had lost her nerve; she had spent a minute too long around Garp, and now that she thought she rather *liked* him, it was hard for her to imagine giving him this news.

"Your knee's not too bad," Garp said, "but let me get something to clean you up." He went inside for

351

antiseptic for her cut, and bandages, but she took this opportunity to limp away. She could not face him with this news, but she could not withhold it from him, either. She left her note for him. The mailman watched her hobble down the side street toward the corner where the buses stopped; he wondered briefly what the Garps were up to. They seemed to get more mail than other families, too.

It was all those letters Garp wrote, which poor John Wolf, his editor, struggled to answer. And there were copies of books to review; Garp gave them to Helen, who at least read them. There were Helen's magazines; it seemed to Garp there were a great many. There were Garp's two magazines, his only subscriptions: *Gourmet* and *Amateur Wrestling News*. There were, of course, bills. And a letter rather frequently from Jenny; it was all she wrote these days. And a letter now and then, short and sweet, from Ernie Holm.

Sometimes Harry Fletcher wrote them both, and Alice still wrote with exquisite fluency, about nothing at all, to Garp.

And now among the usual was a note, reeking of perfume and wet with tears. Garp put down the bottle of antiseptic and the bandages; he did not bother to look for the girl. He held the crumpled note and thought he knew, more or less, what it would be about.

He wondered why he hadn't thought of it before, because there were so many things that pointed to it; now that he thought of it, he supposed he *had* thought of it before, only not quite this consciously. The slow unwrapping of the note—so it wouldn't tear—made sounds as crisp as autumn, though all around Garp it was a cold March, the hurt ground thawing to mud. The little note snapped like bones as he opened it. With the escaping perfume, Garp imagined he could still hear the girl's sharp little yelp: *"What?"*

He knew "what"; what he *didn't* know was "with whom"—that name, which had kicked around in his mind, one morning, but then was gone. The note, of course, would provide him with the name: Michael Milton. It sounded to Garp like a special kind of new ice cream at that shop he took the boys to. There was Strawberry Swirl, Chock-full of Chocolate, Mocha Madness, and Michael Milton. It was a *disgusting* name—a flavor Garp could taste—and Garp tramped to the storm sewer and wadded the vile-smelling note into pieces and stuffed them through the grate. Then he went inside the house and read the name in a phone book, over and over again.

It seemed to him now that Helen had been "involved with" someone for a long time; it seemed that he had known it for some time, too. But the *name!* Michael Milton! Garp had classified him—to Helen—at a party where Garp had been introduced to him. Garp had told Helen that Michael Milton was a "wimp"; they had discussed his mustache. Michael Milton! Garp read the name so many times, he was still peering into the phone book when Duncan got home from school and assumed that his father was once more searching a directory for his make-believe people.

"Didn't you get Walt yet?" Duncan asked.

Garp had forgotten. And Walt has a cold, too, Garp thought. The boy shouldn't have to wait for me, with a *cold*.

"Let's go get him together," Garp said to Duncan. To Duncan's surprise, Garp threw the phone book into the trash barrel. Then they walked to the bus stop.

Garp was still in his track clothes, and it was still raining; Duncan found this odd, too, but he didn't say anything about it. He said, "I got two goals today." For some reason, all they played at Duncan's school was soccer—fall, winter, and spring, they played only soccer. It was a small school, but there was another reason for all the soccer; Garp forgot what it was. He had never liked the reason, anyway. "Two goals," Duncan repeated.

"That's great," Garp said.

"One was a header," Duncan said.

"With your head?" Garp said. "That's wonderful."

"Ralph gave me a perfect pass," Duncan said.

"That's *still* wonderful," Garp said. "And good for Ralph." He put his arm around Duncan, but he knew Duncan would be embarrassed if he tried to kiss him; it is Walt who lets me kiss him, Garp thought. Then he thought of kissing Helen and almost stepped in front of the bus.

"Dad!" Duncan said. And in the bus he asked his father, "Are you okay?"

"Sure," Garp said.

"I thought you'd be up at the wrestling room," Duncan said. "It *is* raining."

From Walt's day care you could look across the river and Garp tried to place the exact location, there, of Michael Milton's address, which he had memorized from the phone book.

"Where were you?" Walt complained. He coughed; his nose dripped; he felt hot. He expected to go wrestling whenever it rained.

"Why don't we *all* go to the wrestling room, as long as we're downtown?" Duncan said. He was increasingly logical, but Garp said no, he didn't want to wrestle today. "Why not?" Duncan wanted to know.

"Because he's got his running stuff on, dummy," Walt said.

"Oh, shut up, Walt," Duncan said. They more or less fought on the bus, until Garp told them they couldn't. Walt was sick, Garp reasoned, and fighting was bad for his cold.

"I'm not sick," Walt said.

"Yes, you are," Garp said.

"Yes, you are," Duncan teased.

"Shut up, Duncan," Garp said.

"Boy, you're in a great mood," Duncan said, and Garp wanted to kiss him; Garp wished to assure Duncan that he wasn't really in a bad mood, but kissing embarrassed Duncan, so Garp kissed Walt instead.

"Dad!" Walt complained. "You're all wet and sweaty."

"Because he's got his running stuff on, dummy," Duncan said.

"He called me a dummy," Walt told Garp.

"I heard him," Garp said.

"I'm not a dummy," Walt said.

"Yes, you are," Duncan said.

"Shut up, both of you," Garp said.

"Dad's in a great mood, isn't he, Walt?" Duncan asked his brother.

"Sure is," Walt said, and they decided to tease their father, instead of fight among themselves, until the bus deposited them—a few blocks from the house in the increasing rain. They were a soggy threesome when they were still a block from home, and a car that had been going too fast slowed suddenly beside them; the window was rolled down, after a struggle, and in the steamy interior Garp saw the frazzled, glistening face of Mrs. Ralph. She grinned at them.

"You seen Ralph?" she asked Duncan.

"Nope," Duncan said.

"The moron doesn't know enough to come out of the rain," she said. "I guess *you* don't, either," she said sweetly, to Garp; she was still grinning and Garp tried to smile back at her, but he couldn't think of anything to say. He must have had poor control of his expression, he suspected, because Mrs. Ralph wouldn't usually pass up the opportunity to go on teasing him in the rain. Yet, instead, she looked suddenly shocked by Garp's ghastly smile; she rolled her window back up.

"See ya," she called, and drove off. Slowly.

"See ya," Garp mumbled after her; he admired the woman but he was thinking that maybe even *this* horror would eventually come to pass: that he *would* see Mrs. Ralph.

In the house he gave Walt a hot bath, slipping into the tub with him—an excuse, which he often took, to

355

wrestle with that little body. Duncan was too big for Garp to fit in the tub with him anymore.

"What's for supper?" Duncan called upstairs.

Garp realized he had forgotten supper.

"I forgot supper," Garp called.

"You *forgot?*" Walt asked him, but Garp dunked Walt in the tub, and tickled him, and Walt fought back and forgot about the issue.

"You forgot *supper?*" Duncan hollered from downstairs.

Garp decided he was not going to get out of the tub. He kept adding more hot water; the steam was good for Walt's lungs, he believed. He would try to keep the child in the tub with him as long as Walt was content to play.

They were still in the bath together when Helen got home.

"Dad forgot supper," Duncan told her immediately.

"He forgot supper?" Helen said.

"He forgot all about it," Duncan said.

"Where *is* he?" Helen asked.

"He's taking a bath with Walt," Duncan said. "They've been taking a bath for *hours.*"

"Heavens," said Helen. "Maybe they've drowned."

"Wouldn't you love *that?*" Garp hollered from his bath, upstairs. Duncan laughed.

"He's in a great mood," Duncan told his mother.

"I can see that he is," Helen said. She put her hand softly on Duncan's shoulder, being careful not to let him know that she was actually leaning on him for support. She felt suddenly unsure of her balance. Poised at the bottom of the stairs, she called up to Garp, "Had a bad day?"

But Garp slipped underwater; it was a gesture of control, because he felt such hatred for her and he didn't want Walt to see it or hear it.

There was no answer and Helen tightened her grip on Duncan's shoulder. Please, *not in front of the children,* she thought. It was a new situation for her—

that she should find herself in the defensive position in a matter of some contention with Garp—and she felt frightened.

"Shall I come up?" she called.

There was still no answer; Garp could hold his breath a long time.

Walt shouted back downstairs to her, "Dad's underwater!"

"Dad is so *weird*," Duncan said.

Garp came up for air just as Walt yelled again, "He's holding his breath!"

I hope so, Helen thought. She didn't know what to do, she couldn't move.

In a minute or so, Garp whispered to Walt, "Tell her I'm *still* underwater, Walt. Okay?"

Walt appeared to think this was a fiendishly clever trick and he yelled downstairs to Helen, "Dad's *still* underwater!"

"Wow," Duncan said. "We should time him. It must be a record."

But now Helen felt panicked. Duncan moved out from under her hand—he was starting up the stairs to see this breath-holding feat—and Helen felt that her legs were lead.

"He's *still* underwater!" Walt shrieked, though Garp was drying Walt with a towel and had already started to drain the tub; they stood naked on the bathmat by the big mirror together. When Duncan came into the bathroom, Garp silenced him by putting a finger to his lips.

"Now, say it *together*," Garp whispered. "On the count of three, 'He's still under!' One, two, three."

"He's *still* under!" Duncan and Walt howled together, and Helen felt her own lungs burst. She felt a scream escape her but no sound emerged, and she ran up the stairs thinking that only her husband could have conceived of such a plot to pay her back: *drowning* himself in front of their children and leaving her to explain to them why he did it.

She ran crying into the bathroom, so surprising Duncan and Walt that she had to recover almost immediately—in order not to frighten them. Garp was naked at the mirror, slowly drying between his toes and watching her in a way she remembered that Ernie Holm had taught his wrestlers how to *look* for openings.

"You're too late," he told her. "I already died. But it's touching, and a little surprising, to see that you *care*."

"We'll talk about this later?" she asked him, hopefully—and smiling, as if it had been a good joke.

"We fooled you!" Walt said, poking Helen on that sharp bone above her hip.

"Boy, if we'd pulled that on *you*," Duncan said to his father, "you'd have really been pissed at us."

"The children haven't eaten," Helen said.

"Nobody's eaten," Garp said. "Unless you have."

"I can wait," she told him.

"So can I," Garp told her.

"I'll get the kids something," Helen offered, pushing Walt out of the bathroom. "There must be eggs, and cereal."

"For *supper?*" Duncan said. "That sounds like a *great* supper," he said.

"I just forgot, Duncan," Garp said.

"I want toast," Walt said.

"You can have toast, too," Helen said.

"Are you sure you can handle this?" Garp asked Helen.

She just smiled at him.

"God, even *I* can handle *toast*," Duncan said. "I think even *Walt* can fix cereal."

"The eggs are tricky," Helen said; she tried to laugh.

Garp went on drying between his toes. When the kids were out of the bathroom, Helen poked her head back in. "I'm sorry, and I love you," Helen said, but he wouldn't look up from his deliberate procedure with the towel. "I never wanted to hurt you," she went on. "How did you find out? I have *never* once stopped thinking of you. Was it that girl?" Helen whispered, but Garp gave all his attention to his toes.

When she had set out food for the children (as if they were *pets!* she would think to herself, later), she went back upstairs to him. He was still in front of the mirror, sitting naked on the edge of the tub.

"He means nothing; he never took anything away from you," she told him. "It's all over now, really it is."

"Since when?" he asked her.

"As of now," she said to Garp. "I just have to tell him."

"*Don't* tell him," Garp said. "Let him guess."

"I can't do that," Helen said.

"There's shell in my egg!" Walt hollered from downstairs.

"My toast is burnt!" Duncan said. They were plotting together to distract their parents from each other—whether they knew it or not. Children, Garp thought, have some instinct for separating their parents when their parents ought to be separated.

"Just eat it!" Helen called to them. "It's not so bad."

She tried to touch Garp but he slipped past her, out of the bathroom; he started to dress.

"Eat up and I'll take you to a movie!" he called to the kids.

"What are you doing that for?" Helen asked him.

"I'm not staying here with you," he said. "We're going out. You call that wimpish asshole and say good-bye."

"He'll want to see me," Helen said, dully—the reality of having it over, now that Garp knew about it, was working on her like Novocain. If she had been sensitive to how much she'd hurt Garp, at first, now her feelings for him were deadening slightly and she was feeling for herself again.

"Tell him to eat his heart out," Garp said. "You won't see him. No last fucks for the road, Helen. Just tell him good-bye. On the phone."

"Nobody said anything about 'last fucks,'" Helen said.

"Use the phone," Garp said. "I'll take the kids out. We'll see a movie. Please have it over with before we come back. You *won't* see him again."

"I won't, I promise," Helen said. "But I *should* see him, just once—to tell him."

"I suppose you feel you've handled this very decently," Garp said.

Helen, to a point, *did* feel so; she didn't say anything. She felt she had never lost sight of Garp and the children during this indulgence; she felt justified in handling it *her* way, now.

"We should talk about this later," she said to him. "Some perspective will be possible, later."

He would have struck her if the children hadn't burst into the room.

"One, two, three," Duncan chanted to Walt.

"The cereal is stale!" Duncan and Walt hollered together.

"Please, boys," Helen said. "Your father and I are having a little fight. Go downstairs."

They stared at her.

"Please," Garp said to them. He turned away from them so they wouldn't see him crying, but Duncan probably knew, and surely Helen knew. Walt probably didn't catch it.

"A fight?" Walt said.

"Come on," Duncan said to him; he took Walt's hand. Duncan pulled Walt out of the bedroom. "Come *on,* Walt," Duncan said, "or we won't get to see the movie."

"Yeah, the movie!" Walt cried.

To his horror, Garp recognized the attitude of their leaving—Duncan leading Walt away, and down the stairs; the smaller boy turning and looking back. Walt waved, but Duncan pulled him on. Down and gone, into the bomb shelter. Garp hid his face in his clothes and cried.

When Helen touched him, he said, "Don't touch me," and went on crying. Helen shut the bedroom door.

"Oh, *don't*," she pleaded. "He isn't worth this; he wasn't *any*thing. I just *enjoyed* him," she tried to explain, but Garp shook his head violently and threw his pants at her. He was still only half dressed—an attitude that was perhaps, Helen realized, the most compromising for men: when they were not one thing and also not another. A woman half dressed seemed to have some power, but a man was simply not as handsome as when he was naked, and not as secure as when he was clothed. "Please get dressed," she whispered to him, and handed him back his pants. He took them, he pulled them on; and went on crying.

"I'll do just what you want," she said.

"You won't see him again?" he said to her.

"No, not once," she said. "Not ever again."

"Walt has a cold," Garp said. "He shouldn't even be going out, but it's not too bad for him at a movie. And we won't be late," he added to her. "Go see if he's dressed warmly enough." She did.

He opened her top drawer, where her lingerie was, and pulled the drawer from the dresser; he pushed his face into the wonderful silkiness and scent of her clothes—like a bear holding a great trough of food in his forepaws, and then losing himself in it. When Helen came back into the room and caught him at this, it was almost as if she'd caught him masturbating. Embarrassed, he brought the drawer down across his knee and cracked it; her underwear flew about. He raised the cracked drawer over his head and smacked it down against the edge of the dresser, snapping what felt like the spine of an animal about the size of the drawer. Helen ran from the room and he finished dressing.

He saw Duncan's fairly well finished supper on Duncan's plate; he saw Walt's uneaten supper on Walt's plate, and on various parts of the table and floor. "If you don't eat, Walt," Garp said, "you'll grow up to be a *wimp*."

"I'm not going to grow up," Walt said.

That gave Garp such a shiver that he turned on Walt and startled the child. "Don't *ever* say that," Garp said.

"I don't *want* to grow up," Walt said.

"Oh, I see," Garp said, softening. "You mean, you *like* being a kid?"

"Yup," Walt said.

"Walt is *so* weird," Duncan said.

"I am *not!*" Walt cried.

"You are so," Duncan said.

"Go get in the car," Garp said. "And stop fighting."

"*You* were fighting," Duncan said, cautiously; no one reacted and Duncan tugged Walt out of the kitchen. "Come on," he said.

"Yeah, the *movie!*" Walt said. They went out.

Garp said to Helen, "He's not to come here, under any circumstances. If you let him in this house, he won't get out alive. And you're not to go out," he said. "Under any circumstances. Please," he added, and he had to turn away from her.

"Oh, darling," Helen said.

"He's such an *asshole!*" Garp moaned.

"It could never be anyone like *you*, don't you see?" Helen said. "It could *only* be someone who wasn't at all like you."

He thought of the baby-sitters and Alice Fletcher, and his inexplicable attraction to Mrs. Ralph, and of course he knew what she meant; he walked out the kitchen door. It was raining outside, and already dark; perhaps the rain would freeze. The mud in the driveway was wet but firm. He turned the car around; then, by habit, he edged the car to the top of the driveway and cut the engine and the lights. Down the Volvo rolled, but he knew the driveway's dark curve by heart. The kids were thrilled by the sound of the gravel and the slick mud in the growing blackness, and when he popped the clutch at the bottom of the driveway, and flicked on the lights, both Walt and Duncan cheered.

"What movie are we going to see?" Duncan asked.

362

"Anything you want," Garp said. They drove downtown to have a look at the posters.

It was cold and damp in the car and Walt coughed; the windshield kept fogging over, which made it hard to see what was playing at the movie houses. Walt and Duncan continued to fight about who got to stand in the gap between the bucket seats; for some reason, this had always been the prime spot in the back seat for them, and they had always fought over who got to stand or kneel there—crowding each other and bumping Garp's elbow when he used the stick shift.

"Get out of there, both of you," Garp said.

"It's the only place you can see," Duncan said.

*"I'm* the only one who has to see," Garp said. "And this defroster is such *junk,"* he added, "that *no* one can see out the windshield anyway."

"Why don't you write the Volvo people?" Duncan suggested.

Garp tried to imagine a letter to Sweden about the inadequacies of the defrost system, but he couldn't sustain the idea for very long. On the floor, in back, Duncan kneeled on Walt's foot and pushed him out of the gap between the bucket seats; now Walt cried *and* coughed.

"I was here first," Duncan said.

Garp downshifted, hard, and the uncovered tip of the stick-shift shaft bit into his hand.

"You see this, Duncan?" Garp asked, angrily. "You see this gearshift? It's like a *spear.* You want to fall on that if I have to stop hard?"

"Why don't you get it fixed?" Duncan asked.

"Get *out* of the goddamn gap between the seats, Duncan!" Garp said.

"The stick shift has been like that for months," Duncan said.

"For *weeks,* maybe," Garp said.

"If it's dangerous, you should get it fixed," Duncan said.

"That's your mother's job," Garp said.

"She says it's *your* job, Dad," Walt said.

"How's your cough, Walt?" Garp asked.

Walt coughed. The wet rattle in his small chest seemed oversized for the child.

"Jesus," Duncan said.

"That's great, Walt," Garp said.

"It's not *my* fault," Walt complained.

"Of course it isn't," Garp said.

"Yes, it is," Duncan said. "Walt spends half his life in *puddles*."

"I do not!" Walt said.

"Look for a movie that looks interesting, Duncan," Garp said.

"I can't see unless I kneel between the seats," Duncan said.

They drove around. The movie houses were all on the same block but they had to drive past them a few times to decide upon *which* movie, and then they had to drive by them a few more times before they found a place to park.

The children chose to see the only film that had a line waiting to see it, extending out from under the cinema marquee along the sidewalk, streaked now with a freezing rain. Garp put his own jacket over Walt's head, so that very quickly Walt resembled some ill-clothed street beggar—a damp dwarf seeking sympathy in bad weather. He promptly stepped in a puddle and soaked his feet; Garp then picked him up and listened to his chest. It was almost as if Garp thought the water in Walt's wet shoes dripped immediately into his little lungs.

"You're so *weird*, Dad," Duncan said.

Walt saw a strange car and pointed it out. The car moved quickly down the soaked street; splashing through the garish puddles, it threw the reflected neon upon itself—a big dark car, the color of clotted blood; it had wooden slats on its sides, and the blond wood glowed in the streetlights. The slats looked like the ribs of the long, lit skeleton of a great fish gliding through moonlight. "Look at that car!" Walt cried.

"Wow, it's a *hearse,*" Duncan said.

"No, Duncan," Garp said. "It's an old Buick. Before your time."

The Buick that Duncan mistook for a hearse was on its way to Garp's house, although Helen had done all she could to discourage Michael Milton from coming.

"I *can't* see you," Helen told him when she called. "It's as simple as that. It's over, just the way I said it would be if he ever found out. I won't hurt him any more than I already have."

"What about me?" Michael Milton said.

"I'm sorry," Helen told him. "But you *knew*. We both knew."

"I want to *see* you," he said. "Maybe tomorrow?"

But she told him that Garp had taken the kids to a movie for the sole purpose that she finish it tonight.

"I'm coming over," he told her.

"Not here, no," she said.

"We'll go for a drive," he told her.

"I can't go out, either," she said.

"I'm coming," Michael Milton said, and he hung up.

Helen checked the time. It would be all right, she supposed, if she could get him to leave quickly. Movies were at least an hour and a half long. She decided she wouldn't let him in the house—not under any circumstances. She watched for the headlights to come up the driveway, and when the Buick stopped—just in front of the garage, like a big ship docking at a dark pier—she ran out of the house and pushed herself against the driver's-side door before Michael Milton could open it.

The rain was turning to a semisoft slush at her feet, and the icy drops were hardening as they fell—they had some sting as they struck her bare neck, when she bent over to speak to him through the rolled-down window.

He immediately kissed her. She tried to lightly peck his cheek but he turned her face and forced his tongue into her mouth. All over again she saw the corny bedroom of his apartment: the poster-sized print above his bed—Paul Klee's *Sinbad the Sailor*. She supposed this was how he saw himself: a colorful adventurer, but sensitive to the beauty of Europe.

Helen pulled back from him and felt the cold rain soak her blouse.

"We can't just *stop*," he said, miserably. Helen couldn't tell if it was the rain through the open window or tears that streaked his face. To her surprise, he had shaved his mustache off, and his upper lip looked slightly like the puckered, undeveloped lip of a child—like Walt's little lip, which looked lovely on Walt, Helen thought; but it wasn't her idea of the lip for a lover.

"What did you do to your mustache?" she asked him.

"I thought you didn't like it," he said. "I did it for you."

"But I *liked* it," she said, and shivered in the freezing rain.

"Please, get in with me," he said.

She shook her head; her blouse clung to her cold skin and her long corduroy skirt felt as heavy as chain mail; her tall boots slipped in the stiffening slush.

"I won't take you anywhere," he promised. "We'll just sit here, in the car. We can't just *stop*," he repeated.

"We knew we'd have to," Helen said. "We knew it was just for a little while."

Michael Milton let his head sink against the glinting ring of the horn; but there was no sound, the big Buick was shut off. The rain began to stick to the windows—the car was slowly being encased in ice.

"Please get *in*," Michael Milton moaned. "I'm not leaving here," he added, sharply. "I'm not afraid of him. I don't have to do what he says."

"It's what *I* say, too," Helen said. "You have to go."

"I'm not going," Michael Milton said. "I know about your husband. I know everything about him."

They had never talked about Garp; Helen had forbidden it. She didn't know what Michael Milton meant.

"He's a minor writer," Michael said, boldly. Helen

looked surprised; to her knowledge, Michael Milton had never read Garp. He'd told her once that he never read living writers; he claimed to value the perspective he said one could gain only when a writer had been dead for a while. It is fortunate that Garp didn't know *this* about him—it would certainly have added to Garp's contempt for the young man. It added somewhat to Helen's disappointment with poor Michael, now.

"My husband is a very good writer," she said softly, and a shiver made her twitch so hard that her folded arms sprang open and she had to fold them closed at her breasts again.

"He's not a *major* writer," Michael declared. "Higgins said so. You certainly must be aware of how your husband is regarded in the department."

Higgins, Helen was aware, was a singularly eccentric and troublesome colleague, who managed at the same time to be dull and cloddish to the point of sleep. Helen hardly felt Higgins was representative of the department—except that like many of her more insecure colleagues, Higgins habitually gossiped to the graduate students about his fellow department members; in this desperate way, perhaps, Higgins felt he gained the students' trust.

"I was not aware that Garp *was* regarded by the department, one way or another," Helen said coolly. "Most of them don't read anything very contemporary."

"Those who do say he's minor," Michael Milton said.

This competitive and pathetic stand did not warm Helen's heart to the boy and she turned to go back inside the house.

"I won't go!" Michael Milton screamed. "I'll *confront* him about us! Right now. He can't tell us what to do."

"*I'm* telling you, Michael," Helen said.

He slumped against the horn and began to cry. She went over and touched his shoulder through the window.

"I'll sit with you a minute," Helen told him. "But you

*must* promise me that you'll leave. I won't have him or my children see this."

He promised.

"Give me the keys," Helen said. His look of baleful hurt—that she didn't trust him not to drive off with her—touched Helen all over again. She put the keys in the deep flap pocket of her long skirt and walked around to the passenger side and let herself in. He rolled up his window, and they sat, not touching, the windows fogging around them, the car creaking under a coat of ice.

Then he completely broke down and told her that she had meant more to him than all of France—and she knew what France had meant to him, of course. She held him, then, and wildly feared how much *time* had passed, or was passing there in the frozen car. Even if it was not a long movie, they must still have a good half hour, or forty-five minutes; yet Michael Milton was nowhere near ready to leave. She kissed him, strongly, hoping this would help, but he only began to fondle her wet, cold breasts. She felt all over as frozen to him as she had felt outside in the hardening sleet. But she let him touch her.

"Dear Michael," she said, thinking all the while.

"How can we stop?" was all he said.

But Helen had already stopped; she was only thinking about how to stop *him*. She shoved him up straight in the driver's position and stretched across the long seat, pulling her skirt back down to cover her knees, and putting her head in his lap.

"Please *remember*," she said. "Please try. This was the nicest part for me—just letting you drive me in the car, when I knew where we were going. Can't you be happy—can't you just remember that, and let it go?"

He sat rigid behind the steering wheel, both hands struggling to stay gripped to the wheel, both thighs tensed under her head, his erection pressing against her ear.

"Please try to just let it go at that, Michael," she

said softly. And they stayed this way a moment, imagining that the old Buick was carrying them to Michael's apartment again. But Michael Milton could not sustain himself on imagination. He let one hand stray to the back of Helen's neck, which he gripped very tightly; his other hand opened his fly.

"Michael!" she said, sharply.

"You said you always wanted to," he reminded her.

"It's *over*, Michael."

"Not yet, it isn't," he said. His penis grazed her forehead, bent her eyelashes, and she recognized that this was the old Michael—the Michael of the apartment, the Michael who occasionally liked to treat her with some *force*. She did not appreciate it now. But if I resist, she thought, there will be a scene. She had only to imagine *Garp* as part of the scene to convince herself that she should avoid *any* scene, at any cost.

"Don't be a bastard, don't be a prick, Michael," she said. "Don't spoil it."

"You always said you wanted to," he said. "But it wasn't safe, you said. Well, now it's safe. The car isn't even moving. There can't be any accidents now," he said.

Oddly, she realized, he had suddenly made it easier for her. She did not feel concerned anymore with letting him down gently; she felt grateful to him that he had helped her to sort her priorities so forcefully. Her priorities, she felt enormously relieved to know, were Garp and her children. Walt shouldn't be out in this weather, she thought, shivering. And Garp was more *major* to her, she knew, than all her minor colleagues and graduate students together.

Michael Milton had allowed her to see himself with what struck Helen as a necessary vulgarity. *Suck him off*, she thought bluntly, putting him into her mouth, and *then* he'll leave. She thought bitterly that men, once they had ejaculated, were rather quick to abandon their demands. And from her brief experience in Michael

Milton's apartment, Helen knew that this would not take long.

Time was also a factor in her decision; there was at least twenty minutes remaining in even the shortest movie they could have gone to see. She set her mind to it as she might have done if it were the last task remaining to a messy business, which might have ended better but could also have turned out worse; she felt slightly proud that she had at least proved to herself that her family *was* her first priority. Even Garp might appreciate this, she thought; but one day, not right away.

She was so determined that she hardly noticed Michael Milton's grip loosen on her neck; he returned both hands to the steering wheel, as if he were actually piloting this experience. Let him think what he wants to think, she thought. She was thinking of her family, and she did not notice that the sleet was now nearly as hard as hail; it rattled off the big Buick like the tapping of countless hammers, driving little nails. And she did not sense the old car groaning and snapping under its thickening tomb of ice.

And she did not hear the telephone, ringing in her warm house. There was too much weather, and other interference, between her house and where she lay.

It was a stupid movie. Typical of the children's taste in films, Garp thought; typical of the taste in a university town. Typical of the entire country. Typical of the *world!* Garp raged, in his heart, and paid more attention to Walt's labored breathing—the thick rivulets of snot from his tiny nose.

"Be careful you don't choke on that popcorn," he whispered to Walt.

"I won't choke," Walt said, never taking his eyes from the giant screen.

"Well, you can't *breathe* very well," Garp complained, "so just don't put too much in your mouth. You might inhale it. You can't breathe through your nose, at all—that's perfectly clear." And he wiped the child's nose again. "Blow," he whispered. Walt blew.

"Isn't this great?" Duncan whispered. Garp felt how hot Walt's snot was; the child must have a temperature of nearly 102°! he thought. Garp rolled his eyes at Duncan.

"Oh, just great, Duncan," Garp said. Duncan had meant the movie.

"You should relax, Dad," Duncan suggested, shaking his head. Oh, I *should,* Garp knew; but he couldn't. He thought of Walt, and what a perfect little ass he had, and strong little legs, and how sweet his sweat smelled when he'd been running and his hair was damp behind his ears. A body that perfect should not be sick, he thought. I should have let *Helen* go out on this miserable night; I should have made her call that twerp from her office—and tell him to put it in his ear, Garp thought. Or in a light socket. And turn on the juice!

I should have called that candy-ass myself, Garp thought. I should have visited him in the middle of the night. When Garp walked up the aisle to see if they had a phone in the lobby, he heard Walt still coughing.

If she hasn't already gotten in touch with him, Garp thought, I'll tell her *not* to keep trying; I'll tell her it's *my* turn. He was at that point in his feelings toward Helen where he felt betrayed but at the same time honestly loved and important to her; he had not had time enough to ponder *how* betrayed he felt—or how much, truly, she had been trying to keep him in her mind. It was a delicate point, between hating her and loving her terribly—also, he was not without sympathy for whatever she'd wanted; after all, he knew, the shoe on the other foot had also been worn (and was certainly thinner). It even seemed unfair, to Garp, that Helen, who had always meant so well, had been caught like this; she was a good woman and she certainly deserved better luck. But when Helen did not answer the phone, this point of delicacy in Garp's feelings toward

371

her quite suddenly escaped him. He felt only rage, and only betrayal.

Bitch! he thought. The phone rang and rang.

She went out, to meet him. Or they're even doing it in our house! he thought—he could hear them saying, "One last time." That puny fink with his pretentious short stories about fragile relationships, which *almost* developed in badly lit European restaurants. (Perhaps someone wore the wrong glove and the moment was lost forever; there was one where a woman decides *not* to, because the man's shirt was too tight at his throat.)

How could Helen have read that crap! And how *could* she have touched that foppish body?

"But the movie isn't half over," Duncan protested. "There's going to be a duel."

"I want to see the duel," Walt said. "What's a duel?"

"We're leaving," Garp told them.

"No!" Duncan hissed.

"Walt's sick," Garp mumbled. "He shouldn't be here."

"I'm not sick," Walt said.

"He's not *that* sick," Duncan said.

"Get out of those seats," Garp told them; he had to grab the front of Duncan's shirt, which made Walt get up and stumble into the aisle first. Duncan, grumbling, scuffed after him.

"What's a *duel?*" Walt asked Duncan.

"It's real neat," Duncan said. "Now you won't ever see it."

"Cut it out, Duncan," Garp said. "Don't be mean."

"*You're* the one who's mean," Duncan said.

"Yeah, Dad," said Walt.

The Volvo was shrouded in ice, the windshield solid with it; there were various scrapers and broken snow brushes and junk of that sort, somewhere in the trunk, Garp supposed. But by March the winter driving had worn out much of this equipment, or the children had played with it and lost it. Garp wasn't going to take the time to clean the windshield, anyway.

"How can you see?" Duncan asked.

"I live here," Garp said. "I don't have to see."

But, in fact, he had to roll down the driver's-side window and stick his face out into the raining sleet, as hard as hail; he drove toward home that way.

"It's *cold*," Walt shivered. "Shut the window!"

"I need it open to see," Garp said.

"I thought you didn't have to see," Duncan said.

"I'm too cold!" Walt cried. Dramatically, he coughed.

But all of this, as Garp saw it, was Helen's fault. She was to blame—for however Walt suffered his cold, or for its growing worse: it was *her* fault. And for Duncan's disappointment in his father, for that unforgivable way in the theater that Garp had grabbed the boy and stood him up out of his seat: *she* was to blame. The bitch with her runt lover!

But at the moment his eyes were teary in the cold wind and the sleet, and he thought to himself how he loved Helen and would *never* be unfaithful to her again—never hurt her like this, he would promise her that.

At the same moment Helen felt her conscience clear. Her love for Garp was very fine. And she sensed that Michael Milton was about to be released; he was exhibiting the familiar signs. The angle that he bent at the waist and the peculiar way he pointed his hips; the straining of that muscle, used for little else, on the inside of his thigh. It's almost over, Helen thought. Her nose touched the cold brass of his belt buckle and the back of her head bumped the bottom of the steering wheel, which Michael Milton gripped as if he expected the three-ton Buick to suddenly leave the ground.

Garp hit the bottom of his driveway at about forty miles per hour. He came off the downhill road in third gear and accelerated just as he exited; he glimpsed how the driveway was glazed with frozen slush, and he worried momentarily that the Volvo might slip on the short uphill curve. He held the car in gear until he felt what grip he had of the road; it was good enough, and he popped the sharp stick shift into neutral—a second before he killed the engine and flicked out the headlights.

They coasted up, into the black rain. It was like that moment when you feel an airplane lift off the runway; the children both cried out in excitement. Garp could feel the children at his elbow, crowding each other for the one favored position in the gap between the bucket seats.

"How can you see *now?*" Duncan asked.

"He doesn't have to see," Walt said. There was a high thrill in Walt's voice, which suggested to Garp that Walt wished to reassure himself.

"I know this by heart," Garp assured them.

"It's like being underwater!" cried Duncan; he held his breath.

"It's like a dream!" said Walt; he reached for his brother's hand.

# 14

## The World According to
## Marcus Aurelius

THAT was how Jenny Fields became a kind of
nurse again; after all her years in her white uniform, nursing the women's movement, Jenny was
appropriately dressed for her role. It was at Jenny's
suggestion that the Garp family moved into the Fields
estate at Dog's Head Harbor. There were many rooms
for Jenny to take care of them in, and there was the
healing sound of the sea, rushing in and out, rinsing
everything clean.

All his life, Duncan Garp would associate the sound
of the sea with his convalescence. His grandmother
would remove the bandage; there was a kind of tidal
irrigation of the hole where Duncan's right eye had
been. His father and mother could not stand the sight of
that empty hole, but Jenny was an old hand at staring
down wounds until they went away. It was with his
grandmother, Jenny Fields, that Duncan would see his
first glass eye. "See?" Jenny said. "It's big and brown;
it's not quite as pretty as your left one, but you just
make sure the girls see your left one first." It was not

a very feminist thing to say, she supposed, but Jenny always said that she was, first and foremost, a nurse.

Duncan's eye was gouged out when he was flung forward between the bucket seats; the uncovered tip of the stick-shift shaft was the first thing to break his fall. Garp's right arm, reaching into the gap between the seats, was too late; Duncan passed under it, putting out his right eye and breaking three fingers of his right hand, which was jammed into the seat-belt release mechanism.

By no one's estimate could the Volvo have been moving faster than twenty-five—at the most, thirty-five—miles per hour, but the collision was astonishing. The three-ton Buick did not yield quite an inch to Garp's coasting car. Inside the Volvo the children were like eggs out of the egg box—loose inside the shopping bag—at the moment of impact. Even inside the Buick, the jolt had surprising ferocity.

Helen's head was flung forward, narrowly missing the steering column, which caught her at the back of her neck. Many wrestlers' children have hardy necks, because Helen's did not break—though she wore a brace for almost six weeks, and her back would bother her the rest of her life. Her right collarbone was broken, perhaps by the rising slam of Michael Milton's knee, and her nose was gashed across the bridge—requiring nine stitches—by what must have been Michael Milton's belt buckle. Helen's mouth was snapped shut with such force that she broke two teeth and required two neat stitches in her tongue.

At first she thought she had bitten her tongue off, because she could feel it swimming in her mouth, which was full of blood; but her head ached so severely that she didn't dare open her mouth, until she had to breathe, and she couldn't move her right arm. She spat what she thought was her tongue into the palm of her left hand. It wasn't her tongue, of course. It was what amounted to three quarters of Michael Milton's penis.

The warm wash of blood over her face felt, to Helen, like gasoline; she began to scream—not for her own

safety, but for Garp's and the children's. She knew what
had hit the Buick. She struggled to get out of Michael
Milton's lap because she had to see what had happened
to her family. She dropped what she thought was her
tongue on the floor of the Buick and with her good
left arm she *punched* Michael Milton, whose lap pinned
her against the steering column. It was only then that
she heard other screams above her own. Michael Milton
was screaming, of course, but Helen heard beyond
him—to the Volvo. That was *Duncan* who was screaming, she was sure, and Helen fought her left arm across
Michael Milton's bleeding lap to the door handle. When
the door opened, she pushed Michael out of the Buick;
she felt incredibly strong. Michael never once corrected
his bent-double, sitting-up position; he lay on his side
in the freezing slush as if he were still in the driver's
seat, though he bellowed and bled like a steer.

When the door light came on in the huge Buick,
Garp could dimly see the gore in the Volvo—Duncan's
steaming face, split with his gaping wail. Garp began to
bellow, too, but his bellow issued forth no louder than
a whimper; his own, odd sound scared him so much
that he tried to talk softly to Duncan. It was then
Garp realized he couldn't talk.

When Garp had flung out his arm to break Duncan's
fall, he had turned almost sideways in the driver's seat
and his face had struck the steering wheel hard
enough to break his jaw and mangle his tongue (twelve
stitches). In the long weeks of Garp's recovery, at Dog's
Head Harbor, it was fortunate for Jenny that she'd
had much experience with Ellen Jamesians, because
Garp's mouth was wired shut and his messages to his
mother were written ones. He sometimes wrote pages
and pages, on the typewriter, which Jenny would then
read aloud to Duncan—because, although Duncan could
read, he was instructed not to strain his remaining eye
more than was necessary. In time, the eye would com-
pensate for the other eye's loss, but Garp had much to
say that was immediate—and no way to say it. When

he sensed that his mother was editing his remarks—to Duncan, and to Helen (to whom he also wrote pages and pages)—Garp would grunt his protest through his wires, holding his sore tongue very still. And Jenny Fields, like the good nurse she was, would wisely move him to a private room.

"This is the Dog's Head Harbor Hospital," Helen said to Jenny once. Although Helen could talk, she said little; she did not have pages and pages to say. She spent most of her convalescence in Duncan's room, reading to the boy, because Helen was a much better reader than Jenny, and there were only two stitches in Helen's tongue. In this period of recovery, Jenny Fields could deal with Garp better than Helen could deal with him.

Helen and Duncan often sat side by side in Duncan's room. Duncan had a fine, one-eyed view of the sea, which he watched all day as if he were a camera. Getting used to having one eye is something like getting used to the world through a camera, there are similarities in depth of field, and in the problems of focus. When Duncan seemed ready to discover this, Helen bought him a camera—a single-lens reflex camera; for Duncan, that kind made the most sense.

It was in this period of time, Duncan Garp would recall, that the thought of being an artist, a painter and a photographer, first occurred to him; he was almost eleven. Although he had been athletic, his one eye would make him (like his father) forever leery of sports involving balls. Even running, he said, he was bothered by the lack of peripheral vision; Duncan claimed it made him clumsy. It was eventually added to Garp's sadness that Duncan did not care for wrestling, either. Duncan spoke in terms of the camera, and he told his father that one of his problems with depth of field included not knowing how far away the mat was. "When I wrestle," he told Garp, "I feel like I'm going downstairs in the dark; I don't know when I get to the bottom until I *feel* it." Garp concluded, of course, that the accident had made Duncan insecure about sports, but Helen pointed out to him that Duncan had always had a certain timidity, a reserve—even though he was good at games, and clearly well coordinated, he'd always had a tendency not to participate. Not as energetically, certainly, as Walt—who was intrepid, who flung his body into every new circumstance with faith and grace and with temerity. Walt, Helen said, was the real athlete between them. After a while, Garp supposed she was right.

"Helen *is* often right, you know," Jenny told Garp one night at Dog's Head Harbor. The context of this remark could have been anything, but it was sometime soon after the accident, because Duncan had his own room, and Helen had her own room, and Garp had *his* own room, and so forth.

Helen is often right, his mother had told him, but Garp looked angry and wrote Jenny a note.

*Not* this *time, Mom,*

said the note, meaning—perhaps—Michael Milton. Meaning: the whole thing.

It was not expressly because of Michael Milton that Helen resigned. The availability of Jenny's big hospital on the ocean, as both Garp and Helen would come to think of it, was a way to leave the unwanted familiarity of their house, and of that driveway.

And in the faculty code of ethics, "moral turpitude" is listed as one ground for revoking tenure—though this never came to debate; sleeping with students was not generally treated too harshly. It might be a hidden reason why a faculty member wasn't given tenure; it would rarely be a reason for revoking someone's tenure. Helen may have supposed that biting off three quarters of a student's penis was fairly high on the scale of conceivable abuse to students. Sleeping with them simply happened, though it was not encouraged;

379

there were many worse ways of evaluating students and categorizing them for life. But amputation of their genitalia was certainly severe, even for bad students, and Helen must have felt inclined to punish herself. So she denied herself the pleasure of continuing at the task she had prepared for, so well, and she removed herself from the arousement that books and their discussion had always meant to her. In her later life, Helen would spare herself considerable unhappiness by refusing to feel guilty; in her later life, the whole business with Michael Milton would more often make her angry than it would make her sad—because she was strong enough to believe that she was a good woman, which she was, who'd been made to suffer disproportionately for a trivial indiscretion.

But at least for a time, Helen would heal herself and her family. Never having had a mother, and having had little chance to use Jenny Fields in that way, Helen submitted to this period of hospitalization at Dog's Head Harbor. She calmed herself by nursing Duncan, and she hoped that Jenny could nurse Garp.

This aura of the hospital was not new to Garp, whose earliest experiences—with fear, with dreams, with sex— had all occurred in the infirmary atmosphere of the old Steering School. He adapted. It helped him that he had to write out what he wanted to say, because this made him careful; it made him reconsider many of the things he might have *thought* he wanted to say. When he saw them written down—these raw thoughts—he realized that he couldn't or shouldn't say them; when he went to revise them, he knew better and threw them away. There was one for Helen, which read:

*Three quarters is not enough.*

He threw it away.

Then he wrote one for Helen that he *did* give to her.

*I don't blame you.*

Later, he wrote another one.

*I don't blame me, either,*

the note said.

*Only in this way can we be whole again,*

Garp wrote to his mother.

And Jenny Fields padded whitely through the salt-damp house, room to room with her nursing ways and Garp's notes. It was all the writing he could manage.

Of course, the house at Dog's Head Harbor was used to recoveries. Jenny's wounded women had gotten hold of themselves there; these sea-smelling rooms had histories of sadnesses outlived. Among them, the sadness of Roberta Muldoon, who had lived there with Jenny through the most difficult periods of her sex reassignment. In fact, Roberta had failed at living alone—and at living with a number of men—and she was back living at Dog's Head Harbor with Jenny again when the Garps moved in.

As the spring warmed up, and the hole that had been Duncan's right eye slowly healed and was less vulnerable to sticking bits of sand, Roberta took Duncan to the beach. It was on the beach that Duncan discovered his depth-of-field problem as it was related to a thrown ball, because Roberta Muldoon tried playing catch with Duncan and very soon hit him in the face with the football. They gave up the ball, and Roberta contented Duncan with diagraming, in the sand, all the plays she once ran at the tight end position for the Philadelphia Eagles; she focused on the part of the Eagles offense that concerned her, when she was Robert Muldoon, No. 90, and she relived for Duncan her occasional touchdown passes, her dropped balls, her offside penalties, her most vicious hits. "It was against the Cowboys," she told Duncan. "We were playing in Dallas, when that snake in the grass—Eight Ball, everyone called him—

came up on my blind side . . ." And Roberta would regard the quiet child, who had a blind side for life, and she would deftly change the subject.

To Garp, Roberta's subject was the ticklish detail of sex reassignment, because Garp seemed interested and Roberta knew that Garp probably liked hearing about a problem so thoroughly removed from his own.

"I always knew I should have been a girl," she told Garp. "I dreamed about having love made to me, by a man, but in the dreams I was always a woman; I was *never* a man having love made to me by another man." There was more than a hint of distaste in Roberta's references to homosexuals, and Garp thought it strange that people in the process of making a decision that will plant them firmly in a minority, forever, are possibly less tolerant of other minorities than we might imagine. There was even a bitchiness about Roberta, when she complained of the other troubled women who came to get well at Dog's Head Harbor with Jenny Fields. "That damn lesbian crowd," Roberta said to Garp. "They're trying to make your mother into something she isn't."

"I sometimes think that's what Mom is *for*," Garp teased Roberta. "She makes people happy by letting them think she is something she isn't."

"Well, they tried to confuse me," Roberta said. "When I was preparing myself for the operation, they kept trying to talk me out of it. 'Be gay,' they said. 'If you want men, have them as you are. If you become a woman, you'll just be taken advantage of,' they told me. They were all cowards," Roberta concluded, though Garp knew, sadly, that Roberta *had* been taken advantage of, over and over again.

Roberta's vehemence was not unique; Garp pondered how these other women in his mother's house, and in her care, had *all* been victims of intolerance—yet most of them he'd met seemed especially intolerant of each other. It was a kind of infighting that made no sense to Garp and he marveled at his mother sorting them all out, keeping them happy and out of each

other's hair. *Robert* Muldoon, Garp knew, had spent
several months in drag before his actual operation.
He'd go off in the morning dressed as Robert Muldoon;
he went out shopping for women's clothes, and almost
no one knew that he paid for his sex change with the
banquet fees he collected for the speeches he gave to
boys' clubs and men's clubs. In the evenings, at Dog's
Head Harbor, Robert Muldoon would model his new
clothes for Jenny and the critical women who shared
her house. When the estrogen hormones began to en-
large his breasts and shift the former tight end's shape
around, Robert gave up the banquet circuit and
marched forth from the Dog's Head Harbor house in
mannish women's suits and rather conservative wigs; he
tried *being* Roberta long before he had the surgery.
Clinically, now, Roberta had the same genitalia and
urological equipment as most other women.

"But of course I can't conceive," she told Garp. "I
don't ovulate and I don't menstruate." Neither do millions of other women, Jenny Fields had reassured her.
"When I came home from the hospital," Roberta said to
Garp, "do you know what *else* your mother told me?"

Garp shook his head; "home" to Roberta, Garp knew,
was Dog's Head Harbor.

"She told me I was less sexually ambiguous than most
people she knew," Roberta said. "I really needed that,"
she said, "because I had to use this horrible dilator all
the time so that my vagina wouldn't close; I felt like a
*machine.*"

*Good old mom,*

Garp scribbled.

"There's such sympathy for people, in what you
*write,*" Roberta told him, suddenly. "But I don't see
that much sympathy in you, in your real life," she said.
It was the same thing Jenny had always accused him of.

But now, he felt, he had more. With his jaw wired
shut, with his wife with her arm in a sling all day—and

Duncan with only half his pretty face intact—Garp felt more generous toward the other wretches who wandered into Dog's Head Harbor.

It was a summer town. Out of season, the bleached shingled house with its porches and garrets was the only occupied mansion along the gray-green dunes and the white beach at the end of Ocean Lane. An occasional dog sniffed through the bone-colored driftwood, and retired people, living some miles inland, in their former summer houses, occasionally strolled the shore, scrutinizing the shells. In summer there were lots of dogs and children and mothers' helpers all over the beach, and always a bright boat or two in the harbor. But when the Garps moved in with Jenny, the shoreline seemed abandoned. The beach, littered with the debris washed in with the high tides of winter, was deserted. The Atlantic Ocean, through April and through May, was the livid color of a bruise—was the color of the bridge of Helen's nose.

Visitors to the town, in the off-season, were quickly spotted as lost women in search of the famous nurse, Jenny Fields. In summer, these women often spent a whole day in Dog's Head Harbor trying to find someone who knew where Jenny lived. But the permanent residents of Dog's Head Harbor all knew: "The last house at the end of Ocean Lane," they told the damaged girls and women who asked for directions. "It's as big as a hotel, honey. You can't miss it."

Sometimes these searchers would trudge out to the beach first and view the house for a long time before they got up the nerve to come see if Jenny was home; sometimes Garp would see them, single or in twos and threes, squatting on the windy dunes and watching the house as if they were trying to read the degree of sympathy therein. If there were more than one, they conferred on the beach; one of them was elected to knock on the door while the others huddled on the dunes, like dogs told to stay! until they're called.

Helen bought Duncan a telescope, and from his room

with a sea view Duncan spied on the trepid visitors and often announced their presence hours before the knock on the door. "Someone for Grandma," he'd say. Focusing, always focusing. "She's about twenty-four. Or maybe fourteen. She has a blue knapsack. She has an orange with her but I don't think she's going to eat it. Someone's with her but I can't see her face. She's lying down; no, she's being sick. No, she's wearing a kind of mask. Maybe she's the other one's mother—no, her sister. Or just a friend.

"Now she's eating the orange. It doesn't look very good," Duncan would report. And Roberta would look, too; and sometimes Helen. It was often Garp who answered the door.

"Yes, she's my mother," he'd say, "but she's out shopping right now. Please come in, if you want to wait for her." And he would smile, though all the time he would be scrutinizing the person as carefully as the retired people along the beach looked at their seashells. And before his jaw healed, and his mauled tongue grew back together, Garp would answer the door with a ready supply of notes. Many of the visitors were not in the least surprised by being handed notes, because this was the only way they communicated, too.

*Hello, my name is Beth. I'm an Ellen Jamesian.*

And Garp would give her his:

*Hello, my name is Garp. I have a broken jaw.*

And he'd smile at them, and hand them a second note, depending on the occasion. One said:

*There's a nice fire in the wood stove in the kitchen; turn left.*

And there was one that said:

385

*Don't be upset. My mother will be back very soon.
There are other women here. Would you like to see
them?*

It was in this period that Garp took to wearing a
sport jacket again, not out of nostalgia for his days at
Steering, or in Vienna—and certainly not out of any
necessity to be well dressed at Dog's Head Harbor,
where Roberta seemed the only woman who was concerned with what she wore—but only because of his
need for pockets; he carried so many notes.

He tried running on the beach but he had to give it
up; it jarred his jaw and jangled his tongue against his
teeth. But he walked for miles along the sand. He was
returning from a walk the day the police car brought the
young man to Jenny's house; arm in arm, the policemen
helped him up the big front porch.

"Mr. Garp?" one of the policemen asked.

Garp dressed in running gear for his walks; he didn't
have any notes on him, but he nodded, yes, he was Mr.
Garp.

"You know this kid?" the policeman asked.

"Of course he does," the young man said. "You cops
don't ever believe anybody. You don't know how to
*relax.*"

It was the kid in the purple caftan, the boy Garp had
escorted from the boudoir of Mrs. Ralph—what seemed
to Garp like years ago. Garp considered not recognizing him, but he nodded.

"The kid's got no money," the policeman explained.
"He doesn't live around here, and he's got no job. He's
not in school anywhere and when we called his folks,
they said they didn't even know where he *was*—and
they didn't sound very interested to find out. But he says
he's staying with you—and you'll speak up for him."

Garp, of course, couldn't speak. He pointed to his
wire mesh and imitated the act of writing a note on his
palm.

386

"When'd you get the braces?" the kid asked. "Most people have them when they're younger. They're the craziest-looking braces I ever saw."

Garp wrote out a note on the back of a traffic violation form that the policeman handed him.

*Yes, I'll take responsibility for him. But I can't speak up for him because I have a broken jaw.*

The kid read the note over the policeman's shoulder.

"Wow," he said, grinning. "What happened to the *other* guy?"

He lost three quarters of his prick, Garp thought, but he did not write this on a traffic violation form, or on anything else. Ever.

The boy turned out to have read Garp's novels while he was in jail.

"If I'd known you were the author of those books," the kid said, "I would never have been so disrespectful." His name was Randy and he had become an ardent Garp fan. Garp was convinced that the mainstream of his fans consisted of waifs, lonely children, retarded grownups, cranks, and only occasional members of the citizenry who were not afflicted with perverted taste. But Randy had come to Garp as if Garp were now the only guru Randy obeyed. In the spirit of his mother's home at Dog's Head Harbor, Garp couldn't very well turn the boy away.

Roberta Muldoon took on the task of briefing Randy on the accident to Garp and his family.

"Who's the great big lovely chick?" Randy asked Garp in an awed whisper.

*Don't you recognize her?*

Garp wrote.

*She was a tight end for the Philadelphia Eagles.*

But even Garp's sourness could not dim Randy's likable enthusiasm; not right away. The boy entertained Duncan for hours.

*God knows how,*

Garp complained to Helen.

*He probably tells Duncan about all his drug experiences.*

"The boy's not on anything," Helen assured Garp. "Your mother asked him."

*Then he relates to Duncan the exciting history of his criminal record,*

Garp wrote.

"Randy wants to be a writer," Helen said.

*Everyone wants to be a writer!*

Garp wrote. But it wasn't true. *He* didn't want to be a writer—not anymore. When he tried to write, only the deadliest subject rose up to greet him. He knew he had to forget it—not fondle it with his memory and exaggerate its awfulness with his art. That was madness, but whenever he thought of writing, his only subject greeted him with its leers, its fresh visceral puddles, and its stink of death. And so he did not write; he didn't even try.

At last Randy went away. Though Duncan was sorry to see him go, Garp felt relieved; he did not show anybody else the note Randy left for him.

*I'll never be as good as you—at anything. Even if that's true, you could be a little more generous about how you rub that in.*

So I'm not kind, Garp thought. What else is new? He threw Randy's note away.

When the wires came off and the rawness left his tongue, Garp ran again. As the weather warmed up, Helen swam. She was told it was good for restoring her muscle tone and strengthening her collarbone, though this still hurt her—especially the breaststroke. She swam for what seemed to be miles, to Garp: straight out to sea, and then along the shoreline. She said she went out so far because the water was calmer there; closer to shore, the waves interfered with her. But Garp worried. He and Duncan sometimes used the telescope to watch her. What am I going to do if something happens? Garp wondered. He was a poor swimmer.

"Mom's a good swimmer," Duncan assured him. Duncan was also becoming a good swimmer.

"She goes out too far," Garp said.

By the time the summer people arrived, the Garp family took its exercise in slightly less ostentatious ways; they played on the beach or in the sea only in the early morning. In the crowded moments of the summer days, and in the early evenings, they watched the world from the shaded porches of Jenny Fields' home; they withdrew to the big cool house.

Garp got a little better. He began to write—gingerly, at first: long plot outlines, and speculations about his characters. He avoided the main characters; at least he thought they were the main characters—a husband, a wife, a child. He concentrated instead on a detective, an outsider to the family. Garp knew what terror would lurk at the heart of his book, and perhaps for that reason he approached it through a character as distant from his personal anxiety as the police inspector is distant from the crime. What business do *I* have writing about a police inspector? he thought, and so he made the inspector into someone even Garp could understand. Then Garp stood close to the stink itself. The bandages came off Duncan's eye hole and the boy wore a black patch, almost handsome against his summer tan. Garp took a deep breath and began a novel.

It was in the late summer of Garp's convalescence that *The World According to Bensenhaver* was begun. About that time, Michael Milton was released from a hospital, walking with a postsurgical stoop and a woebegone face. Due to an infection, the result of improper drainage—and aggravated by a common urological problem—he had to have the remaining quarter of his penis removed in an operation. Garp never knew this; and at this point, it might not even have cheered him up.

Helen knew Garp was writing again.

"I won't read it," she told him. "Not one word of it. I know you have to write it, but I never want to see it. I don't mean to hurt you, but you have to understand. *I* have to forget it; if *you* have to write about it, God help you. People bury these things in different ways."

"It's not about 'it,' exactly," he told her. "I do not write autobiographical fiction."

"I know that, too," she said. "But I won't read it just the same."

"Of course, I understand," he said.

Writing, he always knew, was a lonely business. It was hard for a lonely thing to feel that much lonelier. Jenny, he knew, would read it; she was tough as nails. Jenny watched them all get well; she watched new patients come and go.

One was a hideous young girl named Laurel, who made the mistake of sounding off about Duncan one morning at breakfast. "Could I sleep in another part of the house?" she asked Jenny. "There's this creepy kid—with the telescope, the camera, and the eye patch? He's like a fucking pirate, spying on me. Even little boys like to paw you over with their eyes—even with *one* eye."

Garp had fallen while running in the predawn light on the beach; he had hurt his jaw again, and was—again—wired shut. He had no old notes handy for what he wanted to say to this girl, but he scribbled very hastily on his napkin.

*Fuck you,*

he scribbled, and threw the napkin at the surprised girl.

"Look," the girl said to Jenny, "this is just the kind of routine I had to get away from. Some *man* bullying me all the time, some ding-dong threatening me with his big-prick violence. Who needs it? I mean, especially *here*—who needs it? Did I come here for more of the same?"

*Fuck you to death,*

said Garp's next note, but Jenny ushered the girl outside and told her the history of Duncan's eye patch, and his telescope, and his camera, and the girl tried very hard to avoid Garp during the last part of her stay.

Her stay was just a few days, and then someone was there to get her: a sporty car with New York plates and a man who *looked* like a ding-dong—and someone who had, actually, threatened poor Laurel with "big-prick violence," all the time.

"Hey, you dildos!" he called to Garp and Roberta, who were sitting on the large porch swing, like old-fashioned lovers. "Is this the whorehouse where you're keeping Laurel?"

"We're not exactly 'keeping' her," Roberta said.

"Shut up, you big dyke," said the New York man; he came up on the porch. He'd left the motor running to his sports car, and its idle charged and calmed itself —charged and calmed itself, and charged again. The man wore cowboy boots and green suede bell-bottom pants. He was tall and chesty, though not quite as tall and chesty as Roberta Muldoon.

"I'm not a dyke," Roberta said.

"Well, you're no vestal virgin either," the man said.

"Where the fuck is Laurel?" He wore an orange T-shirt with bright green letters between his nipples.

## SHAPE UP!

the letters read.

Garp searched his pockets for a pencil to scribble a note, but all he came up with was old notes: all the old standbys, which did not seem to apply to this rude person.

"Is Laurel expecting you?" Roberta Muldoon asked the man, and Garp knew that Roberta was having a sex-identity problem again; she was goading the moron in hopes that she could then feel justified in beating the shit out of him. But the man, to Garp, looked as if he might make a fair match for Roberta. All that estrogen had changed more than Roberta's shape, Garp thought —it had unmuscled the former Robert Muldoon, to a degree that Roberta seemed prone to forget.

"Look, sweethearts," the man said, to both Garp and Roberta. "If Laurel doesn't get her ass out here, I'm going to clean house. What kind of fag joint is this, anyway? Everyone's heard of it. I didn't have any trouble finding out where she went. Every screwy bitch in New York knows about this cunt hangout."

Roberta smiled. She was beginning to rock back and forth on the big porch swing in a way that was making Garp feel sick to his stomach. Garp clawed through his pockets at a frantic rate, scanning note after worthless note.

"Look, you clowns," the man said. "I *know* what sort of douche bags hang out here. It's a big lesbian scene, right?" He prodded the edge of the big porch swing with his cowboy boot and set the swing to moving oddly. "And what are *you?*" he asked Garp. "You the *man* of the house? Or the court eunuch?"

Garp handed the man a note.

*There's a nice fire in the wood stove in the kitchen; turn left.*

But it was August; that was the wrong note.

"What's this shit?" the man said. And Garp handed him another note, the first one to fly out of his pocket.

*Don't be upset. My mother will be back very soon. There are other women here. Would you like to see them?*

"*Fuck* your mother!" the man said. He started toward the big screen door. "Laurel!" he screamed. "You in there? You bitch!"

But it was Jenny Fields who met him in the doorway. "Hello," she said.

"I know who *you* are," the man said. "I recognize the dumb uniform. My Laurel's not your type, sweetie; she *likes* to fuck."

"Perhaps not with you," said Jenny Fields.

Whatever abuse the man in the SHAPE UP! T-shirt was then prepared to deliver to Jenny Fields went unsaid. Roberta Muldoon threw a cross-body block on the surprised man, hitting him from behind and a little to one side of the backs of his knees. It was a flagrant clip, worthy of a fifteen-yard penalty in Roberta's days as a Philadelphia Eagle. The man hit the gray boards of the porch deck with such force that the hanging flowerpots were set swinging. He tried but could not get up. He appeared to have suffered a knee injury common to the sport of football—the very reason, in fact, why clipping was a fifteen-yard penalty. The man was not plucky enough to hurl further abuse, at anyone, from his back; he lay with a calm, moonlike expression upon his face, which whitened slightly in his pain.

"That was too *hard,* Roberta," Jenny said.

"I'll get Laurel," Roberta said, sheepishly, and she went inside. In Roberta's heart of hearts, Garp and Jenny knew, she was more feminine than anyone; but in her body of bodies, she was a highly trained rock.

Garp had found another note and he dropped it on

the New York man's chest, right where it said SHAPE UP! It was a note Garp had many duplicates of.

*Hello, my name is Garp. I have a broken jaw.*

"My name is Harold," the man said. "Too bad about your jaw."

Garp found a pencil and wrote another note.

*Too bad about your knee, Harold.*

Laurel was fetched.

"Oh, baby," she said. "You *found* me!"

"I don't think I can drive the fucking car," Harold said. Out on Ocean Lane the man's sport car still chugged like an animal interested in eating sand.

"*I* can drive, baby," Laurel said. "You just never *let* me."

"Now I'll let you," Harold groaned. "Believe me."

"Oh, baby," Laurel said.

Roberta and Garp carried the man to the car. "I think I really need Laurel," the man confided to them. "Fucking bucket seats," the man complained, when they had gingerly squeezed him in. Harold was large for his car. It was the first time in what seemed like years, to Garp, that Garp had been this near to an automobile. Roberta put her hand on Garp's shoulder, but Garp turned away.

"I guess Harold needs me," Laurel told Jenny Fields, and gave a little shrug.

"But why does *she* need *him?*" said Jenny Fields, to no one in particular, as the little car drove away. Garp had wandered off. Roberta, punishing herself for her momentarily lapsed femininity, went to find Duncan and mother him.

Helen was talking on the phone to the Fletchers, Harrison and Alice, who wanted to come visit. That might help us, Helen thought. She was right, and it must have boosted Helen's confidence in herself—to be right about something again.

The Fletchers stayed a week. There was at last a child for Duncan to play with, even if it was not his age and not his sex; it was, at least, a child who knew about his eye, and Duncan lost most of his self-consciousness about the eye patch. When the Fletchers left, he was more willing to go to the beach by himself, even at those times of the day when he might encounter other children —who might ask him or, of course, tease him.

Harrison provided Helen with a confidant, as he had been for her before; she was able to tell Harrison things about Michael Milton that were simply too raw to tell Garp, and yet she needed to say them. She needed to talk about her anxieties for her marriage, now; and how she was dealing with the accident so differently from Garp. Harrison suggested another child. Get pregnant, he advised. Helen confided that she was no longer taking the pills, but she did not tell Harrison that Garp had not slept with her—not since it had happened. She didn't really need to tell Harrison that; Harrison noted the separate rooms.

Alice encouraged Garp to stop the silly notes. He could talk if he tried, if he wasn't so vain about how he sounded. If *she* could talk, certainly he could spit the words out, Alice reasoned—teeth wired together, delicate tongue, and all; he could at least try.

"Alish," Garp said.

"Yeth," said Alice. "That'th my name. What'th yours?"

"Arp," Garp managed to say.

Jenny Fields, passing whitely to another room, shuddered like a ghost and moved on.

"I *mish* him," Garp confessed to Alice.

"You mith him, yeth, of *courth* you do," said Alice, and she held him while he cried.

It was quite some time after the Fletchers left when Helen came to Garp's room in the night. She was not surprised to find him lying awake, because he was listening to what she'd heard, too. It was why she couldn't sleep.

Someone, one of Jenny's late arrivals—a new guest—was taking a bath. First the Garps had heard the tub being drawn, then they'd heard the plunking in the water—now the splashing and soapy sounds. There was even a little light singing, or the person was humming.

They remembered, of course, the years Walt had washed himself within their hearing, how they would listen for any telltale slipping sounds, or for the most frightening sound of all—which was no sound. And then they'd call, "Walt?" And Walt would say, "What?" And they would say, "Okay, just checking!" To make sure that he hadn't slipped under and drowned.

Walt liked to lie with his ears underwater, listening to his fingers climbing the walls of the tub, and often he wouldn't hear Garp or Helen calling him. He'd look up, surprised, to see their anxious faces suddenly above him, peering over the rim of the tub. "I'm all right," he'd say, sitting up.

"Just *answer*, for God's sake, Walt," Garp would tell him. "When we call you, just answer us."

"I didn't hear you," Walt said.

"Then keep your head out of the water," Helen said.

"But how can I wash my hair?" Walt asked.

"That's a lousy way to wash your hair, Walt," Garp said. "Call me. *I'll* wash your hair."

"Okay," said Walt. And when they left him alone, he'd put his head underwater again and listen to the world that way.

Helen and Garp lay beside each other on Garp's narrow bed in one of the guest rooms in one of the garrets at Dog's Head Harbor. The house had so many bathrooms—they couldn't even be sure which bathroom they were listening to, but they listened.

"It's a woman, I think," Helen said.

"Here?" Garp said. "Of *course* it's a woman."

"I thought at first it was a child," Helen said.

396

"I know," Garp said.

"The humming, I guess," Helen said. "You know how he used to talk to himself?"

"I know," Garp said.

They held each other in the bed that was always a little damp, so close to the ocean and with so many windows open all day, and the screen doors swinging and banging.

"I want another child," said Helen.

"Okay," Garp said.

"As soon as possible," Helen said.

"Right away," said Garp. "Of course."

"If it's a girl," Helen said, "we'll name her Jenny, because of your mother."

"Good," said Garp.

"I don't know, if it's a boy," said Helen.

"Not Walt," Garp said.

"Okay," Helen said.

"Not *ever* another Walt," said Garp. "Although I know some people do that."

"I wouldn't want to," Helen said.

"Some other name, if it's a boy," Garp said.

"I hope it's a girl," said Helen.

"I won't care," Garp said.

"Of course. Neither will I, really," said Helen.

"I'm so sorry," Garp said; he hugged her.

"No, *I'm* so sorry," she said.

"No, *I'm* so sorry," said Garp.

"*I* am," Helen said.

"*I* am," he said.

They made love so carefully. Helen imagined that she was Roberta Muldoon, fresh out of surgery, trying out a brand-new vagina. Garp tried not to imagine anything.

Whenever Garp began imagining, he only saw the bloody Volvo. There were Duncan's screams, and outside he could hear Helen calling; and someone else. He twisted himself from behind the steering wheel and kneeled on the driver's seat; he held Duncan's face in his hands, but the blood would not stop and Garp couldn't see everything that was wrong.

"It's okay," he whispered to Duncan. "Hush, you're going to be all right." But because of his tongue, there were no words—only a soft spray.

Duncan kept screaming, and so did Helen, and someone else kept groaning—the way a dog dreams in its sleep. But what did Garp hear that frightened him so? What *else?*

"It's all right, Duncan, believe me," he whispered, incomprehensibly. "You're going to be all right." He wiped the blood from the boy's throat with his hand; nothing at the boy's throat was cut, he could see. He wiped the blood from the boy's temples, and saw that they were not bashed in. He kicked open the driver's-side door, to be sure; the door light went on and he could see that one of Duncan's eyes was darting. The eye was looking for help, but Garp could see that the eye could see. He wiped more blood with his hand, but he could not find Duncan's other eye. "It's okay," he whispered to Duncan, but Duncan screamed even louder.

Over his father's shoulder, Duncan had seen his mother at the Volvo's open door. Blood streamed from her gashed nose and her sliced tongue, and she held her right arm as if it had broken off somewhere near her shoulder. But it was the *fright* in her face that frightened Duncan. Garp turned and saw her. Something else frightened him.

It was not Helen's screaming, it was not Duncan's screaming. And Garp knew that Michael Milton, who was grunting, could grunt himself to death—for all Garp cared. It was something else. It was not a sound. It was *no* sound. It was the absence of sound.

"Where's Walt?" Helen said, trying to see into the Volvo. She stopped screaming.

"Walt!" cried Garp. He held his breath. Duncan stopped crying.

They heard nothing. And Garp knew Walt had a cold

you could hear from the next room—even two rooms away, you could hear that wet rattle in the child's chest.

"Walt!" they screamed.

Both Helen and Garp would whisper to each other, later, that at that moment they imagined Walt with his ears underwater, listening intently to his fingers at play in the bathtub.

"I can still see him," Helen whispered, later.

"All the time," Garp said. "I know."

"I just shut my eyes," said Helen.

"Right," Garp said. "I know."

But Duncan said it best. Duncan said that sometimes it was as if his missing right eye was not entirely gone. "It's like I can still see out of it, sometimes," Duncan said. "But it's like memory, it's not real—what I see."

"Maybe it's become the eye you see your dreams with," Garp told him.

"Sort of," Duncan said. "But it seems so real."

"It's your *imaginary* eye," Garp said. "That can be very real."

"It's the eye I can still see Walt with," Duncan said. "You know?"

"I know," Garp said.

Many wrestlers' children have hardy necks, but not all the children of wrestlers have necks that are hardy enough.

For Duncan and Helen, now, Garp seemed to have an endless reservoir of gentleness; for a year, he spoke softly to them; for a year, he was never impatient with them. They must have grown impatient with his delicacy. Jenny Fields noticed that the three of them needed a year to nurse each other.

In that year, Jenny wondered, what did they do with the *other* feelings human beings have? Helen hid them; Helen was very strong. Duncan saw them only with his missing eye. And Garp? He was strong, but not that strong. He wrote a novel called *The World According to Bensenhaver,* into which all his *other* feelings flew.

When Garp's editor, John Wolf, read the first chapter of *The World According to Bensenhaver*, he wrote to Jenny Fields. "What in hell is going on out there?" Wolf wrote to Jenny. "It is as if Garp's grief has made his heart perverse."

But T. S. Garp felt guided by an impulse as old as Marcus Aurelius, who had the wisdom and the urgency to note that "in the life of a man, his time is but a moment . . . his sense a dim rushlight."

# 15

### ⊪⊪⊪⊪⊪⊪⊪

# The World According to
# Bensenhaver

HOPE STANDISH was at home with her son, Nicky, when Oren Rath walked into the kitchen. She was drying the dishes and she saw immediately the long, thin-bladed fisherman's knife with the slick cutting edge and the special, saw-toothed edge that they call a disgorger-scaler. Nicky was not yet three; he still ate in a high chair, and he was eating his breakfast when Oren Rath stepped up behind him and nudged the ripper teeth of his fisherman's knife against the child's throat.

"Set them dishes aside," he told Hope. Mrs. Standish did as she was told. Nicky gurgled at the stranger; the knife was just a tickle under his chin.

"What do you want?" Hope asked. "I'll give you anything you want."

"You sure will," said Oren Rath. "What's your name?"

"Hope."

"Mine's Oren."

"That's a nice name," Hope told him.

Nicky couldn't turn in the high chair to see the stranger who was tickling his throat. He had wet cereal on his fingers, and when he reached for Oren Rath's hand, Rath stepped up beside the high chair and touched the fine, slicing edge of his fisherman's blade to the fleshy pouch of the boy's cheek. He made a quick cut there, as if he were briefly outlining the child's cheekbone. Then he stepped back to observe Nicky's surprised face, his simple cry; a thread-thin line of blood appeared, like the stitching for a pocket, on the boy's cheek. It was as if the child had suddenly developed a gill.

"I mean business," said Oren Rath. Hope started toward Nicky but Rath waved her back. "He don't need you. He just don't care for his cereal. He wants a cookie." Nicky bawled.

"He'll choke on it, when he's crying," Hope said.

"You want to argue with me?" said Oren Rath. "You want to talk about choking? I'll cut his pecker off and stuff it down his throat—if you want to talk about choking."

Hope gave Nicky a zwieback and he stopped crying.

"You see?" said Oren Rath. He picked up the high chair with Nicky in it and hugged it to his chest. "We're going to the bedroom now," he said; he nodded to Hope. "You first."

They went down the hall together. The Standish family lived in a ranch house then; with a new baby, they had agreed ranch houses were safer in the case of a fire. Hope went into the bedroom and Oren Rath put down the high chair with Nicky in it, just outside the bedroom door. Nicky had almost stopped bleeding; there was just a little blood on his cheek; Oren Rath wiped this off with his hand, then wiped his hand on his pants. Then he stepped into the bedroom after Hope. When he closed the door, Nicky started to cry.

"Please," Hope said. "He really might choke, and he knows how to get out of that high chair—or it might tip over. He doesn't like to be alone."

Oren Rath went to the night table and slashed through the phone cord with his fisherman's knife as easily as a man halving a very ripe pear. "You don't want to argue with me," he said.

Hope sat down on the bed. Nicky was crying, but not

hysterically; it sounded as if he might stop. Hope started crying, too.

"Just take off your clothes," Oren said. He helped her undress. He was tall and reddish-blond, his hair as lank and as close to his head as high grass beaten down by a flood. He smelled like silage and Hope remembered the turquoise pickup she'd noticed in the driveway, just before he appeared in her kitchen. "You've even got a rug in the bedroom," he said to her. He was thin but muscular; his hands were large and clumsy, like the feet of a puppy who's going to be a big dog. His body seemed almost hairless, but he was so pale, so very blond, that his hair was hard to see against his skin.

"Do you know my husband?" Hope asked him.

"I know when he's home and when he ain't," Rath said. "Listen," he said suddenly; Hope held her breath. "You hear? Your kid don't even mind it." Nicky was murmuring vowel sounds outside the bedroom door, talking wetly to his zwieback. Hope began crying harder. When Oren Rath touched her, awkward and fast, she thought she was so dry that she wouldn't even get big enough for his horrible finger.

"Please wait," she said.

"No arguing with me."

"No, I mean I can help you," she said. She wanted him in and out of her as fast as possible; she was thinking of Nicky in the high chair in the hall. "I can make it nicer, I mean," she said, unconvincingly; she did not know how to say what she was saying. Oren Rath grabbed one of her breasts in such a way that Hope knew he had never touched a breast before; his hand was so cold, she flinched. In his awkwardness, he butted her in the mouth with the top of his head.

"No arguing," he grunted.

"Hope!" someone called. They both heard it and froze. Oren Rath gaped at the cut phone cord.

"Hope?"

It was Margot, a neighbor and a friend. Oren Rath touched the cool, flat blade of his knife to Hope's nipple.

"She's going to walk right in here," Hope whispered. "She's a good friend."

"My God, Nicky," they could hear Margot say, "I see you're eating all over the house. Is your mother getting dressed?"

"I'll have to fuck you both and kill everybody," whispered Oren Rath.

Hope scissored his waist with her good legs and hugged him, knife and all, to her breasts. "Margot!" she screamed. "Grab Nicky and run! *Please!*" she shrieked. "There's a crazy man who's going to kill us all! Take Nicky, take Nicky!"

Oren Rath lay stiffly against her as if it were the first time he'd ever been hugged. He did not struggle, he did not use his knife. They both lay rigid and listened to Margot dragging Nicky down the hall and out the kitchen door. One leg of the high chair was snapped off against the refrigerator, but Margot didn't stop to remove Nicky from the chair until she was half a block down the street and kicking open her own door.

"Don't kill me," Hope whispered. "Just go, quickly, and you'll get away. She's calling the police, right now."

"Get dressed," said Oren Rath. "I ain't had you yet, and I'm going to." Where he'd butted her with the oval crown of his head, he had split her lip against her teeth and made her bleed. "I mean business," he repeated, but uncertainly. He was as rough-boned and graceless as a young steer. He made her put her dress on without any underwear, he shoved her barefoot down the hall, carrying his boots under his arm. Hope didn't realize until she was beside him in the pickup that he had put on one of her husband's flannel shirts.

"Margot has probably written down the license number of this truck," she told him. She turned the rear-view mirror so that she could see herself; she dabbed at her split lip with the broad, floppy collar of her dress. Oren Rath stiff-armed her in the ear, rapping the far side of her head off the passenger door of the cab.

"I need that mirror to see," he said. "Don't mess around

or I'll really hurt you." He'd taken her bra with him and he used it to tie her wrists to the thick, rusty hinges of the glove-compartment door, which gaped open at her.

He drove as if he were in no special hurry to get out of town. He did not seem impatient when he got stuck at the long traffic light near the university. He watched all the pedestrians crossing the street; he shook his head and clucked his tongue when he saw how some of the students were dressed. Hope could see her husband's office window from where she sat in the truck's cab, but she didn't know if he would be in his office or actually, at that moment, teaching a class.

In fact, he was in his office—four floors up. Dorsey Standish looked out his window and saw the lights change; the traffic was allowed to flow, the hordes of marching students were temporarily restrained at the gates to the crosswalks. Dorsey Standish liked watching traffic. There are many foreign and flashy cars in a university town, but here these cars were contrasted with the vehicles of the natives: farmers' trucks, slat-sided conveyors of pigs and cattle, strange harvesting machinery, everything muddy from the farms and county roads. Standish knew nothing about farms, but he was fascinated by the animals and the machines—especially the dangerous, baffling vehicles. There went one, now, with a chute—for what?—and a latticework of cables that pulled or suspended something heavy. Standish liked to try to visualize how everything worked.

Below him a lurid turquoise pickup moved ahead with the traffic; its fenders were pockmarked, its grille bashed in and black with mashed flies and—Standish imagined—the heads of imbedded birds. In the cab beside the driver Dorsey Standish thought he saw a pretty woman—something about her hair and profile reminded him of Hope, and a flash of the woman's dress struck him as a color his wife liked to wear. But he was four floors up; the truck was past him, and the cab's rear window was so thickly caked with mud that he couldn't glimpse more of her. Besides, it was time for his nine-thirty class. Dorsey Standish decided it was unlikely that a woman riding in such an ugly truck would be at all pretty.

"I bet your husband is screwing his students all the time," said Oren Rath. His big hand, with the knife, lay in Hope's lap.

"No, I don't think so," Hope said.

"Shit, you don't know *nothing*," he said. "I'm going to fuck you so good you won't even want it to stop."

"I don't care what you do," Hope told him. "You can't hurt my baby now."

"I can do things to *you*," said Oren Rath. "Lots of things."

"Yes. You mean business," Hope said, mockingly.

They were driving into the farm country. Rath didn't say anything for a while. Then he said, "I'm n~t as crazy as you think."

"I don't think you're crazy at all," Hope lied. "I think you're just a dumb, horny kid who's never been laid."

Oren Rath must have felt at this moment that his advantage of terror was slipping away from him, fast. Hope was seeking *any* advantage she might find, but she didn't know if Oren Rath was sane enough to be humiliated.

They turned off the county road, up a long dirt driveway toward a farmhouse whose windows w~re blurred with plastic insulation; the scruffy lawn was strewn with tractor parts and other metal trash. The mailbox said: R, R, W, E & O RATH.

These Raths were not related to the famous sausage Raths, but it appeared that they were pig farmers. Hope saw a series of outbuildings, gray and slanted with rusted roofs. On the ramp by the brown barn a full-grown sow lay on her side, breathing with difficulty; beside the pig were two men who looked to Hope like mutants of the same mutation that had produced Oren Rath.

"I want the black truck, now," Oren said to them. "People are out looking for this one." He used his knife matter-of-factly to slice through the bra that bound Hope's wrists to the glove compartment.

"Shit," one of the men said.

The other man shrugged; he had a red blotch on his face

—a kind of birthmark, which was the color and nubbled surface of a raspberry. In fact, that is what his family called him: Raspberry Rath. Fortunately, Hope didn't know this.

They had not looked at Oren or at Hope. The hard-breathing sow shattered the barnyard calm with a rippling fart. "Shit, there she goes again," the man without the birthmark said; except for his eyes, *his* face was more or less normal. His name was Weldon.

Raspberry Rath read the label on a brown bottle he held out toward the pig like a drink: " 'May produce excessive gas and flatulence,' it says."

"Don't say anything about producing a pig like *this*," Weldon said.

"I need the black truck," Oren said.

"Well, the key's in it, Oren," said Weldon Rath. "If you think you can manage by yourself."

Oren Rath shoved Hope toward the black pickup. Raspberry was holding the bottle of pig medicine and staring at Hope when she said to him, "He's kidnapping me. He's going to rape me. The police are already looking for him."

Raspberry kept staring at Hope, but Weldon turned to Oren. "I hope you ain't doing nothing too stupid," he said.

"I ain't," Oren said. The two men now turned their total attention to the pig.

"I'd wait another hour and then give her another squirt," Raspberry said. "Ain't we seen enough of the vet this week?" He scratched the mud-smeared neck of the sow with the toe of his boot; the sow farted.

Oren led Hope behind the barn where the corn spilled out of the silo. Some piglets, barely bigger than kittens, were playing in it. They scattered when Oren started the black pickup. Hope started to cry.

"Are you going to let me go?" she asked Oren.

"I ain't had you yet," he said.

Hope's bare feet were cold and black with the spring muck. "My feet hurt," she said. "Where are we going?"

She'd seen an old blanket in the back of the pickup, matted and flecked with straw. *That's* where she imagined she was going: into the cornfields, then spread on the spongy spring ground—and when it was over and her throat was slit, and she'd been disemboweled with the fisherman's knife, he'd wrap her up in the blanket that was lumped stiffly on the floor of the pickup as if it covered some still-born livestock.

"I got to find a good place to *have* you," said Oren Rath. "I would of kept you at home, but I'd of had to share you."

Hope Standish was trying to figure out the foreign machinery of Oren Rath. He did not *work* like the human beings she was accustomed to.

"What you're doing is wrong," she said.

"No, it isn't," he said. "It *ain't*."

"You're going to rape me," Hope said. "That's wrong."

"I just want to *have* you," he said. He hadn't bothered to tie her to the glove compartment this time. There was nowhere she could go. They were driving only on those mile-long plots of county roads, driving slowly west in little squares, the way a knight advances on a chessboard: one square ahead, two sideways, one sideways, two ahead. It seemed purposeless to Hope, but then she wondered if he didn't know the roads so very well that he knew how to cover a considerable distance without ever passing through a town. They saw only the signposts for towns, and although they couldn't have moved more than thirty miles from the university, she didn't recognize any of the names: Coldwater, Hills, Fields, Plainview. Maybe they *aren't* towns, she thought, but only crude labels for the natives who lived here—identifying the land for them, as if they didn't know the simple words for the things they saw every day.

"You don't have any right to do this to me," Hope said.

"Shit," he said. He pumped his brakes hard, throwing her forward against the truck's solid dashboard. Her forehead bounced off the windshield, the back of her hand was mashed against her nose. She felt something like a small muscle or a very light bone give way in her chest. Then he tromped on the accelerator and tossed her back into the seat. "I hate arguing," he said.

Her nose bled; she sat with her head forward, in her hands, and the blood dripped on her thighs. She sniffed a little; the blood dripped over her lip and filmed her teeth. She tipped her head back so that she could taste it. For some reason, it calmed her—it helped her to think. She knew there was a rapidly blueing knot on her forehead, swelling under her smooth skin. When she ran her hand up to her face and touched the lump, Oren Rath looked at her and laughed. She spit at him—a thin phlegm laced pink with blood. It caught his cheek and ran down to the collar of her husband's flannel shirt. His hand, as flat and broad as the sole of a boot, reached for her hair. She grabbed his forearm with both her hands, she jerked his wrist to her mouth and bit into the soft part where the hairs don't always grow and the blue tubes carry the blood.

She meant to kill him in this impossible way but she barely had time to break the skin. His arm was so strong that he snapped her body upright and across his lap. He pushed the back of her neck against the steering wheel—the horn blew through her head—and he broke her nose with the heel of his left hand. Then he returned that hand to the wheel. He cradled her head with his right hand, holding her face against his stomach; when he felt that she wasn't struggling, he let her head rest on his thigh. His hand lightly cupped her ear, as if to hold the sound of the horn inside her. She kept her eyes shut against the pain in her nose.

He made several left turns, more right turns. Each turn, she knew, meant they had driven one mile. His hand now cupped the back of her neck. She could hear again, and she felt his fingers working their way into her hair. The front of her face felt numb.

"I don't want to kill you," he said.

"*Don't, then*," Hope said.

"*Got to*," Oren Rath told her. "After we do it, I'll *have* to."

This affected her like the taste of her own blood. She knew he didn't care for arguing. She saw that she had lost a step: her rape. He was going to do it to her. She had to consider that it was done. What mattered now was *living*;

she knew that meant outliving him. She knew that meant getting him caught, or getting him killed, or killing him.

Against her cheek, she felt the change in his pocket; his blue jeans were soft and sticky with farm dust and machine grease. His belt buckle dug into her forehead; her lips touched the oily leather of his belt. The fisherman's knife was kept in a sheath, she knew. But where was the sheath? She couldn't see it; she didn't dare to hunt for it with her hands. Suddenly, against her eye, she felt his penis stiffening. She felt then—for really the first time— almost paralyzed, panicked beyond helping herself, no longer able to sort out the priorities. Once again, it was Oren Rath who helped her.

"Look at it this way," he said. "Your kid got away. I was going to kill the kid, too, you know."

The logic of Oren Rath's peculiar version of sanity made everything sharpen for Hope; she heard the other cars. There were not many, but every few minutes or so there was a car passing. She wished she could see, but she knew they were not as isolated as they had been. *Now,* she thought, before he gets to where we're going—if he even knows where we're going. She thought he did. At least, before he gets off this road—before I'm somewhere, again, where there aren't any people.

Oren Rath shifted in his seat. His erection was making him uncomfortable. Hope's warm face in his lap, his hand in her hair, was reaching him. *Now,* Hope thought. She moved her cheek against his thigh, just slightly; he did not stop her. She moved her face in his lap as if she were making herself more comfortable, against a pillow— against his *prick,* she knew. She moved until the bulge under his rank pants rose untouched by her face. But she could reach it with her breath; it stuck up out of his lap near her mouth, and she began to breathe on it. It hurt too much to breathe out of her nose. She drew her lips into an O-shaped kiss, she focused her breathing, and, very softly, she blew.

Oh, Nicky, she thought. And Dorsey, her husband. She would see them again, she hoped. To Oren Rath she gave

410

her warm, careful breath. On him she focused her one, cold thought: I'm going to *get* you, you son of a bitch.

It was apparent that the sexual experience of Oren Rath had not previously involved such subtleties as Hope's directed breathing. He tried to move her head in his lap so that he would once again have contact with her hot face, but at the same time he didn't want to disturb her soft breath. What she was doing made him want *more* contact, but it was excruciating to imagine losing the teasing contact he now had. He began to squirm. Hope didn't hurry. It was his movement that finally brought the bulge of sour jeans to touch her lips. She closed them there, but didn't move her mouth. Oren Rath felt only a hot wind passing through the crude weave of his clothes; he groaned. A car approached, then passed him; he corrected the truck. He was aware he was beginning to wander across the center of the road.

"What are you doing?" he asked Hope. She, very lightly, applied her teeth to his swollen clothes. He brought his knee up, pumped the brake, jarred her head, hurt her nose. He forced his hand between her face and his lap. She thought he was going to really hurt her but he was struggling with his zipper. "I've seen pictures of this," he told her.

"Let me," she said. She had to sit up just a little to get his fly open. She wanted to get a look at where they were; they were still out in the country, of course, but there were painted lines on the road. She took him out of his pants and into her mouth without looking at him.

"Shit," he said. She thought she would gag; she was afraid she would be sick. Then she got him into the back of her cheek where she thought she could take a lot of time. He was sitting so stiffly still, but trembling, that she knew he was already far beyond even his imaginary experiences. That steadied Hope; it gave her confidence, and a sense of time. She went ahead with it very slowly, listening for other cars. She could tell he had slowed down. At the first sign she had that he was leaving this road, she would have to change her plans. Could I bite the damn thing off? she wondered. But she thought that she probably couldn't—at least, not quickly enough.

Then two trucks went by them, closely following each other; in the distance she thought she heard another car's horn. She started working faster—he raised his lap higher. She thought their truck had speeded up. A car passed them—awfully close, she thought. Its horn blared at them. "Fuck you!" Oren Rath yelled after it; he was beginning to jounce up and down in the seat, hurting Hope's nose. Hope now had to be careful not to hurt him; she wanted to hurt him very much. Just make him lose his head, she encouraged herself.

Suddenly there was the sound of gravel spraying the underside of the truck. She closed her mouth fast around him. But they were neither crashing nor turning off the road; he was pulling abruptly to the roadside and stopping. The truck stalled out. He put both his hands on either side of her face; his thighs hardened and slapped against her jaw. I'm going to choke on it, she thought, but he was lifting her face up, out of his lap. "No! No!" he cried. A truck, flinging tiny stones, tore by them and cut into his words. "I don't have the *thing* on," he said to her. "If you have any germs, they'll swim right up me."

Hope sat on her knees, her lips hot and sore, her nose throbbing. He was going to put on a rubber, but when he tore it from its little tinfoil package, he stared at it as if it wasn't at all what he expected to see—as if he thought they were bright green! As if he didn't know how to put it on. "Take your dress off," he said; he was embarrassed that she was looking at him. She could see the cornfields on either side of the road, and the back side of a billboard a few yards away from them. But there were no houses, no signs, no intersecting roads. No cars and trucks were coming. She thought her heart would simply stop.

Oren Rath tore himself out of her husband's shirt; he threw it out his window; Hope saw it flap in the road. He scraped his boots off on the brake pedal, whacking his narrow blond knees on the steering wheel. "Shove over!"

he said. She was wedged against the passenger-side door. She knew—even if she could get out the door—that she couldn't outrun him. She didn't have any shoes—and his feet appeared to have a dog's rough pads.

He was having trouble with his pants; he clutched the rolled-up rubber in his teeth. Then he was naked—he'd flung his pants somewhere—and he shoved the rubber down over himself as if his penis were no more sensitive than a turtle's leathery tail. She was trying to unbutton her dress and her tears were coming back, though she was fighting them, when he suddenly caught her dress and began to yank it over her head; it caught on her arms. He jerked her elbows painfully behind her back.

He was too long to fit in the cab. One door had to be open. She reached for the handle over her head but he bit her in the neck. "No!" he hollered. He thrashed his feet around—she saw his shin was bleeding; he'd cut it on the rim of the horn—and his hard heels struck the door handle on the driver's side. With both feet, he launched the door open. She saw the gray smear of the road over his shoulder—his long ankles stuck out into the traffic lane, but there was no traffic now. Her head hurt; she was jammed against the door. She had to wriggle herself back down the seat, farther under him, and her movement made him yell something unintelligible. She felt his rubbered prick slipping over her stomach. Then his whole body braced and he bit into her shoulder fiercely. He'd come!

"Shit!" he cried. "I done it already!"

"No," she said, hugging him. "No, you can do *more*." She knew that if he thought he was through with her, he would kill her.

"Much more," she said in his ear, which smelled like dust. She had to wet her fingers to wet herself. God, I'll never get him inside me, she thought, but when she found him with her hand, she knew that the rubber was the lubricated kind.

"Oh," he said. He lay still on top of her; he seemed surprised by where she'd put him, as if he didn't really know what was where. "Oh," he repeated.

Oh, what now? Hope wondered. She held her breath. A car, a flash of red, whined past their open door—the horn blast and some muffled, derisive hoots fading away from them. Of course, she thought: we look like two farmers fucking off the side of the road; it's probably done all the time. No one will stop, she thought, unless it's the police. She imagined a bread-faced trooper appearing over Rath's lurching shoulder, writing out a ticket. "Not on the road, buddy," he'd be saying. And when she screamed at him, "Rape! He's *raping* me," the trooper would wink at Oren Rath.

The bewildered Rath seemed to be feeling rather cautiously for something inside her. If he's just come, Hope thought, how much time do I have before he comes again? But he seemed more like a goat than a human to her, and the babylike gurgle in his throat, hot against her ear, seemed close to the last sound she imagined she'd hear.

She looked at everything she could see. The keys dangling from the ignition were too far to reach; and what could she do with a set of keys? Her back hurt and she pushed her hand against the dashboard to try to shift his weight on her; this excited him and made him grunt against her. "Don't move," he said; she tried to do what he said. "Oh," he said, approvingly. "That's real good. I'll kill you quick. You won't even know it. You just do like that, and I'll kill you good."

Her hand grazed a metal button, smooth and round; her fingers touched it and she did not even have to turn her face away from him and look at it to know what it was. It opened the glove compartment and she pushed it. The spring-release door was a sudden weight in her hand. She said a long and loud "Aaahhh!" to conceal the sound of the things in the glove compartment that rattled around. Her hand touched cloth, her fingers felt grit. There was a spool of wire, something sharp, but too small—things like screws and nails, a bolt, perhaps a hinge to something else. There was nothing she could use. Reaching around in there was hurting her arm; she let her hand trail to the

floor of the cab. When another truck passed them—catcalls
and bloops from the air horn, and no sign of even slowing
down for a better look—she started to cry.

"I *got* to kill you," Rath moaned.

"Have you done this before?" she asked him.

"Sure," he said, and he thrust into her—stupidly, as if
his brute lunges could impress her.

"And did you kill them, too?" Hope asked. Her hand,
aimless now, toyed with something—some material—on the
floor of the cab.

"They were animals," Rath admitted. "But I had to kill
them, too." Hope sickened, her fingers clutched the thing
on the floor—an old jacket or something.

"Pigs?" she asked him.

"Pigs!" he cried. "Shit, nobody fucks pigs," he told her.
Hope thought that probably *somebody* did. "They was
sheep," Rath said. "And one calf." But this was hopeless,
she knew. She felt him shrinking inside her; she was dis-
tracting him. She choked a sob that felt like it would split
her head if it ever escaped her.

"Please *try* to be kind to me," Hope said.

"Don't talk any," he said. "Move like you did."

She moved, but apparently not the right way. "No!" he
shouted. His fingers dug into her spine. She tried moving
another way. "Yup," he said. He moved, now, determined
and purposeful—mechanical and dumb.

Oh, God, Hope thought. Oh, Nicky. And Dorsey. Then
she felt what she held in her hand: his pants. And her
fingers, suddenly as wise as a Braille reader's, located the
zipper and moved on; her fingers passed over the change
in the pocket, they slipped around the wide belt.

"Yup, yup, yup," said Oren Rath.

Sheep, Hope thought to herself; and one calf. "Oh,
*please* concentrate!" she cried aloud to herself.

"Don't talk!" said Oren Rath.

But now her hand held it: the long, hard, leather sheath.
That is the little hook, her fingers told her, and that is the
little metal clasp. And that—oh, yes!—is the head of the

thing, the bony handle of the fisherman's knife he had used to cut her son.

Nicky's cut was not serious. In fact, everyone was trying to figure out how he got it. Nicky was not talking yet. He enjoyed looking in the mirror at the thin, half-moon slit that was already closed.

"Must have been something very sharp," the doctor told the police. Margot, the neighbor, had thought she'd better call a doctor, too; she'd found blood on the child's bib. The police had found more blood in the bedroom; a single drop on the cream-white bedspread. They were puzzled about it; there was no other sign of violence, and Margot had seen Mrs. Standish leave. She had looked all right. The blood was from Hope's split lip—from the time Oren Rath had butted her—but there was no way any of them could know that. Margot thought there might have been sex, but she wasn't suggesting it. Dorsey Standish was too shocked to think. The police did not think there had been time for sex. The doctor knew no blow had been connected with Nicky's cut—probably not even a fall. "A razor?" he suggested. "Or a very sharp knife."

The police inspector, a solidly round and florid man, a year away from his retirement, found the cut phone cord in the bedroom. "A knife," he said. "A sharp knife with some *weight* to it." His name was Arden Bensenhaver, and he had once been a police superintendent in Toledo, but his methods had been judged as unorthodox.

He pointed at Nicky's cheek. "It's a flick wound," he said. He demonstrated the proper wrist action. "But you don't see many flick knives around here," Bensenhaver told them. "It's a flick-type of wound, but it's probably some kind of hunting or fishing knife."

Margot had described Oren Rath as a farm kid in a farm truck, except that the truck's color revealed the unnatural influence of the town and the university upon the farmers: turquoise. Dorsey Standish did not even associate this with the turquoise truck he had seen, or the woman in the cab

416

whom he'd thought had resembled Hope. He still didn't understand anything.

"Did they leave a note?" he asked. Arden Bensenhaver stared at him. The doctor looked down at the floor. "You know, about a *ransom*?" Standish said. He was a literal man struggling for a literal hold. Someone, he thought, had said "kidnap"; wasn't there ransom in the case of kidnap?

"There's no note, Mr. Standish," Bensenhaver told him. "It doesn't look like that kind of thing."

"They were in the bedroom when I found Nicky outside the door," Margot said. "But she was all right when she left, Dorsey. I saw her."

They hadn't told Standish about Hope's panties, discarded on the bedroom floor; they'd been unable to find the matching bra. Margot had told Arden Bensenhaver that Mrs. Standish was a woman who usually wore a bra. She had left barefoot; they knew that, too. And Margot had recognized Dorsey's shirt on the farm kid. She'd got only a partial reading of the license plate; it was an in-state, commercial plate, and the first two numbers placed it within the county, but she hadn't gotten them all. The rear plate had been spattered with mud, the front plate was missing.

"We'll find them," Arden Bensenhaver said. "There's not much in the way of turquoise trucks around here. The county sheriff's boys will probably know it."

"Nicky, what happened?" Dorsey Standish asked the boy. He sat him on his lap. "What happened to Mommy?" The child pointed out the window. "So he was going to rape her?" Dorsey Standish asked them all.

Margot said, "Dorsey, let's wait until we know."

"Wait?" Standish said.

"You got to excuse me asking you," said Arden Bensenhaver, "but your wife wasn't seeing anybody, was she? You know."

Standish was mute at the question, but it seemed as if he were importantly considering it. "No, she wasn't," Margot told Bensenhaver. "Absolutely not."

"I got to ask Mr. Standish," Bensenhaver said.

"God," Margot said.

"No, I don't think she was," Standish told the inspector.

"Of course she wasn't, Dorsey," Margot said. "Let's go take Nicky for a walk," she said to him. She was a busy, businesslike woman whom Hope liked very much. She was in and out of the house five times a day; she was always in the process of finishing something. Twice a year she had her phone disconnected, and connected again; it was like trying to stop smoking is for some people. Margot had children of her own but they were older—they were in school all day—and she often watched Nicky so that Hope could do something by herself. Dorsey Standish took Margot for granted; although he knew she was a kind and generous person, those were not qualities that especially arrested his attention. Margot, he realized now, wasn't especially attractive, either. She was not *sexually* attractive, he thought, and a bitter feeling rose up in Standish: he thought that no one would ever try to rape Margot—whereas Hope was a beautiful woman, anyone could see. Anyone would want her.

Dorsey Standish was all wrong about that; he didn't know the first thing about rape—that the victim hardly ever matters. At one time or another, people have tried to force sex on almost anyone imaginable. Very small children, very old people, even dead people; also animals.

Inspector Arden Bensenhaver, who knew a good deal about rape, announced that he had to get on with his job.

Bensenhaver felt better with lots of open space around him. His first employment had been the nighttime beat in a squad car, cruising old Route 2 between Sandusky and Toledo. In the summers it was a road speckled with beer joints and little homemade signs promising BOWLING! POOL! SMOKED FISH! and LIVE BAIT! And Arden Bensenhaver would drive slowly over Sandusky Bay and along Lake Erie to Toledo, waiting for the drunken carfuls of teen-agers and fishermen to play chicken with him on that

418

unlit, two-lane road. Later, when he was the police superintendent of Toledo, Bensenhaver would be driven, in the daytime, over that harmless stretch of road. The bait shops and beer palaces and fast-food services looked so exposed in the daylight. It was like watching a once-feared bully strip down for a fight; you saw the thick neck, the dense chest, the wristless arms—and then, when the last shirt was off, you saw the sad, helpless paunch.

Arden Bensenhaver hated the night. Bensenhaver's big plea with the city government of Toledo had been for better lighting on Saturday nights. Toledo was a workingman's city, and Bensenhaver believed that if the city could afford to light itself, brightly, on Saturday night, half the gashings and maimings—the general bodily abusings—would stop. But Toledo had thought the idea was dim. Toledo was as unimpressed with Arden Bensenhaver's ideas as it was questioning of his methods.

Now Bensenhaver relaxed in all this open country. He had a perspective on the dangerous world that he always wanted to have: he was circling the flat, open land in a helicopter—above it all, the detached overseer observing his contained, well-lit kingdom. The county deputy said to him, "There's only one truck around here that's *turquoise*. It's those damn Raths."

"Raths?" Bensenhaver asked.

"There's a whole family of them," the deputy said. "I hate going out there."

"Why?" Bensenhaver asked; below him, he watched the shadow of the helicopter cross a creek, cross a road, move alongside a field of corn and a field of soybeans.

"They're all weird," the deputy said. Bensenhaver looked at him—a young man, puffy-faced and small-eyed, but pleasant; his long hair hung in a hunk under his tight hat, almost touching his shoulders. Bensenhaver thought of all the football players who wore their hair spilling out under their helmets. They could *braid* it, some of them, he thought. Now even lawmen looked like this. He was glad he was retiring soon; he couldn't understand why so many people wanted to look the way they did.

419

" 'Weird'?" said Bensenhaver. Their language was all the same, too, he thought. They used just four or five words for almost everything.

"Well, I got a complaint about the younger one just last week," the deputy said. Bensenhaver noted this casual use of "I"—as in "I got a complaint"—when in fact Bensenhaver knew that the sheriff, or his office, would have received the complaint, and that the sheriff probably thought it was simple enough to send this young deputy out on it. But why did they give me such a young one for *this?* Bensenhaver wondered.

"The youngest brother's name is Oren," the deputy said. "They all have weird names, too."

"What was the complaint?" Bensenhaver asked; his eyes followed a long dirt driveway to what appeared to be a random dropping of barns and outbuildings, one of which he knew was the main farmhouse, where the *people* lived. But Arden Bensenhaver couldn't tell which one that might be. To him, all the buildings looked vaguely unfit for animals.

"Well," the deputy said, "this kid Oren was screwing around with someone's dog."

" 'Screwing around'?" Bensenhaver asked patiently. That could mean anything, he thought.

"Well," the deputy said, "the people whose dog it was thought that Oren was trying to *fuck* it."

"*Was* he?" Bensenhaver asked.

"Probably," the deputy said, "but I couldn't tell anything. When I got there, Oren wasn't around—and the dog *looked* all right. I mean, how could I tell if the dog had been fucked?"

"Should've *asked* it!" said the copter pilot—a kid, Bensenhaver realized, even younger than the deputy. Even the deputy looked at him with contempt.

"One of these half-wits the National Guard gives us," the deputy whispered to Bensenhaver, but Bensenhaver had spotted the turquoise truck. It was parked out in the open, alongside a low shed. No attempt had been made to conceal it.

In a long pen a tide of pigs surged this way and that, driven crazy by the hovering helicopter. Two lean men in overalls squatted over a pig that lay sprawled at the foot of a ramp to a barn. They looked up at the helicopter, shielding their faces from the stinging dirt.

"Not so close. Put it down over on the lawn," Bensenhaver told the pilot. "You're scaring the animals."

"I don't see Oren, or the old man," the deputy said. "There's more of them than those two."

"You ask those two where Oren is," Bensenhaver said. "I want to look at that truck."

The men obviously knew the deputy; they hardly watched him approach. But they watched Bensenhaver, in his dull dun-colored suit and tie, crossing the barnyard toward the turquoise pickup. Arden Bensenhaver didn't look at them, but he could see them just the same. They are *morons*, he thought. Bensenhaver had seen all kinds of bad men in Toledo—vicious men, unjustifiably angry men, dangerous men, cowardly and ballsy thieves, men who murdered for money, and men who murdered for sex. But Bensenhaver had not seen quite such benign corruption as he thought he saw on the faces of Weldon and Raspberry Rath. It gave him a chill. He thought he'd better find Mrs. Standish, quickly.

He didn't know what he was looking for when he opened the door of the turquoise pickup, but Arden Bensenhaver knew how to look for unknowns. He saw it immediately—it was easy: the slashed bra, a piece of it still tied to the hinge of the glove-compartment door; the other two pieces were on the floor. There was no blood; the bra was a soft, natural beige; very classy, Arden Bensenhaver thought. He had no style himself, but he'd seen dead people of all kinds, and he could recognize something of a person's style in the clothes. He put the pieces of the silky bra into one hand; then he put both hands into the floppy, stretched pockets of his suit jacket and started across the yard toward the deputy, who was talking to the Rath brothers.

"They haven't seen the kid all day," the deputy told

421

Bensenhaver. "They say Oren sometimes stays away overnight."

"Ask them who's the last one who drove that truck," Bensenhaver said to the deputy; he wouldn't look at the Raths; he treated them as if they couldn't possibly understand him, directly.

"I already asked them that," the deputy said. "They say they don't remember."

"Ask them when's the last time a pretty young woman rode in that truck," Bensenhaver said, but the deputy didn't have time; Weldon Rath laughed. Bensenhaver felt grateful that the one with the blotch on his face, like a wine spill, had kept quiet.

"Shit," Weldon said. "There's no 'pretty young woman' around here, no pretty young woman ever sat her ass in that truck."

"Tell him," said Bensenhaver to the deputy, "that he is a liar."

"You're a liar, Weldon," the deputy said.

Raspberry Rath said to the deputy, "Shit, who is he, coming in here, telling us what to do?"

Arden Bensenhaver took the three pieces of the bra from his pocket. He looked at the sow lying beside the men; she had one frightened eye, which appeared to be looking at all of them at once, and it was hard to tell where her other eye was looking.

"Is that a boy pig or a girl pig?" asked Bensenhaver.

The Raths laughed. "Anyone can see it's a sow," Raspberry said.

"Do you ever cut the balls off the boy pigs?" Bensenhaver asked. "Do you do that yourselves or do you have others do it for you?"

"We castrate them ourselves," said Weldon. He looked a little like a boar himself, with wild tufts of hair sprouting upward, out of his ears. "We know all about castrating. There's nothing to it."

"Well," said Bensenhaver, holding up the bra for them and the deputy to see. "Well, that's exactly what the new law provides for—in the case of these sexual crimes."

Neither the deputy nor the Raths spoke. "Any sexual crime," Bensenhaver said, "is now punishable by castration. If you fuck anybody you shouldn't," said Bensenhaver, "or if you assist in the act of getting a person fucked—by not helping us to stop it—then we can castrate you."

Weldon Rath looked at his brother, Raspberry, who looked a little puzzled. But Weldon leered at Bensenhaver and said, "You do it yourselves or do you have others do it for you?" He nudged his brother. Raspberry tried to grin, pulling his birthmark askew.

But Bensenhaver was deadpan, turning the bra over and over in his hands. "Of course we don't do it," he said. "There's all new equipment for it now. The National Guard does it. That's why we got the National Guard helicopter. We just fly you right out to the National Guard hospital and fly you right back home again. There's nothing to it," he said. "As you know."

"We have a big family," Raspberry Rath said. "There's a lot of us brothers. We don't know from one day to the next who's riding around in what truck."

"There's *another* truck?" Bensenhaver asked the deputy. "You didn't tell me there was another truck."

"Yeah, it's black. I forgot," the deputy said. "They have a black one, too." The Raths nodded.

"Where is it?" Bensenhaver asked. He was contained but tense.

The brothers looked at each other. Weldon said, "I haven't seen it in a while."

"Might be that Oren has it," said Raspberry.

"Might be our father who's got it," Weldon said.

"We don't have time for this shit," Bensenhaver told the deputy, sharply. "We'll find out what they weigh—then see if the pilot can carry them." The deputy, thought Bensenhaver, is almost as much of a moron as the brothers. "Go on!" Bensenhaver said to the deputy. Then, with impatience, he turned to Weldon Rath. "Name?" he asked.

"Weldon," Weldon said.

"Weight?" Bensenhaver asked.

"Weight?" said Weldon.

"What do you weigh?" Bensenhaver asked him. "If we're going to lug you off in the copter, we got to know what you weigh."

"One-eighty-something," Weldon said.

"You?" Bensenhaver asked the younger one.

"One-ninety-something," he said. "My name's Raspberry." Bensenhaver shut his eyes.

"That's three-seventy-something," Bensenhaver told the deputy. "Go ask the pilot if we can carry that."

"You're not taking us anywhere, now, are you?" Weldon asked.

"We'll just take you to the National Guard hospital," Bensenhaver said. "Then if we find the woman, and she's all right, we'll take you home."

"But if she ain't all right, we get a lawyer, right?" Raspberry asked Bensenhaver. "One of those people in the courts, right?"

"If who *ain't* all right?" Bensenhaver asked him.

"Well, this woman you're looking for," Raspberry said.

"Well, if she's not all right," Bensenhaver said, "then we already got you in the hospital and we can castrate you and send you back home the same day. You boys know more about what's involved than I do," he admitted. "I've never seen it done, but it doesn't take long, does it? And it doesn't bleed much, does it?"

"But there's courts, and a lawyer!" Raspberry said.

"Of course there is," Weldon said. "Shut up."

"No, no more courts for this kind of thing—not with the new law," Bensenhaver said. "Sex crimes are special, and with the new machines, it's just so easy to castrate someone that it makes the most sense."

"Yeah!" the deputy hollered from the helicopter. "The weight's okay. We can take them."

"Shit!" Raspberry said.

"Shut up," said Weldon.

"They're not cutting *my* balls off!" Raspberry yelled at him. "I didn't even get to *have* her!" Weldon hit Raspberry so hard in the stomach that the younger man pitched over sideways and landed on the prostrate pig. It squealed, its

424

short legs spasmed, it *evacuated* suddenly, and horribly, but otherwise it didn't move. Raspberry lay gasping beside the sow's stenchful waste, and Arden Bensenhaver tried to knee Weldon Rath in the balls. Weldon was too quick, though; he caught Bensenhaver's leg at the knee and tossed the old man over backwards, over Raspberry and the poor pig.

"Goddamnit," Bensenhaver said.

The deputy drew his gun and fired one shot in the air. Weldon dropped to his knees, holding his ears. "You all right, Inspector?" the deputy asked.

"Yes, of course I am," Bensenhaver said. He sat beside the pig and Raspberry. He realized, without the smallest touch of shame, that he felt toward them more or less equally. "Raspberry," he said (the name itself made Bensenhaver close his eyes), "if you want to keep your balls on, you tell us where the woman is." The man's birthmark flashed at Bensenhaver like a neon sign.

"You keep still, Raspberry," Weldon said.

And Bensenhaver told the deputy, "If he opens his mouth again, *shoot* his balls off, right here. Save us the trip." Then he hoped to God that the deputy was not so stupid that he would actually do it.

"Oren's got her," Raspberry told Bensenhaver. "He took the black truck."

"Where'd he take her?" Bensenhaver asked.

"Don't know," Raspberry said. "He took her for a ride."

"Was she all right when she left here?" Bensenhaver asked.

"Well, she was all right, I guess," Raspberry said. "I mean, I don't think Oren had hurt her yet. I don't think he'd even *had* her yet."

"Why not?" Bensenhaver asked.

"Well, if he'd already had her," Raspberry said, "why would he want to keep her?" Bensenhaver again shut his eyes. He got to his feet.

"Find out how long ago," he told the deputy. "Then fuck up that turquoise truck so they can't drive it. Then get your ass back to the copter."

425

"And leave them here?" the deputy asked.

"Sure," Bensenhaver said. "There'll be plenty of time to cut their balls off, later."

Arden Bensenhaver had the pilot send a message that the abductor's name was Oren Rath, and that he was driving a black, not a turquoise, pickup. This message meshed interestingly with another one: a state trooper had received a report that a man all alone in a black pickup had been driving dangerously, wandering in and out of his rightful driving lane, "looking like he was drunk, or stoned, or something else." The trooper had not followed this up because, at the time, he'd thought he was supposed to be more concerned about a *turquoise* pickup. Arden Bensenhaver, of course, couldn't know that the man in the black pickup hadn't really been alone—that, in fact, Hope Standish had been lying with her head in his lap. The news simply gave Bensenhaver another of his chills: if Rath was alone, he had already done something to the woman. Bensenhaver yelled to the deputy to hurry over to the copter—that they were looking for a black pickup that had last been seen on the bypass that intersects the system of county roads near the town called Sweet Wells.

"Know it?" Bensenhaver asked.

"Oh, yeah," the deputy said.

They were in the air again, below them the pigs once more in a panic. The poor, medicated pig that had been fallen on was lying as still as when they'd come. But the Rath brothers were fighting—it appeared, quite savagely— and the higher and farther from them that the helicopter moved, the more the world returned to a level of sanity of which Arden Bensenhaver approved. Until the tiny fighting figures, below and to the east, were no more than miniatures to him, and he was so far from their blood and fear that when the deputy said he thought that Raspberry could whip Weldon, if Raspberry just didn't allow himself to get scared, Bensenhaver laughed his Toledo deadpan laugh.

"They're *animals*," he said to the deputy, who, despite whatever young man's cruelty and cynicism were in him,

426

seemed a little shocked. "If they both killed each other," Bensenhaver said, "think of the food they would have eaten in their lifetimes that other human beings could now eat." The deputy realized that Bensenhaver's lie about the new law—about the instant castration for sexual crimes—was more than a farfetched story: for Bensenhaver, although he knew it was clearly *not* the law, it was what he thought the law *should* be. It was one of Arden Bensenhaver's Toledo methods.

"That poor woman," Bensenhaver said; he wrung the pieces of her bra in his thick-veined hands. "How old is this Oren?" he asked the deputy.

"Sixteen, maybe seventeen," the deputy said. "Just a kid." The deputy was at least twenty-four himself.

"If he's old enough to get a hard-on," Arden Bensenhaver said, "he's old enough to have it cut off."

But *what* should I cut? Oh, *where* can I cut him? wondered Hope—the long, thin fisherman's knife now snug in her hand. Her pulse thrummed in her palm, but to Hope it felt as if the knife had a heartbeat of its own. She brought her hand very slowly up to her hip, up over the edge of the thrashed seat to where she could glimpse the blade. Should I use the saw-toothed edge or the one that looks so sharp? she thought. How do you kill a man with one of these? Alongside the sweating, swiveling ass of Oren Rath that knife in her hand was a cool and distant miracle. Do I slash him or stick him? She wished she knew. Both his hot hands were under her buttocks, lifting her, jerking up. His chin dug into the hollow near her collarbone like a heavy stone. Then she felt him slip one of his hands out from under her, and his fingers, reaching for the floor, grazed her hand that held the knife.

"Move!" he grunted. "Now move." She tried to arch her back but couldn't; she tried to twist her hips, but she couldn't. She felt him groping for his own peculiar rhythm, trying to find the last pace that would make him come. His hand—under her now—spread over the small of her back; his other hand clawed the floor.

427

Then she knew: he was looking for the knife. And when his fingers found the empty sheath, she would be in trouble.

"Aaahhh!" he cried.

Quick! she thought. Between the ribs? Into his side—and slide the knife up—or straight down as hard as she could between the shoulder blades, reaching all the way through his back to a lung, until she felt the point of the thing poking her own crushed breast? She waved her arm in the air above his hunching back. She saw the oily blade glint—and *his* hand, suddenly rising, flung his empty pants back toward the steering wheel.

He was trying to push himself up off her, but his lower half was locked into his long-sought rhythm; his hips shuddered in little spasms he couldn't seem to control, while his chest rose up, off her chest, and his hands shoved hard against her shoulders. His thumbs crawled toward her throat. "My knife?" he asked. His head whipped back and forth; he looked behind him, he looked above him. His thumbs pried her chin up; she was trying to hide her Adam's apple.

Then she scissored his pale ass. He could not stop pumping down there, though his brain must have known there was suddenly another priority. "My knife?" he said. And she reached over his shoulder and (faster than she herself could see it happen) she slid the slim-edged side of the blade across his throat. For a second, she saw no wound. She only knew that he was choking her. Then one of his hands left her throat and went to find his own. He hid from her the gash she'd expected to see. But at last she saw the dark blood springing between his tight fingers. He brought his hand away—he was searching for *her* hand, the one that held the knife—and from his slashed throat a great bubble burst over her. She heard a sound like someone sucking the bottom of a drink with a clogged straw. She could breathe again. Where were his hands? she wondered. They seemed, at once, to loll beside her on the seat and to be darting like panicked birds behind his back.

She stabbed the long blade into him, just above his waist, thinking that perhaps a kidney was there, because the blade went in so easily, and out again. Oren Rath laid his cheek against her cheek like a child. He'd have screamed then, of course, but her first slash had cut cleanly through his windpipe and his vocal cords.

Hope now tried the knife higher up, but encountered a rib, or something difficult; she had to probe and, unsatisfied, withdrew the knife after only a few inches. He was flopping on her now, as if he wanted to get off her. His body was sending distress signals to itself, but the signals were not getting all the way through. He heaved himself against the back of the seat, but his head wouldn't stay up and his penis, still moving, attached him still to Hope. She took advantage of this opportunity to insert the knife again. It slipped into his belly at the side and moved straightaway to within an inch of his navel before engaging some major obstruction there—and his body slumped back on top of her, trapping her wrist. But this was easy; she twisted her hand and the slippery knife came free. Something to do with his bowels relaxed. Hope was overwhelmed with his wetness and with his smell. She let the knife drop to the floor.

Oren Rath was emptying, by quartfuls—by gallons. He felt actually lighter on top of her. Their bodies were so slick that she slipped out from under him easily. She shoved him over on his back and crouched beside him on the truck's puddled floor. Hope's hair was gravid with blood —his throat had fountained over her. When she blinked, her eyelashes stuck to her cheeks. One of his hands twitched and she slapped it. "Stop," she said. His knee rose, then flopped down. "Stop it, stop now," Hope said. She meant his heart, his life.

She would not look at his face. Against the dark slime coating his body, the white, translucent condom hugged his shrunken cock like a congealed fluid quite foreign to the human matter of blood and bowel. Hope recalled a zoo, and a gob of camel spit upon her crimson sweater.

His balls contracted. That made her angry. "Stop," she hissed. The balls were small and rounded and tight; then they fell slack. "*Please stop,*" she whispered. "*Please die.*"

There was a tiny sigh, as if someone had let out a breath too small to bother taking back. But Hope squatted for some time beside him, feeling her heart pound and confusing her pulse with his own. He had died fairly quickly, she realized later.

Out the open door of the pickup, Oren Rath's clean white feet, his drained toes, pointed upward in the sunlight. Inside the sun-baked cab, the blood was coagulating. Everything clotted. Hope Standish felt the tiny hairs on her arms stiffen and tug her skin as her skin dried. Everything that was slick was turning sticky.

I should get dressed, Hope thought. But something seemed wrong with the weather.

Out the truck windows Hope saw the sunlight flicker, like a lamp whose light is shone through the blades of a fast fan. And the gravel at the roadside was lifted up in little swirls, and dry shards and stubble from last year's corn were whisked along the flat, bare ground as if a great wind was blowing—but not from the usual directions: *this* wind appeared to be blowing straight down. And the noise! It was like being in the afterblow of a speeding truck, but there was still no traffic on the road.

It's a tornado! Hope thought. She hated the Midwest with its strange weather; she was an Easterner who could understand a hurricane. But tornadoes! She'd never seen one, but the weather forecasts were always full of "tornado watches." What does one *watch* for? she'd always wondered. For *this,* she guessed—this whirling din all around her. These clods of earth flying. The sun turned brown.

She was so angry, she struck the cool, viscid thigh of Oren Rath. After she had lived through *this,* now there was a fucking tornado, too! The noise resembled a train passing over the pelted truck. Hope imagined the funnel descending, other trucks and cars already caught up in it. Somehow, she could hear, their engines were still running. Sand flew in the open door, stuck to her glazed body; she groped for her dress—discovered the empty armholes where the sleeves had been; it would have to do.

But she would have to step outside the truck to put it on.

There was no room to maneuver beside Rath and his gore, now dappled with roadside sand. And out there, she had no doubt, her dress would be torn from her hands and she would be sucked up naked into the sky. "I am not sorry," she whispered. "I am *not* sorry!" she screamed, and again she struck at the body of Rath.

Then a voice, a terrible voice—loud as the loudest loud-speaker—shook her in the cab. "IF YOU'RE IN THERE, COME OUT! PUT YOUR HANDS OVER YOUR HEAD. COME OUT. CLIMB INTO THE BACK OF THE PICKUP AND LIE THE FUCK DOWN!"

I am actually dead, thought Hope. I'm *already* in the sky and it's the voice of God. She was not religious and it seemed fitting, to Hope: if there were a God, God *would* have a bullying, loudspeaker voice.

"COME OUT NOW," God said. "DO IT NOW."

Oh, why not? she thought. You big fucker. What can you do to me next? Rape was an outrage even God couldn't understand.

In the helicopter, shuddering above the black truck, Arden Bensenhaver barked into the megaphone. He was sure that Mrs. Standish was dead. He could not tell the sex of the feet he saw protruding from the open door of the cab, but the feet hadn't moved during the helicopter's descent, and they seemed so naked and drained of any color in the sunlight that Bensenhaver was sure that they were *dead* feet. That Oren Rath could be the one who was dead had not crossed the deputy's or Bensenhaver's mind.

But they couldn't understand why Rath would have abandoned the truck, after performing his foul acts, and so Bensenhaver had told the pilot to hold the helicopter just above the pickup. "If he's still in there with her," Bensenhaver told the deputy, "maybe we can scare the bastard to death."

When Hope Standish brushed between those stiff feet and huddled alongside the cab, trying to shield her eyes from the flying sand, Arden Bensenhaver felt his finger go limp against the trigger of the megaphone. Hope tried to wrap her face in her flapping dress but it snapped around her like a torn sail; she felt her way along the truck toward the tailgate, cringing against the stinging gravel that clung to the places on her body where the blood hadn't quite dried.

"It's the woman," the deputy said.

"Back off!" Bensenhaver told the pilot.

"Jesus, what happened to her?" the deputy asked, frightened. Bensenhaver roughly handed him the megaphone.

"Move away," he said to the pilot. "Set this thing down across the road."

Hope felt the wind shift, and the clamor in the tornado's funnel seemed to pass over her. She kneeled at the side of the road. Her wild dress quieted in her hands. She held it to her mouth because the dust was choking her.

A car came along, but Hope was unaware of it. The driver passed in the proper lane—the black pickup off the road to his right, the helicopter settling down off the road to his left. The bloody, praying woman, naked and caked with grit, took no notice of him driving past her. The driver had a vision of an angel on a trip back from hell. The driver's reaction was so delayed that he was a hundred yards beyond everything he'd seen before he surprisingly attempted a U-turn in the road. Without slowing down. His front wheels caught the soft shoulder and slithered him across the road ditch and into the soft spring earth of a plowed bean field, where his car sank up to his bumpers and he could not open his door. He rolled down his window and peered across the mire to the road—like a man who'd been sitting peacefully on a dock when the dock broke free from the shore, and he was drifting out to sea.

"Help!" he cried. The vision of the woman had so terrified him that he feared there might be more like her around, or that whoever had made her look that way might be in search of another victim.

"Jesus Christ," said Arden Bensenhaver to the pilot, "you'll have to go see if that fool is all right. Why do they let everyone drive a car?" Bensenhaver and the deputy

432

dropped out of the helicopter and into the same lush muck that had trapped the driver. "Goddamnit," Bensenhaver said.

"Mother," said the deputy.

Across the road, Hope Standish looked up at them for the first time. Two swearing men were wallowing toward her out of a muddy field. The blades of the helicopter were slowing down. There was also a man peeping witlessly out the window of his car, but that seemed far away. Hope stepped into her dress. One armhole, where a sleeve had been, was torn open and Hope had to pin a flap of material to her side with her elbow, or else leave her breast exposed. It was then that she noticed how sore her shoulders and her neck were.

Arden Bensenhaver, out of breath and soaked with mud from his knees down, was in front of her suddenly. The mud made his trousers hug his legs so that, to Hope, he looked like an old man wearing knickers. "Mrs. Standish?" he asked. She turned her back to him and hid her face, nodding. "So much blood," he said, helplessly. "I'm sorry we took so long. Are you hurt?"

She turned and stared at him. He saw the swelling around both eyes and her broken nose—and the blue bulge on her forehead. "It's mostly *his* blood," she said. "But I was raped. He did it," she told Bensenhaver.

Bensenhaver had his handkerchief out; he seemed about to dab at her face with it, as he might wipe the mouth of a child, but then he despaired at what a job it would be to clean her up and he put his handkerchief away. "I'm sorry," he said. "I'm so sorry. We got here as fast as we could. We saw your baby and he's fine," Bensenhaver said.

"I had to put him in my mouth," Hope said to him. Bensenhaver shut his eyes. "And then he fucked me and fucked me," she said. "He was going to kill me, later—he told me he would. I *had* to kill him. And I'm not sorry."

"Of course you're not," Bensenhaver said. "And you *shouldn't* be, Mrs. Standish. I'm sure you did the very best thing." She nodded her head to him, then stared down at her feet. She put one hand out toward Bensenhaver's shoulder and he let her lean against him, though she was slightly taller than Bensenhaver and in order to rest her head against him, she had to scrunch down.

Bensenhaver was aware of the deputy then; he had been to the cab to look at Oren Rath and had vomited all over the truck's front fender and in full view of the pilot who was walking the shocked driver of the stuck car across the road. The deputy, with his face the bloodless color of Oren Rath's sunlit feet, was imploring Bensenhaver to come see. But Bensenhaver wanted Mrs. Standish to feel every possible reassurance.

"So you killed him after he raped you, when he was relaxed, not paying attention?" he asked her.

"No, *during*," she whispered against his neck. The awful reek of her almost got to Bensenhaver, but he kept his face very close to her, where he could hear her.

"You mean, *while* he was raping you, Mrs. Standish?"

"Yes," she whispered. "He was still inside me when I got his knife. It was in his pants, on the floor, and he was going to use it on me when he was finished, so I *had* to," she said.

"Of course you did," Bensenhaver said. "It doesn't matter." He meant that she should have killed him anyway— even if he hadn't been planning to kill her. To Arden Bensenhaver there was no crime as serious as rape—not even murder, except perhaps the murder of a child. But he knew less about that; he had no children of his own.

He had been married seven months when his pregnant wife had been raped in a Laundromat while he waited outside for her in the car. Three kids had done it. They had opened one of the big spring-doored dryers and sat her ass on the open door, pushed her head into the warm dryer where she could only scream into the hot, muffling sheets and pillowcases and hear her own voice boom and bounce around the great metal drum. Her arms were in the dryer with her head, so she was helpless. Her feet couldn't even reach the floor. The spring door made her jounce up and down under all three of them, although she probably tried not to move. The boys had no idea, of course, that they were raping the police superintendent's wife. And all the bright lighting possible for downtown Toledo on a Saturday night would not have saved her.

They were an early-morning couple, the Bensenhavers. They were young still, and they took their laundry to the Laundromat together, Monday morning before breakfast; they read the newspapers during the wash cycle. Then they put their laundry in the dryer and went home and had breakfast. Mrs. Bensenhaver picked it up on her way downtown to the police station with Bensenhaver. He would wait in the car while she went inside to get it; sometimes, someone would have taken it out of the dryer while they were having breakfast and Mrs. Bensenhaver would have to run it for another few minutes. Bensenhaver then waited. But they liked the early morning because there was rarely anyone else in the Laundromat.

Only when Bensenhaver saw the three kids leaving did he start to worry about how long his wife had been collecting the dry laundry. But it does not take very long to rape someone, even three times. Bensenhaver went into the Laundromat where he saw his wife's legs sticking out of the dryer; her shoes had fallen off. Those were not the first dead feet Bensenhaver had seen, but they were very important feet to him.

She had suffocated in her own clean wash—or she had vomited, and choked—but they had not meant to kill her. That part had been an accident, and at the trial a great deal had been made of the unplanned nature of Mrs. Bensenhaver's death. Their attorney had said that the boys had planned "to just rape her—not kill her, too." And the phrase *"just rape"*—as in "She was *just raped*, lucky thing, a wonder she wasn't killed!"—appalled Arden Bensenhaver.

"It's good that you killed him," Bensenhaver whispered to Hope Standish. "We couldn't have done nearly enough to him," he confided to her. "Nothing like he deserved. Good for you," he whispered. "Good for you."

Hope had expected another sort of police experience, a more critical investigation—at least, a more suspicious cop, and certainly a man very different from Arden Bensenhaver. She was so grateful, for one thing, that Bensenhaver was an *old* man, clearly in his sixties—like an uncle to her, or even more sexually remote: a grandfather. She said she felt better, that she was all right; when she straightened up and stood away from him, she saw she had smeared his shirt collar and his cheek with blood, but Bensenhaver hadn't noticed or didn't care.

"Okay, show me," Bensenhaver said to the deputy, but again he smiled gently at Hope. The deputy led him to the open cab.

"Oh, my God," the driver of the stuck car was saying. "Dear Jesus, look at this, and what's *that*? Christ, look, I think that's his *liver*. Isn't that what a liver looks like?" The pilot gawked in mute wonder and Bensenhaver caught both men by their coat shoulders and steered them roughly away. They started toward the rear of the truck, where Hope was composing herself, but Bensenhaver hissed at them, "Stay away from Mrs. Standish. Stay away from the truck. Go radio our position," he told the pilot. "They'll need an ambulance or something here. We'll take Mrs. Standish with us."

"They'll need a plastic bag for *him*," said the deputy, pointing to Oren Rath. "He's all over the place."

"I can see with my own eyes," said Arden Bensenhaver. He looked inside the cab and whistled admiringly.

The deputy started to ask, "Was he doing it when . . ."

"That's right," said Bensenhaver. He put his hand into a horrible mess by the accelerator pedal, but he didn't seem to mind. He was reaching for the knife on the floor of the passenger's side. He picked it up in his handkerchief; he looked it over carefully, wrapped it in the handkerchief, and put it in his pocket.

"Look," the deputy whispered, conspiratorially. "Did you ever hear of a *rapist* wearing a rubber?"

"It's not common," Bensenhaver said. "But it's not unknown."

"It's weird to me," said the deputy. He looked amazed as Bensenhaver pinched the prophylactic tight, just below its bulge; Bensenhaver snapped the rubber off and held it, without spilling a drop, up to the light. The sack was as large as a tennis ball. It hadn't leaked. It was full of blood.

Bensenhaver looked satisfied; he tied a knot in the condom, the way you'd knot a balloon, and he flung it so far into the bean field that it was out of sight.

"I don't want someone suggesting that it might *not* have been a rape," Bensenhaver said softly to the deputy. "Got it?"

He didn't wait for the deputy to answer; Bensenhaver went to the back of the truck to be with Mrs. Standish.

"How old was he—that boy?" Hope asked Bensenhaver.

"Old enough," Bensenhaver told her. "About twenty-five or twenty-six," he added. He did not want anything to diminish her survival—particularly, in her own eyes. He waved to the pilot, who was to help Mrs. Standish aboard. Then he went to clear things with the deputy. "You stay here with the body and the bad driver," he told him.

"I'm not a bad driver," the driver whined. "Christ, if you'd seen that lady there—in the road . . ."

"And keep anyone away from the truck," Bensenhaver said.

On the road was the shirt belonging to Mrs. Standish's husband; Bensenhaver picked it up and trotted to the helicopter in his funny, overweight way of running. The two men watched Bensenhaver climb aboard the helicopter and rise away from them. The weak spring sun seemed to leave with the copter and they were suddenly cold and didn't know where to go. Not in the truck, certainly, and sitting in the driver's car meant crossing that field of muck. They went to the pickup, lowered the tailgate, and sat on it.

"Will he call a tow truck for my car?" the driver asked.

"He'll probably forget," the deputy said. He was thinking about Bensenhaver; he admired him, but he feared him, and he also thought that Bensenhaver was not to be totally trusted. There were questions of orthodoxy, if that's what it was, which the deputy had never considered. Mainly, the deputy just had too many things to think about at one time.

The driver paced back and forth in the pickup, which irritated the deputy because it jounced him on the tailgate.

The driver avoided the foul, bunched blanket crammed in the corner next to the cab; he cleared a see-through spot on the dusted and caked rear window so that he could, occasionally, squint inside the cab at the rigid and disemboweled body of Oren Rath. All the blood was dry now, and through the mottled rear window the body looked to the driver to be similar, in color and in gloss, to an eggplant. He went and sat down on the tailgate beside the deputy, who got up, walked back in the truck, and peered in the window at the gashed corpse.

"You know what?" the driver said. "Even though she was all messed up, you could tell what a really good-looking woman she was."

"Yes, you could," the deputy agreed. The driver now paced around in the back of the truck with him, so the deputy went to the tailgate and sat down.

"Don't get sore," the driver said.

"I'm not sore," the deputy said.

"I don't mean that I can sympathize with anyone who'd want to rape her, you know," the driver said.

"I know what you don't mean," said the deputy.

The deputy knew he was over his head in these matters, but the simple-mindedness of the driver forced the deputy to adopt what he imagined was Bensenhaver's attitude of contempt for *him*.

"You see a lot of this, huh?" the driver asked. "You know: rape and murder."

"Enough," the deputy said with self-conscious solemnity. He had never seen a rape or murder before, and he realized that even now he had not actually seen it through his own eyes as much as he'd been treated to the experience through the eyes of Arden Bensenhaver. He had seen rape and murder according to Bensenhaver, he thought. The deputy felt very confused; he sought some point of view all his own.

"Well," said the driver, peering in the rear window again, "I seen some stuff in the service, but nothing like this."

The deputy couldn't respond.

"This is like war, I guess," the driver said. "This is like a bad hospital."

The deputy wondered if he should let the fool look at Rath's body, if it mattered or not, and to whom? Certainly it couldn't matter to Rath. But to his unreal family? To the deputy?—he didn't know. And would Bensenhaver object?

"Hey, don't mind my asking you a personal question," the driver said. "Don't get sore, okay?"

"Okay," said the deputy.

"Well," the driver said. "What happened to the rubber?"

"*What* rubber?" asked the deputy; he might have had some questions concerning Bensenhaver's sanity, but the deputy had no doubt that, in this case, Bensenhaver had been right. In the world according to Bensenhaver, no trivial detail should make less of rape's outrage.

Hope Standish, at that moment, felt safe at last in Bensenhaver's world. She floated and dipped over the farmlands beside him, trying not to be sick. She was beginning to notice things about her body again—she could smell herself and feel every sore spot. She felt such disgust, but here was this cheerful policeman who sat there admiring her—his heart touched by her violent success.

"Are you married, Mr. Bensenhaver?" she asked him.

"Yes, Mrs. Standish," he said. "I am."

"You've been awfully nice," Hope told him, "but I think I'm going to be sick now."

"Oh, sure," said Bensenhaver; he grabbed a waxy paper bag at his feet. It was the pilot's lunch bag; there were some uneaten french-fried potatoes at the bottom and the grease had turned the waxed paper translucent. Bensenhaver could see his own hand, through the french fries and through the bottom of the bag. "Here," he said. "You go right ahead."

She was already retching; she took the bag from him and turned her head away. The bag did not feel big enough to contain what vileness she was sure she held inside her. She felt Bensenhaver's hard, heavy hand on her back. With his other hand, he held a strand of her matted hair out of her way. "That's right," he encouraged her, "keep it coming, get it all out and you'll feel much better."

Hope recalled that whenever Nicky was being sick, she told him the same thing. She marveled how Bensenhaver could even turn her vomiting into a victory, but she *did* feel much better—the rhythmic heaving was as soothing to her as his calm, dry hands, holding her head and patting her back. When the bag ripped and spilled, Bensenhaver said, "Good riddance, Mrs. Standish! You don't need the bag. This is a National Guard helicopter. We'll let the National Guard clean it up! After all—what's the National Guard for?"

The pilot flew on, grimly, his expression never changing.

"What a day it's been for you, Mrs. Standish!" Bensenhaver went on. "Your husband is going to be so proud of you." But Bensenhaver was thinking that he'd better make sure; he'd better have a talk with the man. It was Arden Bensenhaver's experience that husbands and other people did not always take a rape in the right way.

# 16

❊❊❊❊❊❊❊

# The First Assassin

WHAT do you mean, 'This is Chapter One'?" Garp's editor, John Wolf, wrote him. "How can there be any more of *this?* There is entirely too much as it stands! How can you possibly go on?"

"It goes on," Garp wrote back. "You'll see."

"I don't *want* to see," John Wolf told Garp on the phone. "Please drop it. At least put it aside. Why don't you take a trip? It would be good for you—and for Helen, I'm sure. And Duncan can travel now, can't he?"

But Garp not only insisted that *The World According to Bensenhaver* was going to be a novel; he insisted that John Wolf try to sell the first chapter to a magazine. Garp had never had an agent; John Wolf was the first man to deal with Garp's writing, and he managed everything for him, just as he managed everything for Jenny Fields.

*"Sell* it?" John Wolf said.

"Yes, sell it," Garp said. "Advance publicity for the novel."

This had happened with Garp's first two books; excerpts had been sold to magazines. But John Wolf tried to tell Garp that *this* chapter was (1) unpublishable and (2) the worst possible publicity—should anyone be fool enough to publish it. He said that Garp had a "small but serious" reputation as a writer, that his first two novels had been decently reviewed—had won him respected supporters and a "small but serious" audience. Garp said he *hated* the reputation of "small but serious," though he could see that this appealed to John Wolf.

"I would rather be rich and wholly outside *caring* about what the idiots call 'serious,' " he told John Wolf. But who is ever outside caring about that?

Garp actually felt that he could buy a sort of isolation from the real and terrible world. He imagined a kind of fort where he and Duncan and Helen (and a new baby) could live unmolested, even untouched by what he called "the rest of life."

"What *are* you talking about?" John Wolf asked him.

Helen asked him, too. And so did Jenny. But Jenny Fields *liked* the first chapter of *The World According to Bensenhaver*. She thought it had all its priorities in order—that it knew whom to heroize in such a situation, that it expressed the necessary outrage, that it made properly grotesque the vileness of *lust*. Actually, Jenny's fondness for the first chapter was more troubling to Garp than John Wolf's criticism. Garp suspected his mother's literary judgment above all things.

"My God, look at *her* book," he kept saying to Helen, but Helen, as she promised, would not allow herself to be drawn in; she would not read Garp's new novel, not one word of it.

"Why does he suddenly want to be *rich?*" John Wolf asked Helen. "What's all this about?"

"I don't know," Helen said. "I think he believes it will protect him, and all of us."

"From *what?*" John Wolf said. "From *whom?*"

"You'll have to wait until you read the whole book," Garp said to his editor. "Every business is a shitty business. I am trying to treat this book like business, and I want you to treat it that way, too. I don't care if you *like* it; I want you to *sell* it."

"I am not a vulgar publisher," John Wolf said. "And you are not a vulgar writer, either. I'm sorry I have to remind you." John Wolf's feelings were hurt, and he was angry at Garp for presuming to talk about a business that John Wolf understood far better than Garp. But he knew Garp had been through a bad time, he knew Garp was a good writer who would write more and (he thought) better books, and he wanted to continue publishing him.

"Every business is a shitty business," Garp repeated. "If you think the book is vulgar, then you should have *no* trouble selling it."

"That's not the only way it works," Wolf said, sadly. "No one knows what makes books sell."

"I've heard that before," Garp said.

"You have no call to speak to me like this," John Wolf said. "I'm your friend." Garp knew that was true, so he hung up the telephone and answered no mail and finished *The World According to Bensenhaver* two weeks before Helen delivered, with only Jenny's help, their third child—a daughter, who spared Helen and Garp the problem of having to agree upon a boy's name that in no way resembled the name of Walt. The daughter was named Jenny Garp, which was the name Jenny Fields would have had if she had gone about the business of having Garp in a more conventional way

Jenny was delighted to have someone at least partially named after her. "But there's going to be some confusion," she warned, "with two of us around."

"I've always called you 'Mom,'" Garp reminded her. He did not remind his mother that a fashion designer had already named a dress after her. It was popular in New York for about a year: a white nurse's uniform with a bright red heart sewn over the left breast. A JENNY FIELDS ORIGINAL, the heart said.

When Jenny Garp was born, Helen said nothing. Helen was grateful; she felt for the first time since the accident that she was delivered from the insanity of grief that had crushed her with the loss of Walt.

*The World According to Bensenhaver,* which was
Garp's deliverance from the same insanity, resided in
New York, where John Wolf read it over and over
again. He had arranged to have the first chapter published in a porno magazine of such loathsome crudity
that he felt sure even Garp would be convinced of the
book's doom. The magazine was called *Crotch Shots,*
and it was full of exactly that—those wet, split beavers
of Garp's childhood, between the pages of his story of
violent rape and obvious revenge. At first Garp accused
John Wolf of deliberately placing the chapter there, of
not even trying the better magazines. But Wolf assured
Garp that he had tried them all; that this was the bottom
line of the list—this was exactly how Garp's story was
interpreted. Lurid, sensational violence and sex of no
redeeming value whatsoever.

"That's not what it's about," Garp said "You'll see."

But Garp often wondered about the first chapter of
*The World According to Bensenhaver,* which had been
published in *Crotch Shots.* If it had been read at all. If
anyone who bought those magazines ever looked at the
words.

"Perhaps they read some of the stories after they
masturbate to the pictures," Garp wrote to John Wolf.
He wondered if that was a good mood to be read in:
after masturbation, the reader was at least relaxed, possibly lonely ("a good state in which to read," Garp told
John Wolf). But maybe the reader felt guilty, too; and
humiliated, and overwhelmingly responsible (that was
*not* such a good condition in which to read, Garp
thought). In fact, he knew, it was not a good condition
in which to *write.*

*The World According to Bensenhaver* is about the
impossible desire of the husband, Dorsey Standish, to
protect his wife and child from the brutal world; thus
Arden Bensenhaver (who is forced to retire from the
police, for repeated unorthodoxy in his methods of arrest) is hired to live like an armed uncle in the house

with the Standish family—he becomes the lovable family bodyguard, whom Hope must finally reject. Though the worst of the real world has been visited upon Hope, it is her husband who *fears* the world most. After Hope insists that Bensenhaver not live with them, Standish continues to support the old policeman as a kind of hovering angel. Bensenhaver is paid to tail the child, Nicky, but Bensenhaver is an aloof and curious kind of watchdog, subject to fits of his own awful memories; he gradually seems more of a menace to the Standishes than he seems a protector. He is described as "a lurker at the last edge of light—a retired enforcer, barely alive on the rim of darkness."

Hope counters her husband's anxiety by insisting they have a second child. The child is born, but Standish seems destined to create one monster of paranoia after another; now more relaxed about possible assaults upon his wife and children, he begins to suspect that Hope is having an affair. Slowly, he realizes that this would wound him more than if she were raped (again). Thus he doubts his love for her, and doubts himself; guiltily, he begs Bensenhaver to spy on Hope and determine if she is faithful. But Arden Bensenhaver will no longer do Dorsey's worry work for him. The old policeman argues that he was hired to protect Standish's family from the outside world—not to restrict the free choices of the family to live as it wants. Without Bensenhaver's support, Dorsey Standish panics. One night he leaves the house (and the children) unprotected while he goes out to spy on his wife. While Dorsey is gone, the younger child chokes to death on a piece of Nicky's chewing gum.

Guilt abounds. In Garp's work, guilt always abounds. With Hope, too—because she *was* seeing someone (although who could blame her). Bensenhaver, morbid with responsibility, has a stroke. Partially paralyzed, he moves back in with the Standishes; Dorsey feels responsible for him. Hope insists they have *another* child, but the events have made Standish determinedly sterile.

He agrees that Hope should encourage her lover—but merely to "impregnate" herself, as he puts it. (Ironically, this was the *only* part of the book that Jenny Fields called "farfetched.")

Once again, Dorsey Standish seeks "a control situation—more like a laboratory experiment at life than life itself," Garp wrote. Hope cannot adjust to such a clinical arrangement; emotionally, either she has a lover or she doesn't. Insisting that the lovers meet for the sole purpose of "impregnating" Hope, Dorsey tries to control the whereabouts, the number and length of their meetings. Suspecting that Hope is meeting her lover clandestinely, as well as according to plan, Standish alerts the senile Bensenhaver to the existence of a prowler, a potential kidnapper and rapist, whose presence in the neighborhood has already been detected.

Still not satisfied, Dorsey Standish takes to sudden, unannounced visits at his own house (at times when he's least expected home); he never catches Hope at anything, but Bensenhaver, armed and deadly with senility, catches Dorsey. A cunning invalid, Arden Bensenhaver is surprisingly mobile and silent in his wheelchair; he is also still unorthodox in his methods of arrest. In fact, Bensenhaver shoots Dorsey Standish with a twelve-gauge shotgun from a distance of less than six feet. Dorsey had been hiding in the upstairs cedar closet, stumbling among his wife's shoes, waiting for her to make a phone call from the bedroom, which—from the closet—he could overhear. He deserves to be shot, of course.

The wound is fatal. Arden Bensenhaver, thoroughly mad, is taken away. Hope is pregnant with her lover's child. When the child is born, Nicky—now twelve—feels unburdened by the relaxing tension in the family. The terrible anxiety of Dorsey Standish, which has been so crippling to all their lives, is at last lifted from them. Hope and her children live on, even cheerfully dealing with the wild rantings of old Bensenhaver, too tough to die, who goes on and on with his versions of the nightmarish world from his wheelchair in an old-age home for the criminally insane. He is seen, finally, as belonging where he is. Hope and her children visit him often, not merely out of kindness—for they are kind—but also to remind themselves of their own precious sanity. Hope's endurance, and the survival of her two children, make the old man's ravings tolerable, finally even comic to her.

That peculiar old-age home for the criminally insane, by the way, bears an astonishing resemblance to Jenny Fields' hospital for wounded women at Dog's Head Harbor.

It is not so much that "the world according to Bensenhaver" is *wrong,* or even misperceived, as it is out of proportion to the world's need for sensual pleasure, and the world's need and capacity for warmth. Dorsey Standish "is not true to the world," either; he is too vulnerable to how *delicately* he loves his wife and children; he is seen, together with Bensenhaver, as "not well suited for life on this planet." Where immunity counts.

Hope—and, the reader hopes, her children—may have better chances. Somehow implicit in the novel is the sense that women are better equipped than men at enduring fear and brutality, and at containing the anxiousness of feeling how vulnerable we are to the people we love. Hope is seen as a strong survivor of a weak man's world.

John Wolf sat in New York, hoping that the visceral reality of Garp's language, and the intensity of Garp's characters, somehow rescued the book from sheer soap opera. But, Wolf thought, one might as well call the thing *Anxiousness of Life;* it would make a fantastic series for daytime television, he thought—if suitably edited for invalids, senior citizens, and preschool children. John Wolf concluded that *The World According to Bensenhaver,* despite the "visceral reality of Garp's language," and so forth, was an X-rated soap opera.

Much later, of course, even Garp would agree; it was

his worst work. "But the fucking world never gave me credit for the first two," he wrote to John Wolf. "Thus I was owed." That, Garp felt, was the way it worked most of the time.

John Wolf was more basically concerned: that is, he wondered if he could justify the book's publication. With books he did not absolutely take to, John Wolf had a system that rarely failed him. At his publishing house, he was envied for his record of being right about those books destined to be popular. When he said a book was going to be popular—distinct from being good or likable or not—he was almost always right. There were many books that were popular without his saying so, of course, but no book he'd ever claimed *would* be popular was ever *un*popular.

Nobody knew how he did it.

He did it first for Jenny Fields—and for certain, surprising books, every year or two, he had been doing it ever since.

There was a woman who worked in the publishing house who once told John Wolf that she never read a book that didn't make her want to close it and go to sleep. She was a challenge to John Wolf, who loved books, and he spent many years giving this woman good books and bad books to read; the books were alike in that they put this woman to sleep. She just didn't like to read, she told John Wolf; but he would not give up on her. No one else in the publishing house ever asked this woman to read anything at all; in fact, they never asked this woman's opinion of *any*thing. The woman moved through the books lying all around the publishing house as if these books were ashtrays and she was a nonsmoker. She was a cleaning woman. Every day she emptied the wastebaskets; she cleaned everyone's office when they went home at night. She vacuumed the rugs in the corridors every Monday, she dusted the display cases every Tuesday, and the secretaries' desks on Wednesdays; she scrubbed the bathrooms on Thursdays and sprayed air freshener on everything on Fridays—so that, she told John Wolf, the entire publishing house had the whole weekend to gather up a good smell for the next week. John Wolf had watched her for years and he'd never seen her so much as glance at a book.

When he asked her about books and she told him how unlikable they were to her, he kept using her to test books he wasn't sure of—and the books he thought he was *very* sure of, too. She was consistent in her dislike of books and John Wolf had almost given up on her when he gave her the manuscript of *A Sexual Suspect,* the autobiography of Jenny Fields.

The cleaning woman read it overnight and asked John Wolf if she could have a copy of her very own to read —over and over again—when the book was published.

After that, John Wolf sought her opinion scrupulously. She did not disappoint him. She did not like most things, but when she liked something, it meant to John Wolf that nearly everybody else was at least sure to be able to read it.

It was almost by rote that John Wolf gave the cleaning woman *The World According to Bensenhaver.* Then he went home for the weekend and thought about it; he tried to call her and tell her not even to try to read it. He remembered the first chapter and he didn't want to offend the woman, who was somebody's grandmother, and (of course) somebody's mother, too—and, after all, she never knew she was *paid* to read all the stuff John Wolf gave her to read. That she had a rather whopping salary for a cleaning lady was known only to John Wolf. The woman thought *all* good cleaning ladies were well paid, and *should* be.

Her name was Jillsy Sloper, and John Wolf marveled to note that there was not one Sloper with even the first initial of J. in the New York phone directory. Apparently Jillsy didn't like phone calls any more than she liked books. John Wolf made a note to apologize to Jillsy the first thing Monday morning. He spent the rest of a miserable weekend trying to phrase to himself exactly how he would tell T. S. Garp that he believed it was in his own best interests, and certainly in the best interests of the publishing house, NOT to publish *The World According to Bensenhaver.*

It was a hard weekend for him, because John Wolf liked Garp and he believed in Garp, and he also knew that Garp had no friends who could advise him against embarrassing himself—which is one of the valuable things friends are for. There was only Alice Fletcher, who so loved Garp that she would love, indiscriminately, everything he uttered—or else she would be silent. And there was Roberta Muldoon, whose literary judgment, John Wolf suspected, was even more newfound and awkward (if existent at all) than her adopted sex. And Helen wouldn't read it. And Jenny Fields, John Wolf knew, was not biased toward her son in the way a mother is usually biased; she had demonstrated the dubious taste to *dis*like some of the better things her son had written. The problem with Jenny, John Wolf knew, was one of subject matter. A book *about* an important subject was, to Jenny Fields, an important book. And Jenny Fields thought that Garp's new book was all about the stupid male anxieties that women are asked to suffer and endure. How a book was written never mattered to Jenny.

That was one thread that interested John Wolf in publishing the book. If Jenny Fields liked *The World According to Bensenhaver,* it was at least a potentially controversial book. But John Wolf, like Garp, knew that Jenny's status as a political figure was due largely to a general, hazy misunderstanding of Jenny.

Wolf thought and thought about it, all weekend, and he completely forgot to apologize to Jillsy Sloper the first thing Monday morning. Suddenly there was Jillsy, red-eyed and twitching like a squirrel, the ratted manuscript pages of *The World According to Bensenhaver* held fast in her rough brown hands.

"Lawd," Jillsy said. She rolled her eyes; she shook the manuscript in her hands.

"Oh, Jillsy," John Wolf said. "I'm sorry."

"Lawd!" Jillsy crowed. "I never had a worse weekend. I got *no* sleep, I got *no* food, I got *no* trips to the cemetery to see my family and my friends."

The pattern of Jillsy Sloper's weekend seemed strange to John Wolf but he said nothing; he just listened to her, as he had listened to her for more than a dozen years.

"This man's *crazy*," Jillsy said. "Nobody sane ever wrote a book like this."

"I shouldn't have given it to you, Jillsy," John Wolf said. "I should have remembered that first chapter."

"*First* chapter ain't so bad," Jillsy said. "That first chapter ain't *nothin'*. It's that nine*teenth* chapter that got me," Jillsy said. "Lawd, Lawd!" she crowed.

"You read nineteen chapters?" John Wolf asked.

"You didn't give me no more than nineteen chapters," Jillsy said. "Jesus Lawd, is there *another* chapter? Do it keep goin' *on?*"

"No, no," John Wolf said. "That's the end of it. That's all there is."

"I should hope so," Jillsy said. "Ain't nothin' left to go on *with.* Got that crazy old cop where he belongs—at long last—and that crazy husband with his head blowed off. That's the *only* proper state for that husband's head, if you ask me: blowed off."

"You *read* it?" John Wolf said.

"Lawd!" Jillsy screamed. "You'd think it was *him* who got raped, the way he went on and on. If you ask me," Jillsy said, "that's just like men: rape you half to death one minute and the next minute go crazy fussin' over who you're *givin'* it to—of your own free will! It's not *their* damn business, either way, is it?" Jillsy asked.

"I'm not sure," said John Wolf, who sat bewildered at his desk. "You didn't like the book."

"*Like* it?" Jillsy cawed. "There's nothin' to like about it," she said.

"But you *read* it," John Wolf said. "Why'd you read it?"

"Lawd," Jillsy said, as if she were sorry for John Wolf —that he was so hopelessly stupid. "I sometimes wonder if you know the first thing about all these books you're makin'," she said; she shook her head. "I sometimes wonder why you're the one who's makin' the books and *I'm* the one who's cleanin' the bathrooms. Except I'd rather clean the bathrooms than read most of them," Jillsy said. "Lawd, Lawd."

"If you hated it, why'd you read it, Jillsy?" John Wolf asked her.

"Same reason I read anythin' for," Jillsy said. "To find out what *happens*."

John Wolf stared at her.

"Most books you *know* nothin's gonna happen," Jillsy said. "Lawd, *you* know that. Other books," she said, "you know just *what's* gonna happen, so you don't have to read them, either. But *this* book," Jillsy said, "this book's so *sick* you *know* somethin's gonna happen, but you can't imagine *what*. You got to be sick yourself to imagine what happens in *this* book," Jillsy said.

"So you read it to find out?" John Wolf said.

"There surely ain't no other reason to read a book, is there?" Jillsy Sloper said. She put the manuscript heavily (for it was large) on John Wolf's desk and hitched up the long extension cord (for the vacuum cleaner) which Jillsy wore on Mondays like a belt around her broad middle. "When it's a book," she said, pointing to the manuscript, "I'd be happy if I could have a copy of my own. If it's okay," she added.

"You want a copy?" John Wolf asked.

"If it's no trouble," Jillsy said.

"Now that you know what happens," John Wolf said, "what would you want to read it *again* for?"

"Well," Jillsy said. She looked confused; John Wolf had never seen Jillsy Sloper look confused before— only sleepy. "Well, I might *lend* it," she said. "There might be someone I know who needs to be reminded what men in this world is like," she said.

"Would you ever read it again yourself?" John Wolf asked.

"Well," Jillsy said. "Not *all* of it, I imagine. At least not all at once, or not right away." Again, she looked confused. "Well," she said, sheepishly, "I guess I mean there's *parts* of it I wouldn't mind readin' again."

"Why?" John Wolf asked.

"Lawd," Jillsy said, tiredly, as if she were finally impatient with him. "It feels so *true*," she crooned, making the word *true* cry like a loon over a lake at night.

"It feels so true," John Wolf repeated.

"Lawd, don't you *know* it is?" Jillsy asked him. "If you don't know when a book's *true*," Jillsy sang to him, "we really *ought* to trade jobs." She laughed now, the stout three-pronged plug for the vacuum-cleaner cord clutched like a gun in her fist. "I do wonder, Mr. Wolf," she said, sweetly, "if you'd know when a bathroom was *clean*." She went over and peered in his wastebasket. "Or when a wastebasket was empty," she said. "A book feels true when it feels true," she said to him, impatiently. "A book's true when you can say, 'Yeah! That's just how damn people *behave* all the time.' *Then* you know it's true," Jillsy said.

Leaning over the wastebasket, she seized the one scrap of paper lying alone on the bottom of the basket; she stuffed it into her cleaning apron. It was the crumpled-up first page of the letter John Wolf had tried to compose to Garp.

Months later, when *The World According to Bensenhaver* was going to the printers, Garp complained to John Wolf that there was no one to dedicate the book to. He would not have it *in memory of* Walt, because Garp hated that kind of thing: "that cheap capitalizing," as he called it, "on one's autobiographical accidents—to try to hook the reader into thinking you're a more serious *writer* than you are." And he would not dedicate a book to his mother, because he hated, as he called it, "the free ride everyone else gets on the name of Jenny

Fields." Helen, of course, was out of the question, and Garp felt, with some shame, that he couldn't dedicate a book to Duncan if it was a book he would not allow Duncan to read. The child wasn't old enough. He felt some distaste, as a father, for writing something he would forbid his own children to read.

The Fletchers, he knew, would be uncomfortable with a book dedicated to them, as a couple; and to dedicate a book to Alice, alone, might be insulting to Harry.

"Not to *me,*" John Wolf said. "Not this one."

"I wasn't thinking of you," Garp lied.

"How about Roberta Muldoon?" John Wolf said.

"The book has absolutely nothing to *do* with Roberta," Garp said. Though Garp knew that Roberta, at least, wouldn't object to the dedication. How funny to write a book really no one would like to have dedicated to them!

"Maybe I'll dedicate it to the Ellen Jamesians," Garp said, bitterly.

"Don't make trouble for yourself," John Wolf said. "That's just plain stupid."

Garp sulked.

*For Mrs. Ralph?*

he thought. But he still didn't know her real name. There was Helen's father—his good old wrestling coach, Ernie Holm—but Ernie wouldn't understand the gesture; it would hardly be a book Ernie would like. Garp hoped, in fact, that Ernie wouldn't read it. How funny to write a book you hope someone doesn't read!

*To Fat Stew*

he thought.

*For Michael Milton*
*In Memory of Bonkers*
454

He bogged down. He could think of no one.

"I know someone," John Wolf said. "I could ask her if she'd mind."

"Very funny," Garp said.

But John Wolf was thinking of Jillsy Sloper, the person, he knew, who was responsible for getting this book of Garp's published at all.

"She's a very special woman who *loved* the book," John Wolf told Garp. "She said it was so 'true.' "

Garp was interested in the idea.

"I gave her the manuscript for one weekend," John Wolf said, "and she couldn't put it down."

"Why'd you give her the manuscript?" Garp asked.

"She just seemed *right* for it," John Wolf said. A good editor will not share all his secrets with anyone.

"Well, okay," Garp said. "It seems *naked,* having no one. Tell her I'd appreciate it. She's a *close* friend of yours?" Garp asked. Garp's editor winked at him and Garp nodded.

"What's it all mean, anyway?" Jillsy Sloper asked John Wolf, suspiciously. "What's it mean, he wants to 'dedicate' that terrible book to me?"

"It means that your response was valuable to him," John Wolf said. "He thinks the book was written almost with you in mind."

"Lawd," Jillsy said. "With me in mind? What's *that* mean?"

"I told him how you responded to his book," John Wolf said, "and he thinks you're the perfect audience, I guess."

"The perfect audience?" Jillsy said. "Lawd, he *is* crazy, isn't he?"

"He's got no one else to dedicate it to," John Wolf admitted.

"Kind of like needin' a witness for a weddin'?" Jillsy Sloper asked.

"Kind of," John Wolf guessed.

"It don't mean I *approve* of the book?" Jillsy asked.

"Lord, no," John Wolf said.

"Lawd, no, huh?" Jillsy said.

"No one's going to blame you for anything in the book, if that's what you mean," John Wolf said.

"Well," said Jillsy.

John Wolf showed Jillsy where the dedication would be; he showed her other dedications in other books. They all looked nice to Jillsy Sloper and she nodded her head, gradually pleased by the idea.

"One thing," she said. "I won't have to *meet* him, or anythin', will I?"

"Lord, no," said John Wolf, so Jillsy agreed.

There remained only one more stroke of genius to launch *The World According to Bensenhaver* into that uncanny half-light where occasional "serious" books glow, for a time, as also "popular" books. John Wolf was a smart and cynical man. He knew about all the shitty autobiographical associations that make those rabid readers of gossip warm to an occasional fiction.

Years later, Helen would remark that the success of *The World According to Bensenhaver* lay entirely in the book jacket. John Wolf was in the habit of letting Garp write his own jacket flaps, but Garp's description of his own book was so ponderous and glum that John Wolf took matters into his own hands; he went straight to the dubious heart of the matter.

*"The World According to Bensenhaver,"* the book jacket flap said, "is about a man who is so fearful of bad things happening to his loved ones that he creates an atmosphere of such tension that bad things are almost certain to occur. And they do.

"T. S. Garp," the jacket flap went on, "is the only child of the noted feminist Jenny Fields." John Wolf shivered slightly when he saw this in print, because although he had written it, and although he knew very well *why* he had written it, he also knew that it was information Garp *never* wanted mentioned in connection with his own work. "T. S. Garp is also a father," the jacket flap said. And John Wolf shook his head in shame to see the garbage he had written there. "He is a father who has recently suffered the tragic loss of a five-year-old son. Out of the anguish that a father endures in the aftermath of an accident, this tortured novel emerges. . . ." And so forth.

It was, in Garp's opinion, the cheapest reason to read of all. Garp always said that the question he most hated to be asked, about his work, was how much of it was "true"—how much of it was based on "personal experience." *True*—not in the good way that Jillsy Sloper used it, but true as in "real life." Usually, with great patience and restraint, Garp would say that the autobiographical basis—if there even was one—was the least interesting level on which to read a novel. He would always say that the art of fiction was the act of *imagining* truly—was, like any art, a process of selection. Memories and personal histories—"all the recollected traumas of our unmemorable lives"—were suspicious models for fiction, Garp would say. "Fiction has to be better made than life," Garp wrote. And he consistently detested what he called "the phony mileage of personal hardship"—writers whose books were "important" because something important had happened in their lives. He wrote that the *worst* reason for anything being part of a novel was that it really happened. "*Everything* has really happened, sometime!" he fumed. "The only reason for something to happen in a novel is that it's the perfect thing to have happen at that time.

"Tell me *any*thing that's ever happened to you," Garp told an interviewer once, "and I can improve upon the story; I can make the details better than they were." The interviewer, a divorced woman with four young children, one of whom was dying of cancer, had her face firmly fixed in disbelief. Garp saw her determined unhappiness, and its terrible importance to her, and he said to her, gently, "If it's sad—even if it's *very* sad—I can make up a story that's sadder." But he saw in her face that she would never believe him; she wasn't even writing it down. It wouldn't even be a part of her interview.

And John Wolf knew this: one of the first things most readers *want* to know is everything they can about a writer's *life*. John Wolf wrote Garp: "For most people, with limited imaginations, the idea of improving on reality is pure bunk." On the book jacket flap of *The World According to Bensenhaver,* John Wolf created a bogus sense of Garp's importance ("the only child of the noted feminist Jenny Fields") and a sentimental sympathy for Garp's personal experience ("the tragic loss of a five-year-old son"). That both pieces of information were essentially irrelevant to the *art* of Garp's novel did not deeply concern John Wolf. Garp had made John Wolf sore with all his talk about preferring riches to seriousness.

"It's not your best book," John Wolf wrote Garp, when he sent the galleys for Garp to proofread. "One day you'll know that, too. But it *is* going to be your biggest book; just wait and see. You can't imagine, yet, how you're going to hate many of the reasons for your success, so I advise you to leave the country for a few months. I advise you to read only the reviews *I* send to you. And when it blows over—because everything blows over—you can come back home and pick up your considerable surprise at the bank. And you can hope that *Bensenhaver*'s popularity is big enough to make people go back and read the first two novels—for which you *deserve* to be better known.

"Tell Helen I am *sorry,* Garp, but I think you must know: I have always had your own interests at heart. If you want to *sell* this book, we'll sell it. 'Every business is a shitty business,' Garp. I am quoting *you.*"

Garp was very puzzled by the letter; John Wolf, of course, had not shown him the jacket flaps.

"Why are you *sorry?*" Garp wrote back. "Don't weep; just sell it."

"Every business is a shitty business," Wolf repeated.

"I know, I *know,*" Garp said.

"Take my advice," Wolf said.

"I *like* reading the reviews," Garp protested.

"Not these, you won't," John Wolf said. "Take a trip. Please." Then John Wolf sent the jacket flap copy to Jenny Fields. He asked her for her confidence, and her help in getting Garp to leave the country.

"Leave the country," Jenny said to her son. "It's the best thing you can do for yourself and your family." Helen was actually keen on the idea; she'd never been abroad. Duncan had read his father's first story, "The Pension Grillparzer," and he wanted to go to Vienna.

"Vienna's not *really* like that," Garp told Duncan, but it touched Garp very much that the boy liked the old story. Garp liked it, too. In fact, he was beginning to wish that he liked everything else he had written half as much.

"With a new baby, why go to Europe?" Garp complained. "I don't know. It's complicated. The passports —and the baby will need lots of shots, or something."

"You need some shots yourself," said Jenny Fields. "The baby will be perfectly safe."

"Don't you want to see Vienna again?" Helen asked Garp.

"Ah, just imagine, the scene of your old crimes!" John Wolf said heartily.

"Old crimes?" Garp mumbled. "I don't know."

"Please, Dad," Duncan said. Garp was a sucker to what Duncan wanted; he agreed.

Helen cheered up and even took a glance at the galleys of *The World According to Bensenhaver,* though it was a quick, nervous glance, and she had no intention of doing any real reading therein. The first thing she saw was the dedication.

*For Jillsy Sloper*

"Who in God's name is Jillsy Sloper?" she asked Garp.

"I don't know, really," Garp said; Helen frowned at

him. "No, *really*," he said. "It's some girl friend of John's; he said she loved the book—couldn't put it down. Wolf took it as a kind of omen, I guess; it was *his* suggestion, anyway," Garp said. "And I thought it was nice."

"Hm," said Helen; she put the galleys aside.

They both imagined John Wolf's girl friend in silence. John Wolf had been divorced before they met him; though the Garps had gotten to meet some of Wolf's grown-up children, they had never met his first and only wife. There had been a conservative number of girl friends, all smart and sleekly attractive women— all younger than John Wolf. Some working girls, in the publishing business, but mostly young women with divorces of their own, and money—always money, or always the *look* of money. Garp remembered most of them by how nicely they smelled, and how their lipstick tasted—and the high-gloss, touchable quality of their clothes.

Neither Garp nor Helen could ever have imagined Jillsy Sloper, the offspring of a white person and a quadroon—which made Jillsy an octoroon, or one-eighth Negro. Her skin was a sallow brown, like a lightly stained pine board. Her hair was straight and short and waxy-black, beginning to gray at her bangs, which were coarsely chopped above her shining, wrinkled forehead. She was short, with long arms, and her ring finger was missing from her left hand. By the deep scar on her right cheek, one could imagine that the ring finger had been cut off in the same battle, by the same weapon—perhaps during a bad marriage, for she had certainly had a bad marriage. Which she never spoke of.

She was about forty-five and looked sixty. She had the trunk of a Labrador retriever about to have puppies, and she shuffled whenever and wherever she walked because her feet killed her. In a few years she would so long ignore the lump she could feel in her own breast, which no one else ever felt, that she would die needlessly of cancer.

She had an unlisted phone number (as John discovered) only because her former husband threatened to kill her every few months, and she tired of hearing from him; the reason she had a phone at all was that her children needed a place to call collect so that they could ask her to send them money.

But Helen and Garp, when they imagined Jillsy Sloper, did not for a moment see anyone approximating this sad, hard-working octoroon.

"John Wolf seems to be doing everything for this book except writing it," Helen said.

"I wish he *had* written it," Garp suddenly said. Garp had reread the book, and he felt full of doubt. In "The Pension Grillparzer," Garp thought, there was a certainty concerning how the world behaved. In *The World According to Bensenhaver*, Garp had felt less certain— an indication he was getting older, of course; but artists, he knew, should also get *better*.

With baby Jenny and one-eyed Duncan, Garp and Helen left for Europe out of a cool New England August; most transatlantic travelers were headed the other way.

"Why not wait until after Thanksgiving?" Ernie Holm asked them. But *The World According to Bensenhaver* would be published in October. John Wolf had received various responses to the uncorrected proofs he circulated through the summer; they had all been enthusiastic responses—enthusiastically praising the book, or enthusiastically condemning it.

He'd had difficulty keeping Garp from seeing the advance copies of the actual book—the book jacket, for example. But Garp's own enthusiasm for the book was so sporadic, and generally low, that John Wolf had been able to stall him.

Garp was now excited about the trip, and he was talking about other books he was going to write. ("A good sign," John Wolf told Helen.)

Jenny and Roberta drove the Garps to Boston, where

they took a plane to New York. "Don't worry about the airplane," Jenny said. "It won't fall."

"Jesus, Mom," Garp said. "What do you know about airplanes? They fall all the time."

"Keep your arms in constant motion, like wings," Roberta told Duncan.

"Don't scare him, Roberta," Helen said.

"I'm not scared," Duncan said.

"If your father keeps *talking,* you can't fall," Jenny said.

"If he keeps talking," Helen said, "we'll never *land.*" They could see that Garp was all wound up.

"I'll *fart* all the way, if you don't leave me alone," Garp said, "and we'll go in a great explosion."

"You better write often," Jenny said.

Remembering dear old Tinch, and his last trip to Europe, Garp told his mother, "This time I'm just going to ab-ab-ab*sorb* a lot, Mom. I'm not going to write a w-w-word." They both laughed at this, and Jenny Fields even cried a little, although only Garp noticed; he kissed his mother good-bye. Roberta, whose sex reassignment had made her a dynamite kisser, kissed everyone several times.

"Jesus, Roberta," Garp said.

"I'll look after the old girl while you're gone," Roberta said, her giant arm dwarfing Jenny, who looked so small and suddenly very gray beside her.

"I don't need any looking after," Jenny Fields said.

"It's Mom who looks after everyone else," Garp said.

Helen hugged Jenny, because she knew how true that was. From the airplane, Garp and Duncan could see Jenny and Roberta waving from the observation deck. There had been some seat changes because Duncan had wanted a window seat on the left-hand side of the plane. "The right-hand side is just as nice," a stewardess said.

"Not if you don't have a right eye," Duncan told her, pleasantly, and Garp admired how the boy was feeling so bold about himself.

Helen and the baby sat across the aisle from them. "Can you see Grandma?" Helen asked Duncan.

"Yes," Duncan said.

Although the observation deck was suddenly overrun with people wanting to see the takeoff, Jenny Fields— as always—stood out in her white uniform, even though she was short. "Why does Nana look so tall?" Duncan asked Garp, and it was true: Jenny Fields towered head and shoulders above the crowd. Garp realized that Roberta was lifting his mother up as if his mother were a child. "Oh, *Roberta's* got her!" Duncan cried. Garp looked at his mother hefted up in the air to wave good-bye to him, safe in the arms of the old tight end; Jenny's shy, confident smile touched him, and he waved out the window to her, although Garp knew that Jenny couldn't see inside the plane. For the first time, his mother looked old to him; he looked away—across the aisle, at Helen with their new child.

"Here we go," Helen said. Helen and Garp held hands across the aisle when the plane lifted off, be-cause, Garp knew, Helen was terrified of flying.

In New York, John Wolf put them up in his apart-ment; he gave Garp and Helen and baby Jenny his own bedroom and graciously offered to share the guest room with Duncan.

The grownups had a late dinner and too much cognac. Garp told John Wolf about the next three novels he was going to write.

"The first one is called *My Father's Illusions,*" Garp said. "It's about an idealistic father who has many chil-dren. He keeps establishing little utopias for his kids to grow up in, and after his kids grow up he becomes a founder of small colleges. But all of them go broke— the colleges and the kids. The father keeps trying to give a speech at the U.N., but they keep throwing him out; it's the same speech—he keeps revising and revising it. Then he tries to run a free hospital; it's a disaster. Then he tries to institute a nationwide free-transportation sys-tem. Meanwhile, his wife divorces him and his children keep growing older, and turning out unhappy, or fucked-up—or just perfectly normal, you know. The only thing the children have in common are these dreadful memories of the utopias their father tried to have them grow up in. Finally, the father becomes the governor of Vermont."

"Vermont?" John Wolf asked.

"Yes, Vermont," Garp said. "He becomes governor of Vermont, but he really thinks of himself as a king. More utopias, you see."

*The King of Vermont!* John Wolf said. "That's a better title."

"No, no," Garp said. "That's another book. No relation. The second book, after *My Father's Illusions,* will be called *The Death of Vermont.*"

"Same cast of characters?" Helen asked.

"No, no," Garp said. "Another story. It's about the death of Vermont."

"Well, I like something that is what it says it is," John Wolf said.

"One year spring doesn't come," Garp said.

"Spring never does come to Vermont, anyway," Helen said.

"No, no," Garp said, frowning. "This year summer doesn't come, either. Winter never stops. It warms up one day and all the buds appear. Maybe in May. One day in May there are buds on the trees, the next day there are leaves, and the next day the leaves have all turned. It's fall already. The leaves fall off the trees."

"A short foliage season," Helen said.

"Very funny," Garp said. "But that's what happens. It's winter again; it will be winter forever."

"The people die?" John Wolf asked.

"I'm not sure about the people," Garp said. "Some leave Vermont, of course."

"Not a bad idea," Helen said.

"Some stay, some die. Maybe they all die," Garp said.

"What's it mean?" John Wolf asked.

"I'll know when I get there," Garp said. Helen laughed.

"And there's a *third* novel, after that?" John Wolf asked.

"It's called *The Plot against the Giant*," Garp said.

"That's a poem by Wallace Stevens," Helen said.

"Yes, of course," Garp said, and he recited the poem for them.

#### The Plot against the Giant

##### First Girl

*When this yokel comes maundering,*
*Whetting his hacker,*
*I shall run before him,*
*Diffusing the civilest odors*
*Out of geraniums and unsmelled flowers.*
*It will check him.*

##### Second Girl

*I shall run before him,*
*Arching cloths besprinkled with colors*
*As small as fish-eggs.*
*The threads*
*Will abash him.*

##### Third Girl

*Oh, la . . . le pauvre!*
*I shall run before him,*
*With a curious puffing.*
*He will bend his ear then.*
*I shall whisper*
*Heavenly labials in a world of gutturals.*
*It will undo him.*

"What a nice poem," Helen said.

"The novel is in three parts," Garp said.

"Girl One, Girl Two, Girl Three?" John Wolf asked.

"And *is* the giant undone?" Helen asked.

"Is he ever," Garp said.

"Is he a *real* giant, in the novel?" John Wolf asked.

"I don't know, yet," Garp said.

"Is he *you?*" Helen asked.

"I hope not," Garp said.

"I hope not, too," said Helen.

"Write that one first," John Wolf said.

"No, write it last," Helen said.

"*The Death of Vermont* seems the logical one to write last," John Wolf said.

"No, I see *The Plot against the Giant* as last," Garp said.

"Wait and write it after I'm dead," Helen said.

Everyone laughed.

"But there are only three," John Wolf said. "What then? What happens after the three?"

"I die," Garp said. "That will make six novels altogether, and that's enough."

Everyone laughed again.

"And do you also know *how* you die?" John Wolf asked him.

"Let's stop this," Helen said. And to Garp she said, "If you say, 'In an airplane,' I will not forgive you." Behind the lightly drunk humor in her voice, John detected a seriousness; it made him stretch his legs.

"You two better go to bed," he said. "And get rested for your trip."

"Don't you want to know how I die?" Garp asked them.

They didn't say anything.

"I kill myself," Garp said, pleasantly. "In order to become fully established, that seems almost necessary. I mean it, *really,*" Garp said. "In the present fashion, you'll agree this is one way of recognizing a writer's seriousness? Since the *art* of the writing doesn't always make the writer's seriousness apparent, it's sometimes necessary to reveal the depth of one's personal anguish by other means. Killing yourself seems to mean that you were serious after all. It's *true,*" Garp said, but his sarcasm was unpleasant and Helen sighed; John Wolf stretched again. "And thereafter," Garp said, "much seriousness is suddenly revealed in the work—where it had escaped notice before."

Garp had often remarked, irritably, that this would be his final duty as a father and provider—and he was fond of citing examples of the middling writers who were now adored and read with great avidity *because* of their suicides. Of those writer-suicides whom he, too—in some cases—truly admired, Garp only hoped that, at the moment the act was accomplished, at least some of them had known about this lucky aspect of their unhappy decision. He knew perfectly well that people who really killed themselves did not romanticize suicide in the least; *they* did not respect the "seriousness" that the act supposedly lent to their work—a nauseating habit in the book world, Garp thought. Among readers *and* reviewers.

Garp also knew *he* was no suicide; he knew it somewhat less surely after the accident to Walt, but he knew it. He was as distant from suicide as he was from rape; he could not imagine actually doing it. But he liked to imagine the suicidal writer grinning at his successful mischief, while once more he read and revised the last message he would leave—a note aching with despair, and appropriately humorless. Garp liked to imagine that moment, bitterly: when the suicide note was perfect, the writer took the gun, the poison, the plunge—laughing hideously, and full of the knowledge that he had at last got the better of the readers and reviewers. One note he imagined was: "I have been misunderstood by you idiots for the last time."

"What a sick idea," Helen said.

"The perfect writer's death," said Garp.

"It's late," John Wolf said. "Remember your flight."

In the guest room, where John Wolf wanted to fall asleep, he found Duncan Garp still wide-awake.

"Excited by the trip, Duncan?" Wolf asked the boy.

"My father's been to Europe before," Duncan said. "But *I* haven't."

"I know," John Wolf said.

"Is my father going to make a lot of money?" Duncan asked.

"I hope so," John Wolf said.

"We don't really need it, because my grandmother has so much," Duncan said.

"But it's nice to have your own," John Wolf said.

"Why?" Duncan asked.

"Well, it's nice to be famous," John Wolf said.

"Do you think my father's going to be famous?" Duncan asked.

"I *think* so," John Wolf said.

"My grandmother's already famous," Duncan said.

"I know," John Wolf said.

"I don't think she likes it," Duncan said.

"Why?" John Wolf asked.

"Too many strangers around," Duncan said. "That's what Nana says; I've heard her. 'Too many strangers in the house.'"

"Well, your dad probably won't be famous in quite the same *way* that your grandmother is," John Wolf said.

"How many different ways are there to be famous?" Duncan asked.

John Wolf expelled a long, restrained breath. Then he began to tell Duncan Garp about the differences between very popular books and just successful ones. He talked about political books, and controversial books, and works of fiction. He told Duncan the finer points of book publishing; in fact, he gave Duncan the benefit of more of his personal opinions about publishing than he had ever given Garp. Garp wasn't really interested. Duncan wasn't, either. Duncan would not remember *one* of the finer points; he fell asleep rather quickly after John Wolf started explaining.

It was simply John Wolf's tone of voice that Duncan

loved. The long story, the slow explanation. It was the voice of Roberta Muldoon—of Jenny Fields, of his mother, of Garp—telling him stories at night in the house at Dog's Head Harbor, putting him to sleep so soundly that he wouldn't have any nightmares. Duncan had gotten used to that tone of voice, and he had been unable to fall asleep in New York without it.

In the morning, Garp and Helen were amused by John Wolf's closet. There was a pretty nightgown belonging, no doubt, to one of John Wolf's recent, sleek women—someone who had *not* been asked to spend last night. There were about thirty dark suits, all with pinstripes, all quite elegant, and all failing to fit Garp by about three extra inches in the pantlegs. Garp wore one he liked to breakfast, with the pants rolled up.

"Jesus, you have a lot of suits," he said to John Wolf.

"Take one," John Wolf said. "Take two or three. Take the one you're wearing."

"It's too long," Garp said, holding up a foot.

"Have it shortened," John Wolf said.

"You don't have *any* suits," Helen told Garp.

Garp decided he liked the suit so well that he wanted to wear it to the airport, with the pantlegs pinned up.

"Jesus," Helen said.

"I'm slightly embarrassed to be seen with you," John Wolf confessed, but he drove them to the airport. He was making absolutely certain that the Garps got out of the country.

"Oh, your book," he said to Garp, in the car. "I keep forgetting to get you a copy."

"I noticed," Garp said.

"I'll send you one," John Wolf said.

"I never even saw what went on the jacket," Garp said.

"A photograph of you, on the back," John Wolf said. "It's an old one—it's one you've seen, I'm sure."

"What's on the front?" Garp said.

"Well, the title," John Wolf said.

"Oh, really?" Garp said. "I thought maybe you decided to leave the title off."

"Just the title," John Wolf said, "over a kind of photograph."

" 'A kind of photograph,' " Garp said. *What* kind of photograph?"

"Maybe I have one in my briefcase," Wolf said. "I'll look, at the airport."

Wolf was being careful; he had already let it slip that he thought *The World According to Bensenhaver* was an "X-rated soap opera." Garp hadn't seemed bothered. "Mind you, it's awfully well *written,*" Wolf had said, "but it's still, somehow, soap opera; it's too *much,* somehow." Garp had sighed. *"Life,"* Garp had said, "is too much, somehow. *Life* is an X-rated soap opera, John," Garp had said.

In John Wolf's briefcase was a snip-out of the front cover of *The World According to Bensenhaver,* missing the back-jacket photograph of Garp and, of course, the jacket flaps. John Wolf planned to hand this snip-out to Garp just moments before they said good-bye. This snip-out of the front cover was sealed in an envelope; the envelope was sealed in another envelope. John Wolf felt pretty certain that Garp would not be able to undo the thing and look at it until he was safely seated in the plane.

When Garp got to Europe, John Wolf would send him the rest of the book jacket for *The World According to Bensenhaver.* Wolf felt certain that it would not make Garp quite angry enough to fly home.

"This is bigger than the other plane," Duncan said, at the window on the left-hand side, a little in front of the wing.

"It has to be bigger because it's going all the way across the ocean," Garp said.

"Please don't mention that again," Helen said. Across the aisle from Duncan and Garp, a stewardess was fashioning an intriguing sling for baby Jenny, who hung on the back of the seat in front of Helen like someone else's baby or a papoose.

"John Wolf said you were going to be rich and famous," Duncan told his father.

"Hm," Garp said. He was involved in the tedious process of opening the envelopes John Wolf had given him; he was having a hell of a time with them.

"Are you?" Duncan asked.

"I *hope* so," Garp said. At last he looked at the cover of *The World According to Bensenhaver*. He could not tell if it was the sudden, apparent weightlessness of the great airplane, leaving the ground, that gave him such a chill—or if it was the photograph.

Blown up in black and white, with grains as fat as flakes of snow, was a picture of an ambulance unloading at a hospital. The glum futility on the gray faces of the attendants expressed the fact that there was no need to hurry. The body under the sheet was small and completely covered. The photograph had the quick, fearful quality of the entrance marked EMERGENCY at any hospital. It *was* any hospital, and any ambulance— and any small body arriving too late.

A kind of wet finish glazed the photograph, which— with its grainy aspect, and the fact that this accident appeared to have happened on a rainy night—made it a picture out of *any* cheap newspaper; it was any catastrophe. It was *any* small death, anywhere, anytime. But of course it only reminded Garp of the gray despairing on all their faces when they were struck by the sight of Walt lying broken.

The cover of *The World According to Bensenhaver,* an X-rated soap opera, shouted a grim warning: this was a disaster story. The cover called for your cheap but immediate attention; it got it. The cover promised you a sudden, sickening sadness; Garp knew that the book would deliver it.

If he could have read the jacket-flap description of his novel and his life, at that time, he might very well have taken the next plane back to New York as soon as he landed in Europe. But he would have time to resign himself to this kind of advertising—just as John Wolf had planned. By the time Garp read the jacket flaps, he'd already have absorbed that horrible front-cover photograph.

Helen would never absorb it, and she never forgave John Wolf for it, either. Nor would she ever forgive him for the back-cover photograph of Garp. It was a picture, taken several years before the accident, of Garp with Duncan and Walt. Helen had taken the picture, and Garp had sent it to John Wolf instead of a Christmas card. Garp was on a dock in Maine. He was wearing nothing but a bathing suit and he looked in terrific physical shape. He was. Duncan stood behind him, his lean arm rested on his father's shoulder; Duncan also wore a bathing suit, he was very tan, with a white sailor's cap cocked jauntily on his head. He grinned into the camera, staring it down with his beautiful eyes.

Walt sat on Garp's lap. Walt was so fresh out of the water that he was as slick as a seal puppy; Garp was trying to wrap him warmly in a towel, and Walt was squirming. Wildly happy, his clownish, round face beamed at the camera—at his mother taking the picture.

When Garp looked at that picture, he could feel Walt's cold, wet body growing warm and dry against him.

Beneath the photograph, the caption cashed in on one of the least noble instincts of human beings.

### T. S. GARP WITH HIS CHILDREN
#### (BEFORE THE ACCIDENT)

The implication was that if you read the book, you would find out *what* accident. Of course, you wouldn't. *The World According to Bensenhaver* would tell you nothing about that accident, really—although it is fair to say that accidents play an enormous part in the novel. The only thing you would really learn about the accident referred to under the photograph was contained in the garbage that John Wolf wrote on the jacket flap. But, even so, that photograph—of a father with his doomed children—had a way of *hook*ing you.

People bought the book by the sad son of Jenny Fields in droves.

On the airplane to Europe, Garp had only the picture of the ambulance to use his imagination on. Even at that altitude, he could imagine people buying the book in droves. He sat feeling disgusted at the people he imagined buying the book; he also felt disgusted that he had written the kind of book that could attract people in droves.

"Droves" of anything, but especially of people, were not comforting to T. S. Garp. He sat in the airplane wishing for more isolation and privacy—for himself and for his family—than he would ever know again.

"What will we do with all the money?" Duncan asked him suddenly.

"All the money?" Garp said.

"When you're rich and famous," Duncan said. "What will we do?"

"We'll have lots of fun," Garp told him, but his handsome son's one eye pierced him with doubt.

"We'll be flying at an altitude of thirty-five thousand feet," the pilot said.

"Wow," said Duncan. And Garp reached for his wife's hand across the aisle. A fat man was making his unsure way down the aisle to the lavatory; Garp and Helen could only look at each other and convey a kind of hand-in-hand contact with their eyes.

In his mind's eye, Garp saw his mother, Jenny Fields, all in white, held up in the sky by the towering Roberta Muldoon. He did not know what it meant, but his vision of Jenny Fields raised above a crowd chilled him in the same way that the ambulance on the cover of *The World According to Bensenhaver* had chilled him. He began talking to Duncan, about anything at all.

Duncan began talking about Walt and the undertow—a famous family story. For as far back as Duncan could remember, the Garps had gone every summer to Dog's Head Harbor, New Hampshire, where the miles of beach in front of Jenny Fields' estate were ravaged by a fearful undertow. When Walt was old enough to venture near the water, Duncan said to him—as Helen and Garp had, for years, said to Duncan—"Watch out for the undertow." Walt retreated, respectfully. And for three summers Walt was warned about the undertow. Duncan recalled all the phrases.

"The undertow is bad today."

"The undertow is strong today."

"The undertow is *wicked* today." *Wicked* was a big word in New Hampshire—not just for the undertow.

And for years Walt watched out for it. From the first, when he asked what *it* could do to you, he had only been told that it could pull you out to sea. It could suck you under and drown you and drag you away.

It was Walt's fourth summer at Dog's Head Harbor, Duncan remembered, when Garp and Helen and Duncan observed Walt watching the sea. He stood ankle-deep in the foam from the surf and peered into the waves, without taking a step, for the longest time. The family went down to the water's edge to have a word with him.

"What are you doing, Walt?" Helen asked.

"What are you looking for, dummy?" Duncan asked him.

"I'm trying to see the Under Toad," Walt said.

"The what?" said Garp.

"The Under Toad," Walt said. "I'm trying to *see* it. How *big* is it?"

And Garp and Helen and Duncan held their breath; they realized that all these years Walt had been dreading a giant *toad,* lurking offshore, waiting to suck him under and drag him out to sea. The terrible Under Toad.

Garp tried to imagine it with him. Would it ever surface? Did it ever float? Or was it always down under, slimy and bloated and ever-watchful for ankles its coated tongue could snare? The vile Under Toad.

Between Helen and Garp, the Under Toad became their code phrase for anxiety. Long after the monster was clarified for Walt ("Under*tow*, dummy, not Under Toad!" Duncan had howled), Garp and Helen evoked the beast as a way of referring to their own sense of danger. When the traffic was heavy, when the road was icy—when depression had moved in overnight—they said to each other, "The Under Toad is strong today."

"Remember," Duncan asked on the plane, "how Walt asked if it was green or brown?"

Both Garp and Duncan laughed. But it was neither green nor brown, Garp thought. It was me. It was Helen. It was the color of bad weather. It was the size of an automobile.

In Vienna, Garp felt, the Under Toad was strong. Helen did not seem to feel it, and Duncan, like an eleven-year-old, passed from one feeling to the next. The return to the city, for Garp, was like returning to the Steering School. The streets, the buildings, even the paintings in the museums, were like his old teachers, grown older; he barely recognized them, and they did not know him at all. Helen and Duncan saw everything. Garp was content to walk with baby Jenny; he strolled her through the long, warm fall in a carriage as baroque as the city itself—he smiled and nodded to all the tongue-clucking elderly who peered into the carriage and approved of his new baby. The Viennese appeared well fed and comfortable with luxuries that looked new to Garp; the city was years away from the Russian occupation, the memory of the war, the reminders of ruins. If Vienna had been dying, or already dead, in his time there with his mother, Garp felt that something new but common had grown in the old city's place.

At the same time, Garp liked showing Duncan and Helen around. He enjoyed his personal history tour, mixed with the guidebook history of Vienna. "And this is where Hitler stood when he first addressed the city. And this is where I used to shop on Saturday mornings.

"This is the fourth district, a Russian zone of occupation; the famous Karlskirche is here, and the Lower and Upper Belvedere. And between the Prinz-Eugen-Strasse, on your left, and the Argentinierstrasse is the little street where Mom and I . . ."

They rented some rooms in a nice pension in the fourth district. They discussed enrolling Duncan in an English-speaking school, but it was a long drive, or a long Strassenbahn ride every morning, and they didn't really plan on staying even half the year. Vaguely, they imagined Christmas at Dog's Head Harbor with Jenny and Roberta and Ernie Holm.

John Wolf finally sent the book, complete book jacket and all, and Garp's sense of the Under Toad grew unbearably for a few days, then kicked deeper, beneath the surface. It appeared to be gone. Garp managed a restrained letter to his editor; he expressed his sense of personal hurt, his understanding that this had been done with the best intentions, businesswise. But . . . and so forth. How angry could he really be—at Wolf? Garp had provided the package; Wolf had only promoted it.

Garp heard from his mother that the first reviews were "not nice," but Jenny—on John Wolf's advice—did not enclose any reviews with her letter. John Wolf clipped the first rave from among the important New York reviews: "The women's movement has at last exhibited a significant influence on a significant male writer," wrote the reviewer, who was an associate professor of women's studies somewhere. She went on to say that *The World According to Bensenhaver* was "the first in-depth study, by a man, of the peculiarly *male* neurotic pressure many women are made to suffer." And so forth.

"Christ," Garp said, "it sounds as if I wrote a *thesis*. It's a fucking *novel*, it's a *story*, and I made it up!"

"Well, it sounds as if she *liked* it," Helen said.

"It's not *it* she liked," Garp said. "She liked something else."

But the review helped to establish the rumor that

*The World According to Bensenhaver* was "a feminist novel."

"Like me," Jenny Fields wrote her son, "it appears you are going to be the beneficiary of one of the many popular misunderstandings of our time."

Other reviews called the book "paranoid, crazed, and crammed with gratuitous violence and sex." Garp was not shown most of those reviews, but they probably didn't hurt the sales, either.

One reviewer admitted that Garp was a serious writer whose "tendencies toward baroque exaggeration have run amuck." John Wolf couldn't resist sending Garp that review—probably because John Wolf agreed with it.

Jenny wrote that she was becoming "involved with" New Hampshire politics.

"The New Hampshire gubernatorial race is taking all our time," Roberta Muldoon wrote.

"How could anyone give all her time to a New Hampshire governor?" Garp wrote back.

There was, apparently, some feminist issue at stake, and some generally illiberal nonsense and crimes the incumbent governor was actually proud of. The administration boasted that a raped fourteen-year-old had been denied an abortion, thus stemming the tide of nationwide degeneracy. The governor truly *was* a crowing, reactionary moron. Among other things, he appeared to believe that poor people should not be helped by the state or federal government, largely because the condition of the poor seemed to the governor of New Hampshire to be a deserved punishment—the just and moral judgment of a Superior Being. The incumbent governor was obnoxious and clever; for example, the sense of *fear* that he successfully evoked: that New Hampshire was in danger of being victimized by *teams* of New York divorcees.

The divorced women from New York allegedly were moving into New Hampshire in droves. Their intentions were to turn New Hampshire women into lesbians, or at the very least to encourage them to be unfaithful to their New Hampshire husbands; their intentions also included the seduction of New Hampshire husbands, and New Hampshire high school boys. The New York divorcees apparently represented widespread promiscuity, socialism, alimony, and something ominously referred to, in the New Hampshire press, as "Group Female Living."

One of the centers for this alleged Group Female Living was Dog's Head Harbor, of course, "the den of the radical feminist Jenny Fields."

There had also been a widespread increase, the governor said, of venereal disease—"a known problem among these Liberationists." He was a terrific liar. The candidate running for governor against this well-liked fool was, apparently, a woman. Jenny and Roberta and (Jenny wrote) "teams of New York divorcees" were running her campaign.

Somehow, in the sole New Hampshire newspaper of statewide distribution, Garp's "degenerate" novel was referred to as "the new feminist Bible."

"A violent hymn to the moral depravity and sexual danger of our time," wrote one West Coast reviewer.

"A pained protest against the violence and sexual combat of our groping age," said another newspaper, somewhere else.

Whether it was liked or disliked, the novel was largely looked upon as *news*. One way for novels to be successful is for the fiction to resemble somebody's version of the news. That is what happened to *The World According to Bensenhaver;* like the stupid governor of New Hampshire, Garp's book became news.

"New Hampshire is a backwoods state with base politics," Garp wrote his mother. "For God's sake, don't get involved."

"That's what you always say," Jenny wrote. "When you come home, you're going to be famous. Then let me see *you* try not to get involved."

"Just watch me," Garp wrote her. "Nothing could be easier."

His involvement with the transatlantic mail had momentarily distracted Garp from his sense of the awesome and lethal Under Toad, but now Helen told him that she detected the presence of the beast, too.

"Let's go home," she said. "We've had a nice time."

They got a telegram from John Wolf. "Stay where you are," it said. "People are buying your book in droves."

Roberta sent Garp a T-shirt.

### NEW YORK DIVORCEES ARE GOOD
### FOR NEW HAMPSHIRE

the T-shirt said.

"My God," Garp said to Helen. "If we're going home, let's at least wait until after this mindless election."

Thus he missed, thankfully, the "dissenting feminist opinion" of *The World According to Bensenhaver,* published in a giddy, popular magazine. The novel, the reviewer said, "steadfastly upholds the sexist notion that women are chiefly an assemblage of orifices and the acceptable prey of predatory males. . . . T. S. Garp continues the infuriating male mythology: the good man is the bodyguard of his family, the good woman never willingly lets another man enter her literal or figurative door."

Even Jenny Fields was cajoled into "reviewing" her son's novel, and it is fortunate that Garp never saw this, either. Jenny said that although it was her son's best novel—because it was his most serious subject—it was a novel "marred by repeated male obsessions, which could become tedious to women readers." However, Jenny said, her son was a good writer who was still young and would only get better. "His heart," she added, "is in the right place."

If Garp had read that, he might have stayed in Vienna a lot longer. But they made their plans to leave. As usual, anxiousness quickened the Garps' plans. One night Duncan was not home from the park before dark

479

and Garp, running out to look for him, called back to Helen that this was the final sign; they would leave as soon as possible. City life, in general, made Garp too fearful for Duncan.

Garp ran along the Prinz-Eugen-Strasse toward the Russian War Memorial at the Schwarzenbergplatz. There was a pastry shop near there, and Duncan liked pastry, although Garp had repeatedly warned the child that it would ruin his supper. "Duncan!" he ran calling, and his voice against the stolid stone buildings bounced back to him like the froggy belching of the Under Toad, the foul and warty beast whose sticky nearness he felt like breath.

But Duncan was munching happily on a Grillparzer-torte in the pastry shop.

"It gets dark earlier and earlier," he complained. "I'm not *that* late."

Garp had to admit it. They walked home together. The Under Toad disappeared up a small, dark street—or else it's not interested in Duncan, Garp thought. He imagined he felt the tug of the tide at his own ankles, but it was a passing feeling.

The telephone, that old cry of alarm—a warrior stabbed on guard duty, screaming his shock—startled the pension where they lived and brought the trembling landlady like a ghost to their rooms.

*"Bitte, bitte,"* she came pleading. She conveyed, with little shakes of excitement, that the call was from the United States.

It was about two in the morning, the heat was off, and Garp shivered after the old woman, down the corridor of the pension. "The hall rug was thin," he recalled, "the color of a shadow." He had written that, years ago. And he looked for the rest of his cast: the Hungarian singer, the man who could only walk on his hands, the doomed bear, and all the members of the sad circus of death he had imagined.

But they were gone; only the old woman's lean, erect

body guided him—her erectness unnaturally formal, as
if she were overcorrecting a stoop. There were no
photographs of speed-skating teams on the walls, there
was no unicycle parked by the door to the W.C. Down
a staircase and into a room with a harsh overhead light,
like a hasty operating room set up in a city under siege,
Garp felt he followed the Angel of Death—midwife to
the Under Toad whose swampy smell he sniffed at the
mouthpiece of the phone.

"Yes?" he whispered.

And for a moment was relieved to hear Roberta Muldoon—another sexual rejection; perhaps that was all.
Or perhaps an update on the New Hampshire gubernatorial race. Garp looked up at the old, inquiring face
of the landlady and realized that she had not taken the
time to put in her teeth; her cheeks were sucked into her
mouth, the loose flesh drooped below her jawline—her
whole face was as slack as a skeleton's. The room
reeked of toad.

"I didn't want you to see it on the news," Roberta
was saying. "If it would be on TV over there—I couldn't
know for sure. Or even the newspapers. I just didn't
want you to find out that way."

"Who won?" Garp asked, lightly, though he knew
that this call had little to do with the new or old governor of New Hampshire.

"She's been *shot*—your mother," Roberta said.
"They've killed her, Garp. A bastard shot her with a
deer rifle."

"Who?" Garp whispered.

"A *man!*" Roberta wailed. It was the worst word
she could use: a *man*. "A man who hated women,"
Roberta said. "He was a hunter," Roberta sobbed. "It
was hunting season, or it was almost hunting season,
and no one thought there was anything wrong about
a man with a rifle. He shot her."

"Dead?" Garp said.

"I caught her before she fell," Roberta cried. "She

never struck the ground, Garp. She never said a word. She never knew what happened, Garp. I'm sure."

"Did they get the man?" Garp asked.

"Someone shot him, or he shot himself," Roberta said.

"Dead?" Garp asked.

"Yes, the bastard," Roberta said. "He's dead, too."

"Are you alone, Roberta?" Garp asked her.

"No," Roberta wept. "There are a lot of us here. We're at *your* place." And Garp could imagine them all, the wailing women at Dog's Head Harbor—their leader murdered.

"She wanted her body to go to a med school," Garp said. "Roberta?"

"I hear you," Roberta said. "That's just so awful."

"That's what she wanted," Garp said.

"I know," Roberta said. "You've got to come home."

"Right away," Garp said.

"We don't know what to *do*," Roberta said.

"What *is* there to do?" Garp asked. "There's nothing to do."

"There should be *some*thing," Roberta said, "but she said she never wanted a funeral."

"Certainly not," Garp said. "She wanted her body to go to a med school. You get that accomplished, Roberta: that's what Mom would have wanted."

"But there ought to be *some*thing," Roberta protested. "Maybe not a *religious* service, but something."

"Don't you get involved in anything until I get there," Garp told her.

"There's a lot of talk," Roberta said. "People want a rally, or something."

"I'm her only family, Roberta," Garp said. "You tell them that."

"She meant a lot to a *lot* of us, you know," Roberta said, sharply.

Yes, and it got her killed! Garp thought, but he said nothing.

"I tried to look after her!" Roberta cried. "I told her not to go in that parking lot!"

"Nobody's to blame, Roberta," Garp said, softly.

"*You* think somebody's to blame, Garp," Roberta said. "You always do."

"Please, Roberta," Garp said. "You're my best friend."

"*I'll* tell you who's to blame," Roberta said. "It's *men,* Garp. It's your filthy murderous sex! If you can't *fuck* us the way you want to, you kill us in a hundred ways!"

"Not *me,* Roberta, please," Garp said.

"Yes, you too," Roberta whispered. "No man is a woman's friend."

"I'm *your* friend, Roberta," Garp said, and Roberta cried for a while—a sound as acceptable to Garp as rain falling on a deep lake.

"I'm so sorry," Roberta whispered. "If I'd seen the man with the gun—just a second sooner—I could have blocked the shot. I *would* have, you know."

"I know you would have, Roberta," Garp said; he wondered if *he* would have. He felt love for his mother, of course; and now an aching loss. But did he ever feel such *devotion* to Jenny Fields as the followers among her own sex?

He apologized to the landlady for the lateness of the phone call. When he told her that his mother was dead, the old woman crossed herself—her sunken cheeks and her empty gums were mute but clear indications of the family deaths she had herself outlived.

Helen cried for the longest time; she would not let Jenny's namesake, little Jenny Garp, out of her arms. Duncan and Garp searched the newspapers, but the news would be a day getting to Austria—except for the marvel of television.

Garp watched his mother's murder on his landlady's TV.

There was some election nonsense at a shopping plaza in New Hampshire. The landscape had a vaguely seacoast appearance, and Garp recognized the place as being a few miles from Dog's Head Harbor.

The incumbent governor was in favor of all the same, swinish, stupid things. The woman running against him seemed educated and idealistic and kind; she also seemed to barely restrain her anger at the same, swinish, stupid things the governor represented.

The parking lot at the shopping plaza was circled by pickup trucks. The pickups were full of men in hunting coats and caps; apparently they represented local New Hampshire interests—as opposed to the interest in New Hampshire taken by the New York divorcees.

The nice woman running against the governor was also a kind of New York divorcee. That she had lived fifteen years in New Hampshire, and her children had gone to school there, was a fact more or less ignored by the incumbent governor, and by his supporters who circled the parking lot in their pickup trucks.

There were lots of signs; there was a steady jeering.

There was also a high school football team, in uniform—their cleats clacking on the cement of the parking lot. One of the woman candidate's children was on the team and he had assembled the football players in the parking lot in hopes of demonstrating to New Hampshire that it was perfectly manly to vote for his mother.

The hunters in their pickup trucks were of the opinion that to vote for this woman was to vote for faggotry—and lesbianism, and socialism, and alimony, and New York. And so forth. Garp had the feeling, watching the telecast, that those things were not tolerated in New Hampshire.

Garp and Helen and Duncan, and baby Jenny, sat in the Viennese pension about to watch the murder of Jenny Fields. Their bewildered old landlady served them coffee and little cakes; only Duncan ate anything.

Then Jenny Fields had her turn to speak to the assembled people in the parking lot. She spoke from the back of a pickup truck; Roberta Muldoon lifted her up to the tailgate and adjusted the microphone for her. Garp's mother looked very small in the pickup truck, especially beside Roberta, but Jenny's uniform was so white that she stood out, bright and clear.

"I am Jenny Fields," she said—to some cheers and some whistles and some hoots. There was a blaring of horns from the pickup trucks circling the parking lot. The police were telling the pickup trucks to move on; they moved on, and came back, and moved on again. "Most of you know who I am," Jenny Fields said. There were more hoots, more cheers, more blowing of horns— and a single sharp gunshot as conclusive as a wave breaking on the beach.

No one saw where it came from. Roberta Muldoon held Garp's mother under her arms. Jenny's white uniform seemed struck by a small dark splash. Then Roberta dropped down from the tailgate with Jenny in her arms and knifed through the breaking crowd like an old tight end carrying the ball for a hard first down. The crowd parted; Jenny's white uniform was almost concealed in Roberta's arms. There was a police car moving to intercept Roberta; when they neared each other, Roberta held out the body of Jenny Fields toward the squad car. For a moment Garp saw his mother's unmoving white uniform lifted above the crowd and into the arms of a policeman, who helped her and Roberta into the car.

The car, as they say, sped away. The camera was distracted by an apparent shoot-out taking place among the circling pickup trucks and several more police cars. Later, there was the still body of a man in a hunting coat lying in a dark puddle of what looked like oil. Later still, there was a closeup of what the newsmen would only identify as "a deer rifle."

It was pointed out that the deer season had not officially opened.

Except for the fact that there had been no nudity in the telecast, the event was an X-rated soap opera from start to finish.

Garp thanked the landlady for allowing them to watch the news. Within two hours they were in Frankfurt, where they changed planes for New York. The Under Toad was not on the plane with them—not even for Helen, who was so afraid of planes. For a while, they knew, the Under Toad was elsewhere.

All Garp could think, somewhere over the Atlantic Ocean, was that his mother had delivered some adequate "last words." Jenny Fields had ended her life saying, "Most of you know who I am." On the airplane, Garp tried out the line.

"Most of you know who I am," he whispered. Duncan was asleep, but Helen overheard him; she reached across the aisle and held Garp's hand.

Thousands of feet above sea level, T. S. Garp cried in the airplane that was bringing him home to be famous in his violent country.

# 17

# The First Feminist Funeral,
# and Other Funerals

E VER since Walt died," wrote T. S. Garp, "my life has felt like an epilogue."

When Jenny Fields died, Garp must have felt his bewilderment increase—that sense of time passing with a plan. But what was the plan?

Garp sat in John Wolf's New York office, trying to comprehend the plethora of plans surrounding his mother's death.

"I didn't authorize a funeral," Garp said. "How can there be a funeral? Where is the body, Roberta?"

Roberta Muldoon said patiently that the body was where Jenny wanted her body to go. It was not her body that mattered, Roberta said. There was simply going to be a kind of memorial service; it was better not to think of it as a "funeral."

The newspapers had said it was to be the first feminist funeral in New York.

The police had said that violence was expected.

"The first feminist funeral?" Garp said.

487

"She meant so much to so many women," Roberta said. "Don't be angry. You didn't *own* her, you know."

John Wolf rolled his eyes.

Duncan Garp looked out the window of John Wolf's office, forty floors above Manhattan. It probably felt to Duncan a little like being on the plane he had just got off.

Helen was making a phone call in another office. She was trying to reach her father in the good old town of Steering; she wanted Ernie to meet their plane out of New York when it landed in Boston.

"All right," Garp said, slowly; he held the baby, little Jenny Garp, on his knee. "All right. You know I don't approve of this, Roberta, but I'll go."

"You'll *go?*" John Wolf said.

"No!" Roberta said. "I mean, you don't *have* to," she said.

"I know," Garp said. "But you're right. She probably would have liked such a thing, so I'll go. What's going to happen at it?"

"There's going to be a lot of speeches," Roberta said. "You don't want to go."

"And they're going to read from her book," John Wolf said. "We've donated some copies."

"But *you* don't want to go, Garp," Roberta said, nervously. "Please don't go."

"I want to go," Garp said. "I promise you I won't hiss or boo—no matter what the assholes say about her. I have something of hers I might read myself, if anyone's interested," he said. "Did you ever see that thing she wrote about being called a feminist?" Roberta and John Wolf looked at each other; they looked stricken and gray. "She said, 'I hate being called one, because it's a label I didn't choose to describe my feelings about men or the way I write.'"

"I don't want to argue with you, Garp," Roberta said. "Not now. You know perfectly well she said other things, too. She *was* a feminist, whether she liked the label or not. She was simply one for pointing out all the injustices to women; she was simply for allowing women to live their own lives and make their own choices."

"Oh?" said Garp. "And did she believe that *everything* that happened to women happened to them *because* they were women?"

"You have to be stupid to believe that, Garp," Roberta said. "You make us all sound like Ellen Jamesians."

"Please stop it, both of you," John Wolf said.

Jenny Garp squawked briefly and slapped Garp's knee; he looked at her, surprised—as if he'd forgotten she was a live thing there in his lap.

"What is it?" he asked her. But the baby was quiet again, watching some pattern in the landscape of John Wolf's office that was invisible to the rest of them.

"What time is this wingding?" Garp asked Roberta.

"Five o'clock in the afternoon," Roberta said.

"I believe it was chosen," John Wolf said, "so that half the secretaries in New York could walk off their jobs an hour early."

"Not all the working women in New York are secretaries," Roberta said.

"The secretaries," said John Wolf, "are the only ones who'll be *missed* between four and five."

"Oh boy," Garp said.

Helen came in and announced that she could not reach her father on the phone.

"He's at wrestling practice," Garp said.

"The wrestling season hasn't begun yet," Helen said. Garp looked at the calendar on his watch, which was several hours out of sync with the United States; he had last set it in Vienna. But Garp knew that wrestling at Steering did not officially begin until after Thanksgiving. Helen was right.

"When I called his office at the gym, they said he was at home," Helen told Garp. "And when I called home, there was no answer."

"We'll rent a car at the airport," Garp said. "And

anyway, we can't leave until tonight. I have to go to this damn funeral."

"No, you *don't* have to," Roberta insisted.

"In fact," Helen said, "you *can't*."

Roberta and John Wolf again looked stricken and gray; Garp simply looked uninformed.

"What do you mean, I *can't?*" he asked.

"It's a feminist funeral," Helen said. "Did you *read* the paper, or did you stop at the headlines?"

Garp looked accusingly at Roberta Muldoon, but she looked at Duncan looking out the window. Duncan had his telescope out, spying on Manhattan.

"You can't go, Garp," Roberta admitted. "It's true. I didn't tell you because I thought it would really piss you off. I didn't think you'd *want* to go, anyway."

"I'm not *allowed?*" Garp said.

"It's a funeral for *women,*" Roberta said. *"Women* loved her, women will mourn her. That's how we wanted it."

Garp glared at Roberta Muldoon. *"I* loved her," he said. "I'm her only child. Do you mean I can't go to this wingding because I'm a *man?*"

"I wish you wouldn't call it a wingding," Roberta said.

"What's a wingding?" Duncan asked.

Jenny Garp squawked again, but Garp didn't listen to her. Helen took her from him.

"Do you mean no men are allowed at my mother's funeral?" Garp asked Roberta.

"It's not exactly a funeral, as I told you," Roberta said. "It's more like a rally—it's a kind of reverent demonstration."

"I'm going, Roberta," Garp said. "I don't care what you *call* it."

"Oh boy," Helen said. She walked out of the office with baby Jenny. "I'm going to try to get my father again," she said.

"I see a man with one arm," Duncan said.

"Please don't go, Garp," Roberta said softly.

"She's right," John Wolf said. "I wanted to go, too.

I was her editor, after all. But let them have it their way, Garp. I think Jenny would have liked the idea."

"I don't care what she would have liked," Garp said.

"That's probably true," Roberta said. "That's another reason you shouldn't be there."

"You don't know, Garp, how some of the women's movement people have reacted to your *book*," John Wolf advised him.

Roberta Muldoon rolled her eyes. The accusation that Garp was cashing in on his mother's reputation, and the women's movement, had been made before. Roberta had seen the advertisement for *The World According to Bensenhaver*, which John Wolf had instantly authorized upon Jenny's assassination. Garp's book appeared to cash in on that tragedy, too—the ad conveyed a sick sense of a poor author who's lost a son "and now a mother, too."

It is fortunate Garp never saw that ad; even John Wolf regretted it.

*The World According to Bensenhaver* sold and sold and sold. For years it would be controversial; it would be taught in colleges. Fortunately, Garp's other books would be taught in colleges, sporadically, too. One course taught Jenny's autobiography together with Garp's three novels and Stewart Percy's *A History of Everett Steering's Academy*. The purpose of that course, apparently, was to figure out everything about Garp's *life* by hunting through the books for those things that appeared to be *true*.

It is fortunate Garp never knew anything about that course, either.

"I see a man with one leg," announced Duncan Garp, searching the streets and windows of Manhattan for all the crippled and misarranged—a task that could take years.

"Please stop it, Duncan," Garp said to him.

"If you really want to go, Garp," Roberta Muldoon whispered to him, "you'll have to go in drag."

"If it's all that tough for a man to get in," Garp

snapped at Roberta, "you better hope they don't have a chromosome check at the door." He felt instantly sorry he'd said that; he saw Roberta wince as if he'd slapped her and he took both her big hands in his and held them until he felt her squeeze him back. "Sorry," he whispered. "If I've got to go in drag, it's a good thing you're here to help me dress up. I mean, you're an old hand at that, right?"

"Right," Roberta said.

"This is ridiculous," John Wolf said.

"If some of those women recognize you," Roberta told Garp, "they'll tear you limb from limb. At the very least, they won't let you in the door."

Helen came back in the office with Jenny Garp squawking on her hip.

"I've called Dean Bodger," she told Garp. "I asked him to try to reach Daddy. It's just not like him, to be nowhere."

Garp shook his head.

"We should just go to the airport now," Helen told him. "Rent a car in Boston, drive to Steering. Let the children rest," she said. "Then if you want to run back to New York on some crusade, you can do it."

"*You* go," Garp said. "I'll take a plane and rent my own car later."

"That's silly," Helen said.

"And needlessly expensive," Roberta said.

"I have a lot of money now," Garp said; his wry smile to John Wolf was not returned.

John Wolf volunteered to take Helen and the kids to the airport.

"One man with one arm, one man with one leg, two people who limped," said Duncan, "and someone without any nose."

"You should wait awhile and get a look at your father," Roberta Muldoon said.

Garp thought of himself: a grieving ex-wrestler, in drag for his mother's memorial service. He kissed Helen and the children, and even John Wolf. "Don't worry about your dad," Garp told Helen.

"And don't worry about Garp," Roberta told Helen. "I'm going to disguise him so that everyone will leave him alone."

"I wish *you'd* try to leave everyone alone," Helen told Garp.

There was suddenly another woman in John Wolf's crowded office; no one had noticed her, but she had been trying to get John Wolf's attention. When she spoke, she spoke out in a single, clear moment of silence and everyone looked at her.

"Mr. Wolf?" the woman said. She was old and brown-black-gray, and her feet appeared to be killing her; she wore an electrical extension cord, wrapped twice around her thick waist.

"Yes, Jillsy?" John Wolf said, and Garp stared at the woman. It was Jillsy Sloper, of course; John Wolf should have known that writers remember names.

"I was wonderin'," Jillsy said, "if I could get off early this afternoon—if you'd say a word for me, because I want to go to that funeral." She spoke with her chin down, a stiff mutter of bitten words—as few as possible. She did not like to open her mouth around strangers; also, she recognized Garp and she didn't want to be introduced to him—not ever.

"Yes, of course you can," John Wolf said, quickly. He didn't want to introduce Jillsy Sloper to Garp any more than *she* wanted it.

"Just a minute," Garp said. Jillsy Sloper and John Wolf froze. "Are you Jillsy Sloper?" Garp asked her.

"No!" John Wolf blurted. Garp glared at him.

"How do you do?" Jillsy said to Garp; she would not look at him.

"How do *you* do?" Garp said. He could see at a glance that this sorrowful woman had *not,* as John Wolf said, "loved" his book.

"I'm sorry about your mom," Jillsy said.

"Thank you very much," Garp said, but he could see

—they *all* could see—that Jillsy Sloper was seething about something.

"She was worth two or three of *you!*" Jillsy suddenly cried to Garp. There were tears in her muddy-yellow eyes. "She was worth four or five of your terrible books!" she crooned. "Lawd," she muttered, leaving them all in John Wolf's office. "Lawd, Lawd!"

Another person with a limp, thought Duncan Garp, but he could see that his father did not want to hear about his body count.

At the first feminist funeral held in the city of New York, the mourners appeared unsure how to behave. This was perhaps the result of the gathering's being not in a church but in one of these enigmatic buildings of the city university system—an auditorium, old with the echo of speeches no one had listened to. The giant space was slightly seedy with the sense of past cheering—for rock bands, and for the occasional, well-known poet. But the space was also serious with the certain knowledge that large lectures had taken place there; it was a room in which hundreds of people had taken notes.

The name of the space was School of Nursing Hall—thus it was oddly appropriate as a place of tribute to Jenny Fields. It was hard to tell the difference between the mourners wearing their Jenny Fields Originals, with the little red hearts stitched over the breast, and the real nurses, forever white and unfashionable, who had other reasons to be in the environs of the nursing school but had paused to peek in on the ceremonies—either curious or genuinely sympathetic, or both.

There were many white uniforms among the enormous, milling, softly mumbling audience, and Garp immediately cursed Roberta. "I *told* you I could have dressed as a nurse," Garp hissed. "I could have been a little less conspicuous."

"I thought you'd be conspicuous as a nurse," Roberta said. "I didn't know there'd be so many."

"It's going to be a fucking national trend," Garp muttered. "Just wait and see," he said, but he said no more; he huddled small and garish beside Roberta, feeling that everyone was looking at him and somehow sensing his maleness—or at least, as Roberta had warned him, his hostility.

They sat dead-center in the massive auditorium, only three rows back from the stage and the speakers' platform; a sea of women had moved in and sat behind them—rows and rows of them—and farther back, at the wide-open rear of the hall (where there were no seats), the women who were less interested in seating themselves for the entire ritual, but who'd wanted to come pay their respects, filed slowly in one door and slowly out another. It was as if the larger, seated audience were the open casket of Jenny Fields that the slow-walking women had come to observe.

Garp, of course, felt that *he* was an open casket, and all the women were observing him—his pallor, his hue, his preposterous disguise.

Roberta had done this to him, perhaps to get even with him for his bullying her into letting him come at all—or for his cruel crack concerning her chromosomes. Roberta had dressed Garp in a cheap turquoise jump suit, the color of Oren Rath's pickup truck. The jump suit had a gold zipper that ran from Garp's crotch to Garp's throat. Garp did not adequately fill the hips of the suit, but his breasts—or, rather, the falsies Roberta had fashioned for him—strained against the snap-flap pockets and twisted the vulnerable zipper askew.

"What a set you have!" Roberta had told him.

"You animal, Roberta," Garp had hissed to her.

The shoulder straps of the huge, hideous bra dug into his shoulders. But whenever Garp felt that a woman was staring at him, perhaps doubting his sex, he would simply turn himself sideways to her and show off. Thus eliminating any possible doubt, or so he hoped.

He was less sure of the wig. A tousled whore's head of honey-blond hair, under which his own scalp itched.

A pretty green silk scarf was at his throat.

His dark face was powdered a sickly gray, but this concealed, Roberta said, his stubble of beard. His rather thin lips were cherry-colored, but he kept licking them and had smeared the lipstick at one corner of his mouth.

"You look like you've just been kissed," Roberta reassured him.

Though Garp was cold, Roberta had not allowed him to wear his ski parka—it made his shoulders look too thick. And on Garp's feet was a towering pair of knee-high boots—a kind of cherry vinyl that matched, Roberta said, his lipstick. Garp had seen himself reflected in a storefront window and he'd told Roberta that he thought he looked like a teen-age prostitute.

"An *aging* teen-age prostitute," Roberta had corrected him.

"A faggot parachutist," Garp had said.

"No, you look like a woman, Garp," Roberta had assured him. "Not a woman with especially good taste, but a woman."

So Garp sat squirming in School of Nursing Hall. He twisted the itchy rope braids of his ridiculous purse, a scraggily hemp thing with an oriental design, barely big enough to hold his wallet. In her large, bursting shoulder bag, Roberta Muldoon had hidden Garp's real clothes —his other identity.

"This is Manda Horton-Jones," Roberta whispered, indicating a thin, hawk-nosed woman speaking nasally and with her rodential head pointed down; she read a stiff, prepared speech.

Garp didn't know who Manda Horton-Jones was; he shrugged, enduring her. The speeches had ranged from strident, political calls for unity to disturbed, painful, personal reminiscences of Jenny Fields. The audience did not know whether to applaud or to pray—whether to voice approval or to nod grimly. The atmosphere was both one of mourning and one of urgent togetherness —with a strong sense of marching forth. Thinking about it, Garp supposed this was natural and fitting, both to his mother and to his dim perception of what the women's movement *was*.

"This is Sally Devlin," Roberta whispered. The woman now climbing to the speakers' platform looked pleasant and wise and vaguely familiar. Garp felt immediately the need to defend himself from her. He didn't mean it, but solely to goad Roberta, Garp whispered, "She has nice legs."

"Nicer than yours," Roberta said, pinching his thigh painfully between her strong thumb and her long, pass-catching index finger—one of the fingers, Garp supposed, that had been broken so many times during Roberta's fling as a Philadelphia Eagle.

Sally Devlin looked down on them with her soft, sad eyes as if she were silently scolding a classroom of children who were not paying attention—not even sitting still.

"That senseless murder does not really merit all this," she said, quietly. "But Jenny Fields simply helped so many *individuals,* she simply was so patient and generous with women who were having a bad time. Anyone who's ever been helped by someone else should feel terrible about what's happened to her."

Garp felt truly terrible, at that moment; he heard a combined sigh and sob of hundreds of women. Beside him, Roberta's broad shoulders shook against him. He felt a hand, perhaps of the woman sitting directly behind him, grip his own shoulder, cramped in the terrible turquoise jump suit. He wondered if he was about to be slapped for his offensive, inappropriate attire, but the hand just held on to his shoulder. Perhaps the woman needed support. At this moment, Garp knew, they all felt like sisters, didn't they?

He looked up to see what Sally Devlin was saying, but his own eyes were teary and he could not see Ms. Devlin clearly. He could *hear* her, though: she was sobbing. Great heartfelt and heaving cries! She was trying to get back to her speech but her eyes couldn't find her place on the page; the page rattled against the microphone. Some very powerful-looking woman, whom Garp thought he had seen before—one of those bodyguard types he had often seen with his mother—tried to help Sally Devlin off the platform, but Ms. Devlin didn't want to leave.

"I wasn't going to do this," she said, still crying— meaning her sobs, her loss of control. "I had more to say," she protested, but she could not get hold of her voice. "Damn it," she said, with a dignity that moved Garp.

The big tough-looking woman found herself alone at the microphone. The audience waited quietly. Garp felt a tremble, or maybe a tug, from the hand on his shoulder. Looking at Roberta's large hands, folded in her lap, Garp knew that the hand on his shoulder must be very small.

The big tough-looking woman wanted to say something, and the audience waited. But they would wait forever to hear a word from her. Roberta knew her. Roberta stood up beside Garp and began to applaud the big, hard-looking woman's silence—her exasperating quiet in front of the microphone. Other people joined Roberta's applause—even Garp, though he had no idea why he was clapping.

"She's an Ellen Jamesian," Roberta whispered to him. "She *can't* say anything." Yet the woman melted the audience with her pained, sorry face. She opened her mouth as if she were singing, but no sound came out. Garp imagined he could see the severed stump of her tongue. He remembered how his mother supported them —these crazies; Jenny was wonderful to every single one of them who came to her. But Jenny had finally admitted her disapproval of what they had done—perhaps only to Garp. "They're making victims of themselves," Jenny had said, "and yet that's the same thing they're angry at men for doing to them. Why don't they just take a vow of silence, or never speak in a man's presence?" Jenny said. "It's not logical: to maim yourself to make a point."

But Garp, now touched by the mad woman in front of him, felt the whole history of the world's self-mutilation—though violent and illogical, it expressed, perhaps like nothing else, a terrible hurt. "I am really *hurt*," said the woman's huge face, dissolving before him in his own swimmy tears.

Then the little hand on his shoulder hurt *him;* he remembered himself—a man at a ritual for women—and he turned around to see the rather tired-looking young woman behind him. Her face was familiar, but he didn't recognize her.

"I know you," the young woman whispered to him. She did not sound *happy* that she knew him, either.

Roberta had warned him not to open his mouth to anyone, not even to *try* to speak. He was prepared for handling that problem. He shook his head. He took a pad of paper out of the flap pocket, which was crushed against his mammoth, false bosom, and he snatched a pencil out of his absurd purse. The sharp, clawlike fingers of the woman bit into his shoulder, as if she were keeping him from running away.

*Hi! I'm an Ellen Jamesian,*

Garp scribbled on the pad; he tore the slip off and handed it to the young woman. She didn't take it.

"Like hell you are," she said. "You're T. S. Garp."

The word *Garp* bounced like the burp of an unknown animal into the silence of the suffering auditorium, still conducted by the quiet Ellen Jamesian on stage. Roberta Muldoon turned around and looked panic-stricken; she had never seen this particular young woman in her life.

"I don't know who your big playmate is," the young woman told Garp, "but you're T. S. Garp. I don't know where you got that dumb wig or those big tits, but I'd know you anywhere. You haven't changed a bit since you were fucking my sister—fucking her to *death*," the young woman said. And Garp knew who his enemy was: the last and youngest of the Percy Family Horde.

Bainbridge! Little Pooh Percy, who was wearing diapers as a preteen, and, for all Garp knew, might be wearing them still.

Garp looked at her; Garp had bigger tits than she did. Pooh was asexually attired, her haircut was similar to a popular and unisexual style, her features were neither delicate nor coarse. Pooh wore a U.S. Army shirt with sergeant stripes and a campaign button for the woman who'd hoped to be the new governor of the State of New Hampshire. With a shock, Garp realized that the woman running for governor was Sally Devlin. He wondered if she'd won!

"Hello, Pooh," Garp said, and saw her wince—a *hated* nickname, obviously, and one she was never called anymore. "Bainbridge," Garp muttered, but it was too late to make friends. It was *years* too late. It was too late from the night Garp had bitten off Bonkers' ear, had violated Cushie in the Steering School infirmary, had not ever really loved her—had not come to her wedding, and not to her funeral.

Whatever grudge against Garp this was, or whatever loathing for men in general, Pooh Percy had *her* enemy at her mercy—at last.

Roberta's big warm hand was at the small of Garp's back and her heavy voice urged him, "Get out of here, move fast, don't say a word."

"There's a *man* here!" Bainbridge Percy shouted to the grieving silence of School of Nursing Hall. That even brought a small sound—perhaps a grunt—from the troubled Ellen Jamesian on stage. "There's a man here!" Pooh screamed. "And he's T. S. Garp. *Garp* is here!" she cried.

Roberta tried to lead him to the aisle. A tight end is chiefly a good blocker, secondarily a pass-receiver, but even the former Robert Muldoon could not quite move all these women.

"Please," Roberta said. "Excuse us, please. She was his *mother*—you must know that. Her only child."

My only *mother!* Garp thought, plowing against

Roberta's back; he felt Pooh Percy's needlelike claws rake his face. She snatched his wig off; he snatched it back and clutched it to his big bosom, as if it mattered to him.

"He fucked my sister to *death!*" Pooh Percy wailed. How *this* perception of Garp had convinced her, Garp would never know—but convinced of it Pooh clearly was. She climbed over the seat he had abandoned and moved in behind him and Roberta—who finally broke through, into the aisle.

"She was my mother," Garp said to a woman he was passing, a woman who looked like a potential mother herself. She was pregnant. In the woman's scornful face Garp saw reason and kindness; he also saw restraint and contempt.

"Let him pass," the pregnant woman murmured, but without much feeling.

Others seemed more sympathetic. Someone cried out that he had a right to be there—but there were other things shouted, rather lacking sympathy of any kind.

Farther up the aisle he felt his falsies punched; he put his hand out for Roberta and realized Roberta had (as they say in football) been taken out of the play. She was down. Several young women wearing navy pea coats appeared to be sitting on her. It occurred to Garp that they might think Roberta was *also* a man in drag; their discovery that Roberta was real could be painful.

"Take off, Garp!" Roberta cried.

"Yes, *run*, you little fucker!" one woman in a pea coat hissed.

He ran.

He was almost up to the milling women at the rear of the hall when someone's blow landed where it was aimed. He had not been hit in the balls since a wrestling practice at Steering—so many years ago, he realized he had forgotten the total incapacity that resulted. He covered himself and lay curled on one hip. They kept trying to rip his wig out of his hands. And his tiny purse. He held on as if this were some mugging. He felt a few shoes, a few slaps, and then the minty breath of an elderly woman breathing in his face.

"Try to get up," she said, gently. He saw she was a nurse. A real nurse. There was no fashionable heart sewn above her breast; there was just the little brass-and-blue nameplate—she was R. N. So-and-So.

"My name is Dotty," the nurse told him; she was at least sixty.

"Hello," Garp said. "Thank you, Dotty."

She took his arm and led him at a fast pace through the remaining mob. No one appeared to want to hurt him when he was with her. They let him go.

"Do you have money for a cab?" the nurse named Dotty asked him when they were outside School of Nursing Hall.

"Yes, I think so," Garp said. He checked his horrid purse; his wallet was safely there. And his wig—tousled still further—was under his arm. Roberta had Garp's real clothes and Garp looked in vain for any sign of Roberta emerging from the first feminist funeral.

"Put that wig on," Dotty advised him, "or you'll be mistaken for one of those transvestites." He struggled to put it on; she helped him. "People are really rough on transvestites," Dotty added. She took several bobby pins from her own gray head of hair and fastened Garp's wig more decently in place.

The scratch on his cheek, she told him, would stop bleeding very soon.

On the steps of School of Nursing Hall, a tall black woman who looked like an even match for Roberta shook her fist at Garp but said not a word. Perhaps she was another Ellen Jamesian. A few other women were gathering there and Garp feared they might be thinking over the advisability of an open attack. Oddly at the fringe of their group, but seeming to have no connection with them, was a wraithlike girl, or barely grown-up child; she was a dirty blond-headed girl with piercing eyes the color of coffee-stained saucers—like a drug-user's eyes, or someone long involved in hard tears.

Garp felt frozen by her stare, and frightened of her—as
if she were *really* crazy, a kind of teen-age hit man for
the women's movement, with a gun in her oversized
purse. He clutched his own ratty bag, recalling that his
wallet was at least full of credit cards; he had enough
cash for a cab to the airport and the credit cards could
get him a flight to Boston and the bosom, so to speak,
of his remaining family. He wished he could relieve himself of his ostentatious tits, but there they were, as if he'd
been born with them—and born, too, in this alternately
tight and baggy jump suit. It was all he had and it would
have to do. From the din escaping from School of Nursing Hall, Garp knew that Roberta was deep in the throes
of debate—if not combat. Someone who had fainted, or
had been mauled, was carried out; more police went in.

"Your mother was a first-rate nurse and a woman
who made every woman proud," the nurse named Dotty
told him. "I'll bet she was a good mother, too."

"She sure was," Garp said.

The nurse got him a cab; the last he saw of her, she
was walking away from the curb, back toward School of
Nursing Hall. The other women who'd seemed so threatening, on the steps outside the building, appeared to be
not interested in molesting her. More police were arriving; Garp looked for the strange saucer-eyed girl, but
she was not among the other women.

He asked the cabby who the new governor of New
Hampshire was. Garp tried to conceal the depth of his
voice, but the cabby, familiar with the eccentricities of
his job, seemed unsurprised at both Garp's voice and
Garp's appearance.

"I was out of the country," Garp said.

"You didn't miss nothin', sweetie," the cabby told
him. "That broad broke down."

"Sally Devlin?" said Garp.

"She cracked up, right on the TV," the cabby said.
"She was so flipped out over the assassination, she
couldn't control herself. She was givin' this speech but
she couldn't get through it, you know?

503

"She looked like a real idiot to me," the cabby said. "She couldn't be no governor if she couldn't control herself no better than that."

And Garp saw the pattern of the woman's loss emerging. Perhaps the foul incumbent governor had remarked that Ms. Devlin's inability to control her emotions was "just like a woman." Disgraced by her demonstration of her feelings for Jenny Fields, Sally Devlin was judged not competent enough for whatever dubious work being a governor entailed.

Garp felt ashamed. He felt ashamed of other people.

"In my opinion," the cabby said, "it took something like that shooting to show the people that the woman couldn't handle the job, you know?"

"Shut up and drive," Garp said.

"Look, honey," the cabby said. "I don't have to put up with no *abuse*."

"You're an asshole and a moron," Garp told him, "and if you don't drive me to the airport with your mouth shut, I'll tell a cop you tried to paw me all over."

The cabby floored the accelerator and drove for a while in furious silence, hoping the speed and recklessness of his driving would scare his passenger.

"If you don't slow down," Garp said, "I'll tell a cop you tried to rape me."

"Fucking weirdo," the cabby said, but he slowed down and drove to the airport without another word. Garp put the money for the tip on the taxi's hood and one of the coins rolled into the crack between the hood and fender. "Fucking *women*," the cabby said.

"Fucking *men*," said Garp, feeling—with mixed feelings—that he had done his duty to ensure that the sex war went on.

At the airport they questioned Garp's American Express card and asked for further identification. Inevitably, they asked him about the initials T. S. The airline ticket-maker was clearly not in touch with the literary world—not to know who T. S. Garp was.

He told the ticket-maker that T. was for Tillie, S. was for Sarah.

"Tillie Sarah Garp?" the ticket-maker said. She was a young woman, and she clearly disapproved of Garp's oddly fetching but whorish appearance. "Nothing to check, and no carry-on luggage?" Garp was asked.

"No, nothing," he said.

"You have a coat?" the stewardess asked him, also giving him a condescending appraisal.

"No coat," Garp said. The stewardess gave a start at the deepness of his voice. "No bags and nothing to hang up," he said, smiling. He felt that all he had was *breasts* —these terrific knockers Roberta had made for him— and he walked slouched and stoop-shouldered to try to hold them back. There was no holding them back, though.

As soon as he chose a seat, some man chose to sit beside him. Garp looked out the window. Passengers were still hurrying to his plane. Among them, he saw a wraithlike, dirty blond-haired girl. She had no coat and no carry-on luggage, either. Just that oversized purse— big enough for a bomb. Thickly, Garp sensed the Under Toad—a wriggle at his hip. He looked toward the aisle, so that he would notice where the girl chose to sit, but he looked into the leering face of the man who'd taken the aisle seat beside him.

"Perhaps, when we're in the air," the man said, knowingly, "I could buy you a little drink?" His small, close-together eyes were riveted on the twisted zipper of Garp's straining turquoise jump suit.

Garp felt a peculiar kind of unfairness overwhelm him. He had not asked to have such an anatomy. He wished he could have spent a quiet time, just talking, with that wise and pleasant-looking woman, Sally Devlin, the failed gubernatorial candidate from New Hampshire. He would have told her that she was too good for the rotten job.

"That's some *suit* you got," said Garp's leering seat partner.

"Go stick it in your ear," Garp said. He was, after all, the son of a woman who'd slashed a masher at a movie in Boston—years ago, long ago.

The man struggled to get up, but he couldn't; his seat belt would not release him. He looked helplessly at Garp. Garp leaned over the man's trapped lap; Garp gagged on his own dose of perfume, which he remembered Roberta slathering over him. He got the seat-belt clasp to operate properly and released the man with a sharp snap. Then Garp growled a menacing whisper in the man's very red ear. "When we're in the air, cutie," he whispered to the frightened fellow, "go blow yourself in the bathroom."

But when the man deserted Garp's company, the aisle seat was vacant, inviting someone else. Garp glared challengingly at the empty seat, daring the next man on the make to sit there. The person who approached Garp shook his momentary confidence. She was very thin, her girlish hands bony and clutching her oversized purse. She didn't ask first; she just sat down. The Under Toad is a very young girl today, Garp thought. When she reached into her purse, Garp caught her wrist and pulled her hand out of the bag and into her lap. She was not strong, and in her hand there was no gun; there was not even a knife. Garp saw only a pad of paper and a pencil with the eraser bitten down to a nub.

"I'm sorry," he whispered. If she was not an assassin, he guessed he knew who or what she was. "Why is my life so full of people with impaired speech?" he wrote once. "Or is it only because I'm a writer that I notice all the damaged voices around me?"

The nonviolent waif on the airplane beside him wrote hastily and handed him a note.

"Yes, yes," he said, wearily. "You're an Ellen Jamesian." But the girl bit her lip and fiercely shook her head. She pushed the note into his hand.

*My name is Ellen James,*

the note informed Garp.

*I am* not *an Ellen Jamesian.*

"You're *the* Ellen James?" he asked her, though it was unnecessary and he knew it—just looking at her, he should have known. She was the right age; not so long ago she would have been that eleven-year-old child, raped and untongued. The dirty-saucer eyes were, up close, not dirty; they were simply bloodshot, perhaps insomniac. Her lower lip was ragged; it looked like the pencil eraser—bitten down.

She scribbled more.

*I came from Illinois. My parents were killed in an auto accident, recently. I came East to meet your mother. I wrote her a letter and she actually an-*swered *me! She wrote me a wonderful reply. She invited me to come stay with her. She also told me to read all your books.*

Garp turned these tiny pages of notepaper; he kept nodding; he kept smiling.

*But your mother was killed!*

From the big purse Ellen James pulled a brown bandanna into which she blew her nose.

*I went to stay with a women's group in New York. But I already knew too many Ellen James-ians. They're* all *I know; I get* hundreds *of Christmas cards,*

she wrote. She paused for Garp to read that line.
"Yes, yes, I'm sure you do," he encouraged her.

*I went to the funeral, of course. I went because I* knew *you'd be there. I knew you'd come,*

she wrote; she stopped, now, to smile at him. Then she hid her face in her dirty brown bandanna.

507

"You wanted to see *me?*" Garp said.

She nodded, fiercely. She pulled from the big bag her mangled copy of *The World According to Bensenhaver*.

*The best rape story I have ever read,*

wrote Ellen James. Garp winced.

*Do you know how many times I have read this book?*

she wrote. He looked at her teary, admiring eyes. He shook his head, as mutely as an Ellen Jamesian. She touched his face; she had a childlike inability with her hands. She held up her fingers for him to count. All of one little hand and most of the other. She had read his awful book eight times.

"Eight times," Garp murmured.

She nodded, and smiled at him. Now she settled back in the plane seat, as if her life were accomplished, now that she was sitting beside him, en route to Boston—if not with the woman she had admired all the way from Illinois, at least with the woman's only son, who would have to suffice.

"Have you been to college?" Garp asked her.

Ellen James held up one dirty finger; she made an unhappy face.

"One year?" Garp translated. "But you didn't like it. It didn't work out?"

She nodded eagerly.

"And what do you want to be?" he asked her, barely keeping himself from adding: *When you grow up.*

She pointed to him and blushed. She actually touched his gross breasts.

"A writer?" Garp guessed. She relaxed and smiled; he understood her so easily, her face seemed to say. Garp felt his throat constricting. She struck him as one of those doomed children he had read about: the ones

508

who have no antibodies—they have no natural immunities to disease. If they don't live their lives in plastic bags, they die of their first common cold. Here was Ellen James of Illinois, out of her sack.

"*Both* your parents were killed?" Garp asked. She nodded, and bit again her chewed lip. "And you have no other family?" he asked her. She shook her head.

He knew what his mother would have done. He knew Helen wouldn't mind; and of course Roberta would always be of help. And all those women who'd been wounded and were now healed, in their fashion.

"Well, you have a family *now*," Garp told Ellen James; he held her hand and winced to hear himself make such an offer. He heard the echo of his mother's voice, her old soap-opera role: The Adventures of Good Nurse.

Ellen James shut her eyes as if she had fainted for joy. When the stewardess asked her to fasten her seat belt, Ellen James didn't hear; Garp fastened her belt for her. All the short flight to Boston the girl wrote her heart out.

*I hate the Ellen Jamesians,*

she wrote.

*I would never do this to myself.*

She opened her mouth and pointed to the wide absence in there. Garp cringed.

*I want to talk; I want to say everything,*

wrote Ellen James. Garp noticed that the gnarled thumb and index finger of her writing hand were easily twice the size of the unused instruments on her other hand; she had a writing muscle such as he'd never seen. No writer's cramp for Ellen James, he thought.

*The words come and come,*

509

she wrote. She waited for his approval, line by line. He would nod; she would go on. She wrote him her whole life. Her high school English teacher, the only one who mattered. Her mother's eczema. The Ford Mustang that her father drove too fast.

*I have read everything,*

she wrote. Garp told her that Helen was a big reader, too; he thought she would like Helen. The girl looked very hopeful.

*Who was your favorite writer when you were a boy?*

"Joseph Conrad," Garp said. She sighed her approval.

*Jane Austen was mine.*

"That's fine," Garp said to her.

At Logan Airport she was almost asleep on her feet; Garp steered her up the aisles and leaned her on the counters while he filled out the necessary forms for the rental car.

"T. S.?" the rental-car person asked. One of Garp's falsies was slipping sideways and the rental-car person appeared anxious that this entire turquoise body might self-destruct.

In the car north, on the dark road to Steering, Ellen James slept like a kitten curled in the back seat. In the rear-view mirror Garp noted that her knee was skinned, and that the girl sucked her thumb while she slept.

It had been a proper funeral for Jenny Fields, after all; some essential message had passed from mother to son. Here he was, playing nurse to someone. More essentially, Garp finally understood what his mother's talent had been; she had right instincts—*Jenny Fields always did what was right*. One day, Garp hoped, he would see the connection between this lesson and his own writing, but that was a personal goal—like others, it would take a little time. Importantly, it was in the car north to Steering, with the real Ellen James asleep and in his care, that T. S. Garp decided he would try to *be* more like his mother, Jenny Fields.

A thought, it occurred to him, that would have pleased his mother greatly if it had only come to him when she was alive.

"Death, it seems," Garp wrote, "does not like to wait until we are prepared for it. Death is indulgent and enjoys, when it can, a flair for the dramatic."

Thus Garp, with his defenses down and his sense of the Under Toad fled from him—at least, since his arrival in Boston—walked into the house of Ernie Holm, his father-in-law, carrying the sleeping Ellen James in his arms. She might have been nineteen, but she was easier to carry than Duncan.

Garp was not prepared for the grizzled face of Dean Bodger, alone in Ernie's dim living room, watching TV. The old dean, who would soon retire, seemed to accept that Garp was dressed as a whore, but he stared with horror at the sleeping Ellen James.

"Is she . . ."

"She's asleep," Garp said. "Where's everyone?" And with the voicing of his question, Garp heard the cold hop of the Under Toad thudding across the cold floors of the silent house.

"I tried to reach you," Dean Bodger told him. "It's Ernie."

"His heart," Garp guessed.

"Yes," Bodger said. "They gave Helen something to help her sleep. She's upstairs. And I thought I'd stay until you got here—you know: so that if the children woke up and needed anything, they wouldn't disturb her. I'm sorry, Garp. These things sometimes come all at once, or they seem to."

Garp knew how Bodger had liked his mother, too. He put the sleeping Ellen James on the living-room couch and turned off the sickly TV, which was turning the girl's face bluish.

"In his sleep?" Garp asked Bodger, pulling off his wig. "Did you find Ernie here?"

Now the poor dean looked nervous. "He was on the bed upstairs," Bodger said. "I called up the stairs, but I knew I'd have to go up and find him. I fixed him up a little before I called anyone."

"Fixed him up?" Garp said. He unzipped the terrible turquoise jump suit and ripped off his breasts. The old dean perhaps thought this was a common traveling disguise of the now-famous writer.

"Please don't ever tell Helen," Bodger said.

"Tell her what?" Garp asked.

Bodger brought out the magazine—out from under his bulging vest. It was the issue of *Crotch Shots* where the first chapter of *The World According to Bensenhaver* had been published. The magazine looked very worn and used.

"Ernie had been looking at it, you know," Bodger said. "When his heart stopped."

Garp took the magazine from Bodger and imagined the death scene. Ernie Holm had been masturbating to the split-beaver pictures when his heart quit. There was a joke during Garp's days at Steering that this was the preferred way to "go." So Ernie had gone that way, and the kindly Bodger had pulled up the coach's pants and hidden the magazine from the coach's daughter.

"I had to tell the medical examiner, you know," Bodger said.

A nasty metaphor from his mother's past came up to Garp in a wave, like nausea, but he did not express it to the old dean. Lust lays another good man low! Ernie's lonely life depressed Garp.

"And your mom," sighed Bodger, shaking his head under the cold porch light that glowed into the black Steering campus. "Your mom was someone special," the old man mused. "She was a real fighter," the scrappy

Bodger said, with pride. "I still have copies of the notes she wrote to Stewart Percy."

"You were always nice to her," Garp reminded him.

"She was worth a hundred Stewart Percys, you know, Garp," Bodger said.

"She sure was," Garp said.

"You know *he's* gone, too?" Bodger said.

"Fat Stew?" said Garp.

"Yesterday," Bodger said. "After a long illness—you know what that usually means, don't you?"

"No," Garp said. He hadn't ever thought about it.

"Cancer, usually," Bodger said, gravely. "He had it for a long time."

"Well, I'm sorry," Garp said. He was thinking of Pooh, and of course of Cushie. And his old challenger, Bonkers, whose ear in his dreams he could still taste.

"There's going to be some confusion about the Steering chapel," Bodger explained. "Helen can tell you, she understands. Stewart has a service in the morning; Ernie has his later in the day. And, of course, you know the bit about Jenny?"

"What bit?" Garp asked.

"The memorial?"

"God, no," Garp said. "A memorial *here?*"

"There are girls here now, you know," Bodger said. "I should say *women,*" he added, shaking his head. "I don't know; they're awfully young. They're girls to me."

"Students?" Garp said.

"Yes, students," Bodger said. "The girl students voted to name the infirmary after her."

"The infirmary?" Garp said.

"Well, it's never had a name, you know," Bodger said. "Most of our buildings have names."

"The Jenny Fields Infirmary," Garp said, numbly.

"Sort of nice, isn't it?" Bodger asked; he wasn't too sure if Garp would think so, but Garp didn't care.

In the long night, baby Jenny woke up once; by the time Garp had moved himself away from Helen's warm and deeply sleeping body, he saw that Ellen James had already found the crying baby and was warming a bottle. Odd cooing and grunting sounds, appropriate to babies, came softly out of the tongueless mouth of Ellen James. She had worked in a day-care center in Illinois, she had written Garp on the plane. She knew all about babies, and could even make noises like them.

Garp smiled at her and went back to bed.

In the morning he told Helen about Ellen James and they talked about Ernie.

"It was good that he went in his sleep," Helen said. "When I think of your mother."

"Yes, yes," Garp told her.

Duncan was introduced to Ellen James. One-eyed and no-tongued, thought Garp, my family will pull together.

When Roberta called to describe her arrest, Duncan —who was the least-tired talking human in the house— explained to her about Ernie's heart attack.

Helen found the turquoise jump suit and the huge, loaded bra in the kitchen wastebasket; it seemed to cheer her up. The cherry-colored vinyl boots actually fit her better than they had fit Garp, but she threw them out, anyway. Ellen James wanted the green scarf, and Helen took the girl shopping for some more clothes. Duncan asked for and received the wig, which—to Garp's irritation—he wore most of the morning.

Dean Bodger called, to ask to be of use.

A man who was the new director of Physical Facilities for the Steering School stopped at the house to talk confidentially with Garp. The Physical Facilities director explained that Ernie had lived in a school house, and as soon as it was convenient for Helen, Ernie's things should be moved out. Garp had understood that the original Steering family house, Midge Steering Percy's house, had been given back to the school some years ago—a gift of Midge and Fat Stew, for which a ceremony had been arranged. Garp told the Physical Facilities director that he hoped Helen had as much time to move out as Midge would be given.

"Oh, we'll *sell* that albatross," the man confided to Garp. "It's a lemon, you know."

The Steering family house, in Garp's memory, was no lemon.

"All that history," Garp said. "I should think you'd want it—and it was a gift, after all."

"The plumbing's terrible," the man said. He implied that, in their advancing senility, Midge and Fat Stew had let the place fall into a wretched state. "It may be a lovely old house, and all that," the young man said, "but the school has to look ahead. We've got enough *history* around here. We can't sink our housing funds into history. We need more buildings that the school can *use*. No matter what you do with that old mansion, it's just another family house."

When Garp told Helen that the Steering Percy house was going to be sold, Helen broke down. Of course she was really crying for her father, and for everything, but the thought that the Steering School did not even *want* the grandest house of their childhood years depressed both Garp and Helen.

Then Garp had to check with the organist at the Steering chapel so that the same music would not be played for Ernie that, in the morning, would be played for Fat Stew. This mattered to Helen; she was upset, so Garp didn't question the seeming meaninglessness, to him, of his errand.

The Steering chapel was a squat Tudor attempt at a building; the church was so wreathed in ivy that it appeared to have thrust itself up out of the ground and was struggling to break through the matted vines. The pant-legs of John Wolf's dark, pin-striped suit dragged under Garp's heels as he peered into the musty chapel—he had never delivered the suit to a proper tailor, but had attempted to take up the pants himself. The first wave of gray organ music drifted over Garp like smoke. He thought he had come early enough, but to his dread he

515

saw that Fat Stew's funeral had already begun. The audience was old and hardly recognizable—those ancients of the Steering School community who would attend *any*one's death, as if, in double sympathy, they were anticipating their own. *This* death, Garp thought, was chiefly attended because Midge was a Steering; Stewart Percy had made few friends. The pews were pockmarked with widows; their little black hats with veils were like dark cobwebs that had fallen on the heads of these old women.

"I'm glad you're here, Jack," a man in black said to Garp. Garp had slipped almost unnoticed into a back pew; he was going to wait out the ordeal and then speak to the organist. "We're short some muscle for the casket," the man said, and Garp recognized him—he was the hearse driver from the funeral home.

"I'm not a pallbearer," Garp whispered.

"You've *got* to be," the driver said, "or we'll never get him out of here. He's a *big* one."

The hearse driver smelled of cigars, but Garp had only to glance about the sun-dappled pews of the Steering chapel to see that the man was right. White hair and baldness winked at him from the occasional male heads; there must have been thirteen or fourteen canes hooked on the pews. There were two wheelchairs.

Garp let the driver take his arm.

"They said there'd be more *men*," the driver complained, "but nobody healthy showed up."

Garp was led to the pew up front, across from the family pew. To his horror an old man lay stretched out in the pew Garp was supposed to sit in and Garp was waved, instead, into the Percy pew, where he found himself seated next to Midge. Garp briefly wondered if the old man stretched out in the pew was another body waiting his turn.

"That's Uncle Harris Stanfull," Midge whispered to Garp, nodding her head to the sleeper, who looked like a dead man across the aisle.

"Uncle *Horace Salter*, Mother," said the man on

Midge's other side. Garp recognized Stewie Two, red-faced with corpulence—the eldest Percy child and sole surviving son. He had something to do with aluminum in Pittsburgh. Stewie Two hadn't seen Garp since Garp was five; he showed no signs of knowing who Garp was. Neither did Midge indicate that she knew *any*body, any-more. Wizened and white, with brown blotches on her face the size and complexity of unshelled peanuts, Midge had a jitter in her head that made her bob in her pew like a chicken trying to make up its mind what to peck.

At a glance Garp saw that the pallbearing would be handled by Stewie Two, the hearse driver, and himself. He doubted that they could manage it. How awful to be this unloved! he thought, looking at the gray ship that was Stewart Percy's casket—fortunately closed.

"I'm sorry, young man," Midge whispered to Garp; her gloved hand rested as lightly on his arm as one of the Percy family parakeets. "I don't recall your *name,*" she said, gracious into senility.

"Uh," Garp said. And somewhere between the names "Smith" and "Jones," Garp stumbled on a word that escaped him. "Smoans," he said, surprising both Midge and himself. Stewie Two did not appear to notice.

"Mr. Smoans?" Midge said.

"Yes, Smoans," Garp said. "Smoans, class of '61. I had Mr. Percy in history." My Part of the Pacific.

"Oh, yes, Mr. Smoans! How thoughtful of you to come," Midge said.

"I was sorry to hear of it," Mr. Smoans said.

"Yes, we *all* were," Midge said, looking cautiously around the half-empty chapel. A convulsion of some kind made her whole face shake, and the loose skin on her cheeks made a soft slapping noise.

"Mother," Stewie Two cautioned her.

"Yes, yes, Stewart," she said. To Mr. Smoans, she said, "It's a pity not all of our children could be here."

Garp, of course, knew that Dopey's strained heart had already quit him, that William was lost in a war, that Cushie was a victim of making babies. Garp guessed he knew, vaguely, where poor Pooh was. To his relief, Bainbridge Percy was *not* in the family pew.

It was there in the pew of remaining Percys that Garp remembered another day.

"Where do we go after we die?" Cushie Percy once asked her mother. Fat Stew belched and left the kitchen. All the Percy children were there: William, whom a war was waiting for; Dopey, whose heart was gathering fat; Cushie, who could not reproduce, whose vital tubes would tangle; Stewie Two, who turned into aluminum. And only God knows what happened to Pooh. Little Garp was there, too—in the sumptuous country kitchen of the vast, grand Steering family house.

"Well, after death," Midge Steering Percy told the children—little Garp, too—"we all go to a big *house,* sort of like this one."

"But *bigger,*" Stewie Two said, seriously.

"I hope so," said William, worriedly.

Dopey didn't get what was meant. Pooh was not old enough to talk. Cushie said she didn't believe it—only God knows where *she* went.

Garp thought of the vast, grand Steering family house —now for sale. He realized that he wanted to buy it.

"Mr. Smoans?" Midge nudged him.

"Uh," Garp said.

"The coffin, Jack," whispered the hearse driver. Stewie Two, bulging beside him, looked seriously toward the enormous casket that now housed the debris of his father.

"We need four," the driver said. "At least four."

"No, I can take one side myself," Garp said.

"Mr. Smoans looks very strong," Midge said. "Not very *large,* but strong."

"Mother," Stewie Two said.

"Yes, yes, Stewart," she said.

"We need four. That's all there is to it," the driver said.

Garp didn't believe it. *He* could lift it.

"You two on the other side," he said, "and up she goes."

A frail mutter reached Garp from the mourners at Fat Stew's funeral, aghast at the apparently unmovable casket. But Garp believed in himself. It was just death in there; of course it would be heavy—the weight of his mother, Jenny Fields, the weight of Ernie Holm, and of little Walt (who was the heaviest of all). God knows what they all weighed together, but Garp planted himself on one side of Fat Stew's gray gunboat of a coffin. He was ready.

It was Dean Bodger who volunteered to be the necessary fourth.

"I never thought *you'd* be here," Bodger whispered to Garp.

"Do you know Mr. Smoans?" Midge asked the dean.

"Smoans, '61," Garp said.

"Oh, yes, *Smoans,* of course," Bodger said. And the catcher of pigeons, the bandy-legged sheriff of the Steering School, lifted his share of the coffin with Garp and the others. Thus they launched Fat Stew into another life. Or into another house, hopefully bigger.

Bodger and Garp trailed behind the stragglers limping and tottering to the cars that would transport them to the Steering cemetery. When the aged audience was no more around them, Bodger took Garp to Buster's Snack and Grill, where they sat over coffee. Bodger apparently accepted that it was Garp's habit to disguise his sex in the evening and change his name during the day.

"Ah, Smoans," Bodger said. "Perhaps now your life will settle down and you'll be happy and prosperous."

"At least prosperous," Garp said.

Garp had completely forgotten to ask the organist not to repeat Fat Stew's music for Ernie Holm. Garp hadn't noticed the music, anyway; he wouldn't recognize it if it were repeated. And Helen hadn't been there; she wouldn't know the difference. Neither, Garp knew, would Ernie.

"Why don't you stay with us awhile?" Bodger asked Garp; with his strong, pudgy hand, sweeping the bleary windows in Buster's Snack and Grill, the dean indicated the campus of the Steering School. "We're not a *bad* place, really," he said.

"You're the only place I know," Garp said, neutrally.

Garp knew that his mother had chosen Steering once, at least for a place to bring up children. And Jenny Fields, Garp knew, had right instincts. He drank his coffee and shook Dean Bodger's hand affectionately. Garp had one more funeral to get through. Then, with Helen, he would consider the future.

# 18

⊰|⊱ ⊰|⊱ ⊰|⊱ ⊰|⊱ ⊰|⊱ ⊰|⊱ ⊰|⊱

# Habits of the Under Toad

ALTHOUGH she received a most cordial invitation from the Department of English, Helen was not sure about teaching at the Steering School.

"I thought you wanted to teach again," Garp said, but Helen would wait awhile before accepting a job at the school where girls were not admitted when she was a girl.

"Perhaps, when Jenny's old enough to go," Helen said. "Meanwhile, I'm happy to read, just read." As a writer, Garp was both envious and mistrustful of people who read as much as Helen.

And they were both developing a fearfulness that worried them; here they were, thinking so cautiously about their lives, as if they were truly old people. Of course Garp had always had this obsession about protecting his children; now, at last, he saw that Jenny Fields' old notion of wanting to continue living with her son was not so abnormal after all.

The Garps would stay at Steering. They had all the money they would ever need; Helen didn't *have* to do anything, if she didn't want to. But Garp needed something to do.

"You're going to write," Helen said, tiredly.

"Not for a while," Garp said. "Maybe never again. At least not for a while."

This really did strike Helen as a sign of rather premature senility, but she had come to share his anxiousness—his desire to keep what he had, including sanity—and she knew that he shared with her the vulnerability of conjugal love.

She did not say anything to him when he went to the Steering Athletic Department and offered himself as Ernie Holm's replacement. "You don't have to pay me," he told them. "Money doesn't matter to me; I just want to be the wrestling coach." Of course they had to admit he would do a decent job. What had been a strong program would begin to slump without a replacement for Ernie.

"You don't want any money?" the chairman of the Athletic Department asked him.

"I don't *need* any money," Garp told him. "What I need is something to *do*—something that's *not* writing." Except for Helen, no one knew that there were only two things in this world that T. S. Garp ever learned to do: he could write and he could wrestle.

Helen was perhaps the only one who knew why he couldn't (at the moment) write. Her theory would later be expressed by the critic A. J. Harms, who claimed that Garp's work was progressively weakened by its closer and closer parallels to his personal history. "As he became more autobiographical, his writing grew narrower; also, he became less comfortable about doing it. It was as if he knew that not only was the work more *personally* painful to him—this memory dredging—but the work was slimmer and less imaginative in every way," Harms wrote. Garp had lost the freedom of *imagining* life truly, which he had so early promised himself, and us all, with the brilliance of "The Pension Grillparzer." According to Harms, Garp could now be truthful only by *remembering,* and that method—as distinct from imagining—was not only psychologically harmful to him but far less fruitful.

But the hindsight of Harms is easy; Helen knew this was Garp's problem the day he accepted the job as wrestling coach at the Steering School. He would be nowhere near as good as Ernie, they both knew, but he would run a respectable program and Garp's wrestlers would always win more than they would lose.

"Try fairy tales," Helen suggested; she thought of his writing more often than *he* did. "Try making something up, the whole thing—completely made up." She never said, "Like 'The Pension Grillparzer' "; she never mentioned it, although she knew that he now agreed with her: it was the best he had done. Sadly, it had been the first.

Whenever Garp would try to write, he would see only the dull, undeveloped facts of his personal life: the gray parking lot in New Hampshire, the stillness of Walt's small body, the hunters' glossy coats and their red caps —and the sexless, self-righteous fanaticism of Pooh Percy. Those images went nowhere. He spent a great deal of time fussing with his new house.

Midge Steering Percy never knew who bought her family's mansion, and her gift to the Steering School. If Stewie Two ever found it out, he was at least smart enough never to tell his mother, whose memory of Garp was clouded by her fresher memory of the nice Mr. Smoans. Midge Steering Percy died in a nursing home in Pittsburgh; because of what Stewie Two had to do with aluminum, he had moved his mother into a nursing home not far from where all that metal was made.

God knows what happened to Pooh.

Helen and Garp fixed up the old Steering mansion, as it was called by many in the school community. The name Percy faded fast; in most memories, now, Midge was always referred to as Midge *Steering*. Garp's new home was the classiest place on or near the Steering campus, and when the Steering students gave guided tours of the campus to parents, and to prospective Steering students, they rarely said, "And this is where T. S. Garp, the writer, lives. It was the original Steering family house, circa 1781." The students were more playful than that; what they usually said was, "And this is where our wrestling coach lives." And the parents would look at one another politely, and the prospective student would ask, "Is wrestling a *big* sport at Steering?"

Very soon, Garp thought, Duncan would be a Steering student; it was an unembarrassed pleasure that Garp looked forward to. He missed Duncan's presence in the wrestling room, but he was happy that the boy had found his place: the swimming pool—where either his nature or his eyesight, or both, felt completely comfortable. Duncan sometimes visited the wrestling room, swaddled in towels and shivering from the pool; he sat on the soft mats under one of the blow heaters, getting warm.

"How you doing?" Garp would ask him. "You're not wet, are you? Don't drip on the mat, okay?"

"No, I won't," Duncan would say. "I'm just fine."

More frequently, Helen visited the wrestling room. She was reading everything again, and she would come to the wrestling room to read—"like reading in a sauna," she often said—occasionally looking up from what she was reading when there was an unusually loud slam or a cry of pain. The only thing that had ever been hard for Helen, about reading in a wrestling room, was that her glasses kept fogging up.

"Are we already middle-aged?" Helen asked Garp one night in their beautiful house, from the front parlor of which, on a clear night, they could see the window squares of light in the Jenny Fields Infirmary; and look over the green-black lawn to the solitary night light above the door of the infirmary annex—far away—where Garp had lived as a child.

"Jesus," Garp said. "Middle-aged? We are already *retired*—that's what we are. We skipped middle age altogether and moved directly into the world of the *elderly*."

"Does that depress you?" Helen asked him, cautiously.

"Not yet," Garp said. "When it starts to depress me, I'll do something else. Or I'll do *some*thing, anyway. I figure, Helen, that we got a head start on everyone else. We can afford to take a long time-out."

Helen grew tired of Garp's wrestling terminology, but she had grown up with it, after all; it was water off a duck, for Helen Holm. And although Garp wasn't writing, he seemed, to Helen, to be happy. Helen read in the evenings, and Garp watched TV.

Garp's work had developed a curious reputation, not altogether unlike what he would have wanted for himself, and even stranger than John Wolf had imagined. Although it embarrassed Garp and John Wolf to see how politically *The World According to Bensenhaver* was both admired and despised, the book's reputation had caused readers, even if for the wrong reasons, to return to Garp's earlier work. Garp politely refused invitations to speak at colleges, where he was wanted to represent one side or another of so-called women's issues; also, to speak on his relationship to his mother and her work, and the "sex roles" he ascribed to various characters in his books. "The destruction of art by sociology and psychoanalysis," he called it. But there were an almost equal number of invitations for him simply to read from his own fiction; an occasional one or two of these—especially if it was somewhere Helen wanted to go—he accepted.

Garp was happy with Helen. He wasn't unfaithful to her, anymore; that thought seldom occurred to him. It was perhaps his contact with Ellen James that finally cured him of ever looking at young girls in that way. As for other women—Helen's age, and older—Garp exercised a willpower that was not especially difficult for him. Enough of his life had been influenced by lust.

Ellen James, who was eleven when she was raped and untongued, was nineteen when she moved in with the

Garps. She was immediately an older sister to Duncan, and a fellow member of the maimed society to which Duncan shyly belonged. They were so close. She helped Duncan with his homework, because Ellen James was very good at reading and writing. Duncan interested Ellen in swimming, and in photography. Garp built them a darkroom in the Steering mansion, and they spent hours in the dark, developing and developing—Duncan's ceaseless babble, concerning lens openings and light, and the wordless *oooh*'s and *aaah*'s of Ellen James.

Helen bought them a movie camera, and Ellen and Duncan wrote a screenplay together and acted in their own movie—the story of a blind prince whose vision is partially restored by kissing a young cleaning woman. Only one of the prince's eyes is restored to sight because the cleaning woman allows the prince only to kiss her on the cheek. She is embarrassed to let anyone kiss her on the lips because she has lost her tongue. Despite their handicaps, and their compromises, the young couple marries. The involved story is told through pantomime and subtitles, which Ellen wrote. The best thing about the film, Duncan would say later, is that it's only seven minutes long.

Ellen James was also a great help to Helen with baby Jenny. Ellen and Duncan were expert baby-sitters with the girl, whom Garp took to the wrestling room on Sunday afternoons; there, he claimed, she would learn to walk and run and fall without hurting herself, although Helen claimed that the mat would give the child the misconception that the world underfoot felt like a barely firm sponge.

"But that is what the world *does* feel like," Garp said.

Since he had stopped writing, the only ongoing friction in Garp's life concerned his relationship with his best friend, Roberta Muldoon. But Roberta was not the *source* of the friction. When Jenny Fields was dead and gone, Garp discovered that her estate was tremendous, and that Jenny, as if to plague her son, had designated *him* to be the executor of her last wishes for her fabulous loot and the mansion for wounded women at Dog's Head Harbor.

"Why *me?*" Garp had howled. "Why not *you?*" Garp yelled at Roberta. But Roberta Muldoon was rather hurt that it *hadn't* been her.

"I can't imagine. Why you, indeed?" Roberta admitted. "Of all people."

"Mom was out to get me," Garp decided.

"Or she was out to make you *think,*" Roberta suggested. "What a good mother she was!"

"Oh boy," Garp said.

For weeks he puzzled over the single sentence that stated Jenny's intentions for the spending of her money and the use of her enormous seacoast house.

I want to leave a place where worthy women can go to collect themselves *and just be themselves, by themselves.*

"Oh boy," Garp said.

"A kind of foundation?" Roberta guessed.

"The Fields Foundation," Garp suggested.

"That's terrific!" Roberta said. "Yes, *grants* for women—and a place to go."

"To go do *what?*" Garp said. "And grants *for* what?"

"To go get well, if they have to, or to go be by themselves, if that's what they need," Roberta said. "And to write, if that's what they do—or paint."

"Or a home for unwed mothers?" Garp said. "A *grant* for 'getting well'? Oh boy."

"Be serious," Roberta said. "This is important. Don't you see? She wanted *you* to understand the need, she wanted you to have to deal with the problems."

"And who decides if a woman is 'worthy'?" Garp asked. "Oh boy, Mom!" he cried out. "I could wring your neck for this shit!"

"*You* decide," Roberta said. "*That's* what will make you think."

"How about *you?*" Garp asked. "This is your kind of thing, Roberta."

Roberta was clearly torn. She shared with Jenny Fields the desire to educate Garp and other men concerning the legitimacy and complexity of women's needs. She also thought Garp would be rather terrible at this, and she knew she would do it very well.

"We'll do it together," Roberta said. "That is, you're in charge, but I'll advise you. I'll tell you when I think you're making a mistake."

"Roberta," Garp said, "you're *always* telling me I'm making a mistake."

Roberta, at her most flirtatious, kissed him on the lips and clubbed him on the shoulder—in both cases, so hard that he winced.

"Jesus," Garp said.

"The Fields Foundation!" Roberta cried. "It's going to be wonderful."

Thus was *friction* kept in the life of T. S. Garp, who without friction of some kind would probably have lost his senses and his grip upon the world. It was friction that kept Garp alive, when he wasn't writing; Roberta Muldoon and the Fields Foundation would provide him with friction, at the very least.

Roberta became the in-residence administrator of the Fields Foundation at Dog's Head Harbor; the house became, all at once, a writers' colony, a recovery center, and a birth-advisory clinic—and the few well-lit garret rooms provided light and solitude for painters. Once women knew that there was a Fields Foundation, there were many women who wondered who was eligible for aid. Garp wondered, too. All applicants wrote Roberta, who assembled a small staff of women who alternately liked and disliked Garp—but always argued with him. Together, twice a month, Roberta and her Board of Trustees would assemble in Garp's grouchy presence and choose among the applicants.

In good weather they sat in the balmy side-porch

room of the Dog's Head Harbor estate, although Garp increasingly refused to go there. "All the weirdos-in-residence," Garp told Roberta. "They remind me of other times." So then they met at Steering, in the Steering family mansion, the wrestling coach's home, where Garp felt slightly more comfortable in the company of these fierce women.

He would have felt *more* comfortable, no doubt, to have met them all in the wrestling room. Though even there, Garp knew perfectly well, the former Robert Muldoon would have made Garp struggle for his every point.

Applicant No. 1,048 was named Charlie Pulaski.

"I thought they had to be *women*," Garp said. "I thought there was at least *one* firm criterion."

"Charlie Pulaski *is* a woman," Roberta told Garp. "She's just always been called Charlie."

"I should say that was enough to disqualify her," someone said. It was Marcia Fox—a lean, spare poet with whom Garp frequently crossed swords, although he admired her poems. He could never be that economical.

"What does Charlie Pulaski *want?*" Garp asked, by rote. Some of the applicants only wanted money; some of them wanted to live at Dog's Head Harbor for a while. Some of them wanted lots of money *and* a room at Dog's Head Harbor, forever.

"She just wants money," Roberta said.

"To change her name?" asked Marcia Fox.

"She wants to quit her job and write a book," Roberta said.

"Oh boy," said Garp.

"Advise her to keep her job," said Marcia Fox; she was one of those writers who resented other writers, and would-be writers.

"Marcia even resents *dead* writers," Garp told Roberta.

But Marcia and Garp both read a manuscript submitted by Ms. Charlie Pulaski, and they agreed that she should hold on to whatever job she could get.

Applicant No. 1,073, an associate professor of microbiology, wanted time off from her job to write a book, too.

"A novel?" Garp asked.

"Studies in molecular virology," said Dr. Joan Axe; she was on leave from the Duke University Medical Center to do some research of her own. When Garp asked her what it was, she had told him, mysteriously, that she was interested in "the unseen diseases of the bloodstream."

Applicant No. 1,081 had an uninsured husband who was killed in a plane crash. She had three children under the age of five and she needed fifteen more semester hours to complete her M.A. degree, in French. She wanted to go back to school, get the degree, and find a decent job; she wanted money for this—and rooms enough for her children, and for a baby-sitter, at Dog's Head Harbor.

The Board of Trustees unanimously decided to award the woman sufficient money to complete her degree and to pay a live-in baby-sitter; but the children, the baby-sitter, *and* the woman would all have to live wherever the woman chose to complete her degree. Dog's Head Harbor was *not* for children and baby-sitters. There were women there who would go crazy upon the sight or sound of a single child. There were women there whose lives had been made miserable by baby-sitters.

That was an easy one to decide.

No. 1,088 caused some problems. She was the divorced wife of the man who had killed Jenny Fields. She had three children, one of whom was in a reform school for preteens, and her child-support payments had stopped when her husband, Jenny Fields' assassin, was shot by a barrage from the New Hampshire State Police and some other hunters with guns who had been cruising the parking lot.

The deceased, Kenny Truckenmiller, had been divorced less than a year. He'd told friends that the child support was breaking his ass; he said that women's lib had screwed up his wife so much that she divorced him. The lawyer who got the job done, in favor of Mrs. Truckenmiller, was a New York divorcee. Kenny Truckenmiller had beaten his wife at least twice weekly for almost thirteen years, and he had physically and mentally abused each of his three children on several occasions. But Mrs. Truckenmiller had not known enough about herself, or what rights she might possibly have, until she read *A Sexual Suspect,* the autobiography of Jenny Fields. That started her thinking that perhaps the suffering of her weekly beatings, and the abuse of her children, was actually Kenny Truckenmiller's fault; for thirteen years she had thought it was *her* problem, and her "lot in life."

Kenny Truckenmiller had blamed the women's movement for the self-education of his wife. Mrs. Truckenmiller had always been self-employed, a "hair stylist" in the town of North Mountain, New Hampshire. She went right on being a hair stylist when Kenny was forced, by the court, to move out of her house. But now that Kenny was no longer driving a truck for the town, Mrs Truckenmiller found the support of her family difficult by hair styling alone. She wrote in her nearly illegible application that she had been forced to compromise herself "to make ends meet," and that she did not care to repeat the act of compromising herself in the future.

Mrs. Truckenmiller, who never once referred to herself as having a first name, realized that the loathing for her husband was so great as to prejudice the board against her. She would understand, she wrote, if they chose to ignore her.

John Wolf, who was (against his will) an honorary member of the board—and valued for his shrewd financial head—said immediately that nothing could be better or wider publicity for the Fields Foundation than awarding "this unfortunate relation of Jenny's killer" what she asked for. It would be instant news; it would pay for itself, John Wolf decided, in that it would surely gain the foundation untold sums in gift donations.

"We're already doing pretty well on gift donations," Garp hedged.

"Suppose she's just a whore?" Roberta suggested of the unfortunate Mrs. Truckenmiller; they all stared at her. Roberta had an advantage among them: of being able to think like a woman *and* like a Philadelphia Eagle. "Just think a minute," Roberta said. "Suppose she's just a floozy, someone who *compromises herself* all the time, and always has—and thinks nothing of it. Then, suddenly, we're a *joke;* then we've been had."

"So we need a character reference," said Marcia Fox.

"Someone's got to see the woman, talk with her," Garp suggested. "Find out if she's honorable, if she's really *trying* to live independently."

They all stared at him.

"Well," Roberta said, *"I'm* not about to discover whether she's a whore or not."

"Oh no," Garp said. "Not *me.*"

"Where's North Mountain, New Hampshire?" asked Marcia Fox.

"Not *me,*" John Wolf said. "I'm out of New York too much of the time as it is."

"Oh boy," Garp said. "Suppose she recognizes me? People *do,* you know."

"I doubt *she* will," said Hilma Bloch, a psychiatric social worker whom Garp detested. "Those people most motivated to read autobiographies, such as your mother's, are rarely attracted to fiction—or only tangentially. That is, if she read *The World According to Bensenhaver* she would have done so only because of who you are. And that would not have been sufficient reason to cause her to finish the book; in all probability—and given the fact that she's a hair stylist, after all—she would have bogged down and *not* read it. And

not remembered your picture on the cover, either—
only your face, and only vaguely (you *were* a face in
the news, of course, but really only around the time of
Jenny's murder). Surely, at that time, Jenny's face was
the face to recall. A woman like this watches a lot of
television; she's not a book-world person. I strongly
doubt that a woman like this would even have a picture of you in her mind."

John Wolf rolled his eyes away from Hilma Bloch.
Even Roberta rolled her eyes.

"Thank you, Hilma," said Garp, quietly. It was
decided that Garp would visit Mrs. Truckenmiller "to
determine something more concrete about her character."

"At least find out her first name," said Marcia Fox.

"I'll bet it's Charlie," Roberta said.

They passed on to the reports: who was living,
presently, at Dog's Head Harbor; whose tenancy was
expiring; who was about to move in. And what were
the problems there, if any?

There were two painters—one in the south garret,
one in the north. The south-garret painter coveted the
north-garret painter's *light,* and for two weeks they
didn't get along; not a word to each other at breakfast,
and accusations concerning lost mail. And so forth.
Then, it appeared, they became lovers. Now only the
north-garret painter was painting at all—studies of the
south-garret painter, who modeled all day in the good
light. Her nakedness, about the upstairs of the house,
bothered at least one of the writers, an outspoken anti-
lesbian playwright from Cleveland who had trouble
sleeping, she said, because of the sound of the waves.
It was probably the lovemaking of the painters that
bothered her; she was described as "overextended,"
anyway, but her complaints ceased once the other
writer-in-residence suggested that all the Dog's Head
Harbor guests read aloud the parts of the dramatist's
play in progress. This was done, successfully for all, and
the upper floors of the house were now happy.

The "other writer," a good short-story writer whom Garp had enthusiastically recommended a year ago, was about to move out, however; her term of residency was expiring. Who would go in her room?

The woman whose mother-in-law had just won custody of her children, following the suicide of her husband?

"I *told* you not to accept her," Garp said.

The two Ellen Jamesians who just, one day, showed up?

"Now wait a minute," Garp said. "What's this? Ellen Jamesians? Showing up? That's not allowed."

"Jenny always took them in," Roberta said.

"This is *now,* Roberta," Garp said.

The other members of the board were more or less in agreement with him; Ellen Jamesians were not much admired—they never had been, and their radicalism (now) seemed growingly obsolete and pathetic.

"It's almost a tradition, though," Roberta said. She described two "old" Ellen Jamesians, who'd been back from a bad time in California. Years ago they had stayed at Dog's Head Harbor; returning there, Roberta argued, was a kind of sentimental recovery for them.

"Jesus, Roberta," Garp said. "Get rid of them."

"They were people your mother always took care of," Roberta said.

"At least they'll be *quiet,*" said Marcia Fox, whose economy of tongue Garp *did* admire. But only Garp laughed.

"I think you should get them to leave, Roberta," Dr. Joan Axe said.

"They really resent the entire *society,*" Hilma Bloch said. "That could be infectious. On the other hand, they are almost the essence of the *spirit* of the place."

John Wolf rolled his eyes.

"There is the doctor researching cancer-related abortions," Joan Axe said. "What about her?"

"Yes, put *her* on the second floor," Garp said. "I've

*met* her. She'll scare the shit out of anyone who tries to come upstairs." Roberta frowned.

The downstairs of the Dog's Head Harbor mansion was the largest part, containing two kitchens and four complete baths; as many as twelve could sleep, very privately, downstairs, and there were still the various conference rooms, as Roberta now called them—they were parlors and giant dens in the days of Jenny Fields. And a vast dining room where food, mail, and whoever wanted company collected all during the day and night.

It was the most social floor of Dog's Head Harbor, usually not suited for the writers and painters. It was the best floor for the potential suicides, Garp had told the board, "because they'll be forced to drown themselves in the ocean rather than jump out the windows."

But Roberta ran the place in a strong, motherly, tight-end fashion; she could talk almost anyone out of anything, and if she couldn't, she could overpower anybody. She had been much more successful at making the local police her allies than Jenny ever had been. Occasional unhappies were picked up by the police, far down the beach, or wailing on the boardwalks of the village; they were always gently returned to Roberta. The Dog's Head Harbor Police were all football fans, full of respect for the savage line play and the vicious downfield blocking of the former Robert Muldoon.

"I would like to make a motion that *no* Ellen Jamesian be eligible for aid and comfort from the Fields Foundation," Garp said.

"Second," said Marcia Fox.

"This is open to discussion," Roberta told them all. "I don't see the necessity of having such a rule. We are not in the business of supporting what we largely would agree is a stupid form of political expression, but that doesn't mean that one of these women without a tongue couldn't be genuinely in need of help—I'd say, in fact, they have already demonstrated a definite need to locate themselves, and we can expect to go on hearing from them. They are truly needful people."

"They are insane," Garp said.

"This is too general," said Hilma Bloch.

"There *are* productive women," Marcia Fox said, "who have *not* given up their voices—in fact, they are fighting to *use* their voices—and I am not in favor of rewarding stupidity and self-imposed silence."

"There are virtues in silence," Roberta argued.

"Jesus, Roberta," Garp said. And then he saw a light in this dark subject. For some reason, the Ellen Jamesians made him angrier than his image, even, of the Kenny Truckenmillers of this world; and although he saw that the Ellen Jamesians were fading from fashion, they could not fade fast enough to suit Garp. He wanted them gone; he wanted them more than gone—he wanted them disgraced. Helen had already told him that his hatred of them was inappropriate to what they were.

"It's just madness, and simple-minded—what they've done," Helen said. "Why can't you ignore them, and leave them alone?"

But Garp said, "Let's ask Ellen James. That's fair, isn't it? Let's ask Ellen James for *her* opinion of the Ellen Jamesians. Jesus, I'd like to *publish* her opinion of them. Do you know how they've made *her* feel?"

"This is too personal a matter," Hilma Bloch said. They had all met Ellen; they all knew that Ellen James *hated* being tongueless and hated the Ellen Jamesians.

"Let's back off this, for now," John Wolf said. "I move we table the motion."

"Damn," Garp said.

"All right, Garp," Roberta said. "Let's vote it, right now." They all knew they would vote it down. That would get rid of it.

"I withdraw the motion," Garp said, nastily. "Long live the Ellen Jamesians."

But *he* did not withdraw.

It was madness that had killed Jenny Fields, his mother. It was extremism. It was self-righteous, fanatical, and monstrous self-pity. Kenny Truckenmiller was only a special kind of moron: a true believer who was also a thug. He was a man who pitied himself so blindly that he could make absolute enemies out of people who contributed only the ideas to his undoing.

And how was an Ellen Jamesian any different? Was not her gesture as desperate, and as empty of an understanding of human complexity?

"Come *on*," John Wolf said. "They haven't *murdered* anyone."

"Not yet," Garp said. "They have the equipment. They are capable of making mindless decisions, and they believe they are so *right*."

"There's more to killing someone than that," Roberta said. They let Garp seethe. What else could they do? It was not one of Garp's better points: tolerance of the intolerant. Crazy people made him crazy. It was as if he personally resented them giving in to madness—in part, because he so frequently labored to behave sanely. When some people gave up the labor of sanity, or failed at it, Garp suspected them of not trying hard enough.

"Tolerance of the intolerant is a difficult task that the times asks of us," Helen said. Although Garp knew Helen was intelligent, and often more far-seeing than he was, he was rather blind about the Ellen Jamesians.

They, of course, were rather blind about him.

The most radical criticism of Garp—concerning his relationship to his mother *and* his own works—had come from various Ellen Jamesians. Baited by them, he baited them back. It was hard to see why it should have started, or *if* it should have, but Garp had become a case of controversy among feminists largely through the goading of Ellen Jamesians—and Garp goading them in return. For the very *same* reasons, Garp was liked by many feminists and disliked by as many.

As for the Ellen Jamesians, they were no more complicated in their feelings for Garp than they were complicated in their symbology: their tongues hacked off for the hacked-off tongue of Ellen James.

Ironically, it would be Ellen James who escalated this long-time cold war.

She was in the habit, constantly, of showing Garp her writing—her many stories, her remembrances of her parents, of Illinois; her poems; her painful analogies to speechlessness; her appreciations of the visual arts, and swimming. She wrote wisely and craftily and with penetrating energy.

"She's the real thing," Garp kept telling Helen. "She's got the ability, but she's also got the passion. And I believe she'll have the stamina."

The aforementioned "stamina" was a word Helen let slide away, because she feared for Garp that he had given up his. He certainly had the ability, and the passion; but she felt he'd also taken a narrow path—he'd been misdirected—and only stamina would let him grow back in all the other ways.

It saddened her. For the time being, Helen kept thinking, she would content herself with whatever Garp got passionate about—the wrestling, even the Ellen Jamesians. Because, Helen believed, energy begets energy—and sooner or later, she thought, he would write again.

So Helen did not interfere too vehemently when Garp got excited about the essay Ellen James showed him. The essay was: "Why I'm Not an Ellen Jamesian," by Ellen James. It was powerful and touching and it moved Garp to tears. It recounted her rape, her difficulty with it, her parents' difficulty with it; it made what the Ellen Jamesians did seem like a shallow, wholly political imitation of a very private trauma. Ellen James said that the Ellen Jamesians had only prolonged her anguish; they had made her into a very public casualty. Of course, Garp was susceptible to being moved by public casualties.

And of course, to be fair, the better of the Ellen Jamesians had *meant* to publicize the general dread that so brutally menaced women and girls. For many of the Ellen Jamesians, the imitation of the horrible untonguing had not been "wholly political." It had been a most personal identification. In some cases, of course, Ellen Jamesians were women who had also been raped; what they meant was that they *felt* as if their tongues were gone. In a world of men, they felt as if they had been shut up forever.

That the organization was full of crazies, no one would deny. Not even some Ellen Jamesians would have denied that. It was generally true that they were an inflammatory political group of feminist extremists who often detracted from the extreme seriousness of other women, and other feminists, around them. But Ellen James' attack on them was as inconsiderate of the occasional individuals among the Ellen Jamesians as the action of the group had been inconsiderate of Ellen James—not really thinking how an eleven-year-old girl would have preferred to get over her horror more privately.

Everyone in America knew how Ellen James had lost her tongue, except the younger generation, just now growing up, who often confused Ellen with the Ellen Jamesians; this was a most painful confusion for Ellen, because it meant that she was suspected of having done it to herself.

"It was a necessary rage for her to have," Helen said to Garp, about Ellen's essay. "I'm sure she needed to write it, and it's done her a world of good to say all this. I've told her that."

*"I've* told her she should publish it," Garp said.

"No," Helen said. "I really don't think so. What good does it do?"

"What *good?"* Garp asked. "Well, it's the *truth.* And it will be good for Ellen."

"And for *you?"* Helen asked, knowing that he wanted a kind of public humiliation of the Ellen Jamesians.

"Okay," he said, "okay, okay. But she's *right,* goddamnit. Those nuts ought to hear it from the original source."

"But why?" said Helen. "For whose good?"

"Good, good," Garp muttered, though in his heart he must have known that Helen was right. He told Ellen she should file her essay. Ellen wouldn't communicate with either Garp or Helen for a week.

It was not until John Wolf called Garp that either Garp or Helen realized Ellen had sent the essay to John Wolf.

"What am I suppose to do with it?" he asked.

"God, send it back," Helen said.

"No, damn it," Garp said. "Ask *Ellen* what she wants you to do with it."

"Old Pontius Pilate, washing his hands," Helen said to Garp.

"What do *you* want to do with it?" Garp asked John Wolf.

"*Me?*" John Wolf said. "It means nothing to me. But I'm sure it's publishable. I mean, it's very well written."

"That's not why it's publishable," Garp said, "and you know it."

"Well, no," John Wolf said. "But its also *nice* that it's well said."

Ellen told John Wolf she wanted it published. Helen tried to talk her out of it. Garp refused to get involved.

"You *are* involved," Helen told him, "and by saying nothing, you know you'll get what you want: that painful attack published. That's what you want."

So Garp spoke to Ellen James. He tried to be enthusiastic in his reasoning to her—why she shouldn't publicly say all those things. These women were sick, sad, confused, tortured, abused by others, and now self-abused—but what point was there in criticizing them? Everyone would forget them in another five years. They'll hand out their notes and people will say, "What's an Ellen Jamesian? You mean you can't talk? You got no tongue?"

Ellen looked sullen and determined.

*I won't forget them!*

she wrote Garp.

*Not in 5 years, not in 50 years will I ever forget them; I will remember them the way I remember my tongue.*

Garp admired how the girl liked to use the good old semicolon. He said softly, "I think it's better not to publish this, Ellen."

*Will you be angry with me if I do?*

she asked.

He admitted he would not be angry.

*And Helen?*

"Helen will only be angry with *me*," Garp said.

"You make people too angry," Helen told him, in bed. "You get them all wound up. You *inflame*. You should lay off. You should do your own work, Garp. Just your own work. You used to say politics were stupid, and they meant nothing to you. You were right. They *are* stupid, they *do* mean nothing. You're doing this because it's *easier* than sitting down and making something up, from scratch. And you know it. You're building bookshelves all over the house, and finishing floors, and fucking around in the *garden*, for Christ's sake.

"Did I marry a handyman? Did I ever expect you to be a crusader?

"You should be writing the books and letting other people make the shelves. And you know I'm right, Garp."

"You're right," he said.

He tried to remember what had enabled him to imagine that first sentence of "The Pension Grillparzer."

"My father worked for the Austrian Tourist Bureau."

Where had it come from? He tried to think of sentences like it. What he got was a sentence like this: "The boy was five years old; he had a cough that seemed deeper than his small, bony chest." What he got was memory, and that made muck. He had no pure imagination anymore.

In the wrestling room, he worked out three straight days with the heavyweight. To punish himself?

"More fucking around in the garden, so to speak," said Helen.

Then he announced he had a mission, a trip to make for the Fields Foundation. To North Mountain, New Hampshire. To determine if a Fields Foundation Fellowship would be wasted on a woman named Truckenmiller.

"More fucking around in the garden," Helen said. "More bookshelves. More politics. More crusades. That's the kind of thing people do who *can't* write."

But he was gone; he was out of the house when John Wolf called to say that a very well read and much seen magazine was going to publish "Why I'm Not an Ellen Jamesian," by Ellen James.

John Wolf's voice over the phone had the cold, unseen, quick flick of the tongue of old You-Know-Who—the Under Toad, that's who, Helen thought. But she didn't know why; not yet.

She told Ellen James the news. Helen forgave Ellen, immediately, and even allowed herself to be excited with her. They took a drive to the shore with Duncan and little Jenny. They bought lobsters—Ellen's favorite—and enough scallops for Garp, who was not crazy about lobster.

*Champagne!*

Ellen wrote in the car.

*Does champagne go with lobster and scallops?*

"Of course," Helen said. "It *can*." They bought champagne. They stopped at Dog's Head Harbor and invited Roberta to dinner.

"When will Dad be back?" Duncan asked.

"I don't know where North Mountain, New Hampshire, *is*," Helen said, "but he *said* he'd be back in time to eat with us."

*That's what he told me, too,*

said Ellen James.

NANETTE'S BEAUTY SALON in North Mountain, New Hampshire, was really the kitchen of Mrs. Kenny Truckenmiller, whose first name was Harriet.

"Are you Nanette?" Garp asked her timidly, from the outside steps, frosted with salt and crunchy with melting slush.

"There ain't no Nanette," she told him. "I'm Harriet Truckenmiller." Behind her, in the dark kitchen, a large dog strained and snarled; Mrs. Truckenmiller kept the dog from getting to Garp by thrusting her long hip back against the lunging beast. Her pale, scarred ankle wedged open the kitchen door. Her slippers were blue; in her long robe, her figure was lost, but Garp could see she was tall—and that she had been taking a bath.

"Uh, do you do *men's* hair?" he asked her.

"No," she said.

"But *would* you?" Garp asked her. "I don't trust barbers."

Harriet Truckenmiller looked suspiciously at Garp's black knit ski hat, which was pulled down over his ears and concealed all his hair but the thick tufts that touched his shoulders from the back of his short neck.

"I can't see your hair," she said. He took the stocking hat off, his hair wild with static electricity and tangled in the cold wind.

"I don't want just a haircut," Garp said, neutrally, eyeing the woman's sad, drawn face and the soft wrinkles beside her gray eyes. Her own hair, a washed-out blond, was in curlers.

"You don't have no appointment," Harriet Truckenmiller said.

The woman was no whore, he could plainly see. She was tired and frightened of him.

"What exactly do you want done to your hair, anyway?" she asked him.

"Just a trim," Garp mumbled, "but I like a slight curl in it."

"A curl?" said Harriet Truckenmiller, trying to imagine this from Garp's crown of very straight hair. "Like a permanent, you mean?" she asked.

"Well," he said, running his hand sheepishly through the snarls. "Whatever you can do with it, you know?"

Harriet Truckenmiller shrugged. "I have to get dressed," she said. The dog, devious and strong, thrust most of his stout body between her legs and jammed his broad, grimacing face into the opening between the storm and the main door. Garp tensed for the attack, but Harriet Truckenmiller brought her big knee up sharply and staggered the animal with a blow to its muzzle. She twisted her hand into the loose skin of its neck; the dog moaned and melted into the kitchen behind her.

The frozen yard, Garp saw, was a mosaic of the dog's huge turds captured in ice. There were also three cars in the yard; Garp doubted if any of them ran. There was a woodpile, but no one had stacked it. There was a TV antenna, which at one time might have been on the roof; now it leaned against the beige aluminum siding of the house, its wires running like a spider web out a cracked window.

Mrs. Truckenmiller stepped back and opened the door for Garp. In the kitchen he felt his eyes dry from the heat of the wood stove; the room smelled of baking cookies and hair rinse—in fact, the kitchen seemed divided between the functions of a kitchen and the paraphernalia of Harriet's business. A pink sink with a shampoo hose; cans of stewed tomatoes; a three-way mirror framed with stage lights; a wooden rack with spices and meat tenderizer; the rows of ointments, lotions, and goo. And a steel stool over which a hair dryer hung suspended from a steel rod—like an original invention of an electric chair.

The dog was gone, and so was Harriet Truckenmiller; she had slipped away to dress herself, and her surly companion appeared to have gone with her. Garp combed his hair; he looked in the mirror as if he were trying to remember himself. He was about to be altered and rendered unrecognizable to all, he imagined.

Then the door to the outside opened and a big man in a hunting coat with a hunter's red cap walked in; he had an enormous armload of wood, which he carried to the wood box by the stove. The dog, who all along had been crouched under the sink—inches away from Garp's trembling knees—moved quickly to intercept the man. The dog slunk quietly, not even growling; the man was known here.

"Go lie down, you damn fool," he said, and the dog did as it was told.

"Is that you, Dickie?" called Harriet Truckenmiller, from somewhere in another part of the house.

"Who else was you expectin'?" he shouted; then he turned and saw Garp in front of the mirror.

"Hello," Garp said. The big man called Dickie stared. He was perhaps fifty; his huge red face looked scraped by ice, and Garp recognized immediately, from his familiarity with Duncan's expressions, that the man had a glass eye.

" 'Lo," Dickie said.

"I got a customer!" Harriet called.

"I see you do," said Dickie. Garp nervously touched his hair, as if he could suggest to Dickie how important his hair was to him—to have come all the way to North Mountain, New Hampshire, and NANETTE'S BEAUTY SALON, for what must have appeared to Dickie to be the simple need of a haircut.

"He wants a *curl!*" called Harriet. Dickie kept his red cap on, though Garp could plainly see that the man was bald.

"I don't know what you *really* want, fella," Dickie whispered to Garp, "but a curl is all you get. You hear?"

"I don't trust barbers," Garp said.

"I don't trust *you*," Dickie said.

"Dickie, he hasn't done anything," Harriet Truckenmiller said. She was dressed in rather tight turquoise slacks, which reminded Garp of his discarded jump suit, and a print blouse full of flowers that never grow in New Hampshire. Her hair was tied back with a scarf of unmatching plants, and she had done her face, but not overdone it; she looked "nice," like somebody's mother who bothered to keep herself up. She was, Garp guessed, a few years younger than Dickie, but just a few.

"He don't want no *curl*, Harriet," Dickie said. "What's he want to have his hair played with for, huh?"

"He don't trust barbers," Harriet Truckenmiller said. For a brief moment Garp wondered if Dickie were a barber; he didn't think so.

"I really don't mean any disrespect," Garp said. He had seen all he needed to see; he wanted to go tell the Fields Foundation to give Harriet Truckenmiller all the money she needed. "If this makes anyone uncomfortable," Garp said, "I'll just forget it." He reached for his parka, which he'd put on an empty chair, but the big dog had the parka pinned down on the floor.

"Please, you can stay," Mrs. Truckenmiller said. "Dickie's just lookin' after me." Dickie looked ashamed of himself; he stood with one mighty boot on top of the other.

"I brung you some dry wood," he said to Harriet. "I guess I shoulda *knocked*." He pouted by the stove.

"*Don't*, Dickie," Harriet said to him, and she kissed him fondly on his big pink cheek.

He left the kitchen with one last glare for Garp.

"Hope you get a good haircut," Dickie said.

"Thank you," said Garp. When he spoke, the dog shook his parka.

"Here, stop that," Harriet told the dog; she put Garp's parka back on the chair. "You can go if you want to,"

Harriet said, "but Dickie won't bother you. He's just lookin' after me."

"Your husband?" Garp asked, though he doubted it.

"My husband was Kenny Truckenmiller," Harriet said. "Everybody knows that, and no matter who you are, you know who *he* was."

"Yes," Garp said.

"Dickie's my brother. He just worries about me," Harriet said. "Some guys have been messin' around, since Kenny's gone." She sat at the bright counter of mirrors, beside Garp, and leaned her long, veiny hands on her turquoise thighs. She sighed. She did not look at Garp when she spoke. "I don't know what you heard, and I don't care," she said. "I do *hair—just* hair. If you really want somethin' done to your hair, I'll do it. But that's all I do," Harriet said. "No matter what anybody told you, I don't mess around. Just hair."

"Just hair," Garp said. "I just want my hair done, that's all."

"That's good," she said, still not looking at him.

There were little photographs stuck under the molding and framed against the mirrors. One was a wedding picture of young Harriet Truckenmiller and her grinning husband, Kenny. They were awkwardly maiming a cake.

Another photograph was of a pregnant Harriet Truckenmiller holding a young baby; there was another child, maybe Walt's age, leaning his cheek against her hip. Harriet looked tired but not daunted. And there was a photograph of Dickie; he was standing next to Kenny Truckenmiller, and they were both standing next to a gutted deer, hung upside-down from the branch of a tree. The tree was in the front yard of NANETTE'S BEAUTY SALON. Garp recognized that photograph quickly; he had seen it in a national magazine after Jenny's assassination. The photograph apparently demonstrated to the simple-minded that Kenny Truckenmiller was a born-and-raised killer: besides shooting Jenny Fields, he had at one time shot a deer.

547

"Why *Nanette?*" Garp asked Harriet later, when he dared look only at her patient fingers and not at her unhappy face—and not at his hair.

"I thought it sounded sort of French," Harriet said, but she knew he was from somewhere in the outside world—outside North Mountain, New Hampshire— and she laughed at herself.

"Well, it *does*," Garp said, laughing with her. "Sort of," he added, and they both laughed in a friendly way.

When he was ready to go, she wiped the slobber of the dog off his parka with a sponge. "Aren't you even going to look at it?" she asked him. She meant the hair-do; he took a breath and confronted himself in the three-way mirror. His hair, he thought, was beautiful! It was his same old hair, the same color, even the same length, but it seemed to fit his head for the first time in his life. His hair clung to his skull, yet it was still light and fluffy; a slight wave in it made his broken nose and his squat neck appear less severe. Garp seemed to himself to fit his own face in a way he had never thought possible. This was the first beauty salon he had ever been to, of course. In fact, Jenny had cut his hair until he married Helen, and Helen had cut his hair after that; he had never even been to a barber.

"It's lovely," he said; his missing ear remained artfully hidden.

"Oh, go on," Harriet said, giving him a pleasant little shove—but, he would tell the Fields Foundation, *not* a suggestive shove; not at all. He wanted to tell her then that he was Jenny Fields' son, but he knew that his motive for doing so would have been wholly self-ish—to have been personally responsible for moving someone.

"It is unfair to take advantage of anyone's emotional vulnerability," wrote the polemical Jenny Fields. Thus Garp's new creed: capitalize not on the emotions of others. "Thank you and good-bye," he said to Mrs. Truckenmiller.

Outside, Dickie wielded a splitting ax in the woodpile. He did it very well. He stopped splitting when Garp appeared. "Good-bye," Garp called to him, but Dickie walked over to Garp—with the ax.

"Let's get a look at the hairdo," Dickie said.

Garp stood still while Dickie examined him.

"You were a friend of Kenny Truckenmiller's?" Garp asked.

"Yup," Dickie said. "I was his *only* friend. I introduced him to Harriet," Dickie said. Garp nodded. Dickie eyed the new hairdo.

"It's tragic," Garp said; he meant everything that had happened.

"It ain't bad," Dickie said; he meant Garp's hair.

"Jenny Fields was my mother," Garp said, because he wanted someone to know, and he felt certain he was taking no emotional advantage of Dickie.

"You didn't tell *her* that, did you?" Dickie said, pointing toward the house, and Harriet, with his long ax.

"No, no," Garp said.

"That's good," Dickie said. "She don't want to hear nothin' like that."

"I didn't think so," Garp said, and Dickie nodded approvingly. "Your sister is a very nice woman," Garp added.

"She *is,* she is," Dickie said, nodding fiercely.

"Well, so long," Garp said. But Dickie touched him lightly with the handle of the ax.

"I was one of them who shot him," Dickie said. "You know that?"

"You shot Kenny?" Garp said.

"I was *one* of them who did," Dickie said. "Kenny was crazy. Somebody had to shoot him."

"I'm very sorry," Garp said. Dickie shrugged.

"I liked the guy," Dickie said. "But he got crazy at Harriet, and he got crazy at your mother. He wouldn't ever have got well, you know," Dickie said. "He just got sick about women. He got sick for good. You could tell he wasn't ever going to get over it."

"A terrible thing," said Garp.

"So long," Dickie said; he turned back to his wood-pile. Garp turned toward his car, across the frozen turds that dotted the yard. "Your hair looks good!" Dickie called to him. The remark seemed sincere. Dickie was splitting logs again when Garp waved to him from the driver's seat of his car. In the window of NANETTE'S BEAUTY SALON Harriet Truckenmiller waved to Garp: it was not a wave meant to encourage him, or anything, he was quite sure. He drove back through the village of North Mountain—he drank a cup of coffee in the one diner, he got gas at the one gas station. Everyone looked at his pretty hair. In every mirror, *Garp* looked at his pretty hair! Then he drove home, arriving in time for the celebration: Ellen's first publication.

If it made him as uneasy as the news had made Helen, he did not admit it. He sat through the lobster, the scallops, and the champagne, waiting for Helen or Duncan to comment on his hair. It was only when he was doing the dishes that Ellen James handed him a soggy note.

*You had your hair done?*

He nodded, irritably.

"I don't like it," Helen told him, in bed.

"I think it's terrific," Garp said.

"It's not like you," Helen said; she was doing her best to muss it up. "It looks like the hair on a corpse," she said in the darkness.

"A corpse!" Garp said. "Jesus."

"A body prepared by an undertaker," said Helen, almost frantically running her hands through his hair. "Every little hair in place," she said. "It's too perfect. You don't look alive!" she said. Then she cried and cried and Garp held her and whispered to her—trying to find out what the matter was.

Garp did not share her sense of the Under Toad—

not this time—and he talked and talked to her, and made love to her. Finally, she fell asleep.

The essay by Ellen James, "Why I'm Not an Ellen Jamesian," appeared to engender no immediate fuss. It takes a while for most Letters to the Editor to be printed.

There were the expectable personal letters to Ellen James: condolences from idiots, propositions from sick men—the ugly, antifeminist tyrants and baiters of women who, as Garp had warned Ellen, would see themselves as being on *her* side.

"People will always make sides," Garp said, "—of everything."

There was not a written word from a single Ellen Jamesian.

Garp's first Steering wrestling team produced an 8–2 season as it approached its final dual meet with its arch rival, the bad boys from Bath. Of course, the team's strength rested on some very well coached wrestlers whom Ernie Holm had brought along for the last two or three years, but Garp had kept everyone sharp. He was trying to estimate the wins and losses, weight class by weight class, in the upcoming match with Bath—sitting at the kitchen table in the vast house now in memory of Steering's first family—when Ellen James burst upon him, in tears, with the new issue of the magazine that had published her a month ago.

Garp felt he should have warned Ellen about magazines, too. They had, of course, published a long, epistolary essay written by a score of Ellen Jamesians, in response to Ellen's bold announcement that she felt used by them and she disliked them. It was just the kind of controversy magazines love. Ellen felt especially betrayed by the magazine's editor, who had obviously revealed to the Jamesians that Ellen James now lived with the notorious T. S. Garp.

Thus the Ellen Jamesians had *that* to get their teeth

into: Ellen James, poor child, had been brainwashed into her antifeminist stance by the male villain, Garp. The betrayer of his mother! The smirking capitalizer on women's-movement politics! In the various letters, Garp's relationship with Ellen James was referred to as "seductive," "slimy," and "underhanded."

*I'm sorry!*

Ellen wrote.
"It's okay, it's okay. Nothing's your fault," Garp assured her.

*I'm not an antifeminist!*

"Of course you're not," Garp told her.

*They make everything so black and white.*

"Of course they do," said Garp.

*That's why I hate them. They force you to be like them—or else you're their enemy.*

"Yes, yes," Garp said.

*I wish I could talk.*

And then she dissolved, crying on Garp's shoulder, her wordless, angry blubber rousing Helen from the far-off reading room of the great house, driving Duncan from the darkroom, and waking baby Jenny from her nap.

So, foolishly, Garp decided to take them on, these grown-up crazies, these devout fanatics who—even when their chosen symbol rejected them—insisted they knew more about Ellen James than Ellen James knew about herself.

"Ellen James is *not* a symbol," Garp wrote. "She is a rape victim who was raped and dismembered before she was old enough to make up her own mind about sex and men." Thus he began; he went on and on. And, of course, they published it—liking any fuel to any fire. It was also the first published piece of *any*thing by T. S. Garp since the famous novel, *The World According to Bensenhaver*.

Actually, it was the second. In a little magazine, shortly after Jenny's death, Garp published his first and only poem. It was a strange poem; it was about condoms.

Garp felt his life was marred by condoms—man's device to spare himself and others the consequences of his lust. Our lifetime, Garp felt, was stalked by condoms—condoms in the parking lots in the early mornings, condoms discovered by children in the playing sand of the beaches, condoms used for messages (one to his mother, on the door knob of their tiny wing apartment in the infirmary annex). Condoms unflushed down the dormitory toilets of the Steering School. Condoms lying slick and cocky in public urinals. Once a condom delivered with the Sunday paper. Once a condom in the mailbox at the end of the driveway. And once a condom on the stick-shift shaft of the old Volvo; someone had used the car overnight, but not for driving.

Condoms found Garp the way ants found sugar. He traveled miles, he changed continents, and there—in the bidet of the otherwise spotless but unfamiliar hotel room . . . there—in the back seat of the taxi, like the removed eye of a large fish . . . there—eyeing him, from the bottom of his shoe, where he picked it up, somewhere. From *every*where condoms came to him and vilely surprised him.

Condoms and Garp went way back. They were somehow joined at the beginning. How often he recalled his first condom shock, the condoms in the cannon's mouth!

It was a fair poem, but almost no one read it because it was gross. Many more people read his essay on Ellen

James vs. the Ellen Jamesians. That was news; that was a contemporary event. Sadly, Garp knew, that is more interesting than art.

Helen begged him not to be baited, not to get involved. Even Ellen James told him that it was *her* fight; she did not ask for his support.

"More fucking around in the garden," Helen warned. "More bookshelves."

But he wrote angrily and well; he said more firmly what Ellen James had meant. He spoke with eloquence for those serious women who suffered, by association, "the radical self-damage" of the Ellen Jamesians—"the kind of shit that gives feminism a bad name." He could not resist putting them down, and though he did it well, Helen rightly asked, "For *whom?* Who is serious who doesn't already *know* the Ellen Jamesians are crazy? No, Garp, you've done this for *them*—not for Ellen, either. You've done it for the fucking Ellen Jamesians! You've done it to *get* to them. And why? Jesus, in another year no one would have remembered them—or why they did what they did. They were a *fashion,* a stupid fashion, but you couldn't just let them pass by. *Why?"*

But he was sullen about it, with the predictable attitude of someone who has been *right*—at all costs. And, therefore, wonders if he was wrong. It was a feeling that isolated him from everyone—even from Ellen. She was ready to be quits with it, she was sorry she had started it.

"But *they* started it," Garp insisted.

> *Not really. The first man who raped someone, and tried to hurt her so she couldn't tell*—he *started it,*

said Ellen James.

"Okay," Garp said. "Okay, okay." The girl's sad truth hurt him. Hadn't he only wanted to defend her?

The Steering wrestling team whipped Bath Academy in the season's final dual meet and finished 9-2, with a second-place team trophy in the New England tournament and one individual champion, a 167-pounder whom Garp had personally done the most work with. But the season was over; Garp, the retired writer, once more had too much time on his hands.

He saw a lot of Roberta. They played endless games of squash; between them, they broke four rackets in three months and the little finger on Garp's left hand. Garp had an unmindful backswing that accounted for nine stitches across the bridge of Roberta's nose; Roberta hadn't had any stitches since her Eagle days and she complained about them bitterly. On a cross-court charge, Roberta's long knee gave Garp a groin injury that had him hobbling for a week.

"Honestly, you two," Helen told them. "Why don't you just go off and have a torrid affair. It would be *safer*."

But they were the best of friends, and if ever such urges occurred—for either Garp or Roberta—they were quickly made into a joke. Also, Roberta's love life was at last coolly organized; like a born woman, she valued her privacy. And she enjoyed the directorship of the Fields Foundation at Dog's Head Harbor. Roberta reserved her sexual self for not infrequent but never excessive flings upon the city of New York, where she kept a calm number of lovers on edge for her sudden visits and trysts. "It's the only way I can manage it," she told Garp.

"It's a good enough way, Roberta," Garp said. "Not everyone is so fortunate—to have this separation of power."

And so they played more squash, and when the weather warmed, they ran on the curvy roads that stretched from Steering to the sea. On one road, Dog's Head Harbor was a flat six miles from Steering; they often ran from one mansion to the other. When Roberta did her business in New York, Garp ran alone.

He was alone, nearing the halfway point to Dog's

Head Harbor—where he would turn around and run back to Steering—when the dirty-white Saab passed him, appeared to slow down, then sped ahead of him and out of sight. That was the only thing strange about it. Garp ran on the left-hand side of the road so that he could see the cars approaching closest to him; the Saab had passed him on the right, in its proper lane—nothing funny about it.

Garp was thinking about a reading he had promised to give at Dog's Head Harbor. Roberta had talked him into reading to the assembled Fields Foundation fellows and their invited guests; he was, after all, the chief trustee—and Roberta frequently organized small concerts and poetry readings, and so forth—but Garp was leery of it. He disliked readings—and especially now, to women; his put-down of the Ellen Jamesians had left so many women feeling raw. Most serious women, of course, agreed with him, but most of them were also intelligent enough to recognize a kind of personal vindictiveness in his criticisms of the Ellen Jamesians, which was stronger than logic. They sensed a kind of killer instinct in him—basically male and basically intolerant. He was, as Helen said, too intolerant of the intolerant. Most women surely thought Garp had written the truth about the Ellen Jamesians, but was it necessary to have been so rough? In his own wrestling terminology, perhaps Garp was guilty of unnecessary roughness. It was his roughness many women suspected, and when he read now, even to mixed audiences—at colleges, mainly, where roughness seemed presently unfashionable—he was aware of a silent dislike. He was a man who had publicly lost his temper; he had demonstrated that he could be cruel.

And Roberta had advised him not to read a sex scene; not that the Fields Foundation fellows were essentially hostile, but they *were* wary, Roberta said. "You have lots of other scenes to read," Roberta said, "besides sex." Neither of them mentioned the possibility that he might have anything *new* to read. And it was mainly for this reason—that he had nothing new to read—that Garp had grown increasingly unhappy about giving readings, anywhere.

Garp topped the slight hill by a farm for black Angus cattle—the only hill between Steering and the sea—and passed the two-mile mark on his run. He saw the blue-black noses of the beasts pointed at him, like double-barreled guns over a low stone wall. Garp always spoke to the cattle; he mooed at them.

The dirty-white Saab was now approaching him, and Garp moved into the dust of the soft shoulder. One of the black Angus mooed back at Garp; two shied away from the stone wall. Garp had his eyes on them. The Saab was not going very fast—did not appear reckless. There seemed no reason to keep an eye on it.

It was only his memory that saved him. Writers have very selective memories, and fortunately, for Garp, he had chosen to remember how the dirty-white Saab had slowed—when it first passed him, going the other way —and how the driver's head appeared to be lining him up in the rear-view mirror.

Garp looked away from the Angus and saw the silent Saab, engine cut, coasting straight at him in the soft shoulder, a trail of dust spuming behind its quiet white shape and over the intent, hunched head of the driver. The driver, aiming the Saab at Garp, was the closest visual image Garp would ever have of what a ball turret gunner who was at work *looked* like.

Garp took two bounds to the stone wall and vaulted it, not seeing the single line of electric fencing above the wall. He felt the tingle in his thigh as he grazed the wire, but he cleared the fence, and the wall, and landed in the wet green stubble of the field, chewed and pockmarked by the herd of Angus.

He lay hugging the wet ground, he heard the croak of the vile-tasting Under Toad in his dry throat—he heard the explosion of hooves as the Angus thundered away from him. He heard the rock-and-metal meeting of the dirty-white Saab with the stone wall. Two boulders, the size of his head, bounced lazily beside him. One wild-eyed Angus bull stood his ground, but the Saab's horn was stuck; perhaps the steady blare kept the bull from charging.

Garp knew he was alive; the blood in his mouth was only because he had bitten his lip. He moved along the wall to the point of impact, where the bashed Saab was imbedded. Its driver had lost more than her tongue.

She was in her forties. The Saab's engine had driven her knees up around the mangled steering column. She had no rings on her hands, which were short-fingered and reddened by the rough winter, or winters, she had known. The Saab's door post on the driver's side, or else the windshield's frame, had struck her face and dented one temple and one cheek. This left her face a little lopsided. Her brown, blood-matted hair was ruffled by the warm summer wind, which blew through the hole where the windshield had been.

Garp knew she was dead because he looked in her eyes. He knew she was an Ellen Jamesian because he looked in her mouth. He also looked in her purse. There was only the predictable note pad and pencil. There were lots of used and new notes, too. One of them said:

*Hi! My name is . . .*

and so forth. Another one said:

*You asked for this.*

Garp imagined that this was the note she had intended to stick under the bloody waistband of his running shorts when she left him dead and mangled by the side of the road.

Another note was almost lyrical; it was the one the newspapers would love to use, and reuse.

*I have never been raped, and I have never wanted to be. I have never been with a man, and I have never wanted to be, either. My whole life's meaning has been to share the suffering of Ellen James.*

Oh boy, Garp thought, but he left that note to be discovered with her other things. He was not the sort of writer, or the sort of man, who concealed important messages—even if the messages were insane.

He had aggravated his old groin injury by vaulting the stone wall and the electric fence, but he was able to jog back toward town until a yogurt truck picked him up; Garp and the yogurt driver went to tell the police together.

By the time the yogurt driver passed the scene of the accident, on his way to discover Garp, the black Angus had escaped through the rent in the stone wall and were milling around the dirty-white Saab like large, beastly mourners surrounding this fragile angel killed in a foreign car.

Maybe *that* was the Under Toad I felt, Helen thought, lying awake beside the soundly sleeping Garp. She hugged his warm body; she nestled in the smell of her own rich sex all over him. Maybe that dead Ellen Jamesian was the Under Toad, and now she's gone, thought Helen; she squeezed Garp so hard that he woke up.

"What is it?" he asked. But, wordless as Ellen James, Helen hugged his hips; her teeth chattered against his chest and he hugged her until she stopped shivering.

A "spokesperson" for the Ellen Jamesians remarked that this was an isolated act of violence, not sanctioned by the society of Ellen Jamesians but obviously provoked by the "typically male, aggressive, rapist personality of T. S. Garp." They were not taking responsibility for this "isolated act," the Jamesians declared, but they were not surprised or especially sorry about it, either.

Roberta told Garp that, under the circumstances, if he didn't feel like reading to a group of women, she would understand. But Garp read to the assembled

Fields Foundation fellows and their assorted guests at Dog's Head Harbor—a crowd of less than one hundred people, cozily comfortable in the sun room of Jenny's estate. He read them "The Pension Grillparzer," which he introduced by saying, "This is the first and best thing I ever wrote, and I don't even know how I thought it up. I think it is about death, which I didn't even know very much about when I wrote it. I know more about death now, and I'm not writing a word. There are eleven major characters in this story and seven of them die; one of them goes mad; one of them runs away with another woman. I'm not going to give away what happens to the other two characters, but you can see that the odds for surviving this story aren't great."

Then he read to them. Some of them laughed; four of them cried; there were lots of sneezes and coughs, perhaps because of the ocean dampness; nobody left and everyone applauded. An older woman in the back, by the piano, slept soundly through the entire story, but even she applauded at the end; she woke up to the applause and joined in it, happily.

The event seemed to charge Garp. Duncan had attended the reading—it was his favorite among his father's works (actually one of the few things his father had written that Duncan had been allowed to read). Duncan was a talented young artist and he had more than fifty drawings of the characters and situations in his father's story, which he revealed to Garp after Garp drove them both home. Some of the drawings were fresh and unpretentious; all of them were thrilling to Garp. The old bear's withered flanks engulfing the absurd unicycle; the grandmother's matchstick ankles appearing frail and exposed under the W.C. door. The evil mischief in the dream man's excited eyes! The floozy beauty of Herr Theobald's sister (". . . as if her life and her companions had never been exotic to *her*—as if they had always been staging a ludicrous and doomed effort at reclassification"). And the brave optimism of the man who could only walk on his hands.

"How long have you been doing this?" Garp asked Duncan; he could have wept, he felt so proud.

It charged him, very much. He proposed to John Wolf a special edition, a *book* of "The Pension Grill-parzer," illustrated by Duncan. "The story's good enough to be a book all by itself," Garp wrote John Wolf. "And I'm certainly well known enough for it to sell. Except for a little magazine, and an anthology or two, it's really never been published before. Besides, the drawings are lovely! And the story really holds up.

"I hate it when a writer starts cashing in on a reputation—publishing all the shit in his drawers, and republishing all the *old* shit that deserved to be missed. But this isn't a case of that, John; you know it isn't."

John Wolf knew. He thought Duncan's drawings *were* fresh and unpretentious, but also not really very good; the boy was not yet thirteen—no matter how talented he was. But John Wolf also knew a good idea for publishing when he saw it. To be sure, of course, he gave the book the Secret Jillsy Sloper Test; Garp's story, and especially Duncan's drawings, passed Jillsy's scrutiny with the highest praise. Her only reservations concerned Garp's using too many words she didn't know.

A father and son book, John Wolf thought, would be nice for Christmas. And the sad gentleness of the story, its full pity and its mild violence, would perhaps ease the tension of Garp's war with the Ellen Jamesians.

The groin healed, and Garp ran the road from Steering to the sea all summer, nodding his recognition to the brooding Angus every day; they now had the safety of that fortunate stone wall in common, and Garp felt forever identified with these large, lucky animals. Happily grazed, and happily bred. And slaughtered, one day, quickly. Garp did not think of their slaughter. Or his own. He watched out for cars, but not nervously.

"An isolated act," he told Helen and Roberta and Ellen James. They nodded, but Roberta ran with him whenever she could. Helen thought she would feel more at ease when the weather got cold again and Garp ran on the indoor track in the Miles Seabrook Field House. Or when he started wrestling again, and rarely went out at all. Those warm mats and that padded room were a safety symbol to Helen Holm, who had grown up in such an incubator.

Garp, too, looked forward to another wrestling season. And to the father and son publication of *The Pension Grillparzer*—a tale by T. S. Garp, illustrated by Duncan Garp. At last, a Garp book for children *and* for grownups! It was also, of course, like starting over. Going back to the beginning and getting a fresh start. What a world of illusions blossoms with the idea of "starting over."

Suddenly, Garp started writing again.

He started by writing a letter to the magazine that had published his attack on the Ellen Jamesians. In the letter he apologized for the vehemence and self-righteousness of his remarks. "Although I believe Ellen James was used by these women, who had little concern for the real-life Ellen James, I can see that the *need* to use Ellen James in some way was genuine and great. I feel, of course, at least partially responsible for the death of that very needful and violent woman who felt provoked enough to try to kill me. I am sorry."

Of course, apologies are rarely acceptable to true believers—or to anyone who believes in *pure* good, or in pure evil. The Ellen Jamesians who responded, in print, all said that Garp was obviously afraid for his own life; they said he obviously feared an endless line of hit men (or "hit persons") whom the Ellen Jamesians would send after him until they got him. They said that along with being a male swine, and a bully of women, T. S. Garp was clearly "a yellow chickenshit coward with no balls."

If Garp saw these responses, he appeared not to care; it is likely that he never read them. He wrote to apologize, mainly, because of his *writing;* it was an act meant to clear his desk, not his conscience; he meant to rid his mind of the garden-tending, bookshelf-making trivia that had occupied his time while he was waiting to write seriously again. He thought he would make peace with the Ellen Jamesians and then forget them, although Helen could *not* forget them. Ellen James certainly could not forget them, either, and even Roberta was alert and edgy whenever she was out with Garp.

About a mile beyond the bull farm, one fine day when they were running toward the sea, Roberta felt suddenly convinced that the approaching Volkswagen housed another would-be assassin; she threw a magnificent cross-body block on Garp and belted him off the soft shoulder and down a twelve-foot embankment into a muddy ditch. Garp sprained an ankle and sat howling at Roberta from the stream bed. Roberta seized a rock, with which she threatened the Volkswagen, which was full of frightened teen-agers returning from a beach party; Roberta talked them into making room for Garp, whom they drove to the Jenny Fields Infirmary.

"You are a *menace!*" Garp told Roberta, but Helen was especially happy for Roberta's presence—her tight end's instinct for blind-side hits and cheap shots.

Garp's sprained ankle kept him off the road for two weeks and stepped up his writing. He was working on what he called his "father book," or "the book of fathers"; it was the first of the three projects he had jauntily described to John Wolf the night before he left for Europe—this one was the novel to be called *My Father's Illusions*. Because he was inventing a father, Garp felt more in touch with the spirit of pure imagination that he felt had kindled "The Pension Grillparzer." A long way from which he had been falsely led. He had been too impressed by what he now called the "mere accidents and casualties of daily life, and the understandable trauma resulting therefrom." He felt cocky again, as if he could make up anything.

"My father wanted us all to have a better life," Garp began, "but better than *what*—he was not so sure. I do not think that he knew what life was; only that he wanted it *better*."

As he did in "The Pension Grillparzer," he *made up* a family; he gave himself brothers and sisters and aunts—both an eccentric and an evil uncle—and he felt he was a novelist again. A plot, to his delight, thickened.

In the evenings Garp read aloud to Ellen James and Helen; sometimes Duncan stayed up and listened, and sometimes Roberta stayed for supper, and he would read to her, too. He became suddenly generous in all matters concerning the Fields Foundation. In fact, the other board members were exasperated with him: Garp wanted to give *every* applicant something. "She sounds sincere," he kept saying. "Look, she's had a hard life," he told them. "Isn't there enough money?"

"Not if we spend it this way," Marcia Fox said.

"If we don't discriminate between these applicants more than you suggest," said Hilma Bloch, "we are lost."

"Lost?" Garp said. "How could *we* get lost?" Overnight, it seemed to them all (except Roberta), Garp had become the weakest sort of liberal: he would evaluate no one. But he was full of imagining the whole, sad histories of his fictional family; thus full of sympathy, he was a soft touch in the real world.

The anniversary of Jenny's murder, and of the sudden funerals for Ernie Holm and Stewart Percy, passed quickly for Garp in the midst of his renewed creative energy. Then the wrestling season was again upon him; Helen had never seen him so taken up, so completely focused and relentless. He became again the determined young Garp who had made her fall in love, and she felt so drawn to him that she often cried when she was alone—without knowing why. She was alone too much; now that Garp was busy again, Helen realized she had kept herself inactive too long. She agreed to let the Steering School employ her, so that she could teach and use her mind for her own ideas again.

She also taught Ellen James to drive a car and Ellen drove twice a week to the state university, where she took a creative writing course. "This family isn't big enough for two writers, Ellen," Garp teased her. How they all cherished the good mood he was in! And now that Helen was working again, she was much less anxious.

In the world according to Garp, an evening could be hilarious and the next morning could be murderous.

Later, they would often remark (Roberta, too) how good it was that Garp got to see the first edition of *The Pension Grillparzer*—illustrated by Duncan Garp, and out in time for Christmas—before he saw the Under Toad.

# 19

❖❖❖❖❖❖❖

# Life After Garp

H E loved epilogues, as he showed us in "The Pension Grillparzer."

"An epilogue," Garp wrote, "is more than a body count. An epilogue, in the disguise of wrapping up the past, is really a way of warning us about the future."

That February day, Helen heard him telling jokes to Ellen James and Duncan at breakfast; he certainly sounded as if he felt good about the future. Helen gave little Jenny Garp a bath, and powdered her and oiled her scalp and clipped her tiny fingernails and zipped her into a yellow playsuit that Walt once wore. Helen could smell the coffee Garp had made, and she could hear Garp hurrying Duncan off to school.

"Not *that* hat, Duncan, for Christ's sake," Garp said. "That hat couldn't keep a bird warm. It's twelve below."

"It's twelve *above,* Dad," Duncan said.

"That's academic," Garp said. "It's very cold, that's what it is."

Ellen James must have come in through the garage door then, and written out a note, because Helen heard

Garp say that he'd help her in a minute; obviously, Ellen couldn't start the car.

Then it was quiet in the great house for a while; as it from far away, Helen heard only the squeak of boots in the snow and the slow cranking of the car's cold engine. "Have a good day!" she heard Garp call to Duncan, who must have been walking down the long driveway—off to school.

"Yup!" Duncan called. "You, too!"

The car started; Ellen James would be driving off to the university. "Drive carefully!" Garp called after her.

Helen had her coffee alone. Occasionally, the inarticulateness with which baby Jenny talked to herself reminded Helen of the Ellen Jamesians—or of Ellen, when she was upset—but not this morning. The baby was playing quietly with some plastic things. Helen could hear Garp's typewriter—that was all.

He wrote for three hours. The typewriter would burst for three or four pages, then be silent for such a long time that Helen imagined Garp had stopped breathing; then, when she had forgotten about it and was lost in her reading, or in some task with Jenny, the typewriter would burst out again.

At eleven-thirty in the morning Helen heard him call Roberta Muldoon. Garp wanted a squash game before wrestling practice, if Roberta could get away from her "girls," as Garp called the Fields Foundation fellows.

"How are the girls today, Roberta?" Garp said.

But Roberta couldn't play. Helen heard the disappointment in Garp's voice.

Later, poor Roberta would repeat and repeat how she *should* have played; if only she had played, she went on saying, maybe she would have spotted it coming—maybe she would have been around, alert and edgy, recognizing the spoor of the real world, the paw prints Garp had always overlooked or ignored. But Roberta Muldoon could not play squash.

Garp wrote for another half hour. Helen knew he was writing a letter; somehow she could tell the difference in the sound of the typing. He wrote to John Wolf about *My Father's Illusions;* he was pleased with how the book was coming along. He complained that Roberta took her job too seriously and was letting herself get out of shape; *no* administrative job was worth as much time as Roberta gave to the Fields Foundation. Garp said that the low sales figures on *The Pension Grillparzer* were about what he expected; the main thing was that it was "a lovely book"—he liked looking at it, and giving it to people, and its rebirth had been a rebirth for him. He said he expected a better wrestling season than last year, although he had lost his starting heavyweight to a knee operation and his one New England champion had graduated. He said that living with someone who read as much as Helen was both irritating and inspiring; he wanted to give her something to read that would make her close her other books.

At noon he came and kissed Helen, and fondled her breasts, and kissed baby Jenny, over and over again, while he dressed her in a snowsuit that had also been worn by Walt—and before Walt, even Duncan had gotten some wear out of it. Garp drove Jenny to the day-care center as soon as Ellen James came back with the car. Then Garp showed up at Buster's Snack and Grill for his customary cup of tea with honey, his one tangerine, and his one banana. That was all the lunch he ran or wrestled on; he explained why to a new teacher in the English Department—a young man fresh out of graduate school who adored Garp's work. His name was Donald Whitcomb, and his nervous stutter reminded Garp, affectionately, of the departed Mr. Tinch and the race in his pulse he still felt for Alice Fletcher.

This particular day, Garp was eager to talk about writing to anyone, and young Whitcomb was eager to listen. Don Whitcomb would remember that Garp told him what the act of starting a novel felt like. "It's like trying to make the dead come alive," he said. "No, no, that's not right—it's more like trying to keep everyone alive, forever. Even the ones who must die in the end. They're the most important to keep alive." Finally, Garp said it in a way that seemed to please him. "A novelist is a doctor who sees only terminal cases," Garp said. Young Whitcomb was so awed that he wrote this down.

It would be Whitcomb's biography, years later, that the would-be biographers of Garp would all envy and despise. Whitcomb reflected that this Bloom Period in Garp's writing (as Whitcomb called it) was really due to Garp's sense of mortality. The attempt on Garp's life by the Ellen Jamesian in the dirty-white Saab, Whitcomb claimed, had given Garp the urgency necessary to make him write again. Helen would endorse that thesis.

It was not a bad idea, although Garp would surely have laughed at it. He really had forgotten the Ellen Jamesians, and he was not on the lookout for more of them. But unconsciously, perhaps, he might have been feeling that urgency young Whitcomb expressed.

In Buster's Snack and Grill, Garp held Whitcomb enthralled until it was time for wrestling practice. On his way out (leaving Whitcomb to pay, the young man later recalled, good-naturedly), Garp ran into Dean Bodger, who had just spent three days hospitalized with some heart complaint.

"They found nothing wrong," Bodger complained.

"But did they find your heart?" Garp asked him.

The dean, young Whitcomb, and Garp all laughed. Bodger said he'd brought only *The Pension Grillparzer* with him to the hospital, and since it was so short a book, he'd been able to read it completely three times. It was a gloomy story to read in a hospital, Bodger said, though he was glad to report that he had not yet had the grandmother's dream; thus he knew he would live awhile longer. Bodger said he had loved the story.

Whitcomb would remember that Garp then grew embarrassed, though he was obviously pleased by Bodger's praise. Whitcomb and Bodger waved good-bye to him. Garp forgot his skier's knit hat, but Bodger told Whitcomb he would bring it to Garp—at the gym. Dean Bodger said to Whitcomb that he liked dropping in on Garp in the wrestling room, occasionally. "He is so in his element there," Bodger said.

Donald Whitcomb was no wrestling fan but he talked enthusiastically about Garp's writing. The young and the old man agreed: Garp was a man with remarkable energy.

Whitcomb recalled that he returned to his small apartment in one of the dormitories and tried to write down everything that had impressed him about Garp; he had to stop, unfinished, in time for supper. When Whitcomb went to the dining hall, he was one of the few people at the Steering School who'd heard nothing about what had happened. It was Dean Bodger—his eyes red-rimmed, his face suddenly years older—who stopped young Whitcomb going into the dining hall. The dean, who had left his gloves at the gym, clutched Garp's ski hat in his cold hands. When Whitcomb saw that the dean still had Garp's hat, he knew—even before looking in Bodger's eyes—that something was wrong.

Garp missed his hat as soon as he trotted out on the snowy footpath that led from Buster's Snack and Grill to the Seabrook Gymnasium and Field House. But rather than go back for it, he stepped up his usual pace and ran to the gym. His head was cold when he got there, in less than three minutes; his toes were cold, too, and he warmed his feet in the steamy trainer's room before putting on his wrestling shoes.

He talked briefly with his 145-pounder in the trainer's room. The boy was getting his little finger taped to his ring finger so that he would give some support to what the trainer said was only a sprain. Garp asked if there'd been an X ray; there had been, and it was negative. Garp tapped his 145-pounder on the shoulder, asked him what he weighed in at, frowned at the answer—which was probably a lie, and still about five pounds too heavy—and went to suit up.

He stopped again in the trainer's room before going to practice. "Just to put some Vaseline on one ear," the trainer recalled. Garp had a cauliflower ear in progress, and the Vaseline made his ear slippery; he thought this protected it. Garp did not like wrestling in a headgear; those ear guards had not been part of the required uniform when he'd been a wrestler, and he saw no reason to wear one now.

He jogged a mile around the indoor track with his 152-pounder before opening the wrestling room. Garp challenged the boy to a sprint in the last lap, but the 152-pounder had more left than Garp and beat him by six feet at the end. Garp then "played" with the 152-pounder—in lieu of warming up—in the wrestling room. He took the kid down easily, about five or six times, then rode him around the mat for about five minutes—or until the boy showed signs of tiring. Then Garp allowed the boy to reverse him; Garp let the 152-pounder try to pin him while he defended himself on the bottom. But there was a muscle in Garp's back that was tight, that would not stretch enough to suit him, so Garp told the 152-pounder to go play with someone else. Garp sat by himself against the padded wall, sweating happily and watching the room fill up with his team.

He let them warm up on their own—he hated organized calisthenics—before demonstrating the first of the drills he wanted them to practice. "Get a partner, get a partner," he said, by rote. And he added, "Eric? Get a *harder* partner, Eric, or you'll work with me."

Eric, his 133-pounder, had a habit of coasting through workouts with the second-string 115-pounder, who was Eric's roommate and best friend.

When Helen came in the wrestling room, the temperature was up to 85° or so, and climbing. The coupled boys upon the mat were already breathing hard. Garp was intently watching a time clock. "One minute left!" Garp yelled. When Helen walked by him, he had a whistle in his mouth—so she did not kiss him.

She would remember that whistle, and not kissing

him, for as long as she would live—which would be a long time.

Helen went to her usual corner of the wrestling room, where she could not easily be fallen on. She opened her book. Her glasses fogged up; she wiped them off. She had her glasses on when the nurse entered the wrestling room, at the farthest end of the room from Helen. But Helen never looked up from her book unless there was a loud body slam upon the mat or an unusually loud cry of pain. The nurse closed the wrestling-room door behind her and moved quickly past the grappling bodies toward Garp, with his time clock in his hands and his whistle in his mouth. Garp took the whistle out and hollered, "Fifteen seconds!" That was all the time *he* had left, too. Garp put the whistle back in his mouth and got ready to blow.

When he saw the nurse, he mistook her for the kindly nurse named Dotty who had helped him escape from the first feminist funeral. Garp was simply judging her by her hair, which was iron-gray and in a braid, coiled like a rope around her head—it was a wig, of course. The nurse smiled at him. There was probably no one Garp felt as comfortable with as a nurse; he smiled back at her, then glanced at the time clock: ten seconds.

When Garp looked up at the nurse again, he saw the gun. He had just been thinking about his mother, Jenny Fields, and how she must have looked when she walked into the wrestling room, not quite twenty years ago. Jenny was younger than this nurse, he was thinking. If Helen had looked up and seen this nurse, Helen might have been fooled again into thinking that her missing mother had finally decided to come out of hiding.

When Garp saw the gun, he also noticed that it wasn't a real nurse's uniform; it was a Jenny Fields Original with the characteristic red heart sewn over the breast. It was then that Garp saw the nurse's breasts—they were small but they were too firm and youthfully erect for a woman with iron-gray hair; and her hips were too slim, her legs too girlish. When Garp looked again at her face, he saw the family resemblance: the square jawline that Midge Steering had given to all her children, the sloping forehead that had been the contribution of Fat Stew. The combination gave all the Percys' heads the shape of violent navy vessels.

The first shot forced the whistle out of Garp's mouth with a sharp *tweet!* and caused the time clock to fly from his hands. He sat down. The mat was warm. The bullet had traveled through his stomach and had lodged in his spine. There were fewer than five seconds remaining on the time clock when Bainbridge Percy fired a second time; the bullet struck Garp's chest and drove him, still in a sitting position, back against the padded wall. The stunned wrestlers, who were only boys, seemed incapable of motion. It was Helen who tackled Pooh Percy to the mat and kept her from firing a third shot.

Helen's screams aroused the wrestlers. One of them, the second-string heavyweight, pinned Pooh Percy belly down to the mat and ripped her hand with the gun in it out from under her; his pumping elbow split Helen's lip, but Helen hardly felt it. The starting 145-pounder, with his little finger taped to his ring finger, wrenched the gun out of Pooh's hand by breaking her thumb.

At the moment her bone *clicked,* Pooh Percy screamed; even Garp saw what had become of her—the surgery must have been recent. In Pooh Percy's open, yelling mouth, anyone near her could see the black gathering of stitches, like ants clustered on the stump of what had been her tongue. The second-string heavyweight was so frightened of Pooh that he squeezed her too hard and cracked one of her ribs; Bainbridge Percy's recent madness—to become an Ellen Jamesian—was certainly painful to her.

"Igs!" she screamed. "Ucking igs!" An "ucking ig" was a "fucking pig," but you had to be an Ellen Jamesian to understand Pooh Percy now.

The starting 145-pounder held the gun at arm's length, pointed down to the mat and into an empty corner of the wrestling room. "Ig!" Pooh gagged at him, but the trembling boy stared at his coach.

Helen held Garp steady; he was starting to slide against the wall. He could not talk, he knew; he could not feel, he could not touch. He had only a keen sense of smell, his brief eyesight, and his vivid memory.

Garp was glad, for once, that Duncan wasn't interested in wrestling. By virtue of his preference for swimming, Duncan had missed seeing this; Garp knew that Duncan would either just be getting out of school or already at the swimming pool.

Garp was sorry for Helen—that she was here—but he was happy to have her scent nearest him. He savored it, among those other intimate odors in the Steering wrestling room. If he could have talked, he would have told Helen not to be frightened of the Under Toad anymore. It surprised him to realize that the Under Toad was no stranger, was not even mysterious; the Under Toad was very familiar—as if he had always known it, as if he had grown up with it. It was yielding, like the warm wrestling mats; it smelled like the sweat of clean boys—and like Helen, the first and last woman Garp loved. The Under Toad, Garp knew now, could even look like a nurse: a person who is familiar with death and trained to make practical responses to pain.

When Dean Bodger opened the wrestling-room door with Garp's ski hat in his hands, Garp had no illusions that the dean had arrived, once again, to organize the rescue party—to catch the body falling from the infirmary annex, four floors above where the world was safe. The world was not safe. Dean Bodger, Garp knew, would do his best to be of service; Garp smiled gratefully to him, and to Helen—and to his wrestlers; some of them were weeping now. Garp looked fondly at his sobbing second-string heavyweight who lay crushing Pooh Percy to the mat; Garp knew what a difficult season the poor, fat boy was about to experience.

Garp looked at Helen; all he could move was his eyes. Helen, he saw, was trying to smile back at him. With his eyes, Garp tried to reassure her: don't worry—so what if there is no life after death? There is life after Garp, believe me. Even if there is only death after death (after death), be grateful for small favors—sometimes there is birth after sex, for example. And, if you are very fortunate, sometimes there is sex after birth! Oh yeth, as Alice Fletcher would have said. And if you have life, said Garp's eyes, there is hope you'll have energy. And never forget, there is memory, Helen, his eyes told her.

"In the world according to Garp," young Donald Whitcomb would write, "we are obliged to remember everything."

Garp died before they could move him from the wrestling room. He was thirty-three, the same age as Helen. Ellen James was just starting her twenties. Duncan was thirteen. Little Jenny Garp was going on three. Walt would have been eight.

The news of Garp's death promoted the immediate printing of a third and fourth edition of the father and son book, *The Pension Grillparzer*. Over a long weekend, John Wolf drank too much and contemplated leaving publishing; it sometimes nauseated him to see how a violent death was so good for business. But it comforted Wolf to realize how Garp would have taken the news. Even Garp could not have imagined that his own death would be *better* than a suicide at establishing *his* literary seriousness and his fame. Not bad for someone who, at thirty-three, had written one good short story and perhaps one and a half good novels out of three. Garp's rare manner of dying was, in fact, so perfect that John Wolf had to smile when he imagined how pleased Garp would have been with it. It was a death, Wolf thought, which in its random, stupid, and unnecessary qualities—comic and ugly and bizarre—underlined everything Garp had ever written about how the world works. It was a death scene, John Wolf told Jillsy Sloper, that only Garp could have written.

Helen would remark bitterly, but only once, that

Garp's death was really a kind of suicide, after all. "In the sense that his whole *life* was a suicide," she said, mysteriously. She would later explain that all she meant was, "He made people too angry."

He had made Pooh Percy too angry; at least that was clear.

He made others pay him tribute, small and strange. The Steering School cemetery got the honor of his gravestone, if not his body; like his mother's, Garp's body went to medicine. The Steering School also chose to honor him by naming after him its one remaining building that was not named after anybody else. It was old Dean Bodger's idea. If there was a Jenny Fields Infirmary, the good dean argued, then there should be a Garp Infirmary Annex.

In later years the functions of these buildings would alter slightly, although they would remain, in name, the Fields Infirmary and the Garp Annex. The Fields Infirmary would one day become the old wing of the new Steering Health Clinic and Laboratories; the Garp Annex would become a building used chiefly for storage —a kind of warehouse for medical, kitchen and classroom supplies; it could also be used for epidemics. Of course, there weren't many epidemics anymore. Garp probably would have liked the idea: to have a storage building named after him. He wrote once that a novel was "only a place for storage—of all the meaningful things that a novelist isn't able to use in his life."

He would have liked the idea of an epilogue, too— so here it is: an epilogue "warning us about the future," as T. S. Garp might have imagined it.

ALICE and HARRISON FLETCHER would remain married, through thick and through thin—in part, their marriage lasted because of Alice's difficulty with finishing anything. Their only child, a daughter, would play the cello—that large and cumbersome and silken-voiced instrument—in a manner so graceful that the pure, deep sound of it aggravated Alice's speech defect for hours after each performance. Harrison, who would get and hold his tenure after a while, would outgrow his habits with his prettier students about the time his talented daughter began to assert herself as a serious musician.

Alice, who would never complete her second novel, or her third or fourth, would never have a second child, either. She remained smoothly fluent on the page, and agonizing in the flesh. Alice never again took to "other men" to the degree that she had taken to Garp; even in her memory, he was a passion that was strong enough to keep her from ever becoming close to Helen. And Harry's old fondness for Helen seemed to fade with each of his fast-fading affairs, until the Fletchers rarely kept track of the surviving Garps at all.

Once Duncan Garp met the Fletcher daughter in New York, after her maiden cello solo in that dangerous city; Duncan took her to dinner.

"Does he look like his mother?" Harrison asked the girl.

"I don't remember her very well," the daughter said.

"Did he make a *path* at you?" Alice asked.

"I don't *think* so," said her daughter, whose first-chosen and best-loved partner would always be that big-hipped cello.

The Fletchers, both Harry and Alice, would die in their ripe middle age, when their airplane—to Martinique—crashed during the Christmas holidays. One of Harrison's students had driven them to the airport.

"If you live in New England," Alice confided to the student, "you owe yourthelf a holiday in the *thun*. Right, Harrithon?"

Helen had always thought that Alice was "a little loony."

HELEN HOLM, who most of her life would be known as Helen Garp, would live a long, long time. A slim, dark woman with an arresting face and precise language, she would have her lovers but never remarry. Each lover suffered the presence of Garp—not only in Helen's relentless memory, but in the articles of fact that Helen surrounded herself with in the Steering mansion, which she rarely left: for example, Garp's books, and all of Duncan's photographs of him, and even Garp's wrestling trophies.

Helen maintained that she could never forgive Garp for dying so young and leaving her to live so much of her life alone—he had also spoiled her, she claimed, for ever considering seriously the possibility of living with another man.

Helen would become one of the most respected teachers the Steering School ever had, though she would never lose her sense of sarcasm about the place. She had some friends there, though they were few: old Dean Bodger, until he died, and the young scholar, Donald Whitcomb, who would become as enchanted with Helen as he was enchanted with the work of Garp. There was also a woman, a sculptor, who was an artist-in-residence—someone Roberta had introduced Helen to.

John Wolf was a lifelong friend whom Helen forgave in small pieces, but never completely, for his success at making Garp a success. Helen and Roberta remained close, too—Helen occasionally joining Roberta for Roberta's famous flings upon the city of New York. The two of them, growing older and more eccentric, were guilty of lording it over the Fields Foundation for years. In fact, the wit of their running commentary on the outside world became almost a tourist attraction at Dog's Head Harbor; from time to time, when Helen was lonely or bored at Steering—when her children were grown up and pursuing their own lives, elsewhere—she went to stay with Roberta at Jenny Fields' old estate. It was always lively there. When Roberta died, Helen appeared to age twenty years.

Very late in her life—and only after she had complained to Duncan that she had survived all her favorite contemporaries—Helen Holm was stricken suddenly with an illness that affects the body's mucous membranes. She would die in her sleep.

She had successfully outlived many cutthroat biographers who were waiting for her to die so that they could swoop in on the remains of Garp. She had protected his letters, the unfinished manuscript of *My Father's Illusions,* most of his journals and jottings. She told all the would-be biographers, exactly as *he* would have, "Read the work. Forget the life."

She herself wrote several articles, which were respected in her field. One was called "The Adventurer's Instinct in Narration." It was a comparative study of the narrative technique of Joseph Conrad and Virginia Woolf.

Helen always considered herself as a widow left with *three* children—Duncan, baby Jenny, and Ellen James, who all survived Helen and wept copiously at her death. They had been too young and too astonished to weep as much for Garp.

DEAN BODGER, who wept almost as much as Helen at Garp's death, remained as loyal as a pit bull, and as tenacious. Long after his retirement, he still stormed the Steering campus by night, unable to sleep, fitfully capturing lurkers and lovers who slunk along the footpaths and hugged each other to the spongy ground—under the soft bushes, alongside the beautiful old buildings, and so forth.

Bodger remained active at Steering for as long as it took Duncan Garp to graduate. "I saw your father through, boy," the dean told Duncan. "I'll see you through, too. And if they let me, I'll stay to see your sister through." But they finally forced his retirement; they cited to themselves, among other problems, his habit of talking to himself during chapel, and his bizarre arrests, at midnight, of the boys and girls caught out after hours. They also mentioned the dean's recurring fantasy: that it had been the young Garp he caught in his arms—one night, years ago—and not a pigeon. Bodger refused to move from the campus, even when he was retired, and despite—or, perhaps, because of—his obstinacy, he became Steering's most honored emeritus. They would drag him out for all the school's ceremonies; they would totter him up to the stage, introduce him to people who didn't know who he was, and then they would lead him away. Perhaps because they could display him on these dignified occasions, they tolerated his odd behavior; long through his seventies, for example, Bodger would be convinced—sometimes for weeks at a time—that he was *still* the dean.

"You *are* the dean, really," Helen liked to tease him. "Of course I am!" Bodger roared.

They saw each other often, and as Bodger grew deafer, and deafer, he was more frequently seen on the arm of that nice Ellen James, who had her ways of talking to people who couldn't hear.

Dean Bodger remained loyal even to the Steering wrestling team, whose glory years soon faded from the memories of most. The wrestlers were never again to have a coach the equal of Ernie Holm, or even the equal of Garp. They became a losing team, yet Bodger always supported them, hollering through the last bout to the poor Steering boy flopping on his back, about to be pinned.

It was at a wrestling match that Bodger died. In the unlimited class—an unusually close match—the Steering heavyweight lay floundering with his equally exhausted and out-of-shape opponent; like beached baby whales, they groveled for the upper hand and the winning points as the clock ran down. "Fifteen seconds!" the announcer boomed. The big boys struggled. Bodger rose to his feet, stamping and urging. *"Gott!"* he squawked, his German emerging at the end.

When the bout ended and the stands emptied, there was the retired dean—dead in his seat. It took much comforting from Helen for the sensitive young Whitcomb to gain control of his grief at Bodger's loss.

DONALD WHITCOMB would never sleep with Helen, despite rumors among the envious would-be biographers who longed to get their hands on Garp's property and Garp's widow. Whitcomb would be a monkish recluse all his life, which he spent in virtual hiding at the Steering School. It was his happy fortune to have discovered Garp there, moments before Garp's death, and his happy fortune, too, to find himself befriended and looked after by Helen. She trusted him to adore her husband perhaps even more uncritically than she did.

Poor Whitcomb would always be referred to as "the young Whitcomb," even though he would not always be young. His face would never grow a beard, his cheeks would be forever pink—under his brown, his gray, his finally frost-white hair. His voice would remain a stuttering, eager yodel; his hands would wring themselves forever. But it would be Whitcomb whom Helen would trust with the family and literary record.

He would be Garp's biographer. Helen would read all but the last chapter, which Whitcomb waited for years to write; it was the chapter eulogizing her. Whitcomb was *the* Garp scholar, the final Garp authority. He had the proper meekness for a biographer, Duncan always joked. He was a good biographer from the Garp family's point of view; Whitcomb believed everything that Helen told him—he believed every note that Garp left—or every note that Helen *told* him Garp left.

"Life," Garp wrote, "is sadly *not* structured like a good old-fashioned novel. Instead, an ending occurs when those who are meant to peter out have petered out. All that's left is memory. But even a nihilist has a memory."

Whitcomb even loved Garp at his most whimsical and at his most pretentious.

Among Garp's things, Helen found this note.

"No matter what my fucking last words were, please say they were these: 'I have always known that the pursuit of excellence is a lethal habit.'"

Donald Whitcomb, who loved Garp uncritically—in the manner of dogs and children—said that those indeed were Garp's last words.

"If Whitcomb said so, then they were," Duncan always said.

Jenny Garp and Ellen James—they agreed about this, too.

> *It was a family matter—keeping Garp from the biographers,*

wrote Ellen James.

"And why not?" asked Jenny Garp. "What does he owe the *public?* He always said he was only grateful for other artists, and to the people who *loved* him."

> *So who else deserves to have a piece of him, now?*

wrote Ellen James.

Donald Whitcomb was even faithful to Helen's last wish. Although Helen was old, her final illness was sudden, and it had to be Whitcomb who defended her deathbed request. Helen did not want to be buried in the Steering School cemetery, alongside Garp and Jenny, her father and Fat Stew—and all the others. She said that the *town* cemetery would do her just fine. She did not want to be left to medicine, either; since she was so old, she was sure there was little left of her body that anyone could possibly use. She wanted to be cremated, she told Whitcomb, and her ashes were to remain the property of Duncan and Jenny Garp and Ellen James. After burying some of her ashes, they could do anything they chose with what ashes remained, but they could *not* scatter them anywhere on the property of the Steering School. She would be damned, Helen told Whitcomb, if the Steering School, which did not admit women students when she had been of age, would get to have any part of her now.

The gravestone in the town cemetery, she told Whitcomb, should say simply that she was Helen Holm, daughter of the wrestling coach Ernie Holm, and that she had not been allowed to attend the Steering School because she was a girl; furthermore, she was the loving wife of the novelist T. S. Garp, whose gravestone could be seen in the Steering School cemetery, because he was a boy.

Whitcomb was faithful to this request, which amused Duncan especially.

"How Dad would have loved *this!*" Duncan kept saying. "Boy, I can just hear him."

How Jenny Fields would have applauded Helen's decision was a point made most often by Jenny Garp and Ellen James.

ELLEN JAMES would grow up to be a writer. She was "the real thing," as Garp had guessed. Her two mentors—Garp and the ghost of his mother, Jenny Fields—would somehow prove overbearing for Ellen, who because of them both would not ever write much nonfiction or fiction. She became a very good poet— though, of course, she was not much on the reading circuit.

Her wonderful first book of poems, *Speeches Delivered to Plants and Animals,* would have made Garp and Jenny Fields very proud of her; it did make Helen very proud of her—they were good friends, and they were also like mother and daughter.

Ellen James would outlive the Ellen Jamesians, of course. Garp's murder drove them deeper underground, and their occasional surfacing over the years would be largely disguised, even embarrassed.

*Hi! I'm mute,*

their notes finally said. Or:

*I've had an accident—can't talk. But I write good, as you can see.*

"You aren't one of those Ellen Somebodies, are you?" they were occasionally asked.

584

*A what?*

they learned to reply. And the more honest among them would write:

*No. Not now.*

Now they were just women who couldn't speak. Un-ostentatiously, most of them worked hard to discover what they *could* do. Most of them turned, constructively, to helping those who also couldn't do something. They were good at helping disadvantaged people, and also good at helping people who felt too sorry for themselves. More and more their labels left them, and one by one these speechless women appeared under names more of their own making.

Some of them even won Fields Foundation fellowships for the things they did.

Some of them, of course, went on trying to be Ellen Jamesians in a world that soon forgot what an Ellen Jamesian was. Some people thought that the Ellen Jamesians were a criminal gang who flourished, briefly, near mid-century. Others, ironically, confused them with the very people that the Ellen Jamesians had originally been protesting: rapists. One Ellen Jamesian wrote Ellen James that she stopped being an Ellen Jamesian when she asked a little girl if she knew what an Ellen Jamesian was.

"Someone who rapes little boys?" the little girl replied.

There was also a bad but very popular novel that followed Garp's murder by about two months. It took three weeks to write and five weeks to publish. It was called *Confessions of an Ellen Jamesian* and it did much to drive the Ellen Jamesians even wackier or simply away. The novel was written by a man, of course. His previous novel had been called *Confessions of a Porn King,* and the one before that had been called *Confessions of a Child Slave Trader.* And so forth. He was a sly, evil man who became something different about every six months.

One of his cruelly forced jokes, in *Confessions of an Ellen Jamesian,* was that he conceived of his narrator-heroine as a lesbian who doesn't realize until *after* she's cut off her tongue that she has made herself undesirable as a *lover,* too.

The popularity of this vulgar trash was enough to embarrass some Ellen Jamesians to death. There were, actually, suicides. "There are *always* suicides," Garp wrote, "among people who are unable to say what they mean."

But, in the end, Ellen James sought them out and befriended them. It was, she thought, what Jenny Fields would have done. Ellen took to giving poetry readings with Roberta Muldoon, who had a huge, booming voice. Roberta would read Ellen's poems while Ellen sat beside her, looking as if she were wishing very hard that she could say her own poems. This brought out of hiding a lot of Ellen Jamesians who had been wishing *they* could talk, too. A few of them became Ellen's friends.

Ellen James would never marry. She may have known an occasional man, but more because he was a fellow poet than because he was a man. She was a good poet and an ardent feminist who believed in living like Jenny Fields and believed in writing with the energy and the personal vision of T. S. Garp. In other words, she was stubborn enough to have personal opinions, and she was also kind to other people. Ellen would maintain a lifelong flirtation with Duncan Garp—her younger brother, really.

The death of Ellen James would cause Duncan much sorrowing. Ellen, at an advanced age, became a long-distance swimmer—about the time she succeeded Roberta as the director of the Fields Foundation. Ellen worked up to swimming several times across the wide neck of Dog's Head Harbor. Her last and best poems used swimming and "the ocean's pull" as metaphors. But Ellen James remained a girl from the Midwest who never thoroughly understood the undertow; one cold fall day, when she was too tired, it got her.

"When I swim," she wrote to Duncan, "I am reminded of the strenuousness, but also the gracefulness, of arguing with your father. I can also feel the sea's eagerness to get *at* me—to get at my dry middle, my landlocked little heart. My landlocked little ass, your father would say, I'm sure. But we tease each other, the sea and I. I suppose *you* would say, you raunchy fellow, that this is my substitute for sex."

FLORENCE COCHRAN BOWLSBY, who was best known to Garp as Mrs. Ralph, would live a life of larkish turmoil, with no substitute for sex in sight—or, apparently, in need. She actually completed a Ph.D. in comparative literature and was eventually tenured by a large and confused English Department whose members were only unified by their terror of her. She had, at various times, seduced and scorned nine of the thirteen senior members—who were alternately admitted to and then ridiculed from her bed. She would be referred to by her students as "a dynamite teacher," so that she at least demonstrated to other people, if not to herself, some confidence in an area other than sex.

She would hardly be referred to at all by her cringing lovers, whose tails between their legs were all remindful to Mrs. Ralph of the manner in which Garp had once left her house.

In sympathy, at the news of Garp's shocking death, Mrs. Ralph was among the very first to write to Helen. "His was a seduction," Mrs. Ralph wrote, "whose nonoccurrence I have always regretted but respected."

Helen came to rather like the woman, with whom she occasionally corresponded.

Roberta Muldoon also had occasion to correspond with Mrs. Ralph, whose application for a Fields Foundation fellowship was rejected. Roberta was quite surprised by the note sent the Fields Foundation by Mrs. Ralph.

*Up yours,*

the note said. Mrs. Ralph did not appreciate rejection.

Her own child, Ralph, would die before her; Ralph became quite a good newspaperman and, like William Percy, was killed in a war.

BAINBRIDGE PERCY, who was best known to Garp as Pooh, would live a long, long time. The last of a train of psychiatrists would claim to have rehabilitated her, but Pooh Percy may simply have emerged from analysis —and a number of institutions—too thoroughly *bored* with rehabilitation to be violent anymore.

However it was achieved, Pooh was, after a great while, peaceably reintroduced to social intercourse; she reentered public life, a functioning if not speaking member of society, more or less safe and (finally) useful. It was in her fifties that she became interested in children; she worked especially well and patiently with the retarded. In this capacity, she would frequently meet other Ellen Jamesians, who in their various ways were also rehabilitated—or, at least, vastly changed.

For almost twenty years Pooh would not mention her dead sister, Cushie, but her fondness for children eventually confused her. She got herself pregnant when she was fifty-four (no one could imagine how) and she was returned to institutional observation, convinced, as she was, that she would die in childbirth. When this didn't occur, Pooh became a devoted mother; she also continued her work with the retarded. Pooh Percy's own child, for whom her mother's violent history would be a severe shock in her later life, was fortunately *not* retarded; in fact, she would have reminded Garp of Cushie.

Pooh Percy, some said, became a positive example for those who would forever put an end to capital punishment: her rehabilitation was so impressive. Only not to Helen, and to Duncan Garp, who would wish to their graves that Pooh Percy had died at that moment when she last cried "Ig!" in the Steering wrestling room.

One day Pooh *would* die, of course; she would succumb to a stroke in Florida, where she was visiting her daughter. It was a small consolation to Helen that Helen would outlive her.

The faithful Whitcomb would choose to describe Pooh Percy as Garp had once described her, following his escape from the first feminist funeral. "An androgynous twerp," Garp said to Dean Bodger, "with a face like a ferret and a mind completely sodden by spending nearly fifteen years in diapers."

That official biography of Garp, which Donald Whitcomb titled *Lunacy and Sorrow: The Life and Art of T. S. Garp*, would be published by the associates of JOHN WOLF, who would not live to see the good book in print. John Wolf had contributed much effort to the book's careful making, and he had worked in the capacity of an editor to Whitcomb—over most of the manuscript—before his untimely demise.

John Wolf died of lung cancer in New York at a relatively young age. He had been a careful, conscientious, attentive, even elegant man—most of his life—but his deep restlessness and unrelieved pessimism could only be numbed and disguised by smoking three packs of unfiltered cigarettes per day from the time he was eighteen. Like many busy men who maintain an otherwise calm and managed air about themselves, John Wolf smoked himself to death.

His service to Garp, and to Garp's books, is inestimable. Although he may from time to time have held himself responsible for the fame which, in the end, provoked Garp's own violent killing, Wolf was far too sophisticated a man to dwell on such a narrow view. Assassination, in Wolf's opinion, was "an increasingly popular amateur sport of the times"; and "political true believers," as he called nearly everybody, were always the sworn enemy of the artist—who insisted, however arrogantly, on the superiority of a *personal* vision. Besides, Wolf knew, it was not only that Pooh Percy had become an Ellen Jamesian, and had responded to Garp's baiting; hers was a grievance as old as childhood, possibly aggravated by politics but basically as deep as her long need for diapers. Pooh had gotten it into her head that Garp's and Cushie's love for fucking each other had finally been lethal to Cushie. At least, it is true, it was lethal to Garp.

A professional in a world that too often worshiped the contemporaneity it had created, John Wolf insisted to his end that his proudest publication was the father and son edition of *The Pension Grillparzer*. He was proud of the early Garp novels, of course, and came to speak of *The World According to Bensenhaver* as "inevitable—when you consider the violence Garp was exposed to." But it was "Grillparzer" that elevated Wolf —it and the unfinished manuscript of *My Father's Illusions,* which John Wolf looked upon, lovingly and sadly, as "Garp's road back to his right way to write." For years Wolf edited the messy first draft of the unfinished novel; for years he consulted with Helen, and with Donald Whitcomb, about its merits and its faults.

"Only after I'm dead," Helen insisted. "Garp would let nothing go if he didn't think it was finished." Wolf agreed, but he died before Helen. Whitcomb and Duncan would be left to publish *My Father's Illusions*— considerably posthumously.

It was Duncan who spent the most time with John Wolf during Wolf's torturous dying of lung cancer. Wolf lay in a private hospital in New York, sometimes smoking a cigarette through a plastic tube inserted in his throat.

"What would your father say to this?" Wolf asked Duncan. "Wouldn't it suit one of *his* death scenes? Isn't it properly grotesque? Did he ever tell you about the prostitute who died in Vienna, in the Rudolfinerhaus? What was her name?"

"Charlotte," Duncan said. He was close to John Wolf. Wolf had even come to like the early drawings Duncan had done for *The Pension Grillparzer*. And Duncan had moved to New York; he told Wolf that his first sense of knowing he wanted to be a painter, as well as a photographer, was his view of Manhattan from John Wolf's office—the day of the first feminist funeral in New York.

In a letter John Wolf dictated to Duncan from his deathbed, Wolf left word for his associates that Duncan Garp was to be allowed to come look at Manhattan from his office for as long as the publishing company occupied the building.

For many years after John Wolf died, Duncan took advantage of the offer. A new editor moved into Wolf's office, but the name of Garp made all the editors in that publishing house scurry.

For years secretaries would come in and say, "Excuse me, it's that young *Garp*. To look out the window again."

Duncan and John Wolf spent the many hours it took John Wolf to die discussing how good a writer Garp was.

"He would have been very, very special," John Wolf told Duncan.

"*Would* have been, maybe," Duncan said. "But what else could you say to me?"

"No, no, I'm not lying; there's no need," Wolf said. "He had the vision, and he always had the language. But mainly vision; he was always personal. He just got sidetracked for a while, but he was back on the beam with that new book. He was back to the good impulses again. 'The Pension Grillparzer' is his most charming, but it's not his most original; he was still too young; there are other writers who could have written that story. *Procrastination* is an original idea, and a brilliant first novel—but it's a first novel. *Second Wind of the Cuckold* is very funny, and his best title; it's also very original, but it's a novel of manners—and rather narrow. Of course, *The World According to Bensenhaver* is his most original, even if it *is* an X-rated soap opera— which it is. But it's so harsh; it's raw food—good food, but *very* raw. I mean, who wants it? Who needs to suffer such abuse?

"Your father was a difficult fellow; he never gave an inch—but that's the point: he was always following his nose; wherever it took him, it was always *his* nose. And he was ambitious. He started out daring to write about the *world*—when he was just a *kid,* for Christ's sake, he still took it on. Then, for a while—like a lot of writers —he could only write about himself; but he also wrote about the world—it just didn't come through as cleanly. He was starting to get bored with writing about his life and he was beginning to write about the whole world again; he was just starting. And Jesus, Duncan, you must remember he was a *young* man! He was thirty-three."

"And he had energy," Duncan said.

"Oh, he would have written a lot, there's no question," John Wolf said. But he began to cough and had to stop talking.

"But he could never just relax," Duncan said. "So what was the point? Wouldn't he have just burned himself out, anyway?"

Shaking his head—but delicately, not to loosen the tube in his throat—John Wolf went on coughing. "Not him!" Wolf gasped.

"He could have just gone on and on?" Duncan asked. "You think so?"

The coughing Wolf nodded. He would die coughing.

Roberta and Helen would attend his funeral, of course. The rumor-mongers would be hissing, because it was often speculated in the small town of New York that John Wolf had looked after more than Garp's *literary* estate. Knowing Helen, it seems unlikely that she would ever have had such a relationship with John Wolf. Whenever Helen heard how she was linked with someone, Helen would just laugh. Roberta Muldoon was more vehement.

"With John Wolf?" Roberta said. "Helen and Wolf? You've got to be kidding."

Roberta's confidence was well founded. On occasion,

when she flung herself upon the city of New York, Roberta Muldoon had enjoyed a tryst or two with John Wolf.

"And to think I used to watch you play!" John Wolf told Roberta once.

"You can *still* watch me play," Roberta said.

"I mean football," John Wolf said.

"There are better things than football," said Roberta.

"But you do so many things well," John Wolf told her.

"Ha!"

"But you *do,* Roberta."

"All men are liars," said Roberta Muldoon, who *knew* this was true because she had once been a man.

ROBERTA MULDOON, formerly Robert Muldoon, No. 90 of the Philadelphia Eagles, would outlive John Wolf —and most of her lovers. She would not outlive Helen, but Roberta lived long enough to grow at last comfortable with her sex reassignment. Approaching fifty, she would remark to Helen that she suffered the vanity of a middle-aged man *and* the anxieties of a middle-aged woman, "but," Roberta added, "this perspective is not without advantages. Now I always know what men are going to say before they say it."

"But *I* know, too, Roberta," Helen said. Roberta laughed her frightening boomer of a laugh; she had a habit of bear-hugging her friends, which made Helen nervous. Roberta had once broken a pair of Helen's glasses.

Roberta had successfully dwarfed her enormous eccentricity by becoming responsible—chiefly to the Fields Foundation, which she ran so vigorously that Ellen James had given her a nickname.

*Captain Energy.*

"Ha!" Roberta said. "Garp was Captain Energy."

Roberta was also greatly admired in the small community of Dog's Head Harbor, for Jenny Fields' estate had never been so respectable, in the old days, and Roberta was a far more outgoing participant in the affairs of the town than Jenny had ever been. She spent ten years as the chairperson of the local school board—although, of course, she could never have a child of her own. She organized, coached, and pitched on the Rockingham County Women's Softball Team—for twelve years, the best team in the state of New Hampshire. Once upon a time, the same, stupid, swinish governor of New Hampshire suggested that Roberta be given a chromosome test before she be allowed to play in the title game; Roberta suggested that the governor should meet her, just before the start of the game—on the pitcher's mound—"and see if he can fight like a man." Nothing came of it, and—politics being what they are—the governor threw out the first ball. Roberta pitched a shutout, chromosomes and all.

And it is to the credit of the athletic director of the Steering School that Roberta was offered the position of offensive line coach for the Steering football team. But the former tight end politely refused the job. "All those young boys," Roberta said sweetly. "I'd get in terrible trouble."

Her favorite young boy, all her life, was Duncan Garp, whom she mothered and sistered and smothered with her perfume and her affection. Duncan loved her; he was one of the few male guests ever allowed at Dog's Head Harbor, although Roberta was angry with him and stopped inviting him for a period of almost two years—following Duncan's seduction of a young poet.

"His father's son," Helen said. "He's charming."

"The boy is *too* charming," Roberta told Helen. "And that poet was not stable. She was also far too old for him."

"You sound jealous, Roberta," Helen said.

"It was a violation of *trust*," Roberta said loudly. Helen agreed that it was. Duncan apologized. Even the poet apologized.

"*I* seduced *him*," she told Roberta.

"No you didn't," Roberta said. "You *couldn't*."

All was forgiven one spring in New York when Roberta surprised Duncan with a dinner invitation. "I'm bringing this smashing girl, just for you—a friend," Roberta told him, "so wash the paint off your hands, and wash your hair and look nice. I've told her you're nice, and I know you *can* be. I think you'll like her."

Thus having set Duncan up with a date, who was a woman of *her* choice, Roberta felt somehow better. Over a long period it came out that Roberta had *hated* the poet whom Duncan had slept with, and that was the worst of the problem.

When Duncan crashed his motorcycle within a mile of a Vermont hospital, Roberta was the first to get there; she had been skiing farther north; Helen had called her, and Roberta beat Helen to the hospital.

"Riding a motorcycle in the snow!" Roberta roared. "What would your father say?" Duncan could barely whisper. Every limb appeared in traction; there was a complication involving a kidney, and unknown to both Duncan and Roberta—at the time—one of his arms would have to come off.

Helen and Roberta and Duncan's sister, Jenny Garp, waited for three days until Duncan was out of danger. Ellen James was too shaken to come wait with them. Roberta railed the whole time.

"What should he *be* on a motorcycle for—with only one eye? What kind of peripheral vision is *that*?" Roberta asked. "One side is always blind."

That had been what had happened, exactly. A drunk had run a stoplight and Duncan had seen the car too late; when he'd tried to outmaneuver the car, the snow had locked him in place and held him, an almost motionless target, for the drunken driver.

Everything had been broken.

"He is too much like his father," Helen mourned. But, Captain Energy knew, in some ways Duncan was *not* like his father. Duncan lacked *direction*, in Roberta's opinion.

When Duncan was out of danger, Roberta broke down in front of him.

"If you get killed before I die, you little son of a bitch," she cried, "it will *kill* me! *And* your mother, probably—and Ellen, possibly—but you can be sure about me. It will absolutely *kill* me, Duncan, you little bastard!" Roberta wept and wept, and Duncan wept, too, because he knew it was true: Roberta loved him and was terribly vulnerable, in that way, to whatever happened to him.

Jenny Garp, who was only a freshman at college, dropped out of school so that she could stay in Vermont with Duncan while Duncan got well. Jenny had graduated from the Steering School with the highest honors; she would have no trouble returning to college when Duncan recovered. She volunteered her help to the hospital as a nurse's aide, and she was a great source of optimism for Duncan, who had a long and painful convalescence ahead of him. Duncan, of course, had some experience with convalescence.

Helen came from Steering to see him every weekend; Roberta went to New York to look after the deplorable state of Duncan's live-in studio. Duncan was afraid that all his paintings and photographs, and his stereo, would be stolen.

When Roberta first went to Duncan's studio-apartment, she found a lank, willowy girl living there, wearing Duncan's clothes, all splattered with paint; the girl was not doing such a hot job with the dishes.

"Move out, honey," Roberta said, letting herself in with Duncan's key. "Duncan's back in the bosom of his family."

"Who are you?" the girl asked Roberta. "His mother?"

"His *wife,* sweetheart," Roberta said. "I've always gone for younger men."

"His *wife?*" the girl said, gawking at Roberta. "I didn't know he was *married.*"

"His kids are coming up in the elevator," Roberta told

the girl, "so you better use the stairs. His kids are prac-
tically as big as me."

"His *kids?*" the girl said; she fled.

Roberta had the studio cleaned and invited a young
woman she knew to move in and watch after the place;
the woman had just undergone a sexual transformation
and she needed to match her new identity with a new
place to live. "It will be perfect for you," Roberta told
the new woman. "A luscious young man owns it, but he'll
be away for months. You can take care of his things,
and have dreams about him, and I'll let you know when
you have to move out."

In Vermont, Roberta told Duncan, "I hope you clean
up your life. Stop the motorcycles and the mess—and
stop the girls who don't know the first thing about you.
My God: sleeping with strangers. You're not your father yet; you haven't gotten down to *work*. If you were
really *being* an artist, Duncan, you wouldn't have *time*
for all the other shit. All the self-destruction shit, particularly."

Captain Energy was the only one who could talk to
Duncan that way—now that Garp was gone. Helen
could not criticize him. Helen was too happy just to
have Duncan alive, and Jenny was ten years younger
than Duncan; all she could do was look up to him, and
love him, and be there while he took so long to heal.
Ellen James, who loved Duncan fiercely and possessive-
ly, became so exasperated with him that she would
throw her note pad and her pencil in the air; and then,
of course, she had nothing to say.

"A one-eyed, one-armed painter," Duncan complained. "Oh boy."

"Be happy you've still got one head and one heart,"
Roberta told him. "Do you know many painters who
hold the brush in *both* hands? You need two eyes to
drive a motorcycle, dummy, but only one to paint."

Jenny Garp, who loved her brother as if he were her
brother *and* her father—because she had been too young
to know her father, really—wrote Duncan a poem while

he recuperated in the hospital. It was the first and only poem young Jenny Garp ever wrote; she did *not* have the artistic inclination of her father and her brother. And only God knows what inclination Walt might have had.

> *Here lies the firstborn, lean and long,*
> *with one arm handy and one arm gone,*
> *with one eye lit and one gone out,*
> *with family memories, clout by clout.*
> *This mother's son must keep intact*
> *the remains of the house that Garp built.*

It was a lousy poem, of course, but Duncan loved it. "I'll keep myself intact," he promised Jenny.

The young transsexual, whom Roberta had placed in Duncan's studio-apartment, sent Duncan get-well postcards from New York.

> *The plants are doing okay, but the big yellow painting by the fireplace was warping—I don't think it was stretched properly—so I took it down and leaned it with the others in the pantry, where it's colder. I love the blue painting, and the drawings— all the drawings! And the one Roberta tells me is a self-portrait, of you—I love that especially.*

"Oh boy," Duncan groaned.

Jenny read him all of Joseph Conrad, who had been Garp's favorite writer when Garp was a boy.

It was good for Helen that she had her teaching duties to distract her from worrying about Duncan.

"That boy will straighten out," Roberta assured her.

"He's a young *man*, Roberta," Helen said. "He's not a *boy* anymore—although he certainly acts like one."

"They're all boys to me," Roberta said. "Garp was a boy. *I* was a boy, before I became a girl. Duncan will always be a boy, to me."

"Oh boy," Helen said.

"You ought to take up some sport," Roberta told Helen. "To relax you."

"Please, Roberta," Helen said.

"Try *running*," Roberta said.

"*You* run, I'll read," Helen said.

Roberta ran all the time. In her late fifties she was becoming forgetful of using her estrogen, which must be used for the whole of a transsexual's life to maintain a female body shape. The lapses in her estrogen, and her stepped-up running, made Roberta's large body change shape, and change back again, before Helen's eyes.

"I sometimes don't know what's *happening* to you, Roberta," Helen told her.

"It's sort of exciting," Roberta said. "I never know what I'm going to feel like; I never know what I'm going to *look* like, either."

Roberta ran in three marathon races after she was fifty, but she developed problems with bursting blood vessels and was advised, by her doctor, to run shorter distances. Twenty-six miles was too much for a former tight end in her fifties—"old Number Ninety," Duncan occasionally teased her. Roberta was a few years older than Garp and Helen, and had always looked it. She went back to running the old six-mile route she and Garp used to take, between Steering and the sea, and Helen never knew when Roberta might suddenly arrive at the Steering house, sweaty and gasping and wanting to use the shower. Roberta kept a large robe and several changes of clothes at Helen's house for these occasions, when Helen would look up from her book and see Roberta Muldoon in her running costume—her stopwatch held like her heart in her big pass-catching hands.

Roberta died that spring Duncan was hospitalized in Vermont. She had been doing wind sprints on the beach at Dog's Head Harbor, but she'd stopped running and had come up on the porch, complaining of "popping sounds" in the back of her head—or possibly in her temples; she couldn't exactly locate them, she said. She sat on the porch hammock and looked at the ocean and let Ellen James go get her a glass of ice tea. Ellen sent a note out to Roberta with one of the Fields Foundation fellows.

*Lemon?*

"No, just sugar!" Roberta called.

When Ellen brought the ice tea, Roberta downed the whole glass in a few gulps.

"That's perfect, Ellen," Roberta said. Ellen went to fix Roberta another glass. "Perfect," Roberta repeated. "Give me another one just like that one!" Roberta called. "I want a *whole life* just like that one!"

When Ellen came back with the ice tea, Roberta Muldoon was dead in the hammock. Something had popped, something had burst.

If Roberta's death struck Helen and made her feel low, Helen had Duncan to worry about—for once, a grateful distraction. Ellen James, whom Roberta had supported so much, was spared an overdose of grief by her sudden responsibilities—she was busy taking over Roberta's job at the Fields Foundation; she had big shoes to fill, as they say. In fact, size 12. Young Jenny Garp had never been as close to Roberta as Duncan had been; it was Duncan, still in traction, who took it the hardest. Jenny stayed with him and gave him one pep talk after another, but Duncan could remember Roberta and all the times she had bailed out the Garps before—Duncan especially.

He cried and cried. He cried so much, they had to change a cast on his chest.

His transsexual tenant sent him a telegram from New York.

I'LL GET OUT NOW. NOW THAT R. IS GONE. IF YOU DON'T FEEL COMFORTABLE ABOUT MY BEING HERE. I'LL GO. I WONDER. COULD I HAVE THAT PICTURE OF HER. THE ONE OF R. AND YOU. I ASSUME THAT'S

YOU. WITH THE FOOTBALL. YOU'RE IN THE JERSEY
WITH THE 90 THAT'S TOO BIG FOR YOU.

Duncan had never answered her cards, her reports on
the welfare of his plants and the exact location of his
paintings. It was in the spirit of old No. 90 that he answered her now, whoever she was—this poor confused
boy-girl whom Roberta, Duncan knew, would have been
kind to.

*Please stay as long as you want to* [he wrote to
her]. *But I like that photograph, too. When I get
back on my feet, I'll make a copy just for you.*

Roberta had told him to pull his life together and
Duncan regretted he would not be able to *show* her that
he could. He felt a responsibility now, and wondered at
his father, *being* a writer when he was so young—having
children, having *Duncan,* when he was so young. Duncan made lots of resolutions in the hospital in Vermont;
he would keep most of them, too.

He wrote Ellen James, who was still too upset at his
accident to come see him all plastered and full of pins.

*Time we both got to work, though I have some
catching up to do—to catch up to you. With 90
gone, we're a smaller family. Let's work at not
losing anybody else.*

He would have written to his mother that he intended
to make her proud of him, but he would have felt silly
saying it and he knew how tough his mother was—how
little *she* ever needed pep talks. It was to young Jenny
that Duncan turned his new enthusiasm.

"Goddamnit, we've got to have energy," Duncan told
his sister, who had plenty of energy. "That's what you
missed—by not knowing the old man. Energy! You've
got to get it on your own."

*"I've* got energy," Jenny said. "Jesus, what do you think I've been *doing*—just taking care of *you?"*

It was a Sunday afternoon; Duncan and Jenny always watched the pro football on Duncan's hospital TV. It was a further good omen, Duncan thought, that the Vermont station carried the game, that Sunday, from Philadelphia. The Eagles were about to get creamed by the Cowboys. The game, however, didn't matter; it was the before-the-game ceremony that Duncan appreciated. The flag was at half-mast for the former tight end Robert Muldoon. The scoreboard flashed 90! 90! 90! Duncan noted how the times had changed; for example, there were feminist funerals everywhere now; he had just read about a big one in Nebraska. And in Philadelphia the sports announcer managed to say, without snickering, that the flag flew at half-mast for *Roberta* Muldoon.

*"She* was a fine athlete," the announcer mumbled. "A great pair of hands."

"An extraordinary person," agreed the co-announcer.

The first man spoke again. "Yeah," he said, "she didda lot for . . ." and he struggled, while Duncan waited to hear for *whom*—for freaks, for weirdos, for sexual disasters, for his father and his mother and himself and Ellen James. "She didda lot for people wid *complicated* lives," the sports announcer said, surprising himself *and* Duncan Garp—but with dignity.

The band played. The Dallas Cowboys kicked off to the Philadelphia Eagles; it would be the first of many kickoffs that the Eagles would receive. And Duncan Garp could imagine his father, appreciating the announcer's struggle to be tactful and kind. Duncan actually imagined Garp whooping it up with Roberta; somehow, Duncan felt that Roberta would be there—privy to her own eulogy. She and Garp would be hilarious at the awkwardness of the news.

Garp would mimic the announcer: "She didda lot for refashioning da vagina!"

"Ha!" Roberta would roar.

"Oh boy!" Garp would holler. "Oh boy."

When Garp had been killed, Duncan remembered, Roberta Muldoon had threatened to have her sexual reversal *reversed*. "I'd rather be a lousy *man* again," she wailed, "than think there are women in this world who are actually *gloating* over this filthy murder by that filthy *cunt!*"

*Stop it! Stop it! Don't ever say that* word!

scribbled Ellen James.

*There are only those of us who loved him, and those of us who didn't* know *him—men* and *women,*

wrote Ellen James.

Then Roberta Muldoon had picked them all up, one by one; she gave to them—formally, seriously, and generously—her famous bear hug.

When Roberta died, some *talking* person among the Fields Foundation fellows at Dog's Head Harbor called Helen on the phone. Helen, gathering herself—once again—would be the one to call Duncan in Vermont. Helen would advise young Jenny how to break the news to Duncan. Jenny Garp had inherited a fine bedside manner from her famous grandmother, Jenny Fields.

"Bad news, Duncan," young Jenny whispered, kissing her brother on the lips. "Old Number Ninety has dropped the ball."

DUNCAN GARP, who survived both the accident that cost him an eye and the accident that cost him an arm, became a good and serious painter; he was something of a pioneer in the artistically suspect field of color photography, which he developed with his painter's eye for color and his father's habit of an insistent, *personal* vision. He did not make nonsense images, you can be sure, and he brought to his painting an eerie, sensual, almost narrative realism; it was easy, knowing who he was, to say that this was more of a *writer's* craft than it was a craft that belonged in a picture—and to criticize him, as he was criticized, for being too "literal."

"Whatever *that* means," Duncan always said. "What do they expect of a one-eyed, one-armed artist—and the son of Garp? No flaws?"

He had his father's sense of humor, after all, and Helen was very proud of him.

He must have made a hundred paintings in a series called *Family Album*—the period of his work he was best known for. They were paintings modeled from the photographs he had taken as a child, after his eye accident. They were of Roberta, and his grandmother, Jenny Fields; his mother swimming at Dog's Head Harbor; his father running, with his healed jaw, along the beach. There was one series of a dozen small paintings of a dirty-white Saab; the series was called *The Colors of the World,* because, Duncan said, all the colors of the world are visible in the twelve versions of the dirty-white Saab.

There were baby pictures of Jenny Garp, too; and in the large, group portraits—largely imagined, not from any photograph—the critics said that the blank face, or the repeated figure (very small) with its back to the camera, was always Walt.

Duncan did not want children of his own. "Too vulnerable," he told his mother. "I couldn't stand watching them grow up." What he meant was, he couldn't stand watching them *not* grow up.

Since he felt that way, Duncan was fortunate not to have children be an issue in his life—they weren't even a worry. He came home from his four months of hospitalization in Vermont and found an extremely lonely transsexual living in his New York studio-apartment. She had made the place look as if a real artist already lived there, and by a curious process—it was almost a kind of osmosis of his things—she already seemed to know a great deal about him. She was in love with him, too—just from pictures. Another gift to Duncan's life from

Roberta Muldoon! And there were some who said—
Jenny Garp, for example—that she was even beautiful.

They were married, because if ever there was a boy
with no discrimination in his heart about transsexuals,
that boy was Duncan Garp.

"It's a marriage made in Heaven," Jenny Garp told
her mother. She meant Roberta, of course; Roberta was
in Heaven. But Helen was a natural at worrying about
Duncan; since Garp had died, she'd had to take over
much of the worrying. And since Roberta had died,
Helen felt she'd had to take over *all* the worrying.

"I don't know, I don't know," Helen said. Duncan's
marriage made her anxious. "That damn Roberta,"
Helen said. "She always got her way!"

> *But this way there's no chance of unwanted
> pregnancy,*

wrote Ellen James.

"Oh, stop it!" Helen said. "I sort of *wanted* grand-
children, you know. One or two, anyway."

"*I'll* give them to you," Jenny promised.

"Oh boy," Helen said. "If I'm still alive, kid."

Sadly, she wouldn't be, although she would get to see
Jenny pregnant and be able to *imagine* she was a grandmother.

"Imagining something is better than remembering
something," Garp wrote.

And Helen certainly had to be happy with how Duncan's life straightened out, as Roberta had promised.

After Helen's death, Duncan worked very hard with
the meek Mr. Whitcomb; they made a respectable presentation out of Garp's unfinished novel, *My Father's
Illusions*. Like the father and son edition of *The Pension Grillparzer*, Duncan illustrated what there was of
*My Father's Illusions*—a portrait of a father who plots
ambitiously and impossibly for a world where his children will be safe and happy. The illustrations Duncan
contributed were largely portraits of Garp.

Sometime after the book's publication, Duncan was visited by an old, old man whose name Duncan could not remember. The man claimed to be at work on "a critical biography" of Garp, but Duncan found his questions irritating. The man asked over and over again about the events leading up to the terrible accident where Walt was killed. Duncan wouldn't tell him anything (Duncan didn't *know* anything), and the man went away empty-handed—biographically speaking. The man was Michael Milton, of course. It had appeared to Duncan that the man was missing something, though Duncan couldn't have known that Michael Milton was missing his penis.

The book he supposedly was writing was never seen, and no one knows what happened to him.

If the world of the reviewer seemed content, after the publication of *My Father's Illusions,* to call Garp merely an "eccentric writer," a "good but not a great writer," Duncan didn't mind. In Duncan's own words, Garp was "original" and "the real thing." Garp had been the type, after all, to compel blind loyalty.

*"One-eyed* loyalty," Duncan called it.

He had a long-standing code with his sister, Jenny, and with Ellen James; the three of them were as thick as thieves.

"Here's to Captain Energy!" they would say, when they were drinking together.

"There's no sex like transsex!" they would shout, when they were drunk, which occasionally embarrassed Duncan's wife—although she certainly agreed.

"How's the energy?" they would write and phone and telegraph each other, when they wanted to know what was up. And when they had plenty of energy, they would describe each other as "full of Garp."

Although Duncan would live a long, long time, he would die unnecessarily and, ironically, *because* of his good sense of humor. He would die laughing at one of his own jokes, which was surely a Garp-family thing to do. It was at a kind of coming-out party for a new transsexual, a friend of his wife's. Duncan aspirated an olive and choked to death in just a few seconds of violent laughter. That is a horrible and stupid way to die, but everyone who knew him said that Duncan would not have objected—either to that form of death, or to the life he'd had. Duncan Garp always said that his father suffered the death of Walt more than anyone in the family suffered anything else. And among the chosen forms of death, death finally was the same. "Between men and women," as Jenny Fields once said, "only death is shared equally."

Jenny Garp, who in the field of death had much more specific training than her famous grandmother, would not have agreed. Young Jenny knew that, between men and women, not even death gets shared equally. Men get to die more, too.

JENNY GARP would outlive them all. If she had been at the party where her brother choked to death, she probably could have saved him. At least she would have known exactly what to do. She was a doctor. She always said it was her time in the Vermont hospital, looking after Duncan, that had made up her mind to turn to medicine—not her famous grandmother's history of nursing, because Jenny Garp knew that only second-hand.

Young Jenny was a brilliant student; like her mother, she absorbed everything—and everything she learned she could redeliver. Like Jenny Fields, she got her feeling for people as a roamer of hospitals—inching what kindness was possible, and recognizing what wasn't.

While she was an intern, she married another young doctor. Jenny Garp would not give up her name, however; she stayed a Garp, and, in a frightful war with her husband, she saw that her three children would all be Garps, too. She would divorce, eventually—and remarry, but in no hurry. That second time would suit her. He was a painter, much older than herself, and if any of her family had been alive to nag her, they would have no doubt warned her that she was imagining something of Duncan in the man.

"So what?" she would have said. Like her mother, she had her own mind; like Jenny Fields, she kept her own name.

And her father? In what way was Jenny Garp even slightly like him—whom she never really knew? She was only a baby, after all, when he died.

Well, she *was* eccentric. She made a point of going into every bookstore and asking for her father's books. If the store was out of stock, she would order. She had a writer's sense of immortality: if you're in print and on the shelves, you're alive. Jenny Garp left fake names and addresses all over America; the books she ordered would be sold to *someone,* she reasoned. T. S. Garp would not go out of print—at least not in his daughter's lifetime.

She was also avid in her support of the famous feminist, her grandmother, Jenny Fields; but like her father, Jenny Garp did not put much stock in the *writing* of Jenny Fields. She did not bother bookstores about keeping *A Sexual Suspect* on the shelves.

Most of all, she resembled her father in the *kind* of doctor she became. Jenny Garp would turn her medical mind to research. She would not have a private practice. She would go to hospitals only when *she* was sick. Instead, Jenny spent a number of years working closely with the Connecticut Tumor Registry; she would eventually direct a branch of the National Cancer Institute. Like a good writer, who must love and worry each detail, Jenny Garp would spend hours noticing the habits of a single human cell. Like a good writer, she was ambitious; she hoped she would get to the bottom of cancer. In a sense, she would. She would die of it.

Like other doctors, Jenny Garp took that sacred oath of Hippocrates, the so-called father of medicine, wherein she agreed to devote herself to something like the life Garp once described to young Whitcomb—although Garp was concerned with a *writer's* ambitions (". . . trying to keep everyone alive, forever. Even the ones who must die in the end. They're the most important to keep alive"). Thus, cancer research did not depress Jenny Garp, who liked to describe herself as her father had described a novelist.

"A doctor who sees only terminal cases."

In the world according to her father, Jenny Garp knew, we must have energy. Her famous grandmother, Jenny Fields, once thought of us as Externals, Vital Organs, Absentees, and Goners. But in the world according to Garp, we are all terminal cases.